The Voice of Kings

Copyright © 2022 Matthew de Lacey
All rights reserved

Print: 978-1-7391087-0-0
EBook: 978-1-7391087-1-7

Proofing by Nicola Saitch & Dallas Wilcox
Cover art by Jeff Brown
Cartography by Robert Altbauer

matthewdelacey.com

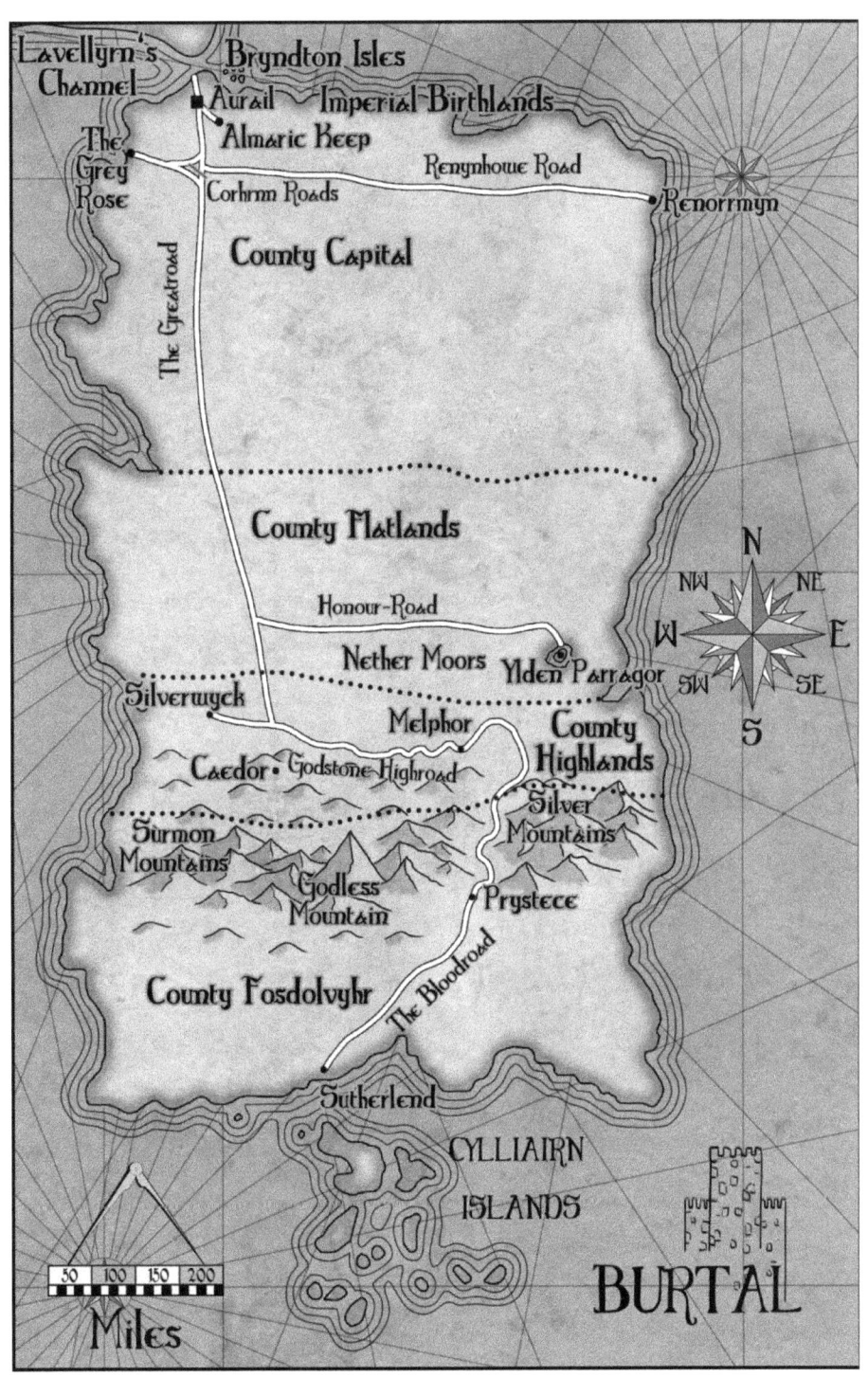

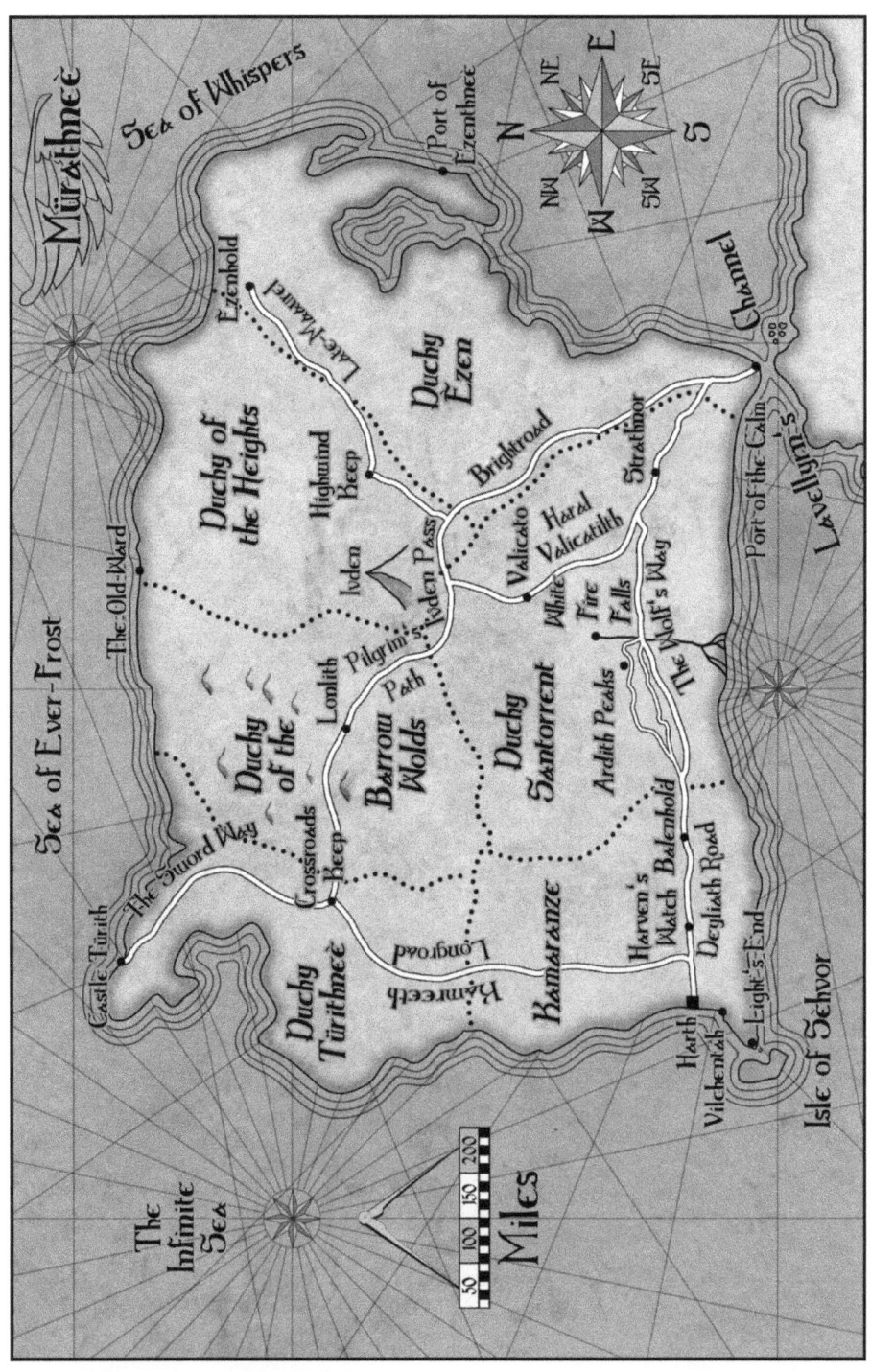

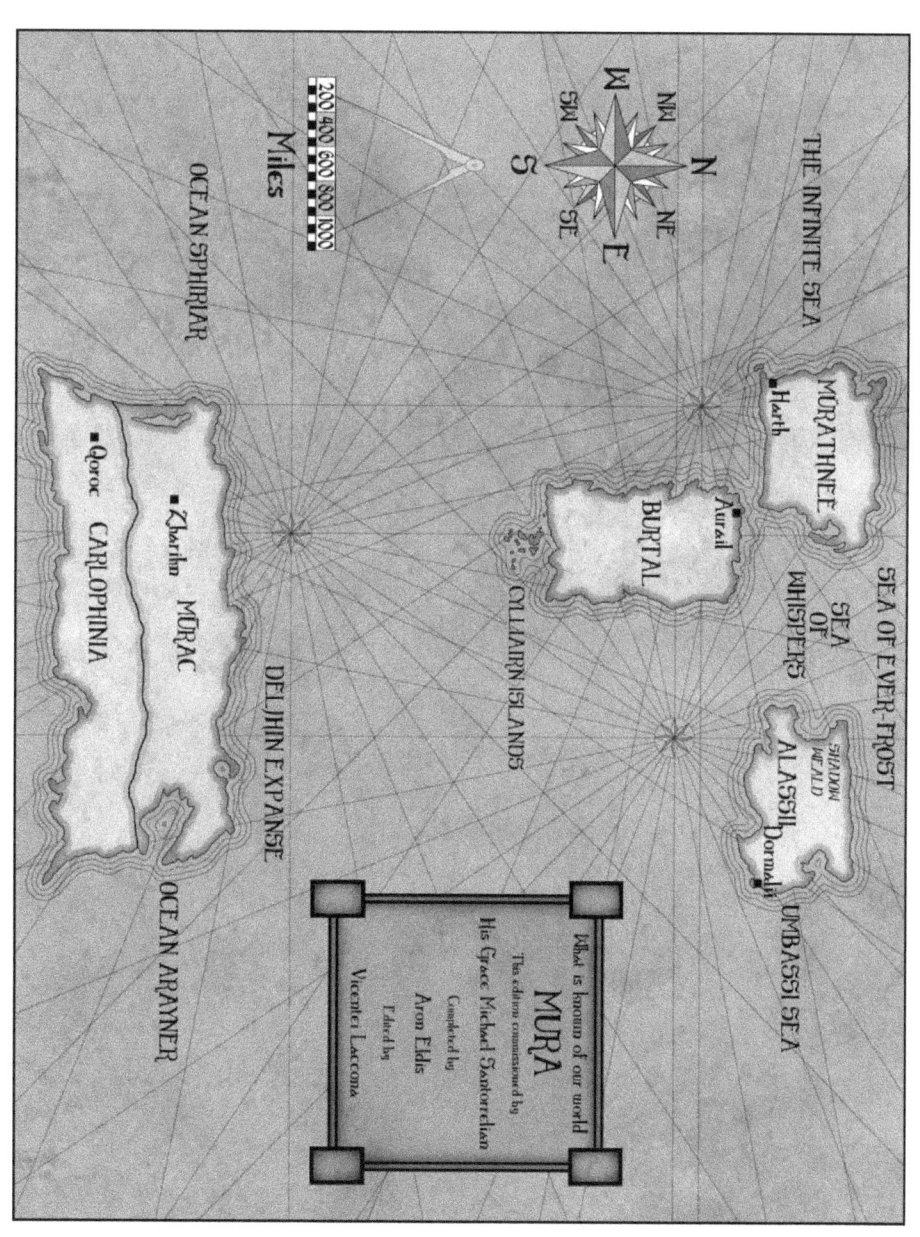

-Precursor to
Shadows of Gods and Men-

To think of victory was as hollow as could be. The thoughts of Harræmina festered on the wrath of the nightmare beyond the manse walls. For it was a nightmare, and no creature could act so wild and not be fuelled by passion. At the rumble it birthed came the fears. Always at the rumble. This one was more distant and, such was her counting that, for all her fears, she had time to ponder its spontaneity in doing so. Close, it was before, then distant, collapsing her world with its fluster all the same, before circling round to shake this hill once more. No creature of reason acted like this. So, it was of higher intellect; like a human, capable of emotion, of rage, but also tactics. She'd feared as much since she first set eyes on it.

The rattle shook dust from the ceiling of the tight staircase that seemed to spiral ever upward, as her boots continued to drum on the stone, sabatons of her Royal Guard hammering away in her wake in urgent rhythm. As the world rumbled again, so soon after the last, and angrier still, the beating of feet ended just as quickly, all four behind her bracing each other as they'd been so trained to do in the shield wall. Dust rained to drown them, tall sconces half-embedded to the stone quivered and died, the ceiling flaked with flecks of its mortar. Even this modest world, away from the world, would wither and be lain to waste before long. No lord ever *really* believed his castle could be brought low until it happened. Harræmina still wondered if she believed it.

"Is this wise?" Defender Prince Horyce's thick voice broke their silence; agitated, fearful, yet not driven by it. He was being pragmatic.

And she would defy it so long as she could. She *needed* the opposition, the advocate to steady her belief. In the wan light, she drew herself up, tall as half her guards and, though they couldn't possibly have been able to properly comprehend the subtleties of it, she made effort to correct her gait to what she was, not who she was. Her eyes grew stark and hard…and bold too? *Yes, bold, brave Harræmina, for the people,* she declared to the void in her head, hoping it would evoke more feeling in them than for her. Her back was straight, unique armour complementing her posture as it glimmered faintly before a feeble flame. She knew it was dirtied all over, blood and dirt and more besides, and so she made to look the warrior queen.

"The people need their leaders," she replied, fierce in her quiet and, without turning, sprinted onward. Her mouth opened to prattle on, but she heard the terror again outside; even the *screaming* again mounted so high as they all combined, and her tongue fell dry and heavy. Bloody hell, would it never stop? "If this was a poor decision my friends, it would be

Prelude

all the poorer to turn back so close to the Lord's Solar, after all we've been through. We'll keep going."

She had to force her mouth shut or she would have blabbered on in her hot-blooded fervour forever. And..."friends", had she just called them? What in gods' names...? True enough, but she'd never spoken to them like that before. Such times of pain were as good a time as any for a queen to play contrition, she conceded.

The bronze door met her at the top of the stairs and she barraged through. And there, sunlight, streaming sickly in dust-filled beams from her left side. It didn't feel good on her face today. There was barely enough to dazzle her now that the dark clouds had closed in on them. For it all, the corridor she ran through proudly shined its marble; it was clean, not tampered but for the splintered glass afoot the grand oval windows, framed with leaves of gold that represented holy lordship, in its absence, unfortunately. The ceiling of curved frame blurred overhead, the curved arches too, and the angled, polished silver rings and spears extending rigid beneath, but to her flew like a shower of steel, such was her frantic mind that all and sundry became a weapon to her. She couldn't stop thinking about how to kill it.

Rumbling, again. Shouting, panic, arrows nocked, arrows loosed, steeds falling with their masters, all together. A crashing sounded far off, like thunder but heavier. The Queen shook her head and lowered it in shame. In the curved tiled marble, her reflection bobbed along, cloak fluttering even with the thin ringlets, enamelled silver of steel that patterned its rim.

"Gods below, why have you done this to me?" her own voice whispered.

"Keep moving, Holiness," Defender Garet urged, again pushing her where the others couldn't, if only by virtue of his ever insistent tone.

She didn't need encouragement from anyone though. The dread drove her on, and it mounted at the tension of her voice and, quite honestly, she knew the reason why. A curse made in passing might very well have been the truth of it; if this was her fault, her punishment, or perhaps all those who ruled, for offences unknown...

If that was a demon, then there could be few explanations for its presence, none of them good.

The Queen burst through another door, stumbling through a small hall on cue of the shaking, and barging her way into the Lord's Solar. Sunlight streamed brighter here, and the reason for that was clear too. She slowed on sight of the gaping hole in the far wall, almost stopping but for the dread again that she begged to be dispelled. As, at great speed, she navigated the rubble through the long hall of stolen majesties, her eyes searched maniacally to the edges. Corpses were pushed against both sides, or hurled, more accurately. No, swept aside, like dirt, for the stone table that once sat beside the balcony was splintered all about one wall from great impact. The bodies were broken; not split apart, but lain about with their chests collapsed and limbs twisted.

"Holiness, there!" Horyce cried in surprise, belting past her. The sight of him alone made her twitch, as she suspected many a man and beast and falling leaf would do for her now.

On the meadow between the city's two halves, where the troops gathered, black death shot from the ground, making her skid to a halt this time. She'd seen it before but would never get used to it; a claw rising from the shadowed earth, not breaking it but slipping from the very shadow of the storm clouds that hung strangely low to slash apart her men before retreating. But, *from* it or *of* it?

No matter, she could worry about that later, if later ever came to be spoken of. She ran to her Defender Prince, lowering to one knee at his side as he pushed aside the body of the lord's steward without decorum. She would have done the same, but her heart panged in guilt as she looked up and saw that the fussy, noble man had thrown himself before his lord, arms wrapped around him by the look of it, for there, against the wall, the Lord Keeper of this realm was slumped, so bloodied she couldn't even properly make out the injuries.

"Laveltth Morna," she incanted solemnly, placing her left hand to his chest to make herself heard to the God of Souls, should it be needed, or should he even be listening, for that matter. That really sent a shiver down her spine. What if they were all alone now?

"Laveltth Morna," three of her guards chanted. "Laveltth Byyra."

Horyce didn't partake, merely tugging gently on her arm as he rose, but she resisted on a whim, grabbing a ring of keys from the steward's body and slinging them over the hilt of her guard's sword. He tugged a second time, not concerned with proper form this time. His straight lip fell crooked disapprovingly but, more than that, he seemed desperate beneath his stoicism to find something in looking at her, as if he'd finally come to question her leadership. Who could blame him? If he was cracking, he was in good company.

"Will that be all, Holiness?" he asked more calmly than he looked. An armoured hand clutched her shoulder when she didn't answer. She eyed it suspiciously for a second.

"Not quite."

Rightfully, he was taken aback, just as the others were. An almighty crash shut him up before he could speak, and they both jumped back, heads zipping around to face this new destruction. In the great meadow there stood natural formations of rock that jutted high, jagged, and around them clustered the shattered fragments of the once great host that struggled to organise but, now, one less formation pierced the sky, for she saw one crumble at its base, unable to turn away as, for an age, it toppled, and smashed down, clouding the field with dust of grey. She flinched as the echo assaulted her ears, but little more, stricken sick and pale as the creature crawled from its shadow burrow, glistening with blackness, as

Prelude

if pooled of ink, before engulfing itself in the cloud, even wrapping the grey mass around it like a cloak, or so it seemed. And the death screams resumed; the Red Field made red again. She could always tell them apart from the others. Its own cry drowned them all; like a deep horn, it was, that bellowed its warning to the skies and ocean near, but too organic to be mistaken as such, too...emotional. Horns couldn't chill the soul, like frozen steel the heart.

Her attention was whipped away; fires springing up both sides of the city the beast had raped, creeping through the battered streets...and distracted *again*; at the city aft where the domed temple stood, heaved, quivered at the pillar bases, fell inwards sanctum by sanctum with the five of them watching, speechless. Despite it all, her features were locked hard and still, that she made sure of.

"Blasphemy," Garet hissed.

So it was. People had told her the idea of so many sanctums for so many different kinds of people was fussy, divisive and archaic and, what's more, she'd agreed, damn it all, and done nothing. Now, this. She looked to her knights for comfort and barely restrained a laugh. Horyce, Garet, Daved, Domanne. There they all were, repressing their emotions as a clam shut itself away at the approach of serpents, just as she'd been doing, trying to be oh so strong, but what was the gods' damn point? Strong for whom? Is this what her land's nobility boiled down to – lots of men so concerned with bravery that they were too afraid to show anything else?

The temple's inner sanctum fell and Queen Harræmina gulped to relieve her heart from her throat. Her worst fears returned, so, hastily, she strode to the broken overhang, just to be away from her knights. She couldn't openly reveal her logic. Just saying it aloud might break her, never mind the others. Nonetheless, the thoughts couldn't be withheld.

If this was a demon raging on the Red Field, then their dearest hope stood with the blessing of the Hanaverë, or even the gods themselves. But there was a demon here, and the lack of either blessing contradicted all she knew of her faith. Either the demon had fought its way on to the human plane, in which case the gods now lay broken in the ether for all eternity, or they'd grown weary of fighting for people who they perceived to have failed them and let it through. In which case, it came back to sins.

"Gods, no!" she growled, stepping to the very edge of the collapsed balcony, as if considering ending her part in this play right now.

She squinted as the winds picked up, howling so melancholy they might have belonged to the creature, flapping the royal cloak of leather and silk that extended beneath the spaulder flaps of a hauberk steel and leather that otherwise had no gaps, clinking the metal links faintly. In the face of imminent death, on the precipice, she was sent a burst of courage and, with it, anger. Anger was good. It was something she knew how to use.

"No," she repeated. "No, no!" Harræmina paused only to embitter herself at the monster's work. Still it showed no rhyme or reason, its only purpose destruction. "Is it me

The Voice of Kings

you want?!" she yelled, throwing her arms out. "You've killed the King, are you here for the Queen? *I* am the Queen, demon!"

"It's hopeless," Horyce said softly. "If it could understand you, it would only defy you further. Now, please, we have to go."

True enough, she might as well have been addressing the wind, but it felt good all the same, and maybe she'd even believed something would come of it. Turning, she made to beckon her guards who clustered behind, stopping as she saw the expressions of longing upon Garet and Domanne, temperamentally cagey and quietly contemplative respectively. She followed their gaze into the fell cloud.

"Do you want to fight?" she posed.

"I'll only fight beside you," Garet replied stiffly, creasing his features as if deeply offended.

"I'm serious." She saw Horyce's scepticism and pivoted to shoot it down. There was tension in her neck and shoulders. "Tell me it's prudent to fight, convince me it's the right thing to do, friend, and we'll go out there together, all of us. Say the words and I'll follow."

"I would do it," Daved said flatly, sadly denying her the confrontation.

"There's nothing prudent about that," Horyce replied awkwardly. He slowed his voice as if speaking to a child. "Gods' sakes, Holiness. With respect, you just risked your life to save a Lord Keeper. I can't let you let throw your life away on a fancy now. It's not even the noblest thing you could do."

"And so it isn't." She sighed because she knew it was true.

"Good. So now..."

"I still need my sword."

They, all of them, glanced at her sword by instinct, but the dark shifts that overcame them showed they understood. The dark of their faces objected, in each their different ways, subtleties popping in ways they never could before, when she'd sat complacently on her throne.

"It's just a sword," Horyce responded.

"It's the only blessed weapon I have. What sort of idiot would I be to run and leave it when I'm this close? It carries magic that might one day kill that *thing*; it's a symbol of strength, it will give strength, it..."

"I know," the Defender Prince interrupted, shocking her out of her volatile tirade with those simple words subdued. "But it's just a sword."

That made her hesitate, if only for a moment. Everything else made her ignore that advice. The spirits of these dead men begged her not to waste the visit to their fastness. So she ran, and ran some more, ever trying to go faster, to blur all destruction but that which lay ahead.

"I don't ask you to come," the Queen called out.

Prelude

Their boots hammering heavy on the tiles were all the answer she needed. Truthfully, they'd probably thought her disingenuous but, today, they would be wrong in thinking it. She barged through a side door into a dim hallway centred with a five-pointed altar, trying to think where the sword might be. The opposite door, she decided without stopping. She couldn't stop, not while she felt this strong, and so barged her way into the next room, just as before.

Black smoke rushed up at her from where it had pushed against the door, wreathing her. Against her wishes, she skidded to a halt, heart thumping as if it might explode. A croak escaped from her throat, her eyes widening despite the sting and, across her body, she found her hand had reached for the sword at her waist. Flames, that somehow thrived on stone, lapped up all across the room, thickly exhaling the smoke that had strangled her. So, yes, she'd been right to despair, in a way, for the monster had to have made this, through the hole in this room's wall, just like it made fires spring in the city below. But, apart from that, nothing. She was still alive. If paranoia was going to assail her like this from now on...

She resumed her sprint, turning left into the room, furious at the weakness. Fury was good, she told herself.

"There!" Horyce shouted. He shot up alongside her, pointing. At his continued vigilance, she smiled weakly.

Near the back of the room there stood a display case and, inside it, her prize, safe as the good Lord Keeper had promised. At that, everything else warped into focus through the flames; the half pillars embedded into the green and gold walls, the round wooden table that smouldered black, the crisscrossing arches overhead...the Lord Keeper's study.

Harræmina jumped in surprise as Domanne rushed alongside too, courting danger with the fiery wall on his other side and, as if to prove an even closer allegiance, Horyce threw an arm round her shoulder and sheltered her as she ran the open path. It crept inwards, near its end. *No, too close,* she shouted inwardly, but her companions seemed not to care. Both of them were swept through it, the smoke, again, obscuring her vision. The heat reached out, such that she heard it singe the fine silk over the leather of her cloak. She gasped, for herself, and for them, all she had left, so held her breath while she waited to know if the grips on her were merely a desperate cling to life.

The fire vanished behind and her knights emerged with her, armour now dressed in black. Their helmed heads rose from hiding, red but unburned, and she bolted ahead of them to the glass cabinet, colliding with it and employing her remaining momentum to drag it from its pedestal, collapsing hard with it, landing a punch with a gauntleted fist as it fell. For all the pain she might feel later, right now her blood pumped like fire all its own; a lesser monarch maybe, not worthy of the sword, but she was going to give it a try anyway. If one could get close enough to the beast without being sundered and without it slipping away, there was a chance it could harm it. So she laid another punch, cracking the thick sheet, reaching right through at the third. Her fingers fell around the smooth hilt and she leaped up.

I'm on fire, she thought triumphantly. This momentum was the only way she knew how to feel in control. Stop, and she risked having to deal with her feelings properly.

When Harræmina pulled the blade free by half, it repelled her with its mysticism, eerie in such light. The red smoke, waving thick beneath the glass-like surface, grew bold before the fire.

"The way out..." she demanded as she looked back to her men.

They glanced back the way they'd come. There was another door, but reaching it would be treacherous and they couldn't guarantee it wasn't locked. Funny, her blade could singe hotter than these flames at its most eager but, on the door, it would but chip it bit by bit.

And her blood slowed, so she ran.

The brine smelled strong when she walked through the front doors of the manse, sword hanging by its sash around her neck and armpit. There were no seabirds though. The courtyard gave her a strange feeling, being so lifeless with its wagons and carts abandoned. She might have believed the world had already ended, if not for that chilling crashing repeating over and over in the distance.

There was something almost cathartic about the finality, as her realm became only memory and her burden lightened, isolating her from her duty. Perhaps, if she found some suitable island to live on in the sea, she would build a house like a common worker and dress in drab clothes again, unnoticed as simply 'Mina', like being a child again. A deep breath escaped when she looked up at the terrible sky. She'd remembered something.

"Horyce, when we're past the walls, lock the...no, give me the keys."

The Defender Prince frowned but flicked the ring from his hilt and held them out. He seemed to understand.

"You're staying behind?" Daved said.

"Not me," she forced the words out. They stepped past the perimeter, there staring both ways at the wall extending into the distance before the coastline. The Queen shook her head. This would require courage, and it would have to be hers.

"No one else can leave. They're most likely doomed anyway if they stay in plain sight and, even if they reach the sea, the boats will have already left. All it will do is get us *all* killed instead of most of us, right?"

"As you say," Horyce spoke for the rest of them.

She smiled through a grimace, suppressing tears. The battle thrill was dying and she could only stand by, helpless.

"Friends," she called them one last time, "if you have unfinished business beyond the walls, I suggest you go now."

Prelude

Her guards shuffled where they stood.

"Don't lock up now and regret it later. The world has changed; we've run out of land to flee on. I won't think less of you if you go. My safety isn't your priority any longer. If you want to be released from your bonds, then you're released, gladly."

Garet strode away from his brothers in arms, not bowing as he approached, but staring dumbstruck straight at her face as if it was the first time he'd seen her. He hesitated, lips dry.

"Holiness, I...sorry, I have to..."

She waved a hand at him vigorously to stop him. *I hope you find who you're looking for*, the words caught in her throat. *Good luck my friend. Farewell.*

Before she could wipe away her blank expression and get used to speaking to her knight this way, he simply strode past and, when he'd done so, broke into a run. Domanne came next.

"My Queen," he thus revered her in the deep voice he reserved for when his words mattered.

He passed also.

Short of closing the huge metal gates locked against the other side of the wall, they instead pushed in the lattice bronze gates that rested on the outside of that brick barrier. Harræmina fiddled with the keys in the lock, doubt sown just as she heard that dreadful click. *Was it, perhaps, this sort of behaviour that had got them into this mess in the first place? Why would a god bother with a people so heartless?* But no, she couldn't afford to second guess herself. After hesitating, she took a great step back and dropped the keys, which clunked on the stone. There, a compromise. *Gods, save me.*

Domanne turned back, lowered his head, ashamed, before carrying on his way in haste.

"Well now..." Daved breathed in awe as he watched his companions leave, as if he hadn't seen a more shocking sight all day.

Suddenly he froze; they all did, they lonely three. The beast was crying out again. No, she decided; she'd changed her mind. It sounded like a horn well enough but, now that it boomed again, she likened it more to a male choir, holding a deep note of monotone and lonely, like the silver wolf that used to howl outside her chambers. Either way, it made her hairs stand on end. So she ran on, toward the sea, scanning the coastline as she did so. Many ships had already left, but others floated limp against the horizon in their docks, not a sail or sailor in sight. Had so few made it here?

When she made it to the jetty of her grand eight-decked vessel, her seafaring captain rushed to the plank, biting his lip, and he frowned when he caught her dirtied visage up close. Up the tilted plank she ran, on to her ship of smooth wide curves and bright sails.

"This is it? You lost two more guards?"

"Not as such...For all intents and purposes," she added when the captain did nothing.

The Voice of Kings

At that, he barked orders and the ship lurched forward, dozens of oarsmen desperately heaving away until safer waters were reached, the prow now scything the water into the west. Behind the Queen, her guards rushed up before the plank fell.

"Your kin?" the captain pressed nervously. "Did any of them survive?"

"Possibly so." It was true.

Daved murmured, passively aggressive toward the captain, "Never mind that. Is the cargo safe? It's very important."

"Safe and sound in the treasury deck, Holiness. Your friends were quite insistent on that, worry not."

It would be interesting to see if anything came of that, as indeed many things would, come to think of it. To the aft of her ship she ran, up the first sterncastle and to the rear of the second, watching the walls of the city slowly sink away into the distance. Too slowly, but kicking up a fuss wouldn't help anyone. Her hands squeezed the handrail in anger, but her heart wasn't in it anymore and she didn't feel she could crush the wood as, in her hubris, she would have some minutes ago.

"I don't suppose we'll be back," Horyce said as he arrived alongside her with Daved.

Obviously not, Defender Prince, she thought. Then again, the demon's purpose was destruction. Surely it wasn't planning on actually living here. The very idea of it was absurd. When it had laid waste to all in its path, perhaps it would simply...go away?

Queen Harræmina, Mina, leaned over the railing, staring into the watery abyss that darkened with the clouds, wondering on the infinite journey before them, yet her head was so clouded with her experiences that she was dizzied by it and seemed to think nothing at all. She jumped as Horyce shouted in alarm, drawing himself back from the stern to shout some more. Her face creased up in annoyance but, quickly, she remembered what she'd thought just before.

The waters darkened with the clouds. Instinctively, her right hand clasped the mystical sword hanging out before her and her breathing grew fast. She despaired: *Come, demon. Finish it.*

SHADOWS OF GODS AND MEN

BOOK ONE

THE VOICE OF KINGS

Chapter One: The Shadow Tongue

Along a stone road, paved through a valley in the highlands, the carriage trundled on, its wooden wheels grating and scraping against the smooth cobbles. Tristan Almaric had come to rely on this, in part, almost as a form of hypnosis, keeping him at peace and on one train of thought. The rhythmic hammering of rain on the tiny window, and the condensation blocking all view to the outside world, had created a sense of safety and belonging, as if no one could interrupt him here. A single lantern swung gently in the peripheral of his vision, in time with the movement of the carriage; the moody light of its dim flickering flame and its limited warmth holding fast his feeling of pleasant isolation.

Thoughts of home, and his woman, and the empire, such as it was, crossed his mind. Since leaving his hectic duties in the capital behind, he'd had time to think about the future of the realm and his standing, stretched out in a long, long life before him. The thoughts cycled past his mind's eye like artwork for his perusal, analysed with growing scrutiny each time they arrived back at the forefront of his consciousness.

The heavy rain was fast dying down. The comforting pattering of water droplets on glass was slowing and, with it, the many threads of Tristan's thoughts drifted from his reach, and he awoke from his daydream. He blinked in reflex. Then again, this time consciously. The world, and its many sights and sounds, warped back into focus around him. He noticed the comfort of the seat beneath him, the clopping of hooves outside, and the pinging sound of the rain deflecting off the armour of the soldiers whose steeds bore them.

Sidling over to the left edge of his seat, he wiped the tiny window with the back of his hand and peered through the distortion of the rain. The last he had seen of the outside world, they were on flatter ground, and there was not another soul around them. Now, hills rose up and rolled into the distance, and there, beside the road, were houses spread sparse and random. He also realised, now, that he was a little hot around the neck and untied his long, woollen, embroidered coat at the neck to reveal the collar of a prim linen suit. He yawned and dug the index finger from each hand into his eyes, rubbing them, and shaking the stiffness from his shoulders, stopping only as his attention was drawn by a spectacular sight through his window.

A vale opened on the skies, sunlight streaming through cracks in the clouds and lighting up the highlands. A rainbow could be seen between two of the hills, only now as the rain was stopping. He stared for some time, and then paid attention to everything else passing by, reorienting himself.

The carriage hit an uneven patch in the road, causing him to jolt up and fall down, just short of colliding with the ceiling. He looked to the old man sitting opposite, who had been sleeping the whole time. It appeared as if he might wake up but, with that hiccup out of the way, he continued breathing quietly, and his eyes remained shut. Tristan tapped one knee in unrest, bejewelled ring his passive plaything. Suddenly, he began to feel a little claustrophobic. The door opened at his behest and he climbed out, the carriage still moving, and shut the door behind him, holding on in a precarious manner while the tips of his shoes held his weight on the rim which ran below the door, all the way round the carriage.

The two guards riding this side of the carriage instinctively looked at him with some concern and began searching his vicinity for signs of trouble, a job they'd been trained to do so thoroughly that they probably began the procedure before they even realised it. The guard at the back tugged at the reins and pulled in a little closer.

"Is there a problem, Sir?" the soldier said.

"No problem. I just thought I'd get some fresh air."

He gave the guard a toothy grin and clambered his way around to the front, emerging much to the surprise of the driver, and sank himself down, adjusting his position for comfort.

"Sir Tristan," the driver said with some uncertainty, nodding politely.

"I'm just getting some fresh air," Tristan replied while consciously taking a deep breath.

The driver looked slightly to his right and in some awe at a giant stone statue of a man; proud and straight he was, with sword held firm affront him, perched atop the tallest hill in sight. Tristan followed the driver's line of sight and recoiled when he spotted the monolith, feeling uneasy at not having spotted it before. His lips lifted into a smile on one side of his face.

"You're not using that old thing for directions are you?"

"Of course not."

The driver observed Tristan's uncertain smile with much interest, looking away only so not to make him feel uncomfortable, which was good of him because the knight, Tristan, was beginning to feel it.

"You're not feeling nervous are you, Sir Tristan?"

Tristan grinned again and then chuckled, half to himself, pleasantly surprised that such a person without noble standing would speak to him with that kind of casual mannerism. He was new to his job, and had not yet gotten accustomed to being knighted either. Regardless of a blue blooded upbringing, it was humbling. *Thank you for that, my friend*, Tristan said in his head, amused.

"Nervous is not the word I would use," he said with a self-mocking smile. "Less than two weeks ago, at the Emperor's coronation, I fought and arrested three armed drunks and that was really not so bad, but...well, I am not quite so used to making social calls to strangers."

"It's a good thing you're not here for a social call then."

The Voice of Kings

Tristan sighed and shook his head from side to side in consideration at this, finally conceding playfully with a snort, and rubbing his eyes again so that it would be known he was tired and this was the reason why he had perhaps not spoken straight. He remained silent for a time, leisurely breathing in the clean highland air and composing himself for his meeting.

The flat land either side of the road was widening out and, there, more houses were seen of hardy brick, simple but well-constructed. Tristan watched with vague interest as a hairy dog barked at him, as if it wanted something, and tried in vain to run at him, shooed away by one of the guards at its lunge. And, there, a large wooden sign was jutting out of the ground, reading "Caedor". This was, indeed, the place then.

He rolled his shoulders back and released the remaining leather ties on his coat, now fully revealing just how expensive and regal his clothes really were; as true an indication of his status as any, from a distance. He pulled back the coat around his knees also, feeling much less stuffy already.

"It's not nearly as cold down here as I'd expected."

"Well, it's only the mountains where it gets really cold this time of year," the driver replied confidently, as if he were an expert. "The highlands filter the warm air from the sea with the cold from the mountains, I suppose. I don't know."

He shrugged, no longer appearing quite so confident. *You are a traveller. You know. My status does not diminish truth. Good enough though,* Tristan thought. That would do.

"I can see that now, obviously, but because it's colder for a patch down south, people exaggerate it like folklore, apparently. Seriously, you'd think it was fucking magic from the way some people talk about it."

"Forgive me, Sir Tristan, if I'm too bold, but it sounds like you've been talking to the wrong people."

Tristan's eyebrows shot up and a smirk materialised, easing the driver's newfound nervousness at having said such a thing. He patted him on the back.

"No need to apologise. No points of favour deducted for speaking the truth. Not while our Emperor rules."

The carriage rumbled round a sharp corner to the left, the flat land now opening up. There were many buildings here, a few of them considerably bigger than others. He spotted the spire of a church, sharp on new found sunlight, the roof of what might have been a granary, tall and rounded. As the carriage was pulled along down the long, straight road, people outside their houses stopped and stared, while others came out from their houses just to see what the commotion was all about.

It occurred to Tristan that an imperial carriage flanked by four horsemen clad in Aurailian armour entering their isolated little town must have been quite a sight. He smiled at the thought, and imagined what might have been going through their heads as he stared into their eyes. He of noble stock, of a southerly complexion, and indeed by his thin nose and smooth face identifiable as the son of a lathe-man; there was no mistaking his outlandish comport for that of even a highland lord. He was feeling good about this all of a sudden. He nodded at each and every one of them and, in return, a few of them bowed and curtseyed to him. From the opposite direction, a young child of seven or eight years ran towards them with great enthusiasm in his bound. As seemed to be a theme of this place, he wore a simple, yet smart, leather getup, and his length of dark blonde hair was swept back neatly at either side of his head, wind-whipped where it hung just below his ears.

When the boy reached them, he paused for breath, and then walked backwards in a charming fashion, rather than simply turn around, keeping level with the carriage, and Tristan in particular.

"Afternoon, young man," Tristan said with gusto, tipping an imaginary hat.

"Are you here to see my father?" the boy said excitedly.

"Who's your father then?"

"He's called Lennord Brodie," the boy informed him.

"In that case, I most definitely am here to see your father."

"You'll want to see his inventions then?"

"That *is* why I'm here."

"My name is Isaac, by the way," the young boy continued, obviously eager to please.

"Sir Tristan, at your service."

Tristan leaned in to the driver and patted him on the shoulder, at the same time keeping an eye out for the man he was supposed to be meeting.

"Just steer this thing over here and set it steady."

"What about your sleepy friend back there?"

"Leave him be for now; I'll wake him when I need him. Besides, he'll probably get terribly vexed if we disturb his hibernation before it's time," Tristan snorted in jest.

He clambered down from the carriage and brushed his jacket down, smoothing it out that he might look appropriately smart, running finger and thumb down the wavy folds either side of the buttons. He tilted his head on one side and smiled at the boy.

"Lead the way, young master Isaac."

The boy called Isaac laughed at the tall man's forced peculiarities, and hurried on ahead, with Tristan striding in tow, doing his best to uphold his status with his presence and posture alone.

At the end of the straight road, before it veered into a sharp right turn, a door opened, and in the doorway stood an ordinary-looking, blonde man of few more than thirty years, seeming extremely anxious. The anxiousness turned to puzzlement the moment he got a good look at the man he was supposedly going to be doing business with. Sir Tristan's mind worked to anticipate his thoughts: jet black hair slicked back, posture as straight as could be, and his clothes, his ring, and a ceremonial shortsword he wore on his belt were probably worth as much as his house. Most notably of all though, he was very young indeed; no older than, say, twenty, and his face showed supreme confidence. The inventor called Lennord Brodie was right to be sceptical.

"Good to meet you," Sir Tristan said pre-emptively as he crossed the border of the road and onto the man's land.

Young Isaac stepped out of his way and watched tentatively from the sidelines. Tristan stuck out his hand forcefully and the bewildered man in the doorway shook it.

"I am Sir Tristan Almaric."

"And I am Lennord Brodie, Sir."

His brow furrowed, and he grasped for the right words.

"You are...much younger than I had been told to expect."

"Ah," Tristan replied energetically, if nervously. "That's because I'm not a representative of Count Andrews."

Lennord's gaze was drawn beyond Tristan, who smiled at the further surprise befalling the man. Above the carriage, a dark green flag of deceptively wispy cloth fluttered in the wind, bearing an image of the great red castle tower of Aurail, Harmony, rising up from a green field, flanked by two smaller towers, Heart and Blood, which bore its likeness of colour. The four guards surrounding it wore grey armour like flint, if flint could cast a shine like the sun that peeked through the clouds, just in time for a fortuitous meeting, and the same picture motif took centre stage on their breastplates.

"I see you carry the Emperor's banner with you."

Tristan nodded excitedly in recognition.

"That's right. I herald from the capital, under direct orders from my liege, Emperor Richard Llambert, fourth of that name, which is why I'm later than you probably expected. The city's been abuzz with energy recently, very hectic, but now that the coronation is over, the Emperor is keen to get to work at once."

"Very good. Well, anyway, come in, come in."

Lennord ushered him in and offered him a chair at the dining table. A brown-haired woman of about the same age as Lennord stood waiting with a steaming pitcher already in hand and cups lined up in a row in front of her.

"Would you like some tea?" the woman hurried the words. "It's a local blend, so it might not be like the glamorous stuff you're used to up in Aurail."

"No, I'm sure that would be fine. I quite enjoy sampling different cuisines anyway."

The three of them were seated at the table now, and Isaac was sitting on a chair at the edge of the room, watching proceedings with barely restrained excitement. Tristan was back to twiddling his fingers on his lap now, playing with words in his mind for an appropriate icebreaker.

"So, I hear you want to do a service for the Emperor," he settled on.

"I really just want the means to conduct my research properly," Lennord replied more bluntly than he had probably intended.

"Fine by me. The Emperor wants you to do just that anyway. As someone who knows him exceptionally well, I can tell you he is quite a relaxed, modern man. He wouldn't be offended by your bluntness and, truth be told, is very uncomfortable with this accepted notion that the gods will one day bestow him or his ancestors with...magical powers, and many of the other questionable beliefs."

He waved a hand as if his mocking tone weren't emphasis enough, very conscious that both husband and wife took stock of this, for better or worse. Tact was required. Lennord and his wife sat awkwardly in silence, seemingly hoping Tristan would have more to say.

"So, Lennord, tell me about yourself," Tristan continued. "The Emperor is keen on the idea that the people at the forefront of his renaissance should be more than just names churning out work for him. All men have stories."

"Well, I'm not sure what of interest there is to tell but, okay, I'll try," Lennord said, already frantically searching his memories for some nuggets that might intrigue his guest. "I grew up in County Flatlands, actually. I always wanted to be an inventor I suppose, always playing around with any mechanical devices I could get my hands on, looking for faults in them, and in everything around me, really. I came to County Highlands because I'd heard about some strange metals being dug up around here. Didn't know exactly how significant it was at the time, of course."

"No one did," Tristan interjected helpfully.

"No, I suppose not. But it was here that I met my lovely wife, Gèyll."

Lennord put an arm around her and squeezed her arm. She grinned at Lennord, then at Tristan, with such sweetness that he couldn't help but smile back. Lennord pointed outside to two children playing with a leather ball which was well made considering it was, essentially, a sack.

"That brown-haired boy is our eldest son, Lucian. He turned eleven just a couple of months ago."

"And the blonde boy?" Tristan said of the other child, who looked to be a tad younger than Lucian.

"Oh, that's Lucian's friend."

"And my friend," Isaac said, from his spot in the corner.

"And your friend, yes," Gèyll replied softly. "Why don't you go outside and play with him then?"

"In a minute I will."

Isaac fell silent again, still watching the three of them, interest fast waning.

"That's Isaac. He's our second eldest; he's seven."

The Voice of Kings

"Yes, we've been introduced already. A fine young man, by my reckoning," Tristan said, raising his eyebrows at Isaac, who did the same back at him.

Lennord leaned round in his chair and pointed through to one of the bedchambers, to an even younger boy with dark blonde hair, like Isaac's, hunched over a book, meticulously following the words with a finger and silently mouthing each one.

"I don't know if you can see from where you're sitting, but that boy there is our youngest son, Marcel. He'll be five soon. And that's it. For now, anyway."

"Good man," Tristan said with a smirk. "No, honestly, your passion for your family is quite touching. And then there are your supposed talents to consider. The perfect renaissance man, as I think the Emperor would say. Speaking of which..."

"Ah, I have a number of showcases prepared already."

As Lennord carefully lifted a large wooden crate onto the table, Tristan finally took the opportunity to have a long swig of his tea. He had done it out of courtesy, but realised as the steaming drink touched his lips and swept over his tongue that he had been quite parched and continued to drink until it was nearly all gone, conscious to maintain noble composure as he did so. He gasped for air, with his belly now ablaze with warmth he had not expected to find in this place. He lifted the mug to Gèyll and nodded in satisfaction.

"Where would you like me to start?" Lennord asked.

"Just do as you wish. It's your work; I can't tell you how best to pitch it."

Lennord reached into the crate and began dumping lumps of metal on the table, some small, some quite large, and of varying shapes, with colours ranging from a dull grey to a shimmering white. Tristan tapped his fingers in time with a silent rhythm in his head, watching with simultaneous interest and amusement in equal measure as the man opposite him started arranging the metals into rows, but kept his mouth firmly shut. Sitting back in his chair, the inventor cocked his head back. His eyes scanned the metals to make sure they were arranged correctly. At Lennord's side, Gèyll sat calmly, unfazed by her husband's behaviour. Tristan wrote another mental note; Gèyll appeared to have some involvement, or at least understanding, in his work, and was not a clueless bystander as he had thought.

"This is probably not news to you," Lennord said, "but we had better be clear now, to avoid any misunderstandings later. These pieces of metal look different but, as far as I can tell, are all Sèhvorian steel. The pure white one on the end there is the purest of the lot, and somehow stronger for it. All the others seem to have been diluted into alloys of some kind, naturally, mind. Some of them might even be a different kind altogether. Are we on the same level so far, Sir?"

"Of course," Tristan said, remembering to straighten his back and place his hands over his knees for a more lordly impression.

"I only ask because I've heard reports from as far as northern Alassii of other differences still, in Sèhvorian steel."

The Shadow Tongue

Tristan sniffed, and scratched his nose. He noticed, once again, that he was quite thirsty. The last of his drink seared down his throat and that warm feeling ran through his body again so that, now, the knight was fully content in the welcome he'd been given. Nodding all the while, he placed the mug on the table with deliberate care. In his current state of empathy, he also noticed that the house was quite bare of life, and wished for Lennord to impress him so that he could be granted the money he deserved. This, he chose not to mention, and thought back to the task at hand.

"Yes, I've heard that too. And, thus, it bears even less relevance to the Isle of Sèhvor if it's true."

"I'm sure I could look into it if I had the resources. And even these, maybe."

Lennord reached into the crate. There was a rustling of a paper and objects clanging together and, when he removed his hand, he was holding a crystal, fairly spherical, if notched, and about the size of a large apple. For the most part, it was a pure white, like the one piece of Sèhvorian steel on the table, though with a flat effect, not shiny, and smudges of red and blue visible below the surface. Tristan's regal mannerisms slacked and he leaned in, his chair creaking as he peered at the stone, now sitting in the middle of the table, with fascination.

"That's a fine specimen. Not that I'm as qualified as I hope you are, you understand, but it certainly looks quite special. I travelled here with one of the Emperor's inventors. I'm sure he'll have something to say about this."

"I have some notes written down which I hope he'd find interesting as well. I've been experimenting a lot with these things, and the chemical reactions you can make or prolong with them, so I've had to write things down. Most of it's drivel, of course. Most people would find it very tiresome."

"The crystals and steel are at the heart of Lennord's fascinations, really."

Gèyll spoke with some excitement, but the simple fact she had decided to speak had piqued Isaac's interest, who now was looking very bored and whose attention had been shifting to various points around the room for some inspiration.

"There's a lot going on at the mine," Gèyll continued. "It looks like there could be something really intriguing down there."

"Ah, we do have strict safety measures in place, of course," Lennord defended.

There was silence. Isaac was looking away from everything else in the room, and now back at the group again. Tristan grinned and shrugged to ease the tension.

"You know, you really don't need to feel so nervous around me. If you can do what you say you can do, you have nothing to worry about. Why don't you show me what else you've got in there?"

"Oh, of course."

The Voice of Kings

This time, Lennord took from the box a handful of parchment rolls and unravelled them on the table, overlapping them and pinning down the edges with the lumps of metal. Tristan dragged one at random to his side of the table and studied it while Lennord was finishing his arrangements.

In the centre was a cross-section of a cannon, with various annotations linked to it with arrows. He squinted and scanned the paper with scrutiny, not understanding much of the technical explanations. There were two major components, from what he could tell, to these schematics, one being a cut on the weight, and the other, being the most highlighted factor, was a series of mechanical workings linked to a pump which, supposedly of ease, could be used to adjust the height and trajectory of the cannon while its base remained firmly on the ground. It also appeared to have a wider base than most cannons, and stronger wheels to compensate for the added downward force when using the pump.

A curiosity struck Tristan's mind. Out of nervousness, he'd read his brief more thoroughly than most would. Pushing the paper away, he leaned back in and placed his elbows on the table, interlinking his fingers in a manner he assumed looked very professional.

"When I read your application, there was no mention of designs such as this one. Why are you branching out?" Tristan enquired.

"The application instructions said the Emperor would be looking out for military applications, so I spent a few weeks working on that. It could probably use some tweaking, but…I don't know yet."

"You should really just take those official statements with a pinch of salt. As far as I can tell, they're almost always run through the Emperor's council first, so the wording is not precisely his own. Still, it would be a waste not to use this."

Twice he slapped his hand on the cannon schematics and grinned in appreciation. In the corner, Isaac sighed and was now impatiently waiting for something interesting to happen.

"I told you that you'd get bored," his mother said. "You don't have to stay here. Why don't you go outside and play for a while?"

Isaac jumped from his chair and ran to the door. Outside, Lucian and his friend were still playing with the ball, having set up rocks against, presumably, the house of the friend as a means of scoring their little game. Isaac hesitated. He turned back to Tristan and bowed earnestly, if briefly. He cleared his throat.

"Good day, Sir."

~

He darted out the door like a shot and didn't look back. First of all, the royal carriage was too fascinating not to be drawn to. Aware that he was gawping at the gold and silver swirling patterns, crawling all over it like vines, he, nevertheless, kept running at his own risk. And the guards, too, were high and mighty on their horses that contentedly kicked at the dirt. Lucian was guarding between the rocks, and held the misshapen ball under his foot as Isaac rushed over to them. Isaac skidded to a halt and looked between the two of them expectantly.

"Why were you in there so long?" Lucian asked. "It can't have been that interesting."

"I got bored, so I came out here."

"So nothing at all then?" Kester said hopefully.

"They're just talking about royal stuff. But they don't get bored by it. Oh, but there's something going on at the mine. That's what I heard anyway."

Lucian frowned at him disapprovingly and shook his head as if he had done something wrong. He kicked the ball up and caught it.

"That's not news."

Isaac fired the same look back at his brother.

"There's a wall of Sèhvorian steel stuck in the rock, somewhere down there," Lucian continued, now juggling the round piece of sack. "Father told me a couple of days ago."

"Is it the proper stuff? I mean, proper white steel?"

Kester's curiosity had peaked now, and there was a twinkle in the eye of Isaac. Lucian had seen this and his shoulders drooped at what he knew was about to happen. He sighed deeply in disappointment that he was going to have to tag along. The ball fell, and this time he tucked his hands in so that it would hit the ground. He stamped his foot on it but didn't look at it, being too busy weighing up the intentions of the two boys standing opposite him. Noticing his brother's fussiness awakening, Isaac thought simply to run right now.

"I don't know what it looks like," Lucian said at last.

"We could always look into it ourselves," Kester, inevitably, replied.

"Why would we want to?" Lucian insisted half-heartedly, already giving up. "We'll probably stop caring the second we get there."

"You're being uptight again," Kester said with a daring smirk.

"I'm *not* uptight."

"You are," Isaac chimed in.

Lucian took another deep breath and looked down at his feet, which were now lightly kicking the ball back and forth between them. *This is a lost cause for him*, Isaac shouted very loudly in his own head, as if drowning out his own thoughts might be enough to make Lucian listen. *You may as well make the most of it Lucian*, his silent words pleaded to dead air.

"I'll show you why you shouldn't care. A few seconds down there, and that's it."

Lucian was careful to direct his scorn only at Isaac, not Kester Irvyng, by keeping his sight locked on him.

"You've been down there longer than that," Isaac grumbled, now in tow behind the agitated Lucian, who was swiftly leading at the fore.

"Yes. Because I'm older than you."

The Voice of Kings

They veered off the stone road and cut between two houses to where the next stretch of road intersected. Most of the houses in this section of the village had vaguely been built to line up with one another and save space, by his father's designs, with enough room for gardens and for the road to cycle round the rows. One could see where his father's influence ended, and where the older part of the village began, because the houses were scattered haphazardly across the field.

The group of children made their way through the last row of houses and, as they stepped into the wide open space behind the village where the farms spread out, a strong gust of wind funnelled through the gap between two tall hills ahead, at Caedor's rear, and raised the dirt around their legs in miniature whirlwinds. A further gust raised it to Isaac's eye level, and he squinted as he waited for it to settle once more.

Before the heavy rainfall earlier in the day, it had been surprisingly dry here and, with the amount of miners coming and going, the ground had cracked under their boots. Isaac knew that his father had been helping make a more stable water pump system from the streams in the caves but, apparently, it hadn't paid off yet. Lucian swerved left and headed for the wooden door set into the hill, now wearing regret plainly for setting a precedent by leading at such a fast pace and for lots of other things, Isaac hoped, but he was determined to see it through.

He arrived at the door and swivelled round, now also surprised that he was somewhat interested to go inside but, being his older brother who tried too hard to be their father, took comfort in the fact that his interest was reasonable, unlike Isaac's.

"Having fun yet, Isaac?" he said plainly.

"Let's just go in," Kester suggested, stroking his blonde hair back absentmindedly.

The door opened fairly quietly as Lucian proceeded into the mine, much to Isaac's disappointment. He had expected it to creak ominously but, apparently, his father had meant it when he said he looked after everything. Whatever that had meant. Now he thought he knew. The inside, too, was not nearly as dark as he had expected. There were many lanterns hanging from hooks embedded into the wooden beams in the ceiling, which cast a warm light on the dark brown rock throughout the entire tunnel, or at least that of which he could see.

It was almost completely straight, for far beyond the counting of his thoughts which jumped back and forth to this and that, it caught his attention when, gradually, it curved out of sight. The three of them could see clearly all the way down, with only the immense amount of dust in the air to provide any obscurity in their vision. A short distance ahead, there was a hole in the ground, a makeshift wooden barrier, and a ladder leading deeper into the complex. Isaac fidgeted. Time to see what the fuss was about. Kester and Isaac ran to gather around the hole, while Lucian casually wandered over, not wishing to appear too childish or excitable.

The Shadow Tongue

"I wager there's something down here," Kester said.

Lucian forced a sigh, but argued no further and followed Kester and Isaac down the shaft, allowing them to take the lead for now. The lower level was even dustier than above, if equally well lit, and they three, not used to this environment, covered their mouths with their hands as they walked blindly through corridors, rocky and thin.

The others seemed to have the same idea as Isaac. The passageways sloped down at certain points, and they assumed this would lead them to their destination. It was paying off as well, for as the passages widened out, there were varying qualities of white steel ore embedded in the walls in fragments. There weren't many people down here today either, because his father wanted it cleared to give the Emperor's funny knight an unhindered tour, at a guess. They only spotted a few men, one alone further down one of the shafts, but they turned off into a different area, immediately short of him noticing them.

Finally, the white metal fragments got bigger and bigger until, eventually, they came to a dead end and, there before them, was a giant wall with less than half the obscuring rock chipped away, but what had been removed showed what appeared to be one giant, connected sheet of pure Sèhvorian steel, the light of the flames nearby gleaming off its perfectly smooth surface. As the three of them drew closer, the light, from their perspectives, continued to creep all across it, amplified back at them. Kester, who was now stroking his dirt ridden hair once more, flicked one of the lanterns nearest to the wall, and the light ricocheted with stunning majesty all around the cave, shooting through the pile of dust riled from the lantern's top in what looked like a thick, white beam.

The lantern's joyous swaying was slowing and, with it, the light on the shimmering wall seemed still once more. They were all impressed by this discovery, including Lucian, who stared at it with his mouth slightly ajar in awe before he realised this was not how he should be acting. Luckily for him, Isaac was transfixed to the white steel and, though his brother's amazement was plain to him, it was at his vision's edge where nothing mattered, for nothing there was white of magic sheen.

"Are we done here then?" Lucian managed to spurt out with a certain forced degree of impatience.

"Why would I?" is how Isaac replied, blankly.

Kester saw a pickaxe on the ground and smiled to himself. He stopped stroking his hair and held it down at the back with both hands, relaxing himself for the ensuing hilarity.

"Ho, Isaac, I bet you could smash through that rock if you tried," Kester suggested.

Even Isaac was sceptical of this, but picked up the pickaxe, with some difficulty, and put his whole weight into swinging it forward, nearly tripping in the process. The axe chipped a few pieces of rock away, mostly just by the fact that it hit, with little to do with anything Isaac did, having stumbled back and dropped the axe. Kester raised his eyebrows and grinned in amusement, and Lucian barely restrained a laugh before remembering none of this was appropriate and cleared his throat, ready to make a point, and make it well. Except, he wouldn't, because Isaac's brother didn't know what he was talking about.

"Isaac, you could hurt yourself doing that. I'm going to tell father, unless you leave with me now."

"But..." he started to plead.

"Don't worry, I'm going to walk, so you'll have plenty of time to catch me up and stop me."

Lucian was already striding away and, before long, he was out of sight and his muffled footsteps were just a dull echo. Kester smiled and shrugged, hurrying after his friend, and soon he was out sight, out of earshot, and out of mind.

Isaac considered going with them at first, but was enthralled by this sheet of shimmering metal. He wasn't entirely sure what he would do even if he uncovered the entire sheet, but there were a few details in particular which grabbed his attention. Lines were carved in patterns in the steel, gravitating towards the centre, which was, as of now, completely covered by rock, and where he had chipped away at it, there appeared to him to be the edge of a picture carving. Such was Isaac's way that, when he found intrigue in something, he would see it through to a conclusion, be it a proper conclusion, or if the intrigue value was lost for some reason, or otherwise was forced to stop by his parents.

Though he had not taken in much of what had been said in the house today, the promise of a discovery, the meaning of which was not yet understood by anybody else, had caught his ear. It was that which led him here, even with his brother at the lead, and it was these markings on the metal sheet which towered above him, waiting to be uncovered, which kept his attention now. Such was his temperament that he wasn't going to allow it to elude him until it more visibly became a bad idea.

He hauled the pickaxe from the ground and swung as he had before; not learning from his previous mistake, but attacking with determination. The same happened again, with Isaac tripping and falling to his knees, but he had landed the axe well enough, though again not to his credit, and the picture was now ever so slightly more complete. Then more rock crumbled away.

He continued this process, to hack away haphazardly, sometimes even managing to keep a grip on the handle which, to him, was a sign that he was learning quickly. It made him feel stronger, gave him motivation, as did the image that he was slowly unveiling. The energy he was throwing into this endeavour tired him quickly and, in draining so much energy, he lost track of time before too long. He was absorbed by it, literally in part, for dust and soot settled on his face, like snow unperturbed, piling up on the hills in midwinter, the means by which he understood his extended term down here and, within Isaac's mind, he was making progress.

The Shadow Tongue

He flung himself at the obstacle and embedded the end of the axe into the softened rock, before rending it free with an almighty tug. Isaac was impressed that his blow had caused such an effect. He touched the lines on the steel. They were incredibly smooth, not remotely hoarse or sharp as he'd expected. He now saw that the part of the drawing visible was that of a head, possibly of a griffin from lands afar, and, as he ran a finger on the lines, a white light began to shine from the cracks. It blended with the reflections so well that he didn't notice it at first, but soon its colour changed, dark of brown it was, a leaf green flourishing as it brightened, and finally darkening into crimson.

The light seeped from all crevices. The wall began to rumble. Isaac took large, cautious steps back, *fleeing* halfway down the tunnel, as his mind already labelled his action. Rock began to fall from the wall, at first around the edge, the trail of destruction spiralling towards the centre. The picture was clearer now, its brightness defying the dust cloud, as was the context. The head had been that of a griffin. There were other large animal carvings, all arranged in an arc around something that was not yet clear. Isaac spotted a sea serpent, a drakeel, a horse of horned head, and many others which he did not recognise or that his excited eyes refused to focus on.

Now, as the rock around the bottom crumbled away to join the pile on the ground, there was visible what looked like water, connected to the arc of animals in some unseen way. It stood upright with the wall of white steel, shimmering eerily, and swaying at its fancy with more weight and density to it than water did. Finally, the last of the rock crumbled away, revealing in full the semi-circle anomaly. It rippled, the steel rippling smoothly with it, cracking as it undulated like a wave, and something tumbled out that made Isaac flinch, gawp, gasp. A skeleton it was, cloaked in a grey robe, old and worn. It fell onto its back and was still.

Isaac, again against his better judgement, could have sworn there was something strange about it that he couldn't quite place and, with his eyes open as wide as they could be, unblinking, he tiptoed through the mass of rock, grey rain stinging him, and took a closer look at the skeleton, as close as he dared. It was much taller than any human he'd ever seen. Seven feet? More than eight feet? Definitely, he decided, his stomach knotting, definitely. And he thought he saw extra bones and layers to the ribcage, though, of course, he was no expert. The skull was not quite the same shape; that he could see clearly, for it had been dented and cracked. A giant, Isaac assumed, half in wonder, half disgusted. Disgust won out. He was going to be sick.

In addition to all of this, Isaac could have sworn he smelt some sort of gas, pungent like a flower, itchy on his skin, and, suddenly, an immense wave of heat whirled through the portal at him, like a campfire being directed toward him by mountain winds, startling his black-coated hair. It clawed through smoke and, for but a second, through that grey sheet, his eyes perceived the steel itself seem to shiver. This was as much as he could handle. He jumped to his feet, nearly tripping in his desperation several times, and sprinted from the otherworldly device, muttering, in part, every prayer he knew. At the connection between the next two tunnels, he ran straight into a large man who, as he looked upon, he realised was the man they had evaded earlier, and he was in quite a rush also.

"What the bloody hell is going on down here? Why are you here?"

Isaac realised now just how terrified he was, his voice failing to obey him, his mouth thick with phlegm. But he didn't need to speak. The miner was already gawping at the bizarre event occurring, whose light was mirrored on his rough face, and Isaac was on the run again. The miner's gait was heavy behind him. Even he was scared, big and tough as he was.

By the time he made it up the ladder, he felt as if he might make it and, yet, at that same time, there was another rumble from below which almost cost him his footing. And then the tunnel heated up to almost unbearable temperatures. His legs whirred, such that he felt them eating themselves from the inside out, an ache, like acid. They took him for the door and he barged his way through, well aware of the roaring of fire behind him, sweeping through the tunnel far faster than he could ever run. He leapt to one side, throwing his hands out, and he unexpectedly rolled, with a jet of flame ejecting from the cave at a terrifying speed, blowing the door from its hinges and vaporising it to smouldering ash before it could so much as touch the ground. The ground was on fire, fast spreading over the dry earth. Isaac rolled onto his back and crawled away, staring into the abyss of fire from which he knew the miner must not have escaped. *Miners*, he despaired, and he might join them. Despair laughed, for at the tip of the wave there were flames of utter blackness, just little shoots, ever leading the destruction, licking the cool air like the tongue of a demon's mouth, intent to cause only pain. Isaac saw despair in the blackness.

Even from this distance, his hair was singed, and the air all around him rippled with such immense heat that pushed him to impart a shrill scream and, in unison, his lungs screamed for the torment it inflicted. So frightened was he- but a boy that the entire world seemed to melt around. There was just him and the catastrophe before his eyes that could not shut, already playing out in his mind one hundred times the speed, and at the same time a hundred times slow. In that moment, he felt he had been transported to the nameless realm itself, a shadow demon's toy, and how it loved his terror.

Chapter Two: Of the Brodies' Quests

Atop the tallest hill in the vicinity of the town of Caedor, the orange light of the midday sun that had bathed Isaac in its rays was now cloaked in the shadows of an overcast sky. The grey mass had moved in quickly over the land and was taking with it the shadow of the figure that loomed above him, ever holding its sword out to the north. Isaac looked up from his papers and out across the hills to the town as he waited for the light of the sun to return. He'd sat on the plinth at the foot of the great statue many times in the past and stared out across the wilderness but, this time, it seemed not such an ordinary experience. This time it brought back many memories of his childhood; of playing with his friends when he was younger, of being schooled by his father and following him up to this statue, where he would watch him contemplating the town as a queer, funny little thing that was always one step from perfection, hoping to devise new improvements and inventions.

And then, of course, at the back of the town there was the entrance to the exhausted and abandoned mine set dead in the hillside, his bane of youth eighteen years past, but not eighteen years dead, not to him. Isaac sat, unflinching, with one leg bunched up as he contemplated this place in his memories. Strange, it was, looking back now, almost quaint; like a dream he could still, somehow, remember from years long past. He had devoted so much time to understanding the phenomenon that had taken a hold of his mind that day and, even now, continued to make efforts to attain further enlightenment, conducting the final pieces of research before he made his move. His father would be leaving sometime soon, for the capital on business for the Emperor, and Lucian would be heading even farther north, to Mürathneè, for ambassadorial research. He intended to go with them.

So it was that such nostalgia was forced upon him. The town had truly evolved under his father's guidance, more than he had ever considered. It was such a gradual process but, now that he was on the cusp of leaving it for gods knew how long, he realised just how much better built the houses were, and how much more convenient the amenities were, how piping a fixed chamber pot from a dozen houses into an iron-lined underground reservoir must have been a nightmare to bring his sanity into question, that poor, stubborn, ingenious fool of a father.

He cracked a smile as he spotted two figures of roughly the same height outside his house that appeared to be gardening; matchsticks to him. He stood up, dumping the papers that were in his hand into the satchel by his feet, and squinted. One had vaguely fair hair, the other dark, being the only major distinction between his sister and mother at this range. His mother was wearing one of her quite plain, green dresses, and Kate was wearing one which she had insisted on making on the basis of expressing creativity but, really, she was an unimaginative young woman and had just copied the design of her mother's dress, with a few added frills and flower patterns.

Isaac stretched his arms and took in a long breath of the cool summer air, staring up at the sky where the clouds were condensing to the point where, soon, it would be black as night and, with it, there would be a downpour. To his right, an animal growled. Isaac turned and jumped at the sight of a wildcat staring straight at him, baring its teeth, still scowling and keeping its body to the ground, as if ready to spring at him. Isaac cocked his head to one side and stared directly into the cat's eyes in a vague attempt to understand it. It was unusual, he thought, for a wildcat to deliberately approach and provoke a human. It looked lost and confused at that, and was probably threatening him in fear.

He knelt in both respect and caution, and reached for his sword, which was lying on the stone plinth. At first, he held it out, still, and then, in a flash, half unsheathed it, and the cat shot him one last scowl and scurried away. Isaac's eyes followed it as it disappeared over a sharp dip in the landscape and snorted in amusement at nothing in particular but the randomness of the encounter. He looked east, back to the town again, standing perfectly still on the hill as if tempting the swirling clouds to drench him.

From the left, something distant entered his peripheral vision, distracting him once more from his nostalgia. A horse was being ridden into town with the great haste that, generally speaking, only a courier, a race, or a soldier's horse could attain. So, presumably a courier's horse then. As well as this, the horse was caparisoned, unless his eyes deceived him with imagined refineries; perhaps the banner of the Count, then. He wracked his brain for any more information he had ordered, but could think of nothing. Puzzled, he scratched his head. There was the chance, of course, that the rider was here for another person, despite how little most people around these parts used the Count's courier service.

Without real need, he straightened his clothes in an attempt to look more presentable; even at times such as these, where he wore but a simple, brown, leather doublet and a woollen overcoat, he would often unconsciously smarten his appearance. When he'd finished tightening the ties on his studded boots, he leapt to his feet, swung the satchel over his shoulder, and ran for town.

No more than two or three minutes later, Isaac arrived at the last small hill and slid down the, now damp, slope dexterously, holding his arms out either side to balance himself, before arriving at a slightly clumsy landing where the town proper began. At the end of the road, opposite to where Isaac now stood hunched over, panting for air, the rider was adjusting the saddle on his horse, just outside his house where his sister and mother were now contemplating going inside, as the density and speed of the rain increased at an alarming rate.

Isaac made slow steps down the middle of the road, trying to work out if he might have seen the rider before. The cloth on display was clear now; a clean cut silk, by the look of it, depicting Count Andrews' crude, abstract standard of a black falcon on a grey-green background. Next to it, smaller than the primary picture, was printed a picture of an opened envelope, signifying his status as a courier.

The man mounted his horse, a great black stallion, and, without further ado, tugged at the reins, and he came roaring down the road at Isaac at such speed that he wondered if he was being expected to take the initiative and move.

"Woah, woah!" Isaac shouted, standing firmly in place and throwing his arms out.

The horse skidded to a halt and reared with a distressed whinny, slamming its hooves down hard on the cobbles. The rider, Isaac now noticed, was a burly hulk of a man who looked like he would come across stern and intimidating even when relaxed at an informal function and, now, he was just one step from dismounting and correcting the young fool who'd interrupted his busy schedule.

"What?" the man snapped, surprisingly reserved.

Isaac was very conscious, now, that the rain was sullying his image, though remained eerily calm in the presence of this man who grew ever more restless by the second. Something sprung to life inside him. He shifted his weight into a relaxed, yet authoritative, stance, and arranged his parted, medium-length hair in a way he thought made him smarter, without appearing overly obsessive to the irritated courier.

"I understand you must have a busy schedule; I've played the part myself in the past, but I'm wondering, what is your business here, if you don't mind me asking?"

The courier pulled his reins tight and dug the stirrups into the horse's sides, such that it jerked round and the horse's head nearly smacked into Isaac. Isaac, who saw in his stiff facial response how difficult a person he was, nonchalantly avoided the horse and stroked it, ignoring its somewhat rancid breath, and smiled to deliberately provoke the courier further. Might as well, he wasn't likely to remove the stick from his arse any time soon. The courier raised a hint of a passive-aggressive grin back at him.

"I have no further business here," he replied.

He reared the horse, very nearly kicking Isaac in the process, and galloped away without another word. Isaac didn't turn to see him off, or even to see what havoc he might cause on the way out. He just smiled softly, striking a balance between amusement and bemusement, and continued down the road to his house while brushing his coat clean of the wet mud that had caked it during the courier's smug theatricality.

Kate, who was still gathering vegetables, expressed an over-exaggerated frown at Isaac's muddy aesthetic.

"Never you mind," Isaac said offhandedly, and hurried inside while emulating the very same expression to the young woman.

In his room, an expansion at the far front left of the original building built half a decade ago, he slung his coat over a hook on the door and slumped into a chair by a small desk on

The Voice of Kings

the other side of the bed. From his bag he took several sheets of parchment, protected by a waterproof inner lining, and dumped them on the desk in a pile. He would ask around about the courier later. For now, he would continue with what might prove to be last minute research on the capital of Mürathneè.

He was interrupted almost immediately by the high pitched screeching of a bird of prey from outside. Though his window was right beside him to his left, the rain was now falling so strongly that he could see but halfway down the road, and his window was beginning to mist up anyway. Again, he blocked it out of his mind for now with the intention of revisiting that oddity later, but even as he turned his attention to his work, the front door shut and the same bird screeched its loud declaration, from inside the dining room this time.

Isaac dropped the piece of parchment and leaned back in his chair, folding his arms and staring up at the ceiling with an inkling of a smile in humorous defeat, as if the world was trying its very hardest to interrupt him. There was a knock at his door. Isaac shifted his eyes as far right as they could go to accommodate the door in his vision without having to break from his relaxed stance. He paused for thought to humour himself with the possibilities before finally sighing and answering.

"Yes?" he said.

The door opened and Isaac sat bolt upright. In the doorway stood Marcel, his entirely black clothes drenched, his blonde hair sagging over his face, and clutching a bag in one hand. Most notably though, a great eagle, bigger than any falcon he had ever seen, sat comfortably on his shoulder. It stretched out its wings, revealing murky white, downy feathers, and shook all the pent up water from its body. Marcel hid his face from the spray, half-delighted, half-disgusted.

When the eagle drew in its wings, it assumed a noble pose, its head held high; a posture it may have been trained to do. Or perhaps this was just its way. Marcel shut the door and fell into a chair on the other side of the desk, placing his bag there just as Isaac was scooping his papers into his satchel.

Marcel looked extremely pleased about something, even through his very sorry appearance. He pushed back the hair from his eyes and used the same hand to wipe the water from his face. The eagle twisted its head and observed with its watchful eyes in what might as well have been admiration at Marcel's movements, for all the grandness in its stance. Marcel now reached into his bag and removed an envelope made of an expensive and embroidered paper. He placed it on the desk and pushed it towards Isaac, who noticed the seal had been broken.

"What's wrong?" Marcel said in jest.

One of Isaac's brows was sharply raised. He stared at the letter and deflated.

"How many people have read this?" Isaac said.

"Everyone except you."

"Alright, but hold on. I'll get some light first. It's like the middle of the night in here."

Isaac opened a drawer and rummaged through the cluttered contents for flint and fire striker.

"Is that a Mürathneèan eagle?" Isaac asked, not looking up.

"That it is. It landed at Melphor originally, of course, and the courier took it from there."

Isaac finally retrieved the striker box, but didn't light his desk lamp at once. He lightly bit his lower lip and leaned back into his relaxed position again.

"Why would he bring that bird with him?"

"The cathedral considers it a matter of courtesy that the receiver of the message should see the bird that carried it. I don't quite understand it myself. I think, maybe, it's just them showing off, when it comes down to it. Must be a pain, having to escort this eagle across half the county. He was very clear that he had to pay for its food with his own money too."

Isaac struck steel and flint in the lamp with a ponderous expression, almost as if offended by being enriched with such unique information from a land he had recently been researching so diligently. The fire leapt up and illuminated the magnificent, golden coat of the eagle, and the brilliant green strips on its wings; a sight for sore eyes in what was, by and large, a relatively drab room. Isaac felt warmer already, and at that, was feeling better about his ignorance. Ignorance was the best motivator there was, after all.

"I did not know that," Isaac whispered, half to himself. "Still, that might go some way to explaining why that courier was such an arse, having to look out for that eagle for fifty miles of uneven ground."

"I'm sure he was already an arse, long before this eagle came into his life," Marcel added.

Isaac stared intently with a deadpan expression, so deeply that it seemed as if he was trying to look straight through his younger brother. He spoke plainly and clearly, and with a stern sensibility.

"You'll make a terrible priest, you know that, don't you?"

Marcel's initial confusion and apprehension at how Isaac knew why he was here, and the severity of his tone, took him aback at first, but Isaac cracked a grin and Marcel laughed in relief.

"No, but I have no intention of being a priest anyway; I'll be an apprentice. That means no giving services, just learning the creed and medicinal ken. And travelling, lots of travelling, I think. A lot of churches, nowadays, are teaching in lessons to benefit humankind."

Isaac nodded, burying his doubts in their old grave. It told Marcel that Isaac was happy for him, but there was also an undercurrent that told him that he knew this and didn't need to be lectured again. Marcel smiled meekly and considered, again, what Isaac had just said to him. His jaw dropped a little.

The Voice of Kings

"How did you know what was in the letter?" he quizzed Isaac.

"I guessed what it was, the moment you showed it to me, and I knew where it was from, the moment I saw the seal. Speaking of which..."

Isaac snatched up the letter and held it beside his head.

"This isn't just from any old nowhere town in Mürathneè, is it? This is from Harth," Isaac stated with absolute certainty.

Marcel shrugged and nodded. Isaac was aware that *he* was aware that he could be quite shrewd and couldn't be bothered to press him further, Marcel probably assuming that he would let him in on the workings of his mind soon enough. The letter read, and even looked, more or less as Isaac guessed it would. It was written exceedingly well and the handwriting was immaculate, scribed with a high quality ink. It outlined that Harth Cathedral would be very pleased to take on Marcel as an apprentice, and gave a short list of duties so vague they might not have bothered as a reminder, and a passively pushy "we expect to hear from you soon" sentiment, underscored by the signature of the cathedral's guide, its ruler, the duceverëe, so named.

Isaac carefully folded the letter and put it back in its envelope.

"Congratulations," Isaac said sincerely. "It looks like redrafting your application six times paid off after all."

"Thank you," Marcel replied in surprise at Isaac's genuine blessing.

"You will need to write back to all the others, of course. So, have fun with that."

The corners of Marcel's lips rose in a wry smile, and he shook his head.

"Another time, yes. It looks like I'll be leaving with Father tomorrow."

"*Tomorrow?*" Isaac spat out.

"When Harth Cathedral asks you to show up promptly, you take it seriously if you want to be taken seriously yourself."

"And Lucian? Is he travelling to Harth with you?"

"As I understand it, he'll be following a few days later."

Isaac swished his tongue around his mouth and gazed out the window for no particular reason, deep in thought. Suddenly, though, there was a subtle shift in his expression, at the moment he decided he would take advantage of this opportunity. He had already pressed his father about them going together, but hadn't expected to leave this early. Still, this wasn't an opportunity he could pass up. His face lit up and there was a sparkle in his eyes. The recognition was on Marcel's face. Marcel knew his look; a look that occurred when he was scheming something, when he thought he was being clever which, in this case, he prayed he truly was.

"That's quite a coincidence, now that I think about it," Isaac said, slowly and carefully. "I shall be leaving for Harth tomorrow as well."

Marcel folded his arms, and the eagle jumped in surprise. Marcel was not entirely surprised, however, though he was curious.

"Alright, I'll bite," Marcel said in animated fashion. "Why are you leaving for Harth tomorrow?"

"Father wants materials to mess around with while he stays in Aurail. I volunteered to find some for him. And where better to find top quality Sèhvorian steel than the very heart of the renaissance? It's a damn efficient society, or so I've heard. The Isle of Sèhvor ships over ten tonnes of Sèhvorian steel to the mainland every year. Duds included, but no matter. The prices should be very respectable."

"And I suppose this is what you've learned from reading all those documents you keep having delivered, is it?"

"In part," Isaac said vaguely with a wave of his hand.

"And another part is trying to explain what you saw eighteen years ago, correct?"

Isaac looked only mildly surprised, and shrugged.

"Well, I know you're more intrusive about this than the others, anyway. I'm not surprised you've caught on. You knew I'd never let it drop."

"Let's face it, you can't keep taking deliveries from couriers from around the country without people getting suspicious, no matter how much you insist how it's of "personal interest". You've stored enough paperwork in here to start your own library."

Something more simple to do upon my return, he mused.

They were now aware of someone moving cutlery in the dining room, and both leaned in over the desk. Isaac, in his paranoia, lowered his tone. If someone heard that he was still on this case, his father would certainly not give him the money he needed to go about his business in Harth.

"Suspicious to you only, as far I can tell," Isaac whispered. "Besides, that's my lot, I'm going to Harth with you. And there's only so much I can learn here. It's about time I got off my arse and actually conducted my own firsthand research. Nor am I too keen on embarrassing myself for the fiftieth time in front of Father, trying to find a shred of evidence in that damn mine."

Isaac was now conscious that he'd become a little hot-headed and his whisper had developed a sharp sting to it. He recoiled and put his hands up in apology, that Marcel must surely have noticed his loss of control.

"I get the feeling Father doesn't entirely disbelieve you," Marcel said softly.

"He knows something happened there. And he believes that I didn't lie. But not that I remembered the truth. Still, I learned my persistence from him, by my money, and, for every day that goes by, I have even less of an excuse to give up."

"How ironic," Marcel said dryly.

As two brothers, they sat in increasingly awkward silence, both of them frantically racing for a way to break it. Marcel's chair creaked as he shifted closer to the window and pushed it open to hold his arm out. The bird on his shoulder stared blankly at the intense rainfall but didn't move.

"How do I get rid of this thing?"

Isaac said nothing at first and held out a finger, the bird toying with it in its beak affectionately. With the other hand, he stroked its sleek feathers and, somehow, perceived the feel of raw power from the beast.

"I think they're trained to respond to exaggerated movements," he said at last.

Marcel jerked his hand in the direction of the outside world and, simultaneously, pointed to the sky. It leapt from its perch and majestically took to the skies with extraordinary swiftness and a quietness he had heard only owls achieve.

~

Lucian and his father saw a great eagle spring out from Isaac's window, take a sharp turn upwards, and soon disappear in the thick coverage of rain and mist. They were walking home from the end of the other road at the time, and watched it until they could see it no more. They both wore long, dark, hooded, woollen coats, covered with mud that the wind had thrown at them, and carried pitchforks, having worked on the farm for much of the day on behalf of another. *On behalf of all*, Lucian told himself, for personal posterity. From the confines of his hood, Lucian looked about with a kind of stern interest, as much as his large head covering would allow.

"Do you know where Isaac's been today?" his father said loudly, to counteract the rain. "I haven't seen him anywhere where he would be doing work, that's for sure."

"Probably doing his *own* work," Lucian replied vaguely, glancing back to the spot where he last saw the eagle. "Whatever that entails."

They made their way to the house and hurried in, hanging their coats up on a hook by the door. Both of them having short hair, they looked much more respectable than the wet dogs that Marcel and Isaac looked, groomed as they were, regardless.

His father and he turned, quietly startled, to find that the rest of the family were arranged throughout the dining room; siblings Marcel and Kate sitting at the table, and Isaac and their mother leaning against two separate worktops. They were all eyeing the two of them in silence, having obviously been waiting for them.

"What is it?" Lennord said at once, a hint of worry laced with his voice.

Mother shook her head back and her long hair was flung back gracefully, but there was a look of concern on her face, and an ironic smile.

"Apparently, another of my children will be leaving," she said. "Isaac tells me he's going to Harth, on business for you."

Of the Brodies' Quests

The smile became more apparent, as did her intrigue. His father glared at Isaac without an ounce of surprise. Isaac didn't respond.

"So he's told me," Lennord said.

"I've heard you're leaving tomorrow, so it would be best if I accompanied you," Isaac suggested.

His father tried to interject, but Isaac hurriedly continued, much to the amusement of Marcel and Kate, who bore smug smiles, knowing Isaac was now going to fight to get his way.

"I've handled business transactions before, at various locations some miles from Caedor. It seems to me that the only point of dispute here is that Harth is even further from home, which is logic I don't fully understand. The setup is simple, really. You give me a purse of money and I will find an appropriate seller. If I need extra money, I'll just make use of some of my other skills..."

"By which, you mean all the things you've tried your hand at and gotten bored with?" Marcel added casually.

Even Lucian smirked at this remark, and stared at his feet lest anyone notice. Isaac grinned sarcastically, his being the smugger of the two smiles.

"Shockingly, Marcel, your words don't inspire confidence."

"What makes you think you can stand out in Harth?" his father pressed.

"Lucian, how would you describe my negotiating?" Isaac asked confidently.

Lucian looked deep into Isaac's eyes, relentless and powerful, like some sort of test to break him. When Isaac's expression remained static, Lucian loosened up.

"Shrewd, I'd say," he finally replied. "But never unfair."

Their father rolled his eyes before fixing his focus on Isaac to complete his interrogation.

"One last question, and this is very important: Why?"

"I need a new challenge to sink my teeth into. I always need an interesting pursuit. Besides, I'll be interested to know if Kester's got his commission while I'm in Aurail."

Isaac straightened up and became serious all of a sudden. A sincere, yet pleasant, plea crossed his face.

"Give me a chance, and some credit, and I'll find you the best deal in all of Harth."

There was silence in the room. All heads turned to his father in anticipation at his judgement. He appeared tired all of a sudden, as if he had given up, but at the same time, there was a look of approval creeping on his face, and a slow nod of admiration.

"Fine," he concluded.

It occurred to Lucian that his mother and Kate may find it difficult to cope with the work requirements after they were left behind, especially after Lucian had left also, something his father was not far behind on, naturally.

The Voice of Kings

"If that's not a trouble for you," his father posed to her. He cupped his hands, as if in prayer, and a softer conversation seemed to weave through the air between their eyes.

"I'm sure we'll be fine, dear," she replied assuredly, if reluctantly. "I could always hire someone to help us if need be."

"It's not like Isaac is much use anyway," Kate added.

Isaac was pleased to see the proof, once again, that his smarminess was apparently spreading to other people. He ignored her in favour of closing the deal properly, however.

"I will not let you down," he said to their father.

~

It was an odd and awkward start to dinner, later that evening, as it could only have been. Isaac was far away, already there, white towers high all around him, there in grandest Harth. Marcel he judged to imagine it more fey, like the calling that would bring him there. If Marcel thought himself a pious man, then Isaac would have laughed and gone along with it as many times as needs be, but Isaac had scarcely asked the question why. Secrets he intended to conquer while leaving Marcel well enough alone, for he suspected his dreams were nondescript and based on a different promise of the unexpected. Now would have been the perfect opportunity to bring it up again. *It doesn't matter yet*, Isaac comforted himself with an inward smile. They all stuck to their own thoughts, not intruding on those of others, until the silence subsided; gradually, it felt like, starting with his mother politely scolding the lot of them.

"This is an unusual way of spending our last dinner together for gods know how long."

"A fair observation," Lucian admitted sternly on behalf of the rest of the family, nodding heavily as if he'd been about to say the same thing.

From that point on, the weight was wound up from their shoulders until, eventually, they could appreciate the succulent meat on their plates, surrounded by a variety of vegetables picked that very morning, some bought from the market, some farmed by his mother and Kate, from their own tiny patch of farmland.

And soon, Isaac was drawn in by his father's talk of his previous trips away from home, of which he always thought he'd heard everything in the past, but was, again, surprised to hear new details; interesting little details of building docks, and fixing roads and watchtowers, and the, ultimately, doomed attempt to reinvigorate Aurail. And, of course, there was his trip to Harth, where he praised their ingenuity and, yet, told it as it was to him, not realising he was romanticising any of it. Isaac's brain translated that romanticism for him, pondering this distant city while keeping an ear open for what was being said around him. To wit, in the heart of every Burtalian aristocrat lived a mythical figure called Áurǎíla, inoffensive enough to lend her name to a nation capital without ever being relevant, important enough to represent anything one wanted. Why, Isaac must have been a nobleman at heart, for that was a forceful way of thinking familiar to him.

"It's strange to think this house will have so little life left in just a few days," his mother said dotingly at one point, smiling reassuringly at his sister, young Kate.

"So it is," Isaac agreed in a loud toast that he hadn't intended, and repeated it silently, this time sounding far away once more.

The night brought with it stillness and, with that a silence, that even the leaves of the trees could not be heard rustling, nor the rain, which had stopped some hours ago. The road outside Isaac's window was illuminated by only the faintest rays of moonlight, barely visible but for a silver sheen on the cobbles and thatched roofs.

Within his room, lit by several wall lanterns spread evenly about the place, Isaac loaded the last of his baggage into two saddlebags, roughly balanced to make it easier on the horse, as it would carry one on either side. Lastly, he inserted his sword into an additional pouch on the side of the bag closest to the rider, concealed so that it could not be seen, but easily accessible should a wild animal attack while he was on the road and with no clear escape. Or a bandit. *Not a bandit*, he scowled to himself, old wounds peeling open at the proposal. That wasn't the way to think.

With this completed, he stood back and took in the emptiness of the room. It hadn't been bursting with life and colour before, especially, but now it was almost completely bare. Though he wasn't particularly fond of this room and had been meaning to further equip it and stylise it for more homeliness and comfort, he felt now that he would miss it, in some small way.

On the bedside table, he'd left out some cream and a razor, something which had slipped his mind until he saw it now. Taking both to the mirror beside his wardrobe, he began shaving half a week's worth of facial hair from him, and doing so more delicately than usual, so as not to leave any mark. During a business transaction, he thought, there should be no irregularities or unwanted distractions about his person. They should see and hear only what he chose them to. He was going to be dealing with a variety of strange and important people, if his research was any indication, and it was vital that he imprinted the right impression upon them.

There was a rapping at his door.

"Come in," he said absentmindedly, not breaking eye contact with the reflection of his razor.

His sister opened the door but didn't enter, instead inspecting his room from the entrance with mild interest.

"Are you going to commandeer my room while I'm away?" Isaac said.

"Maybe," she replied quietly. "I'd quite like the extra space."

The Voice of Kings

"Are any arrangements being made to help you and Mother with the workload while we're away? I'm sure I could find a servant in one of the towns if need be, and point him this way."

Kate was quite taken aback at his earnest tone, devoid of all sarcasm or ulterior meaning. Not that she had come to expect such a response per se. Rather, his mood had been, from her perspective, randomly changeable as of late, and the way he would respond to any given scenario would often be the opposite of what she had come to expect. He spent much time alone when not performing assigned duties;, he was conscious of this, reading mystery documents and records that were delivered on a regular basis. When he came out, sometimes he would act withdrawn and thoughtful while, other times, lively and excitable. He knew that, and it worried him that he might be casting an unruly shadow on his family. If they were to but stand aside into the light, they would discover his subterfuge.

"Um, no," she replied. "Lucian said he planned to stay and help for a few days. He'll sort something out on his own."

"Apparently he decided on that the moment Marcel said he needed to leave tomorrow. Reliable as ever..." Isaac trailed off.

Isaac dropped the razor in the basin below the mirror and stroked his chin in satisfaction.

"Your hair's still a mess," Kate pre-empted.

It was true; he hadn't really arranged it since arriving home from his hilltop read, and it had been deranged and deformed by the rain. Short of rummaging through his bag for a comb, he forcibly ran his fingers through his hair to make himself reasonably more presentable.

"You think I'm a bit strange, don't you?" Isaac said without taking his eyes from the mirror.

Kate recoiled a second time; this time more in embarrassment that he had nonchalantly stated more or less what she was thinking.

"I *have* been acting a bit odd," Isaac went on. "I acknowledge that. With any luck, I'll prove to you why when I return. What did you want anyway? You wanted to ask something about my trip?"

"Yes. Why?"

She shrugged and smiled politely. Isaac ceased what he was doing and watched Kate curiously. She didn't have a clue as to what he was hoping to achieve, of this he was certain, but had something on her mind.

"I could ask you the same question," he said.

"Oh, I was just thinking that you and Marcel seem up to something, that's all."

"Not Marcel, little sister. Just me."

Her eyes became slits as she tried to figure him out, though she was not malicious in her manner, that being outside her emotional vocabulary. Isaac knew she would not pursue the matter, or so much as mention it to their parents, so long as he didn't give her much to work with. She was a shy, but curious, young woman and was probably too proud to ask about this.

"Maybe you should go to Harth one day," Isaac said sincerely, after a short silence. "You're already showing promise in healing. I imagine you could learn a lot. And teach some things while you're at it," he jested. "The ducevereë's wife is a holy mirror, so you shouldn't be out of place as a woman."

She contemplated this idea in silence, and seemed to reach some entertaining conclusions which flashed bright across her face. It was obvious to him she had often considered that medicine and healing would be a more constructive pursuit for her than menial housework and farming, even having never put it in to words.

Surprisingly, he only, now, truly realised that he would miss his sister and mother, but what about them precisely, he could not yet tell.

~

"He's a 25-year-old man. I continually have to remind myself of that. I don't think he's immature, let's be clear, but..."

Lennord searched for the words, still pacing up and down the length of the statue; a purposeful and powerful stride, as it had to be to stride through the soaked mud. His own irritability peaked so much that the squelching of his boots was like cannons being fired next to his ears in pure spite. He huffed and put his hands on his hips, throwing his head back. He was not used to fumbling over words, but Isaac had provoked him, if inadvertently. It was inevitable really. It was the subtle, underlying smugness of his tone, and the hint that he had some master plan but, in reality, he was probably acting simply as he pleased.

"It's true that he can handle himself," Lennord went on, "but I still wonder why he's so eager to go. Certainly not to shirk duties here, I'm sure. He's perfectly capable when he puts his mind to it. I don't want to say he's hedonistic, but..."

"Don't say it then," Gèyll snapped.

Lennord's head fell forward and he stared startled at his wife. She was still resting on the thick cotton sheet but had sat up, leaning back on her elbows. The two lanterns still shone brightly on the statue's plinth, but the ordinary flame flickered and almost vanished at every gust of the wind, whereas, the moderate Sèhvorian crystal, nestled in the other lantern, provided a great flame which rose up at random intervals in a thin streak and, at the strongest gusts of wind, merely flinched, hissing a shower of beautiful embers into the night.

The Voice of Kings

It even showed many of the features of the giant statue with superb clarity and, now, a peculiar thought crossed his mind, as the oranges and yellows of the candles danced across his wife's face so elegantly. There was his wife, the marrying of whom being one of his greatest accomplishments, along with their children, and there, on the plinth, was the crystal, which was at the root of what might, one day, be his greatest work, his legacy. He tried in vain to calculate why such a thought had come to him in the first place, but he could discover neither the reason nor a way to conclude it and, like so many other threads of thought that evening, was lost and he was left with stress clawing at him again.

"I'll tell you what I think," Gèyll said, causing Lennord to snap from his daze. "I think he's a man who's had some tough patches in his life and has come through it all seeing things a bit differently than other men he's known. And that's basically all there is to it."

Lennord nodded wearily but didn't answer. Though his mind was scrambled from stress and over-thinking a predicament which may not even exist, he could see, even now, that she hadn't finished yet, and he kept quiet because she was almost certainly going to be completely correct in her assessment.

"Now I'll tell you what you think you're thinking," she carried on firmly, holding her curled hair back in place with royal grace as a gust picked up. "Lucian is doing some impressive work handling trade agreements and will, no doubt, one day soon, become a full ambassador for the Emperor. Marcel, of course, has chosen an honourable route of directly helping those less fortunate than himself, and then, of course, Kathrynne is merely 16 years old and few, besides us, would expect anything of her.

"Isaac, though, he has no master plan. Not that you and I can see, at any rate. He wants to disappear to the far side of another country for a purpose which, frankly, should be praised, and you can't understand exactly why, at a time when everything needs to make sense to you. So, you take out your frustration on him when, of course, you should be venting what *really* frustrates you."

Lennord pulled his coat in, suddenly feeling cold and vulnerable. Gèyll had given him the pieces he needed, now the truth that had become lost in his mind slotted together nicely. Suddenly, he felt like he was seeing clearer now; the storm that was his headache fading already. It was not uncommon that Gèyll would unscramble him when too many ideas vied for space in his head. She usually managed to put into words what he was thinking but couldn't quite access somehow, especially when trying to organise ideas for several inventions at once. She didn't disappoint, which, in thinking so, was a little like applauding the stars for showing themselves, only stars didn't want applause, nor did they deserve as much as Gèyll. His shoulders sagged and he let on a smile that combined relief and frustration as he spoke the truth that Gèyll had prompted.

"Aurail," he whispered under his breath.

Of the Brodies' Quests

He lay down next to Gèyll, the mud underneath the cloth parting as he did so, but not breaking through the thick blanket. The moonlight of Refeer forced through the dark clouds in thin increments and the odd star cluster shone brightly where it could but, for the most part, there was darkness.

"Aurail," he said again, loud enough for her to hear this time.

"You'll be gone some time, won't you? That's why you're frustrated, isn't it?" she prompted.

"At least they'll no doubt let me start as early as I wish. Travelling with Marcel and Isaac, I'll probably arrive a week early."

"From Lord Almaric's tone in his letter, they'll usher you in the moment you arrive, I imagine."

"He *did* seem quite worried, didn't he? Gods know how long the Emperor will need me, but I'd rather not guess. Tristan's letter gave me the impression that Aurail's economy dies a little for every day that King Michael introduces some grand new perk or scheme for his people, every time he has another cathedral or spectacular statue commissioned, and every time his citizens leave for Harth, the balance is tipped even further, with the Emperor taking it as some manner of personal offence."

With each word Lennord spat out, a fear arose with a subtlety that Gèyll could have spotted half asleep; a fear that he would be implemented directly in to the Emperor's plans. The Emperor had seen firsthand how talented Lennord was when he put his mind to something. He had an enthusiasm for him that made him nervous.

"Worst case scenario, he'll use me as his trump card to demonstrate the worth of our country. Or his wife will, rather," he added, a detail that he should not have missed.

Gèyll locked eyes with Lennord in sympathy, but also in hypnotic sincerity; a gesture that he didn't have the heart to look away from.

"Lennord," she commanded softly. "Do not get embroiled in the politics of the realm if, by the grace of the gods, you can *possibly* avoid it. Keep your head down when in the castle and do your job, and you might be home sooner than you think."

"Oh, I will try, you have my word on that," Lennord laughed meekly.

They gazed into the night sky together and, together, remembered other times they had done this. Even as Lennord opened his mouth to voice this, Gèyll spoke up with more or less the same sentiment.

"I think we can both agree that we came up here with more the intention to be at peace and probably, accidentally, romantically reminisce about the past than get bent out of shape about problems which are far bigger than us."

She was right again. He loosened up, and the candlelight offered new warmth as he considered this. Her face was warm also, not merely to the touch, but in its complexion. She wasn't young, here, such that, when her hair blew before her face, he was taken aback by an off-colour hair. *Is that strand silver?* And so she seemed to reply, *Don't be ridiculous.*

"Romance?" Lennord said hurriedly, trying to force it. Perhaps that was charming, in its own way.

"Like, how one beautiful day, 30 years ago," she said, "we hiked through these hills for hours, and talked about our ambitions for the town, and a thousand wonderfully irrelevant topics, and, in the evening, we made love behind this very statue?"

She paused for breath and a flurry of emotion rushed through the two of them.

"Is that what you had in mind?" she added with a hint of playful sarcasm.

"Something like that," he said wistfully, grateful of the memory that had been brought to life again, skin constricting him at the reaction of the large part of him that was actually his age. "Is that the unicorn constellation?" Lennord said, deciding it was his turn to evoke buried memories.

Gèyll shut one eye and lined her finger up with Lennord's. The dark clouds still swept through the sky like inky surf, constantly obscuring her view, making it even more difficult than it already was. When she finally acquired a clear line of sight, she squinted and shook her head.

"I have no idea," she said. "I was never any good at this and time has not improved my perception of it."

She deflated, beaten, but was sucked back in a moment later. Her eyes scanned the sky with scrutiny that, to her, seemed futile, but failed to stop her regardless. She ran her finger from the purported unicorn cluster up and left, and drew with it the shape of another animal.

"Is that the bear?" she said. "If it is, you were right."

She nudged him with her elbow in congratulation. Lennord nudged her back. The clouds parted quickly, as if by command, to allow the light of the scarred moon to shine through in all its glory. The enormous oceans on its surface glistened, its silver lands bright, and the stars either side of it sparkled such that they both kept deathly silent and were drawn in by the universe at large.

~

The morning was a warm one, and the sun was brighter than it had been for some time. Isaac stood in the doorway, adjusting the straps of the bags on either shoulder, taking in the scenery around him. It felt more final, now that he knew that he would leave his home just minutes from now but, at the same time, there was serenity in him, almost apathy, as if he had exhausted all feelings on the matter.

He considered, for a moment, the statue of Sir Martin Caedor, pointing to where he would soon be going. Now that he thought about it, he couldn't really remember the story behind it beyond vague mythical gestures, but what stuck out in his mind was how, one day as a child, while playing beneath it, his father's genius had struck him cold. It was he who had noticed that the body could not support the sword arm for many more years. It was he who had thought of the idea of stripping the outer coating and entrapping the body and arm in a metal mesh before seamlessly replacing the outer rock.

He remembered how amazed he was at his father's astuteness and the swiftness with which he sought to prove and act upon his suspicion. As he remembered this, he couldn't help but compare himself to him. His father was an open-minded man but, naturally, would never believe the stories Isaac spouted in the past, not when all his proof was naught but dust, and that dust had long since developed fractal dust, like a withered tree of truth. Evidence was the key, and he had a mind to get to the bottom of this, after so many years of wishing it to prove itself.

He imagined himself here, younger, and younger again. He imagined himself a fool, and worse. Like pleasant summer heat turning slick beneath his clothes, his joy was infused with anxiety. In his mind he killed the devil again, and smiled.

Before setting out, he adjusted the collar of his jacket; a smart-fitting jacket of light brown, boiled leather, its shined copper buttons left undone. Beneath it, he wore a loose, white shirt, the frills of which on the end of each sleeve just showed through beyond his jacket sleeves. His hair had been properly cleaned as well, and his boots sacrificed hiking efficiency for looks, though not so much as to be a detriment to his riding. Still, if this was as smart as people ever were in Caedor, he would still need a completely new getup to make an impression in Harth.

When he arrived at the stables on the west side of town, Marcel and his father were already waiting for him, though, thankfully, not to the point of boredom.

"Everything packed and ready to go?" his father said.

"Ready," Isaac replied.

Isaac remarked on his horse. These were highland beauties that would fly swiftly for long miles, even on the cobbled roads. As he affixed his saddlebags, his father watched him with beady eyes, probably weighing up how jovially he was taking the situation. Meanwhile, Marcel appeared to be in such a mood himself, absentmindedly patting his horse while deriving some small amusement from Isaac's fumbling with the straps on his saddle. Upon adjusting the positioning of the bags to his satisfaction, Isaac and his father and brother walked their horses back onto the road, through the town, and stopped outside the house where the other members of the family stood waiting to bid their farewells.

Lucian watched, with his arms crossed, as the others said goodbye a dozen times and hugged each other. Mother and Father held each other tightly for a time that, to them, would be just another flicker from the flame, like a drop of sand in an hourglass, but seemed to Isaac an eternity. They kissed with a passion that he hadn't seen in a long time, embracing one another as if neither was prepared to let the other one go.

The Voice of Kings

"Watch where you put your feet," his mother said fiercely.

Lennord nodded. All of a sudden, Isaac had the strangest feeling that he would regret not wishing farewell again.

"Goodbye, Mother," he said. "I'll make you proud." *Just watch.*

He added a hint of pride to his voice, so not to shock them too much.

"That shouldn't be too hard," she replied, more earnest than he had been.

Isaac ruffled Kate's hair as he walked by; an action which mildly annoyed her but she opted not to respond to, only smiling, as being such an emotional young woman, she, too, would surely regret him leaving without her letting him know, for once, that she would miss him. He stopped before Lucian. Although Isaac was no higher than five feet nine and Lucian was the tallest of the Brodies at over six feet, with his emotions subtle and his face serious, Isaac stared confidently up at him, while others might be intimidated by his stare alone.

"But we'll see *you* in a few weeks, I hope," Isaac said short of a proper goodbye.

"That you will," Lucian replied.

~

They mounted their horses, took off with a cloud of dust with their father roaring ahead at the fore, and soon disappeared round the bend in the road. It truly felt as quick as that, as if they had rushed to leave home. Kate blinked to make sure.

Lucian and her mother parted from the group, leaving only Kate, whereupon she sought to correct the damage done to her hair, listening to their conversation for she could not concentrate on herself until they had gone.

"This is more saddening than I'd anticipated," her mother said. "And sadder still, it becomes. Good will come of all this, though, I know it. I just have to keep telling myself that."

"I hope we'll all be wiser when we return," Lucian conceded.

"Perhaps you will return with a loving woman also, and be wiser yet for that," she laughed softly, gently patting him on the arm. What her mother didn't express was desperation, as Kate had perked her ears to hear.

It was to be expected, Kate thought, that her mother would bring that up somehow, before she missed her chance and immediately regretted it. But they were gone, now inside, and Kate remained, playing with the most preposterous of ideas, awoken suddenly by this startling turn of events. She had an inexplicable urge now to read upon the practice of medicine, ignoring the fact she did not know where to even begin looking, or that she would give up, if she discovered how. She didn't consider herself strong-minded in the slightest, and Isaac, in particular, had an annoying habit of inadvertently getting alluring ideas fixed in her head that she wasn't really prepared to deal with. In this case, she had an urge to emulate Isaac's example, and expand on her knowledge by way of courier delivery.

She bit her lip. She really couldn't tell if she was going to ignore her own fascinations or not at this point. It would be quite something if she didn't.

Chapter Three: Echoes in the Night

On the evening of the second day, the trio slowed to a trot at the approach of an inn; a three-storey brick building with a thatched roof by the left side of the road. A heavy wooden sign swung gently above the door with the words "The Emperor's Crown" carved above a generic picture of a golden crown beset with jewels. On the right, there was a large pond, bubbling with energy from the movement of hundreds of fish, and plant life resting on the surface, flapping lightly in the breeze. A brothel sat some safe distance from the inn, where the guests of each couldn't see the others rolling their eyes at one another.

"Always a place to rely on," Isaac's father said, nodding at the inn.

Isaac nodded back in recognition that he'd heard him. He half shut his eyes and slowly breathed in until his chest was fully inflated. He'd passed by here before, but had forgotten just how much warmer the air was down here, how the texture was so much smoother. Out before him, there was an expanse of land with bumps on the landscape, but no real hills, not as he experienced them day-to-day. Beyond the tall green grass and patches of woodland in the west, he could see the fiery ball that was the sun descending in its entirety on the horizon; a sight which he was not used to seeing when not upon Sir Martin's hill.

A quick look at the sign told him that this was, indeed, their heading; directly north through County Flatlands and finally arriving at Aurail. To the southeast was Melphor, Count Andrews' city, the grand library of which was one of his sources of research for his mission. As he stared down this road, he considered how far away his destination must still be; the so-called greatest city in the known world, a haven and showcase of all the brilliance of industry, society and the endless stretch of the imagination, in the purest form humankind had yet attained. And here he was, in the middle of the wilderness in another country, the only semblance of civilisation being a quaint roadside traveller's inn.

His purpose had never been far from his thoughts on his journey so far, but he'd spent much of it in a daze, half asleep, surprised to see the sun so low in the sky after what seemed like two hours since dawn. He concentrated, and breathed with great care. He played in his mind's eye his discovery 18 years ago, and everything he had experienced to get here now, all the emotions that had driven him, the people that had influenced him with even the smallest of nudges in the right direction. He shivered as a thought passed him by, and he concentrated further, to reaffirm that this was not in vain. He had to do this every so often of late, to ensure that it was a valid expedition and not a meaningless obsession, born from the fear of a young child, embedded in his psyche.

He came to a satisfying conclusion and relaxed, burying the complex machinations of his plan. As he dismounted his horse in the stable, his attention was drawn to Marcel, who patted his horse on the head. In varying ways, each member of his family had been an invaluable anchor for him, without any of which he would not be quite so sane, but Marcel was the only one who seemed fully aware of this fact, having spoken openly with him about his quest. Quest. A fey quality accompanied that word in this context, but all would be well so long as he didn't let the word pass his lips.

Inside, Isaac remained unusually quiet, studying the people around the room, from a seat beside a window, with fleeting interest, listening to the soothing flute music while keeping an ear out for key words in the conversation his brother and father were having that he might want to divert his attention to. Compared to Aurail, even, this building was like a relic. There was no indication of the passage of time, as was the case with all the other inns he'd ever visited, really. There had been no attempt to update it in any way, but the wooden girders holding the ceiling up had so little wear or rot that the tree they were made from might have been felled today, as was the case with many of the wooden appliances about the room. Even the window to his right, made up of many tiny panels, was so clean he could see a clear reflection of himself from some angles, and it was as smooth as it could be without it having been created with more modern methods.

The middle-aged couple that owned this inn were doing a damn fine job and worked well together, so what they could do with modernisation could really make them stand out. Such was the problem of getting comfortable with a fixed chamber pot.

It now registered with him that the conversation his brother and father had been having had met its closure and he turned sharply when Marcel spoke.

"Cat got your tongue?"

Isaac shrugged.

"I had nothing to say."

"That's probably the biggest lie I've heard," Marcel retorted without as much as a second to think about it.

"I'm really not so arrogant to think that every thought that crosses my mind needs to be heard by whoever is near me at the time," Isaac replied in a straight tone but with the hint of a smile.

He cut a large chunk out of his fish pie, and steam jetted out of the opening along with the delicious smell of all the unseen morsels inside. As he ate it, his father patted his pockets. His face creased and wrinkles morphed all over his face as he tried to remember something. Before long, he took out a rolled up scroll and unravelled it a crack, to check if it was correct.

"What's that?" Isaac said after hurriedly swallowing a piece of food.

"A letter to a woman in Harth. An old friend of mine actually, who used to live in Burtal. Assuming she's still doing what she was when I was there, she rents out rooms. I'll have it sent ahead to have her save one for you."

The Voice of Kings

"What's her name?" Isaac said snappily, tapping the table, now entering a serious business mode.

"Rosalynn."

His father thought deeply.

"What was her surname...?" he whispered to himself, lost in the emptiness where his memories should be.

"How much did it cost you, when you were there?" Isaac asked when his father appeared to be at the point of giving up.

"I will not discuss prices with you now," his father replied quickly and firmly. "I don't want to give you too much time to think about how you're going to con me out of more money."

Though he was undeniably serious, the look on his face suggested he found amusement in this, as did Marcel. This was not unprecedented, and his father called one of the owners over before Isaac had a chance to truly respond.

"Artoria, is it? Can you send a letter to Harth for me, madam?" he said politely.

"Of course!" the woman replied. She was too weary to be enthusiastic, but she gave it a go anyway; Isaac winced at the results. "It'll cost you five florin though."

His father rummaged in a leather purse and withdrew three coins; not pure gold but copper, as all but the highest valued currency had only so much as a pinch of gold or silver anywhere in it, laden on the surface with a minting press, which also printed its numerical worth and an image of the great castle tower at Aurail on the obverse, making it difficult to forge.

"I don't want to be rude, but I'd rather you didn't use that one," Isaac said with excessive politeness, charming with a grin as his finger pressed against the window, pointing at the bird cages outside, specifically at a very sorry-looking pigeon with its feathers ruffled and its form droopy and tired.

"Oh, no!" the woman laughed. "We just look after him now. He'd probably get lost over the channel to Mürathneè, poor thing, or eaten. No, we have a Mürathneèan eagle. Bought and trained it ourselves."

She skittered away before any of them could get a word in edgeways, to behind the drinks counter and took, from underneath it, a thin tube for keeping scrolls and letters in. She ran back to them in much the same excitable manner, and took Lennord's letter.

"My husband and I tried training a falcon first. As it turns out, most birds of prey don't have a homing instinct."

His father was not even mildly surprised, and indulged in laughter without a hint of irony, having met her before. Marcel nonchalantly sunk in his chair, as if trying to blend in with the wood, simply nodding in approval.

Outside, she held out the tube, coloured silver, in front of the eagle, for it to bite and inspect, this being the crux of the situation, and when she strapped the letter to the bird's foot, it felt the ridges and bumps in the material with its talons, all of these things indicating where it was required to go. The eagle took flight and Lennord stood, stretching his arms painfully. Though not aging at all badly, he was not as athletic as he once was, and the rough ride up until now had not made him feel any better. Isaac and Marcel had to accept blame, being eager to roar ahead.

"I'm turning in early," he said quietly.

Marcel watched him like a hawk as he plodded up the stairs, and stared a new hole in Isaac's head the second he was out of sight.

"So, why now? Why pick this back up after so many years?" Marcel interrogated.

As before, Isaac was not remotely shocked. He stroked his hair back thoughtfully, shaking out the dirt that the wind had accumulated there over the course of the day, and swished his tongue against his teeth.

"I'd rather not leave this any longer. As you said, it's been a long time. I always said to myself that I'd look into it properly some day. But the term "some day", I've noticed, is more a personal excuse for laziness than any sort of genuine aim. I want to show the world what I saw that day," Isaac said with rising enthusiasm, a steadfast passion brewing in his eyes, letting it have its fun to quash any doubts. "I want to know *exactly* what happened and, who knows, maybe there's a revelation somewhere here that could change the way we look at the white steel *and* the crystals."

His stare was that of absolute certainty. Certainty that what he was doing was not only of personal curiosity, but of historical importance. When he was younger, he wondered if that arch in the mine was a regular discovery; if the explosion that had obliterated the miner fleeing not 30 feet behind was an occurrence that, at least, was not unheard of.

Eventually, it had dawned on him, at first in increments but, one day, as an epiphany, that he held one piece of knowledge that possibly no other person did. Marcel recognised this in Isaac's expression and couldn't help but nod in admiration. Even he, surely, couldn't get so excited about his vocation at the grand cathedral in Harth. He sipped his ale and mulled it.

"Good answer," he replied.

"What is this, a test?" Isaac said with deliberate passiveness.

"I'm just very, very interested. You have a plan, I take it?" Marcel asked, shrugging and holding his arms out exaggeratedly.

Isaac sat bolt upright. This was something he'd considered a great deal within the confines of his head but, ideally, wanted to pass it with someone else verbally, before putting it through its paces. He was bustling with fervour. He felt an irritation in his fingers, as if they wanted to tap the table, but he remained still.

"I have three people I'd like to speak to, to start with," Isaac started. "The first is the Captain of the Mercenary Guild, Martello Jacart. You may have heard of him. He was found in a longboat off the coast of Harth, many years ago, when he was a just a boy. When he was oriented and shown a map of where he was, he didn't recognise any of our countries, and claimed to have crossed the Infinite Sea."

Marcel sat in silence, amazingly patient, occasionally taking a swig out of his tankard, but making no effort to interrupt, despite how odd this might have seemed to him; a trait which had first led him to listen to Isaac's story with an open mind a long time ago, and he'd become no more sceptical since.

"I came across various records by accident, initially. The ship he claimed to have travelled on, the Salet Antonia, purportedly never existed, I saw in some old documents. Its remains from the accident it was supposedly involved in were never found either. I would have left it at that but I came across other reports that a ship was spotted off the coast which matched the description Martello gave, at around the time he said. Only later was it accepted as fact that, yea, there was a ship of some description."

Marcel squinted, attempting to understand where his brother might be going with this, but he looked as though he'd forgotten that they did not share a single mind. He put a hand up firmly, but with reservations. Marcel couldn't read people like he could.

"Sorry, I'm not following. What does this have to do with what you're doing?"

"I was getting to that," Isaac replied calmly. "Supposedly, the ship was carrying not only large quantities of what Martello came to know as Sèhvorian steel, but also a number of revolutionary technologies created with it, as well as other materials; materials, by the way, that people could only guess as to what he was talking about. The way I see it, he could be like me. Obviously, something happened to him, and it was mighty strange, but none would ever believe a story like that. It would be a difficult situation for him, especially if he *did*, *indeed*, have memory problems *as well*, as was the explanation for his story."

"But he is a mercenary," Marcel supplied, as if Isaac had forgotten.

Isaac sighed and, after a flash of confused contempt, looked sullen all of a sudden. He dug into his pie and chewed it, savouring the taste before continuing.

"Yes," he whispered, staring out the window. "I have heard he can be a particularly difficult person to talk to. A very unpredictable man, I've read. I can only hope he will prove responsive."

He brightened up and moved on, forgetting all about Martello through sheer force of will.

"The second man is Vicentei Laccona. I know you've heard of him."

Even as Isaac released the words, Marcel was smiling and nodding eagerly. Their father thought quite highly of him.

"He's a true genius; a visionary without bounds, they say. That's the undercurrent of everything I've read about him. Admittedly, my interest in him is a much broader one, and possibly circumstantial, depending on what I can coax from Martello and my third man, Michael Santorellian."

Isaac's lips rose ever so slightly in pre-emptive amusement at Marcel's response. Marcel was lifting his tankard at the time, but almost dropped it when he heard those words.

"The King?" Marcel blurted, barely a question so much as a statement.

He laughed so loudly that people on nearby tables turned to see what the commotion was about, and he covered his forehead with one hand, the lute player smiling forcedly from his bench by the empty hearth pit to compensate for this euphoric rise. Marcel's face was rosy red now, evidence that the strong ale was getting to him, but Isaac remained stiff as a statue for now, waiting for him to find some composure before replying.

"I'm being serious."

"What cause would I have to laugh if you weren't?"

"He's the King. He has contacts with the best and brightest Harth has to offer. He has to maintain those relations to stay ahead of the pack. I'm not running blind here. I have an idea as to how I might attract his attention," he added obliquely.

"You're not making it easy for yourself."

"It was not made easy for *me*," Isaac replied plainly, and grinned when he could hold back the ironic joy no longer.

There was a glint in Isaac's eye and the way he relished the very thought of the plan that he was weaving at this moment, so vivid, it was, that Isaac almost wondered if Marcel could see the cogs of the meticulous machine in his brain running through every stage of it. Another curiosity caught Marcel's eye.

"Forgive me for being blunt," Marcel went on pleasantly, decidedly not blunt, "but how, exactly, do you expect people to help you if they don't know what you're talking about? Alas, if they knew what you were talking about, none of this would be necessary anyway, and fuck, Isaac, where technicalities are concerned, you can name little more than naught regarding that arch. So an uphill struggle awaits you, just to make people understand your position."

Marcel stopped for air. Isaac regarded the world beyond the window casually, fully aware that he was not being nearly as blunt as he would perceive. There was still an air of mischief in his voice, very distinct to his ear.

"I am so confident, dear brother, because knowledge can be viewed like a jigsaw puzzle, really. I have one piece, useless individually, we've established that, and if we assume the men I have mentioned each have a piece, or the means to acquire one, they might be just as meaningless alone, until I bring them all together. Perhaps, then, I shall see clearly.

The Voice of Kings

"History is littered with people who have assumed others have done what they had sought to do, simply because they thought it was of such importance that others *must* have had the same idea. Trouble is, those others often have that same thought. Eventually, someone must break the chain, of course."

"Fair enough then," Marcel said, more satisfied with the response than he looked to be expecting, as was the point. "You have done your research, I know that. I doubt neither your resolve, nor your intellect."

"Thank you."

There was quietness from their table, punctuated only by the slurping of drinks, and the increasingly raucous behaviour from an inn that was now packed became all the more apparent to them. Even Marcel paused to consider this, noticeably tipsy himself and starting to look drowsy as well. He beamed as another way to quiz Isaac came to him but, more than anything, he spoke with genuine intrigue beyond the hazy and muddled exterior brought on by the strong alcoholic drink. He folded his arms.

"What did you learn about Harth Cathedral on your quest for knowledge?"

Still sober and focused, at least that he could tell, despite having downed most of his ale, Isaac pursed his lips and stared at Marcel.

"Little. I know you won't get on well if you swear in the Ducevereë's presence, as you do with me."

"Duly noted," Marcel replied jovially.

"I believe you may have to cut your mop of hair, but don't quote me on that. And I know there's a degree of diversity throughout the city in how people perceive certain things, more so than here. You won't have to worship the King though, but I expect you know all this anyway."

"I think you're about two hundred years late on that one. That simply does not happen anymore."

"That was a real rumour though," Isaac said with a shrug. "Started here, in Burtal, as propaganda. A small movement, yes, but I'm surprised you haven't heard about it. And the idea of the world leaders being demigods is not entirely scoffed at there. Five gods, five countries, five magisterial family lines. Each god possibly representing one country, as is sometimes woven into the lore, and each family possessing the latent ability to, one day, control not only their people, but the world around them; a gift granted by one of the gods," he recalled as if for the first time, amused. "It's a fanciful prospect, in my opinion, but people still believe their own versions of it."

Perhaps I should start believing for consistency, Isaac mused a little too seriously. Marcel shook his head in tentative agreement, and he showed a fear which suggested he was being accused of being one of those people. Or of not. But he'd tried to make it irrefutably clear to his family, after announcing his intentions to seek a religious career in Mürathneè, that his choice was not influenced by a desire to reform to the half-forgotten old ways, or any of the radical new ways for that matter, but, instead, by a passion to learn and help people, born from whatever fiery drive that pushed Isaac ever onward, sometimes without his permission. That was the Brodie way, perhaps. Again, Isaac was made very conscious of this, and how he really did not appear, on the surface, the sort of person to make such a choice.

"I don't believe any of that," Marcel said strongly. "I certainly wouldn't pray to a king as a demigod. Besides, a king has had the luxury of inheriting his power. The burden is on him to prove he can handle it."

"I know," Isaac reassured calmly.

He tapped his fingers against one another and turned, thoughtfully, to the cackling laughter that drifted across the room from one crowd of drunken merchants, as he so named them, and continued to study them, as if hoping to derive some inspiration.

"Come to think of it, Father mentioned, the last time he came back from Aurail, that there were some wearying sycophants in the Emperor's court. So, maybe there's more of that sort of thing here than we think. We've always known too little."

Marcel shrugged in mildly interested acknowledgement. Outside, the guttural cry of a bird of prey swooped through the window. In an attempt to catch sight of it, Isaac realised now that there was darkness outside, and the only image he could see was the candlelit reflection of the room. When the two brothers made to exit, Isaac rummaged in his purse and placed two coins on the table that, really, he couldn't afford to give away. Between two fingers, he tapped one on the wood. Artoria rushed over upon successfully drawing her interest.

"What's this?" she said. "You've already paid."

"In Mürathneè, it's a courtesy from nobility. It means you've done a good service."

Bewildered, she ran the coins through her fingers as they walked away, but was of no mind to argue.

~

The Emperor rubbed his eyes; bloodshot and underscored by dark bags on his skin, they were, and made a conscious effort to breathe more steadily. A weight crushed his lungs, like a malevolent force, constricting them back each time he dared take in a breath of air. The lack of sleep was giving him yet more problems then, he thought to himself.

In such a state, sagging and hunched, his regal attire was ill-fitting and made his illness further stand out. Dressed in the fur-trimmed mantle robes of royal green, embroidered with interweaving intricate patterns of dark red and brown, and an expertly cut white fur collar, his clothes were well groomed, while the man himself drooped like a sick willow. Even his hair, usually a bright blonde, was so dirty from seeing such little care over the past few days and not being washed but by dirt-sodden rain. It was a mess, despite being short.

The Voice of Kings

He became tired of standing and gave in to the bench situated beside the door leading to the side courtyard. He'd seen better days, and he knew he looked the part. Under better circumstances, he might have been attractive but, such as he was, none could but wince at his drooping face as they passed. At present, he was wrought with gauntness, appearing strangely confused. He tapped the hard heel of a boot on the floor, the echo of which resonated up the tall, slim hall, heard only by the servant who was lighting the candles of a chandelier from the first floor balcony. Each time a fire roared into life, the Emperor further squinted, as if each one was a new sun forming in the sky. The fire lights shimmered up the walls of dark red brick as best they could, and on the reflective floor of diamond-shaped tiles too, either side of the rug that ran from door to door. It was more of notice now than ever, the brooding of the flames, the castle's motif of dark colours shining at him bleakly. At the best of times, this was truly a proud setup to behold, but now it dimmed his mood. He yearned for the fresh open air and the colours of nature. His dreams were filled with alternatives to end the suffering, of him stepping back from Aurail and saying, *What will happen if I leave it?* The city would taunt him and, henceforth, he would never be able to enter. Now he saw it with waking eyes.

~

In Aurail's hour of need, Tristan Almaric appeared.

The door creaked open beneath the stairs and his old friend was there, on the bench below one of the great windows, submerged in the bright charity of his sconces, and he saw it was really Richard's hour of need. Behind Tristan, his cloak, flaunting the green and silver of House Almaric, took sweet flight. His tight-fitting tunic of leather and velvet was lordly indeed, and today he felt it, far sprightlier than Richard, and he hurried over in lordly strides and now huffed to regain his breath, having run through the castle to find him.

"I can only apologise for my lateness, Your Majesty," he said with a short miniature bow. "I have been very busy at my keep, but I dropped what I was doing and came as swiftly as I could."

"Lord Almaric..."

There was an awkward silence as they wondered what to say next, but eventually smiled warmly at one another and embraced, as only old friends do. It might have looked a celebration, and perhaps it was, though their partnership had not always brought a strong yield. *Give it time*, he heard his Lady Evylyn say again and she laughed so: *the man will age like a fine wine!* The question of how to influence that was not yet relevant, that was the agreement.

"How have you been?" Emperor Richard asked.

"Well, very well. Better than you, anyway."

Tristan looked up and down him in jest, with a laugh.

"And your wife?" Richard said.

Echoes in the Night

"She is well also. I don't suppose I'll see her again for some time though. I at court, and her...well, people want her," Tristan said amicably, wishing they wanted her outside of Almaric Keep. Flowers didn't grow so cooped up.

"I wish I could have your problems," Richard laughed bitterly.

Tristan mimicked this, but there was an air of pity about it. Richard was, clearly, in one of his lows. Tomorrow, he might be on top of the world. Tristan allowed the clanging of metal from outside to distract him, and though, at first, he looked worried, Richard, who noticed his distress, was unfazed, and his worry turned to misunderstanding.

"What are we doing here? Making hay?"

"Indeed," Richard said as cheerfully as he could muster. "Come."

They exited the castle through the large wooden door and stopped at once, at the top of the steps. Before them, the path stretched ahead and split apart, weaving around expansive patches of grass, much of which was nicely presented with an array of flowers and shrubs, with the odd oak tree expanding the reach of its branches over benches and stone patios; an action taken to provide more aesthetic variety in an area of constant shade where other plants did not grow anyway. Upon the battlements of the dusty-red wall which arced around the garden and, behind the two men, the castle, guards could be seen patrolling by firelight. To their far left, presented by a significantly more decorated path. most notably because of the two statues of knights kneeling in respect, was the chapel.

All of this was as Tristan would expect it, but for the large area of the garden set aside for combat training. Between the paths, in the middle, a number of squares of grass had been set aside for this purpose, where dozens of men clad in basic steel armour were creating an almighty din, swinging blunt swords at one another and thrusting back with shields. All illuminated by tall candle stands, and presided over by, who appeared to be, Master-at-Arms Havdan Linch, whose usual role was rather more to play practise with soldiers more proficient than he.

Even from this range, however, Tristan could see that half of them were amateurs; this seen by his eyes that were so willingly blind to the subtleties of battle. The Emperor beckoned with a single finger and they began to casually walk towards the group. As they did so, Richard unconsciously straightened up, to appear more kingly; an unmistakable quirk to Tristan.

"What exactly is going on here?" Tristan said.

"We thought we might grow more plants there at first, but it seemed like a waste, so we decided on this instead."

Tristan made himself noticeably unimpressed with this answer but, more than that, he noticed a familiar transition in Richard, as if a different person was controlling his vocal chords. He chose to ignore it.

"But why are you training soldiers here?" Tristan pressed.

The Voice of Kings

"When King Alamier has finished squabbling with his peers in Mūrac, he may decide he'd like a little bit more power and head north to invade Burtal, or, perhaps, enemies will cross from the Infinite Sea. We need to be prepared for anything."

"There is no evidence whatsoever for such an event as that occurring," Tristan replied sourly, already piecing together Richard's point but playing along to make certain.

"I'm aware of that. But that's the line we stand on, and it's our job to convince others of this. And who knows? I may yet, one day, come to believe it myself," he said without the slightest conviction.

Tristan nodded obligingly and with utter patience, but couldn't help but feel that the Emperor was far away somewhere, not really listening to what was being said to him.

"You still haven't answered my question. Why are you training soldiers *here*? There are already designated barracks in and around the city."

"This is just one of many steps we're taking to move out from the squalor. The renaissance is what you can see and what you can hear; what you can experience for yourself. When we have visitors, especially those from other countries, they will see this and many other aesthetically pleasing displays, and they will see that our society is not to be ignored, and that it could be an important part of the new world. King Michael caught on to this a long time ago, and we should have too.

"We're catching up now though, that's what's important. We can bring Aurail into the new age. But if we hide all this away, I may as well grind all the gold I'm spending on this into dust and blow it to the wind from the Tower of Harmony."

The stoop returned as Richard's temper rose and his breathing became more strenuous. Tristan gave him a moment to relax, to regain his composure, taking this time to more closely study the soldiers. They were now level with the first rows of them, sandwiched between the horrific grating noises of solid metal being slammed together, bombarding them from both sides. It appeared that all the inexperienced fighters had been paired with seasoned soldiers.

"I just don't think this is the best pursuit you could commit yourself to," Tristan said after Richard had re-evaluated his posture. "If you want Aurail to get properly noticed on the same level as Harth, you'll need to look at the wider picture, at what's going on outside these walls and, with the greatest respect, I don't think you're fully aware of that."

"Perhaps not," Richard said softly, and trailed off. "We have more planned than this though. I sent you the portfolios of a list of people for you to read through and consider. I hope it reached you."

"Indeed. I sent letters to various people I felt were suitable to give this city a boost, but there weren't many. It might not amount to much."

Tristan frowned but remained patient, and even put on a small smile. He'd never taken their friendship for granted in the past, and didn't plan to start now.

Echoes in the Night

"Oh, don't worry about that. You weren't the only one sending out those letters. There will be many more people than you think."

They stopped to observe the training of a very young man, no older than 18 surely, and skinnier than soldiers generally should be. What was supposed to be a back and forth battle mainly just consisted of this young man holding his shield up desperately and stepping back. Even his footing was wrong.

"Is your old friend from that town in the highlands coming?" Richard said without looking away. "I gave him a high recommendation, I believe. I practically ordered you to summon him."

"Lennord Brodie. Yes, of course. No recommendation needed."

"I'd do it myself but...well, look at me. I obviously haven't been lazing about. I just stamped some folders with vague thoughts applied and sent them packing to you."

"Of course. I understand."

The young man practising, or attempting to practise, sword fighting was quite pale now, from exhaustion and fear of being hit. He tried in vain to parry an incoming blow, but his strength was not enough and the sword knocked his shield down.

It was only now that he noticed the Emperor and Tristan watching him, unimpressed. As his eyes flicked in their direction, for only a moment, his instructor's sword sliced through the air so fast it was just a blur, and became visible again as it stopped almost dead on the young man's lower jaw with a firmness that only an experienced soldier has. There was an agonising scream which sounded more like a yelp, and the distinct sound of bone being cracked, and even shattered in some places.

He span with a thin spray of blood which reached the path, and he protected his fall the best he could with his shield, holding down his half-helm with the other hand. Tristan winced for the poor boy, but Richard sighed and rubbed his forehead, the despair already welling up inside him.

"Why were you looking at me?" Richard asked, trying to strike a balance between concern and firmness.

The man spat a mouthful of blood onto the grass, along with a tooth. As he tried to reply, he gave another yelp and squeezed his eyes shut while he tugged at another tooth which hung by a thread in his mouth. He threw it to the ground in a mix of bitterness and anger, and clumsily stumbled to his feet, nearly tripping over his own shoes.

"I don't know, Your Majesty," he managed. "I'll be okay though."

"You're not okay," the Emperor snapped. "Go and clean yourself up."

The young man looked relieved to be given this order, not thinking for a second to argue, dropping his equipment and heading for the castle in what he hoped passed for a dignified walk.

"I used to train with real swords," Richard added.

When wearing a visor, that was true.

The young man, covering his blood-soaked mouth and looking thoroughly pained at trying to work out the relevance of this, bowed and continued on his way.

"As for you," Richard said to the trainer, "for gods' sakes, watch where you're swinging that thing in future. You should know better."

"Majesty!" the man said with a bow, and took his leave also.

The Emperor shook his head and attempted to gather his thoughts, but he'd let his illness get the better of him and composing himself was like climbing a cliff face now.

"What were you saying, Tristan?" he said distantly.

"I don't believe I was saying anything. However," he added nervously, "I was wondering something. If you're planning on igniting a renaissance here with one swift movement, how are you hoping to fund it? The royal bank is not, shall we say, brimming with excess gold."

"We're taking out substantial loans from the county banks. Nothing fancy."

Tristan saw right through him. It was there again, that subdued and awkward tone which suggested he was not speaking entirely of his own accord, and was manipulating the message.

"You're "loaning"?" Tristan spelled out sarcastically, showing a knowing smile. "What was your initial reaction when the Empress proposed this to you?"

Richard laughed depressively and shook his head in shame. He, himself, had not realised that he was speaking with his wife's tone. Tristan was always the one to acknowledge this when it slipped past his tongue. The laugh turned to a cough, and Tristan patted him on the back. The ruler of Burtal resumed his regal stance, this time consciously so, and looked about to make certain nobody had seen him do this.

"I was sceptical of course, but I scarcely had time to question why with the way she hammers ideas into my head."

"I would say her coercion technique is far too delicate and meticulous to be compared to a hammer."

"Fine. Yes, you're right. I should point out, though, that I fully intend to pay back my debts, the very moment it becomes feasible to do so. I just don't know when that will be."

He trailed off to wallow in his doubt, and his lips shut tight, parched and cracked, his eyes droopy, begging for sleep. In the midst of the mock fighting, one person in particular snapped him out of his trance and brought back the irritation which bubbled inside him. There was a young man who was fighting, not unlike the one whose jaw had been cracked. Richard looked to the instructor, then back again, and, with purpose, made to approach them. Tristan grabbed his arm, having spotted exactly what he was doing.

"Richard, you're ill."

"But not in public. It's better that way."

"Illness happens," Tristan said understandingly with a shrug.

His friend smiled as if he agreed. Part of him did, Tristan knew. *A large part*, the words forced themselves into his mind. But today, Richard chose to ignore it.

The couple ceased their fight as it became obvious that the Emperor was approaching them, turning to him, but careful not to make eye contact. Richard glared and growled silently at the trainer, who was, understandably, confused at the hate being projected onto him.

"You, boy," the Emperor said to the student. "What exactly do you think you're doing?"

"Er, I'm not sure I understand your meaning, Your Majesty."

"I mean, what are you doing with that shield? If you so consistently hold it that close to yourself, it's got nowhere to go but into you. Into your face, that could break all sorts of things, but you'd quickly have more to worry about than that. Or into your ribs, perhaps. Or your sternum; that would take the wind out of you long enough for your enemy to rip your throat open, no question about it."

"If you say so, Your Majesty."

"I do. Hand me your sword and shield."

Tristan watched from a distance, Havdan Linch from the other side, arms crossed. Tristan evaluated this and took a few steps closer, weaving between the combatants so that he would be in a good position to intervene if things got out of hand. Richard looked more comfortable now that he was holding these implements of war. Mistakenly. He took a low stance before the bewildered trainer, his shield out before him and his sword held back, ready to strike.

"I'll show you how to block. Hell, I'll show you how to fight. And you will be the one to fight me," he said to the Master-at-Arms.

"Are you sure you don't want to change into something more appropriate first?" was the reply.

"No need," the Emperor replied with a weak smile. "I have done this before."

The grizzled teacher took a similar stance and, without further warning, Richard lunged at him. He was already acting strategically. Before his sword touched his opponent's shield, he whipped it back and slid out of harm's way, parrying with his shield an incoming blow with tremendous force and a primal grunt.

The tutor staggered back. His face became awash with uncertainty, and even fear, as he tried to comprehend what the Emperor was doing, and to what degree he was allowed to fight back. He struck at Richard, lighter than before by his reckoning, to which the Emperor taunted him cheerfully with blade and shield. Many more people had stopped practising and had formed a wide rim around them. One of them absentmindedly tried to pass Tristan, but was stopped abruptly as Tristan thrust an arm out to barrier him.

Tristan was feeling edgy now. He couldn't be sure, but he thought he noticed Richard slipping up, weakening, and, unfortunately, if this was true, Richard either had not yet noticed himself, or was too proud to let it bother him. Richard's legs worked quicklyand efficiently again, sliding his feet about and, every time he looked to be on the defensive, Havdan lunged in with his shield held firm to meet only black air, the Emperor slamming his shield into his opponent's sword with tremendous force, hurrying forward and pushing it downward. At the same time, he banged the pommel of his sword against the rim of the trainer's shield, leaving him wide open for a finishing blow for but a second before he recovered. Richard cried out triumphantly despite the fact that, as Tristan had spotted, a soldier as adept as he'd fooled himself into believing he was would have ended the fight after that last barrage.

Richard swatted away another blow, but this time, literally, slipped, lost his footing for just the blink of an eye and regained it a mere moment later in such way to make it appear that it was, in some way, deliberate. That was what tipped Tristan off. He was sure now, and there were other signs to accompany it. His breath was running short and the stoop was returning, as if some unseen force was gradually applying a weight onto his back that he could not aptly fight, despite his pretence. His body was engulfing itself in the white hot flames of rage, not at his opponent, but rather a muddled anger born from his own weakness.

As the fighting instructor moved for a short jab, Richard slammed his shield against the incoming strike. The signs were like lightning on pitch to Tristan; the narrowing of the eyes was from blurring vision, and a heart pounding at his chest like a separate entity trying to escape. He brought his shield up again in the general direction of his opponent's weapon, accompanied by a yell from the depths of his lungs which drifted far out through the darkness. A final downward strike was dealt to the shield with gusto, fervour wreathing Richard's blade, which caused the man to drop his weapon and instantly put up his hands. Richard appeared to wake up, suddenly wondering what had come over him, as if his heart had stopped for a moment.

To Tristan's relief, a few members ofthe crowd clapped for his victory and, soon, others started also, Havdan among them. It was possible that they had construed his near breakdown as keenness and fierceness, or a feint if he was lucky.

"Carry on," Tristan heard Richard say.

Tristan hurried the Emperor away from the crowd to allow them to continue in peace.

"You really should get some sleep now, Your Majesty. Just watching you is making me feel tired."

~

The earliest light of dawn was what warmed Isaac's face through the curtains, but it was not this that had woken him. He could have sworn that, even in his sleep, he'd heard loud noises, and that they had carried over to the real world when he awoke. He was proven right when a raw, deep voice screamed outside; in pain or anger he could not quite tell in his drowsy state, but he sat up like a bolt and he, all of a sudden, felt long spent of his drowsiness.

The man's scream was followed by the flailing of a sword or other weapon against what he could not decipher, the cry of an animal, and the distressed whinnying of a horse. Isaac rolled out of bed and crept across the boards, the window his destination. There was the temptation to rush, to get it over with as quickly as possible. Every fibre in his body told him to fire up the pace but, with the benefit of experience in life or death situations, he resisted, watching his feet to see that they did not land on an uneven board which might give his position away, while his body screamed at him to watch the window instead. The unnerving clanging of whatever it was out there continued until he reached the window, and even as he peered through the curtains, the horse could be heard galloping away and could not be seen from his position without leaning out, which he dared not do, despite the situation seeming more or less diffused. He couldn't relax while the second participant of the conflict remained.

He shoved on a pair of boots and ran downstairs, where there was already a crowd of people shuffling outside. He strolled alongside the nervous congregation, waiting patiently for a gap in the line to take advantage of to slip through the door. The trail of destruction was more apparent now, but made little sense still. There were specks and pools of blood about the path and surrounding grass, some of it human blood, much of it a considerably darker fluid from the creature in its death throes that the people were giving a wide berth.

Though he had never seen one so close before, Isaac recognised it as a drakeel. A lizard, perhaps six feet in length or more even, with a kind of segregated shell, stripped plates which could move back and forth, under and over one another, just to give it the flexibility needed to have the edge as a predator. As a whole, it was heavily armoured, but a sword was embedded deeply through the flesh where the shell connected to the body.

His brother and father closed in beside him, but he did not look at them. The drakeel was still dangerous despite its fatal injury. It emitted a constant throaty growl, and snapped its gigantic jaws at anyone that even rocked in its direction, and whipped its tail around upon the ground to warn those who might approach its rear.

Its growl became distorted all of a sudden; a curdling wail which gave the impression that it was probably choking on its own bodily fluids. It heaved, and even managed to lift itself onto its hind legs, then collapsed. Its legs spread under the weight, and it breathed its last. The hilt was pushed deeper still by the extra pressure on the pommel as its lumbering mass collapsed upon it, opening a larger hole from which blood flowed down the sword, quickly colouring it completely red.

The husband of the woman Isaac had spoken to last night, Ewywn, pushed it with his boot from as far away as he could. It did not respond. He and others began to see the tracks of the drakeel, and the now absent horse, stretching not along the road, but out into the plains.

"This is what happens when you cut across country," he sighed.

"Why would it follow a rider all the way across the plain?" Isaac mumbled.

"They can be very vicious," his father mumbled back. "Maybe the rider crossed through its territory."

Ewywn looked at Isaac despairingly and shook his head. Others were asking all manner of questions to one another, while Isaac tried to find a clear line of sight to the road leading south, where splashes of the rider's blood could be seen.

"Listen," Ewywn said, raising his voice. "It doesn't matter. I'll alert the Watch Patrol next they pass through here, and that will be the end of it."

The crowd slowly dispersed at Ewywn's increasingly demanding behest, granting a clear view of the horizon, where the sun clawed its way over a hill on Isaac's right, and its rays streaked across the plains. It should have been mundane, but he'd rarely seen such colours in a sunrise. He'd name it a portent, only he wasn't in the mood.

"We should be setting off soon anyway," his father said, playing the part of the optimist, just as he'd always considered it his duty to be. "We may as well get ready to move."

Isaac found he had to agree. Ideally, he would have liked to stay and investigate to appease his indomitable curiosity. However, therein lay the problem; the problem that had plagued him for so many years, the very reason that he had been so unfocused and had never before uncovered the truth of the mystery that ate at him. He put aside all thoughts of past violence, evoked by this scene of decay, and concentrated on his objective, fiercely so, meeting with his father's concerned look as he awoke from it. It was good to be back in the real world, but to stay there was something he had to take to task.

"Yes, we should go," he replied earnestly.

Chapter Four: The Seamstress' Reverie

In leaving, the family had created a void, an emptiness, from which boredom had swiftly followed. One family member would sometimes leave on business, but Kate had never witnessed four of them leave, let alone within two days of one another. She sat outside the house on the bench by the vegetable patch, swinging her legs back and forth, sewing a pattern onto a new dress which sat across her lap, loom pushed to one side. Quite what the pattern was, she still didn't exactly know. In her head, she had an image of what it should look like, but she couldn't keep a lock on this. It kept changing, and what appeared on the cloth were just basic patterns as results, reactionary manoeuvres to correct her uncertainty, as she didn't want to utterly ruin it.

Technically, the needlework was near flawless, as far as she could see, her hand so steady with such a feel for the motion that she could carry on, even as she swung her head back and gawped at the clouds floating by. Already, she was seriously considering devoting her attention to a more worthwhile cause, or as seriously as she could muster. There was always the niggling feeling that she probably would not bother to break from her routine and would persist in mindlessly floating through each day, as she was already doing in denying her considerations. Her apathy amused her.

She dreamed of this work being done for her instead and, like a twisted blessing from the gods, there appeared a sign a short time later, a harbinger raising dust and fury. Beyond her fantasies, she took no notice of it, assuming the horse roaring down the road to be of another overzealous rider, but the fantasies limped at her feet like a dying fish, and so the commotion caused by it ensured she couldn't divert her eyes from its truth. She froze in place when it entered clearly in her view, mentally glued to the seat by her fear of action.

The rider was white as a sheet and looked not to be even fully conscious of his surroundings. As he raced in her direction, she felt her head split in two. Time seemed to speed up to taunt her into making a rash decision. Before she knew what she was doing, she'd unfixed herself from the chair and flung herself before the horse with her arms outstretched.

"Stop!" she shouted.

As her senses returned to her, regret engulfed her and she jumped back, taking gigantic clumsy steps backwards and covering her head with her hands. The rider was fully aware of her now, so much so that he looked like he might have a heart attack when she shouted.

The horse reared at a sharp signal and it stopped abruptly, the rider shaking badly in his saddle. Kate rushed by the horse's side and looked up at the rider in clueless desperation.

His clothes might have been smart once, but they were torn in several places and were caked in dry blood, to the extent that the weight of them made them heavily sag.

Similarly, she found it difficult to approximate his age in his dreadful state, but he gave her the impression of someone who, until recently, was a very athletic person and, quite possibly, muscular as well, but his recent wounds and, probably, lack of subsistence had shrunken him.

"Can you get off your horse?" she said slowly so that he could understand her, but nonetheless squealed in nervousness.

The man almost certainly understood her. He removed one boot from its foothold with all the efficiency of a dithering old man, and then the other with even more shakiness. Most worryingly, while he was having some difficulty performing this simple task, he also did not look to be feeling any pain at all, for a dying body could sometimes numb from its injuries.

He climbed down with less trouble, but fell to his knees when he let go of the horse. Kate slung one of his arms over her shoulder and was fortunate enough to have him recognise her intent. He groaned as he got his muscles under control and rose. At first, moving was hard going and he nearly tripped more than once but, with Kate's help, he soon found a groove and shuffled along comfortably, barely having to think.

"Where am I?" he mumbled almost incomprehensibly.

"Never mind," she replied.

Kate's mother burst through the front door with such power and purpose that Kate nearly, in her delicate state, allowed herself to be over encumbered from shock and by the man relying on her support. Her mother ran to her aid, but Kate shook her head.

"I've got him," she said with attempted firmness of tone.

"I'll fetch a physician then," her mother replied with an inspiring resolve and quickness.

Kate led the sick man through the kitchen and into Isaac's bedroom. Already he was becoming too drowsy to walk and was dragging his feet. Kate was not a strong girl but, nonetheless, put everything she had into keeping him upright, ignoring the straining of muscles all across her body, the pain that told her she was going too far. When they reached the bed, however, there was nothing she could do to safely set him down, already putting all her strength into simply holding him in place. He rolled onto the bed, and the bed sprung him back up.

Kate clapped a hand to her mouth at what must, surely, have incurred serious internal damage, but, worse still, he barely reacted where he should have been crying in agony. She rushed into the kitchen, the world around her blurring in and out of conventional existence, one moment almost surreally clear, the next a flash of colours and shapes stretched beyond all recognition.

Her hands were shaking and she bit her lower lip hard as she stared pensively into the distance through the window at the outside world where no one was yet bounding down the road to help this poor man. At this time it dawned on her, the real reason she was so frightened.

A kitchen cupboard was flung open and a box removed so hastily and carelessly that it very nearly slipped from Kate's fingers. Without thinking, she opened it and snatched a knife, a suture kit, and as many bandages as she could fit in the other hand before running back to Isaac's room where the man was barely conscious, leaving the plant remedy ingredients for when her brain could hope to process them.

"Who are...?" the man fumbled his words, not even looking at her.

"Don't talk."

He passed out. She knelt down beside the bed and arranged the medicinal items around her. She took the knife and cut open the man's shirt. On his chest were three main injuries, which had been bandaged and held together badly with layers of cloth. She gently pulled at them, but the dried blood glued them to his skin and she wasn't about to take any chances.

She cut around one of the cloth patches and it became clear that, somehow, he had sutured himself with makeshift materials and equipment. The hole was, fortunately, not too deep to be intrinsically fatal, more gash than stab wound, but had gone dangerously long without proper treatment. The sutures needed to be redone. She cut them and took a hold of the suture thread, holding it up to his skin. She gulped and closed her eyes when she saw that her hands still shook so violently. She paused for the peace and calm she needed. In her mind, she stood before the hidden river in the valley behind Caedor. It ran thick and red, but she waited, tensed, and the colour passed to clearness. She was upstream where the river was wider and deep enough to dive in. She lifted a bare foot from the rocky floor and dipped it daintily into the water, smiling at how cold it was, and the soothing nature of the current. She jumped.

When she was back in the real world, her hands no longer vibrated, but were still. Not still as most people's hands were, but like a statue, totally unflinching. Even so, she found she needed to devote a small amount of her consciousness to maintaining correct breathing habits, in order to keep the status quo while she pierced his skin with the needle.

The perturbed wound was bleeding again but, against all regular instincts, Kate did not panic or seek to hurry. Still she locked herself in her place of calmness, got a grip on her emotions and, somehow, rose above her insecurities. She could feel her body on the verge of shaking from the hypnotic threading of the needle through skin, again and again, nausea pushing through her brain tissue like a battering ram but withheld from it by sheer force of will. So long as she didn't stop to consider the mechanisms of this, she would be fine.

Two people ran into the house. One of them came into Isaac's room and loomed over Kate. He coughed as a deliberate diversion, and she nearly fell from her isolated place of serenity.

The Voice of Kings

"I can take over now," said the man whose voice Kate recognised as that of Jyric from the church.

"I'm already doing it. I may as well finish," she said in breathless increments. "You're distracting me."

Even as she spoke these words, it twice occurred to her that she had, in her haste, not taken all the necessary medical implements for the injured man. In trying to preserve her levelheadedness, she spoke to Jyric again with fractured speech.

"Something for the infection. Please. The bottle in the box. In the kitchen. And water too. If it's not clean from the tap, a sieve is on the worktop. And the poker in the embers."

Jyric left, not wishing to provoke her in such a delicate state, but, out of the corner of her eye, Kate saw an approving nod to her suturing. She harnessed this positivity and finished off closing the gash. It no longer bled but it was still a mess. There was a moment of terrifying weakness as she wondered how to progress, but she soon pulled her vital thinking components together and prioritised.

Jyric re-entered while she was working on a second, less serious injury, and placed two bottles and three glasses of water beside her, striking the difficult balance of ensuring she noticed them but not disturbing her. One bottle was of vinegar and trace hemlock, another more gelatinous, and she didn't dare check it. Jyric left a second time and returned with a pail from the hall, possessed of a stench so powerful that scratched at the eyes more than the nose; alcohol, pure, from the church's cellar. One should be nervous about hemlock, she knew, and she also knew there were better medicines to be made, but worrying would only degenerate her hands into nervous wrecks. *Get those later*, she thought. She went for the next jar, peering into it in the despair of ignorance, until Jyric tried to take it from her, and pressure forced her memory. With a scalpel she scooped some of it out, and rubbed it on the wounds. Boar fat, likely, and something pungent from a censer. The scalpel went to the pail, her hand signalled for the length of metal he brandished so carefully, and, through a grimace, she pressed it light as a lover's kiss to the skin, not scraping, but dabbing.

"I can help," he ventured after a while. "I have more experience than you."

"It's already too dim in here, and with no way of projecting light directly onto him, another shadow would hinder rather than help."

Jyric weighed this up against the positive influence of his involvement, but, regretfully, seemed to come to that same conclusion. He allowed her to continue, uninterrupted, from a corner of the room where his presence would not disrupt the procedure. Kate liked to think that, at first, he was apprehensive at best about this, but soon was awash with confidence. Her skills were something to be reckoned with, that was the line she drew.

When Kate finished closing the gashes on the man's stomach, she again soothed them with the purifying heat. She poured all three glasses of water over him, and soaked the now-diluted blood from his chest with Isaac's coverlet, at the same time washing away the loosened cloth that had previously stuck to his skin. Next, she poured vinegar over him and rubbed it gently into the wounds with the bed sheet and her hands. His skin glistened now, and all his arterial fluids were congealing on the sheet below him.

"Now I'll need your help," she whispered, taking a dressing.

Jyric took a chance, taking the poker and handing it to someone out of sight who didn't matter, and she assumed he knew what she had in mind. He lifted the sick man's body, just enough for Kate to weave the bandage around him. After she finished, she tumbled back in exhaustion, the heels of her feet catching her where she would certainly have continued falling. She swung her arms to rebalance herself, and Jyric helped her to her feet. She shivered all over, like leaving the river.

"That was some incredible work you did there," he said, his mouth agape. "Artful, even. Where did you learn to do that? Wasn't all from me, I know that."

"I just have steady hands, is all," she said defensively.

Her protective shell enclosed her and she escaped Jyric's gaze before he could ask more questions. Her mother was given quite a fright when her daughter emerged, dreamy Kathrynne she was, very much a different person. A drop of blood trickled down Kate's index finger and splashed on her foot. Only now did she remember that she had not been wearing shoes, a choice made due to the mild weather. She must really have been engrossed in that case, she thought, if she did not notice until now. Jyric the healer, and Cerddan the apprentice, and Turner the journeyman, each took turns examining her handiwork, and, far away, she took turns staring at nothing, and nothing, then nothing.

The bathroom contained a mirror the height of Kate. Under ordinary circumstances she considered herself decidedly plain, someone who by many accounts would find difficulty arousing anything in the area of one's brain that dealt with memory. Now, though, her green dress was sodden with blood from where she had wiped her hands over and over again, and when the pressure was getting to her even the sweat on her forehead had been substituted with blood at one point. It contrasted with her hair, brunette dark, which hung loose and without uniformity. Of a sudden panic set in, and she no longer recognised the woman before her.

"I know who I am," Kate whispered. "I'm Kate," she snapped.

The bloody maiden in the glass tilted her head uncertainly.

She burst into awkward laughter for reasons she couldn't wrap her head around, as if part of her was possessed. Perhaps, she humoured the thought, at the dramatic irony of shunning Isaac's nudges to become a healer, and then being forced to do so anyway.

Regardless, barely as soon as it had started, the laughter was choked by an awful constriction in her stomach and a feeling of her heart being in her throat. As she gawked at the sordid reflection of her bloodstained visage, she couldn't help but envision herself as a

The Voice of Kings

scared 13-year-old girl again, dodging swords and axes and hammers whizzing through the air. Merely touching a fallen man who used to live not one hundred feet from her house, her hands were drenched with his blood. It was inevitable that she would be reminded of it at some point. The only surprise was that it hadn't happened sooner.

She quivered at the thought. The pump of the bath was slippery in her hands and aching to her arms, but was affected in full in haste. Kate knelt and put her head under the stream of cold mountain water sucked from the well, to drown her, to wash it all away.

"It was the strangest feeling. I couldn't help but act. And before I knew what I was doing, I was performing the operation. So very strange..."

"I don't think so at all," her mother replied. "It's who you are."

Kate removed, from the coals, a pitcher, and from it ran a rich smelling tea into a mug. She rested her nose on the mug and inhaled the aromatic steam that wafted from its rippling surface. The ground-up herbs gave a distinct pungent impression that other teas did not. It was as she remembered it, the last time she was sick. It was, indeed, properly made then. Hopefully this would be of use to the mysterious man, should he ever wake.

A depressing thought, that he very well might not. Kate looked sullen, but she pivoted to see that her mother was sitting upright in an armchair, concerned that no response had been given.

"The exception, not the rule," Kate sighed. "If I was that confident in other walks of life, we wouldn't be having this conversation. If I was that confidant just in medicine even, we would not be talking about this now. What happened today was an extreme situation."

"I still don't agree. If you can have the initiative and the courage to try to fix a dying man where the consequences of failure would fall squarely on you...going up to another woman of your age and saying hello shouldn't be a problem. Or a man, for that matter."

Kate blushed at the mere insinuation that a man might take interest in her. She downed a hefty amount of hot tea to prevent from having to reply to that, and scrabbled on the kitchen worktop for the piece of paper before taking the mug from her lips. The letter, or whatever it was, was instantly recognisable, having more the texture of rock than paper. She brought it before her eyes and scanned the contents yet again, or that which was visible and not obscured by dried blood.

"What do you make of this, Mother? I found it in the man's breeches pocket, but I can't read most of it. The words Aurail, Melphor and Mūrac I can just about see though."

"Kathrynne!" her mother barked. "That's not for you to..."

"I just wanted to find out who he was!" Kate protested, and held the paper out for her mother to read.

Her mother read, or attempted to, while Kate held it still, often putting a finger to it and squinting before shrugging and giving up.

The Seamstress' Reverie

"I'm afraid I can't see any more than you can."

"It was worth a try. Thanks anyway."

Kate carried this item and the mug into Isaac's room, and set herself down on the rickety chair behind his desk, where her brother did all his scheming. The mysterious man was still breathing at least. With Jyric's and her mother's help, the bed sheets and duvet had been replaced by clean ones from Lucian's room, and he was now dressed in Lucian's clothes as well, being roughly the same height as her elder brother, as he was. Protected candles surrounded the bed also, to prevent a draught or coldness from causing more damage to him while unconscious. Satisfied that he wasn't about to drop dead any time soon, she made effort to decipher his letter, but was restless and gave up quickly.

There were too many distractions besides, all originating from Isaac's bed. The heaving of the man's chest, strenuous yet desperately petty, like ripples on a still lake. The pale skin shrugging off the candlelight, akin to a body set for a ritual; dead, already dead. Blonde hair, bedraggled on his scalp, was long and windswept, pushed back that one might see his face, hard set features on a kind face, a young face, handsome but for his plight that ensured only pity welled within when she canted her head to better line her face up. *Who are you, my mysterious friend*, she thought. *What cause is yours?* Noble? It seemed likely, somehow. If she was a spontaneous fool in believing it, perhaps that wasn't so bad. The patient's face alone was cause for consideration, such that she wondered if she could determine him from it; what he liked to do with his time, what he hated. He was her patient for now and, in her mind, that entailed much more than it should have done.

But too much, too soon, too distressing for her tired body. She resorted to rummaging through Isaac's drawers for entertainment or, at the very least, something to keep her occupied. She skimmed through a dozen documents consisting of mining reports from around the country, and some even from Mürathneè, and just about anything from Silverwyck. So wrought with poor crop yield, she mused in jest, that they really couldn't be bothered to humour Isaac with any manner of consistency. But by whole truth, Sèhvorian steel, and the crystals that often accompanied it, was the main focus.

A ludicrous idea came to her, as to why Isaac might want such things; a memory of a tale from years ago, but she was far too beaten and tired to give such ridiculousness the time of day. She threw down the papers and slipped into a deep sleep.

Chapter Five: The Red City

"This is it then," Marcel said in awe, pulling his horse back to a trot.

"You'd have to have lived under a rock your whole life to not know what that is," Isaac mocked jokingly. "Even the drawings I did as a child would be all the reference you'd need to correctly name this."

The road had twisted to the east and so, by the light of the evening sun, the tallest tower of Castle Aurail was gloriously appraised, its outline scorched with orange fire, a cylindrical funnel of dark red brick 700 feet high, piercing the sun. At 45 degree angles to the tower were the other two; one just about visible, almost identical save for having half the height and girth.

Isaac was in silent awe with his brother. A stunning sight and no mistake, even though the castle itself on which they sat could not be seen, being more central and eastern from the central gate, thus quite a walk. The wall which surrounded the whole city, of the same material as the castle, also played its part in blocking the view. Left and right it stretched, not perfectly straight but zigzagging here and there, as if following the blueprints drawn down by a jittery man. Choice few towers sprung up from it at irregular intervals, in themselves of irregular designs; some being tall things, a couple little more than a series of squat boxes with a dome of yet darker red, shielding the lookouts who must have gazed from within.

Isaac was so dumbstruck by all this that, at first, he failed to notice the horseback soldiers, 20 or more, trotting in single line by the wall.

"What's going on?" Marcel asked.

Father's face screwed up as it often did when he was working things out, those same wrinkles forming. His eye searched the top of the great tower and panned down, but there was no sign of alarm. A merchant wagon trundled from the south-east gate. A quick glance at the last watch outpost they passed yielded no cause for concern either.

"It's probably nothing to worry about. Maybe they're doing training exercises."

The horses broke in to full pelt at the all-clear and galloped the last stretch of the plain. They stopped before one of the gates and were subjected to a brief visual search from the guards. The grey armour they wore looked familiar to Isaac; he'd seen it before. If what his memory told him was correct, the armour was the same now as it was years ago, the last he had seen it, and perhaps had not been changed for a long time before *that* as well.

The immense gates of heavy wood and strips of red iron were already agape, as opening and closing them for each and every party that passed through would slow down business in the city more than he'd already heard it was. So far, Isaac had been thoroughly impressed

The Red City

with everything he'd seen but braced himself to be disappointed, or even disgusted, by what was to follow. This was Aurail.

Having been to Melphor in the past, on more than one occasion, the adjustment to being part of such a large community was not such a stretch but, at first, he found it difficult to understand what he was looking at. He truly felt alien and was unable to analyse the society.

Many of the buildings were old of course, but this made it more difficult to immediately tell what area of the city he was in, whether they were poor or rich. Soon enough however, he was given the context he needed. A nobleman trotted by on a decorated horse with head held high, and it was clear that he did not live in this area.

The clothes the people were wearing was what put him off initially. There was a wide variety of them; some of which those native to Caedor would call very smart, some of which looked as if they were old ripped clothes that had been taken out of want for something better and attempted, badly, to be fixed by the wearers themselves, while reading a book. And while asleep.

Yet here they were together, on the same streets together. There could be no mistake that they all lived in this area either, as he took note of them walking in and out of what were, clearly, houses. Some of the houses and shops were part-way modified, or updated as the intention no doubt was, but most of the work was unfinished. Scaffolding poles had been discarded in alleys; probably a temporary action, though of course the word temporary was not a measure of time, which people had either forgotten, or they didn't have the means to act upon this crucial information.

Even the old cobbled streets, much of which were not in bad condition, had seen an attempt at reform to flatter stone, and yet, some of it had been left unfinished and, in some places, very obviously rebuilt with the old cobbles.

A picture was being painted to Isaac, a very vivid one at that, of a district which, at one time, had no monetary worries and had even received various commissions to improve its infrastructure but, very suddenly, that funding had been cut and, for whatever reason, the district became poorer almost as quickly. The loss of funding possibly factored into this. Perhaps there was also inflation to deal with at around the same time, and perhaps also the citizens had been spending without a thought that trouble might blow their way.

"I have to say, I'm not seeing the influence of the renaissance anywhere here," Isaac said.

His father veered his horse closer to Isaac so he could aptly reply above the din of the crowded street without raising his voice.

"I gather from the letter Lord Almaric sent me that the Emperor is probably planning to exact his renaissance plans all at once, or as close together as possible, so I imagine we'd know if it was in effect. That being said, I already have my work cut out for me. If what we're seeing now was the best he could muster, I'd have no hope."

"I wish you luck with that, Father," Marcel said. "I should attend to my matters for now though. I'll check up on you whenever I can."

"You're leaving already?" Isaac laughed, not entirely sure if his brother was being serious. "We only just got here. Surely you can take out ten minutes from your busy schedule to have a quick dinner with us."

"The duceveree will pay little mind if I arrive in good time; he'll only notice if I make effort to arrive extra early. That should get me a few points early on. I can come back here when I have free time organised."

Isaac was pleasantly surprised at this reaction and patted Marcel on the back for at least having thought about it.

"Ah. Now you're thinking like me."

"I shall endeavour not to in future," Marcel replied snidely before washing his expression and replacing it with a more earnest one. "Will you join me?"

Isaac craned his neck at a flock of gulls flying in formation high in the sky. He'd never seen any before but they fit all the descriptions he'd ever seen of them, and bore strong similarities to drawings in picture books he'd read as a child. He released the reins of his horse and casually sat back, ruffling his hair and swishing his tongue in his cheek. He jumped from his horse energetically and, remembering to smile, stopped a man in the street with the wave of a hand who he thought might respond politely and easily.

"Excuse me, I was wondering if you might help with a little something. This shouldn't take long," he added when he saw the man's gaunt expression. "Per chance, could you tell me where I could find a weather chart for Lavellyrn's Channel? One that shows what the weather has been like recently, and perhaps the tides, that sort of thing."

"The channel doesn't often see bad weather if that's what you're worried about. Were a few storms not long ago but it's calmed down now, I understand."

"Ah. Thank you. Have a good day."

Isaac remounted his horse with just as much energy. Marcel gave him a bemused look. He shrugged and looked all around for clues as to what had him perturbed.

"What?"

"Why did you get off your horse just to ask that man what the weather is like?"

"I didn't know if he would be any help, and getting, not to mention keeping, the full attention of a random person in a crowded street is so much easier if you're on the same level."

"So what's the verdict?" his father said, undecided on whether he disapproved of Isaac's behaviour, interjecting his horse between the two of them. "Are you going or staying?"

Isaac admitted to himself that he had probably spoken to that man in the street because he'd wanted an excuse to stay and take in more of what the city had to offer and to understand its workings, not so he could help make it better, but as a curiosity. He then thought of how he might help, but managed to stop this line of thought quickly. There were only so many tasks he could juggle at one time. There was Kester to consider as well, and Lucian who would be arriving shortly, he remembered, but there would be time for that any other time.

"I think I'll go with Marcel. It's a very long journey to Harth without any company."

They arrived in a large clearing only marginally less packed with citizens than the tiny streets they'd just traversed through. As well as shops lining the outer rim of the square, there were market stalls here and there, the owners of which were heckling passersby. In the centre of the square was a fountain of simple design spouting crystal clear water and, at one edge, to his right, was an old building entranced by an arched tunnel which was slowly but surely crumbling away, in spite of the signs and congregations outside which suggested that it was still in use.

One of the signs in particular caught Isaac's eye. A trade embassy was somewhere in this building. When Lucian did arrive, he would undoubtedly pay a visit here, involving a series of dull and drawn out meetings, the likes of which Isaac had no intention of enduring.

"You don't want to see Kester before you leave then?" his father said.

"I want to. It's fortunate that I have you to relay other means of interacting with him, if nothing else."

"How would you go about finding Kester?" Marcel asked. "Gods know how many thousands of people live in this city."

"It would be easy I bet. Father, is the opera theatre still under construction?"

"I think it is. Why?"

"Kester has a vested interest in it, and of the musicians who would perform there. Therefore, I would find the opera house and ask the construction workers of any musicians that have visited. Vocalists in particular will want to know how their voice carries. So I would find a musician or singer, and surely one of them must know Kester."

He paused and, still steering the horse with one hand, dug into a saddlebag. His hand pushed aside clothes which, by now, were in no particular arrangement until, eventually, there was a faint knocking from within as his knuckles clashed against wood.

"That's what I *would* have done."

He removed his hand holding a tiny wooden box about the size of a candlestick and thrust it out for his father to take.

"What's this?" he said in a manner that forcibly described his dissatisfaction.

"Just a little present for Kester. I anticipated that I might not find time to meet with him, so I packed this. Finding him shouldn't be too hard. Lord Almaric would do it if you asked, if he's as good a friend as you say, even if Kester isn't already in the Emperor's employ."

"Fine," his father replied, making sure to highlight in this single word that he was being generous.

The Voice of Kings

Father led them out of the square, which seemed to act as a sort of threshold between the rich and poor. Though considerably smaller, the next district got noticeably richer in appearance alarmingly quickly; not five minutes' walk from a place where citizens were watching their step for holes in the ground.

The streets were wider, giving them the leeway to fan out at their leisure. Though still relics of the last age, everything was well kempt and groomed here. The houses were bigger and more luxurious. Curtains made of fine linens and other expensive fabrics framed scenes of warmth and comfort within.

Isaac took the same tentative care analysing this district as he had the previous one. While it must have been awfully nice for the people living here, there was something missing. He was hesitant to label it as soulless, but that was how it must appear to a person used to the pleasures and efficiency of Harth. There was nothing that suggested that it was moving with the times. It may have been clean and physically outstanding in a technical sense but, when viewed through the lens of renaissance progression, it was all being left to wither away at the mercy of time.

A sympathetic smile came about upon Isaac. His father really did have his work cut out for him.

The sun was still not touching the horizon when they pulled up outside the north gate, where a grand steppe waited to start their next journey. The sky was clear too, so clear that Refeer could be faintly seen opposite to the sun. Even this was peculiar to Isaac. Clear days in Caedor still rarely yielded such a sight.

"I've put this off long enough," his father said to Isaac. "Here's your money. Four hundred florins: a reserve of mine. You've got some money of your own to boot, so that should be enough. You won't pay full price to the seller. Castle Aurail should deal with the rest; I'm counting on it. All the money in Caedor wouldn't help if they thought you were buying it for yourself."

Isaac felt his eyelids fly up in surprise. He retracted them, but his father was aware of the game he was about to play anyway, and he knew it. He gripped the reins, just as he had been, and didn't even adjust them for comfort, so he could not be construed in any way as making to grab the bag of coins his father was holding out for him.

"Five hundred florins and I'll give you a valuable return on your investment. I promise you that."

"You should be more careful when you make promises."

"I promise it so you know, and I know, that I'll try my very best to do just that. And my best should be enough."

Naivety, or knowing, steely resolve, his father could not instantly tell from this statement, but he generously seemed to decide on a combination of the two. His dark gaze dug deep into Isaac's features, so much so that even Isaac began to feel discomfort and an itch at the back of his neck. He was sure his father was going to decline but, instead, he shook his head in self-mocking laughter.

His father's cognitive dissonance prevented him from acquiescing even though he had decidedto help his son. He hesitantly counted out a hundred more florins and plunked them into the bag which now sagged beneath the weight, to the extent that he was forced to hold it two-handed.

"What the bloody hell am I doing?" Isaac's father said.

"A very generous thing," Isaac replied. "But also wise."

Marcel deliberately laughed for a second.

"Seriously though," their father said, ignoring the jibing of his sons. "Good luck to both of you. You can make it to the port by nightfall; it's only a couple of hours ride from here if you're at a good pace. Just follow the road north and you can't miss it."

Their worlds were to be so very different, and though his father didn't know the context, he seemed to understand Isaac's resolve and nodded his blessing. *You'll do well*, the tight expression said. They hugged and, before long, Isaac and Marcel were back on the road. Their father, the inventor, was like an ignored statue outside the city gates, for he would not turn nor divert his gaze.

Isaac was happy to be out in the open again with the cool wind caressing his face. He took a final glance of the city panorama; splendid, and not far enough away. Harth would change everything. He spurred his horse to a gallop.

There was a hill with a tree atop it with a good view of the docks and the sea. The two horses tied to the tree gorged on fresh grass; it was bright green, and there was a wide open field of it, soothing for the mind and bristly to the touch.

All of this was overwhelmingly beautiful. The salty air was a fresh experience for Isaac too. He felt free in this place, more than he had done in a long time. There was something incredibly final about this. The time for sitting around waiting for couriers to feed him fragments of information was finally over. Marcel must have felt something similar; the time for travelling from town to town to do odd jobs in churches here and there was over. Most likely, neither of them knew exactly what they were doing, but lack of peripheral vision wasn't going to harm them so long as they resolved to only go forward.

Before him, ships of all sizes underwent preparations for the journeys they would soon undertake and, beyond them, the tide swept out the sea to the horizon. The intricacies of the fight outside the Emperor's Crown Inn had left him pondering for some time, as he knew it would, but now he was focused only on this and, like so many other things, would soon forget about it entirely.

The Voice of Kings

The dying sunlight gave it all an orange hue, detailing every ripple, every wave. Even though he knew Mürathneè was somewhere across the channel, to him it appeared endless, and he felt, in this time of quiet thought, that he understood the appeal of the Infinite Sea.

"It's not quite as I imagined it somehow," Marcel said.

"How so?"

"Just everything that's going on. All the little details, every sound; I couldn't have imagined it like this."

Isaac nodded. He kept his gaze locked on one particular transport ship, a shabby but reliable boat, or so he'd been told. Certainly shabby, he could see that much, but he knew nothing whatsoever of maritime engineering and was forced to take the longshoremen's word for it. Marcel also showed interest and had to tear himself away to coax more serious divulgence from Isaac.

"Tell me honestly, why did you need another hundred florins from Father? Don't tell me you've even worked out all your accounts for your visit to Harth."

"I'm going to turn it in to more money, just as I promised. I'm insulted you'd suggest otherwise," he laughed. "No, I haven't accounted anything; I don't trust myself to do that well."

"But what will you do with the extra money?" Marcel pressed weakly, likely already feeling that he could be here for some time.

"If Father thinks I need four hundred florins for his business, then it stands to reason that I'll need more to buy services and information for my purpose, but I don't know how much. Plus, I promised I'd give Father a valuable return. That's it really; nothing sinister."

"If you're planning on generating revenue anyway, how about buying us a ride on that ship?"

Marcel pointed further along the docks to a ship that even Isaac could see, from this distance, was far better built than the sorry looking mishmash of wood they'd been planning on boarding.

"How much more?" Isaac said sceptically.

"Another three gold each, I think. Leaves earlier than the other ship too. Plus, I've heard seasickness can be quite a shitstorm for those who haven't travelled by sea before."

Isaac shrugged in willing submission.

"Suits me. Let's go."

Chapter Six: The House of Llambert

The waiting room was exactly as Lennord remembered it. Everything was clean and undamaged so there must have been refurbishments in order to keep it this way. The fabric on the chairs felt new, as it had the last time he'd sat here waiting to be summoned, and there on the walls, the old paintings still hung just where they had been, honouring kings of ages past, the distant years counted by fineries and painting styles that echoed from their times. Certainly all in the past century looked down on those who sat or whisked themselves through the hall, all but the tyrant. And it was King Paryn who stuck out most of all, faded but magisterial, the cracks not breaking his smile which he had good reason to flaunt for, without him, there would be no Castle Aurail, no lots of things, and topping this history was the possibility that he, of all kings, wielded blessings from beyond the ether.

The court would take after him. But they hadn't yet. Improvisation was perhaps not the strong suit of the servants here, or at least not the ones he had spoken to thus far. The previous night, after seeing off Isaac and Marcel, he'd decided it might be best to make his presence known to the Emperor, but the servants he spoke to couldn't seem to grasp why he was here ahead of schedule and eventually sent him away, telling him to return the next day without so much as consulting the Emperor or an assistant first.

The double doors to the throne room quietly and ominously opened, and a servant scurried out to greet Lennord. But it was not to be. Beyond him, a woman strode past, dark of hair, dark of complexion, dark of mood. Marioyrne Castellon, still learning to smile warmly without irony.

"I am Lady Castellon," she announced. *Lady*? Her tone suggested awareness of his knowing her name and so she was proud to lay the title before him. Not gloatingly though. She could have been condescending like all the others, yet none of that came to pass. "The Emperor will receive you now."

Lennord took a moment to evaluate and correct his clothing before passing through the arched doorway into the familiar windowless hall. Two guards by the door shut it when he'd walked out of range. Guardians beyond, these wearing green cloaks, three on either side of the room, stood stock still before banners hanging from the ceiling over pillars, which bore the Aurailian flag, and, between them, ornate candle stands stood almost as tall as the guards. There were three chandeliers too, all hanging in a row above the designated route to the thrones.

All of this was a perfunctory formality of course, and a discomforting one at that, seeing as there wasn't even a queue for the Emperor's reception. Lennord made his way up the red and green carpet with a strong pace, but not so much as to appear impatient, yet it was an awkward experience with the hall being so empty that it seemed even longer than usual.

The two heavy thrones dominated the back end of the room, needlessly tall at over six feet above the dais which backed on to the rear wall; proportioning that Lennord had never understood, although there was obviously a colourful back story to it that he was not aware of. There were five steps leading to this platform, but Lennord was to stop directly before them. The distance drew shorter and he was afforded a clearer look at the three figures before him. Directly ahead was the Emperor. He wore burgundy and leaf green robes, and his crown which Lennord had seen precious few times in the past. He looked to have seen better days; perhaps recovering from another bout, his head slumped in his hand while his elbow rested on the armrest of the throne.

The Empress, to his right, was the antithesis of this image. There was significant lighting in the hall but much of it was absorbed by the dark colour palette of the room. The Empress, however, basked in it. She shone as a beacon of self-assurance and control. Her blonde hair was so well shined and groomed that it appeared almost golden. Her long, lively face of beauty was perfectly complemented by her rosy complexion and meticulous make-up appliance.

Unlike her husband, she sat as upright as could be, wearing her robes as if she were born to do so. Although she was an inch shorter than him, her presence was significantly more radiant and even though at, from what Lennord could remember, perhaps 35 years of age, three or four years the junior of the Emperor, he looked more like a decade older in his weary state. There was that smile of hers too, a warm and loving smile juxtaposed by eyes that gave nothing away.

Lennord was careful not to stare despite the raw power she exuded, so much that she might have crushed the armrests that buckled in her grip, and looked to the Emperor's right instead, where he knew he could relax. Lord Almaric stood with his hands behind his back, prim like always, beaming elegantly in such a way that Lennord couldn't help but smile back.

"Lennord Brodie!" Tristan boomed. "Welcome back to the court of Aurail. I hope your stay here will be a pleasant one. I present you to His Majesty, Emperor Richard Llambert, fourth of that name, and Her Majesty, the Empress Alycia Llambert, representing House Lyrdred."

Tristan indicated the Emperor enthusiastically with open palms, and Lennord descended to one knee, as was customary, keen to be done with it all.

"Rise, rise," the Emperor said with as much kindly authority as he could muster, almost managing to completely obscure the croak in his throat. "Welcome back. I'm sorry about the way you were treated last night but we honestly didn't expect such a swift arrival."

"I understand, Your Majesty. I hadn't anticipated it myself. It was a good opportunity to escort two of my sons part-way to Harth. My youngest son, Marcel, is being initiated into the cathedral apprenticeship there, and Isaac will be acquiring rare materials on my behalf. I understand supplies are short here."

"Excellent use of initiative for sure."

The Empress raised an eyebrow quizzically so that Lennord could only look over his shoulder to meet her gaze's destination. One of the guards raised his eyebrows and shook his head. There was so much finesse in this that he might have done it to be purposely noticed. The Emperor let out a gloomy sigh and rubbed his forehead in frustration.

"What?" he exhaled weakly. "We're in a state of peace with Mürathneè. Such an act is not treason. Besides, there's a whole island full of Sèhvorian steel not one mile off the south-west coast. Of course we're going to have dealings with them."

The Empress was not pleased with the nod the young guard performed. There was a change in the atmosphere. Though she did not shift from her position, though she continued to clasp the armrests with both hands, and though she did not even move her weight, the Emperor clammed up. It was the eyes; it was like they shot daggers at the guard.

"Sir Yanick, I do believe the Emperor addressed you directly."

She didn't even need to shout. She opened her mouth and, effortlessly, the words slithered out and whipped Yanick like a noose being tightened around his neck. He gulped and stood to attention.

"No, Your Majesty!" he shouted.

She tapped the armrest silently. Her smile remained, yet her eyes projected a different story. Yanick was sincere but not demeaned enough to understand his wrongdoing.

"Sir Yanick, that was not a response to His Majesty's statement. Unless I, in my stupidity, have not picked up on a vital aspect of those three words, in which case, you will no doubt enlighten me and I will retract my scorn as it is fit."

"No, Your Majesty! Sorry, Your Majesty! Emperor, you are correct; I did not think."

"Mister Brodie, I can only apologise for our uncouth behaviour," the Emperor said tiredly. "I hope, at least, you found your boarding house last night."

"It took a bit of coaxing to get one of your servants to hand me the front door key. That aside, I found it easily enough thank you."

"Once again, I can only apologise for your treatment thus far. Truly, everyone is swept off their feet with preparations at the current time."

The Empress cocked her head in her husband's direction, just enough that he could see and interpret her meaning, and only because of Tristan's prior illuminations. No words were necessary, just a disconcerting look accompanied by a demure smile. The message was that the Emperor was not doing justice to his title and was fast running out of things to say, and obviously so. This was a meeting protracted beyond its welcome, demonstrated by

The Voice of Kings

Lennord's speechlessness. The Emperor, not wishing to insinuate his wife as wrong, sought to wrap up the meeting as quickly as possible.

"I'm afraid I don't have anything for you right now, I'm sure you understand, but rest assured I will send a courier to your door the very instant I do."

"Uh, excuse me if I'm being rude, Your Majesty," Lennord said before he could be sent away, "but I have a small favour to ask, if you'll listen."

"Name it."

"There's a young musician living in this city by the name of Kester Irvyng who I'd like a parcel delivered to. I don't know if he's in your employ or not, but I know he applied for a commission."

The Emperor, in dissociative sleep deprivation, rubbed his forehead and tapped his knuckles on the armrest of his throne and, at the same time, bore his teeth, almost in bitter amusement at words which would not roll off his tongue.

"Kester Irvyng. Why do I know that name?"

"I believe he applied several times, in fact," Tristan said. "You recently granted him a commission to compose a symphony."

"A quirky man, ordinary to look at," Alycia said, and put her hand on his and rubbed it. "You quite liked him."

"Yes, of course," the Emperor exclaimed quietly along with the click of his fingers. "Lord Almaric will take it. Assuming, Mister Brodie, you have it with you now?"

Tristan obligingly took the box and tucked it into a pocket. The Emperor's wife was giving him the look again. He was already aware of his mistake. The danger in acting so lazily while in an official meeting in the throne room was that the impact of any demeaning or chastising he might, for whatever reason, be required to inflict would be unavoidably lessened, even if not directed at Lennord. He straightened up and stared thoughtfully at Lennord to make one last impression on him before he left, hopefully without intimidating him at the same time.

"You may go now," he said for want of more to say.

Lennord took all of this in his stride when he left the hall. It was obvious to him, by now, that when the Emperor was feeling vulnerable and speechless, his wife tugged at his strings to kick him into action.

"Lennord!" Tristan called out to him from the doorway as he crossed the waiting room. "Care for a drink in my office?"

"Sure, why not?"

Up a set of winding stairs, Lennord was led to a long, thin hallway which probably stretched most of the length of the castle's face. Tristan's office, unlike many other rooms and halls, was not exactly the same as Lennord remembered it. The wall hanging rugs were of a different design and more colourful, and even the candleholders were stylised to his liking. On the wall, beside the one window, there hung a painting that had not been there before; a portrait of a tall raven-haired woman sitting on the steps of an ancient shrine somewhere in the wilderness. The artist had done a marvellous job at lighting her features, those of Tristan's wife, Evylyn, Lennord now realised. It was the centrepiece of the room, despite its positioning, and truly shone.

From the seat Tristan had indicated to, this was especially true, given that the large window afforded him barely more than a strip of the world outside the castle above the high walls.

"Do you drink whiskey?" Tristan said, running his finger over a variety of glasses in a cabinet.

"I don't think I know what that is, my Lord."

"Just Tristan, if you please. It's a very sorry state of affairs if I can't have a drink with an old friend without my title getting in the way," he laughed. "I understand that you would be wary to address me by my first name after years though. How long has it been? Four...five years?"

"Four years. I passed through on my way to undertake a quick excursion in Harth a couple of years back, but I didn't see you then."

Tristan poured a golden-brown fluid into two stubby glasses and, as he sat down, slid one across the desk to Lennord. As always, his jet black hair was slicked back, not dissimilar to how Lucian had fashioned his in the past in fact, and he wore that very same smile he had had the last time they'd met. His indomitable optimism had aged him well.

Lennord brought the glass of whiskey to eye level and swished it around thoughtfully, as if to reveal all its secrets.

"I remember the last time I was here on business; I stayed in one of the castle bedrooms and, on a bedside cabinet, someone, the Emperor I suppose, had left me a bottle of something. I also remember it tasted putrid, felt thick, and stung in my throat; it had more the texture of porridge than a drink."

"If it *was* whiskey, it must not have been the good stuff, like this. Real whiskey should be silky smooth."

Lennord shrugged loosely and downed a mouthful. He winced and recoiled but extended a hand palm down and waved indecisively. His mouth opened to respond, but he shut it again and pondered on it further as the flavour continued to develop.

"I don't think my wife would like this at all," he said at last.

Tristan smiled gleefully and stroked his pine desk without thinking about it. These little ticks were of no consequence now, so much as leftovers from his early, insecure days of being a knight.

"How is your family, by the way? Living in the lap of luxury from all your hard-earned commission money?"

The Voice of Kings

"It's a nice thought, but no. Not exactly. I had an idea to evolve my house into something grander, like a proper keep, but I abandoned it quite quickly. It didn't seem right when my neighbours couldn't even implement pumps into their homes. Too embarrassing, for that matter. So I put the money into raising Caedor's overall quality instead. Maybe one day though," he ended on a high note.

Tristan thrust a finger at Lennord with surprising restraint and pent up joy, and there was approval brewing inside him as the weight of this deed began to sink in.

"This is why I was right to hire you, my friend. You'll bring everything down to earth."

He smelt and sipped his whiskey as a connoisseur would. He'd taken to politics with a rather more casual attitude than most, and though, at first, this and his affinity for alcohol had gotten him some disfavouring looks as a nervous 20-year-old man, it had all somehow worked in his favour. It was obvious why the Emperor was so fond of him; a jovial yet deceptively level-headed and intelligent man such as he would be all that was needed to bring the elitists at court crashing down.

"You mentioned that young Isaac is travelling to Harth for you," Tristan said in the same relaxed manner that Lennord had once heard him use to negotiate a business transaction with a Mürathneèan baron.

"And probably flirting with a pretty young lady as we speak. He's quite the talker now. A good lad if I'm honest, if a little unfocused."

"All grown up then," Tristan said. "Not quite the sweet boy I met 18 years ago."

"Time will do that, I find," Lennord sighed.

"I did happen on him in an inn a few years ago, and time did not diminish hope. Too briefly, alas."

Tristan tapped the desk rhythmically, perhaps to an old song that always helped him think during their earlier exploits. Every time he met Lennord, he was cautious of this subject but, thankfully, each time his worries were unwarranted, for Lennord did not balk at predicting it.

"I'm glad to hear he's keeping faith," he ventured. "I expect you and Gèyll are the reason for that. What happened to him in that mine could have ruined him, for certain, with less capable parents. I know you never believed his story, but you must have helped him out in other ways."

"He made it quite difficult for me when he started to grow up," Lennord said quietly, so far away in his mind. "He would pester me to investigate and, I'll admit it, it fascinated me. But I never could work out the line where the truth in his memory ended and the irrevocable truth began. Perhaps, one day, such an incident will occur that will renew my interest but...I've made my peace with it, and so has Isaac."

"Would you rather get down to business then?" Tristan said smoothly, unfazed in transitioning to a new subject. "We can discuss your political role if it pleases you."

Silence dropped in the office. Cogs built up momentum in Tristan's mind as it came to him that this was a revelation to Lennord, who also was playing the words back in his mind to ensure he hadn't misunderstood.

"Why in the name of all the gods would I want to involve myself in politics? I'm an inventor, and that's all."

"I'm sorry, Lennord, but it's inevitable," he said with anxiety slipping in now. "You'll get caught up in it one way or another. I'm also sorry to tell you now that the Emperor intends to assign you as a military engineer."

"That's a waste of my talents!" Lennord laughed hollowly. "Why are you only telling me this now?"

"Because it was my intention to sway the Emperor's decision anyway. I will if I can, I assure you."

"But why am I to be involved in politics?"

Tristan smiled sympathetically and Lennord cooled down. Inside him there was still anger, but it was being contained for now, to allow him room to think. From the chapel in the garden, the bell signalling noon rang out and knocked his thoughts back to nothingness. His continued frustration did not go unnoticed by Tristan, who pushed his now empty whiskey glass aside and made clear that Lennord had his full attention.

"Listen to me, Lennord. The Emperor is feeling desperate at the moment and he wants to catch up with King Michael's success quickly. His correspondents in Mürathneè are not helping matters either, feeding him information about strange goings-on over there, and mounting tensions and hushed conspiracy meetings behind their backs. Superstitious drivel really, but the Emperor is feeling rather melancholic and has bought all of it.

"He will use you as one of his front men for his renaissance, and he'll expect you to sell it, maybe even attend court sometimes, whether you like it or not, *but* I know how the Emperor and Empress plan these things inside out. If a messenger sends me orders from one or the other, it's a rare failing if I can't tell, before finishing reading the document, whose idea it was originally, who sent the order, even if they got someone else to write it. I can help make it easy for you, or relatively so."

"You can minimise my exposure to politics then? If I have no other choice, then I gladly accept your help. Must we talk about it now?"

Tristan shook his head side to side.

"Not if you're not ready."

He rose elegantly and strode round the desk to excuse Lennord from having to ask to leave. When Lennord got up, the kindly lord shook his hand furiously. Lennord put his other hand on Tristan's, to make up for the weak handshake on his part.

The Voice of Kings

"You worry now, but you'll feel better about it later, I'm sure," Tristan said. "We're romantics. Even when we're wading through shit, we'll merrily take up a shovel and keep up the pace."

Lennord couldn't help but laugh at this and grabbed his side in painful humour as Tristan escorted him to the door. Followed out, Lennord was secure in the knowledge that he was not alone.

"I'll see you soon, friend," Tristan said, slapping Lennord on the shoulder.

"Goodbye, friend."

Such words were comforting. Tristan strolled off in the other direction, tapping his fingers on the wall absentmindedly.

~

Tristan contemplated where Richard might be right now. He reflected on words exchanged with the Master-at-Arms, Havdan Linch, ensuring in his memory the man had betrayed no tension. "The Emperor is rash and fierce in combat; that served him well enough, but I have to say, I saw him hold back just the same," he remembered. The man had stroked his scars, sage-like, but Tristan had kept an amicable half stare with the man's eyes, and saw no deception. Good man, Havdan, he complimented in hindsight. Such was true of dear Richard in other matters also, yet more besides might rouse his sorrow of now, his wife's ambitions so sad not to align with his. Tristan smiled as he sighed. The look on Alycia's face after Lennord had turned to leave, while unreadable, was unmistakably brimming with a fiery purpose, and he was obligated to see the aftermath of that.

~

In despair, the Emperor stood on a fourth floor battlement staring wistfully into the distance. The wind up here was cooler and had a bit more of a bite to it than the tepid breeze down below. He hoped the combination of this and a view of the city beyond his stronghold would help him think, and perhaps even be blessed with some sort of epiphany.

It was all helping in some fashion, though not as he had anticipated. The city was to him, in this place, now, an unmoving, stubborn, pathetic entity. There was life to be seen on rooftops, smoke billowing from chimneys and birds flying to and from lofts, but there was no energy, no passion to be derived from any of it. His city had collapsed into a dull, empty routine around him, creating his nightmare that he had not even, until recently, been willing to acknowledge.

This drove him to catalyse his anger into something far greater, into ideas for the future. He forced his palms along the coarse battlement merlon before him, sliding his legs apart to distribute his weight as he did so. His fingers, tensed, rose up slowly while his palms remained flat, as if he was trying to take chunks out of the brick. A few loose pieces of the battlement rattled beneath his hands and tumbled to the patio at the fore of the garden. When he looked down, he saw a few men swinging swords at one another on that same patch of his garden as before, their ringing sounds amalgamating into one high-pitched squeal which he had, until now, ignored, as the wind was merciful enough to not blow from their direction.

Someone was watching him. His brain had picked up on it before but, only now, as the world besides the city came back into focus, did it register, as if somehow the sound of their footsteps had only just caught up with him. There were very few people who could so gracefully and quietly sneak up on him, and fewer with the daring not to announce his or her presence and stare at him without remorse, like he was a strange and unique sculpture to be examined.

He tilted his head just enough to confirm his assumption. Alycia was indeed standing behind him. She had a purpose, a will of such power that he couldn't compete with, that sapped all the energy and motivation he'd built up. Even the way her hair flapped in the wind could have been part of her plan for all her confidence. It was of ethereal beauty, hypnotising him into wishing to stroke it and feel its splendour, but a mental block, to his shame, prevented him from making such a move. He looked to the cityscape once more.

"You're a picture of misery," she said serenely.

She had his full attention, begrudgingly. Besides, he was also interested in what scheme she might be planning now, if only to hear the end of it.

"Go ahead," Alycia said. "Speak."

"You're dissatisfied with something. So much of what we're doing was organised by you, yet still you want more. No doubt it's all my fault somehow."

"I'm over here, love. Your argument won't rouse straw men." A pause. "You lack a cohesive vision. If standing here and gazing longingly to the horizon helps, then by all means continue. If not, you're wasting your time and you need to try something else."

"Such as?"

"Listen to me, for a start."

"That is *exactly* what I've been doing," Richard explained meekly.

He wandered away from her in what he hoped would be a subtle way of making his leave. Alycia strode ahead of him, blocking his path, and pivoted to face him. She was but a few inches from him, holding his attention with her beautiful eyes, like a seductress. Shifting back to allow room to breathe, he felt compelled to stay and fight his corner this time. He probably couldn't break eye contact even if he wanted to anyway.

"If you want my honest opinion," he said, "I think such a strong military focus will do us little good. We should follow Lord Almaric's advice and cease this foolishness."

"My dear, your great, great grandfather invaded Mürathneè and Alassii and Mūrac and declared himself Emperor, yet here we are."

"Jorin Llambert was also a lunatic! Besides, he couldn't keep all those countries, and no wonder. What an example he is to follow in the footsteps of."

The Voice of Kings

He was weary at the mention of his despotic predecessor, the self-professed king of kings, the maniac who thought he could provoke the entire world and enslave them when they refused to comply with him, because obviously the gods would be on his side. And then there was his wife, Terryn, who was no better. To hear Alycia speak in her cryptic and condescending way did not help.

A guard marched along the wall towards them. Richard courteously stepped back to allow him passage between them, but Alycia's hands reached out and tugged hard on his robes lest he use this as an opportunity to escape. The guard carried on by them, giving them a short bow without stopping at the same time. A sweet smile veiled a disapproving look. Anyone else might not have noticed but, for him, there were just enough signs to look past the charm and see something else at work, yet so little evidence that he could not be sure. She allowed the unease to fester within him, provoke his brain into doing actual work before finally putting him out of his misery.

"You think my point was to prove to you what a great leader that man was?"

"I did think that's what you were insinuating, though rest assured, it sounded bizarre coming from your lips."

"Of course I agree he was a lunatic," she assured him. "What he did was pure despicable folly, madness even. The lands he dominated might have grounded Burtal into dust after his grip was weakened but we were still strong, we were still *relevant*, and here we are now, still fighting for our right to survive."

She initiated another tactic to fix him in place. She fussed at his tunic, running dainty fingers like a magic wand along his collar, back, and chest. For her, this was as technical and reliable as working the strings on a violin. He knew why, but made no motion either way.

"Carlophinia was an immense military power many generations ago, like the first Emperor, and look at them now. The destitute nation of the known world; a vast expanse of degenerating settlements and, at the centre of it, a king of intelligence, but with no power because corruption festers like a forest of weeds. Are we like them, doomed to descend into oblivion? Are we?"

She spoke forcefully but not for its own sake. She had a passion for this and, in order that her husband might not misconstrue her, she juxtaposed her speech by lovingly wrapping her hands around his neck.

"If that was your point, you should have just come out with it instead of dancing around the issue."

"Oh, that wasn't my point. That was a means by which you might appreciate my point better. My point is that I agree with you, to an extent, but unlike you, I am thinking more clearly. I'm aware that you've not been feeling well and may not have picked up on the nuance in my ideas, and thus passed them off as uninformed tripe."

"So?" the Emperor said, his tiredness becoming ever more apparent, feeling like he would have better luck squeezing blood from a stone.

"So I agree that we should focus on a variety of issues for our renaissance, but we need detailed plans laid out in full before we act, whereas you would have us floundering about in deep water at the very start because of impatience. And let me make perfectly clear that our initial military focus will only do us good. It will make us look strong. There are people who think you're spineless; "an Emperor without an empire" they joke, and but for the Cylliairn Islands, you would be, technically, and those belonged to many a king of Burtal anyway. And there are those who still wonder why you carry the title of Emperor. Jorin's son decided to keep the name, to show that we already have the empire we need, and that it is Burtal, one and only, island lathes to our very south or no. It's just a word, one we'll give new meaning by talking the loudest."

Muffled voices carried from the chamber leading from the battlement walkway and were whisked by the wind like sweet music to Richard's ears, a merciful release. It was Tristan's voice, and that of a guard giving him directions. The voices died down and voices echoed, louder and louder until Tristan appeared in full sight.

He must have known immediately what manner of conversation his Emperor and Empress were undertaking and resolved, as such, not to intervene, so remained quiet as the grave, under the door arch halfway in the light of the candles and the glaring sun at its peak, high in the sky. His arms were behind his back and he did not motion to proceed, so as to make clear he was a bystander.

Richard pointed a finger at Tristan but Alycia did not sever eye contact for a second.

"Lord Almaric had it right though," Richard said. "Our royalty is our bane. We don't perceive the city as those out there do. Your plans could be flawed from the outset because of a skewed perspective."

"Rest assured, Your Majesty, that I do conduct research. Precisely none of it is baseless supposition. Still, an excellent idea. I was having similar thoughts myself." She smiled mischievously. It was a wonderful smile, but gods damn it.

"What?" the Emperor growled.

"To walk the streets and bask in the inadequacies of our city. We could go tonight. If we hide ourselves and minimise our security detail to a couple of expert soldiers, we should encounter no trouble. We should see to the preparations."

She curtseyed to Lord Almaric and glided away. The Emperor was torn between seeking advice from his aide Paramount, and uncovering what was going through his wife's head. In the end, there was only one choice. He scurried after Alycia, as she knew he would.

Chapter Seven: King of Dirt

The hinges of the solid iron gates creaked slowly, at first grating, then turning to a high pitched wail, followed by the understated thud of the two doors sliding in place and the cogs meshing together, locking the parts together and barring the four people standing outside from the castle grounds, facing west.

Richard and Alycia wore simple merchant surcoats bearing low hanging hoods dipping over their foreheads. Richard, resolved to be sullen, took a closer look at the two guards as they walked, in hopes of reassurance. To their left, Sir Pedrig Lannoi strolled like he had no cares in the world but, upon more scrutinised inspection, it became apparent that he was keeping a watchful eye on his surroundings and he held the hilt of his sword at all times, albeit not with the arm one would normally associate with a sword draw; the sword was on his left side, gripped with the left hand like in a public march. Still, he was a capable warrior and had many years of experience, evidenced in his greying hair.

To his right, Sir Doru Byrd, formerly a captain in the army and much else besides, was poised with a more intimidating approach backed by an eerie calmness. He was younger than Pedrig but was still of no fewer years than 45, by Richard's estimation. Committed young soldiers of superior athleticism, expert skills, and unwavering loyalty were hard to come by in Aurail these days, but the experience and loyalty of these two men would do him fine.

So he was safe, yet he was not at ease. There was nothing to indicate that this would not be a wild goose chase around the city. Indeed, the knights did not appear to be leading with any consistency or coherency, in favour of pure randomness. *Alycia's cunning may soon prove otherwise*, he thought, knowing her. It was entirely possible that she'd briefed the knights in private before leaving. Yes, she must have done. Before today, they were merely names on paper to him, and now they wore perfect fitting Guardian armour, similar to that of the City Watch captains, yet stronger forged, of finer filigree, and betraying not the same gaps, showcasing refineries and a golden crown wreathing the three towers on their breastplates, and green capes clasped firmly at their shoulders.

If there was a method to the madness, it was not yet apparent. As, in jarring procession, they passed from an aristocratic district into a poorer area of the city, disgust washed over him for not putting an end to this sooner. It was all depressing and the light rain being spat on them, making for a gloomy picture; it was hardly inspiring. There were potholes everywhere, dilapidated buildings looming over them like a dead ecosystem from which the inhabitants had all disappeared. He failed to restrain a sickly cough.

King of Dirt

There were some lights from within the houses but scarcely many lanterns designated for the roads, practically inviting robbers, or worse, murderers and rapists, to easily pick out innocents, sometimes without so much as the cover of an alley. A crate had been abandoned by the side of the road, for how long he did not care to investigate. Someone who was so inclined could hide behind it without fear of being seen. He felt safer than before, against all reason. The knights created an invisible bubble of protection which made him feel invincible in a place where almost anyone should, otherwise, feel at their most vulnerable.

He made a mental note of this lack of lighting. On Alycia's face, he could almost see her brain whirring away, writing notes more extravagant and intuitive than his that he could not begin to imagine. Hand in hand with his feelings of inadequacy, he sought to prove a point about something in their surroundings, anything that had not occurred to her which would demonstrate his logicality and forethought.

"There might be a fatal flaw in the approach we're taking," he said. "In borrowing so much money from the other counties, we might inflate the same disparity of wealth classes in Aurail to a larger scale throughout Burtal."

"One thing at a time," Alycia cooed. "If the capital becomes an awe-inspiring visual and economic success, reinvesting the money owed to the other counties, and more, will be a breeze. Don't take my word for it though; position more correspondents across Mürathneè if you want a wider view."

Her smooth, snappy response was more than enough to shut him up. A part of him wanted to rebuke this, but he knew if he tried to outsmart her in this way, he would only make a fool of himself, thus he declined to object and made further observations in silence.

The streets all looked the same in this ill light. It did nothing positive for him, only make him more tired. His thoughts drifted from the streets to other things, feeling asleep already, and, as with dreams, when the barking of a dog from someone's house booted him into the real world again, he could not rightly remember anything that had come before, except vaguely defined images and words that could not be grasped in any meaningful way. Not knowing how much time had passed, he felt even more lost. As a consolation, there were lanterns providing appropriate light levels here, not that he could distinguish one house from the next, even if they weren't so shoddy around here. Just when he was about to raise the question of their location, he spotted the outer wall of the city not far to their left.

The sounds of civilisation returned in the form of rowdy shouting and laughter from within, what could only be, an inn. This was confirmed when they turned into a road wider and longer than any other they had yet encountered, where buildings were not badly kept. Starved from a notable lack of human contact on this night, they would have stopped to observe the lives of these drinkers through the taphouse windows anyway, but an argument inside drew them like a siren's call. Two men who'd had too much to drink were in the middle of the room shouting and pointing at one another, flailing their arms incomprehensibly.

Most disturbing of all was that half the people in the inn gave only cursory glances to the bickering idiots and returned to their own conversations, even as the noise level rose higher and the words and meaning of the dispute were lost to vulgar insults. All four of them knew the next step in this escalation was physical violence, and when the first blow was struck to the other man's temple, there was only grave disappointment in them. The man who'd been punched did not take the insult lightly, retaliating with an uppercut to his offender's stomach and a back-fisted strike to his jaw.

"Animals," Sir Pedrig grunted.

Richard blew cool summer air out upon realising that he was holding his breath. He turned away, with the sounds of knuckles beating against bone ongoing, for a real breather. To his left, at the end of the road, not a hundred feet away, half a dozen or so torches lit an iron gate, similar in craftsmanship style to that of Castle Aurail, if less fancy.

It dawned on him, in terror, where they were. His fists clenched so hard they turned white, and he shook his head as if denial could eventually alter the truth.

"Gods, is that the south-east gate?"

"I think you're right, Your Majesty," Sir Doru agreed.

Richard and Alycia shot each other rare looks of mutual understanding. The fight in the inn was now fully disrupting even the hardest-skinned drinkers. It couldn't be ignored any longer, seeing as chairs and a table had been upturned and blood was cascading down the two fighters' faces, not that they cared or possibly even noticed. Attempts had been made to interrupt the fighting, but half-heartedly at best.

It was a fair assumption that some of them may have been too scared to try, but there were a few groups who did not look remotely intimidated, and one of the men tending to the bar merely crossed his arms and shook his head, giving distasteful looks to guests around the room as if in hopes that forced guilt might spur them into action.

"Do you want us to split them up?" Doru said.

"Wait!" Alycia barked, holding a hand out.

They obeyed without hesitation. They didn't even flinch. The fight was all but over now regardless. The man who'd landed the first strike was pummelling his opponent in the chest repeatedly. A great deal of his punches were weak, misjudged, and were going to cause him considerable pain in his hands when he sobered up but, for now, he wasn't feeling a thing and the damage was mounting up.

His opponent collapsed onto a table. The victor staggered an about turn. Already the pain was setting in, and the implication on his horrified face was that he didn't know where he was or, if he did, the world was crashing down around him and he was replaying in his mind how this situation had come to be. The downed man, like a wild beast, screamed, clambered to, and grabbed the backrest of a chair. The temporary winner of their bout turned but not fast enough. A chair leg was thrust into his abdomen, splintering it, and then it was swung into his upper chest, snapping it this time.

Like birds of prey, the knights' heads pivoted in a flash for advice from their superiors.

"Wait!" Alycia said again, forceful but less sure this time.

"To hell with that; he'll fucking kill him."

Richard's resolve was not witnessed as a definitive order, as he had hoped, rather than a statement, striking uncertainty as to whose wishes were to be enacted.

"Go!" Richard shouted, pointing to the door and clicking his fingers. "And bring me the publican!"

The knights stormed through the door and ripped the chair from the bewildered offender's hands. They targeted the group consisting of the most respectable, yet also strongest, citizens and sternly gave them all orders. They helped the two drunken buffoons to their feet and dragged them to the door. From what Richard could infer, they most likely were informed to take the drunkards to a physician, and tell any available at this hour the whole truth.

The knights physically stopped them before they could get far, to issue a strong warning, presumably to threaten them of the consequences of omitting some details from their explanation.

The group left and didn't so much as give the Emperor and Empress a moment's notice. Soon they were gone, to Richard's relief. Doru and Pedrig exited shortly after, pushing ahead of them the apathetic innkeeper. Though aware that he was in trouble, there was an inkling of confidence which Richard was keen to stamp on. Was he drunk too? It would take a drunk or very flustered man not to notice the armour the soldiers wore.

"You're the owner of this inn, are you?" Richard asked commandingly.

"The landlord and proprietor, yes. Have we met before?"

His tone showed recognition. Richard and Alycia glanced at one another to read each other's expressions. Fortune be fair, they were on the same page. There was no reason to conceal the truth any longer. They untied their merchant coats and swished them back to reveal, in complete glory, their magisterial robes. The truth clicked into place, visibly and aesthetically pleasing, like clockwork. His mouth was agape and the despair was engulfing him already; of all the worst of luck, this was one scenario he could never have planned for.

"Your Majesty, I..."

"What happened in there was unacceptable. Do you hear me? Not fucking acceptable!"

The Emperor took a lunging step forward, stamping his boot on the road so hard it echoed throughout the whole street. Alycia looked positively impressed with his passion. Even so, it was obvious she had no intention of following through with his unarticulated shouting.

"Your Majesty, I can only apologise."

"You can do more than that, I promise you," the Empress purred. "I'm afraid I can't tell how many nights you'll be sleeping on a prison mattress if you don't."

"Empress..."

"It simply won't do to hold a conversation from this distance. You show the Emperor great disrespect. Sir Doru, if you please..."

She pointed inconspicuously to Doru's sword and then swept the finger in the landlord's direction. The gamble paid off; he understood her notion. Sir Doru unsheathed his sword in one swift motion and dug the point in the small of the terrified innkeeper's back. Richard was a man of power no longer. His brief stint of menace ended as soon as it started, supplanted by Alycia's terrifying new scheme.

The landlord marched without incident. He said not a word and dared not speak when Alycia commanded him to stop with a hand movement.

"Explain to me, if you will, how this is acceptable. My puny mind can't comprehend it. As I see it, if a merchant enters the city through that gate there, looking for a good trade, the first impression of my husband's city he'll get is two idiots beating the life from one another in a squalid little inn, while a crowd of uncaring spectators lay back and indulge in this despicable barbarism.

"He'll think, *'This place isn't for me, but I've heard Harth is where all the good deals are.'* Is it not so?"

"I suppose it is," the landlord replied weakly, even having overcome his shakes.

"You suppose it, do you?"

Sir Doru twisted his blade so that the tough leather tunic the man wore began to tear. He puffed out his chest and arched his back. He was definitely feeling it now, and he trod very carefully in this verbal arena.

"I won't excuse my own actions, but there is no justice around here."

"Were you praying for mighty Lameeri to materialise from the celestial realm and dispense holy justice?"

He was exactly where she wanted: helpless, frightened, and alone. Nothing he could say would satisfy her, and at the same time, if he did not respond, it would be taken as a grave insult to the crown.

"Guards scarcely ever patrol here. I don't know if they're supposed to, but they don't. When they do happen to check in, they don't always care about lawlessness."

The landlord's voice rose and fell, his breathing exasperated, as if he wasn't sure, with every word, whether he should continue or whether it would be safer to keep his mouth shut. The fear was wrapped with uncertainty when no one responded. It was possible, he thought, that, by accident, he had hit just the right note. Alycia thoughtfully looked to her knights for guidance.

King of Dirt

"Is what this man says true? An entrance to the city going practically unguarded?"

"There are guard patrol routes and times for this area, I'm sure of it," Sir Doru said. "Although, if the guards have been as lax with the law as this man says, I wouldn't be surprised if they've not taken their patrols seriously either."

"There will have to be a full investigation, do you understand? Take as many loyal soldiers from the castle and sweep this whole area first thing tomorrow morning. Question as many guards as you can, report back, and we'll release as many from service as is necessary."

"Yes, Your Majesty."

She glared at the man who, by now, must have been feeling very small and, with the power of her venomous stare, sucked the soul from him and made him feel beyond irrelevant, as if he didn't exist at all.

"Your Majesty," he croaked, "I assure you I will be of no trouble at all if you at least tell your knight to take his sword from my back."

"I hope my point is well illustrated then. When a sword is pressed to your back, one push away from making you a cripple, or, for example, when someone holds a chair over your head with the intent of killing you, it can be very frightening indeed, especially so when time ebbs away and you realise no one is coming to your aid, no one even cares."

He nodded feverishly and licked his lips, though they were as dry as the stone walls inside Castle Aurail. The Empress pointed to Doru's sword, then to his sheath. The innkeeper sagged in relief so much he looked like he might fall over. The pointed metal was graciously pulled back without further incident and sheathed where it couldn't immediately harm him. Then the devil became a god. Alycia glided to the innkeeper, gently placing a hand on one shoulder, stern but pitying. *Very clever, Alycia*, Richard thought. When he'd just been threatened so, the grace that followed was all the more poignant.

"Go on, get out of my sight," the Emperor growled. "I'm quite sick of looking at you."

"You have an obligation to uphold the peace, just as every other citizen of this city does," Alycia added, a second before the man walked back into his inn. "Not just the guards. Your excuses won't hold up the next time this happens."

Richard waited impatiently for the man to return and watched as he picked up the tables and chairs that had been knocked over during the brawl. More than one of them was broken; he scooped up the pieces and carried them into a back room where he could no longer be seen.

"What you're proposing could result in dozens of guards losing their jobs," Richard said.

"Not to worry. If they start a ruckus over it, they can have a nice long think down in the dungeons."

The Voice of Kings

"That's not what I meant," Richard protested angrily. "With everything we've got going on, it's just not feasible to hire and train so many new recruits. And then what? We do the same for the rest of the city?"

Richard put his hands behind his head and looked up into the black abyss that was the sky. The rain was picking up; just another reason to be miserable. He tugged at his hood, even though it was already all the way down, and tied his coat closed. Alycia stroked his back soothingly and there was nothing he could do but let her.

"It will have to be feasible, Your Majesty. We must make a statement that people understand; lay down some principles. Gods know the people here don't have any."

"If you say so. I'll order a script to be written for the city criers first thing in the morning, and have some fliers drawn up as well."

"Tonight," she rebuked as an indisputable fact, not a suggestion.

All the madness of the inn gave her another idea already. Even by her standards, she was absorbing a lot of information. There was much in the way of micro details to log when she returned to the castle. For now, a shrewd smile grew steadily.

"Sir Pedrig, Sir Doru, count the seconds please. In your heads. I need to think."

In unison, they nodded in spite of their reservations. Richard resolved that asking her to explain was expended energy. She was likely mapping out a big reveal already, while he was content to soak in the atmosphere of the place and be ashamed. If there was one thing to be thankful for, it was that he could see where he was going without fear of tripping and splitting his head open. The added illumination provided him with the means to fully appreciate how little his city had moved with the times; a trade of one depressing situation for another.

Before he had time to slip into another daydream, more loutish shouting billowed through the night air, injecting dread into Richard that the four of them might have another incident. Perhaps, this time, someone would be killed.

They followed the din to its source, being a small square with a large well in the middle. Two drunkards sat on a bench, conversing loudly, so disconnected from the real world that they, themselves, probably only had a loose grasp on what they were talking about. Breathless silence followed. The sight of two people of noble blood flanked by two seasoned bodyguards, their armour clunking noisily through the dead of the night, must have been intimidation enough.

They both jumped to their feet, ready to defend themselves from being arrested for a crime they did not yet know. One of them lobbed the tankard he was holding. Richard and Alycia flinched. It shattered on the breastplate of Pedrig. If it scratched the enamel, it couldn't be seen in this light. His friend looked prepared to defend himself.

"Arrest those men," the Empress ordered, solemn.

They were no match for the knights. When they saw them sprinting in their direction, they abandoned all thoughts of self-defence and ran. Pedrig and Doru caught them before they even left the square, and were each disabled with one fell move, being swung around and trapped in an armlock. Alycia smiled bitterly.

"What?" Richard asked. "What does this prove?"

"It doesn't prove anything. They needed to be taken off the streets. The point's already been proven."

"Not to me."

"Good knights, what had you counted to when we encountered these unsavoury characters?"

They all walked on again, the knights pushing the drunken men ahead of them. If there was one positive quality to be said about them, it was that they had truly surrendered, so they weren't completely stupid, even while so inebriated. The knights could be seen working through their hindsight to before the arrest.

"About four and a half minutes," Sir Pedrig said.

"I know what you're thinking, but that doesn't prove anything," Richard protested. "You need an average time."

"We'll put it on our to-do list."

Ideas formed in Richard's head. He fought them at first, not wishing to prove his wife correct that this would be a good idea. The allure was too strong. There was something to it, he was sure of it, and he'd be a fool to bury it, not to mention depriving his dying city of a movement which could change the outlooks of some of its inhabitants.

"I will confess," he said, "I'm having a thought. The people around here are, by my judgement, very private and introverted, even those who go out drinking. They need to be brought together somehow. It's all very well to impress outsiders, but we need different tactics for our own people. They need to be educated."

"You have the right of it," Alycia said, genuinely impressed. "Public seminars could solve more than one problem at once: merging classes into one conglomerate, at least for the duration of the seminars, giving people hope, a way for them to understand the changes being made, the personal and socioeconomic benefits, as well as incentives for getting involved. Exquisite. It requires a level of grandiosity to amuse the public of course. The opera house or the castle will be appropriate locations to consider."

"The opera house isn't even finished!"

"All the better to host them there and let everyone see it being built!"

She laughed and slapped him on the back. What should have been a playful gesture of goodwill was translated by Richard as a diabolical act of mockery. He was a seething vessel of rage and confusion, made worse by his tiredness which blinded him. The grin on Alycia's face could have lulled any other man into a sense of satisfaction, and somewhere in him felt the need to obey that instinct. He fought it off, but said nothing of it nor indicated it in any way.

When the gates of the castle finally warped through the blackness into sight, a weight was lifted from his shoulders, the likes of which he could not before comprehend the weight of. It was a gruelling wait for the gates to open. Sleep was close, yet so far. Blood whizzed through his veins so fast it felt like they would burst. He felt, in that moment, that he wouldn't even be able to fall asleep this night.

On the other side, Richard had only just opened his mouth to utter a command when he was interrupted, before a single syllable could be uttered.

"You may go," Alycia said to the knights.

"As she says."

Alycia stroked Richard's chin affectionately. Real affection, even, may have been the motivating factor behind this. It was still far simpler for him to believe otherwise.

"Good luck exploring new avenues for our realm," she said.

"And you."

They parted in the main hall for their separate research paths. Richard stormed through the castle like an ill-tempered child, thoughts racing through his mind that he couldn't hope to catch up with. He barged through door after door, like a simple brute, until he came upon an elegant chamber decorated with an impressive variety of weapons in cabinets around the edges. Stairs led upwards in right-angled increments, and not far along the corridor up there was Tristan's bedroom. Richard slung his surcoat over the banister and heaved for air.

"Lord Almaric! Lord Almaric! LORD ALMARIC!"

He paced the room furiously. Each weapon he looked at brought his temper down a notch, each containing a memory. There was a cabinet of small swords and daggers, ranging from the smallest on the left to the largest on the far right. The largest was a cinquedea short sword, gifted by King Michael some few years past. It was a decorative piece of marvellous craftsmanship. A ruby sparkled in the pommel.

And then there were two of the biggest weapons in the room; a battleaxe and a war hammer. He had never used them in combat of any sort, but he remembered training with them, how different they were to a broadsword, and how Alycia was in fits of giggles between covering her mouth in shock when he insisted on trying them.

Pride of place, on a wooden plaque, was the preserved head of a chupacabra, the biggest he'd ever seen so close. It was very much like the head of a mountain lion, but the fur was grey and it had four fangs like the sabretooth tigers from the far north. One of its gigantic spines, similar in basic aesthetic to those of a porcupine, protruded from the back of its head.

Beneath it, the bastard sword that felled it was gripped in two wall clasps. Richard reached up and removed it. He took a firm grip with one hand and held it out as far as he could. His breathing was too heavy. The sword was trembling and he could have sworn it had felt half the weight the last time he had used it. The anger, weirdly, was all vented away now, replaced by lethargy.

"Did you summon me, Your Majesty?"

Tristan stood in a nightgown on the landing intersecting the right angle directional change on the stairs. For once, he was not quite so perky. Richard nodded to acknowledge his presence but, for some time, said nothing, merely gazing at the sword in a distant daydream.

"I need your advice, my Lord. I need to assert myself somehow. I need to resolve these issues of tiredness."

"That's hardly an enigma, if you don't mind me saying so. Decrease your workload for a bit. Take some time out to see Rickart, that's what I would do. It's what I, in fact, did. Seeing my son and wife helped me gather my composure."

"Time is one thing I do not have in excess," Richard said sleepily. "I feel like I need to redistribute my skills to something else, but that's just not possible, and I can't even be sure *that's* what I want because my mind is just...mush, right now. Prison is what this is."

"Please tell me you're not referring to your fighting prowess," Tristan groaned.

"Prowess? I can't even hold my sword like I used to. I used to be better than this," Richard said, his voice becoming fiercer and louder. "I defeated *that thing* in combat," he snarled, pointing to the chupacabra head. "It raced at me and I lopped its head off."

"And very impressive it was too, but with the greatest respect, Your Majesty, you were never a soldier. I was more a soldier than you when I was delegated to security management all those years ago, and I never fought on a battlefield either. This idea that fighting is your most proficient skill is maddening. And wrong." He laughed in good nature.

Tristan walked the rest of the way down the stairs and approached the Emperor with caution. There was no chance of him lashing out, that was a statistical impossibility. He was feeling weak and, somehow, holding his old sword was calming him, if depressing him also. However, he had to scrutinise every step, every movement, and every word if he was to help him. It wasn't just about staying in the Emperor's favour, Richard knew of him, it was personal, and that's what separated him from the sycophants in court.

Richard allowed Tristan to take the sword, misjudging even this action somehow and nearly dropping it before the grip had passed hands. Tristan grabbed it immediately, the lightning speed of his early days as a knight rearing its head to ensure Richard did not feel the full disgrace of his clumsiness. The sword was fairly light and, at the same time, well-balanced. It had a good feel to it, and would be an excellent friend in any number of tight combat situations. His friend, Tristan, would never be seen to appear overly proud in taking the great sword. The thinking being that, if he saw that Tristan was handling it so well, he might feel inferior. Perhaps he was right. Understatedly, Tristan placed the sword in its grip and wiped a thin layer of dust from the blade with two fingers.

"You need to stop this," Tristan said firmly, staring unblinkingly into Richard's eyes. "You're the Emperor of Burtal, you have been for many years, and you've ruled well, given the circumstances. There is nothing nobler about fighting than ruling the country."

"Given the circumstances?" Richard mused.

Tristan, fighting a losing battle, reached out his hand, fast like an arrow, and squeezed his arm. Tristan's hand shook him violently and lured him in. The Emperor staggered and thankfully retained his footing. His eyes were so wide they looked like he'd seen a ghost. His mouth dropped too, and then he looked about at random places in the room, as if he had been asleep all this time and was suddenly and rudely awakened.

"Your Majesty, what you're doing is not healthy. I'm your friend and I love you, and we have exciting times ahead of us for which you will need my help, but I can't do that if you continue on this self-demeaning tirade. You're *not* a soldier, you're the Emperor, and you can do great things for your people. It's better this way, believe me."

Richard gawked. Slowly his senses returned to him, and Tristan's meaning sunk in. A confused expression switched to a nervous smirk, and then back again, and finally a laugh broke out. A sadly apologetic smile emerged. Tristan smiled proudly and confidently, spurring him to dreams of success.

"I'm sorry," Richard said. "I thought I was only speaking my mind in jest. I didn't know, myself, that I sounded so serious."

"Spilling your thoughts is a good starting point, I suppose. No good keeping them locked away. Sixteen years married to a very emotional woman has taught me that. If I might make one final suggestion though, I would say check yourself out with one of your physicians. I'm sure good will come of it."

"I might just do that. Oh, you may go back to bed now. We have some very long days ahead of us, as you know. Oh, and thank you," he added as an afterthought when Tristan reached the top of the stairs.

"Pleasant night, Your Majesty."

Tristan, in all his modesty, waved Richard's thanks away with a casual attitude most would not dare use around such a figure. Then he was gone, leaving Richard alone with what thoughts he could piece together, and his tools of reminiscence.

Richard stripped his clothes with disregard for proper function and formality, leaving them in a crumpled heap on the tiled floor of the bathroom. Hot steam billowed from the water in thick clouds, courtesy of the coals and metal pipes hidden beneath, writhing and dancing through the air and all around the room like sentient ethereal entities being born into the world.

As his foot touched the water, it stung all over with the intensity of a wasp sting, but he didn't care. When he lowered the rest of his body, the water scorched him like ravenous animals tearing at his flesh. Despite his flinching, he made no effort to get out of the bath, for it concealed his aches. The reward he reaped was great enough that the pain was almost cancelled out. He felt clean instantly, a weight lifted as if his body had been drenched in mud. His mind, too, repaired its shattered components into a cohesive vision. The peace and quiet contributed nicely. Having sent his servants away, and with his wife undoubtedly working in her own chamber, he knew no one would interrupt him. His eyes shut, vision being wasted energy at this point, and he played out in his mind's eye the events of the day, every relevant little detail.

~

In her own chamber in the castle, Alycia bathed. The temperature was just right for her; she had made sure of that before entering the water. Unlike her husband, who squandered the potential as if in hopes of degeneration, it was a true luxury for her. Even bathing with him would be stilted and strange, against the odds. There was no need to look back on the day in such disjointed and effortful fashion because all information absorbed had been filed correctly in an appropriate mental compartment.

Even so, as the bathwater massaged her body, she studied pages of notes laid out on a table next to the basin, not looking back at the past simply to make basic sense of it, but to organise the future. As she read snippets from various pieces of parchment, she formed a new plan, and everything not relevant to this was buried through force of will, taken over by a new driving force.

"Lady Castellon," she called.

Her serving lady and apprentice in idealism, Marioyrne, eagerly entered from the bedchamber holding two different soaps, just in case.

"That's very thoughtful of you, but no, you can put those down. I need you to bring me whatever files are readily available on Lennord Brodie of Caedor, the inventor the Emperor and I welcomed this morning."

"Yes, Empress."

The lady curtseyed and hurried off. Alycia, agent of change, rubbed aromatic oil into her hair and sank deeper so that, on her face, only her nose protruded from the water. Beneath the surface, she smiled, her face lighting up even out of direct candle view. With her fingers, she flexed, performing a moulding action on opposite shoulders, as if controlling an unseen puppet, the ripples from which created relaxing waves.

Life was good. It would be better.

The Voice of Kings

Chapter Eight: A New City

Kester Irvyng's inspirations had been less in quantity and power here in Aurail than in Caedor. Upon arriving, it seemed to him a beautiful and nuanced city of many wonders and cultures. The truth had set in fast and blocked all positivity like an impenetrable wall. He was even more of an outsider then than he was now. He still often wore baggy shirts of whites and blacks, but he'd learned to present himself differently in how he acted in public.

He was not tall or exceptional and had scruffy hair, and found wonder in daily life far easier than most; he soon came to realise that he was the epitome of a stereotypical artist. Once, when sitting in an inn motioning his fingers like a picture frame and sweeping the place for any miniscule source of inspiration, the man at the next table seriously asked if he was accepting commissions. People in the street would occasionally give him strange looks too. It became increasingly difficult to compose a symphony of triumph and joy when there was so little of it around him. A city of such festering bad will was no place for him.

Aurail had healed this rift just as easily as it had broken it. When he strode through the half-finished opera house, what might have been divine providence descended to bless him with the solution he so desperately needed: that he could inspire the people. The pitch he'd given had been more heartfelt than he could have imagined, so much so that the Empress had been roused by his commitment.

With this burst of positive reinforcement, things were looking up for him. There was still a niggling emptiness which ate away his insides, but its malice was kinder now and he was keen to muffle its outward effect to ambiguity at the absolute least. The native citizens, he now knew, were not as intolerant of him as he had previously perceived. He knew, now, that there were only ever a few who saw shadows on his heart, the impact of which he'd blown out of proportion.

It was a crisp, clear morning and, at this time, he didn't care to obscure his quirks from the world. Hopefully Isaac would be waiting at Lennord's boarding to gleefully discuss old times to further fulfil his spectrum of happiness. The single-storey house was but ten minutes' walk from the castle. At some point every day, the great tower, which could be seen even above the tallest buildings permeating the area, probably cast a dark shadow over the house. If there was one thing that never ceased to amaze him from the outset about Aurail, it was the way the sunlight toyed with the castle, creating a unique look from various angles. If painting was his forte instead of music, he would have portrayed it from a hundred locations in the city. Was it possible to evoke three towers in musical notes then? An interesting thought.

The Voice of Kings

Lennord's house was more than adequate by the dire standards of the city as a whole. It was sturdy, cosy, equipped with all necessary amenities if the view through the dining room window was any indication, and there was a wide street out the front, swept recently and not stinking from a loose sewage plug.

He rapped so enthusiastically that Lennord must have thought guards were trying to smash his door down. A brown horse, tied to a street lantern, grazed on a tiny patch of grass by the boarding. It moaned in distress, as if ill. This was no place for such an animal, especially one reared in a rural environment. The only consolation was that, in this district, it was relatively safe from opportunistic thieves. Incidentally, unless one of them had bought a new horse in the year since leaving Caedor, the horse belonged to neither Lennord nor Isaac.

The door flipped open. Lennord stood in the doorway, looking as though he'd been expecting him.

"Kester, it's good to see you."

Kester took Lennord's hand without warning and shook it, biding time while he considered his next move. Lennord was agreeable to his gesture, having prepared for more spontaneous actions. His face retained a static aura of politeness. He might not have had a wink of sleep, as his features crinkled with every adjustment, like paper under such circumstances, as it did now, in radical comparison to normal when his skin was rather smooth. This didn't stop him being jolly; very little could from his experience. Kester ceased the handshake and whipped his hand to his side with animal instinct, aware that he was abusing the man's goodwill.

"Excuse me if I appear rude," Kester spluttered. "I was nervous to reunite with you and Isaac. Though, I must say, you look like you've been waiting for me."

"We spotted you a mile off," a new voice said. "We weren't even looking for you; you just popped out."

The voice was unmistakeable, deep and powerful, starkly well-suited for the profession he pined for. Lucian leaned against the doorframe of the dining room, darkly suave with his slick chestnut-brown hair and a whiskey glass clasped with a casual grandeur often achieved by noblemen who'd grown up with obsessively strict etiquette rules.

"Fair play," Kester replied. "I admit I'm not the most discreet kind of person."

Lennord stepped aside courteously when Lucian put his arms out. The house's atmosphere welcomed him in. Having already secured accommodation in the city long ago, he had not been given an apartment by the Emperor. He would have to wait until after his symphony was completed to think about getting his own home up to these standards.

He became aware of stares digging into him, patiently waiting for him to respond. He hesitated, even when he overcame his distraction, and when the stares intensified and he felt closed in, he hugged Lucian and patted him on the back for good measure.

A New City

"No Isaac, then?" he said.

"Isaac's headed for Harth on business. Marcel too. And me, soon enough."

"Oh..."

Kester trailed off into a choked silence and rubbed his hands in nervous anticipation until the friction burned him. Beneath Lucian's steely expression, Kester saw him humoured by his quaint old ways.

"I take it you got Isaac's gift, if you're here," Lennord said.

"Ah, yes," Kester said, lighting up. "One of Lord Almaric's minions ran it over to me. Pointed me in your direction. Neglected to tell me Isaac had run so far away though. Very disappointing."

Kester was very much like a puppet when in a good mood, or so it occurred to him. His hands twitched like an overenthusiastic politician and he spoke in distracted short bursts, often pacing or stretching his legs as if juggling a dozen thoughts, writing music even while holding a conversation, which may in fact have not been so far from the truth.

"What was the gift, if you don't mind me asking?" Lennord asked.

"Oh, you don't know?" Kester laughed. "It was a broken acoustic string. Like from an old lute I used to play. And a note saying, "You'll need this"."

"Is that an esoteric joke? I'm afraid that's flown right by me."

"He wasn't very good at it," Lucian supplied. "Hence the broken string."

Lennord provided a smile of mild amusement, just as his nature as an attentive host screamed at him. He strode into the dining room in a gentlemanly fashion and held out a bottle of alcohol for Kester to sample.

"It's whiskey," Lennord said. "I'm not fond of the stuff; especially not this kind. Care for a glass?"

"Oh, very quickly, if you insist. Strong drinks are excellent medicine to me, as it happens. They calm me down, make me more normal."

"Drink the whole bottle if you like," Lennord suggested, offering it in earnest.

"That would be decidedly unhealthy."

Kester poured himself a drink with complete disregard for ordinary drinking conventions, filling the glass to the very top and downing half the contents in one mouthful. He grimaced, shook his head in a circle as if to throw off the effect, and proceeded to swallow the rest. Lucian, who had made himself comfortable in an armchair, watched with morbid interest. He tapped the thick glass, biding his time until Kester's unappetising drinking habit wore off, before reservedly taking a sip.

"*That* is healthy, is it?" he said.

"Obviously I wouldn't dream of drinking like this normally, but I have jitters which need to be controlled. Oh, by the way Lennord, are you here as an engineer? I hear a number of outsiders are being assigned to work on the opera house."

The Voice of Kings

"Military engineer, apparently. I'm not happy about it, but Lord Almaric is an influential man; I can only hope he can get me out of it," Lennord murmured.

Two separate bell towers rang out from opposite directions, marking, with its heavy clanging, the ninth hour of the day as a dictation and reminder that work should be underway. Kester, though somehow giving the impression of being more sober than when he first arrived, was alerted by the bells, initially making, for an instant, to the door like a well-trained dog obeying its master's whistle, then stalling when the cogs in his head clashed.

"I must go, I'm afraid. Those musicians won't hire themselves."

"Why would you be allotted with that job?" Lucian enquired. "I should think there are people in court whose specialty it is to find people."

"Empress's orders," Kester said, and shrugged. "She said it would be more appropriate for the composer to assemble his own team...ah, I should apologise for..."

"Don't fret about it, Kester," Lucian said, standing in respect for his official obligation and providing him permission to leave. "I'm going to Harth for a while, to conduct law research, talk to some officials from Michael's court if I can, that sort of thing, but when I return, we'll meet properly, I promise. Isaac too."

"Thank you kindly. We'll do that, yes. And hopefully you and I will meet again soon Mister Brodie," Kester added, pointing to Lennord as he left.

~

Lucian seated himself again, and his father too in an opposite armchair, stroking his chin sagely. Lucian watched as his friend sauntered down the street. His father did not move, only stared dazedly in Lucian's direction at something which confused him in his head.

"Without meaning offence, I never know where I stand with Kester," Father said.

Lucian muffled his cackling by willing his mouth shut and stared at the people outside thoughtfully while swishing what remained of his swill.

"There is sanity behind the madness, believe it or not. Genius, maybe. We'll have to wait and see."

The silence that followed was not pressurised by the formalities which ordinarily marred speechlessness in social meetings; no obligation to speak up for the sake of voicing an arbitrary observation for only its own sake. From many discussions with his father where he would request a second opinion on trade politics, Lucian learned it best to pause for thought during times like these before saying something outrageous. Likewise, his father had, in the past, misunderstood how Lucian's role was not, as of yet, set in stone: performing odd jobs, overseeing trade transactions, and streamlining costing, and, as such, had embarrassed himself jumping to conclusions about how much power he had as a Highland civilien.

A New City

Silence was good. In itself, it was an expression that thought was underway. That it would be broken was a foregone conclusion, and when it did happen, there was a safe guarantee that it wouldn't be with a barrage of nervous nonsense. Lucian took advantage of this intermission to observe the world as it appeared within the window frame, creating a vague ratio of rich to poor citizens and, perchance, anything in-between, as he had done upon entering the city.

There was a middle class here, of a small, if ill-defined, minority. There was no doubt, too, that the people in this district were living better lives but weren't really showing their appreciation for this. In their minds, they must have thought they were being grouped in with the poor regardless; left to busy themselves in a city distinct only by how grand the citadel was, from which noblemen and noblewomen could watch all, as overseers.

Lucian backpedalled hastily. It was foolish to assume such bitterness was inherent in each and every one of these people, damningly so if he intended to represent them. Isaac would have called him out on that in a second, given half a chance. He sipped the last of his whiskey and was glad of it. The pleasing initial taste was flushed away, choked by an overbearing, new, disgusting flavour wrapping round his tongue and scraping his throat with its coarse texture.

That they would provide such a cheap gift as a welcome present didn't surprise him, and to think they had someone bring it to his father personally. At the same time, it raised a point. The city was about to leap for freedom from the hole it had dug for itself and was looking for new and influential representatives. If he could prove on his expedition, in Harth of all places, his mettle, and show he knew how to operate in a political environment, then being promoted to ambassador might be as simple as having the courage to stand up and present his findings and outlook with the greatest aplomb he could muster. The Empress's shrewdness and ability to think outside of the box had attained near mythical status, or at least that was how he had interpreted it from Caedor and the surrounding towns. She would surely listen and extract the spark of genius in him.

He was fortunate that he would not to be bound by monetary constrictions as his father would constantly be, which itself raised a valuable point.

"Father, when you spoke to Tristan, did he give you any indication that you might eventually be given leeway to perform your own experiments regarding Laccona's theory?"

"Hmm?"

"Vicentei Laccona's theory. You said he thought it might be possible to catalyse Sèhvorian crystals to propel boats without oars or sails, and carriages without horses. It's still insanity to me but...you sounded keen on it before."

"Oh," Lennord said, sitting up and stroking his chin again. "Yes, I've been thinking on that actually. I think it's a lost cause but, on reflection, I was met with no reasonable objection when I mentioned Isaac's mission, so I may get pushed into it, whether I like it or not. I expect the Empress, being the pragmatic woman she is, will push me to go forth with it when she hears it, without so much as consulting her accounts. It's as if she has a second empire bank all to herself, for the casual way she spends money."

Lucian stood, after a brief pause in which to consider the possible influence of this, wherein he quickly admitted to himself his failure to understand the scope of such advancements. Lucian was not an openly excitable man but, nevertheless, his father spotted his eagerness to expand his horizons, thus standing in adulation.

"Will you be going now then?"

"If it pleases you, I will. I'll stay if you want the company."

"No, by all means, do as you like."

His father reached for Lucian's arms and flattened out a few minor creases in his jacket. His proud features gleamed. There was much of himself he seemed to see, along with a strong, honourable sense of individuality, if that wasn't bold.

"I just want you to know that I'm proud of what you're trying to accomplish. You'll succeed, I know it."

It was mildly amusing for Lucian to see his father bestow him with such humble admiration, even if not unprecedented. His father patted his arm and walked him as slowly as possible to the door.

"And you'll keep an eye on Isaac, won't you? Sometimes I think he's too clever for his own good. Just make sure he doesn't do anything rash."

"I was planning on watching him like a hawk anyway. And I'll keep my other eye on Marcel while I'm at it. He's just as naive, to be fair," he added when he spotted his father's questioning expression.

Stepping outside was like shifting into a different dimension for Lucian. The house had felt homely by the very fact of his father's presence and the way he had arranged the furniture to his liking. This was a different world to that place; expansive and misunderstood, even by itself. Still, he was compelled to be the one to untangle it. He suspected himself in the minority, being a country man here. The more complicated the situation was, the more it fascinated him.

"I wish you all the luck in the world, Father. My advice is keep your head down out of the way and do your job well, and you might get out of here sooner than you think."

"Those were your *mother's* words," his father laughed edgily.

Lucian untied his horse from the post, patting its neck to stop its nervous stamping, meanwhile racing through his memories to uncover how in the hell he could have picked up his mother's mannerisms to mirror them so accurately. He concluded it did not matter.

"I shall take that as a compliment, I think."

He smiled briefly and walked his horse away. Long goodbyes were not something he was used to, nor planned on becoming accustomed to.

"Fortune be with you too," Father called after him.

He would be remiss should he not have wished Lucian luck; a strange mentality, as Lucian knew he'd meant what he said when expressing his faith in him. Lucian waved and smiled again in acknowledgement of his father's farewell, and then he was gone, lost in a crowd where his progress could only be tracked by the beautiful brown horse parting the way.

In order to act both amiably and professionally in Harth, he would need points of reference, trade reports and figures, and any other details that might stand out, thus he altered his course south-west to the trade embassy.

For want of something to do on the way, he made effort to analyse the people and the increasingly squalid streets from other perspectives. He found himself, before long, fixed in Isaac's mind, trying to understand everything at a glance, every person, but it was all blurry to him this way; little made sense in any profound way. He was not Isaac. He, to his frustration, needed to be slower, more methodical.

A rundown brothel caught his eye. Despite having such a beaten look to it, wood rotting on its outer walls and on the boards barring its windows, and brick crumbling ever so slowly into dust, it may have only been closed down recently. They shouldn't have needed the renaissance as an excuse to move in on this pathetic creature, engulfing all around it in sordid darkness. It was practically inviting mockery. Even when visiting a brothel, people didn't want to feel that they were debauching, so there was no wonder why it had run such a course. As if a sign of impotence, the eldest Brodie son was reminded that there was no woman to ride beside him to Harth, defensively scowling it away as if it purported to be a premonition.

In the real world, where he was again, he would have hated to see the state of any one of the military garrisons if this was an indication of how the city was looked after, and felt for his father who was charged with fixing likely a near insurmountable plethora of problems.

A ringing of steel, which at first met his ears in one conglomerated echo, indefinable and distant, grew ever louder at an alarming rate until it could be ignored no longer. Every single person bar none stopped what they were doing and consciously drifted to the edges of the road. The immense rhythmic clanging of steel plates banging against one another could be heard from just beyond the buildings to their left where the road forked off, singing triumphantly like a marching brass band playing without concern for tune.

As the air was held down the throats of all these bystanders, and for an inordinately long time, they each imagined what need would have arisen for soldiers to parade through the streets in such force, with such purpose. A wave of guards, more than a dozen at first glance, veered into the road and washed like an unstoppable force of nature, completely disregarding all that might stand in its way, led by a worthy battle veteran, grey-brown of hair, armoured as one of the Guardians. Of no single uniform, most wore half-helms and

The Voice of Kings

byrnies with Watch emblems sown on the sleeves of their undertunics, a few blessed with hauberks, and a couple yet in plate. *A point for conquerors, not for my like*, he assuaged himself. Cobbles shook underfoot, and steel plates and mail rattled, held tightly in place around these guards of mighty purpose.

When they approached, it became very clear that they were not one unified force at all, and not only that, but someone had wanted this to be known by all. The guards in the centre of the formation were holding their peace, tight-lipped and resentful, having been relieved of their weapons. All who confined them in this moving prison wore green capes, he now saw, bearing the Guardian symbol on their armour, in order to differentiate them to the public. Depending on the reasons for such a shamelessly public display, whoever ordered this was either very clever or very stupid.

"Make way!" the captain shouted. "Make way for the Guardian huscarls! Make way for the Watch!"

Lucian's horse fidgeted in distress, even jumping when the stampede swept by. Lucian tugged at its reins and stroked its head to control it. This earned him, momentarily, worried glances from the guards who, even so, did not break pace.

"Easy there," the captain cooed at Lucian. "Calm your friend."

The guards marched north-east, to the castle one would assume, and soon returned to existing, to the sense of these people, as that dull metallic vibration soaring through the streets, still echoing its message long after they were out of sight. People were talking again, in speculation and hope and cynicism. The first phase of the plan was working wonderfully, it seemed, whatever that plan was. Any merchants from Mürathneè witnessing it would be a substantial bonus, was probably their thinking.

Talk of similar tone was being conducted even as Lucian passed through roads that the guards had not left their mark on, the reason for which became abundantly clear upon entering a city square. A crowd of people were gathered before a city crier, who expounded, with joyful energy, news which apparently enraptured his audience.

"If you've noticed changes," he shouted, "it's not your imagination! The Emperor has declared an official declamation of the start of the renaissance in our humble city, this very day! Good citizens of Aurail, the power will be in *your* hands to propel this country into a new, golden age, with excellent pay prospects! Public demonstrations and details on how *you* can be a part of this magnificent turn of events will be administered at the opera house very soon. Listen *here*," he shouted while pointing to the wooden stand beneath his feet, "for instructions to emerge over the coming days. By the Emperor's own words, we will birth a new city!"

It was beginning then. The Emperor couldn't be stupid enough to make public promises without fully intending to back them up. Lucian walked the passage to the Office of Commerce and Trade Embassy beneath the darkness of the arch tunnel. The circular hall was half-packed; each desk presented with long winding queues, a great deal of those waiting being rich nobles with folders and shagreen portfolios tucked under their arms, presumably at the command of the Emperor. His initial sigh of discouragement evaporated when he spotted a sign exclaiming "library" pointing to a back room.

Happily, Lucian diverted his path between the crowds, flashed his Melphor-stamped credentials to the flinty guard in his way, and respectfully pushed open an old oak door, which creaked despite his best intentions, and slipped through the archway into the library. It had a very traditional feel about it, that of decay and must; rows of long shelves, lit from above by chandeliers, hung so high and so protective to decrease chances of fire spreading should they fall, that there was barely enough light to read by.

As he skimmed the records for recent data which he could use for comparisons in Harth, another thunderous storm of metallic apparel roared through the square. If this was but a flavour of things to come, the Emperor obviously understood the principles behind literally showing his people why Harth was not unique.

Turning back to a scroll pertaining to recent trade taxes, he realised he needed to expand his range if he was to stand out. He began grabbing scrolls almost at random, on military technology and recruitment, shipping trade, exploration records, and anything else he assumed might go down well in a conversation with court officials in Harth and Aurail alike. He took a bundle and made himself as comfortable as was humanly possible at a round, wooden table at the back of the room.

Even after a short time distractedly running a finger over important aspects of each document, in his heightened state of alertness, he noticed people around him were shooting him cursory glances and whispering amongst one another. He pretended not to notice but became irritated as it persisted. He sat back and huffed, and in response, everyone rude enough to stare at him looked away. A librarian interpreted Lucian's actions and subsequent penetrating glare as a means of ushering him to his table.

"What the hell is their problem?" Lucian demanded, seeing as he was here anyway.

"I think they view you with suspicion. They see you're not from around here and suspect you might be up to something."

"I'm just as Burtalian as any of those people. And my business is not theirs. They should keep to themselves."

"I understand that," the librarian said coolly, "but you're not from this city. Your clothes don't quite match. Learned men from outside Aurail aren't favourites of the regulars in here. They fear too many outsiders will mean less work for them."

"Less credit, you mean," Lucian scoffed. "There's already far too much work to go round anyway. Perhaps sitting in here has turned their brains soft. Big change is approaching. They really will be out of work if they keep thinking like that."

The Voice of Kings

Lucian was met with an icy stare, and he shifted uncomfortably. He swept the room quickly by sight and decided he would still rather be without the poor ignorant fools watching him. From his pocket, he took out a letter signed by and printed with the seal of Count Andrews, and a bag of gold.

"These records are copies, I take it?" Lucian enquired, noting the parchment quality and raising his eyebrows.

"Well of course."

"Then I'll buy them. Legitimate business, obviously," he said, handing him the letter.

Lucian nodded to the bag of money when he had finished reading the letter, and poured out a handful.

"I am a trade ambassador, I'll be more soon enough," Lucian said. "This, in the long run, could help a lot of people; people in our country. You tell these fine men that, next you speak with them."

"Wait here..."

She hurried away, hopefully to retrieve someone with the authority to grant his request. He didn't wait long. No one was watching him, but he could be sure some of them were thinking of him, and it made him uneasy. He scooped the documents into his hands and strolled off after the librarian, consciously holding his head high, only to be stopped by a wiry, pale man in exquisite, dark clothing who glared at him, lips puckered, and smiled like a reptile would if it could, pointing animatedly at the table from which he'd come. They sat.

"Lord Reid," the man said of himself. "Who is this for?"

It was hard not to regret his lack of tact, now.

"Burtal," Lucian said, because it seemed appropriate.

The lord smiled, mostly for his own benefit.

hurry, I didn't think about how I would control my horse across the marshes and the Nether Moors or, for that matter, any ground I couldn't see. I riled a drakeel somehow. I don't know, maybe it was protecting a nest, but it followed me. I was so focused on getting away, I didn't notice the road drawing in until I was on it. I was too busy looking behind me to see the great big bloody inn I was speeding towards... I fell from my horse as I avoided it, not on my head mind... I tripped on my head a couple times later, but...well, you can guess the rest anyway."

Edwin's stutters gave Kate the impression of paranoia again, as if he consistently wanted to retract his statements, should they contain information pertaining to actions motivated by questionable intent. Whatever the case, this was a man on the edge. A lump formed in her throat when she saw the reality behind his steely eyes, if only for a split second. He was scared, terrified perhaps, and paranoia gripped his soul, even in the presence of a socially inexperienced 16-year-old girl, isolated in a valley of overwhelming natural beauty. Her observation did not go unnoticed by Edwin, who hurriedly blurted out whatever words came to him first, after a short splutter of nonsense.

"Did you heal me, Kate?" he asked with genuine awe. "You mentioned watching over me."

"I did most of the work," Kate said meekly, her pride just about shining through the cracks in her defences. "I stitched you up and I've been your physician ever since."

"Extraordinary. Very impressive for one so young, if I do say so myself."

He sighed strenuously, at a loss of having more to say. His interest in Kate's doctorial skills was that of true astonishment, his wounds having been sewn up with such understanding and desire for perfection, as a master painter controls brush strokes to convey his or her feelings. Still, there was no escaping that he hadn't the mind for small talk, and it was imperative that he complete his mission somehow.

"Where are we, Kate? What town is beyond those hills?"

"We're in Caedor," Kate informed him quietly, in response to his pushiness.

"So it's not all bad news...you may be able to help me then," Edwin said, pulling his composure in place like wrapping a cloak around himself. "Do you, by any chance, know a man by the name of Isaac Brodie? It's of the utmost importance that I speak with him."

By the mere fact of Edwin's paranoid attitude, Kate was now eyeing the man up for clues to his goal, despairingly so as she possessed not an inkling of that gift. Her more severe social quirks returned: her teeth chattering, her eyes widening, and her shoes thudding noisily on the rocks beneath, for want of the most prudent course of action to take. If Isaac was in trouble, she needed to know, but Edwin did not look, to her, in the mood for spilling his thoughts so readily.

"What's your interest, if you don't mind me asking?" Kate said as enigmatically as possible.

The Voice of Kings

"How do you know him?" Edwin said sharply, ever more suspicious that she would attempt to hide her relationship with him.

"Perhaps if you could tell me..."

"That would be unwise of me," Edwin snapped. "I could be in danger and so could Isaac, and I don't know who my friends are as of now, so you'll forgive me if I'm finicky around other people. You tell me what I want to know and we'll see about answering your queries afterwards."

"Isaac is my brother," Kate sighed, crossing her fingers that she'd made the right decision.

Edwin was apprehensive but, not unlike Isaac, he scanned her with great care, and the flickering of his eyes whirring in their sockets showed that he wasn't to take too long a time about it. His decision clicked into place, as did his smile of satisfaction. Kate was a shy maid who had to insert enormous effort and prior planning into lying, so unless he so profoundly missed the point and guessed her to be an extraordinarily blessed con artist, she was, to him, as easy to read as an open book.

"I will trust you, Kate," Edwin said with a level of humility lining his words. "I speak to people for a living, so I don't make that judgement lightly. But you must allow me to speak with your brother."

"That won't be possible..."

"Why not? What's happened?" Edwin blurted out, sensing the urgency in her tone.

"Nothing, I hope," Kate heaved with more confusion than ever before. "If all's well, he'll be halfway to Harth by now."

"Shit..."

Edwin's profanity was spat out in equal parts rage and grievous disappointment. He flung his arms up, only to inflict on to himself a dreadful pain of skin stretching and expanding beyond its threshold, his internal scars tearing like wet paper. A shrill shriek soared upwards, reflecting off the walls of the valley, his agony an echo riding the wind like a ghostly cry. Kate didn't have to think about it; she didn't have time to. She was supporting his weight and, only then, did she regret it, as his build proved too much for her, stamping her boots down and digging them into the rocks so far as was possible to prevent her sliding, and him with her.

Pride kicked Edwin into motion, and dutiful respect of her spirit did the rest. He staggered away, waving to Kate in thanks, and lowered himself to sit on a large rock overlooking the river, his chest beating up and down uncontrollably as he clutched it and gasped uselessly for more air. He appeared to be utilising the swirling of a cluster of tiny green fish to regulate his mood. At least, this is what she would have done. The river fauna was comforting to her in stressful times, and could burn through time such that, when she returned to reality, she was calm once more. However, it was a struggle to understand quite what was going through Edwin's head. She was out of her depth, flailing madly to no avail and no rescue.

By now, she was almost pining for the hard pews of the church as a sanctuary, even fumbling over her prayers and feeling so small in the company of gods being preferable to this uncertainty.

"Did he say why he was going to Harth?" Edwin asked.

"He's just going to buy goods for my father's research. He's an inventor, see."

"You're sure there's nothing else to it? No ulterior motive?"

"Now that you mention it," Kate said energetically, clapping her hands together, "I do remember thinking it was a bit strange how he was ordering so many documents from...all over the place I think. I know he was gathering information about Harth, but beyond that I really can't say. I did confront him actually. He didn't reveal anything, but he was smug, very pleased with himself, not worried at all."

The shoals rippled and fish darted in their wake, in response to Edwin's hands scooping water from the surface. Cupping it as stably as he could, he lifted the water to neck height and flung it over his face, his hands swooping to catch the dregs. His tongue lapped up any of the cool, clear water that connected with it with relish. Such drops were, to such a creature out of time and body, a godsend. She'd provided him with fluids, yet his exhaustion and frailness from lying in bed for so long must have elevated this water to heavenly glory in his mind; fluid imbued with magic that would grant him everlasting hydration.

In that boyish relief, Kate became increasingly impatient, so much so that she wondered if he'd forgotten he wasn't alone. The need for the truth was too high a concern to idly wait for it to be given, like orders to a dog. The skin, which warded off unwanted interactions, was shed in her time of need.

"What kind of trouble has my brother gotten himself into?" she blurted out at high speed.

"I can't be sure," Edwin said in sudden reply, taken aback by Kate's resolve. He blinked back the fruit of his fountain as he returned to the world of the living. "Seeing as he's so far away, he may be free of any danger, if indeed there was ever a direct threat to him. But I tell you now, whatever Isaac was hoping to accomplish, he wasn't doing it through simply researching Harth; he was searching for something specific. I'm not certain of much, but what I do know is that he sent enquiries all over the country, and even Mürathneè, regarding peculiarities and anomalies around Sèhvorian steel, and there was a fixation on mines for reasons I cannot fathom, as they are most bizarre."

"I don't understand," Kate whispered hoarsely. "Do you mean to suggest my brother has been digging for answers to that...*incident* that happened in Caedor mine so many years ago?"

The Voice of Kings

"I'd never even heard about it until recently," said Edwin, who was back to scratching his scalp, "but that seems to be the case, yes. What do you know about it, Kate?"

Kate's jaw, firmly shut, would not let her speak, and her legs were trembling, though she dared not confirm this with her own eyes. Feeling the tremors throughout her body was more than unsettling enough. She would like to have been able to convince herself that it was all a product of anticipation. She was no good at that either. Instead, fear burdened her with an almost insurmountable wealth of possibilities, none of them bearing thinking about, for then she would have no self-control at all. Where, before, she was treading water out of her comfort zone, she was now drowning, being sucked to the depths by the colossal weight of matters that were far beyond her comprehension.

Shuffling, to reduce the risk of tripping caused by her shaking, she made her way to the river bank, beside Edwin, and in a gradual, ladylike fashion, lowered to her knees, careful to preserve the material of her dress from damage incurred by sharp rocks.

Dark blonde hair fluttered before her eyes as she leaned forward to observe the tormented reflection in the water. She folded her hair back behind her ears to make herself more presentable, as if this would somehow elevate her confidence, and dipped her hands in the water. Like newly forged steel in oil, they radically dropped in temperature, so much so that, for a brief moment, it was as if ice encased them, giving a feeling like peace flowing through her veins.

Aware now that Edwin was about to interject, her mind raced back to the subject at hand. He was sure to question her silence and ask how she was feeling, and she didn't want to hear it.

"It's not my place to comment on what happened in that mine," she murmured. "I wasn't even born then. All I know is what I've heard, and what I've heard is a combination of contradicting things from Isaac and my father, some of which sounds quite crazed, but it's not my place to judge. Isaac's not insane," she added sharply when Edwin gave her a look, probing for her opinion.

"I hear you. It's not my place to judge your brother for anything, especially if you won't. I was just wondering what you knew. Kate, listen, I can see you're still apprehensive, and rightly so. I'll clear the air a little by coming totally clean and we'll move on from there. I work for Count Andrews in Melphor. I once was one of the men closest to him. But, a few weeks ago, I discovered a spy in our midst, from Mūrac. I thought it was strange at the time, but apparently he works for the Count as a trade emissary."

"But Mūrac is in civil war!" Kate cried. "Why would they care about what happens up here?"

"I can't answer that for sure. It's a big country, who knows how much of it's affected by the war? I know the Count trusts him, but I don't. I get out more; I see more than he does. This man from Mūrac, he was intensely private, but not only that, he imprisoned himself within the bounds of very specific routines, most of them seemingly pointless. He would receive mail frequently; confidential mail which no one else saw. It tipped me off well enough so, one time when a letter arrived for him, I intercepted it before it reached him. It turned out he, or rather someone in his employ, or perhaps an affiliate, was intercepting your brother's letters before sending them on their way again."

A pause was given so that this could sink in. Kate was being overloaded with information, entrapped in a world of politics that was not her own, and out here there were no distractions, no other people to talk to, no excuses with which to shield herself. The valley was working against her today, a force of tranquillity corrupted to malevolence so that, even in its vast scope, it was claustrophobic. Even the sky might have been falling for how terribly suffocated she felt.

Her body was so tense she could barely move of her own accord. None of this was right; this was news that should have been relayed to her mother first, and then she would enlighten her, supplemented with a cup of tea and an armchair on which to collapse. Her arms sank deeper into the river, which sucked the cuffs of her dress to her skin. The current was not strong enough down here to wash her of all tension. Yet, there were stark differences at the water level, above which her arms and body needed the tension literally wrung from them, or so it felt. With this thought, she suddenly could no longer withstand the torment of the wait.

"Go on!" she snapped, more coarsely than she could have anticipated or said of her own free will.

"With hindsight, I wondered if he might not be a spy," Edwin swiftly continued. "He might, in truth, be a servant of some other. To investigate further, I called him from his chamber when the Count next had need of him, and entered using a spare key. I searched the whole room, and found, under his bed, a chest locked with a padlock, which I pried open with my sword. Inside, I found a pile of letters. In my hurry, I did not commit to reading them in full, but I saw enough to conclude that what he was doing was spying, and he was working with Burtalian traitors for some purpose I could not decipher, yet I know what your brother saw in that mine, all those years ago, was a primary focus."

"But to them, they should just be silly stories!" Kate wailed. "Why would they care what my brother may, or may not, have seen as a child?"

"Maybe they already have evidence to back up his claims."

Second-hand memories overflowed Kate: images of an explosion which, still, she could scarcely imagine, and a wall of Sèhvorian steel embedded beneath rock from the world, gods knew why, crafted into some device. There was a belief that the halves of the gods existing on the mortal plane had sent the white steel and the crystals up from the centre of the planet as gifts for humans to do with them as they wished, which was why they were such enigmas, bringing people together in discovery and exploration.

The Voice of Kings

Such things were not a strain for her to believe. However, the prospect of gods actively intervening, and these beliefs becoming physical, was daunting, to put it mildly. She had considered this in the past, years ago, without suggestions from Isaac, and each time she had dismissed it. Was it possible, though, that some mad group of people had gotten the same idea?

"For one thing, Kate, I don't think they knew of the incident in Caedor mine when they first started...whatever it is they're doing. There was mention of a leak from Aurail of that event, as the Emperor keeps it secret, I inferred. They must have had some idea of what they wanted. Rummaging through the Emperor's records is, by all means, a high risk procedure, so they must have thought the reward would also be high."

"I did not know it was a secret," Kate said quietly, stroking her hair with her still wet hands. "My family rarely speak of it, but there was no gag order that I'm aware of... What did you do after you saw the spy's letters?"

"I fled Melphor; it seemed the only logical option at the time. The spy knew it was I who discovered his secret!" Edwin cried out in defence at Kate's astonished look, which would have been condescending had she the stomach to illustrate it. "Of that I am sure. He suspected me before then, and he even saw me a moment after I left his room. When I sneaked back a short while later and pressed my ear to his door, I heard burning, a fire rising and falling as sheet after sheet of paper was destroyed in it. So I fled, so that he might stay."

"I don't understand," Kate replied in a rush before giving it so much as a second's thought.

"If I had stayed, he would have fled for sure," Edwin explained as calmly as he could, given the circumstances. "It would have been counterproductive. I should have taken that whole bloody chest while I had the chance, I think. A grave folly on my part, I fear," he said bitterly, rubbing a hand across his scalp as he revisited his shame.

"But you had the letter! You had the upper hand!"

"No, Miss, I did not. I let him have it as if it had not been tampered with. It was the wise thing to do at the time."

"But surely you must have informed the Count!" Kate cried out, letting loose her anger, for Isaac, for the truth.

"Count Andrews is proud and stubborn to a fault. I couldn't guarantee that he would understand my argument to wait for the other players to be revealed instead of torturing the answers from him, which may or may not have yielded results. If it did not, his affiliates, or servants, or whatever the bloody hell they are, would be free to operate as they pleased. Be that as it may, I do wonder if I made the right choice. I want you to know I did not make the decision idly. I would not willingly push your brother, or any other innocent man or woman, into hot water, and I have considered that, should this matter ever reach its rightful justice, I may very well be punished for my treason with the death sentence."

The solemnity of Edwin's predicament drifted slowly downward in fragments, unappreciated in full capacity and misunderstood until the truth settled in Kate's mind, like dead autumn leaves, released from their branches and only seen in full when laid bare on the ground. Frantically piecing all that had been said into one image was difficult; it required an emotional detachment for a speedy methodical analysis, and for her to simply not be emotional would be a violation of her very being.

"When I left Melphor, I journeyed to County Flatlands," Edwin recalled painfully, "to Ylden Parragor, for some further sleuthing under a false name, to see if I could gauge the spy activity there, but nothing came of it and...in my frustrations at such wasted time, I sought to stop Isaac sending his letters without delay.

"We have to send a homing bird to my brother to warn him," Kate said forcefully, feeling that his story was at an end and the time for action was at hand.

"No!" Edwin retorted loudly.

His hand grabbed her wrist in reflex, before she had even time to move. His eyes showed, through his petrified features, that it was not merely out of blind fear as to why he reacted so rashly. The light of reason shone in an expression that told so much with so little words. Acknowledgement of what he might have seen as sins, he saw writhing within himself; a soul-destroying illness borne from him by allowing this to progress so far in the first place, yet even so, he had done what he thought was right, and stood by that.

By Kate's reckoning, he couldn't decide whether to blame himself or not, and the cracks in his hard defences began to spread from his impossible rationale. For a few seconds, she remembered that he was a young man, not a wise old sage with all the answers stored safely away, to be acted upon at the most perfect time. She looked at her wrist, which was now white from how tightly Edwin was gripping it. Seeing her distress, he released her and put his hands up in humble apology.

"I'm sorry, Kate, but think about the facts. I came here personally because it was the safest way. The spies already have a method in place to intercept letters from Caedor, as unlikely as that may seem. If you warn Isaac that way, you risk putting him in danger anyway, danger that he may have evaded already."

"We must tell my mother though."

"As you say," Edwin said with pure courtesy. "Help me along will you, please? I promise I won't put too much weight on you."

Edwin needn't have asked, as she was all too keen to jump into action before he had finished speaking. Upon him, a thin smile rose in appreciation of this, apparently, rare trait. Kate wrapped an arm around his back and slung his over her shoulder. Even in this situation, with him using her as a crutch to hobble, he was strong again, as he had been just a minute prior, and deeply thoughtful too; not the indecisive wreck who could not string together his own reasoning.

"You're unduly kind," Edwin said.

"How do you mean?" Kate said in surprise, blushing.

"You act in compassion on instinct alone. You don't see that in many people."

"Not normally I don't."

"I don't believe you. Twice you've done it now, and that's just what I've seen. And the emotion you demonstrated on your brother's behalf, that was something special, the ferociousness of a warrior. I don't mean like a sword fighter," Edwin exclaimed firmly. "Not literally a soldier, but just as strong. What made you want to heal people?"

Never would she have imagined that, of all the subjects from her past, this would be the one that she would be cornered into reliving by a stranger. The two clambered from the valley, up the slope leading back to the town. Before them, there were the farms to traverse, then the town itself, houses, and other obstacles to weave between to reach her house. It was a mighty long walk at this speed to indulge in such antisocial behaviour as to ignore her patient the entire time.

What was most surprising was that, after laying down her options, she really, really wanted to talk about it with this man she had known for all of ten minutes. Ten minutes, or two weeks. She craned her head to the sky, breathing deeply. Nature opened itself freely, claustrophobia evaporating, and though nervous, she did not feel as though she was being slung in prison, sentenced to recall memories to spite her crushing disposition towards not talking.

The sun smiled upon young Kate, blessing her with all its natural glory, unsullied by low clouds which were sparse on a blue-grey sky. She cleared her throat with a raspy cough and, without contemplation, panned her head so that the mine entrance was directly centred for her viewing consideration; a sight neither solicited nor sought, though even now its mysteries offered a morbid attraction. So tragic it was that, even past its expiration, its destructiveness might still linger, holding by mere the existence of memories with the capacity to stir danger.

Only one thing at a time could ably be confronted. She felt it written on her bones, that inescapable sensation to worry, in as many ways, and covering as many subjects as there was to concern her, whether she could process it all or not. She had to focus: one problem at a time.

"I, er...well, I suppose it started a few years back, a short time after The Purification in Mürathneè, when King Michael's army killed all those pirates and bandits. Before it happened, a few of them saw what was coming to them and scattered. You may have heard. Small groups of them hid all about; one of them hid out here. Caedor is worth more than it looks. Someone compromised who they really were..."

As the words were created, so too was a vision of the past they regarded, vague and nondescript in some parts, vivid like the ground she walked on and the air she breathed in others, backed by a soundtrack of screaming. Edwin did not speak for fear of jarringly disrupting a meditation, and, indeed, when she continued speaking, it was with her eyes staring at the horizon, as if what she was describing was being played out there.

"Fighting broke out in the street. Of course, I didn't know why at first. I ran from the house and my father was there, and Isaac, and Lucian, my eldest brother, in the midst of it all. I couldn't tell what was going on, it was madness...chaos...but I could hear familiar voices calling out, in fear I think. I still don't know. I didn't ask in such detail of course."

"Were they hurt at all?" Edwin asked, deathly serious, readjusting his arm on her shoulder respectfully as to not disturb her thought. Wishful thinking, and comforting.

"They were lucky. Others weren't. At the time, I didn't know if they were being hurt or not. I'm told it only lasted a few seconds but, even now, it seemed so much longer. Every time someone got in my way, so I couldn't see my father or brothers, was like an eternity. They could have died there and then for all I knew. I waited for it to end, to run to them, thinking about what I would do if they were hurt. Or what I couldn't do. I rushed in early, actually, tripped on a man's body as the fighting was still going on..."

Ensuing silence wrapped sullenly around the two of them, like a blanket denying them breath. For all the solemnity Edwin showed on Kate's behalf, she found herself relieved. She could have gone into grittier detail if she'd tried, but as it stood, she was satisfied with the outcome, more so than she realistically expected to be, and felt almost ready to confront the ongoing issue.

"This is starting to make sense," Edwin said stiffly. "I'm sorry you had to go through that. That's where you got your urge to heal people then... Who taught you so well?"

"I was taught the basics by my mother, and the rest by a few people around town. I never really discussed my lessons with the other tutors though, nor do any of them have advanced training. I'd need to go elsewhere to broaden my horizons."

"But your skills are beyond the reproach of any others your age," Edwin replied in astonishment.

"If you say so," Kate said tiredly, now feeling the strain of her patient's weight squeezing what strength she had out of her. "To be truthful, I had never put my skills to serious use until you came along, but I just have..."

"You have physician's hands," Edwin finished for her.

Kate nodded vaguely, expressing with an uneasy smile that he was basically correct. She would not have put it like that, but the truth was that, when in the mood, her hands could be commanded to respond to any command, no matter how much precision and patience required.

"What was it like, to finally place your skills to a good cause?" Edwin asked.

The Voice of Kings

There was a strangeness attached to this question that she had already considered, but found difficult to pin down, and therein lay the peculiarity. She felt irrevocably changed now that she had performed such a deed, but the change was not apparent, if, indeed, it was not in her imagination. With a strong gust from the hills, the words came to her, as if whispered by that wind.

"Like waking from a very long dream," Kate said softly.

Soon after, they cut between two buildings and arrived at the road at last, near where Kate's house was situated. Four men clad in armour, mail covered by plate, men of the Watch Patrol, led their horses down the road on foot, talking to everyone in their path as they generally did. It was as quaint a sight as could be nowadays, people only paying mind of them as they were talked to. In lieu of a sheriff, it was wise to keep on good terms with them.

Characterised by steel harness, usually plain save for a white cape which bore the black falcon motif of the county, officers of the Watch would often check in on the towns to ensure lawfulness was being upheld, and dangerous wildlife was not encroaching on human territory. And for the tithes; people remembered that, especially. Additionally, bags attached to their horses contained basic medical equipment and treatments, and an array of survival equipment for living out in the wilderness. In all, a commodity not to be underestimated that had been a service to Caedor in many a time of need, yet somewhat unsurprisingly, Edwin was wide-eyed and suspect of every step they took.

In particular, he watched the captain, his status denoted by decorative cape clasps and the black falcon painted crudely on to his breastplate. Beneath his left arm, he carried his helm, allowing Edwin to recognise him immediately by his short ginger hair, beneath which, on his scalp, there was a long scar.

"I can make it from here," Edwin said coldly.

"It's just the Watch," Kate insisted, upon noticing his scrupulous observations. "What reason have you to be paranoid about them?"

"None, yet. Go talk to them. Gauge their intent."

Edwin hobbled away nonchalantly to Kate's house, underplaying his injuries remarkably well once he got a rhythm going. She held out an arm to stop him and opened her mouth to make profanity, but no words came out. Anger bubbled to boiling point inside, first and foremost at her inability to protest, then more so when, in hindsight, she considered all the things she might have said. The captain, of around 40 years of age or so, swaggered to a halt before her, causing her to jump.

Again, her jaw dropped and she stuttered meaningless noises in fear of speaking out of turn. Her brainpower was more devoted to calculating whether Edwin had seriously considered him a suspect or a mere curiosity. Her mind told her the first option was the most likely, for no logical reason other than because it was the most frightening, and if, indeed, this was the case, she would need to watch what she said, not that she could find the means to do so anyway.

"Something the matter?" the captain said, squinting as if to determine a visual problem.

"Not at all. Sorry. To who am I speaking?" she said quietly but forcefully, now trying to gain the command of her legs which shook so much that the captain must have noticed.

"Captain Olswalt, at your service," he replied in gruff dignity. "This, here, is my sergeant, Patric, and these other two men are officers we met on the road and joined forces with."

Now that Kate began to use her senses at appropriate functionality again, she noticed that the two men the captain had indicated to had checked in not one week ago, and as if reading her mind, he shocked her by bringing up this very subject.

"These two men passed through recently, but forgot to ask around for information regarding a certain incident that occurred at an inn a couple of days ride from here, the incident being a man attacked by a drakeel, and the man in question riding from the scene on his horse. These lads told me it wasn't their business to poke around in those affairs, or that it would waste time, or other such excuses, but I told them no, it's our duty as Watchmen to confront any trouble that comes to pass on the road."

Kate couldn't help but look to Edwin as he described these events, so spontaneously that she hadn't even realised it until she'd done it. Captain Olswalt squinted a second time, then swung his weight round to follow her gaze. Edwin was staring, and her mother was nearby, doing the same.

"I don't know his name," Kate said instinctively.

"Gods, that's Sir Edwin, one of the Count's aides. What the hell is he doing here?"

Captain Olswalt strode towards Edwin and, short of provoking suspicion by attempting to uphold his pathetic charade, he waited for the captain's arrival graciously and without apparent disdain.

"Sir Edwin Meri," the captain said formally. "The Watch Patrol has been instructed to return you to Melphor, where you will answer for your abandonment of the Count, and that's just what I intend to do, Sir."

"You can't!" Kate cried, physically interjecting herself between the two men. "He's hurt. He won't recover on horseback. He was the man you mentioned, attacked by the drakeel..." Kate said with decreasing certainty, and finally trailed off.

Edwin lifted his shirts, in light of Kate's lack of confidence, to quickly confirm her sentiment, peeling back the bandages, to his own pain, to show the scars of the gashes left by the giant lizard's claws. They were well-treated and not miscoloured, to his disadvantage, which he made up for by sagging his weight and wearing a grim expression.

"Two birds with one stone, at least," Olswalt muttered. "Be that as it may, you must return. Sergeant Denkyn, leave with these two Watchmen for Melphor, and bring back a sturdy carriage and a surgeon. I will remain."

The Voice of Kings

"Captain!" Sergeant Denkyn exclaimed his compliance, and climbed on to his horse, pointing to the other soldiers, despite them already complying.

Kate could only watch them ride away, her mind a blank slate, or, at the very least, she could not understand what she was thinking. As the riders reached the halfway point of the road, everything fell back into place with the impact of a lightning storm, burning the truth into her brain, and the consequences striking deep into her heart like a dagger. So literal was this effect to her that her heart did, indeed, appear to skip a beat, maybe two, or even three.

"No!" she declared with passion that made the captain jump. "I hardly think that's necessary. He's not going anywhere, anyway."

Her mother, too, who was observing the goings on of the conversation at a peripheral distance, narrowed her eyes and crossed her arms. Being the least of her worries as things stood, Kate ignored her mother the best she could. Olswalt looked like a man on the edge of taking some extreme action, though what it was, she could not tell. His mail leggings clanged ominously on his sabatons as he tapped his foot to a painfully slow beat. He looked back and forth between Edwin and Kate, each time appearing more enlightened than before until, eventually, he pressed his tongue to his cheek, toying with some idea.

"You're not lovers, are you?" he said darkly. "Would be an awful shame if you ran away for the pleasures of a young lass. Your family would be ashamed, I'm sure."

"She's not a part of this," Edwin snapped. *Sir* Edwin. "And I will answer for what I've done when the time comes, to the Count, not you. I mean no disrespect, but you have no right to interrogate a knight of the realm with impunity when I have not committed any heinous crimes of rape or murder. And Kate, I'll be fine. Don't worry."

Her mother's stare was like a spear now, so intense and intrusive, as if to find the answers she sought through this simple gesture. Kate wanted to run up to her and tug at her dress, as a young girl would. She wanted to scream everything Edwin had said, and demand that she do something about it, as she surely would, rationally and with a plan with different stages, but still Olswalt was an unknown quantity. It was entirely possible that the captain was a good and honest man who lived by the code of justice he had to have pledged to Lameeri to uphold, and this seemed the case to her. However, the chance that he might be a spy, wearing the mask of a righteous man, willing to sanction other despicable men to hunt down Isaac and torture him into submission, so to talk of a haggard old mine, sickened her to the bone; the thought sent shivers down her spine, and Edwin might not be in a position to disconfirm that possibility, for all she knew.

The soldierly Henri emerged from the house to see what commotion was unfolding; rare that he would abandon his chores, though given the circumstances, he couldn't be blamed. Not that this made Kate feel any better, strong presence as he was. On the contrary, the added attention was causing her to lose concentration. Edwin, presumably having seen this, nodded kindly and then flicked his head in a random direction, providing the respite she'd been searching for. It was possible that this meant he had everything under control, and all would be well. She assumed the worst, as this was easier, and decided to formulate her own idea instead, aware that this was considerably simpler to commit to than actually imagine some perfect solution.

Giving her mother an apologetic smile as she turned to leave, she saw the mystery thicken for her in a hard, authoritative glare which said this matter would not be forgotten, mixed with sympathy for what she did not yet understand.

"Technically, I can question you," Olswalt corrected Edwin. "You may hold your peace of course, you're correct about that. I'm not allowed to torture you, and I plan on respecting that rule," was the last Kate heard before she slipped from the real world into one of her own.

Kate needed someplace cold and quiet, where she was guaranteed not to be disturbed and, equally as important, an appropriate avenue of communication. So it was the church, she decided in a flash, and she arrived at the open doors a few minutes later, to seek guidance and peace of mind. The clopping of her boots echoed loudly on the smooth stone floor; the only sound in the building, rising to the rafters and projected all about the room as she dazedly tumbled one foot after the other between two rows of pews, until she reached the final row at the front. She seated herself at the end and waited for the lingering distraction of the echoes to subside and grant her the silence she craved. Isolation was far too alluring.

On one side of the church, stained glass windows of wise folk and other notable historical figures glowed with an orange hue from the sun at near its high point for the day. The otherwise dark and dank interior of brown seats and grey stone was illuminated on Kate's side with the many colours of the windows, framed and spewed across the church benches like heavenly apparitions. Dust drifted in clouds, in and out of these ghostly images, flitting over reminders of deceased heroes, lending them an ethereal quality, like living crowns. Isolation became too comfortable; she was sick with it.

Kate bathed in the sunlit depiction of an old holy knight resting his hands on the pommel of his sword. She, too, cupped her hands, as he did, only in quiet prayer, not in glory, with her eyes so firmly shut that the light could barely pass through her lids. Her prayer, such as it was, was devoted to Isaac, and Marcel too if they travelled together, accompanied by assured muttering to guide the direction of her thoughts.

The eyelids curled back to their default condition and she blinked stupidly, directly ahead of her, feeling horribly unfocused in a situation in which she would already be uncomfortable. Saying prayers was not something she could take lightly. She realised that her focus had landed on the stained glass window of Sir Martin Caedor, at the very back of the church, poised in the same stance as he stood, near-immemorial, on the hilltop. An odd choice for the centrepiece window, she always thought, but then she knew little of the man anyway.

In place of stained glass windows celebrating the gods, a large engraving, painted beautifully, was a major attraction in the open space between the pews and the rear section of the church, where the priest, and choir, and sermon readers sat on their raised chairs. The gods were lined up, depicted as kind-faced, pale humans dressed in white robes. On the far left, Lavellyrn, goddess of love, offered a compassionate smile, cupping her hands over where her heart would be, and her robes were lined with gold strips. The god of truth and justice, Lameeri, stood tall and lean beside her, resting one hand on the pommel of his silver sword and, to his lower chest, he held a swirling mass of energy: a human soul exposed in purity, where irrevocable truths cannot be concealed, even when, to the mortal realm, lies might overrule all else.

In the middle, the god Venlor, keeper of the realms and of nature, gripped tightly in his right hand a black staff as tall as him; for why, Kate could not remember or discern, as surely he should not need to derive power from it. Floating above his other hand was Mura, the world, obviously painted only to show the five countries of the known world, while above him, the heavens were shown by a clear night sky with all the stars shimmering brightly as they rarely did in Caedor. At his feet, a black stallion of a unicorn lay sleeping and, further down still, was a dark, contemptuous mist signifying the evil of the Other Realm, hell, held at bay via Venlor's magic. Next was Saliis, the god of soul, and body, and mind, fronted by a floating strip of ocean and a ship riding the ferocious waves, to her a seemingly random sign of human wilfulness and accomplishment. He stood unwaveringly with his legs wide apart, his arms behind his back, and he gazed longingly into the distance, insofar as this was adequately portrayed. Kate had been told this was the case and, now, could see it no other way.

Finally, Nel, the goddess of faith and fortune, contemplated the heavens above in wondrous awe, throwing her arms out above her to behold the glory. All this was wrapped in an engraved circular frame and, high up in the ceiling, a window had been cleverly positioned and sized to shed the light of the sun on this work of art at midday, as was almost the time, lending a striking and even more memorable quality to it.

Kate was always drawn to pretty Lavellyrn and her sweet smile, as she seemed the most real out of all of them. Perhaps the engraver had had similar ideas, or perhaps it was just her affinity for a romantic deity clouding her objectiveness. Either way, she had strayed from the topic of immediate importance. She studied the artist's interpretations and brought up memories of the gods to prepare a suitable prayer, doing as much good as it usually did. She settled with a spontaneous prayer of favour and guidance, wavering from subject to subject with an unclear objective. Surely the gods would understand.

Heart of the Warrior

Outside of time and space, she slipped once more, and might have fallen into sleep from sheer overwhelming weariness, or into a deeply unfocused daydream at the very least, flitting manically between vague thoughts of Isaac, and Marcel, and Sir Edwin among an array of indecipherable nonsense which was forgotten as soon as it dematerialised.

The presence of another human tore her from this world of nightmares, to the comfort of real sounds and real sights. It was the hard-heeled shoes that gave the presence of this man away, even though he had tried his very best not to be a nuisance.

"I've not disturbed you, have I?" Jyric said reluctantly, now that he knew she was no longer in prayer.

Kate said nothing. There were some basic adjustments to be made before talking could commence. To provide a bearing, she looked to the carving, where the sun had moved beyond its highest point and only a chunk of the artwork was cast in that bright orange illumination. It was entirely possible that sleep had taken her then, in which case, her tribulations had stalked her to her dreams.

"How's your mysterious patient faring?" Jyric asked anxiously.

"He's awake. And well enough. I would ask you, kindly, not to disturb him. He should be in contact with as few people as possible."

"Of course, of course, I'll respect your judgement. Were you praying for him?"

"My prayers are my own," Kate said blearily, now fixedly staring at Jyric, as uncomfortable as it was, to make her point extra clear.

This provided the unexpected bonus of making her appear edgy and unnerved, and at the same time, uncharacteristically confident, and thus, in turn, he was mildly unnerved too, and respectfully backed off to grant her the privacy she needed, disappearing through an alcove door into an office. Though it was bizarre that she could derive enjoyment from unintentionally manipulating Jyric's perception, she afforded herself a wry smile nonetheless, that she had been confident enough to end the conversation.

No tangible achievements had been made, she thought, in coming here, but even as aloneness set in, she realised she was mellower now. At any rate, there was no further use in sitting here, no good to come of it that might not already be in motion.

The kitchen dining table had been moved out the back of the house, where Edwin sat basking in the sunlight, relishing the fresh highland air, and Kate's mother was laying plates of bread and ham. She sat opposite Edwin without saying a word, and without daring to look the Watch captain in the eyes. He was giving her no valid reason for paranoia and, in fact, stood on guard like any noble soldier with no hint of treachery, but still, she couldn't be sure.

"Where did you run off to then?" her mother asked as she seated herself beside her daughter.

"Oh, just the church."

"Really?" she laughed. "Must be something important on your mind then, hmm?"

Kate bit a chunk out of the spongy bread and chewed slowly to excuse herself. Her mother could not be allowed to continue questioning Kate on her unusual disposition. Edwin, whether having the same mindset as Kate or just seeking a way to dispose of the tension between the two of them, coughed and tilted his head in the Watch Patrolman's direction, quickly swallowing his food.

"So, Captain Olswalt," Edwin said brightly, "I've been wondering about a few things, and please don't take this the wrong way, as I'm ignorant of your ways, but tell me, is it standard procedure to disrupt the duties of other Watchmen on such short notice and for such trivial matters?"

"Procedure doesn't factor into it, Sir," Olswalt chuckled darkly. "Besides, one of the Count's advisors riding off into the night with nary a word to his friends or family, let alone his lord, is not a matter any Watchman worth his title would take lightly."

"Fair enough, I didn't mean any disrespect, Captain."

The knight took a long knife and tugged a loaf of very stubborn-looking bread in his direction. As he carefully sawed a slice for himself, it was unclear if he was aware of the Brodie matriarch's suspicious chagrin, or Kate's franticness in eating her food, now too afraid to look anywhere other than her plate for more than a second. To her growing despair, Edwin was bouncier than she had yet seen him, and was not yet finished with Olswalt.

"Still, was it appropriate to send your sergeant away? It doesn't take three people to deliver a message and you might need another man, should anything else crop up here."

"Perhaps," Olswalt said with slow deliberation. "I stand by my decision though."

The captain shifted his weight from side to side in a rare case of his discipline failing him, and his fingers curled halfway to fists before unravelling, as if by a life of their own they attempted to enact their own plans, while his face remained pleasantly stoical.

"Excellent bread, Mistress Brodie," Edwin exclaimed joyfully.

"Thank you very much, Sir," she replied graciously, shrugging her shoulders. "It's nice to be appreciated."

"Are you sure the good captain doesn't want any?"

"Well the offer still stands," she said to Olswalt hopefully.

Captain Olswalt rubbed his hands together, not removing his leather gloves, and adjusted his helm as he eyed the plates of food. When Kate's mother offered an endearing smile, he sighed and nodded. An increasingly jittery Edwin pulled a plate of pre-sliced bread near the edge of the table for him, and Olswalt reached out with his left arm, freezing his hand nearby while he chose.

Heart of the Warrior

The captain flinched at the sound of metal whizzing, slicing through the air, Edwin's knife spinning into a backhanded position before being slammed down. The captain was too slow. The first blow ripped through his glove and embedded the serrated knife deep into his hand, and the second, accompanied by Edwin's free hand brought down on the handle like a hammer, severed the skin with a resistive tearing sound which made Kate and her mother cringe, finally thudding into the wooden table.

She was already out of her seat with her mother following, leaping back with such urgency they nearly tripped over their chairs as they retreated. Olswalt, in his agonising frenzy, fumbled for the hilt of his sword, gritting his teeth with such intensity, to quell his own screams, that the rows scraped together like two swords at a stalemate, screeching in her mind like chalk on a blackboard.

Upon grasping his sword, he swung it as far round as he could manage while still pinned to the table. Edwin was already making his move, ducking, barraging with all his might into the captain's arm, ignoring the rattling of his ribcage and his own arm, and whipping the helm from Olswalt's head while he still had a chance. Olswalt gave up on swinging at Edwin solely, and focused his effort on removing the knife from the table.

He succeeded quickly, but at the cost of further pain; his helm clobbered into the back of his skull, then uppercut into his sword hand when he flailed it to cut at Edwin's neck. His hand flung up, opened in reflex, and the sword spiralled from his reach, rolling softly on the grass. Kate didn't think she could be more shocked by anything right now, yet here her mother was, sweeping the sword up with both hands and holding it out, clearly inexperienced and without the proper knowledge to so much as hold it properly, but even so, it was a wise move. She was being shrewd and, as neither of them was in tip-top condition, might stand a chance should one of them attack her. Hopefully.

Her involvement was ambiguous, probably deliberately so, giving the impression that she could be siding with either one of them. It was obvious, by now, that the Watch captain was fighting a losing battle though. Edwin was still behind him, and now had a grip on the knife handle which he could use to manipulate him however he pleased. He settled for forcing Olswalt to ram it into his own mail leggings, which didn't remotely puncture them as he knew it wouldn't, but Olswalt clutched his hand, blood-soaked, as he hoped he would.

Edwin forced the serrated blade back and forth like a pulley, with blistering speed, before wrenching it to freedom and his complete control, opening the floodgates for the sizeable hole in Olswalt's hand. Blood gushed from the wound, seeping out and over the tear in his glove and on to the grass like rain from each of his fingers and, very soon, soaked his other hand as he attempted to block it up. The blade was at the Watchman's throat, trickling its fluid down his neck and armour, though Edwin had to retract it slightly when the violent throbbing of the man's neck tempted the steel, as his screams and wails in harrowing pain were bringing the skin too close to it.

"You're not as subtle as you think you are," Edwin panted. "You're too nice, for one. It's a little too forced at times. Everyone knows you're a miserable cunt."

Olswalt's screams had ceased but he was gasping for air, breathing five times faster than he should, spluttering phlegm and blood as tears rolled down his cheeks. Surprisingly quickly, he got a firm enough hold on himself to formulate a coherent sentence.

"The Count will have your head on a pike outside the palace for this, you crazy fool," he wheezed.

"Or yours, if you are exposed as a traitor. I think you brought those two Watchmen here as witnesses, to back up how legitimate you are, should it to come to question, and you sent them away so you, alone, could assess me, see how much I know, put me in line if necessary. As for when I saw you speaking to that *spy* in Melphor, I thought nothing of it at the time. I thought you were a decent man."

"Ah, so you *are* lovers," Olswalt choked painfully in laughter, nodding at Kate, the layers of his pleasant mannerisms fast peeling away.

"*Listen* to me," Edwin said impatiently, shaking the man in his grasp. "Why would you sell yourself out? You have a wife and child to look out for. The reward must be pretty substantial, huh?"

"Go to hell," the Watchman replied drunkenly.

It was apparent that he had no mind to answer any questions, or couldn't. He struggled to break free, but his escape was not as he had hoped, Edwin striking his helm upon the right side of his head, knocking him out cold almost instantly. He collapsed and slumped unhindered to the grass.

"Kate, see to him please," Edwin said, panting, his body a vessel of weakness.

She was apprehensive, and even resentful, of being forced into this. What was most frustrating was that she didn't know whether any of that was necessary. Abandoning these doubts in favour of the simple option, to save a man's life, she rushed to the Watchman's aid, finding her inner peace and blocking all the spectators from her world.

"You had better have a damn good reason for bringing this violence to Caedor," she heard her mother's menace. "Speak quickly."

"I assure you, I acted with the best of intentions. You will thank me later, I think. Yes, yes, I shall explain," Edwin sighed, now cautious not to provoke the woman, whose eyes, ablaze, foretold the knight's sundering. "This may take a while."

Chapter Ten: Fire and Steel

In a small grove, which must have been tended to with real passion by expert gardeners on a regular basis, there was a circular clearing, just as well kept, and even the path leading up to it was immaculate save for leaves and twigs which drifted onto it. The clearing was enclosed by a short wall of white brick that one could easily step over, but it was clearly not designed for protection so much as for a beautiful, idyllic image: a frame on a very real landscape painting.

On one of the wooden benches backing onto the wall, Isaac pondered this new world with fascination for each and every detail. *Why*, he thought, *would anyone bother to maintain a shrine in the wilderness so diligently?* In Burtal, things were prioritised very differently, more sensibly, it appeared on the surface, yet work was evidently so much more efficient here that they could afford time and money for these pursuits, which in turn came together to create a superb reputation and generated the attention of visiting merchants, and pilgrims, and immigrants looking for a new life.

The sky was bluer here than he was used to, with whiter, fluffier clouds. Never had he seen so many days go by without grey skies sweeping through at some point in Caedor. As he observed this sight, he stretched out his arms either side of him and rubbed the masterful engravings of the oak bench; just interesting patterns to Isaac, though the artist must have had something specific in mind as nothing here was accidental.

Most prominently, the clearing housed, at its very centre, a shrine to Venlor, a grey-white pillar of rock as smooth as marble, shimmering like salt on water, and nine or ten feet tall with a girth of more than two. Wrapped around it was a vine, carved from the very same rock, winding from the bottom all the way to the top, where atop the monument was a stone unicorn rearing on its hind legs gracefully. All around it there was writing in an old language, that of Mürathneè before the first emperor was even a thought, or an older version of that even, though he couldn't be sure without a guide as he couldn't read it. Supposedly it was ancient, as were other shrines in the wilderness, and housed a very old magic, with the emphasis on *old* most likely, and a little magic on the side, perhaps.

Rarely, someone would report that from a shrine they saw the words gleam ever so slightly, or it would whisper to them but they couldn't hear or remember what was said. If there was godly power in these monuments, they had long since lost it, dissipated after the gods left upon creating the celestial realm as some said, or as a select few theorised, a capsule of magic for the future. Either way, a shrine was all that was left, and that suited Isaac just fine.

Ten steps of the same kind of rock, whether made at the time of the shrine or later he could not immediately tell, led up to it on four sides, while the strips in-between contained a

The Voice of Kings

variety of flowers in full bloom. At the bottom of one of the sets of stairs was stone carved like a headstone with writing on it, also in an old Mürathneèan language, but this was almost certainly a new addition. Still, he knew what it meant even before he read the translation underneath as it was a phrase he'd heard used in Burtal as well. It read: "This land around you, and all other lands everywhere, I will watch over, for you and for everyone, for today and all the days to come. Treat this world with respect and you will be rewarded in the next".

Isaac allowed his eyelids to slide shut, listening intently to the birds, some familiar, some with more exotic screeches and cries. The rustlings of the leaves was far more prominent than before, and as he allowed the sensation to fill him, he could almost hear each individual leaf blowing back and forth in its own way, visualise the trees organised in their rows exactly.

That it was all illusion didn't matter. He was building a precedent for Harth in his mind so that it was less jarring when he finally arrived, utilising the sights and sounds and feel and people of this country as a basis, constantly re-evaluating as was necessary, but he needed his imagination as well, to fill in the blanks.

"What time did you get to bed last night?" he heard Marcel say.

"Late."

"With or without your lady friend from the Strathnor Inn?" Marcel asked after a pause for effect.

One eye opened, and then the other. Marcel was still sitting cross-legged at the bottom of one set of the steps, with his hands on his knees. Isaac smirked and shook his head; only he would bring this up while basking in the awe of Venlor's monument and still claim piety.

"For your information, "my lady friend" is called Mareesse. And you're mistaken. She's due to be wed in just 12 days. Lovely woman though. Did you not see her engagement ring?"

"Engagement ring?" Marcel said, nodding with approval. "What sort of man is she marrying?"

"Well, here's the interesting bit," Isaac said excitedly, sitting up and stroking his hair back from where the wind had deemed fit to place it. "Up until now, he's been a merchant, sometimes travelling, sometimes fixed, and making good money for it, but nothing special, was the message I was getting. And he's an honest trader. But in Mürathneè, engagement rings are not so expensive if you know where to look and what jewels are most common where. And this man should, let's face it. It's less valuable than it looks. But the materials are all here, and they know how to get them out of the ground efficiently."

Marcel rose to stretch his legs. Outwardly he did not seem impressed, or to most he would not. Isaac saw his inner workings as if there was a window on his head. Right about now, he was probably regretting going to bed early the previous night. Isaac sat back to let this settle and lower his expectations. It was always best to be prepared to be proven wrong, as unlikely as it was when it came to reading his younger brother.

"You could do a hell of a lot worse, at any rate," Isaac added thoughtfully. "It had a tiny stone set into the top, fairly smooth, and the ring itself had a thin finish of real gold with the words "Lameeri's Truth" engraved into it."

The memory of her ecstatic grin and bounciness brought a smile to him. Of the people he'd spoken to in this country so far, few were so poetic or pleasant, but it couldn't be denied that there was something special about this land which made its people, in a broader sense, happier. It was something Isaac couldn't quite understand yet, if indeed there was a way to simplify it at all. This was probably more Kester's area of expertise. Not to mention, he'd be better off here than in Aurail, though it might, one day, be better off for having him.

"That sounds like something you'd put on a ring if you ever got married," Marcel chuckled.

He casually made his way to Isaac's bench and sat on the other end of it, and even as Isaac began speaking, another thought begged for his attention, though he shouldn't have been surprised.

"Father would have..." Isaac said.

"She let you touch her invaluable engagement ring?" Marcel asked, scratching his chin, ignoring Isaac entirely. "If you tried that on a woman back home, she'd immediately assume you were trying to seduce or rob her."

"It's true, people are more uptight in Burtal from my experience, but I'm inclined to disagree. You just need to know how to approach different people."

"Perhaps you can teach me to be that trustworthy," Marcel replied, only half-joking.

Isaac sat perfectly still for a moment in confused contemplation, as if all his functions had shut down, before suddenly jumping to his feet and striding across the grove with strong resolve for reasons he had not yet decided upon. Suddenly, the statue spoke to him, not literally, but in the few days he'd spent in this country, the fine, arduous work that was crafting architecture tickled him. There was a chance it would be thrown to the back burner of his interests in a week or two, as so many were, sizzling, burning away, but for now he marvelled at who might have built the monument. Perhaps it was Venlor himself, as legends suggested; an idea perfect for song, no doubt!

Certainly there were sufficient records to vouch for, at least in terms of continuity, the validity of Venlor as a lover of the theatrical, as developing beauty alongside functionality in nature could be perceived.

In that regard, any given detail in the arrangement of this grove could very well be designed by the gardeners to invoke a similar feel, as if specified in blueprints by Venlor himself; the trees correct in their exact quantity and kind, and by that logic, it was probable that he was surrounded by a myriad of obscure metaphors which translated as amazing finds to those keen of religious sight and, fortunately, doubled as a haven to be respected and ingrained in the memory of all who bore witness.

Following a short distance behind with his hands in his pockets, Marcel was only very mildly irritated by Isaac's behaviour, for he was sure he hadn't neglected to respond, and knew Isaac was acutely aware that he knew. Never would strangers hearken to him if he acted so familiar and with so little readily apparent sense, so he only acted as such before family and friends.

"I have no idea how to respond to that," Isaac said, not breaking eye contact with the shrine.

"Let me rephrase that."

"That won't be necessary," Isaac assured.

He looked to Marcel, and as they were the same height, Isaac could see into his soul through one glance of his eyes, and composedly stared at the shrine once more, feeling at that time in an oddly pious mood himself, in his own twisted, untraditional, maverick way, and a thin smile crept into existence, for Marcel was rarely so self-conscious before the past two or three days.

"I know what you meant. And you have many talents just waiting to be appreciated," Isaac said encouragingly, intertwining his words with an appropriate level of kindness, careful not to demean him in the process. "You'll do well in Harth, I know it."

"I didn't say..."

"But you were thinking it," Isaac said with a sly smirk.

Each step Isaac now made towards the shrine was Venlor taking a step closer to him. Where some others, he thought, probably bore such unnecessary, perfunctory humility in close proximity of shrines like these, Isaac carried a confident sense of awe. He placed a hand gently on its surface, slipping ever so slightly, surprised that it was even smoother than he'd imagined, not weathered in the slightest after all these years, as the land around it must have changed almost beyond recognition dozens of times. Caught up in the moment, he wondered how it had been made, and why the gods would need or want it.

Pressing his cheek to the cold rock, it occurred to him that it must not be of a material humans had yet used, however it may look and feel, or else it was combined with something else. Or perhaps there was, indeed, magic here once, outlandish as it did sound as he said it in his mind.

"Are you not nervous at all?" Marcel said with renewed coolness.

"Rest assured, I'm no less nervous than you. This is a massive and important undertaking for me, and I have to try to prepare myself for the, admittedly, unknowable possibility that it may lead me back where I started. You should have no such reservations, Brother."

As ever, Marcel did not openly show his appreciation for Isaac's encouragement, even if, unusually, there was no sarcasm or jibing fun in his tone this time. Not that Isaac needed him to be outwardly grateful to know that he was. Marcel sniffed loudly and puckered his lips at Isaac's new obsession, knowing it would pass very soon, but still, his jitters indicated he was very conscious of time all of a sudden.

"Are you going to pray before this or not? If you're not, then we can make our leave."

Isaac sidled one foot to the next step, then the other to the next, and continued to do this with a certain grace as if he already knew the exact placements of the stairs without turning or looking at his feet, and when he reached the bottom, he thought upon the proud unicorn whinnying to its master in another realm. Strange, it was to him, that praying to a god before a shrine was considered more effective than in a church or any other place. It took commitment to come all the way out here of course, if that was your only intention, travelling as a pilgrim, but it seemed to him the gods should know any given person's sincerity and intent anyway. Already he imagined the answer as long and bewildering, unless, again, these giant stones held an ancient incomprehensible magic. Yes, that would do. They had magic, lots of it.

"What would I say?" Isaac said, keen to brush this subject aside.

"Anything."

"Anything encompasses quite a lot," Isaac replied as straight as was possible.

"I don't know, perhaps think about anything you've appreciated or been inspired by here, and draw some prayer from that. Or think of home, and what might be happening there."

Under his breath, Isaac whispered a nostalgic laugh and mouthed the word "home" as if trying to send a message to be carried on these fine Mūrathneèan winds, across Lavellyrn's Channel, all the way to his mother and sister. In truth, it had not been such a long time since leaving home, but now was the first time he'd really visualised it since then.

"I'll think on it when we're back on the road," Isaac said, backing away from the shrine. "Apologies for not staying," he added with a smile and a short bow. "By your leave."

"That might be blasphemy," Marcel joked, sounding only remotely convinced at his own words.

"I shouldn't have to listen to any of that from you, hypocrite," Isaac said with flat sarcasm and a quizzical smile. "Honourable to the gods as you may be, you're not the most conservative of worshippers either. So it's a good thing you're not going to, say, a Mūraci cathedral. Or Mūrac in general, I guess."

Typically, and thankfully, Marcel let out a miniature laugh and fell silent without rebuke or indication that he'd been offended. Approaching the exit path to the grove, Isaac took in one final panoramic view of the trees in their rows, looping round into separate directions at the back of the grove to black out all the world; the wood of dark, yet not lifeless, greens and browns, and billowing leaves of voluptuous red and golden-brown were signs not of autumn's coming, but summer's strength. All was as it was intended: to uphold the illusion of a paradise outside of the countryside surrounding it. That the countryside was beautiful also was irrelevant. Only that it was a place of solitude.

The shrine was more invariable and unchangeable than it had ever seemed to him before now. At its core, it was a hulking mass of seemingly invincible stone, stubborn in the face of time, juxtaposed with so much flourishing life which could not, in the end, withstand such a force. Even the unicorn, while not timeless, could not be disputed in its visage as a depiction of Venlor could, as it was quite simply one of his creatures.

Isaac was beginning to tire of the nature of his own thoughts, but stored them all away for a future discussion if he should ever need to call upon them, if indeed he could remember it all, as he likely wouldn't. These thoughts brought a smile to his face in what he generally considered as very stiff and conventional thinking, treating the gods as objects to project one's faith unto.

"I'm sure Venlor would understand, at any rate," Isaac remarked. "Surely he must have a sense of humour. No one can be so wise and yet so dull."

Marcel conceded with difficulty that, on principle, Isaac may have had a fair point, nodding slightly. They untied their horses from an area of grass specifically created for them to graze while their masters proceeded into the grove. They pressed on down the narrow winding path where shadows and light sparred, sunlight flickering through the leaves and tree trunks overhead, grown through human intervention to curve to create an archway the whole distance of the path. At the very end, they passed beneath a man-made arch to match the floral theme, fashioned from fine bronze to give the impression of two thin trees entwined together.

The world was theirs again: the fields and rolling hills and the cobble road carved through the landscape. From the east, an expensive-looking merchant wagon, pulled by four horses and guarded by a mercenary horseman, rocketed swiftly over the impressively even road on sturdy wooden wheels, which were held together with brilliantly forged iron, in addition to a form of simple suspension, to protect the goods inside at relatively high speeds.

Isaac and Marcel hauled themselves hastily onto their own horses and pulled out in front with a show of dust, speeding off left, westward. Isaac's horse soared, the scenery whizzing past him at breakneck speeds, and the usual rush of adrenaline shot new life into him as it always did when beginning a horse ride. With all due respect to his father, they could afford to quicken their overall pace without having to slow down for him when he could no longer take the bumpiness of some of the roads in Burtal, despite how much he loved it, apparently, from when he used to ride for miles around Caedor with Mother, relishing getting lost together.

Farms came into view now on both sides of the road, roaring by barely before he could observe them, but there was enough time to take in the major details. Typically effective craftsmanship of these people was brought out through their well built houses, and even such simple things as fences. Cows and sheep roamed freely within these confines and, outside of them, dozens of farmers were ploughing fields for vegetables he couldn't quite make out as, to his vision, they blurred into smudges of pure reds, and greens, and yellows, like an abstract painting.

Further along, there were apple trees which would make his mouth water if he had stopped to think about them for more than five seconds, and he recognised them instantly, even though few grew anywhere near the highlands of his home. Presumably it was not a bad place, technically speaking, to live here, seeing as merchants travelled this, The Wolf's Way, constantly as it split off at both ends to fairly direct routes to several cities.

Beyond, where the farms were more sparse, where the apple orchards and all else beneath and around them zipped into the distance, into a dot and then a memory, cliffs rose up not five miles to his foreright, and stretched as far as he could see. Unlike the gradual rising of the County Highlands, these were steep and sheer, for the most part, from flat ground. *The Ardith Peaks*, he thought to himself, scanning the vague image of a local map in his mind. Not as tall as mountains, they nonetheless looked craggy and rough; a tough chore to pass through its roads, carved in very select places by experts who must have spent months figuring out the safest places to work.

Next in the long line of memorable sights was, to the side of the road, perched atop a rugged rock formation ten feet tall or more, a cylindrical watchtower built from another kind of white rock, tinted red, hardy and with an air of power about it blasting out across the landscape, inspiring obedience in all would-be lawbreakers. Archery loopholes were arranged in lines with seemingly perfect precision all over it, and behind the embrasures, soldiers patrolled around a neat stack of sticks and hay encased in more brick to negate any sliver of a chance of fire spreading when the beacon was lit. He felt he may have been mistaken, but Isaac thought he saw the guards at the top wielding crossbows and flintlock muskets, the latter of which was, as far as he knew, an experimental device not fit to be used in combat, let alone from such range and altitude, unless this was another technology advanced by the spectacular, collaborative skills of the Mürathneèan people.

That such a weapon could exist in a practical format was intensely uncomfortable a notion; Isaac's mouth dried at the thought, his throat constricting his breathing in an instinctive reaction before he had even the time to think about it. He calmed himself quickly and rationalised that it was still scientific advancement, no matter what its purpose was, and the inventors were probably proud just to make something new, as was a recurring theme here.

The Voice of Kings

When so much as a new mineral was discovered on Mürathneèan turf, these patriots were glad to let everyone know it was them, as most famously occurred on the Isle of Sèhvor, by which that white steel was named and remained so to this day. In Burtal, people were less inclined to spread the word of their discoveries; many didn't care, if Aurail was any indication. Where, here, even watchtowers were a declaration of architectural brilliance, along the road to Aurail they were merely functional for their primary purpose which had served them well enough in the past. Times were changing; maybe they wouldn't.

In a hail of blurred stone, Isaac could have sworn to seeing gaol bars near the rim of this watchtower, and an extension at its base for some unseen additional reason that, no doubt, was taken absolutely for granted. For all the finesse and quality of structures like these, Isaac could see, as well as anyone, the temptation of stamping your feet where you stood and proclaiming yourself a part of your own little world. With a genius for a father, he, too, experienced the weariness of having to change, even as he applauded and welcomed it.

The cliffs, too, disappeared again, as the road was now encased by a wooded area, sparsely populated with trees tall and lush. A sign noted a crossroads up ahead as he whizzed by it, wind screaming in his ears, at which point he tugged at the reins to slow the horse right down to a fast trot. Behind him, more hooves clopped ferociously and scraped with a dust cloud to the same speed, Marcel rocking in his saddle uneasily as he pulled beside Isaac. Soon after, they turned a sharp corner into a fork of two directions.

"Was left or right the fastest route?" Isaac asked. "It was left, wasn't it?"

"I think so. I'm not sure though. Just check the map..." Marcel trailed off quietly, noticing a sign for the left road proclaiming it as unfit for their purpose, and he shrugged. "It doesn't matter anyway; it says there's bridge maintenance ahead."

"Left it is then," Isaac said slyly.

Marcel grinned sheepishly, and to humour Isaac looked both ways intently for some sign of his sudden coy enthusiasm. To the south-west road, there was no discernible advantage or lure, and to the north-west, no hindrance made itself apparent to him. In fact, there was little difference between the two, both veering from view after 50 foot stretches. He sighed deeply and squinted at Isaac.

"Nope, you've lost me there."

"Read between the lines, Marcel. It says there is maintenance, not that the bridge is closed. Perhaps there is passage enough for us, and not for a carriage or heavy load. We'd be fools to assume the subtext implies no passage and give up when the river is such short distance from here. This road cuts so many hours from our journey."

"As you please," Marcel said plainly, happy enough to submit to Isaac's judgement over his own and, as always, willing to put his smug intellect to the test with the secret intent of hoping to learn something from his methodology, or else enjoy the spectacle of him crashing and burning.

Fire and Steel

Sure enough, the river drew close but minutes later, first by way of the tremendous gushing of water smashing against rocks and the banks over and over again; gallons of it seething ever onward from north to south. Before it came to be seen, more sounds erupted from the river, smooth in clarity and mechanical in nature, over the rushing of water and the clopping of hooves beating on cobblestones beneath them.

The outer rim of the woodland shot past them, and clearings on both sides of the road led all the way to the bank. Beyond it, the river, five times as wide as the road and filled almost to its brim with freshwater, ran beneath two bridges. The first was the original stone bridge connected to the road, broken and abandoned for all but the lightest of burdens. Wooden planks provided a safe passage across for those working at the encampment on the opposite bank, but for no other, as the sign pitched before it clearly stated in stark contrast to the oblique sentiment of the previous one. Isaac knew he could command his horse to jump the gaps, though whoever erected that sign must have considered that when he was hammering it into the ground.

The second bridge was the source of all the puzzling noises; an industrial experiment, the likes of which the two brothers could not discern at first glance, but so fascinated by it they were that they pulled back on the reins much earlier than was necessary, to cease all movement for the sake of this strange new contraption in their path.

Isaac softly whispered something into his horse's ear, which soothed it, allowing it to slow to a trot without incident, and for Isaac to analyse the monstrosity above the river without his vision being blurred by the antics of a riled beast. He smiled and nodded in approval. His father would have loved to see this. One look to Marcel showed him that he was thinking the same.

At both ends of the bridge were two huge boxes made of metal, one of which was open at the front and being examined by three engineers out of their depth, arguing amongst themselves. The box itself was stuffed full of gears of massively varying sizes and appeared to be connected to mechanisms in the bridge itself, which was far thicker than any bridge of this length and width should reasonably be, which would have tweaked his curiosity, had the area been deserted of all other humans. It was reinforced with layers of steel and iron, further adding to its already immense density, surely weighing twice as much as its stone bridge partner.

The engineers disappeared behind the box into a control booth and, as if by magic, steam was borne and the gears churned and scraped against one another, straining so hard that Isaac winced and waited for the inevitable failure. There was an awesome rumbling as clamps were released and the bridge separated at its exact middle point, creaking in a manner that seemed to disturb the professional engineers around it as much as it did Isaac and Marcel, and caused all of them to jump just the same when the creaking gears could hold it no more and the two segments came crashing down.

The Voice of Kings

Isaac and Marcel tugged hard at the reins of their distressed horses which nearly threw them off in fright from the almighty bang of giant metal and stone slabs slamming together, crumpling and splintering, which echoed through the river, and between every tree, and all the way up to the heavens, as a demon might roar when escaping from its realm. Isaac, suddenly unsettled, spat out the phlegm that had formed in his throat. *What, precisely, was wrong with a normal drawbridge?*

The very ground shook, and people either side of the bridge spread their legs and arms out to maintain balance, shaking their heads that their dismay would be blatantly known to all responsible. The guard at the bridge stood vigilant, eyeing them with muted intrigue and a stiff upper lip, as if trying to scare the duo away with his presence alone which, granted, would have been enough for most people.

"Don't you worry about a thing, Brother," Isaac said confidently. "We may yet talk our way to the other side."

When Isaac inevitably hopped from his horse in staging his confrontation with the guard in the friendliest way possible, Marcel imitated his actions. The immediate solution came to Isaac in the blink of an eye. The guard was utterly serious in defending the bridge with all his honour, and yet Isaac saw uncertainty behind those steely eyes, the voice of reason shouting at him, at present unheard, that perhaps, despite his loyalty and wish to serve only as his job described, it was all rather pointless.

He wore his Watchman's harness with pride, the relief fronting it well-cleaned and gleaming, being an image of two meanings: two swords crossed, one wreathed in flame and the other steaming with grey smoke that encompassed it the same way its counterpart burned merrily away, red hot but soaked in water. It was a rather profound message for one so simple as a guard to bear; the fires of war raging and extinguished at the same precise moment. On the other side of the coin, it doubled as a subtle declaration of Mürathneè's thriving industry, fire and steel fronting this image, a weapon bathing in the fires of war from which it was also made and cooled as all swords must be after forging; the end of one process.

An unnecessary level of detail for a lump of metal, the primary purpose of which was to stop a man being killed, Isaac thought, yet it provoked discussion and reinforced the country's position as the best at everything, when foreigners like to over-thinking came to see it.

"Good day," Isaac said cheerfully, embodying, with stupendous accuracy, both joy and fiery commitment to his business in one tight package.

"No passage to the west bank for civilians, I'm afraid," the guard regurgitated from a list of phrases he must have commanded a hundred times to speak it with such monotony in his tone. "I don't make the rules," he added firmly.

"Could I trouble you to fetch the person who does?"

"He's not here," the guard sighed.

He was already troubled, it would seem, or annoyed, more accurately, and was anxious for the trouble, which was out of his hands, to be resolved as quickly as possible. It was likely it pertained to the snag the engineers had encountered with building this immense contraption in the bridge. No harm could come from squeezing more information from him if Isaac was careful to remain polite.

"Can you not, in that case, bring me the next leader in line?"

"There isn't one," the guard replied bitterly. "Everyone's running around like headless chickens."

Isaac felt his luck waning, but he showed no sign of resignation from his standpoint, as Marcel began to. There was something gravely amiss in this puzzle and there might just be a way to take advantage of it, if luck was still on his side. Not in this country, not anywhere for that matter, could such an ambitious project be undertaken and, without precedent, shatter under the bloated weight of incompetence so close to completion. With this in mind, it would be logical to assume the project leader was the missing link in this scene.

The gears caught his attention in his desperate state, in dire need of finding a solution before the guard realised he had no idea what he was talking about. Some of them were coated in Sèhvorian steel, or possibly even made of it in full, no doubt to strengthen the whole structure; no easy feat as, in spite of how it was heralded with such fanfare, very few really knew how to use it, and of those who did, the best of them admitted that there were yet more secrets to uncover. In the precursory strain, they'd sheared through the standard steel gears around them.

"That's some very clever machinery you've got back there. Or it would be if they could get it working," Isaac said on a whim, pointing in the general direction of the gearbox. "Who is the chief engineer, may I ask? Is it the camp leader you were talking about?"

"That's him," the guard sighed, more strenuously this time. "Man called Vicentei Laccona. If you really want to wait around for him, you're welcome to, but I think you should know the detour road will only take you a few miles out of your way."

Marcel's eyebrows lifted quizzically and his lips puckered into a smug smile on one side of his face, and in return, Isaac tilted his head the absolute minimum amount required to meet his brother's expression with his own knowing look. Confusion beset him as much as excitement did, the two emotions dancing back and forth from the fore of his heart in a bout of indecisiveness, unable to weigh this unexpected encounter; whether this was a blessing, or another hurdle in the endless line of complications.

For all the uncertainty of the debate within him, it lasted only a few seconds before he was raring to return to the delicate matter of how to extract the most useful information. The guard perked up in response to the thrusting mood change.

"What is it? Do you know him?" he asked hopefully.

"Not as such," Isaac replied. "I hope to soon enough. If he's as intelligent and wise as I've heard he is, he will be of true value in my affairs, and I in his. *If* he's really as inquisitive as people say. Do you not know where he is?" Isaac said sharply but softly, noting the guard's bitter pessimism shining like a beacon from his very body now. "Does he no longer live in Harth?"

"Sometimes," the guard replied with a droopy wave of his hand. "He travels a lot. Maybe he's gone there, maybe he's not. He headed west, I can tell you that much, but for what purpose I can't rightly say, and I don't think any of the 30 or so residents of his encampment could either. For all I know, a moth flew over his nose and he chased after it. He has the combined intellect of four people, but the attention span of a five-year-old."

For need of a context for the guard's statement, Isaac sought to inspect the men on the far bank, scurrying here and there between tents, carrying machinery parts. The heels of his boots landed softly on the grass with the subdued precision of strides slow and scrupulous as he paced a short distance from the guard, head held high while a hand brushed through his matted hair and held it flat at the very back. It was increasingly obvious to him that they weren't really sure what they were supposed to be doing. Though he couldn't clearly see their expression or make out all their words, the tone and body language spoke volumes in and of themselves, and there was a pattern to their actions, in that they lacked the cohesion normally associated with these people.

"Am I to take it he left without informing *anyone* here?" Isaac said, unconsciously making eye contact with the guard again.

"That's the truth of it, as far as I know," the guard said, and shrugged, almost past the point of caring now. "Ran away in the night without a clue as to why, and left these mere mortals to finish his job with some near incomprehensible schematics. He was visited by a courier of some description, I've heard a few say, not that any of the witnesses can swear to a single purpose for that courier."

"Do you have no idea why he might have left, then?" Isaac pressed, hoping the assumption of the guard's obliviousness would spur him to recall even the most minor of details.

Indeed, he now appeared thoughtful in his weariness, in regret at this ever having transpired beyond his control. He gazed fondly up the river, cutting through open plains as it was and further blanketed in thicker woodland patches, where it twisted and turned out of sight, gradually rising with the landscape and disappearing at last on the horizon past a gigantic ravine in the sand-coloured Ardith cliffs. To his eyebrows, the guard brought an un-gloved hand, sweat trickling from beneath his vambrace, and squinted, craning his neck for what appeared to be a vain attempt to find something far off, which in reality he needed for peace of mind and perspective.

He sighed, even now retaining his soldierly posture, and his attention drifted back around, where Marcel had his arms crossed and was smiling curiously, standing rather casually, and Isaac was stock still, save for his mind which whirred with energy and thought. His lips curled thinly into a smile of satisfaction and thanks when he saw the man's resolve.

"Well," the guard started, "he did have this idea of creating a floodplain further north. The river can get damned wild here a'times, and far worse up at White Fire Falls, and the whole point of this bridge is to encourage trade boats to pass through instead of clogging the roads, so he set to work on his plans for this clever mechanical dam which sort of siphons off water somehow, even before he'd finished this thing. But like I said, he was headed west, so unless his leaving was all deception in itself, he's not there."

"I see," Isaac said sombrely, putting his hands together as if in contemplative prayer and staring up the river. "There's no chance you can get me through then?" he continued dimly in hope, only for the sake of having said he tried.

"None whatsoever."

And why not? He could make his horse jump the stone bridge; his opinion hadn't changed on that.

The curtains began to close on the meeting; the stagnant atmosphere made this abundantly clear. Still, for all their troubles, Isaac had gained a sympathiser in reward for his tact. The guard even, for a time, seemed like he might be considering the small possibility that passage might be granted for them, but with a final sigh of submission shook his head, perhaps in fear of interfering with his employer's complex plans or for the bridge's safety, but as he did so realised that he trusted this talkative stranger.

"Good luck," he said hesitantly. "If you do find him, just be sure to keep your expectations in check. If it's help you seek, he might not be reliable. Oh, and while you're at it, tell him to get his arse back here where he belongs and face up to his responsibility so the guard at the bridge can go home to his family."

"I will do that. My word is my bond."

There was not so much as the most distant glimpse of japery in Isaac's voice in the face of the guard's slight sarcasm; on the contrary, he was resolute and steadfast, and spoke with forcefulness accompanied by a trusting grin, as if making an unofficial promise.

To quickly cement this impression, he fumbled in the purse strapped to his belt, fingers clasping on one coin, then, after a moment's reconsideration, his index finger thrust through the pile of gold and whipped back into a fist formation with a second coin. This was not Burtal, he reminded himself; wealth was harder to imply. One coin would not suffice to leave a lasting positive impression.

They gleamed as they span through the air, the glare of the sun beaming from their faces with each rotation as they danced over one another in mid-flight. However, it was not this, but the shock of generosity in the guard's otherwise dull day that caused him nearly to miss

The Voice of Kings

them entirely, raising his hands as they neared his chest and catching them well enough nonetheless.

"I thank you for your time and your understanding. You're a good and noble man, I see. If Mister Laccona happens to return, tell him Isaac, son of Lennord Brodie from the town of Caedor, searches for him in Harth, for he proposes a riddle worthy of his gifts."

The guard nodded eagerly and shook Isaac's hand, and then Marcel's too, though he had not been a great presence. They mounted their horses and rode from the scene with no further words exchanged, comforted in the belief that the guard could be relied upon to relay Isaac's message if the need arose.

"That was very generous of you," Marcel said, impressed, when they were out of ear shot.

"Take note: shiny things can be a very effective memory trigger. It's not that I don't trust him," Isaac protested in his defence when Marcel shot him an unsavoury look. "I was just taking out extra insurance, that's all."

"And you learned that how? You've never had anywhere close to that much money to burn on things like that before."

"Alright, I'm only guessing," Isaac said with a forced sigh and a sarcastic, toothy grin. "It wasn't exactly what I'd call a gamble though," he said, tapping his purse which brimmed with only a fraction of the money given to him by his father.

Silence replaced banter, even now as they trotted side by side, each operating on the understanding that the other would shatter the quietness with some query or witty observation, as they both searched their thoughts, hoping that the right words might fall into place.

"You're not going after Vicentei up north then?" Marcel finally interrupted the silence, genuine in his concern for Isaac's plan.

"I'm not in the mood for a wild goose chase; I've spent long enough doing that already. I'll not humour that possibility any more than I need to. We go north, but not as far as White Fire Falls. I have a plan and I'm going to stick with it; it's easier that way. Come," Isaac said more lightly. "We'll still make up for lost time if we hurry."

Their horses leapt into action gleefully at their masters' commands, the two of them, in mental preparation, taking in the sight of the cliffs, which lay a great shadow strewn across the treetops; they cowering more like decorated sticks in its wake, and it would soon test them for all their might. And then horses and riders were gone once more, beneath a blanket of leaves and bark.

~

Long hours of bones rattling within his body, hurtling up the steep slopes of the Ardith cliffs, now belatedly began to set in as pain for Marcel. With how well-lit and patrolled the highroad was at night, they could afford to stop off at inns after nightfall, but today, enough was enough. His body ached and he relished the opportunity for an early rest, leaning on the balcony of his inn room and looking out at the landscape below, lit by the late afternoon sun. The sky streaked a wondrous purple, especially on the horizon where the river, as a thin strip of deep blue water shimmered. Stars already were advancing into view, one by one, without waiting for the leave of the sun, opposed by a ghostly, pale spectre of Refeer on the opposite side of the sky; a confrontation the moon would reign victorious over and, with the night, would smother this land in its cool embrace.

To the west, his right, Marcel gazed aimlessly, to where no significant civilisation could yet be seen with the naked eye. It made him wearier still, that the passage of space through this foreign country, none of which he recognised, could not be measured by any of his senses, save for the uneducated guesses that his mind presumed to bestow on him at the best of times and the want in his heart for progress to be tangibly apparent, more so than the tracking of their miniscule movements on the ink roads of ragged cloth maps.

He flicked away a flake of sandstone which aggravated him between the clutches of two eyelashes and, to be sure there was no more, ruffled his hair, not caring to flatten it or neaten it in any way, and patted his hands together to be final; something he had done fairly frequently on the ride up here, when dustbowls ravaged him from the increasingly harsh winds, whipping yellow rock particles from the cliffside.

All of this was memory now, and the aches that cursed him were a small price to pay for a nice bedchamber such as this to rest in, with a comfortable bed, a plump feather pillow, and a pleasant view from a balcony, of which not all rooms had. With this, he forced happiness upon himself, as he considered himself a simple person all told and was not often bogged down with such melancholy, and even tiredness and the niggling anxiety of how life would change for him in Harth were trumped by his optimism. Besides, it would certainly not do to be complacent, here of all places. He was grateful, as all others were who trekked or rode this far, to be blessed with the sight of a rest stop.

The inn, of convex face, was situated cosily within an alcove by the curving roadside, close to the flat peak of this, the tallest of the cliffs. Marcel could not see much of the cliff as the road before him was convex also, especially by the rocky, uneven terrain, so without this visual context, it gave the impression of being contained in a giant natural tower of sandstone. The owner of this establishment must have been laughing. The road was so rough and relentlessly winding in that one could frequently, frustratingly, see another section of the road 50 feet away which could only be met up with 30 minutes later. Surely even the thriftiest people could not refuse accommodation such as this, regardless that on three walls, the window view was of little more than bare rock, but then most would be too tired to care. You got what you paid for, at any rate. Only masochists and determined, rich, purist hikers and mountain climbers would surely give it the cold shoulder.

The Voice of Kings

The owner was literally laughing now, more a breathless, subdued chuckle than anything else. He was still leaning on the railing at the edge of the road with Isaac, occasionally pointing out specific landmarks and roads to appease Isaac's boundless curiosity, seemingly prioritised, at this time, equally with learning all accessible routes in the area to plan the morrow's journey. He'd heard something about White Fire Falls and how, when the gods had walked Mura, the waterfall had literally thrown water and fire together into the river below, the two elements never affecting one other. He was fascinated by old myths like that.

And it was fascinating to Marcel, Isaac's relentless pursuit of knowledge and the opinions of others. Amidst his awe for his brother, he also saw the other side of this randomness, that Isaac was so lustful for any knowledge that, most of the time, he didn't know what he wanted to know, and passed his lessons into compartments of his mind to be forgotten, the event in Caedor mine standing out as a distinct exception. Though he couldn't say for why, there was something about his brother's aspect that made him sad.

So far, it had done him no harm, Marcel considered, and wasn't likely to so long as he held onto the values he would sometimes discuss with him in his surprising bouts of deep humility. Perhaps, also, there was even more coherence and focus to it all than Marcel could tell. He liked this idea, but still smirked at the thought of him meeting Vicentei Laccona. Presumably they would get on exceptionally well, if the bridge guard's analysis of him was accurate.

Somewhere below on the ground, a silent stirring came to being; an ominous mass of life slithering through the woods on long clawed paws, and was followed by a howl, similar to that of a wolf but shriller, high-pitched, as no dog he'd heard could muster at such volume, with an undercurrent of guttural roughness as he imagined a lion might roar. Definitely, this was not any animal he'd ever come across, and one by one, other creatures in the same pack erupted with the same howl, overlapping and shooting to the skies, higher and higher as if a platform of noise was built up, lifting the mysterious calls of the wild to Marcel's ears.

He shivered, half in awe, half in fear, and Isaac too shot bolt upright, for he was experiencing the very same duality of emotions. The innkeeper chuckled and said something to calm Isaac, quelling Marcel's fears in the process.

Marcel thought he saw the pack of wolf-like creatures darting nimbly as a single congealed silhouette between tree patches, unless his imagination was getting the better of him and, in actuality, it was perhaps just a couple of deer bouncing about. At any rate, the howls alone served as a reminder why they couldn't just cut through the woods, especially when the dark lured beasts such as those out of their pits in the ground. Development could be seen clear enough in this light; a safer path forged through the woods and watchtowers erected, yet he and Isaac elected not to tread there, lest they find themselves alone with a hungry forest creature. For the time being, the owner of this inn would relish the added business, essentially shoved right through his front door, for as long as it lasted. As Isaac kept saying with a raise of an eyebrow and a knowing grin, this was not Burtal; people didn't just twiddle their fingers in the hope that problems would solve themselves, in the deeply ingrained fear that problems meant danger.

His fingers reached back, finding a lazy grip on the balcony doors and shutting them at the exact moment of stepping into his room, the wind generated from this bursting the nearby candles into further exuberance. Closing the door connecting his and Isaac's room, he paused for thought, tapping his fingers on the wall to create a dull, thumping tune, eyebrows locked in a quizzical position as he spotted the sword poking from underneath a cloth on the bed. During their travels, he kept it hidden beneath one of his bags, something he, too, had adopted, as it was frowned upon for individuals such as them to be publicly armed when riding through populated areas, not being soldiers, mercenaries or knights, the exception being when passing a checkpoint when they would display them openly to not arouse suspicion.

Isaac had been positively unnerved, hot around the collar, in telling Marcel to follow his lead. He assumed he could not fight back again if he were attacked by another human, for it was a point of inner contention for him. This was one of the few areas in which Marcel could say Isaac was wrong about something, but he wasn't in the mood for debating his brother's flaws, or indeed anything, he realised. He allowed, slowly, his weight to be distributed back, his arms out, his feet tilting on their heels, and he tumbled, falling softly onto the bed. He threw the coverlets over himself and, before long, drifted into silent sleep.

~

Isaac hoped to find rest in sleep, but it was not certain. Striding down the inn corridor as he would otherwise do, he then hurled himself onto the bed upon arriving at his room. He fell asleep in not too long a time, and as he slept, he dreamed, vividly so. In the dream, he was in Kester's room at his parents' house in Caedor. It was another time he stood in, years ago, when he was 19, or 20, possibly 21; his mind would not let him know in his current state. He knew only what it told him, and what it told him was that the house was on the Ardith cliffs, in a fictional space of land on the way up, big enough to hold it, for his mind was too stressed and strained to generate all of Caedor when he glanced out the window and, thus, latched onto the most recent memories, to grant the accuracy of the important details.

Lucian was leaning against a wall, his arms folded, staring blankly at Kester who sat before a lectern, where he dabbed the finishing, obsessive alterations to a music script, having had a will to show it to them and noticing an indiscretion.

"There," he said with a pleasing nod. "Now I just need to learn all the instruments, see if it makes any sense," he laughed.

"You're joking, aren't you?" Lucian asked, unable to interpret his tone in the moment. "I mean no offence, but that's a massive undertaking. How many was it, 15, 20 different instruments?"

"I was joking, of course. Half, at least," Kester said, faking nervousness for comedy's sake, though the sentiment rang true. "Maybe I should just learn the basics of the major instruments, brush up on my knowledge of the ones I already know; I could get a feel for my own work that way, then search for the musicians later," he added as an afterthought, clearly making this up almost as quickly as the words could slip from his tongue, and taking a liking to it just as fast.

"Do it," Isaac demanded, displaying a sly, miniscule smile; a canned, artificial response of course, derived from his memory. He felt like he was watching events unfold, unclearly, with great interest, with no lucid control. "It would be more than either of us could say we've done."

Isaac pointed briefly to his older brother, then back to himself. Lucian remained on the verge of being a blank slate still, all his emotion condensed into the twitches and minor static creases across his face, calm and unthreatening. He must have been thinking about how wrong Isaac was in ironic amusement, as even then, the gears of his ambitions were slowly grinding into place, appearing stoic at this time in accepting the responsibility of an older brother and friend, as he still viewed himself; a serious countermeasure developed over many years, ever seeing himself as the dominant one, not by intention, not by wish, but by default and necessity. Of course, this had crept into his psyche as a whole, and was influenced by his other friends as well. What, at first, was probably pretentiousness, turned to genuine maturity at some threshold Isaac could not determine, awake or asleep.

Images flashed before Isaac of the first time Lucian had been anointed with some form of official responsibility from a letter written by the Count's knightly young aide. As with all dreams that offered no lucid movement, Isaac saw this with naught but the most fleeting intrigue, the peculiarities to set in when he woke. The conversation continued without a hitch.

"I could do. Then again, maybe not," Kester grumbled ponderously. "If I'm honest, I think I'm too lazy," he continued, laughing at the irony.

"Stop being lazy," Lucian said, and then shrugged and shot him a smirk, that of an aristocrat being forcibly witty, as his stance and features suggested high bearing, somehow.

"It *would* be a shame to abandon it. And this is the best way forward, I suppose. Gods know I've prattled on about being a composer long enough. It's easier to express myself with music than anything else. Cleverly ambiguous too; people interpret it how they like," he said distantly, half to himself, before snapping back to the real world, or the dream simulation of it. "But yes, I will need outside help eventually. Would be foolish to think I could succeed here."

"Indeed," Isaac replied, a glint in his eye. He blinded himself by it.

An unknown distance above him in his bed, atop the cliff, riders rode in haste from the west, finally navigating the craggy landscape, circling round the old watchtower and heading north-west with due haste, to more civilised lands. In his dream, it wrenched control, so seamlessly that he did not think to question it. The tower was blurred and nondescript as he had not yet caught a close look at it in reality, though he'd remembered the unusual design and the two pillars between this tower and another beyond a sheer drop in the cliffs; a tower not 20 metres away, but so very far to walk the path round to it. Each tower had a drawbridge, this he remembered also and they clicked into place on the pillars, and there was a third tower which materialised as he remembered it, with the very same drawbridge connection. They must have had strategic uses if they were so adamant not to build a bridge at ground level.

His mind afforded him a brief glimpse of this, and then it all vanished as he heard the two riders soaring along the path well-travelled beneath one of the bridges, saying something about the High Duke, and some mention of elapsed distance and distance remaining; words without structure. The smashing of the hooves died down to a frail whisper. His dreams, too, were swept from the cliff top, flying majestically now that he had no thoughts to process, carefree as the horses galloped on with all urgency.

Then they rose again like trumpets, only this time it was from within the dream. And he was falling. And he was still. Outside Caedor mine, a hundred people or more were milling about, panicking and whispering in frightened tones, and just outside the gigantic half ring of chaos Isaac waited for the bodies of the miners to be hauled from the charred cave entrance, his imagination crafting the worst solution it could conjure: black and pocked corpses that slowly crumbled to dust, poison to the wind. No such corpse was removed, because there was no corpse to speak of.

After his parents had coddled him and made absolutely sure he was unharmed, they left him in the temporary keeping of Sir Tristan Almaric, as he'd been then, a newly belted knight who was lacking in confidence but relayed, from the depths of his pupils, the same optimism and kindness that Isaac's father had famed him for in the years since then.

"You're a strong lad," Sir Tristan said, dropping to one knee and laying a hand on Isaac's shoulder. "Strong of spirit. Don't let this nastiness change you. You have such fine parents that I needn't worry." He winked and smiled warmly. It was powerful now, as then.

Whether by perfect recollection, or analytical hindsight, or pure imagination, Sir Tristan looked scared of the crowd and out of his depth. It was but a fleeting moment, for then he was Lord Almaric, and he ordered his guardsmen to ease the density of the crowd, and Isaac watched in awe for want of a distraction, where Tristan performed his task perfectly, without a single blade being drawn.

The Voice of Kings

The dream crept away as a mother does her sleeping child. For now, his mind was content with how it had organised his thoughts, and allowed him to sleep in darkness.

Chapter Eleven: Lameeri's Wish

Long days stretching before Lennord in slow motion, the inventor observing, with growing disdain, the city within whose walls he waited with a quiet restlessness for his calling, watching within time so sluggish he felt like ages passed and the city might have fallen from the grace of its glory days before his very eyes; it now culminated with him entering the gigantic square with a contemptuous mix of relief and dread.

Laid with red cobblestones all over, and lined on two sides with old stone statues of prolific and, questionably, heroic soldiers hailing from the days of Aurail as a war obsessed city, the square was merely a precursor to the north barracks, Lameeri's Wish. It bordered the wall of the city, where battlements extended and protected the entire barracks; a huge complex, he presumed, precisely rectangle in shape.

So named because of the first Emperor's, quite literal, god complex: bestowing the army with Lameeri's blessing, claiming to speak for him; the madman; as soldiers exited the barracks gates while their families bid farewell and showered them with petals as they marched to war. Behind the statues, people would stand under the wall of archways, two storeys high, wherein gatherers could congregate and look down on their loved ones from the first or second level, as was preferable should they not find a place at the front of the crowd, whistling and shouting, hoping to be heard amongst the cluster of names being called out. Now it carried no such energy, instead bustling with soldiers and other military men going about their daily mundane business, talking casually around the place, including in the arches where pigeons now nested undisturbed. Considering the alternative, it was certainly for the best.

In the middle of the square, two guards flanked Lord Tristan. Today he wore a suit of rich royal green, flavoured with red. The sleeves were puffed fairly subtly, a gesture which added a touch of Mürathneèan nobility to his already smart Burtalian attire, and a pale cravat which contrasted well with his dark hair. He wore all as gracefully as anything else, there being no real difference between the two men either side of him in that regard. He might have been an imperial soldier if Lennord didn't know better, for all his pride and his posture, so straight that he could have had a splint forcing his back into place, if it weren't for his mischievous element. His early arrival was of no surprise to Lennord whatsoever, his impeccable timing a guarantee, not a probability. Failure to do so quite perplexed him, as Lennord understood it.

"I bid you good morning," Tristan said cheerfully; serious, too, as he did not wish to appear insensitive at such a time, in such a place, given Lennord's task. "So you did receive my message."

"Morning, my Lord," Lennord replied with a short obligatory bow.

The Voice of Kings

He added Tristan's title belatedly but firmly, as was required. He had needed to make their greeting formal for the sake of Tristan's image and to immerse himself in this world, reluctant as he was. Tristan's good name was well-earned and it would take more than an outsider addressing him by his name in public to besmirch his reputation, though it was good practice for the etiquette he was expected to adhere to, especially when, at such a wretched time, he might be forced to mingle with high society. At any rate, Tristan did not object; Tristan understood the way of this world much better than he.

"Well, here we are then," Tristan went on after a short pause, "exactly where I said I could steer you away from."

There were the machinations of some hope in his expression, derived from no clear source, as he no longer spoke with grave apology in his tone, satisfied that there was a consolation he could appease his old friend with. He was an ambitious man, Lennord had always thought, insofar as it was appropriate and honourable, and preferably benefited a cause larger than any man without his stature and connections could comprehend.

"Apologies for the court neglecting you, good friend. It hasn't been sitting around twiddling its thumbs, if that makes you feel any better. Did you find some way of occupying yourself in the meantime?" Tristan said, half sarcastically without a shred of doubt as to the answer.

"There's not much for a man of my age, a married man of my age rather, to do around here, unless I'm looking in the wrong places. Or I'm too boring for this city," he said with a dry half-smile, feeling the spirit of the conversation. "I've wandered about the city for the past four days, scanning all I saw, that I might discern what the hell's gone wrong," he ventured.

"That sounds fairly accurate," was the immediate reply. "Did you hear any announcements regarding our plans for the city?"

"It's hardly possible to escape them, I fear. There are few places I've been where I've not been made acutely aware in some fashion or another."

"That's the idea," Tristan chuckled. "Just so long as people don't get burned out on it. That would be sadly ironic. We are hoping to inject some...excitement into this city though, you'll be pleased to hear. Preferably catering to various demographics, I might add."

He paused and put an index finger over his mouth in thought, some realisation striking him hard on the head.

"Lucian has left the city already then?"

"I can only assume so," Lennord replied slowly, wincing suspiciously and scratching the day-old stubble on his chin. "He visited me at my house the night I was greeted by His Majesty at court, and left the morning after. Why?"

"Oh, just a passing interest. He caused a bit of a fuss at the mercantile embassy, did you know? He wanted to buy a big wad of documents from the library. I think he got away with them in the end, but a few trade ambassadors complained. They do little else, actually."

Tristan rolled his eyes, and for a fraction of a second seemed far away, buried in the affairs of his master's country. Lennord's brow creased into a frown but, quickly, a wide grin vanquished it. Lucian must have had good reason to want those documents, and his detainees must have had pretty poor excuses to deny him his request.

"Good for him," Lennord said triumphantly. "I'm sure he'll put whatever he bought to good use."

"Oh, I'm with you on that. Some of the officials and lords who work at that trade embassy are strange, strange people. They know there's change going on but they don't seem to understand that it's not just going to happen around them. Or else they just don't want to understand. One of them, I'm told, said he thought they weren't supposed to give trade information away in case Mürathneè saw the papers, as if he expects us all to isolate ourselves in starting this renaissance. When, of course, it's the opposite. But people get stuck in their old ways if you leave things to stagnate," he sighed, shaking his head while not actually displaying any real pessimism. "It's how Carlophinia sank so low, and it's worth remembering that the same squalor could befall us. Those people will change of course. They'll have to. Or they'll be flushed out. Yes, the *Empress* will flush them out," he added, smirking softly. "I know you were thinking it."

Lennord nodded quickly, ever impressed at Tristan's perception, at those eyes of his that took in all that there was to see without you even noticing.

Monologue finished, it now occurred to Lennord that they had been standing there talking all this time and Tristan had not been courteous enough to show him his assignment. Lennord was bursting at the seams in anticipation.

"You must think me rude," Tristan said suddenly, bowing his head an inch or two in reverence. "Follow me, I'll show you what you'll be doing."

There was that look again; he was confident about something. Lennord pulled at the bottom of his jacket to straighten out the creases as much as possible before, reluctantly, venturing to follow in the lord's wake, then hurrying to walk alongside him. It was only as good a suit as he was willing to pay for until he received a monetary commission from the court; quite comfortable and not at all flashy or regal as the man beside him was. The two guards followed also, as subtly as they could, given their getup. Lennord got the impression they could have been deathly silent, wearing the proper gear.

The entrance to the barracks was wide open for them; two gigantic wooden slabs as doors, a realistic depiction of the great tower carved deep into the middle, split exactly into two so that each door kept half the picture. Lennord made to touch one of the doors as he passed, purely as a matter of mild interest as to its construction method, and withdrew his hand after a lone second. It was sturdy in its old age, only half down to the craftsmanship and maintenance work. Beyond, there were many dozens of buildings, some the reliable base variety of red stone, some newer of both wood and rock, and some crumbling old buildings which currently were seeing reform. The taller buildings in particular were wrapped with scaffolding, no doubt not a coincidence that it should happen at this time.

A walkway, maybe 300 feet in length, and wide enough for six or seven carriages to move abreast at speed without trouble, stretched directly ahead of them, the full distance to the row of old stone buildings at the back, directly attached to the outer wall of the city. No buildings stood on this path; all of them were in rows either side, arranged surprisingly neatly, he thought at first, until the truth of the matter dawned. The buildings might have been dilapidated, but soldiers strode about with as much purpose as they ever had, darting in and out of these troubled constructions, giving the impression of a rusted machine scraping its gears together under such tremendous pressure without so much as a drip of grease to ease the stress on this enormous failure.

This wasn't entirely incorrect. At the same time, on closer inspection, he concluded that the work being done here was probably the best, if he could put it that way, in the entire city. It was a well-oiled machine with a shabby exterior. This isolated zone was abuzz with energy and progress, from blacksmithing to practising archery, sword and pollarm at the pell, to timed combat formations and horse training, in segregated areas for novices, and pretty much anywhere else, within reason, for the experienced riders. Obstacle courses, too, were laid out, that he could barely see from this range and position, as he couldn't a great many nuances in this machine, but there was real discipline here.

It was an eye-opener, soldiers marching and riding in force about the place for some unknown reason. Lennord's lower lip shuddered while he methodically, if ineffectually, comprehended the meaning for an army thriving so at this time. Out of the corner of one eye, he saw Tristan grimace momentarily. They were in this together, then.

"I'm not getting the impression of an average training regimen from any of this," Lennord muttered. "If I didn't know better, I'd think they were suiting up for war."

"It's a delicate position we stand in, yes. It would be disastrous should it be perceived that way, but don't you worry about a thing. I'm personally keeping an eye on how people see this. I can tell you now that this is just the beginning, one of many avenues of progression. All of this military recruitment business will eventually become all but lost in the spectacular myriad of renaissance wonders, or so goes the plan. It's still not what I would have started with but...well, it's a start nonetheless. Oh, and you'll get what you want too," Tristan said sharply, slyly.

Tristan slowed to stare Lennord in the eyes before speeding to his lordly strides once more. He smirked in self-satisfaction ever so slightly, and it grew in selfless gratification.

"How so?" Lennord enquired levelly, after a short break to ensure he would not sound churlish.

"Surely you must be brimming with ideas. You'll have your hour, I promise you. The Empress wouldn't have it any other way, I think. She's taken a shine to you. Can't say why, exactly. She's a very enigmatic woman when she wants to be."

"Certainly I have ideas," Lennord replied quickly. "In particular, I'm intrigued to experiment with some ideas an inventor called Vicentei Laccona, in Harth, is playing with. There's all sorts of ideas he has about Sèhvorian crystals, as I understood it in a treatise he sent me, and I'd be interested to add my own contributions. Of course, I can't really experiment a whole lot until Isaac returns, but..."

"It sounds splendid," Tristan responded with severely reserved enthusiasm. "I've heard of Mister Laccona, as it happens. The world has me believe he's a great man. I'm sure the court would be more than happy to see you invent something eye-catching before he can; put a notch on their belts for Burtal, as it were. You would garner more respect, and thus more leeway in getting your own way. Speaking of which..." he said hurriedly, excitedly, interrupting Lennord's warning plea of his inferiority to Laccona before he could even speak, and divulged a curiosity that he might forget his doubts, "...it occurred to me that your current title is no longer befitting of your status, given that you require a little more influence."

"I don't understand," Lennord said blankly.

"I suggested to His and Her Majesty that you receive a knighthood for your services."

Lennord carried on walking, not immediately taking this in, and then stopped. His jaw dropped stupidly as he processed these words, as if to ensure he hadn't misheard.

"My Lord, I am honoured," Lennord gasped, genuinely flustered and humbled. "Though how is that even possible?" he said, with reason now returning to his senses. "Surely you must already be a squire, or a soldier of identifiable loyalty, or at least of noble birth?"

"Remember that I am officially the fourth most important person in the entire country, including Rickart Llambert, and being little more than a child, he isn't going to be seen in court any time soon. I know, it's still surreal to me at times," Tristan said with a single breath of laughter. "But it's true; I have a lot of power, and frightful influence. If I say someone deserves a knighthood, people stop and listen, and they damn well take it into consideration. You'll do fine. We'll arrange something. I don't know, maybe you'll have to swing a sword around like you know how to use it, but we'll cross that bridge when we come to it."

Eyes were upon Lennord, the soft eyes of the naive youths mingled with the grim gazes of veterans, their eyes beady and curious, hardy like balls of stone cemented into human sockets that had seen much in the way of violence, one would think. They all were reaching conclusions of varying validity about him and his personality, and in this time, marching

The Voice of Kings

down this road for all to gawp at, as if being displayed like a criminal, he was at his most cautious.

Most strangely, he felt extremely self-conscious, his senses heightening to fully appreciate the situation. Itching with hopefulness was Lennord; that old romanticism that, thanks to Lord Tristan's dreams and the anchor that was his family, could not be rid of even in times like these, where others would succumb to despair at being so far out of their depth. And he was out of his depth. In Caedor, people had naturally flocked to him for his engineering advice, and even a loan on occasion after news had spread, all those years ago, of his affiliation with Sir Tristan, and all the while, they looked down at the dirt before their feet in between shiftily looking into his eyes, and scratching the back of their necks in extreme embarrassment. Over time, it became accepted that he was a conscientious man, and being a stranger asking him for help without paying was viewed as wrong, apparently, as he already did so much work for the town of his own initiative, of the itch that made him act upon any flaw he saw in any given manmade element of daily life.

Here, he had to start that relationship from mistrust once more, and with company he felt would be far harder to get along with, given his limited experience with soldiers. And then there was this idea of having *official* power. *Sir Lennord.* Perhaps this was a strike of fortune. Lord Almaric had orchestrated this with care and thought, no doubt, and he had delivered, with perfect grace, wisdom beyond his years, unless his aura was so deceptive that Tristan himself was ignorant of its influence. It was possible, Lennord contemplated, but poor sport to judge a friend with that manner of scrutiny. The balance of pessimism and hopefulness regarding this affair was restored, and he forced all criticisms of Tristan into the abyss. He would remain cautiously optimistic about this scenario.

"Regrettably, I couldn't sway the Empress to grant you immediate lordship, as I originally proposed as an option," Tristan continued. He was grinning now, the wonderful, mischievous bastard. "She wants you to display a clear arc of progression, make you stand out, so we'll bide our time for a short while after your knighthood. That, and it wouldn't be seen as prudent by other members of the court to be dishing out more precious gold for a lord of such humble beginnings," he trailed off.

Lord Brodie of Caedor. It rang like the three giant bells of Harth's cathedral, encapsulating him with a buzz of impenetrable white noise, thrust by a ferocious hurricane beside his ears, shattering his brain as he attempted to reason with this; a step too far, surely, as he was no more lordly material than Tristan was a peasant. In the midst of deconstructing this revelation, he couldn't help but crack a smile, though he knew not why in the moment.

"I don't know what to say," Lennord replied earnestly.

"It will be an honour well-deserved. Are you feeling well?"

"I think not," Lennord wheezed, only half-joking. "Will I be required to wield power in the same way any other lord would? Would I not be expected to stay here for the long haul?"

"Don't worry about that, my friend, you'll be allowed to leave when you otherwise would. Quicker, if anything, I'd say, with a title like that. Your loving wife will be back in your arms before you know it," Tristan beamed, slowing to a complete halt near one of the old buildings undergoing construction. "And when all is said and done, it won't matter how long it took to arrive home. Once you're there, you're living in the present, appreciating all that you have, not mourning over how long it took to get there."

Lennord got a long, hard look at Tristan at the sound of these words. He was impossibly optimistic at times, such that Lennord wondered if he cloyed at the other lords, putting his own scepticism to shame, and most fascinating of all was the astuteness with which he spoke, a deep understanding that most others did not think as he did, so he took great care in making his point absolutely blatant.

"Wise words," Lennord conceded.

Tristan nodded appreciatively, his hands now in his pockets, his gaze directed to their right at the century-old building nearby, projecting a mild interest. Scaffolding rose from the roof and around its tower, where two dozen soldiers had been contracted to partake in the repairs, do their part to shape the barracks as a whole into an image of order and harmony and togetherness: the necessary illusion of appearing more than the sum of its parts to the rest of the world, which bore just as much importance as its practical purpose.

Lennord stood beside Lord Almaric, eyeing the structure and the building techniques being implemented. It could be done better, faster. Stronger mortar could be created. Stronger bricks too, if he was any judge. They could be made to *look* stronger as well, he wagered. That's what was expected; already he was doing exactly what the Empress wanted of him.

"You really believe things will be better this time, don't you?" Lennord said. "Far be it for me to assume a negative posture, but it's failed before."

"It's true. It might seem that I'm riding on the wings of hope right now; I feel a change in the wind," Tristan said with a faint smile, at which point he looked at his most thoughtful, as contemplative as a philosopher. When Lady Almaric was mentioned, he shouldn't have been surprised. "Evylyn and I have spoken at length...we have the benefit of hindsight this time. Yes. Yes, I believe it is possible that we'll succeed."

They continued on at a leisurely pace, at Tristan's ushering. The lord's focus was on the people around them, whom he regarded with mild fascination. Perhaps doubt crept into him, for his lips were dry and clasped shut.

It was not these people in his line of sight, however, that interested him most. His soldierly senses, honed in yester years, of which Lennord had assumed had become somewhat unreliable over time, now sprang into life. Colour flushed through his face. Lennord, startled, looked up.

"How much farther is..."

Lennord's words were curtailed as he was thrust from his spot with surprising strength, followed up with him being rammed with Tristan's full body weight, so hard that he was flung from the ground, grunting in shock as Tristan crushed him. Behind them, something heavy met the ground with a thud; its cry was heavy then soft, sounding all of a sudden fragile, like the splinters of wood which rained down around it and the length of rope slithering through the air, landing in a heap. Metal pinged, its red gleam bright amongst the wooden rain. When they were able, both Lennord and Tristan leapt to their feet, and there before them lay the soldier who would never rise. He wore no armour even, and so the fall would definitely have finished him off if the dagger that had flown from his throat hadn't killed him first.

They both looked up, as did many others; a perimeter of men frozen in time, it seemed, just for a second, taking one deep breath before the inevitable rush, staring at the equally bewildered man, fixed on the spot at the edge of the scaffolding around the tower, where the safety barrier had been broken. His mouth was agape, in fear and uncertainty. He put his hands up, and gulped. It was, unfortunately, very difficult to discern if he was denying responsibility or not by taking this defensive action, but regardless, every armed man within a 20 foot radius ran straight for him and, in the face of this stampede clambering precariously across the increasingly rickety scaffolding, he fled.

"Surround him!" Lord Almaric bellowed at the men on the ground, causing Lennord to jump at this most jarring shift in tone.

Those who were not immediately aware of what had happened were soon enlightened, and either by recognition of his status or the power with which he fired his order, they too were surprised and did not waste time in pursuing the offender.

"Bring him to me alive," Lord Almaric shouted in response to the contemptuous looks that some of the soldiers wore. "Heed those words or you shall answer for murder just the same."

He waved his fingers and his two guards took formation either side of them, legs apart, ready to dash for the nearest scaffolding entrance at ground level. Even Lennord found himself tensing up, preparing against his better judgement to tackle the murderer should he come at him. That, or to run, he couldn't tell which. Tristan said nothing to discourage him, instead just holding his open palm out and pushing back on thin air in front of Lennord, a simple but effective message which informed him to keep his head on straight and not do anything stupid. The situation would be under control, it said, and so Lennord could only trust him.

The assailant leapt into one soldier, flooring him with all his weight and unbalancing the man behind him, who drew his sword, intending to scare him into submission. Instead, the assailant, crouched upon the boards, barraged into the knees of a soldier of too few years, slicing his own arm open in the process but, for now, barely feeling it, jumping over the soldier and carrying on as if nothing had happened.

"Wait!" Tristan said firmly, noting what appeared to be a more experienced soldier in the process of apprehension, and the two he previously felled now hot on his tail. "It's under control. If that walkway gets any more crowded, you'll be climbing over each other."

From the crowd, now forming a ring around the building, a man clad in full plate stepped forward, not intent on doing anything foolish, just walking close to Tristan and his accomplices, eyes fixed sternly on the events unravelling above, his teeth grinding together and his head shaking violently. He was a captain, his armour being official combat attire for a man of his rank; black beside the red motif of the three towers on a tight-fitting cote shaped as his breastplate, and a fanciful red lining on every lame. His lips quivered into obscene contortions, his dark eyes so hot with rage they might burst aflame at any moment, searching here and there, flitting between hateful glares at no one in particular and a panic he'd meant to conceal.

By now, the murderer was sprinting for the edge with his arms held back like springs to be released, in position to leap atop the barrier and to the next building. He skidded to a halt before it as the distance seemed to rapidly expand, Lameeri's justice, and his body seemed to die in defeat, a useless form swaying on the spot. Two soldiers each grabbed one arm and hauled him down to ground level, and there threw him before Lord Almaric.

"It was an accident, my Lord" was the first thing the man said through spit and deep breaths. "It was an accident. I can explain."

Tristan somehow managed to retain an appropriate level of professionalism. From what Lennord had seen, his claim could have been true. He couldn't show that he believed him, nor could he display any sign of judgement at all, in fact.

"What's your name?" Lord Almaric asked.

"Adrian Mortain, my Lord," the man blurted out, not daring to avert his gaze from the dirt before him.

Lord Almaric glanced around for an affirmative on this, and was quickly rewarded with a nod from the captain, who looked set to intervene but begrudgingly stayed put. Adrian winced, one hand reaching for the opposite arm that he then withdrew with all his willpower. The gash on his arm must have stung as the world came sharply into focus. A world he didn't want to know right now. Quite some effort must have gone into not wiping his wound clean, as his body must have screamed at him to do. Tristan was not impressed by his attempt at sycophancy, whether he was humble in his heart or not. It just communicated itself as foolish.

The Voice of Kings

"Look at me now," Lord Almaric commanded softly, and Adrian obeyed. "You're not helping either of us, hiding your face like that. Tell me, if it was an accident, why did you run?"

"Any man would have. I thought they would kill me," he protested.

"For the record, he had not even been assigned a job on this building," the captain interjected with a malice that threatened to smother Adrian, whose fear would not allow him to look at his superior from more than the very corner of one eye. "And neither should have been here," the captain went on, nodding at the dead man.

~

He was Mürathneèan, as his accent gave away, a fact which caused Tristan to frown heavily, though fortunately no one was to know his true thoughts. The Empress had spoken in recent council meetings of employing personnel from Mürathneè who were experienced in various areas. If the captain's presence here was her doing, then she surprised him yet again, as she always did, no matter how many times he assumed he'd seen all her tricks. He was a tall man, soldierly in appearance and heftily giving the aura of one with official, royal standing. In moving toward Mortain, he came off as *heavy*, in all the most intimidating ways. He was incredibly analytical and methodical, or so Tristan presumed by his demeanour, and the brown hair that crept below his helm was straight and smart, marred only by the sweat dripping from it, courtesy of whatever workout he'd been participating in a few moments prior. Not that it mattered what he thought. If the Empress had indeed given the man permission to be here, she would first have personally assessed his capabilities.

Beside Tristan, Lennord was faring remarkably well. While he, in such close proximity, could hear exasperated breathing from him, it was covered up by a tough, stoic expression which he must have been forcing into place, and his wide eyes could be translated as simply being alert. Tristan could safely ignore him for a minute more then, without it beating on his conscience.

"What he says is true, my Lord," Adrian panted. "But I can explain all of this."

"I'm sure you can," Lord Almaric replied hotly.

"We were arguing, yes, but near as I could tell I caused no offence, or else I would have backed down. Then he just lost his mind and pulled a knife out on me. Touched, my Lord. And not by a god."

Tristan stared at the seemingly pathetic man with growing unrest. He was definitely playing for sympathy, but that didn't necessarily mean he was lying, annoyingly so, as Tristan couldn't quite determine if it was entirely a very well-constructed ruse. He swished his tongue around his mouth and tapped his thighs in an utterly random pattern before pointing at two soldiers with a respectable look about them.

"You two, restrain this man, have him patched up and hand him over to the guards at the castle. You may not, under any circumstances, torture or interrogate him, is that clear? If he shows up at the castle with any but that one wound, I'll know to look here for justice," he said louder now, addressing the crowd as a whole. "Captain, I will be with you in one moment."

~

Tristan placed a comforting hand on Lennord's shoulder and led him from the sickening scene to a small building a little further on. He flipped a cluster of keys attached to a large ring from his jacket pocket and pushed them encouragingly in Lennord's direction.

"The big one opens the front door. The rest open desk drawers and cabinets and things. You'll figure it out."

"You're not staying?" the pale-faced Lennord replied, squinting as he struggled to unravel the lord's motives.

"For a while I will stay, but it will be to clear the facts with these people before it's too late. But if you need anything, don't hesitate to approach me before I make myself scarce. I have a few questions I want answered at the castle before long too."

Tristan was distant, already at the castle it seemed, as he mulled over the best course of action.

"What questions?" Lennord asked confusedly.

"Routine questions really, deemed imperative and to be answered swiftly, I should think, given our current delicate situation of *publicly* bettering ourselves. I have a very basic theory as to what just happened. It shouldn't be anything for you to worry about though. Just get settled here and at least have a look at the work left out for you. It would be most prudent for you to appear humble," Tristan said pointedly, raising a single eyebrow and waving a finger. "I intend to appeal yet again, with this incident in mind, for you to be given more appropriate resources for your talent. You'd give the best impression if you showed you don't mind either way. And I beg, think not of fraud. Such a knighthood would complement you appositely; an inventor who'll fight for his country."

"You really needn't go to such lengths. You must be busy enough as it stands."

"It shouldn't take long though. You really need to stop worrying about my job," Tristan said, and patted him on the shoulder again. "Stay safe. These guards will be in your charge henceforth. I was going to leave them with you at any rate, and now it would seem foolish not to keep them around."

"It's much appreciated."

Tristan nodded, acknowledging his sincerity as he could never hide it anyway, and left Lennord alone with the guards and an old stone shack full of military equipment. He entered hastily, desperate to disassociate himself with the crime scene, and strode to the desk at the back of the room before so much as glancing about the place, tiredness washing over him in a great wave all of a sudden, and with a chair now begging for use before him, he slumped and consciously regained his composure, breathing wildly.

The Voice of Kings

After a time he could neither count nor recall, he noticed the guards looking at him expectantly, patiently. He waved a hand at them, with no intention of appearing rude, but concern immediately befalling him for he thought he had been.

"Just stand either side of the door, thank you. If it suits you fine."

They obliged with extreme courtesy, presumably compensating for his apparent lack of experience giving strict orders. Upon feeling well enough to observe with sufficient interest, with the frightful knot crushing his stomach ignored as much as could be, the room, Lennord now realised, was packed around the edges with drawers and cabinets, many of which had glass doors to display a variety of military tools, aged weapons blunt, rusted, and broken held in clasps alongside specimens as shined and brilliant as the day they were forged. In the midst of all of this conventional weaponry was a nearly bare cabinet housing a flintlock pistol and musket, not so very different from the dreadful designs he'd seen in the past, by all accounts useless contraptions for any practical designation.

In a neat row on the desk were papers detailing his tasks, or more vaguely than that, a list of expectations presented as if to imply the writer knew more about mechanics than he could honestly admit to. The desk itself, an old creation varnished for a remotely new effect, was specifically envisioned for people like him who liked to sprawl their work out before them for a more complete picture; for tinkering with machinery, he presumed, as it was far too wide for any other reasonable office worker.

Sure enough, there were numerous mentions of firearms in the text, and allusions to how he should do something about their performance flaws. He winced and looked up. If he was being purely objective, they were probably no less vulgar than swords, though killing could become dangerously impersonal if one could eventually advance such technology to a point where a solider need only be, to their opponent, but a speck blending into the vegetation in the distance. This responsibility was being placed in his hands. Perhaps, he reasoned after some thought, he should stop thinking on behalf of soldiers, the lives of which he could barely comprehend.

He looked to the papers again and read them carefully. Reading would do no harm, at any rate. It would give perspective on the person who wrote it, if nothing else. And anything that might potentially take his mind off of the frantic activities outside the window, and the tricks of his mind taunting him with devilish flashes of steel in flesh and the ground thickly painted violent crimson, was greatly appreciated.

~

"Lord Carrick, do you know where I might find the Emperor or Empress?"

The middle-aged man turned and waited in silence for Tristan to approach him, swiftly and ghostlike, along the castle corridor, his heavy footsteps absorbed by the thick carpet atop the cold stone floor. Lord Carrick was displaying a highly strained expression, his brow furrowed and his head held high, to ensure his position was entirely unmistakable, and only partly an instinctive reaction to Lord Almaric's alarming pace. Tristan had come to terms, at least in the sense of day by day tolerance, with the fact that lords like Carrick would continue to seek favour from His and Her Majesty, or those already in direct favour with them, namely him, for one could only assume the purpose of further wealth or power, or sadly perhaps because sycophancy had been ingrained into his lifestyle. He'd learned it from his father, surely, in one way or another; another narrow-minded man born into nobility who, somehow, failed to see that there was little more to gain from pandering to Richard's father after receiving his lordship but to be endowed with more riches he would never use. Putting it that way, he could not bring himself to hate the poor fool, even holding into account that he was certainly an intelligent man fully responsible for his actions, and not a witless victim of the imperial court.

Tristan maintained that he would not, however, allow himself to view these things as quaint and common, and would remind people like Carrick of their wrongs even as they could, seemingly, not take a hint. Lord Abram Carrick was capable of creating good work when it was appropriate and wasn't given the opportunity to get in the way. The promise of praise could help or hinder. He threw his weight around nonchalantly, almost artfully, with a subtle quality. People who didn't know him well enough translated it as eagerness. All things considered, that wasn't loyalty at all, but selfishness, ironically, pandering for his own desires even as he may have convinced himself otherwise, and with the way the city was professing to change, the Empress would reveal it to the world in her own clever way soon enough, if he couldn't burn away his self-centredness. He would not be banished or reviled or scolded directly; he would be forgiven profusely, almost as if His and Her Majesty were somehow the ones at fault, and in doing so, he would be forced to exceed their humility. He would retire to his estate and the town he ruled, and have little more than official standing in court, his title a masquerade for the mild contempt the newly appointed lords from respected families would hold towards him, until such time that he could earn trust back or become an obscure blip in Castle Aurail's history.

"I don't believe I've seen the Emperor today," Lord Carrick said pleasingly, in a more self-aware mood at present. "The Empress though, she is hard at work in the council chamber."

"Why would she be working in the council chamber?" Lord Almaric asked, perplexed, attempting to understand what her angle might be on this. It housed only a table, as was required; there was certainly nothing of importance or reference. She must needs find it beneficial, or inspiring.

"I can't answer that, I'm afraid. I can't claim to know, even now, how she thinks. I should say that she mentioned to me that she intends to host a council session sometime soon. Other than that, I'm in the dark."

"Interesting," Tristan breathed. "Thank you, at any rate."

"Of course," the lord replied, wielding that same highly concentrated expression and offering a smile of courtesy, which then dissipated when Lord Almaric saw fit to quiz him further.

"While we're here, there is a message being sent about the castle stating that reports on any and all activities you partake in for the renaissance will be required, failures being equally important for scrutiny as successes. Have you received anything of the like yet?"

"I heard about that earlier today, actually. I can have an initial report on your desk by tomorrow if you wish it."

"How would that be at all relevant?" Lord Almaric said slowly, making certain his wording would induce a semblance of a thoughtful response as opposed to providing a canned reply, probably before he even realised he was doing it. It was the best way to force him in a bold new direction, assuming it was not too late to convert his stubbornness to a more useful outlet. "You haven't done anything yet. Efficiency is a key factor of all that we're doing, but that does not go to say expedition is, also."

"I'm getting ahead of myself again," Abram fumbled.

His composure was regained quickly when Tristan's gesture of uncertainty, unspoken, shot out at him, presenting a clear picture of Tristan's displeasure at his manner, but simultaneously giving a reluctant blessing, a simple nod.

"Thank you again, Lord Carrick."

And so Tristan left him at once, wondering what a strange new world this castle would feel if so many new people were offered placements here, if people like Abram were to fail to change. *Heart-rending. The old Houses must be shown the light.* It had always been a given that the city of Aurail required the grandest of overhauls, yet he had never imagined it would spread within these castle walls, nostalgia flooding him of a time long past when he would play with Richard in these very halls, long before he was Emperor or cared to be, when his worries were few and could never bring him to his knees.

Tristan was, by his nature, a creature of nostalgia; therapy that let him put the future into perspective, thus ensuring each day held some joy or promise of hope. He smiled. If he were still a knight, people would accuse of him taking after his wife too much. If they did it now, they did it very quietly. But what did he care? He allowed himself to indulge, concurrently with present issues, right up until the moment of standing in the council hall doorway. It was beyond the throne room, and not far from it either; another windowless hall seeing as it was even closer to the heart of the castle complex, a room attached to one of several wide corridors, especially ornate and showy. The room itself was rectangular, designed for tables of the same shape, for supposedly more archaic political machinations; archaic, despite the fact this setup was still used for other places around the building. As of only recently, a circular table had been installed, about 50 chairs arranged around it for those rare occasions when that many people were there to attend meetings, and it was created from smoothed grey stone, a temporary measure until the necessary amount of marble was gathered for the final construct. This had not been a truly inspired choice, all things considered. They would need more than superficially mimicking King Michael's court procedures and furniture if they were to make progress.

Ironically, he thought this as Alycia came into view, seated at her place at the back of the room on one of two taller chairs, subtly splendid with an extraordinary raiment cut fine to her contours, mostly a royal green and created with traditional Aurailian techniques, blended perfectly with the puffy, extravagant designs of modern Harth clothing, with a sizeable amount of flair courtesy of her own imagination, naturally. To her left, Lady Castellon, a woman in her late 20s, focused on whatever work had been handed to her, ever diligent and willing. Tristan decided not to question this for the time being; it would be a waste of energy. Sir Pedrig was behind them, so casual he barely appeared to be guarding at all, holding in one hand a piece of paper and scanning it at, again, Empress Alycia's bidding. She picked her loyalists very well, to multitask so seamlessly. How this scene would play out to those with merely fundamental knowledge of castle workings, would be the Empress being assisted by a chamber servant and a bodyguard in important city business. But they would trust there was a reason for it, because she had become such a beloved figure of wisdom and womanly grace.

One chandelier hung above them, and light closed in on them from candelabras positioned plentifully around the room's perimeter, drawing one's gaze to the trio effortlessly, silently seductive Alycia in particular. She registered all around her, even as she concentrated on her work.

"My Lord Almaric, you're looking ravishing today," her voice so soothed him, as she looked up for a fraction of a second. "Is there something I can help you with?"

"I hope so," Tristan replied upon stopping a short distance from her, still standing straight. "What are you doing? Why work here and not in your chamber?" he asked after a pause of confused consideration. "I was told you're planning on holding council soon. Does Richard know?"

"Keep up, please," she japed, carefully scribbling away, only slowing to not appear too rude, as if obsessed by the work arranged tidily before her. "Such behaviour gets people talking, firstly. They know work is being done here, and they assume it is important because they link it to the council hall in which it is being done, and the person at the centre of it. Second of all, these are two highly talented personnel, and conveniently, it also gives them an opportunity to earn their reputation as multitalented, as I hope to create a blanket impression of all castle staff. Not that those assumptions should not be true, mind," she added, raising a finger sharply. "It wouldn't be the first time that a mere soldier or servant has captured the minds of the people on the street. The Knight of the Holy Storm is beloved by the people of Harth and revered across his kingdom by those who've never even seen him."

This was a comparison Tristan had hoped not to hear from Alycia at this early stage, although it was perhaps inevitable. It was a dangerous road to tread.

"King Michael's white knight has earned respect though. I expect his intelligence and combat prowess are overplayed to some extent but the fact remains, he is prodigious in a number of fields, and he won the people's love. You can't just pin that respect on anyone you please and expect it to stick. And I mean no offence to either of you, of course." Sir Pedrig nodded and shrugged, while Lady Castellon seemed barely to register his comment.

"I understand that," Alycia replied calmly. "I have no intention of directly transplanting the white knight's public image onto anyone here. That would be lunacy, and probably impossible at the moment. I'm merely suggesting we alter how castle staff are perceived by visitors. It's not as complex as you make it sound. Where's your lovely sweet optimism when I need it? And Richard does not know," she finished abruptly.

It was like she knew exactly how Tristan would object, as his look of mild surprise conveyed. Certainly, she knew what he would have spoken, and opted to interrupt before he could enquire about the Emperor a second time. She ceased working and extended to him her full attention.

"Are you intending to tell him?"

"I surely will let him know," she replied softly, acknowledging that he asked only from his core of tremendous curiosity and was not accusing her of anything. "He's being examined by another physician at present. It's a waste of time, if you ask me. And it was your idea, I gather. You shouldn't encourage him."

"Another?" Tristan said blankly, eyes narrowing. "Wouldn't that make it the third examination?"

"He's being thorough," Alycia quoted. "It will be the last time, but one was enough. Really, I don't know what you said to him that got him so concerned. If you ask me, the root of all his troubles lies here," she said, and lightly tapped her head.

"Believe me, Your Majesty, I didn't suggest he be so obsessive about it, though I should say I have no immediate desire to stop him now that I know. I'm well aware he's finding it difficult to cope under the pressure, which is why I directed him to a professional. I, like you, never thought there was anything physically wrong. I did it because I thought he would feel better for being told he was fine by a doctor, and on the logic that if, per chance, he is ill, all the better that he be seen to at once. In the end, it's only you and I who have power to give him hope, so we have a responsibility."

"Indeed, yes. Fair enough. That was good of you."

Alycia's lips rose at the edges in true admiration and she nodded for the respect he deserved, as it was something she might also have done. Both Lady Castellon and Sir Pedrig noticed her relax without even directly looking at her, so subtle yet so obvious. They looked to her with intrigue.

"Come, what was it you wanted?"

The tone shifted again, and with it, Tristan darkened also, concentrating on how best to question the Empress.

"Well, there was an incident at Lameeri's Wish, as I was showing Lennord Brodie to his office. A man was stabbed in the neck and fell from the scaffolding he was on."

"Just what we need," the Empress muttered, and then stopped while her brain began arranging and filing this information. "And it was vital you tell me in particular, so urgently, where one would think there are people at the barracks who can handle this. My attention is yours, my Lord."

"There are people who can do it, and they are. There's more to it than that though. Before the murder took place, I caught a glimpse of the murderer and the victim, above me. They were definitely arguing, yet I saw no rage in either of them, no yelling as one would expect to accompany such tension. They were hushed, restrained, paranoid even. They didn't look like they wanted to be overheard. Others I spoke to got the same impression. One of them drew a dagger, with intent to use it...or not. I, again, have no idea, but the other man did. He tore the dagger from his hands and, in the struggle, the dagger found its way to the knife owner's neck. Maybe intentionally, maybe not. He showed remorse, at any rate."

"You suspect conspiracy," the Empress stated, leaning forward.

"In some fashion. Big or small, I can't yet say."

Alycia showed no signs of panic through her concerned expression, just another status of beauty for her. Her neck craned ever so slightly to her right and she lifted a finger as if pointing. It was as close to an order as she needed to give.

"I would have thought the same thing, had I seen what Lord Almaric described," Sir Pedrig said. "I've seen many cases of spontaneous murder in my time, and it's usually accompanied with visible rage, or, rather, rage is the source. On the other hand, if it was premeditated, I don't think he would have chosen a public place to do the deed. It's probably nothing to worry about, from my experience, but best to expect the worst just in case. What did you do with the man, my Lord?" he asked sharply.

"He should be in a cell beneath the castle by now. I've given no further instructions and the guards should have been told I ordered him to be brought here, so no one will do anything but leave him in gaol for now, if they have any sense."

"Very good, then. It's what I would have done."

Alycia gave a sigh: a beautiful, regulated wisp floating free at her command, partially masking her concern. She stared pensively at the mass of shimmering light above her, index finger over her lips, elbow resting on her other hand. After a second or two, she returned her gaze to Tristan.

"Would you care to be seated?"

Tristan sat beside her. There would be no use in refusing even if he'd wanted to; it was less a suggestion and more an order, if one still containing heartfelt courtesy. Now, in such close proximity, he knew at least he had her full attention and was free to speak at his leisure. To be so close was to smell her scented breath, rich like a flower in bloom. It was to see every inflection flicker across her face, like delicate brushstrokes on canvas.

"Go on," the Empress said, sensing his urge to speak.

"Well, I also wondered if there is anything unusual regarding those barracks you already know of, or perhaps have been involved with. It might be of help or consequence."

"You wouldn't be implying anything, my Lord?" she said smoothly, employing mischief to outshine all else, by the silk texture of her tongue; her tongue of silk and thorns.

"Nothing sinister," Tristan replied, wincing in the awkwardness she had beset upon him. "You needn't look for a deep truth in me; everything I am is right on the surface."

"Forgive me, dear lord, I didn't intend to slander you," she breathed, suitably contrite, while maintaining intact the firmest eye contact and that calm smile of hers that would melt the hearts of many. "I am used to dealing with people who are inclined to withhold their thoughts far too often at the slightest fear of offending me or proving me wrong. I sometimes forget how forward and honest you are. Continue."

It was very clever of her. A good deal of her charisma manifested itself in conducting pitch perfect damage control, as any silver-tongued devil knows. This time, Tristan decided, she was probably being completely honest. She was aware her usual tricks wouldn't work on him, even with a number of them being subconscious reactions, this being another great asset he admired, despite her still being so obsessed with her own little schemes; perceptiveness of how any given person views her.

"Thank you, Your Majesty. My concern was of the Mürathneèan man I saw in the barracks, a captain no less. Does his presence have anything to do with you?"

"I'm sorry I didn't clear this up sooner, my Lord. I didn't realise it would be brought into question, but yes, I have already taken it upon myself to recruit people from abroad for many a task. Captain Westrym is a Santorrenti fellow of minor standing and fair instincts, the perfect combination. I don't see how that could be related to the murder you're discussing, but if you suspect something in your gut, I urge you to follow through with it."

"I will take you up on that offer, however it's not that in particular. I thought it may have been an influence." Tristan sighed heavily, scratching his forehead as Alycia watched, unchanging. "I was more wondering, if you've done this much, what else might you be doing of your own accord?"

"Certainly nothing to do with that or any other Aurailian barracks, rest assured. Were you hoping I would say yes?" she quipped, raising her eyebrows in response to the drooping of his shoulders.

"It would have been easier if you had," he chuckled dryly. "In all seriousness though, I often feel you running far, far away from the rest of us. It seemed only logical to ask you about it. It's a wonder you haven't already enacted your renaissance plan by yourself."

The Empress sat back slowly, not sluggishly but gracefully, as if time had been slowed around her, and stroked a few loose strands of hair back with two fingers, regarding him with approval.

"You're the first person to so directly say that to me," Alycia smirked. "I know others have wanted to. The truth is, until now I could not so easily coerce so much money from the Counts. I am a crafty and resourceful woman, but I am no miracle worker. If I can fool people to think otherwise, even for a moment, then I must be fulfilling my role as well as I could ever hope to."

"Gods, you fool even me sometimes," loyal Lady Castellon took a moment from her work to say, a rare undercurrent of humour underlining her tone.

"I shall take that as a compliment, my Lady," the Empress said. "There is something else you wish to say," she observed, peering into Tristan's soul once more.

"Yes, I should like to request a transfer for Lennord, given this recent development. Not to mention he could prove himself elsewhere. When I spoke to him earlier, he had a rather interesting idea of working on the great Vicentei Laccona's theories. It would surely prove a visual feast for the people of Aurail, as well as practical purposes, as you seem to want."

"I thought you might bring this up," she replied, not sounding especially bothered.

Tristan frowned. It was possible she had predicted he would say that. She was a woman of exceptional perception, not that it mattered if she was lying. She was so convincing, he definitely could believe her, and she would know that she could not be proven wrong, at any rate. Alycia leaned forward, both elbows on the table, hands locked together, head held above them still, where most people would subconsciously stoop. She looked serious.

"Listen to me, Tristan. I recognise that, even with the security detail you, as I understand it, left in his charge, you would be worried for his well-being, but I have faith in the men you chose. As for this matter you keep bringing up of him being misused, I hear you, but I give you my word, I'm not trying to insult or spite your good friend. You remember our talk about how we would go about granting him a lordship, of course. This is no different. Part of being human is to dream, and see those dreams fulfilled, rich and destitute alike. I have the rare gift of being able to bestow that fulfilment on people. The real trick is getting everyone else to care, and care they must, in this case, to unify the hopeless wishes of thousands into one vision: a waking dream you can touch, a true revolution exemplified by smoke and mirrors," she said mysteriously, alluringly. "It's how Harth became so powerful, and while it presents itself so effortlessly nowadays, we, too, will attain such status in time. And to think, my Lord, this is but one of many strategies, and it is not only Lennord we must apply this to, though he may be our most treasured asset, but many others.

"In assigning your friend to the barracks, which, as you will not deny, needs help anyway, it allows me to promote him, so to speak, as quickly as I see fit, to provide context for those who, otherwise, would not give him the blindest bit of notice. Because suddenly, in my scenario, he is a great man who has risen in the favour of myself and the Emperor, and will be respected for his talents, not just his titles. "The venerable Lord Brodie", they'll declare in exultant voices. "Remember his deeds from last year? No, neither do I; he must have been great indeed to grow those wings, so." Is this beginning to make sense?"

"Perfect sense. I'm just not sure it's entirely necessary. This could end up being more long-winded and time-consuming than it needs to be. It's quite daunting to think how many people we might have to apply that to."

"We'll agree to differ," Alycia said politely. "Don't worry. I'm sure he won't be spending long there. He'll be flying high with the likes of you soon enough."

Tristan almost felt bad for rebuking her impassioned speech so coldly, though that was perhaps the point. She had been so eloquent and natural in her tone that, for a time, he had forgotten why he approached her in the first place. Indeed, he'd seen her mesmerise others into a state of stupor from which they could not ably respond within a respectable amount of time.

"You may go at your leisure," the Empress said.

"And my Lord, if you ever need help with your investigation, I would be happy to assist you," Sir Pedrig offered with the purest, most dignified respect. "Assuming I have the time."

"I'm sure something could be arranged, yes. Not now," Alycia said sharply, taking note again of Tristan's renewed intent and his eagerness to leave. "I shouldn't think there will be time. Council will convene in, shall we say, 30 minutes? Be a dear and have the other lords informed, if it please."

"I will, Your Majesty," Lord Almaric replied, finally succumbing to using routine phrases.

"Bless you."

Tristan nodded to Sir Pedrig in the briefest of thanks, and left the Empress in all her shrouded secrets and fervour, having to remind himself what exactly had just transpired. All things considered, he saw that she was keeping secrets, a discovery which proved to be of no use. It went without saying that beyond that sparkle in her eyes, ambitions ever grew. What was far more difficult to discern was whether any of it was relevant to his investigation. It was best not to think about it too hard, really. He would just have to hope she was not withholding valuable information, as her pride surely would if she thought she could do it better than he.

~

Lennord dabbed his pen into the inkwell and held it there to contemplate his next move. There were already too many sullied sheets of paper screwed in balls in the bin beside his desk. It only occurred to him as he had begun writing, that he might want to refrain from being so blunt about his situation, lest his words be misconstrued and his wife and daughter fall beside themselves with worry. At the same time, he could not outright lie. A knot formed in his gut at the thought of such a thing, as they deserved better than being fed a version of the truth of which "liberties" had been taken, so he would simply have to indirectly reference his troubles and not outright mention the death of that soldier. His body had been removed now, and the blood stains wiped clean with ferocious force, meticulously as duty demanded, but for him it was still there, an afterimage, a ghost which yet lingered in this world beyond its time. He concentrated on his letter and continued to write the current iteration as the words came to him.

My stay, thus far, has been thoroughly unpleasant in many ways, he wrote, *deplorable even, but there are some who hold much of it together, like Tristan, who thankfully has not changed so very much! I believe I must make the most of my situation, and so I shall, as I shall also remember that, were you here, you would be rapping on the Emperor's chamber yourself to have him give me some other work! Though I already weary of these barracks, Tristan, in his kindness, has suggested a knighthood for me, by gods, so perhaps I can convince them to release me early, or set up a workshop in Caedor.*

At any rate, I don't have specifics of my work to tell you as of now. You'll have to tell me what you and Kate have been doing with yourselves instead.

All my love, Lennord.

He threw the quill down in its inkwell before reading through it again. There was a banging from outside, that of smithing, the source of which he could not see for there were no windows on the sides of the building. It had been happening for some time, and now was doing his splitting headache no favours. And it wasn't just the noise, either. There was something incredibly *wrong* about the sound it gave off. He left his office at once, waving his guards back a little as they followed him without so much as a suggestion, and stormed over to a small smithing establishment nearby, situated beneath a thick straw roof, open at the front, having only three walls.

"Stop that for a moment," Lennord said coarsely, surprising the rugged looking man committing the deed.

"Why?" he replied bluntly.

"Do you know how frustrating it is, listening to that rhythm over and over again? It might not be so bad if you would stop treating the metal like your worst nightmare. You're trying to forge a sword, I take it, not kill it."

The Voice of Kings

There was the feeling growing inside Lennord that he might have stepped into the nest of something entirely unwelcoming. It made him uneasy at first, and then the truth clicked into place as the man confronted him again.

"Are you telling me my technique is wrong? I've been doing this for years," the rugged smith rebuked, wiping the sweat from his face and crossing his arms as he apparently weighed whether to show contempt or interest.

The other smiths were younger than him, and perhaps the only reason Lennord had not taken issue with their technique was that they were too quiet be heard above the din of this man, who judging by the shocked faces of these young men, must have been their superior. Still, it was too late to back out now. Someone might thank him for this later. If he was lucky.

"I'm not saying you're a bad smith, of course. You could have been mistreating the metal for any number or reasons. You might not be functioning at your best, for all I know," he said, taking care to leave out any mention of the dead soldier. "What you were doing was serviceable, at least, but it could be better. It's not your fault, I suppose."

Lennord, now aware that he may have started sounding condescending, took up a hammer and began to lightly tap the half-finished sword on the anvil, at points all along the length of it.

"You must be the inventor," the smith said plainly, conceitedly, taking note of the guards standing like statues nearby.

"That I am. I should take back some of what I just said, by the way. The quality of this steel isn't particularly good."

"I could have told you that. I don't suppose you can do something about that, can you?"

"Maybe. I can't promise anything; I don't know how things work around here. I'll see what I can do. I'll leave you to your work," Lennord added for want of a way out.

He left the blacksmith to his forging, taking precautions not to rush from the scene. He'd already started something now, and there was no way to stop it. In his state of annoyance and his natural, imperative need to expose his knowledge to the world, he'd made a direct impression now, as he inevitably would have had to at some point, so he may as well make it a good one, he thought. Fortunately, the blacksmith was no longer aggravated by his intervention; at worst apathetic, and at best intrigued enough to watch what he was doing more closely.

And this was only the start. He'd probably have to do it again, and prove that he could rise to the challenge of improving the functionality of this place, to meet and exceed expectations of escalation, as morally troublesome as it was here. He didn't need long to think on his next move, as all that was really needed was to do what he would back home. He took from his office a portable lectern, some scraps of paper, and a quill, and headed for the back of the barracks, silent guardians in tow. They were beginning to irritate him now, and so he longed for the moment when it was knowingly safe enough to dismiss them.

Up the tight winding stairs of a watchtower he went, grabbing from the rest room at the top a wooden chair which saw no current use. He emerged, blinking, from the dank darkness atop the battlements where he settled himself before an embrasure. His sight was drawn to the vista of hills tumbling up and down to his far left, and sporadically placed walled houses, so small like dolls' houses, to his right, and further back, the woods that housed the manors of lords, and then there was The Victory Road, built as such during the first Emperor's days, cutting through the steppe between them all. It would make for a fine change of view if he got bored of the other side, and could imagine how far Isaac and Marcel and Lucian had travelled beyond that horizon.

Away from all that, he sat himself down and placed his lectern on an embrasure, peering through the struts of stone either side of him, at the barracks below and the three towers jutting out of a castle unseen.

The air was cleaner here at least, he thought to himself. More agreeable. The time and space alone, or close enough to it, would give him the means to think. The guards, too, had taken a liking to the place he'd chosen to ponder his inventions, standing at ease on the other side of the battlement. Perhaps they were more used to this sort of work then, at altitudes like this. As with Sir Martin's hill in Caedor, he could sit and watch and, hopefully, be inspired by whatever was going on down below, and take more detailed notes later.

It was more difficult this time. Already he had examined the guns in his office and decided to put off adjusting those until absolutely necessary, and, for now, tried in futility to discover an application for this congregation of soldiers and war machines that had no violent purpose, and so he was grateful, if a little concerned, when an imperial courier approached him, flustered as if he'd been running everywhere looking for him, and indeed probably had.

"Lennord Brodie?" the courier asked between two heavy breaths.

"Yes, I am. What is it you wanted?"

The courier breathed a sigh of relief, a short-lived happiness as he noticed the two guards eyeing him, itching to unsheathe their swords. They needn't have bothered, for the courier looked a diligent, pleasant sort of man, thin and young, bearing a few very old scars but being a servant of, presumably, Lord Almaric, was very young in the eyes.

"My name is Marcus Baldwin. Lord Almaric sent me in his stead to inform you he still cannot relieve you of your duties here, but wishes me to reassure you that it remains a temporary measure."

"I see," Lennord mused, feeling all of a sudden much more sullen again. "That was thoughtful of him."

The Voice of Kings

"He is a thoughtful man. And that's not all. I am also instructed to tell you that you're to be kept up to date with the trial of Adrian Mortain, the murderer, as he sees it beneficial to your safety, I think."

"What reason did he give?"

"Nothing specific. I could have probed him further but I trust his judgement. He said for you not to speak of this to anyone, for reasons I'm sure you can ascertain," Marcus said in all seriousness. "I think he fears the involvement of an outsider, as unlikely as that may or may not be."

"What do you mean *you think*? Aren't you supposed to remember these things?"

"I'm just giving you something to work with. I'm telling you I think he withheld some of his thoughts on the matter from me, as he rightly should. Disregard it if you wish. It didn't come from his mouth."

"Very well. I meant no offence," Lennord said, overly contrite in apology, for his own thoughts were already moving on.

Lennord drew his attention to the spot where, until a few hours ago, a man's lifeless body had been splayed over his own vital fluids. A question returned to him that had plagued him earlier in the day, that of identity, the need to make this man matter in some way or to know that he mattered. It was certainly jarring to be in this environment, so perhaps his query would seem strange here. It was worth a shot though.

"Do you know his name? The man who died here?"

"I can't say that I do, I'm afraid. I could look into it if I'm obliged to visit again," Marcus offered, starting to feel thoroughly uncomfortable in the presence of, Lennord noted, an increasingly sombre inventor. "Just bear with us, please. I know this is a bloody mess."

"It is."

"Your safety is in good hands," Marcus gave him, for want of something more appropriate to say. "For now, well, I had best be off then."

"Yes, of course. Thank you Marcus. Don't let me distract you."

Lennord considered briefly going to the other side of the battlement again, to look out across that landscape, ultimately deciding to stay put. It would console him for now, he told himself, to add something of value to this place, however big or small, despite how it might not be appreciated the same way as in Caedor, and so he put quill to paper and it made work for him while his mind was elsewhere.

Chapter Twelve: In Madness and Flames

Smoke and fire had left the wreckages littering what was once fertile farmland as echoes of the past: only a reflection of what had come before, so charred that were it not witnessed, historians and alchemists would have to make a leery search for clues of the function of those black shapes, whether they were once alive or as inanimate as they now were. In place of luscious greenery, vegetable plants and apple trees and the like, there was ashen ground, riled by the wind when it felt like blowing dead earth on the territory of the living.

Atop this barren earth, charred objects rested, untouched as if to memorialise their existence. Some of them were very clearly recognisable as trees and lumps of wood, farm animals, and people even. As one looked further back, they became decidedly less preserved until they were lumps of charcoal; beyond that they faded further still until, eventually, anything that was there had been incinerated, mingling with the ground beneath and whipped up by occasional unruly winds which people feverishly attempted to avoid breathing in. And there at the apparent source was the mouth of a cave. Its innards had been cleansed by tremendous heat.

All the nearby houses, this being the very border of a town, had been evacuated, their residents moved further inward to squat in the homes of others, leaving this field near-desolate save for the few people shaking about its perimeter without much purpose, waiting anxiously for some action to be taken. From the nearby road, the convoy of highly-decorated carriages was setting up a wider perimeter of its own: carriages both containing and backed by men armed to the teeth with halberds and swords, and bowmen too, and some choice few with firearms, not to mention the array of other specialists, covering a number of areas of expertise. A flag was flown from the top of more than one carriage, dancing merrily in the wind, demanding unequivocal respect at every swing, like the crack of a whip. High Duke Dorrin observed their form from his own carriage and was satisfied. He stared gaunt at the horror, and though there was reverence in silence, he heard the flag above his carriage cracking all the louder, for it was the largest of them, bearing the same motif as the others. His sigil, today signalling justice, a dark green escutcheon on a field of dark yellow, within which was a Mürathneèan eagle, close regardant: a striking image as expressed by the armour of the soldiers too. It was unmistakeable who accompanied this convoy, as was the point.

High Duke Dorrin peered through the window at two men, one the Lord Paravail Savello, the other a citizen of the town: not a baron or nobleman, evidently, but he conducted himself confidently, utilising whatever leadership skills he had acquired from whatever social circles he engaged in, and was displaying an appropriate level of humility. A few seconds went by, and the lordling returned to Dorrin. After an interlude, wherein every townsfolk watching held their breath for what must have felt like an eternity, Dorrin emerged to portray what needed to be seen. An incredibly serious-looking man in his late thirties, tall and lean but by no means thin; there was no spare meat on him, nor likewise too little. His build suited him perfectly. He shot looks demanding fealty and obedience about the place, a mere consequence of this gravest of situations, his face hard as stone, not in fact relishing his power too much as one might interpret, for he was none too happy.

He took from his robes, gloriously puffed at the sleeves, with an understated black puff tie around his neck and woven with immaculate care as it had to be, a handkerchief, and covered his mouth as he grimaced slightly, wiping away specks of dirt flung into his short, black beard as he did so. He crossed the uneven terrain, occasionally clutching at the hilt of his sword to shut out its rattling, keeping his dignity remarkably intact despite a lack of proper clothes for this environment, his black boots having flat soles meant for striding down halls, not navigating hilly landscapes. There were few men in the country that could inspire more discipline than he without even speaking, and they were probably all in Harth at this time.

"Maricous, I present to you the High Duke, Dorrin Santorellian," Lord Savello said to the town representative, now stepping back to let the two men converse.

The man was sweating, growing increasingly restless and anxious, and understandably so, Dorrin thought. Besides being naturally imposing, he was intimidating by his very name to a lowly farmer, or whatever this man's profession was. All dukes were lords, but only one born of the royal Santorellian family could be named High Duke, a title designed for the purpose of showing status alone as, in reality, he owned a duchy as any other duke did and had no constitutional power beyond that: any drastic or unusual orders he might choose to issue, on account of his family name, to those other dukes would have to pass through the King's hands eventually, and he with his council of cynics and visionaries would doubtless have a clearer view of any situation than he, or would rule as such.

"I received a great deal of correspondence at Valicato recently, all from your town," the High Duke said flatly. Small talk would feel fundamentally wrong given what he was witnessing, assuming the worst even as he struggled to make out what exactly it was. "Some of them arrived via eagle, some of them via couriers who took different paths to reach me, and all of them carried exactly the same message."

"My Lord Highness... We wanted to be positive that the message would reach you as quick as possible. We also thought it would get your undivided attention," Maricous admitted sheepishly.

"It worked. I couldn't ignore it: you painted it as an attack," Lord Dorrin replied, deliberately blaming this man directly to gauge his response.

"Well, we can't be sure of that yet. All I know is that there was an explosion of some kind, or a fireball, from that cave over there. Men came from Harth recently to mine there."

The High Duke said nothing. His eyes were ablaze in confusion as he scanned the field, his gaze like forks, piercing all that touched it.

"My Lord Duke?" Maricous ventured.

"Why have you not done anything about this?" Lord Dorrin growled. "Why have you left this mess to fester? It's uncouth."

"It wasn't a decision made lightly, believe me," came the nervous reply. "*Or* without opposition. We decided to move as little as possible until you arrived, to show the severity of all this. There was one man working here only killed by his burns a few hours later, so we removed him from the scene without delay."

"Yes, fine," Dorrin sighed, so bitter to admit that there was some logic in the man's words. "But I have seen it now."

Dorrin tilted his head and waved for six ominous figures milling outside one carriage to step forward. They were clad all in black robes designed with as few gaps as possible in the material. Hidden beneath their robes, their trousers were tucked into their boots, and their sleeves beneath their gloves, and they wore masks which extended into a long, curved beak shape. It was a drastic measure, perhaps, to employ plague doctors, and anyone who saw them here who was not educated in the circumstances would misinterpret it to mean the worst it could be, and run a mile before stopping for breath and proceeding to spread nasty rumours to everyone they met.

Or rather, they would without care. If the guards caught wind of an outsider, they would apprehend them and set the record straight immediately. It wouldn't do to have people hear frightful constructions of the imagination as news. As for these doctors, they were broadly and thoroughly trained physicians, and in truth, plague was an extremely rare occurrence in populated areas of Mürathneè. They fanned out and poked around with tools from their belts with the highest regard for anything which once breathed the clean air from before this ghastly event unfolded, cautiously moving their heads in close where they saw fit.

"Stay away from the cave for now," the High Duke barked. "Stick to this patch of land. What were you saying, Maricous?" he said to the man next to him. "You spoke of men from Harth. Proceed."

"There were only a few of them. Four, if I'm right. A couple of them looked very official. They said they came with permission from the King's court, showed us documentation to prove it, to scout out this cave and, if need be, set up a mine. Said there was white steel inside. I don't rightly know how they found out about it. Maybe a traveller tipped them off. You might want to investigate."

"You're sure they were from Harth?" Lord Dorrin pressed, growing impatient as to where this conversation might be going, how it could be remotely relevant to the explosion. If the man was lying, Dorrin's stark and edgy tone would soon make him remember.

"Quite sure. We offered to help, that is, me and some others from in town, but they ordered us to not get involved. Said they'd tell us if they needed our help."

Dorrin hesitated and pocketed the handkerchief. He was getting used to the smell, shameful as that may have been, though he couldn't concentrate on morality at this time. Obviously this man would not dare irritate him on purpose, so he must have been building up to something.

"What does this have to do with the explosion?" the High Duke asked, outwardly showing impressive patience.

"Only that they were all in there at the time, all four of them. I'm not saying it was them that did it, obviously," Maricous pleaded, to cover his bases in case treason was brought up. "But..."

"But what?" Lord Dorrin snapped. "Did you see it for yourself?"

"From afar, Lord. I don't know what weapon could create that kind of force. You should have seen it, Lord. One minute everything's fine, the next this fireball bursts from the cave entrance, and where you'd think it would stop, it just kept on growing, and the air was so hot it shimmered as if...as if bent through curved glass, like. It set things alight before it even touched them. Oh, and its tip was black, pitch black, Lord. I didn't imagine that, unless we all did."

"Everyone in town will be asked to testify to what they've seen or otherwise heard. You understand this, don't you? There is no use in you exaggerating, if that's what you're doing."

"I'm not, I swear! Shadows take me if I lie! I tell you only what I saw, plain and simple."

Dorrin detected no lie or hyperbole in the man's voice and was not best pleased.

"Do you have any idea if those visitors from Harth were doing anything else in the area, anything at all? Or if there were others examining similar caves for Sèhvorian steel?"

"Not that I know of. That's all I can say."

"Would you be likely to know if that were the case?"

"Probably not," the man said helplessly, shrugging.

Dorrin began to stroll round the edge of the field, taking note of the damage done and burn wounds inflicted more than anything else, as per instinctive reaction from his earlier years of meddling in affairs of the City Watch, insisting that he gain experience in all the fields of military. It was true that the fire would need to be unimaginably hot to blacken livestock and people in one burst of flame, so he took to assuming the man, and whoever wrote the letters, wasn't exaggerating. It was insinuated that it had all been over almost as soon as it had started. Perhaps lava could do this, Dorrin contemplated on a whim, wincing as he recognised that he had never seen an active volcano up close before.

The peasant, Maricous, followed closely beside the High Duke's footsteps, whose surcoat billowed at the bottom and edges with an appropriate level of elegance, especially when viewed from afar. Dorrin's lordly assistant followed at his own pace, an unshakable grimace carved into his face, half turning away from the smell of the dead bodies until a flurry of noises reached them and it suddenly became irrelevant. Dorrin's immediate stop and alarming twitch confirmed this fact to them, but he ignored them. Fighting against the current of the wind, the noises yet cut through when they could, those of swords in motion, clashing against flesh and possibly armour. That of swords clashing against swords, however, was something that could not be heard. And there, against his chest, he felt his armour like the throbbing of a heart long-lovelorn; mail and square plates sewn tightly in fine cloth, and atop that, thin plates again sewn over the others like great black diamonds, for he was both lord and soldier. Or soldier and lord, perchance, for he heard the scraping of steel on leather before ever he touched his sword.

"How far out did you order my men to go?" the High Duke snapped.

"All around this half of the town. Those could be your men over there, if that's what you're asking."

Dorrin was already belting towards the source of the combat, leaving his assistant in trust to bring reinforcements. A pistol was fired, and then another, and there were stranger noises than that erupting like wildfire through the wilderness. Animals screeched in pure unbridled rage, imbuing him with dread that he kept tightly in its place even as he fast approached the fighting, these unusual battle cries sending chills down his spine. It was not very far for him to run at the speed he was going, arriving soon enough at the top of a hillock, barely breathless from the sprinting and only gasping for air in shock when he witnessed the bizarre scene unfolding like a confused, messy nightmare battle below. Eight of his men were engaged in the thick of combat, four men at their feet as well: whether dead or alive, Dorrin could not tell through the havoc and the mayhem. Their opponents were animals, not humans, as there was none other to be seen; chupacabras scowling and howling as they leapt, and scratched, and bit at Dorrin's soldiers with their sabre fangs, proud if protective creatures, reduced through madness to blind violence. They were rather wolfish in their movements and colour, and in their shape also, with more than a few similarities to lions, in particular their heads, and as they played out their vicious dance with Dorrin's men, the single row of long black spines on their backs sank and rose in time with their jumps, shivering as they bounded; fast, mad.

They were noticeably larger than wolves, a point made through ever-growing despair and bafflement as Dorrin spotted several timber wolves embroiled in the fighting, and in the trees, like raucous spectators, crows stood in rows cawing loudly, not fleeing in force as they should. Possessed of an eerie element, they fidgeted and jumped around, appearing indecisive as if any moment they would all take to the skies.

Dorrin wasted not a second longer contemplating the particulars: that could wait. His sword was naked on command and, abandoning years of military experience, he was there with his men, swinging with brute force at a charging chupacabra, catching it in its gaping maw, grunting to control his breathing as his blade ripped through the creature's jaw, nearly collapsing backwards from its weight. It was dead almost instantly in a spray of blood and a guttural howl of pain, high-pitched and begging for sympathy as if in its final seconds, it was released from the clutches of its madness. Dorrin left it, both parts of its jaw hanging by threads of muscle where a nudge of the foot might have cut them loose completely. With disregard for his own life, he flung himself into the fray, giving one or two of his soldiers a much-needed burst of energy, while the others scarcely noticed his presence. Just the same, he forgot them, the throng of chaos beating around him in sheathing of metal and layers upon layers of scratchy wails.

And to slay one beast was not to deter another, because as he ran at a wolf that growled the other way and cracked his sword upon its back, the blurs of grey continued to circle around as sharks about a corpse, two mouths clamping onto his leg now, ripping cloth from plate and wailing as their teeth cracked on that segmented metal. Like an amateur again, Dorrin heard a violent scream escape him as he slashed for the head at his right and just as quickly, twisted his left leg around and down, hammering the second chupacabra with his elbow. And again when it did little, and again when the mouth didn't let go. Thus, he found himself at their level, observing their mania as if one of them; concentric circles of fey things moving this way and that, like a whirlpool defying the laws of nature. He saw his men's defence, and was up on two feet.

Rising too fast, dizziness unmanned him, a hundred cries fuzzing around the edges: the hallmarks of a bad dream. Another chupacabra jumped for Dorrin, making a lash for his throat which, surely, could have snapped his neck had his instincts not pulled him aside so nimbly, and had the creature not been so blinded by insanity, as they all were, that it could not focus its violence. But with lightning reflexes, it drew up a clawed foot to strike him again: an almost humanoid hand, comprised of five thick, furry fingers with curved blades poking from the ends, only conforming to the more interconnected structure of a wolf paw nearer the leg. Dorrin was still staggering, swiping at nothing in his fear. Then, again, a straight downward arc, cleaving that very same leg in half, which in his heart felt like a desecration, and the feeling of being in a dream world was heightened even as the gritty reality sank in, whatever that reality was. The mangled screams of people, and frenzied wild beasts circling around him among a flurry of swords slicing through the air, was more than a little disquieting, as he would no doubt feel the full effects of later. The chupacabra bit desperately for his leg, parried by a move fuelled purely by instinct, dazed and flung aside by the flat side of the High Duke's double-edged blade being struck upon its head, followed by a swing which decapitated the beast.

Behind him, a wolf scurried through the grass to pounce on him, curtailed by the surprise attack of one of Dorrin's men: a brutal uppercut to its underbelly, whereupon the screeching animal was upturned and lay helplessly on its back to soon pass on. Dorrin afforded only a cursory glance to ensure the attack had been successful, then held his sword up straight beside his head: a defensive tactic which he only now realised would not work quite so well against opponents so low to the ground. He readjusted its position and moved to intercept another chupacabra, deciding it best to lure the beast into the length of hard steel at the exact moment it lunged for him, twisting his whole body weight as he kept his sword still and his feet flat on the earth.

The shock of the animal's sheer strength barraging into his sword sprung his eyes open, and for a moment he was off balance, one foot off the ground before stamping it down again and swinging madly in the momentarily incapacitated animal's direction: a near miss, to his frustration, quickly corrected by a downward stab, impaling right the way through. His throat let out a battle cry, all darkness and fear for the soul; but souls not of these creatures. When Dorrin heaved his blade from the wound, now caked in bodily fluids and dirt glued near the tip, he repeated his new tactic of lowering it to ground level, as a man of his strength and skill could afford to, where others would be too slow to parry at such a cumbersome angle. On both sides of him, his men whirred their blades frantically, like whips they were, and between them and the bodies strewn bloody and twisted, he saw in the blurred emptiness an opportunity.

"Shield ring!" Lord Dorrin barked, for all but he bore a bloodstained shield, they being Knights of the Herald, bearing devices they'd never thought to use outside parades, and at his command they were made conscious of their surroundings, backing in around him until he was encased. They were six, not eight.

There was a wild beating on the ring of steel, like tribal drums and snarls of beasts being sacrificed. Or sacrificing themselves, as it so appeared, crushing their own skulls. The swords jabbed from behind them in unison; fountains of red when withdrawn. Over the shields was seen a field born of nightmare, creatures of the wild bred with demon blood strewn ill upon the ground. Dorrin lowered his body weight a notch, only his knees, not his back, and for several seconds maintained this position until it sank in that the sounds of the battlefield had dimmed to a dull roar, injured animals crying out for release which, as the truth sank in to all, the High Duke's soldiers were all too eager to provide.

In the trees, the crows were mainly silent, though still fidgeting as if all of them were trying to rid their bodies of some unseen parasite. A few of them flew from their perches, then all of a sudden, the rest followed suit, every one of them cawing as one almighty entity, soaring like a black cloud over their heads. A thought struck the High Duke and he sought to implement a new plan before he had time to consider what it was. He trusted his own judgement.

"Anyone have a shot left?" he shouted to be heard above the almighty din. One of them nodded, taking from his side a pistol: an experimental device Dorrin prayed would not fail as they so often did. "Fire into that flock," the High Duke demanded.

The Voice of Kings

Without a care for aiming... here a crack of gunpowder, and there from the riled flock, a bird dropped. The flock split up, screeching even louder, and flew their separate ways, not even attempting to rejoin as one. It was the sweetest relief for them all when the usual quiet tranquillity of nature resumed its service. Thirty or more of Dorrin's soldiers stood in formation atop the hill from which he had charged, pollaxes at the ready.

"Hold!" Lord Dorrin barked, thrusting an open palm in their direction, where he could safely ignore them and take in the destruction that had been wrought.

It was not a godly sight, wolves and chupacabras splayed dead about the place in discomforting positions. Dorrin didn't enjoy it in the slightest, but dealt with it with the professionalism his men needed. They were gasping for breath, not saying anything.

"What the fuck just happened?" he bellowed, not angry as much as wanting to kick his soldiers back into motion.

"They came out of nowhere," one knight said, stepping forward to show his commanding officer proper respect. "We didn't do anything to provoke them, they just came right at us like they were rabid. A couple of us were killed before we could even react."

"We should not discount that they are not rabid, though it would be a stretch for so many of them to have contracted it. And for them to attack in unison like a gang of ruthless pirates... I will see to it that all of them are examined. Whatever disease they carried, we must put a stop to it now."

One soldier in particular caught his eye as he said this, covering a bite mark on one hand to stop the bleeding. One of the animals must have somehow ripped his gloves from him. All eyes turned to him, and his heart was in his throat as the realisation dropped. But he wasn't the only one: two more bore scratches seared across their cheeks.

"Have those seen to by a physician. Now." Dorrin waited for the three of them to run off, as they were keen to do, before another thought crossed his mind, taking note of the blood splashed across the soldiers' armour. "Did any of you swallow their blood?"

"I'm sure none of us could say for sure," the first soldier said.

"That would be the wisest assumption to make. Return to the convoy, all of you."

After they'd all left, he wandered between the lifeless creatures to one unlucky man who was dead now, but hadn't been when he'd arrived: newly knighted Sir Evras. He kicked a chupacabra from his corpse, knelt beside him, and silently pondered his next move with a dark cloud over him, as if the man's mauled and near unrecognisable face helped him think. *To the five, weigh his soul for its worth, don't let the shadows steal it. May Venlor burn the shadows into nothing before him.*

After a short time spent wiping his sword on a dead wolf, he rose and sheathed it, convinced that it would, at the very least, not stick to his scabbard.

In Madness and Flames

"Lord Savello!" Lord Dorrin shouted at the top of his voice, already trudging back to the convoy as he knew he would not appear. To his surprise, he was swiftly proven wrong by the lordling hurrying over the hilltop at his behest, trying his hardest, for the time being, to avoid looking at the sea of dead bodies.

"My Lord Duke," said he, a statement of his stern eagerness to be subservient.

"Listen carefully, and take mental notes. There is apparently a disease spreading throughout the wildlife in this area, but how I do not know, nor could I hazard as to what it is for that matter. You will have all townsfolk refrain from drinking water until a preliminary check has been performed, and until that time, will be rationed on the water from our flasks. Secondly, you will have more water sent from a town which does not directly connect with any rivers in the area, and you will have plague doctors examine every one of these corpses. They are to show extreme caution."

"Indeed, my Lord."

"I will set up a tighter perimeter and begin having the locals questioned and make sense of this. I'll send for you at such time as I need you," the Duke finished, nodding.

"Yes, my Lord."

And I can only hope that there is, in fact, sense to be found here, Dorrin thought, attempting to run through his mind all that had happened since his arrival. In his heart, he was tired, but in his head, he knew they would find answers. This was not Mūrac or Carlophinia, where truths were left to fade in the depths of time and justice was a pleasant commodity of the rich. The Santorellians had not made this the greatest country in the known world by luck. Not that justice could be had; how did one enact retribution on the world itself?

There was so much to do in so little time, so he could only hope that when he would soon leave for Harth at his brother's summon, its purpose would be compensation enough.

Chapter Thirteen: A Dream of a Dream

When the calm beneath the tree was upset, Kate's gaze drew away from the leaves rustling back and forth overhead, their majestic arms lined with bark. In the daydream, they'd been the ground her feet parted, writhing like a gentle bog of green. And to now look on Jyric was to be startled for a moment. To the fields atop this higher plain she looked again, left to the indented farmland where the soil was richer. The man who'd slipped and sliced his hand upon his scythe was already consumed by work again. To await Jyric's swiftness after her bandaging him would seem the right thing, here by the tor where the leaves tripped down the rocky pass to the stream below. Thinking would be easier here, yet the mind somehow had secret plans when nature worked magic all about, and too many seeds vied for sowing in her thoughts.

At last, her back straightened from the tree trunk on which she slumped, her fingers playing down the creases of her dress as she remembered why she was still here.

"You don't have work to do?" the dutiful vigilant spoke, suspicious of her restfulness at this time of afternoon. His words carried no judgement of course, and so she tried to see him as a mirror: see if that worked. His eyes searched for meaning, a result of time spent in the light of Sèhvorian artefacts at the back of the church.

"I'll find some," replied Kate, giving him a wan smile. "If you'll humour me..." she went on and trailed off just as quickly, making certain to have his consent. "What was this land used for in the past? This space I mean, this bit of land."

She waved an arm to encompass in her meaning the grass and the crops, the highs and the lows away from the cliff above the river.

"I wouldn't know." Jyric sniffed as if trying to smell out her purpose. "I should think not much. Even Martin Caedor didn't build anything here, as I understand."

"Thank you."

With that he bowed reluctantly and turned to leave, and it dawned on her that with her glassy tone, she'd sent him away, off to help someone else. But she didn't call him back. Watching him go, she wondered on that disposition of his, wandering amongst people to and fro, forgetting her soon enough, and his confusion with it. For all the altruism, she didn't want that life for herself either, she suddenly decided, pulling an amused face at her whimsy. To be so passive deterred her, then?

Enough, she told herself, stepping from the shade of the oak, and there in the open, feeling the cold beneath the furs of her coat. She wasn't here to debate the path of her future.

"I'm here to do something a bit odd," she spoke under her breath.

A Dream of a Dream

Her hands fell to her hips, her back straightened. It was stupid to believe she'd see what a hundred thousand others had not, but here she stood nonetheless. *Assume Isaac is only half-right*, she arbitrated. The world of grey and mist looked as tired as she felt, but it couldn't deter her, given the alternatives. And besides, she'd heard right, hadn't she? The town's founder had never built anything up here. Not from a reliable source, perhaps, but she didn't have the patience for reading through her father's collection. Already, she was sure she'd seen somewhere that he'd pitched his men up here once.

"So, if I'm Sir Martin, what am I doing here? My King told me to, of course, to reinforce the despondent lands. Why here though? There are easier routes into the mountains."

The veil to the south took her attention: the greyness that would otherwise afford distant views of the mountains. Before it, the ground was uneven, craggy, and before that, pastures green paled in comparison. Kate breathed deeply, forming the scene in her waking eyes: soldiers by the hundred, or by the thousand, cramped up here, but only the blue sky was clear, and vegetation below that she'd placed there. What did an army look like anyway? All the banners, and the tents, and the armour couldn't be conjured, and how far would it stretch? *Trade the corset and the bodice for the hose and the cuirass, and the greatsword on my back because I'm a man of strength*. And drums too, to rouse the men. Hammering away in her brain as she paced, frantic in its search, as if it stood a chance.

"If I'm Martin," she muttered to the highland air again, for the thoughts in her head became cluttered, "do I know what's in the ground beneath me? Did I put it there? If I did, why don't I write it down for posterity? And if I don't know, then why am I up here? What a funny man I am." She pulled a sickly face as she smiled.

The pressure in her veins rose to the beat of the drum: drumming by count of eight, palm on fist, boots working the earth. If that most significant of visitors didn't know of it, then it must have been older than three hundred years; then barred one way or another, intentionally or otherwise. One who'd stand to benefit, but not the rest of the county, would have been here: a foreigner.

"*How foreign?*"

"Should I disturb you?" said a voice, not her own. Her eyes shut and she deflated. The drums faded, the world calmed, the shining on armour was of scythes once more. "You seem vexed. More than you should be, rather," the pleasant knight corrected.

"Shouldn't you be resting?" Kate said, turning. Oh, but he was *strong*. There was colour in him again.

"I'll be fine. My physician is too protective by half, the lovely lady. She forgets that I'll get cramp again if I sit around waiting for that damn fool to sober."

"Ah. That'd be it. I was just thinking about your friend from Mūrac."

"Haarjo." Edwin's flirtatiousness turned stern and rigid, as if remembering this was somehow proper around her.

The Voice of Kings

Kate ran to the rocky tor before the chasm, hopping up its steps till she was at its peak, and there could look down on the valley. She saw the knight make to protest but that, too, was just a turn, so then he watched curiously, before taking a place at her side, tossing a temporary walking stick into the chasm.

"You didn't get to know him at all before you ran off?"

"At best, I learned him at first sight if I think about it. I went to fetch him from his vessel on Hemryyn River. He wasn't on a Mūraci boat, but he'd arranged some mountain fishing boat to look like his own: a bit over the top it was. Even his men looked embarrassed as they took to the jetty. Pompous bastard... Excuse me."

"Mm?" she said distractedly. "Not at all. Think nothing of it."

Think of something else. If only it wasn't thought of Captain Olswalt that came next.

So it was again, when out the back of the house and out of earshot of the allegedly corrupt Watch captain, Kate walked beside her mother and Sir Edwin, with whom she was compelled to lay her trust, growing day by day, and in doing so, she believed every part of his story. Her mother had been necessarily sceptical where she had not, and while she now gave him the benefit of the doubt, she was not quiet in her dismay at the knight's insistence to not send warning to her sons. Between them Kate walked, to quell her insecurities that it might somehow make them more agreeable, and was slightly ahead of them so that she led them on and on; perhaps to the church where her mother would be calmer, as her legs wanted to carry her forward for as long as this conversation was to continue. It made her feel better, somehow, having some motion, getting her blood moving. One important thing to remember was that her mother had certainly noticed what she was trying to do, which was fine until she would inevitably bring the subject up later. Though Kate could not work out how, she apparently showed her intentions to her mother with a sign above her head when she was nervous.

"I strongly suggest you interrogate him next time he wakes, whether he's ready or not," her mother said sternly. "For every day that we wait, the chances rise for my sons being in peril. I give it until tomorrow and then I will go after them myself."

"As you say. I can't stop you," Edwin said defensively, desperately, with a wave of a hand. "I should also remind you, however, that it is highly unlikely Olswalt or his employers even know Isaac has left his home town."

"That still leaves a margin of error. Until you can prove it is impossible for them to have found out, I will continue to argue this point for as long as it takes. I want to know what my son was doing that could possibly catch the attention of murdering conspirators. You ask a great deal of me. One of the first things you said to me after waking from your coma was that my son had not only endangered himself with his obsession, but that it all comes down to that...damn incident in the mine all those years ago," she cried out in a sudden dismayed burst of anger, still managing to correct her strong language before it could be said. "I thought he'd lost interest in that long ago. And then you ask me not to do anything about it."

Kate noticed, as she strained to make the most out of their conversation, that her mother flitted momentarily to her father's tone a few times, as she sometimes did when she was passionate or otherwise flustered about something. She was sure it wasn't her imagination. They'd even swapped a few character traits, over the years: she was sure of that too, as they must have really worn off on one another. Her father now took closer to the stance of a realist, while it was her mother who did the motivating. He was still a visionary at heart: it would take a lot to change that, but he pretended not to be. It was her mother's job to convince him he was now, not the other way around.

"I will question him today," Edwin reassured them both again. "You're right. I can't keep putting it off. It's not an ideal situation, but the Watch may even return as early as today for my arrest, so I must make it quick."

"So you *are* turning yourself in?" her mother replied, positively disappointed.

"Eventually," Edwin said thoughtfully, gazing into the distance. "I wouldn't word it like that though."

"Just be sure that whatever you choose to do, it doesn't implicate my family in any way."

Her harsh tone made Kate cringe. It always made her wince. It could be chalked up to lack of sleep in this case. In fact, both Kate and her mother sported dark bags under their eyes. It surprised even her how many possible scenarios could be exhausted in the imagination before her body finally gave in to sleep. It was getting better now, at least. One could only lose so much sleep for so long until their body forces them to comply with its needs, regardless of whether the mind was fighting it, even in despair.

"I will assure you again, and a thousand times more if I have to, that my intentions are genuinely as I have stated them: to help your family as best I can and expose the people who crave the information your son carries with him so innocently. Not to mention I've already chosen a side now. There's no going back from that," he added with a hint of regret.

His tone rang with desperation, and that same paranoia flashed across his face that she had grown familiar with. Most subduing of all, his fear carried a deep shame that filled him up for a split second, which caused him to close his eyes, as if he could shut the world out if he couldn't see it. This, too, she recognised. She had seen him at his most vulnerable and clueless, and in a strange way, it was of some comfort to think that she was starting to know him; especially strange at times like this. She thought, perhaps, he had considered running from all this madness with his tail between his legs, and convincing himself that it wasn't his business anyway.

She cringed. It was a theory that threatened to engulf her soul in this dark time. She'd latched onto him for hope: an object of hero worship that she hated to see disrupted.

The Voice of Kings

"It's possible to get to Melphor and back in eight days?" Kate asked, determined to be involved in whatever way she could. Thinking made her too melancholy.

"Eight days and several hours," Edwin corrected. "They could be here before midnight, I think, even having to lug a carriage on the return trip. Especially if the Count was informed. He can be quite..."

"...impatient," Mother finished for him.

"Yes. Sorry I'm so predictable. I must be repeating myself too much," he said, winking at Kate to lighten the pressure any way he could. "But yes, you're correct. This is why I can't go back yet. Even if he believes me, there's a good chance he'll just have Olswalt interrogated and executed, and it could negate everything I've done so far. I had the...I warned you of the situation, where others wouldn't," he said wonkily, hesitating to credit his actions with the word 'courage'.

"I don't mean to insult you. I appreciate what you did could have you executed if bastards like the ones you've described to me would truly seek to harm my Isaac. I've been lacking in sleep lately, as I'm sure you can understand."

"Oh, I understand full well. It's just that when I question the captain, he'll be...well, that will be it. There'll be no going back. If I do it wrong, I can't just hit a reset lever. He'll know my tactics. He'll resist better and better with every interrogation."

He sighed and looked wide-eyed at Kate, afraid again, scratching his near-bald scalp nervously. It was obvious what he would ask her, and now that it came to it, it was so bizarre, to think that she was being consulted as if she were a sagely doctor with years of experience. It felt like having power, and it didn't feel good.

"I will talk to him now, with your permission. Do you think he will be well enough to answer me coherently?"

"I have no love for him," Kate found herself saying in stark contrast to the question posed. "I'm no expert, obviously, but...do what you have to do, I suppose. My brothers deserve no less. But please, don't torture him," she cried out suddenly, eyes wide in fear, almost crying at the thought. "I couldn't bear to see that, having given you permission to question him. I've heard it said that torture makes the victim say only what he thinks wants to be heard. Is there any truth in that?"

Never having considered it before, she found herself desperately wishing it to be true. If Edwin were to tell her torture could be reliable under certain or, indeed, under *any* circumstances, she may yet find herself condoning the act, to her horror.

"I've no doubt. Don't fret, at any rate, Miss Brodie," he replied with clear approval at her resolve. "I had no intention of doing such vile things. Others at Melphor may do it, but my father continues to do his best to ingrain his moral code into my very soul."

"Good then, I suppose. Do as you will with him. If you fail, we'll just have to leave, as my mother said."

A Dream of a Dream

"I don't know if I'd take you," her mother said suddenly. "It could be dangerous."

"I know," was all Kate could say in return.

It was a stupid thing to say in the first place. She had often found herself saying things she would consider out of her character over the past few days. On the day of Edwin's awakening, she recalled describing healing him like waking from a dream, but now she felt she'd only been transplanted into another, more twisted dream, and longed for the dull reality of what already seemed like such a very long time ago: a dream of the mundane. The stress was rather too much for her to comprehend.

Sir Edwin attempted to take the lead as they turned around to stride back to the house, but her mother took over, moving even faster out of some obligation she, no doubt, felt to be at the forefront of any effort to save her sons from any and all the horrible fates she'd imagined could come to pass. Kate realised, seeing this, that half of what she feared now was responsibility. If Edwin failed, she would blame herself. *Don't ever put me on the spot again, you bastard*, she thought: a thought whisked away by the gentle nature that had nurtured her into who she was, and she was left to wallow in her thoughts of what she would do if her mother left; whether she would have the courage to insist on going with her, as she prayed for.

"You do have the credentials for this?" Mother whispered to him.

"I've interrogated people before. You'll just have to trust me."

"Don't worry. I wouldn't have stopped you if you'd said no," she replied with a wry and sad smile at admitting her desperation.

People nearby stopped to look and make their opinions known through their silence as they entered the house bearing grave expressions of trepidation and distress. It was fortunate, at least, that while her father had no official power, he was well respected, and by extension, his wife was trusted also, enough to stop them contacting the authorities, or even plastering her with derogatory terms behind her back and whispering conspiracy theories of their own. If lovely Gèyll Brodie said there was a top secret reason for holding captive an injured Watch captain in her house, there probably was.

Kate glared at the closed door beyond the sitting room, behind which the captain resided. Her house had quickly become the hub of her strange new dream, ever warping into something she did not recognise. She saw at the right side of the house, through the open doorway to her parent's bedroom, her father's work study: another attachment to the house built around the time she was born, as far as she could tell. It was empty, and his equipment gathered dust: a poignant sight really, especially now, when every little thing could push one emotion or another to an extreme.

It was Lucian's room they stopped beside, where just before entering, Edwin, rather predictably, showed second thoughts and ushered them aside to make a point he had otherwise forgotten in that scrambled but brilliant head of his.

"You'll want to watch, I expect," Edwin said.

"Obviously," Kate's mother replied, looking for suspicious activity from the mysterious Melphorian knight. "I don't see a problem with that."

"No, you misunderstand! It would be disrespectful, and even suspect, of me to ask you to leave. I mean only that you should stay out of his sight, and do not interrupt me either. That way it's just me and him. If you please."

Her mother nodded, patting his arm to diffuse any hard feelings that might seem to have developed, and drew up an armchair close to Lucian's room, where she sat with patience no one could have asked from her. Kate did the same, situating herself beside her mother. Sir Edwin entered the room and it was as good as begun, tenser an experience than she could have imagined.

~

The captain woke, as he had done more times than he could count over the past few days in his state of fever, and the sun shone on his face like a hundred torches lit around after a night spent in a dark cave. On his face, beads of cold sweat dripped sluggishly down his cheeks, giving him the natural urge to wipe a hand across his face. As with every time he'd woken from his nightmares before, he seemed not to know who he was or why he couldn't move, desperately tugging at his limbs to break from their cruel bonds. Then he spotted the ropes tying his ankles and wrists to the bed and his confusion was laden with rage, and regret that he had shown fear in case anyone was watching. The pain in his left hand returned like a hammer dropped on it, increasing tenfold as he tried in vain to curl his hand into a fist. There was a certain point where he gave up, as if half his muscles had been stripped out and replaced with unflinching iron.

He quelled his grunts of anguish upon spotting the man sitting to his right, staring almost unblinkingly at him, calm and collected with his fingers interlinking in his lap, squirming in a combination of reluctance and impatience.

"Son of a whore," the captain croaked without thinking about what his choice of words might do for him. He paused for thought. "How long have you been watching me?"

"Hello Elias. You're going to answer a few questions."

"Like hell I will. I've done nothing wrong. I'll answer to the Count if it comes to it."

"You have a lot to answer for, though," Edwin said shakily, as if influenced by the blatant nervousness of the young woman out of the corner of his eye. He regained control. "You'll answer to me as you would the gods. It's a matter of life and death, you see. More than one life," he forced himself to say. "But then I imagine you know what I'm talking about already."

"Get to the point then."

"Take me back to the day you were asked, or *you* asked, gods forbid, to participate in the scheme revolving around a certain mine in this area," Edwin proceeded cautiously so as not to provide the captain with any information he might not know. "Or perhaps you were blackmailed. In which case, I strongly advise that Count Andrews will inflict on you a world of hell, just as your employers can, and likewise, provide protection if you have been wronged."

"Usually in an interrogation, you should explain how you've come to your conclusions, or you're not going to get a straight answer."

"I hardly think..." Edwin spat in anger. He sat back in his chair. "What do you know about Caedor mine?"

"I don't know anything about that."

Edwin clenched a fist. In the sitting room, Kate was growing ever restless at the captain's antics, and Gèyll appeared positively disgusted though did not display her emotions too haughtily. Rather remarkably, she was always setting an example, Edwin had observed, even in dire times such as these.

Kate smiled as best she could when Edwin glanced at her. Most likely, she would not if she knew what he was thinking: if only resorting to violence was so frighteningly easy as he'd once believed. He recalled that unhappy time when he'd tortured a man: the agony expressed on the poor man's face had been so horrific to Edwin that it was like looking into a mirror, and he had imagined himself on that infamous table in the dungeons. He could still see the confusion on the faces of the men around him as he refused to continue, as if he was some petty child. How had he got there? A question he had not dared to ask his sole defender since the event. Such would mean having to think about it.

Despite that, violence would be easy, once his anger was controlled and he could forget about that event until it, inevitably, came back to taunt and haunt him later. That was by far the scariest part. Theoretically, he could grab one of the man's fingers right now and twist it far beyond its designated reach, and maybe that would get him to talk, but Kate brought him down to earth. It made him sick to even think about it while she watched. It occurred to him, in this sobering moment, that it probably wouldn't make a very good case for him if the captain of the Watch Patrol turned up at Melphor with more bruises and broken bones. The long grind it was then.

"But the thing is, I know you do, because if you think back to when I put that hole in your hand, I explained why I already know you're in on it. Or am I to take it you're just a minion in all this, clueless to the motives of your master's orders? That won't save you when you're on your knees in court before the Count's judgement."

"I see. That's just your opinion though."

"The Count's opinion too. He will hold it more strongly than I." Edwin steepled his fingers. "I spoke to Isaac, and the message I got was that you might be in on...whatever it is that's going on."

The Voice of Kings

Elias twitched. It might have been more apparent if he weren't tied down. Belief in that could be a fine thing. He needed some avenue to pursue. The longer this dragged on, the more nervous he'd become.

"There," Edwin cried out triumphantly, to mock him for him for his twitch, almost enjoying himself. "Don't look so surprised, of course I know who you're looking for. I didn't come to this town just to hide from my duties."

"You can't prove anything. All I know is that Isaac has been asking for a lot of information, and that was official information I received from Melphor. It raised a few eyebrows, but he wasn't doing anything illegal."

"Not a chance. The Watch Patrol isn't privy to investigations carried out by Melphor officials unless necessary to the way they function, or if they are required to make an arrest. I think I would know, by the way, being a member of the Count's inner sanctum, if such an investigation were to be undertaken."

"It's so trivial, I don't see why you would," the captain scoffed, still refusing to look his interrogator in the eyes. "You don't know as much as you think you do. You think that, because you answer directly to the Count, nothing gets by you. That's arrogance, plain and simple. The arrogance I'd expect from a young man given so much power."

Edwin breathed deeply and, with his paranoia returning like a recurring illness, couldn't help but flick his eyes back and forth to the sitting room, as if pleading for some direction from his hopeful spectators.

"You can't even read," Edwin snapped, leaning forward in restless anticipation.

"I can read well enough. What does that even..."

"The fact that you sought to defend yourself so readily on something so trivial, in the circumstances, only further indicates that you think it *is* important. And I've seen you, poring over letters and billboards like they're written in code. I'm sure you can read to some extent, but no one's going to send you written messages if they can help it. So, I imagine you must have met your employer, or otherwise an affiliate. The Mūraci man staying in Melphor, perhaps."

"You're still working on the assumption that I am guilty," Elias said snidely, content to stare at the ceiling. Or so the pretentious oaf would have him believe. *You will answer to me.* "You have evidence, not proof, and I shouldn't think you'll resort to torture, being so vain, and dare I say, dainty, so you won't be getting a confession."

~

Kate's mother was already devising how she would interrupt the interrogation, as she was certain it would soon become appropriate. There was a time when she would need more pressure and a different perspective; this she knew, even having never witnessed such a scene. Kate stopped biting her lips long enough to display interest in her mother's express resolve.

A Dream of a Dream

"What is it? You're not thinking of interrupting, are you?" she whispered.

"I'll gladly give Sir Edwin a few minutes more, but that captain is playing games with him, I know it. It might be prudent to change up the formula."

And so it might, Kate conceded reluctantly. She bit her lower lip again and glanced around the room for some prop she could cling to to help her through the tension. Behind them, there was a low table where drinks were often placed, and she wished now she had a steaming cup of tea to clasp in both hands to counter the coldness that gripped her like a malicious force borne from the icy mists on the desolate hills. In better times, they, as a family, would sometimes, on dreary nights, even miraculously tear themselves away from their own interests to sit around this living room, which had been honed to homely perfection over many years, and simply talk, all the while warmed merrily by the fire. Currently, she couldn't quite focus on any one aspect of the room: so little, in fact, that it might as well have been a blur surrounding Lucian's doorway.

Once again, she felt obligated to contribute, feeling so helpless that she attempted, for all her inexperience, to define the ongoing heated exchange well enough that she could help: a motive she, this time, attributed to her mother's drive.

~

"Consider then," Edwin resumed haughtily, one step away from marching up and around the room like a prison guard, "that my intentions must only be for the most moral and just outcome, as you're right, I will not hurt you. I urge you also to consider, though, that should I be forced to hand you over to the Count, I won't be able to guarantee your comfort. You see, I'm also working on the assumption that, because we are in the Brodie household in good faith, any plea you make of innocence will fall on deaf ears if they so desire it, as this town owes all it has to them and trusts them completely. Most definitely, the witnesses of that little incident at lunch the other day will claim I acted in self-defence."

"A poor bluff," Elias retorted, though now he looked at Edwin. Even from the next room, the uncertainty would be detected in his voice.

"Tell that to Lennord Brodie. He's in high favour with the much-loved Lord Almaric of Aurail. That's not a bluff, it's a fact. And if you can, then swear to him that you do not know the particulars of the incident in Caedor mine, and you will be released. He's quite the judge of character, or so I've heard. If you're truthful, he will know."

"This is ridiculous," Elias snorted.

"What's wrong, running out of steam?" Edwin replied triumphantly, almost sadistically, relishing the upper ground like a conqueror sighting victory, though beneath all that he was deeply relieved and knew it was down to luck. His paranoia kicked him into gear, that the captain might yet snatch this victory from him. "So, let's go back to basics. You may recall me asking how a man like you could end up so depraved. You are very dear to your wife and children, and I believe they think you feel the same. I pray you have been manipulated in some way, or else you're really a wretched creature."

"Enough!" the captain barked, struggling for a hopeless second to break free from his confines, lashing his hands with the frayed rope.

"I suggest you reconsider your position then. I do what I do for the goodwill of the Brodie family and all others who might become affected by this ongoing scheme."

"You're going to get me killed," the captain said grimly, relaxing as he seemed to succumb to the seriousness of the scenario.

Only now did his body finally seem awake, and while it had been asleep, Edwin had pulled a number on him. There were sighs of relief from his hosts: the captain had as good as confessed his involvement. Edwin was so caught up in the moment that he needed the baffled expressions of the two women to remind him that it was not yet time to end this interrogation. He took note though: family was a soft spot for Elias.

"You won't get killed if you cooperate. You should know that I'm your best hope by now. Just think, you're not a knight yet, which is almost unheard of for a Watch Patrol captain. You must have done something to antagonise the Count. Is there some truth in that?"

"If you wish there to be," Elias said bleakly, seeing now that he had allowed the knight to take advantage of him. That was good: let him see exactly what was happening.

"Tell me, Captain," Edwin went on, struggling to refrain from commenting on Elias's manner, "if you have an honest fibre left in you, who is so keen on observing Isaac Brodie? Why did they hire you in particular?"

"I don't even know that. You were right about the diplomat from Mūrac, Haarjo Farelli: he's a spy, but for who I don't know. I won't discuss how they hired me," the captain scowled at Edwin's visual prompt. "It is too shameful to speak of and may put my family in danger."

"I see," Edwin replied slowly, eyeing him warily.

~

Beside Kate, her mother rose swiftly and silently, and hesitated to move into Lucian's room. She must have become fed up with Sir Edwin's nervousness, and this most recent lack of firmness was akin to giving the man a free pass. A bit sudden, Kate thought, to intervene so soon, and perhaps unfair. He seemed to be handling himself well enough for now.

"What are you doing?" Kate said in a hushed and hurried tone.

"Nothing yet. I'm just waiting for the right time to move. Captain Olswalt needs more pressure put on him, I fear," she said with the fiery tongue of a riled mother fighting for her child: a tone that both excited and alarmed Kate.

"What should I do?"

A Dream of a Dream

"You've done enough already," her mother doted, taking her eyes off of Edwin for long enough to provide a comforting, if weak, smile. Apparently it occurred to her mother, every so often, that Kate's recent behaviour was to be encouraged, such as it was. "You can come with me if you like. Just don't say anything unless you absolutely have to."

Kate opted not to stand yet, as her nerves would surely get the better of her if she had to command her legs to stay still. Still she watched, practically hearing the gears straining inside the captain, even as she couldn't see him.

"Why is the mine incident being investigated so thoroughly?" Sir Edwin demanded of him. "What reason is there to believe the rumours are any more than a child's overactive imagination?"

"I don't think you would believe me if I told you."

"Why don't you just tell me anyway? Obviously I already think your employer is insane."

"Very well," Elias said reluctantly, taking in a deep breath. "Whoever is behind this operation seems to think it's linked to some old magic planted on Mura for him and his...ilk to use, I gather. His family, perhaps, I don't know. He knows of what happened in that mine, or at least thinks he does, and attributes it to magic made dormant long ago, to be awoken at some unspecified point, and by near impossible means. He believes he can harness it somehow."

Edwin slowly craned forward, licking his lips in anticipation and glaring a hole through the captain's head. Mother was similarly unimpressed, now creeping towards the door, insofar as she made only the faintest sound while not strictly sneaking or moving in a way which might appear suspicious. Kate hopped off of her chair to follow in her footsteps. This was too intriguing now, and she had to hear the captain's ramblings as clearly as possible, as she dared not to miss one breath. She was sure she hadn't misunderstood him, but he had made little sense.

"What you're describing is folklore. What bearing does it have in modern times to a grown man? A grown man who has organised a conspiracy, no less, built on stolen information from the capital."

"I don't know."

"If it were true though, there is only one Mūraci citizen who could bring that magic to heel: none other than King Alamier. He would have to be mad indeed," Sir Edwin mocked, one side of his mouth curling up in a purely ironic and humourless smile.

"If madness is the driving force, it needn't be the King. It could be any other clever enough to orchestrate such an operation."

"What about the myths then? They detail that none other than those of royal blood may obtain said power, and even only he who governs his country as King, or Emperor, or whatever else is eligible."

The Voice of Kings

"They also state it will only be granted at a specific time of need. What of it? He'll believe what he wants to believe."

"Don't play games with me!" Edwin growled, seemingly restraining his temper before rising abruptly, kicking back his chair and marching to the bed, pointing an accusing finger. "You can be sure I will double check everything you've told me, and if you have lied..."

"I haven't!" Elias protested, folding at what might have been a fist coming his way.

"Seeing as you are so knowledgeable on this subject, why don't you tell me the name of the leader of this conspiracy?"

"I don't know."

"That's not good enough!" Edwin bellowed. "Even if that's true, you're still withholding information; I shouldn't have to suck it from you like blood from a stone. We should have a mutual understanding by now."

"I believe you're asking the wrong types of question," Kate's mother said icily, making her presence known with a swish of her dress and a determined look about her.

While the captain was caught up in the immense confusion that ensued, Kate slipped past to Edwin's other side, as if her entry could go unnoticed, yet for all her perceptions of how she blended into the background, the captain's gaze snapped in her direction like a scared animal weighing up its chances in a fight. She felt a sudden burst of anger staring into his eyes, and diverted her attention elsewhere when it became unbearable: to the quaint world painted in greys and greens in the square window frame. No respite would it give today.

It wasn't right, him occupying Lucian's room like this; she constantly had to remind herself while healing him that to not do so would be just as barbaric as he allegedly was. All of Lucian's belongings, all his work, and the few ornaments which had sat reliably in place around the room as if fixed there, had been tucked away so as not to give her patient even the tiniest of clues as to his location. There was nowhere to look but at the edgy ginger-haired criminal on the bed.

Now that they had met face-to-face, she was flooded with renewed feelings of fear, just as she had been with Edwin, only this time there could be no mistaking him. Where, with Edwin, she had been uncertain of his motives, she now boiled with rage at how a captain of the Watch Patrol could saunter around wearing the facade of honour over his black heart, all the while performing, in knowing ignorance no less, deeds for some fetid and godforsaken cause which, regardless, he must have known could bring about pain and despair. It brought to light a stark truth. He had not yet let slip Isaac's part in all this, and whether his whereabouts were known to the conspirators. She could not have cared less about a lunatic in another country skewing old religious text to his own liking, so long as he kept it to himself. And of all the people, the consequences had fallen on her family, making her care more than she ever knew she did for her sometimes perplexing and irritating brother. Sorely tempted to have her opinion heard, she nonetheless trusted her mother and the time she had deemed opportune to strike on the corrupt captain's fortifications.

"Who are you?" the bewildered Elias asked, before the memories came flooding back to him in a torrent which only threw him into further disarray. From his brief waking minutes here and there, he must have pieced together that the young woman before him, so bland of dress and face, was his begrudging rescuer, and though her innards squirmed, she stayed put.

"My name is Gèyll. And this, here, is my daughter, Kate. She brought you back up to strength, which I should think is more than some others might have done after the way you insulted her."

"In more ways than you can imagine," the kindly knight muttered, calming down. "Next time, you might not be so lucky to have someone so compassionate on hand."

The knight of Melphor took comfort, it appeared to Kate, in her close proximity, perhaps because it was her that had helped him initially. Again, she thought, in the new waking dream that she found herself in, that she was only fooling herself, the trouble being that it was so very hard to deny it when the facts were laid bare. She had noticed it happen on a number of occasions, which later reinforced the notion: less of a hunch and more an unavoidable fact. Whenever Sir Edwin became hot-headed, her being nearby would cool him long enough to find serenity of his own accord. He often appeared ashamed, as if her innocence reminded him of their differences, and it had left him so very contrite more than once.

Still, it wouldn't do to dwell on it while the interrogation was ongoing, though it was an oddity to bear thinking about, as never before had someone reacted to her so strongly in such a short time. Or indeed at all, she considered, her family notwithstanding.

Kate's eyes glazed over in self-defence at Elias's stare, and in attempting to show no fear or any emotion at all, leant back on a finely crafted chest of drawers: a collaborative effort between Lucian and their father, her mind supplied to her in the tension of the moment as an escape.

"Have you been listening in all this time?" Elias said in rising anger. "What's your stake in this affair?!"

"Er, Gèyll is understandably vexed," Edwin offered cautiously, his face contorting as he was unsure what expression to display. "You have gravely offended her also."

"That would be an understatement. No words can adequately describe my abhorrence towards your actions."

"Mistress...Gèyll, a moment please," Edwin fumbled urgently, an idea having crossed him, breathing colour into his strong features.

Her mother hesitated for a short time and then nodded, striding out the door with not a glance more at the captain. There was certainly the temptation to shoot him a deathly glare, though it would perhaps have been overkill. Edwin followed her, and after some deliberation, Kate, too, went with them, also not looking at Elias, though in her case it was not for effect. The three of them gathered round conspiratorially in one corner of the living room, hunched and wearing dark frowns that were scarcely lit by the dull rays of the sun through the window, and each cast shadows over one another, as if they wished not to be identified by outsiders.

"There's a problem?" Kate's mother whispered ponderously, mulling the words over as she spoke them.

"I believe you may have your answer as to whether they know of Isaac's relocation. The answer being no," he added at her and Kate's wide-eyed, yet impatient, anticipation.

"How can you know that?" Kate asked, looking between the two of them.

"I believe Sir Edwin is referring to the captain not acknowledging Isaac's disappearance when he lied about having spoken to him," Mother said equally as sluggishly and gently, as if not wishing to disturb the foundations of his logic, just as she caressed the soil beneath her when planting flowers. This being so, she was openly and unashamedly not convinced at this logic.

"That, yes. That, and I mentioned his name more than once, and not even his face gave away the smallest inkling that he knew of Isaac's whereabouts. He is an outspoken man; very opinionated. If he was aware of the truth, I think he would *want* to retaliate and call me a liar if he thought I was. With only the humblest respect for your situation, ma'am," Edwin rushed out, rubbing his hands as if washing them of all misconstrued intent. "I don't expect you to lie down and accept that verdict without unequivocal proof."

"Why would you think that at all though? Surely if he is only an underling in this operation, he would not know everything."

"No, but he is an agent, and agents will know information before their employers do. That is their purpose, after all: to discover things of interest and relay that information. Look, I just wanted to caution you to employ discretion. Allude to Isaac if you must, but don't let him know he is not here, as we may yet have to send him back to Melphor soon enough, where he will be free to spread whatever lies to the Count that he's concocted on the journey there."

"You raise a good point. Thank you, Sir," she managed, to Kate's relief, glad to see the kindness of her mother shine through at a time where she purposely covered all that up.

They silently filed back into Lucian's room, resuming their positions more or less exactly as they had left them. Her mother stroked back her brown hair, as if seeking to look presentable without any apparent urgency to continue, save for a glint in her eyes that flashed by every so often. She stared at Elias, pained, as if doubting the man, or everything that transpired. It was too late for that, Kate urged without speaking. With the benefit of hindsight, her mother would have made the very same choice regardless, surely.

"How were you hired, Captain Olswalt?" she said. "Who approached you and why?"

"I already told him..."

"I don't believe you. If it were the case, your secret would be safe with us, but I think you're afraid of death for yourself, not your family. Again though, we shall hear it, and then decide if it can be kept secret." She knelt beside the bed. "Isaac Brodie is my son. Your exploits may have endangered him, and I will know the truth of it all. I want to know what was worth you engaging with traitors and madmen that my son's health was so worthless besides," she spat with a menace and ferocity, neither planned nor expected, inevitable as it was, delivered with raw emotion straight from the heart.

"Yes, I am a coward!" Elias replied defensively. "It seems that's what you want to hear. I was approached by Haarjo as he had already discovered me letting off a number of my men for minor law-breaking on countless occasions, something the Count would not see so lightly, and so he decided to blackmail and bribe me."

"A blackmail and a bribe?" Edwin said, raising his eyebrows and tightly crossing his arms. "The threat must have been of pretty poor quality if he had to back it up with a reward."

"It was subtle. He spoke to me of my transgressions and of my family in passing, and I got the message. The bribe kept my mouth shut though, I grant you. I probably could have found a way around it, but the amount of money he was promising was too good to refuse. He said nothing of hurting anyone, Sir."

"Just how petty are you?" her mother said, disgusted, standing up, for none should wish to be so close to him. "You could have arrested him there and then. Or even if you let him go, you could have posted 20 guards at your family's house if you wanted. The blackmail was of no consequence."

"Like I said before, it is shameful!" Elias replied in an outburst that shook Kate where she stood. As bad for him that he had to *say* it as anything else, it occurred to Kate. "But as I said, it was not purely selfish. So much money for my family would mean we'd never have to rely on the court to pull in any great tithe. When the land prospers, the tithe is great. When the tithe is great, my family receives a share. It's rarely great enough for Andrews, wouldn't you know? I'm fed up. And now I have you in my way, because there always has to be someone who thinks they're a godsend. And..."

"And what?" Edwin said.

"It was not a direct influence to me, but...he intrigued me. I found his story compelling. He spoke in great detail of his aim, yet, in hindsight, told me very little at all, as men of his kind often do, I suppose. But he was so very sure, and when I questioned him, he spoke excitedly of his master using the power of the gods, for what I don't know. Maybe he doesn't either. Strangest of all, he said he had no reason to *believe*, as he already knew what he spoke was the truth. I couldn't help but wonder if there was something to it after a while.

Are you saying you wouldn't even be tempted?" the captain said, raising his voice again in a barrage of emotion. He seemed to be losing his mind trying to justify his actions.

"Not in the slightest," the woman looming over him replied with crystal clear honesty. "I respect the gods enough not to tarnish their good names by spreading such drivel. Or my own name, for that matter," she added, unblinking, and with a foul taste in her mouth.

"Speaking of which…" Edwin brought forth energetically. "That name. Any name you heard will do. Save yourself some pain and be out with it."

"I know no other name. Haarjo may have been boyishly enthusiastic, but he was not reckless. He let nothing slip by his tongue that he didn't command."

Kate's mother glared at him contemptuously for what seemed like an age, the room growing musty and dank and unwelcoming in her imagination; a chilly draught from the window made ever more prominent in the midst of her darkening mood, Lucian's room transforming into a hellish apparition by its new resident. Kate could not have denied feeling the experience, much as she'd wish to ignore it. Her mother shook her head, and looked down at the floor in disappointment before leaving. Edwin gave Elias one last cautionary expression to think over before following her, an expression that said, *"You haven't gotten away with anything; we'll be back for more"*, and last of all, Kate remained for a few seconds longer, tempting her nerve by staring him in the eyes as if hoping to prove a point, or perhaps find some hidden meaning within them.

Elias would not, or could not, look directly back. Perhaps he, too, saw in her the innocence he wished to have again, and perhaps, also, he was ashamed to know that she had healed him for want of no reward, he who could not have deserved such tender treatment in her mind. There was a lurching in Kate's stomach, not of pain, just that of her body responding in its own way to further attention drawn to her, surreal and unexplainable, like feeling butterflies when nervous. She considered him a moment more. He might also just have been stubborn and cold not to look at her.

She closed the door behind her and joined Edwin and her mother by the kitchen window on the other side of the house.

"Is he sane?" her mother asked in all seriousness. "How did he ever reach captain rank?"

"I couldn't say. I've never seen him act like that before," Edwin said with an almighty, hopeless shrug. "I never knew of his repeated unlawfulness for that matter."

Kate coughed for attention.

"It might be worth taking into account that he's been mostly asleep for the last eight days, and with a nasty injury, so he might be groggy and not himself. Edwin, you, yourself, were not…you weren't quite there when we spoke by the river."

"Agreed," Edwin said, flashing Kate a cheeky smile in response to her remark. Her mother, too, silently agreed. "We should talk to him again when he's recuperated. In the meantime, we should do all that we can to reach the bottom of this."

A Dream of a Dream

"Are you going to turn yourself in when the Watch Patrol returns?" her mother asked with a dying interest that suggested she knew the answer.

"Hell no, I'm not," Edwin replied, almost cheerful in his enthusiasm. "Not after what I just heard."

A beefy fist rapped on the window three times, and they all jumped, whereupon Henri offered a muted apology. The poor hired hand had been told to knock before entering the house, every time without fail. Showing what wisdom he had, he decided instantly not to get involved in the affairs of his masters, graciously accepting the offer of an extra silver piece and half florin per week before he had been given time even to think of haggling, given the new responsibility he had been burdened with. He entered.

"Am I interrupting something?" Henri said, taking care not to appear resentful in any way.

"Not at all. I think we were just finishing up for now."

It became all too apparent now that Kate was the odd one out here, as her mother turned back and frowned. Kate looked beaten and confused, so much so that her mother smiled sympathetically. For both of them. That was less comforting.

"Are you not feeling well, Kate? You look pale."

"I don't really know," Kate answered without thinking.

"Perhaps you'd like some fresh air. It's perfectly okay, we'll be fine without you for a while."

"Yes, I think that would do me good," Kate said wearily, letting her suppressed exhaustion flow freely now.

Stopping at the doorway only to take in the looks on their faces, almost as if considering apologising, she then stepped out into the open air, so fresh and cool. Watching the clouds move as she slowly walked from her house, she felt herself coming back together. It was going to rain again, and the sooner the better.

For all the blessings nature bestowed upon her to break her free from her woes, in the form of strong, cold gusts which splayed her hair behind and before her, and sunlight blinding her momentarily through gaps in the clouds, she could only focus on what the captain had said. It was absurd of course, she knew that well, but all the same, she couldn't shake those words away. No one in their right mind would go running after a myth like that. Never had she known there to be a detailed account of what one might do with this celestial gift, nor a particular reason cited for the gods' undue generosity of granting their gifts to mortal kings besides the all-purpose hand-waving explanation that they were kings. If magic such as that was real, it was so old that records could not be found of its conception, be it through the forces of nature weathering them away over long eons, or perhaps by the weight of the ocean crushing them on a seabed far, far away, or maybe buried beneath hundreds of tons of rock in a cave on a country beyond the borders of any map. If such a record ever existed.

Instinctively, she fought that thought. She could not bring herself to discount it forever, though couldn't say for why. The sheer wonder in it: that was a strong possibility. Believing it was well enough, surely, as in the past she had wondered if Isaac's encounter with the wall of white steel had been related to the gods, and now uncannily, years later, another person had brought forward this theory, not in passing, but in regards to a serious conspiracy movement. It was all well enough to at least want to believe, but to be more than passive about it was, to her, probably a fool's errand. What Olswalt had recalled was a man going too far in his quest for truth, or rather power, as he apparently already "knew" what he was searching for. These days, the myth was mostly relegated to children's stories, and now as she reflected, she remembered reading some when she was a small child, and that the authors had put a spin on it to make it more exciting, or teach a moral.

When she had been deemed old enough, her father had sat her down on his lap and imparted a lesson: "They're all good stories, aren't they? The important thing, the *most* important thing, to remember is that they're all different. Some have tried to keep a historical edge, others have deliberately fantasised, as is the case with even the most detailed texts I know of. We cannot know if there is truth in it," he had said with a wide smile she now realised she missed, "but neither can we rely on any source available to us thus far."

Ironically, Kate now felt the strongest urge to find the truth of this matter, if only to know for certain that her family would be safe once more. Her pace was hurried at the adrenaline rush of the situation, at dreaming foolish dreams that she would not have the will nor the resources to carry out, of riding away there and then to end it all, and at trying to cobble together a plan or discovering some new angle to present to her mother and Edwin when she inevitably returned to them. It was for this reason that she thought people were giving her puzzled looks, a revelation which startled her at first. *Obviously* they were looking at her, she quickly came to accept. Her mother, and by extension, she, was holding prisoner a supposedly corrupt Watchman. It was time to get used to being noticed.

She thought again she might go to the church for help, not that it helped her greatly the last time, but it was a worth a try and, at the very least, she could leave with no less understanding than when she walked in. Trying to think more realistically, she wondered how they would make money if she and her mother were to leave Caedor for weeks. Their primary source of income without her father's earnings was, firstly, selling vegetables and processed crops, as others seemingly didn't have the knack for it as the Brodies did, or were not fortunate enough to have the money to buy the necessary amount of fertile land. Secondly, they would sell all kinds of things that they made, mostly her father's inventions, as well as the odd dress or other item of clothing that someone was willing to buy. Kate felt grown up all of a sudden, only here it didn't feel as good as she'd imagined, and thus, she felt small again.

The raw, instinctive determination that Edwin's half-dead body riding into town had awoken fought back to get her focused again. Even if she was too inexperienced in life to be of use, she would never forgive herself for not trying.

~

With two chairs positioned to face the kitchen window, Gèyll and Edwin sat drinking steaming cups of tea as Gèyll had silently insisted they do, several times over the past few days, as a way to ease the pressure of an awkward situation. Henri drank his at the dining table with his back to them, though Gèyll watched him briefly to ensure she knew where she stood with the two of them. Henri was tall and dark-haired, a man in his 30s who lived on the other side of town, and the sort of respectable man she could generally rely on to just get on with his assigned duties, and not, it seemed, because he had no morals to tether him down. In that sense, he had honour. Gèyll wondered if she might yet find further use for him, and swiftly banished the idea, for it wouldn't be right to involve him, not unless she was desperate. Then, with only strangers around her, she ultimately felt alone, and had to pull herself together where her husband's presence would normally do just that trick. It was her duty and responsibility. She was the matriarch here, much older and wiser than Sir Edwin, and she wasn't about to leave it to him alone to fix that mess. Be that as it may, Edwin, the other mysterious stranger in her house, at least had a stake in the events that would unfold henceforth.

Gèyll was wearing a dress of her own making, perfectly acceptable, comfortable, and imbued with her subtle flair, if not flashy. However, next to Edwin, donning clothes that weren't his own, ever so slightly ill-fitting, and his shoulders sagging as he contemplated his tribulations, and Henri who was content with his hardy, unimpressive green and brown attire, seemingly reflecting his ambitions, she must have really looked like the master of the house, and she was not going to let that standard slip while Lennord was away.

"Sir Edwin," she started delicately, paying no mind to Henri who must have been listening in. "I think I should tell you that I'm grateful for all that you've done and yet promise to do. It may not appear as such, but you have my thanks."

"I know. I fear you still give me too much credit. All your criticisms and scepticisms have been entirely reasonable, and I suspect you will find more foibles with me, if we get to know one another."

"I have another for you now, come to think of it, though do not be offended. My daughter, Kate, looks up to you more than I at the moment. You are an outsider with a heart of gold to her, and it is here that I need to clear the air between us."

"Indeed, you may be right," Edwin said, adjusting himself to more comfortably embrace what he was sure would follow. "I can't do much about that."

The Voice of Kings

"You can do *something*. Don't encourage it, if nothing else."

"I didn't think I was."

"Inadvertently, probably. Just be conscious of what you say and do, is all I'm asking. Have you noticed her taking a fancy to you?" Edwin nearly spat out his drink, and his paranoid twitch made itself present.

"I don't know. Possibly." He scratched his head. "Probably. But I assure you, Mistress Brodie, I have harboured no profane thoughts about her. If I must be honest," he continued briskly as if he could hide no secrets anyway, "I've been known to bed women of many different...dispositions, personalities, sometimes without regard for those personalities, as my father would be ashamed to hear. No, I digress. Ma'am, your daughter is an extraordinary young woman, but if I did have feelings for her, I would not be so insensitive to let them be known at this difficult time."

"I didn't really doubt you, I just wanted to know what you thought. Your quality is beyond reproach, Sir, just not what she needs, as she thinks she does. Another time, it may be different."

Damn it, she couldn't help herself. Ever she burdened herself with this. She wasn't going to be the woman whose children each ended up alone because she had encouraged them in all but marriage. The townsfolk were willing to forgive oddities like that from her because of Lennord's value, but that was too easy an excuse. Failure unspoken was failure left to live into old age.

Gèyll rose and leaned back against the window so that she could address him more directly, and Henri too, who she had been made aware of when the slight creaking of his boiled leather jacket had occurred during Edwin's admission, a sign of his piquing interest, and now he turned back to the dining table to look into his cup.

"It's okay, Henri, I know you can hear us even when you're not looking at us." He turned round once more.

"I suppose you can," Henri said with a nervous grin, speaking as if to say it as a joke and almost bailing out before he had finished.

"If you so bothered me, I would have sent you away," Gèyll clarified before returning her attention to Edwin. "Your honour and good nature never fails to astound me, so much so that I sometimes wonder if you're even tricking yourself. No one forced you to get involved."

"Begging your pardon, but they did. That snake, Haarjo, forced my hand. Because the truth is, my father told me things I wish he hadn't, from a young age. He is in the Count's favour too, less so these days mind, as a nobleman of sorts. He would tell me of beheadings he'd seen, and of murder aftermaths, of dishonourable men, like his own father who would steal petty amounts of tax money for whatever sordid ends, and of far worse betrayers than him. I don't always see eye to eye with him, but I am grateful for that."

A Dream of a Dream

Edwin's temper rose, his blood seething through his veins in excitement, and finally he was near panting. The pains across his chest were brought to life. From the way he curled up, face reddened, the rest of him might have been whipped by red hot knives. He groaned, clutching his stomach, attempting to cover up his pain and remembering a stark truth that could not be ignored.

"I fear you had the right of it when you said I trick myself. I flung myself into this as I often do. But I want you to know that, on the whole, I don't regret it."

"You have passion. So much passion you don't know when it's safe to stop. It's reckless, but admirable. In that sense, you're a bit similar to Isaac I suppose, and that's a compliment, if you like. There aren't many young men like you around."

Silence enveloped them, that of respect and thoughtfulness, where words were efficiently passed to one another without being spoken. Henri sniffed loudly. If he was uncomfortable, it was of no surprise.

"Henri, you look like you're dying to speak. Tell us what makes you want to work for me. I am, after all, housing a fugitive and a corrupt ranger of the Watch Patrol."

"I'm in it for the money, of course. You pay me quite well."

"You'd be safer elsewhere, a little less gold for a lot more comfort."

"I'll take my chances here. Your husband is a respected member of the community and I'm not breaking my code, as I see it. For the right price, I might consider dusting off my sword if it came to it, provided I was expected only to defend. And I don't want to get involved with the Watch Patrol, let me tell you that. I won't fight defenders of the law."

"Don't you have a family to think of?" Gèyll said, her brow creasing immensely at this declaration.

"Not at the moment. I had a woman not long ago, see. Didn't work out, that."

How deeply, then, had Lucian profiled this man before hiring him? He prided himself on being thorough. Before she had time to properly speculate on this, the front door swung open.

~

Kate had been rejuvenated by her highland air, and with a deep breath, strode through the door, immediately noticing her mother's needless relief. Henri, once present in the conversation, was a part of the background again. Dusk was approaching, and they all, in their separate ways, hurried to think of what next to do before the day's end.

"Are you feeling better?" her mother said.

"Better than I was," Kate replied.

"I've been thinking, actually, about how Edwin spoke of your father's popularity, and now our new acquaintance, Henri, has brought it up again."

"And?" the keen knight said with anticipation.

The Voice of Kings

"I don't quite know yet. I think maybe I could rally some of the townsfolk here, create a bias against Elias when the Watch Patrol returns."

"I very much doubt that."

"I said create a bias, not just make up an old, fantastical story. It would help if they didn't see you lounging around my house. It might give us, or more specifically, you, time to do what needs to be done, to give them reason to arrest him as a precaution, before he starts running something dangerous off his tongue."

Sir Edwin was stone-faced, and rocked back and forth, for some reason expecting her to unveil more of her plan. Being so polite, he remained silent, making certain that she was waiting for his verdict, before nodding and rubbing his hands together, flustered.

"Yes, it's worth a shot, I'd say. You had better work out the particulars soon though. As I say, the Watch could arrive at any minute now. I'd like a good vantage point of the road to see them coming."

"There's Sir Martin's statue," Kate offered eagerly.

"That's not ideal. I need somewhere that's heading out of town; somewhere I can get a good look past the entrance road."

"I can think of a hill which might be suitable. I can show you!" Kate said with a little too much fervour.

Edwin's eyes, wide with expectation, darted to seek her mother for her opinion on the matter, or otherwise seek new advice, for he took great stock in her all of a sudden.

"Yes, okay. Just be careful," she said, though quite what Kate was to be careful of, she did not know.

The door was already swinging open, Edwin briskly pacing away without Kate, despite having not the faintest idea where he was going, and right behind him Kate ran, brandishing a long, black wool and fur coat from a wall hook. It was soft, and in her rare vainer moments, she had admired it in front of a mirror. For all her self-perceived blandness, she felt it succeeded in giving her character, and even a royal edge, she liked to pretend. She would have liked to say she'd made it herself, as it complimented her better than her own dresses. Or rather, that would have been her standard mentality. Today, she could not bring herself to care and was happy just to have a nice, warm coat to defend her from the harsh winds.

Right at that time, Kate wanted Edwin to speak up and reassure her that he knew what he was doing, that everything would be fixed, that he'd tell her exactly how this would come to pass. He was looking for a way to comfort her, she could see that, and she couldn't help but think, *"Go on, keep your mouth shut; let someone else put the effort in"*. Her hand was forced to divinity. Edwin stumbled, and now Kate was his minder once more: she the protector to guide him, he the weak one. It should not have been so. When he was healed, it would not be so.

A Dream of a Dream

"How are you holding up?" Edwin said before she could speak first, as in defiance, she was about to. "You still look tired."

"I'm as good as can be expected, thank you."

"Your mother worries about you."

"Of course she does. I worry about her too," Kate laughed meekly, as it was the truth, but it felt wrong to say it out loud. She stopped laughing at once when she realised she should have questioned him by now. "What did she say about me?"

"Oh, not much. I think she wishes she had more power to sort this mess out, as do you and I, Miss. She just approaches it with a protective attitude, and rightly so. In the short term, she'd like to find a way to ease your troubles. For my money, she's a very wise woman, and a kind and experienced mother too. I have no concerns."

As always, Edwin was extra cautious to outline his own opinion in bold so as not to offend, which didn't annoy Kate; in fact, she quite liked it, knowing where he stood at any given time. It was just that it was also food for thought. He couldn't have acted in that manner before the short-tempered Count Andrews, in whose favour he was, until now, very comfortable.

They steadily began climbing a hill which would take them, ultimately, to an even taller rise affording them a fine view of the road. Wet grass would be a problem, although nothing which didn't come as second nature to her, when the rain started to pick up, and it was drizzling fine, cold beads already, which, for now, did wonders for Kate's awareness, making her yet more awake at the touch of each drop. At the same time, the destination wasn't far and they would hopefully arrive before the rain picked up its pace. It didn't require much effort yet, and so she was free to reflect on Edwin's words with a relatively clear head, and fight to be the woman she needed to be. At the knight's use of the word "troubles" in conjunction to her, she wanted to pity herself, but a new part of her cried out for her to stop and think of Isaac. She couldn't force out self-pity entirely, as it was, strangely, of some comfort, but it wouldn't do to actually speak of it. She would surely feel sick again.

"It's good to know my mother has earned your trust," she settled on. "I am more at ease now, though, now that I know Isaac...my brothers are safer. You brought me despair, and hope as well. In that order, I'm happy to say."

"I see," he laughed. "Good of me."

Before too long, before the rain was pouring, they arrived at the appropriate hill, having completed the journey in silence since Edwin had dropped into deep thought. Kate pointed at the road leading out of town on their left, northwards, and then waved her whole hand across the bumpy landscape. The roadside torches, by likeness of thin iron poles, pitched into the ground with brick bases and sheltered from the elements with curved iron sheets, were ablaze: safety beacons that lit up the road at sparse intervals, stretching away onto other roads until they were indistinguishable orange hues, blurred into the setting sun and warped behind streaking rain. If one looked far enough, there was only darkness where the lines of torches met their ends, as no one was willing to attend them beyond those points. Even the County Watch Patrol only put up lights where they considered it to be especially dangerous.

"Look, there, and there, and there, through the gaps in the hills. If you have a good eye and pay attention, you might see your carriage coming to collect you."

Kate allowed herself to drop like a brick, steadying herself when she reached the ground, and crossed her legs, drawing in the coat collar around her neck and wrapping her arms around her knees.

"You're staying then?" Edwin said edgily, refusing the temptation to sit down also.

"I may as well. And when I go back home, at least there'll be a fire waiting for me."

Just as she said these words, Kate couldn't but think she was being foolish. She could be of no use to anyone here. If nothing else, the fresh air was good. Edwin rubbed his hands together in front of his face and, after doing this for a while, held them in position below his nose, as if praying.

"I do remember that road now," he started slowly, and paused contemplatively between each sentence. "I was barely paying attention when I arrived, but I remember it now. It's like looking back on a dream again. I don't recall where I started to lose consciousness."

He lost touch with himself and stopped speaking, whereupon he took a chance and tore his sight from the landscape and turned to the town proper, and to the pale silhouette of the statue. It was a tiny bit eerie. In his brooding mood, his tone changed.

"It's quite something isn't it?"

"What? Oh, yes."

"I suppose you don't really think about it, do you? It's always there. It looks a peaceful town, I've just realised. Must be nice."

"Most of the time. Do you really hate Melphor so much?" she enquired as empathetically as she could, although probably spoke more flatly than she'd hoped. She began to wish he would just sit down.

"No, no, not at all. Melphor is fine. Never mind me, I was just thinking out loud," he said apologetically.

He focused on the horizon once again and, without thinking, rubbed his scalp with one hand, feeling the chilly winds more prevalently now that his full head of hair had been so thoroughly shortened. Now pacing back and forth, also to stay warm, he inadvertently caused Kate even more discomfort in a silence that was awkward only to her, until she had to speak up.

"You like being vague, don't you?"

"How so?" Edwin replied, stopping dead.

A Dream of a Dream

"When you said Melphor is fine, you sounded like you were in a hurry to get the words out. You've done it before as well."

"Really? I hadn't noticed. Without meaning to sound arrogant, I'd put most of that down to our situation, and my injury has made me feel rather rotten. I'll endeavour to be more self-aware, if it bothers you."

"Don't misunderstand me, I'm not any better," Kate protested quickly, smirking nervously. To Edwin's despair, that made it seem like the whole landscape had frozen at the touch of an icy sadness, perceived far worse than it was. "I was merely curious. Well, I am still curious. I know nothing of your home or Melphor, and I find myself wanting to."

"I'm surprised you don't already know."

Finally, Edwin lowered himself beside Kate, making certain his view of the distant roads was not compromised before relaxing. Kate was to be an amicable and conscientious figure, finding it effortless as she took the time to know him, and though when, just now, he'd seemed to shut her out, he was returning to normal now. She pondered. If she was lustful towards him, she was being very subtle about it, even to herself, and so she felt he could have a personal conversation without the reservations that she had been careful to maintain.

"I can tell you about Melphor, if you really want to know. I can't promise it won't be boring though."

"Go on," she said simply, smiling briefly as a sweet idea struck her. "Tell me as if you were literally going home." Edwin took a deep breath.

"Well, if I were going home, I would have to pass through a long ravine first. It's wide enough for an army to fit through, 10 men abreast at best. After leaving the ravine, I'd enter a clearing, and against the cliff on the other side, there would be Melphor; thin towers of dark, dusty brick, an outer wall much the same and covered all over in loopholes. And to get there, I'd have to traipse up a windy, craggy path of my choice, all of which are supposed to make it almost impenetrable for invading forces but, in truth, it really makes it quite difficult for everyone else as well."

"You're not portraying it in a very good light *now*."

"That's as may be so far. When I pass through the gates, it's so much less...militaristic. It's homely. The houses are a mix of stone and thatching. The streets are cobbled and narrow and, at night, are bathed in the candlelight from the houses on either side. And nothing is spare about it. I don't know if that describes it well to you; I've never described it to anyone, come to think of it. There's never been a need, or at least, not a request...but, somehow, I find it welcoming. The Count, in his pomposity, calls it a city without a hint of irony, which makes me laugh. It is, but he likes to point it out a lot. Generally, good people live there, I have to say. Don't let Captain Olswalt and I give you the wrong impression."

"Please don't joke about that!" Kate pleaded, typically scorning him without the heart or menace to back it up. All the same, Edwin looked serious. He laughed.

"I'm sorry, I meant no offence."

"No, it's okay. Maybe I should be sorry," she sighed, and was relieved to see him wave a hand and smile.

Socially astute she most certainly was not, yet even she could see that Edwin was reflecting on his home life as he stared fixedly on the roads again. On closer inspection, she realised that she had really done very little to provoke him, and it evoked a surprisingly warm feeling within her. She'd asked a simple request, and he had done the rest of the work. If only it was so easy all the time. Could it be?

"Actually, it's usually colder in Melphor than much of the highlands, save for the mountains down south of course. That's something to be grateful for, I expect," he reconciled.

"Mm," Kate uttered to be agreeable, and from then, they settled down into a more relaxed quietness, until such time that Edwin was sure of this fact and sought to round off their conversation.

"Don't refrain from asking more questions if you think it will make you feel better. I'll be happy to provide any help you desire. I hope I *have* been of help."

"You have, don't worry about that. I hope I have as well," she said shyly.

"I see."

The knight of Melphor, who was becoming, to Kate's mounting satisfaction, less ambiguous all the time, gave her a cursory glance, one of surprise and, soon after that, respect in the form of a dignified nod. He had figured her out more swiftly than she'd given him credit for.

At least now with that settled, she could wait for a carriage that might not arrive that night with the warm feeling in her heart that she had made another positive impact. This was all very well until something rattled past the gap between two hills, and her brain, which was half asleep from being subjected to the simple boredom of being so still in the rain and the cold dusk light for uncounted minutes, thawed and panicked, as she knew that, if this was the time that they'd come to cart Sir Edwin away for the Count's judgement, she would have to act. She struggled to get her thoughts in order and to organise her plan of action, and in the heat of the moment, leapt to her feet at much the same time as Edwin.

"Is that the one?" Edwin said.

"I don't know," Kate replied honestly.

"I believe it must be. Look closely if you can, at the riders on either side. Their clothes shine. Armour. And there, the falcon. I must take my leave already then," he sighed despairingly, and turned quickly to go.

"Wait!" Kate wailed in confusion. "Go where?"

"Well away from here, I'm sorry to say. It's the only intelligent thing to do."

"That won't be necessary! I know these hills better than any Watchman. I could show you hiding places where they'll never find you."

"Oh, Kate, I fear I've been unclear. It's not a matter of whether I can hide, but whether I should and, sadly, I think not. I should leave now and get a head start on the Watch. I want to see where they go, see if any of them assist their captain in any suspicious manner. Maybe I'll get a message to the Count if I can."

The world around Kate became a mess again as she attempted to decipher this most unexpected turn. In the end, it served to lay bare her reliance on Edwin for support for everything; a sobering fact for which she had no present reaction to greet.

"I should really, shouldn't I?" Edwin continued uncertainly, his head lopsided. "Yes, I think I should go. Of course I should."

"How will you track them without being followed? Have you even thought about that?"

"A little. I'll go off the road as much as I can, and pick up their trail at each inn and town. Don't worry, I have no intention of getting mauled again. I'll be careful this time, I promise. Listen, I know you have your doubts and you should hang onto them until every little detail in this affair has been dealt with. Your mother, most of all, won't want to sit around, but give me...give me five days, let's say. Five days, or four at the very least, to report back, and then you can leave for Aurail, or wherever else you want to go, and I'll catch up to you."

"Right," the breathless Kate said, clambering for something more substantial to say. "You'll be in my prayers, along with Isaac and Marcel."

"You're too kind."

For all the expedition they should have been acting in, and for how their hearts pumped against their chests in the heat of the moment, the embrace that followed was more tender and longer lasting than it really should have been; firstly, Kate hoped to give Edwin another emotional memento of his stay in Caedor to keep his distractible body from giving up and running for the hills, to remind him why he'd meddled in the dangerous affairs of others in the first place, and finally for herself, because Kate needed a reminder that she was not just a bystander watching an accident unfold in slow motion before her.

When they stopped hugging one another, they seemed to make up for the lost time at once, with Edwin sprinting away under the grey sky, not the way they had come, but in an arc around the town, to avoid passing near the Brodie house. Kate watched him until he became a silhouette dancing through the downpour, and then looked back to the road where the carriage and its two riders were fast coming into focus between the opening rows of houses outside the main town, as the streaking rain obscured this picture less and less. She turned in an instant and bounded away, lifting the hem of her dress, and as mud flew up and was plastered to her legs, and although she half-slipped over a few times, she kept running until she was close to home, where a small crowd was already gathered outside:

The Voice of Kings

neighbours and family friends among others. The church Advocate was there, and Jyric beside him, who gave Kate a quizzical look as she weaved her way through them all, and Kester Irvyng's parents. The carriage was already there, and events were in motion, but they hadn't been there long enough to stir up an incident. This must have been what her mother had had in mind.

Her mother and the man Kate recognised as the sergeant, Patric Denkyn, were by the entrance, watching Captain Elias Olswalt being escorted to his transport, looking alarmingly more ill than not so very long before. Kate couldn't help but hold her breath when he passed, flinching terribly and sliding back. He didn't see her, though. He had a contemptuous look about him, yet he did not appear to be directing it at anything in particular, too out of touch with reality to really see her. He was pushed into the carriage; a rugged and unremarkable thing which, nonetheless, had seats comfortable enough to effectively transport an injured person. His harness was thrown in with him and then the door was slammed shut, and she could have sworn to faintly hearing a horse being riled some way off, ridden fast away. She loosened up a little.

"You were ordered to keep an eye on Sir Edwin!" the sergeant said to her mother once the captain was safely tucked away.

"He was here recently. I'm afraid I don't know where he is now. If he's run away, it's because he wanted to get away from you. He knew you wouldn't believe that your captain lost his temper so badly. He is under the impression Captain Olswalt is a loose cannon, I think, but apart from that, Sir Edwin felt he was getting too close to the captain's indiscretions with the law, for his liking. That is to say, allowing Watchmen to break the law. I assume you don't know anything about that?"

"You can be sure as hell I don't!" the sergeant rebuked angrily, cocking his head back as he so clearly took offence at her offhanded remark.

"You'll want to look into it though."

"I will watch out for signs of treachery," Patric answered icily. "How do I know you're telling the truth? Because you're right, I don't see my captain lashing out like that."

"I was just telling these good people what happened before you arrived, for one thing." They nodded in unanimous agreement.

"How do I know you didn't lie to them though?"

"I think that would be quite impossible, Sergeant. There were witnesses to Captain Olswalt's attack on Sir Edwin. They've been watching me like a hawk since then. No lie would get past them."

The sergeant was at a loss for words. He looked like he just wanted to turn in for the night, in a nice, warm bed, and let the matter sort itself out in the morning.

A Dream of a Dream

"Your opinion will be taken into consideration," he said begrudgingly, itching to disprove her as quickly as possible. "Don't you dare leave this town. If I can find proof that you've lied to me, I'll be back for a word."

"My family are spread out across Burtal and Mürathneè. If I leave, they'll never find me. I'm not going anywhere."

The sergeant shook his head from side to side, not out of spite or to be condescending, but just generally at the whole debacle. If he was true to his oath, he would be loyal to his captain, and if he, too, was being manipulated in some way, he would do everything in his power to stop the truth getting out. If that was true, the witnesses had acted as shields.

He climbed his horse, huffing like an angry child, and held one arm out before him, yelling for his men to make a move. The evening was alive with wheels rumbling over the path, hooves colliding with cobbles, and rain playing its music on the armour of the Watchmen, and when this could be heard no longer, the crowd dispersed and filed away, knowing from Gèyll's perturbed and thoughtful expression that they would hear no more from her that day.

Soon, Kate found herself in her home again. All was quiet outside. The captain's ominous presence no longer bore down on them, and Edwin's strength and humility no longer graced them. It felt empty again. Henri was there, but he leaned against a wall with his arms crossed, his eyes glazed over, so he might as well have not been present.

"That was very clever of you," Kate congratulated her mother.

"Thank you. That should keep them off our backs for a while."

"What will happen when Elias talks?"

"Don't worry about that. I have a feeling they'll be obliged not to pay him too much credit for the time being. I think he won't be too coherent for a while. Quite a large quantity of ale found its way into his medicine. For the pain."

Kate could only smile at this. Her mother gently drove her, with a hand on her back, to the sitting room, where a roaring fire greeted her and told her that the fur coat was no longer necessary. All too happily, she removed it and threw it over the back of an armchair.

"Where's Edwin?" her mother asked with extraordinary softness, to ease her back into the real world.

"Gone. I think he means to find out if anyone else has been drawn into this scheme."

"Is he coming back?"

"In four or five days, he says. He pleaded for us to hold off leaving until then."

"I feared he might ask so much of us. We needn't stay in the dark though," she considered delicately, brimming with energy that she controlled so gracefully. "We could do our own investigation in nearby towns until then. Or even just sit in an inn, listening for banter."

The Voice of Kings

There was a stirring on the other side of the room; the creaking of a leather coat as Henri adjusted himself for comfort. Or for attention. Her mother pivoted and a sentiment was exchanged. Henri, relaxed, raised his eyebrows and shrugged. He became ever more curious to Kate, though all he would want was more money, no doubt. Her mother was, surely, extremely pleased to have someone with such simple motives yet such commitment with them, just as long as he didn't get any funny ideas about reporting them to the Watch Patrol.

As Kate's gaze returned to the roaring flames curling and spitting up the chimney, mesmerising her, she couldn't help but reflect on the day gone by, and as she skimmed over the craziness of it, one thing in particular caught her attention. It was a silly thing. Still, it would be interesting.

A few minutes later, she was lining a ladder up to a hatch in the ceiling, and climbed to the loft, brandishing a lantern, while her mother watched with interest. Even she had decided that, at that very moment, she may as well humour her daughter's curiosity. Kate crawled through the small space, waving the light about and opening boxes, brushing years of dust away, occasionally spluttering, until she at last came across what she was looking for. It was madness, she thought, but then so was the captain's story. Before grabbing the few relevant books and making to leave, she had a quick flick through the one on top, a picture book, and saw once again that delightful drawing of the gods before five kings, without shadows, all content with each other's presence, about to receive their long-promised gifts.

~

Sir Edwin Meri lay low down in the deepest hours of the night, on a field like a tracker, when the rain had subsided, eyeing the group of Watchmen through the inn window. It had been a gamble to wait for them at the first inn from Caedor, albeit a very sensible one, and had paid off to that degree. Beyond that, he now wondered what he was doing here, lying on the soaked grass in what must have been the early hours of the morning, so far away from the inn that he could barely even make out who was who through the window, let alone determine what was going on.

What he did know was that they were the only ones in the taproom; the only lit candles in the building being those surrounding the four men, with Elias having been put to bed, as if they were partaking in some shady ritual. He knew that they had been sitting there for some time, and their spirits, which had not been so very high to begin with, had dropped immensely. Before, the occasional laugh could be heard from within their group, headed by Patric Denkyn, who was keen to remind them he was their leader, but now they were tired and irritable yet would not go to bed, still hunched over their flasks which they refilled whenever they wanted, leaving a mound of coins on the front desk. He could only speculate as to why they insisted on sitting so sullenly together at this hour, as he could a great many other things. Sick to the bone from the cold which gnawed at him, and bored to the bounds of insanity, he rose and crawled on all fours like a predator through the darkness, so painfully slowly that he shivered even more. Though the sky was black and the only light source was from indoors, they might still detect him should he move too suddenly.

Eventually he reached a shed of some unseen description, from which earlier in the evening he had heard the squawking of birds. If it housed anything else, he didn't care. He was entirely focused on the conversation within. Frustratingly, the voices he could now hear lacked clarity; just incomprehensible murmurs drifting out into the dank night. The conversation stopped briefly, and he distinctly heard a chair being scraped back. A back door swung open, and there was the lurching of armour. The figure stopped, breathing the cool air heavily, strenuously even; a reminder for Edwin to suspend his own.

The Watchman remained. The best Edwin could do was to gently restart his breathing. Tension rife through his tired body, his foot slipped, the wooden boards he was leaning on creaked, and his eyes slammed shut in a moment of shame and loathing. The Watchman's mail murmured as his upper body shifted slightly in his direction, and then all was quiet again. If he strode round the corner of the shed and found Edwin just standing there, he would arrest him without delay. That left only one option.

Edwin sauntered to the opposite of the shed, in a way he hoped would pass as being casual, and appeared on the other side with his hands behind his head, neck craned back, and licking his lips as he couldn't help but take into account the stable to his right. In the worst case scenario, if the man recognised him, he could use the Count's name and his standing alongside it as a shield to evade arrest, with all the luck in the world.

"A little late to be wandering the hills, isn't it?" the Watchman slurred after jumping from shock.

"I couldn't sleep. I thought I'd take a moonlight stroll to ease my pain. It would seem that was too much to ask for as well, alas."

"I've been sitting downstairs for much of the night, and I've not seen a single person come down those stairs. I know I've not seen you at all. You must have been out here for hours."

"Damn right. I really can't sleep."

The ranger swaggered over to him; so he was lacking urgency at least. Not that this could comfort Edwin. The man was sharp with his wits, even while inebriated. Edwin tried to drift towards the stable, as if to make out he didn't know where he was going.

"Wait there a moment," the Watchman said, and inspected the stranger's face, oblivious. "You don't look well. You should come inside."

"I think I'll be off, actually. I may as well. Maybe it will liven me up."

Hastily, Edwin left the bewildered Watchman, swung the wide gate of the paddock open, and strode to his horse without a moment's delay, counting his blessings until he heard the gate swing open again.

The Voice of Kings

"Am I to take it you arrived without any gear? Or did you leave it attached to your horse?"

His tone was not malicious or sarcastic; slurred, but intrigued. Far too intrigued for Edwin's liking. This wasn't going to end well if that man wouldn't shut his mouth.

"I am carrying no luggage but the money I have on me."

"I think you should come back inside with me," the Watchman suggested, nay, demanded. His voice was close now, and his hand grabbed Edwin's arm from behind.

No, Edwin yelled silently at himself, *don't let them see you*. He swirled and, with his free hand, pushed the Watchman away. He was stunned for only a second, his confusion turning to anger as he grabbed his sword. Edwin had anticipated this, landing both hands on the Watchman's as they grabbed the hilt, slamming the sword back into its sheath before it could be drawn even an inch. Suddenly, his mind came alive, and it told him to slam his elbow into the man's throat. If he let the man unsheathe his sword, it was over. He was a dead man.

As with all cases of life-threatening situations, Edwin's body found strength he didn't know he had, thrusting his opponent to the ground and landing a punch on his face as he did so, feeling it coated thinly with blood all of a sudden, even as he struggled to see it spill from the man's nose. The Watchman, too, was all base instincts, shrugging off the strike to his forehead and throwing Edwin from him, elbowing him in the chest as he tried to fight back. The Watchman aimed to elbow him again, this time to the face, but instead stirred the wet, slippery mud and grunted as his elbow connected with the hard ground beneath it. Edwin had rolled from his reach, at the price of his stomach appearing to rip open. He could have sworn he felt each individual thread snapping one by one, and yet still he functioned beyond his normal aptitude, lunging at his shadow of an enemy and swatting, with the back of his fist, a dagger which had been wrenched in desperation from its scabbard, like a lightning bolt.

At first, the hand would not open and it swung at him again, but through sheer luck, he was sure, Edwin found the man's wrist and forced it back into the Watchman, the knife scraping and pinging off his armour and into the night, obscured by the darkness and a moon which refused to reveal itself in full. The Watchman swore, spat into Edwin's face, and landed a punch on him before staggering to his feet, narrowly avoiding the hand that sought to strike at the balance of his legs with an imprecise, lucky jump. Before Edwin could react, he heard the ghastly scraping of leather, and saw, outlined in inky blackness, the sheen of a blade held in high posture. It may have been a warning, or he may have meant to lay a killer blow. Edwin didn't want to find out, desperately scrabbling in the mud and dirt for a weapon.

His fingers clasped around as much wet mud as he could hold and he flung it at the man's face. The sword-wielding shadow staggered back and wiped it from his face with one hard stroke of his hand. It was all the time Edwin needed, now on his feet and circling him, giving him a wide berth. The Watchman held his sword out cautiously, doing the same, surveying him as any good swordsman will do to an opponent they don't yet understand, if they have the opportunity.

A clanging of more mail and swords being drawn could be heard, ringing as the musical accompaniment to his impending defeat. The other three men were charging across the length of the backyard, led by Patric Denkyn who rushed like a devil unleashed. *I can't let him see my face*, Edwin vowed. *He knows who I am.*

Edwin outstretched his arm, releasing a rock he had scooped from the ground on the way up. The Watchmen skipped back, parried the weapon with his forearm with such a dull thud resounding that had him startled at what it was. Already Edwin was unfastening his horse, it being as reckless and crazed as the rest of them were by now, stamping its feet and crying in protest. When its restraint was unfastened, he held on for dear life as it sped away, just managing to right himself on the saddle in time to swerve it directly at the Watchmen, forcing them to jump out of the way and preventing them from cutting the horse's legs to ribbons from the side. The horse swerved again of its own accord, and when it reached the low wooden fence of the paddock, leapt all too eagerly; Edwin was soon leaving his pursuers in the dust. In that moment, he feared for what the sergeant had seen, for one peek from the moon behind the clouds could betray his identity, and though the thought passed, it still gnawed at him.

They may have mounted their own horses to follow him, although Edwin heard nothing of the sort and was not of a mind to listen. As the sweet mercy of battle instincts began to leave him to his pain, he focused all his energy on riding as hard as he could, kicking the horse again and again, even when it seemed he might have gone so far as to have it throw him off, and his thoughts raced for a destination, as he surely needed one. He was forced to wait for the Watchmen at their next rest stop, and try the same again. But damn it, no, they would expect that, and every night from now on. The only solution was to get far ahead of them. To Melphor.

Chapter Fourteen: The Frozen Wars

In a square in the town of Balenhold, there was an old plinth of red brick from the days of the first Emperor, placed there for the Emperor to spread his madness and lies from a slight vantage point and, in doing so, fatten his bloated ego. Now it was a piece of history, albeit one preserved as if it were brand new, just like the rest of the red brick buildings in town, and unlike those old days, it was now, ironically, a platform for the truth to be shouted from, as the King could apparently not abide by his loyal subjects spouting hideous lies, certainly not outright lies, to the plebeians, every day of the week. He was a man who understood that such nonsense would come back to him eventually. *I shall judge that in sweet time*, Isaac decided.

At the front of the crowd, Isaac considered this and came to the conclusion that it was probably true, at least pertaining to all the things the masses cared about in their day-to-day lives, as no society that thrived like this one could do so on the back of rampant dishonesty. He waited alongside his brother for the crier to continue. The crier, draped in green cotton garments, was running a finger down the board on which his parchment was clipped and tapped it triumphantly upon reaching the desired point. He looked up and reached one arm to the crowd.

"In our High Duke's duchy of Santorrent, it has been reported via official channels that 11 people were killed in an incident near the Ardith Peaks by means of burning, the methods of which have *not* yet been discovered," he said, holding an open palm out firmly. "The High Duke himself took the time out from his busy schedule at Valicato to personally convey his deepest sympathies and offer the finest support to resolve the situation in swift course. He reports, on an unrelated note, that groups of riled wild animals have been found in the area also, which he and his men have clarified as having an illness which they are eradicating as I speak. Additionally, he reports that he will be passing through our town on his way to Harth very soon, and will be happy to listen to requests from businesses and governing bodies during his stay."

The town crier nodded to signify the end of the news and leant back against the lamppost behind the plinth to rest while the next inquisitive crowd arranged themselves before him. Isaac and Marcel took their leave, curiously pondering the true meaning of the crier's news, strolling at a relaxed pace across the white brick square. It was modern, unlike the plinth, and this contrast was present throughout the entire town. Old, red towers which once served as forts for the first Emperor during his invasion were now being maintained as Mürathneèan watchtowers, and between them were the remnants of the fort walls and innards. The fort had been bombarded at some point, and the parts of it deemed too damaged to be worth repairing were demolished completely, and so intertwined with these old buildings were new ones of white and grey brick.

Mingled amidst all this were a few buildings older than both of them, from before Emperor Jorin called this land his own, not dissimilar from the most modern additions in that they had been created with the same rock, but they were clearly not as strong, nor were they as beautiful, and the overall effect was that of different periods of time frozen alongside one another.

It was almost like the town was silently mocking that Emperor's work with far superior, sturdier constructions which reflected the bright sunlight well and gave the whole place an open, airy feel. Most impressive of all was how everything coalesced seamlessly, the structures hailing from various eras lending itself a wonder which might have easily made it garish and muddled in the wrong hands. It was the most modern architecture that held that image together; a town drawn out by visionary artists and translated for the real world by masters of the appropriate crafts. White bridges with ornate handrails arched between rooftops above them, and at ground level, the streets had been proportioned with shops and stalls in mind, also considering how the masses act, to avoid congestion, and it had worked perfectly. All of this efficiency came together to say, "if you're looking for Harth, you're travelling in the right direction".

"Do you suppose the newsreader was being entirely honest?" Marcel wondered.

"How do you mean?" Isaac replied, not tearing his eyes away from his surroundings.

"I mean contrary to the normal order of things, the criers here seem very much the same as in Aurail."

"I expect someone in Aurail realised it was a good way of getting information to the public. The difference being that here they actually have experience with distributing information and in Aurail they could just be copying a winning formula in the hopes of having the same effect. Maybe it would become clear if you listened for long enough. Maybe not. Maybe I'm talking rubbish." Isaac stopped to think on this, staring at an intriguing archway leading to the next wide, bustling street as his muse. "Then again, the crier just then, rather coyly, described 11 deaths as an "incident", did he not?"

"Implying intentional, not accidental?"

"Possibly. That said, it's more a fabrication than a lie, to stop people needlessly worrying about a threat that doesn't exist. The truth is still there after all, just not so obvious."

His voice gave a less convincing argument than he'd thought his heart had supplied. Such was politics to him; a curious diversion which he frequently misunderstood, he felt, and disagreed with himself regarding.

Beneath the archway, they walked aimlessly without any real direction or destination in mind, merely observing the daily lives of the inhabitants of Balenhold for unseen benefits that Isaac had insisted would reveal themselves, should they look hard enough. Whether he was referring to his grand endeavour in Harth, Marcel was not privy, and in truth, Isaac didn't know. He expected only to understand when such benefits of enlightenment were already known. It was then that a new realisation dawned.

"Why were you trying to talk like me just now?" he enquired, raising an eyebrow.

"How do you mean?"

"When you asked about the town crier just now, it sounded like something I would say. I'll not decry you for wanting to expand your horizons, mind, but it did sound like you were emulating my speech."

"Did it? How odd. Well, seeing as you ask, I had hoped to deliberately provoke you into saying something interesting on the matter. In that sense, I suppose I was being like you. As for emulating your speech...that wasn't intentional, believe me," he said honestly, holding a hand up as if to physically defend this allegation.

"Ah. I forget that my opinions amuse you. I do quite think you give me too much credit sometimes though," Isaac said with an undercurrent of a serious point.

"I'll remember not to appraise you too heavily in future then," Marcel said wryly.

At this point, they were in the heart of the town, and in the middle of the street there was a gigantic oak tree, walled in at its base with a short barrier, grey with gilded cement: a tree which was here well before the first Emperor had decided he was the gods' chosen one, before Paryn's epiphanies, and before Ylden Parragor was Burtal's capital. At its base there was small plaque of iron, and carved on it was a tiny portion of the town's history: a snippet to be digested with ease and without the reader having to consciously contemplate too much. Isaac was an exception, he liked to think. He was contemplating it.

Apparently the tree had been cut back, and burned, and pelted with arrows in its life, and though the ground around it had been remade several times, all these years later it continued to flourish. Just like Balenhold, and just like Mürathneè, and unlike Burtal, despite the same treatment. What stood out most was that no one walking by was reading the plaque. The closest to such an occurrence was people looking at him and Marcel, as they must have looked like the strangers they were. So the plaque was not intended for the town's residents, who saw this tree every day; it was for outsiders like Isaac. They wanted outsiders to know their history: a history steeped in barbarity and mayhem, leading to them becoming the greatest power ever recorded in the history of the known world, and peaceably so.

"What are you thinking now?" Marcel said, straining. "You have that look about you; you're fascinated by this tree."

"Not the tree; I'm fascinated by what it represents, and when I think about that, a whole load of possibilities open up for me to explore. Someone wanted this tree to inspire images of Mürathneè past and present, and with me it has worked."

"And do you not ever tire of indulging the history and meaning of everything you come across? Isn't that exhausting?"

"If that history, or the meaning of something, is boring, I daresay it becomes very tiresome to force myself to learn more, but then I would have no one to blame but myself if I did that. Something bothering you?"

"No, not really. I was only wondering," Marcel replied edgily.

Isaac's brow creased as he inspected Marcel. It was obvious he was feeling increasingly nervous as they neared Harth, and who could blame him? From what he could tell, the cathedral offered a lifestyle that was so very different than that his brother had led up until now. Isaac was becoming aware that his brother was depending on him for support, though would not say it plainly. That was fine too. What was most amusing was that Marcel seemed to have no intention of changing and was praying that he could get away with being himself, just as long as he performed well in his duties. It was going to be extremely interesting to watch him try, and Isaac was inclined to back him up, even though it was not his world.

It was bizarre, however, to actually think of himself as Marcel's new mentor in life, though this had been niggling for some time now. He was apparently fulfilling the role of older brother more than he had ever tried to, let alone expected to, in that Marcel was taking advice that he didn't even know he'd given.

"Yes, wondering does the mind good, I expect," Isaac said slightly distantly. "Shall we continue?"

A church bell rang a midday tone to interrupt. Marcel snapped his fingers and winced as memories flooded back to perplex him. Apparently he had been genuinely entranced by this town, then.

"I've just remembered, I'd intended to go to the church here to have them send an eagle to Harth for me, to send word of my impending arrival and show my enthusiasm. I forgot to tell you before now."

"It's not a problem. We'll go there now if you wish."

"I may have to spend some talking with the local priest too, about Harth, and theology, and generally express my enthusiasm: that's the problem I foresee. Otherwise he's not likely to have so many good things to say in his letter, correct?" Marcel asked as if hoping to be proven wrong.

"You may be right," Isaac said, shrugging. "That sounds as though it could be exceedingly boring, I might add," he exclaimed smoothly, looking bemused and humoured at once.

"It probably will be. You don't have to come, of course. It's my business."

"Are you certain? I never meant to imply I wouldn't accompany you, if you think it would help."

The Voice of Kings

"No, I think I'll be fine if I go alone. I'm sure you'll find something to do while I'm gone."

"Undoubtedly," Isaac replied with a subtle smirk. "We'll meet back at the square when we're both finished."

Marcel left to follow the tolling of the bell to its source, leaving Isaac stock still, hands in his pockets, staring at the tree. He frowned as images from his previous stream of thought slotted back together and the tree presented unto him yet more ideas to play with. It made one think, this town. Or just Isaac. That would be typical. It evoked memories of his own past, some of which had caused him considerable grief and now were just passages from another time: lessons to learn from.

"Battle Hold", which he'd not heard a single person here say, but knew was the translation of Balenhold, was simultaneously a memorial and a celebration. In addition to everything else that clouded his vision, it made him think also of his poor father slaving away in Aurail, for it occurred to Isaac that Mürathneè was not deliberately keeping Burtal from progress as people liked to believe. The truth was that, by and large, it was just a side effect of their own success at best, or an excuse at worst, and Mürathneèans didn't laugh about it as they still needed the trade from Burtal, but at the same time, were not in a hurry to compromise their thriving economy to help another country. Unless that country was Alassii, if Lucian's past ranting on the King's allegiances were to be believed. At any rate, the competition between Burtal and Mürathneè was very one-sided.

That being so, Burtal did seem to acquire the leftovers from Mürathneè's triumphs, and so, because of these reminders of war all around him, of the Emperor's self-proclaimed War of the Chosen, Isaac was swept away to three years ago, to a more recent skirmish when an organised gang of pirates had become too brash and arrogant. The King had initiated The Purification, whence his legendary holy knight and his men of valour annihilated the pirates with startling efficiency, and sent the stragglers off to Burtal; more an unfortunate collateral effect than an act of aggression towards Burtal. And Caedor had been unlucky enough to bear the presence of them, whilst Isaac had been unlucky enough to be *right there* when the fighting had broken out. He allowed himself to wince and curl his hands into fists as it would do no good to withhold his feelings from himself and, besides, there was no call to impress any eagle-eyed member of the public at that given time.

Perchance he had missed something, he doubled back to the square, hoping to be distracted from his melancholy in swiftness. In the centre of the square, crystal clear water gushed out of the fountain from its fourth tier at the top and cascaded down each level with the same beautiful ferocity of that which he had seen of White Fire Falls: that being only the base of it, admittedly, from a distance. It was four crystal-crafted serpents that sprayed the water from their mouths here, seeming almost more real here than they had in his picture books. Perhaps the sculptor had seen one with his own eyes.

He sighed and inspected the contents of the square again. The fast-paced journey and the magnitude of the world had taken its toll on him, insofar as it could on one as enlightened as he. Marcel too. Yes, integrating himself into the culture of this foreign land was proving to be a challenge worthy of his attention, and he was learning a great deal of interesting details, but for the occasional moment, it all felt oddly hollow, as if it were shameful to be doing so in light of what his quest was. For that he was also ashamed, if only in embarrassment and in his heart, he knew a few days more should not dent his patience, where years without answers had happily flown him by and not weathered him.

His reservations notwithstanding, he, in his unfocused state, felt his mentality lining up with Mürathneè and its culture, unless he was becoming delusional: a consideration he casually and cheerfully regarded. In Harth, he was fairly certain he could fit in as well as any resident, or better, sooner or later. It was just a feeling, but it was a good one, and so, spurred on in winning his internal debate, he sought to make progress on this front. The crier, then, he thought in a flash of inspiration, spotting the man calling out the news to the masses from his stand. It might have been too much to expect to get much of use from him, though all the same, Isaac was compelled to approach him. It was a means to waste time, if nothing else. Wasting time was an important aspect for him, despite the dedication he knew he had for his cause, as, on reflection, he hadn't gotten to where he was now by shutting out the world, spending his whole life hunched over old musty piles of parchment. It just had to be enjoyable time-wasting, obviously.

He waited at the foot of the stand for the crier to finish reading the news again, glancing about absentmindedly as he listened.

"Excuse me, friend," Isaac said cheerily when he'd finished, stepping onto the stand with him without asking, remaining courteous in his manner as he did so. "I have a few questions, if you'll afford me the time."

"Yes?" the town crier replied, surprised. "Make it quick then, if you please."

"You seem like a man who hears and knows a lot of things. Can you tell me how easy it is to acquire information in Harth?"

"It depends what you're looking for," the crier replied expectantly.

"I have an interest in Sèhvorian steel, and other materials that are connected to it, about its usage and where precisely it is found. I wonder if there is a pattern between the kinds of rock it is found buried in, and if there is anything peculiar to take note of. I also have an interest in reading some old naval records." The town crier was understandably puzzled, tapping his board on the open palm of his other hand, wearing a troubled expression as he tried to figure Isaac out.

"What's your ultimate goal, if I might ask?"

The Voice of Kings

"I fear it would take me rather more time than you'll permit me to explain it, and then more time still to justify myself to your liking as not raving insane, so I'll just say it's a personal matter, and I mean no offence when I don't tell you."

"Whatever you say. It's your business," the crier replied with a weak shrug, implying he cared so little as to even properly communicate this fact. "Yes, to answer your question. I'm no expert, but all that you look for should be there. It may be that you'll have to look around for it, and you may have to pay for it, I warn you. Information is currency, apparently."

"And would you say it's easier to find such information in Harth than most other places? Anywhere in Burtal, if you've ever been there?"

Isaac casually circled the town crier until he was standing before the lamppost, and the crier tilted his body around to face him anew. And so, now, only Isaac could see the crowd congregating at the foot of the stand, which would otherwise distract the man to his job.

"Never been there. You're better travelled than me, I'd guess."

"Balenhold, then. Is it easier to acquire information here or in Harth, in a general sense?"

"Well, Harth takes care to preserve and file records more than most other places, Balenhold included. In that sense, yes, it's probably easier to find information there, I suppose."

"Not surprising. One last question, if I may?" Isaac said before the crier was afforded the chance to redirect his attention elsewhere. "Is there some information or records which are prohibited from public viewing in Harth?"

"What are you suggesting?" the crier said darkly, as if the man was referring to the intention of performing illicit activities.

"I'm not suggesting, I'm asking."

"In that case, I would have to say I don't have a clue. I can only guess that the court might want to refrain from releasing some records to the public. Kings have always done that. Our King is less secretive than most, but if it were important for some reason or other to hide some things, he would do it for the good of the realm, I'd think. Now, can I please be allowed to do my job?"

"Instantly. Thank you for your time."

Isaac hopped from the stand and strolled away at a good pace to match his thoughts. All things considered, he had not taken much from this conversation that he didn't already know, other than a reminder, for which he was grateful. The crier had not been taken aback by him as such, just jarred by the fact that he was clearly a foreigner. That was given, although there were ways to counter that, the most obvious of which being how he dressed. He'd resolved to spend as much as he needed on new attire that was befitting of a man of high status, something he'd avoided doing until now, for fear that he would regret it later, noticing attire more regal and reflective of Harth as he journeyed west.

Balenhold was likened enough to Harth, or so it appeared, that he could now prowl the bustling streets for a suit worthy of how he wished to be noticed. The roads meandered between red, and white, and even black where Jorin Llambert had decided to leave old buildings and archways intact, as these were simultaneously beautifully made and had obviously not had a religious slant accompanying them. Having searched with great aplomb for only a short period, Isaac saw that the stalls which were, nonetheless, attracting good business, were not what he was looking for. What he was looking for presented itself grandly with a well kept exterior: an old building in a part of town where the poorer people probably never bothered to go.

The right attire spoke to him almost instantly, and boots, separate from the suit, which he knew would match with it. He spent some minutes in a changing room trying slight alternatives until, before long, one suit clicked with him. A tremendously snug fit and a perfect look for him, he considered as he looked at his distorted image in a mirror, watched with immense suspicion by the shopkeeper and guard; a scrutiny which turned to shock, which pleased Isaac, when he approached the back desk and laid down the asking price in Burtalian gold, and bought a satchel to put them in as well. It was not to be worn until he needed it, so the merchant folded it. Flaunting it before then would be stupid, and require vanity beyond reason. But his family had been poor once, and he was all too happy to show off to those who would remind him of his place.

Isaac strode the way he had come until, by accident, he finally found himself by the very entrance of the town, where the two bronze statues sat, each eight feet tall and depicting proud, elegant kings on their respective thrones, and clasping sceptres in their own distinct ways. He assumed they were the previous rulers of Mürathneè and Alassii, not those of present, though he knew not what King Michael looked like, so couldn't say for sure. If he was correct, the man on the left would be King Christopher of Mürathneè, Michael's father, and on the right, there was King Erenhart Tallastan.

Obviously, if he was right in his assumption, then it was a remembrance of the War of the Distant Kings, which had finished roughly three years before he'd been born. The war had started because of religious and political squabbling which, ultimately, he knew very little about, but what he did know was that, after tens of thousands had died, it turned out to be a misunderstanding. It was so, ironically, named in hindsight because the Kings of Mürathneè and Alassii had had no contact during the war and, after one final battle, had met and soon become good friends, so much so that peace relations were quickly established. It was still a strange name though, he thought as he stood before the two statues, his hands on his hips and his head tilting from one to the other. Surely that described lots of other wars too.

What did make sense, more than ever now, was how Mürathneè had attained such a shining reputation. It was from things like this, a war costing many lives and an unfathomable amount of gold, which this country had somehow turned around and transformed into glorious fortune, while Burtal had had no major conflicts recently and yet still had not the wealth to throw down for its renascent daydreams.

Isaac returned to the square, sullen and thoughtful. He sat on the bottom tier of the fountain to wait for Marcel, switching between optimistic and sceptical about things he could not remember just ten seconds later, becoming increasingly tired and bored, the citizens of Balenhold little more than blurs as he could no longer analyse them. When Marcel finally did arrive, everything shot back into focus and Isaac stood bolt upright.

"How did it go?"

"Well. A little tedious at times, but it went well. I got the desired result."

"Good, good," Isaac said dreamily, reacquainting himself with his surroundings.

"Something wrong?"

"Oh, no, I was just far away back then. Shall we make a move now?"

"I think so."

"Onwards and upwards then."

And, in a few hours, a soft bed to collect my thoughts, and sleep, to which I greatly look forward to, he thought.

~

Deyliath meant kindness. The Deyliath Road was well named, in light of the prior unpleasantness. Upon this straight and gentle road, Lucian Brodie rode alone, drifting into daydream again. If he had only left with his father and brothers, he would not be travelling this foreign land alone, but it would have been selfish to leave Caedor without having found a reliable man of integrity to serve the Brodie household. He was the elder son and so it fell on him to do it, or so he always said. Besides that, he really felt like the oldest son in that Isaac and Marcel were both so naïve, whereas he was sure of the extent of his shortcomings. And while he wished he could have them here to talk to, or rather here for the company as they were just as likely to annoy him as entertain him, he was also worried about what they were doing by themselves now: if they were misspending their money, or had deliberately gone off the track on a whim at Isaac's bidding. And then there was Isaac's peculiar behaviour before leaving Caedor to consider; hopefully he wasn't planning some stupidity.

For want of a change of scenery and an eagerness to be among civilisation again, Lucian dug his heels into his horse and stormed onwards. The Ardith Cliffs had been a challenge, albeit a painful one, but there had been nothing of the sort since then to stop him fading into daydreams, and so now he roared through the countryside in a manner shortly shy of reckless. A short time later, the sight of an old hilltop fortress some distance off his designated path presented itself, one that looked still to be operational and was perhaps the residence of a duke or baron. It drew his eyes from the road for only a short time, but it was long enough to give him cause for alarm when he returned to standard posture. A maddening mass of horses, and bright, brilliant carriages, and flags of gold and green fast snapped into focus before him, until, barely before he could react, he was almost amongst them, skidding the horse to a trot in good time, but silently scolding himself all the same.

One of the rear horsemen, a soldier like all the rest, pulled back alongside Lucian, looking both calm and mildly annoyed, holding a hand up to ward him back.

"Careful there. Are you in such a rush that you don't have time to look where you're going?"

"I can only offer my sincerest apology," Lucian said with a bow.

When he lifted his head, he saw the flags fluttering again, and for a moment all else was blocked out by the swishing of fine cloth so distinct it might have been all around him, and the fluttering of the proud and noble eagle within its shield of sworn defensive loyalty to king and country.

"I recognise your banner," Lucian added fervently. "I have great respect for your Lord Duke and his duchy, of which I have done research on. I meant to cause no alarm."

"I know. Now please, ride on, and give us a wide berth," the guard warned.

"Wait!" a gruff voice commanded from one carriage, the very back one and the most extravagantly made. A small window had been slid half open and a hand protruded, beckoning. "Slow the carriage," he said with a bang of his fist on the roof.

"My Lord?" the same guard said, just as others were a second from asking this also.

"Come along now, stranger," the man from inside said, and pointed to a spot beside the carriage, to where Lucian nervously rode.

"My Lord, I have not checked him for weapons," the guard insisted.

From inside, the man, a soldierly-type with a short, black beard, eyed him suspiciously while remaining restful and subdued. Beside him sat a woman who Lucian could not make out as well as she was cast in shadow, although she looked as well-dressed as he, as did the man opposite who kept to himself.

"I doubt he will stir trouble. He doesn't look the type. If he does, you will of course arrest or slay him before he can succeed," the man said, and Lucian became, at once, extremely conscious of the image he was presenting. "Excuse the rudeness. I am the High Duke of Mürathneè, Dorrin Santorellian."

"My name is Lucian Brodie, my Lord Highness."

An unlooked-for honour, he'd be bound, and he knew not what to say besides that. A Santorellian. *Here.* He could have mentioned how, when reflecting on the visage of the hilltop castle, that this was neither near Valicato, nor anywhere in his duchy at all for that matter, but refrained from doing so at the risk of casting a dark shadow over himself.

"When you spoke of me, you sounded almost excited."

"Distinctly! I live for politics."

The Voice of Kings

"I see. I must confess," the High Duke went on at his own tangent, "I wanted to speak with you because you are Burtalian, that and you have a gentlemanly bearing. I have heard the Emperor is planning real change for Burtal. Can you confirm if there is any truth in this rumour?"

"My father is working with the Emperor as I speak, as an engineer, and I can confirm that the court is abuzz," Lucian replied, still uptight in his reply and posture, an act which was unintentional and appeared not to go unnoticed by the High Duke.

"Really?" was the reply, sweeping aside the issue of Lucian's current mental state. "I wish them the best of luck. Incidentally, where are you going now?"

"I'm headed for Harth, at present. I plan to do my own political research there. It seemed the most appropriate place."

"A wise conclusion, if not a very taxing decision. Just let me give you some advice if you're planning on getting noticed in your homeland. Politics is a messy game. We hold it together in Mürathneè and Harth in particular, but it's not a magic trick as some like to believe. It's through the wisdom and cautions of my brother, the King, and his advisors all working together and watching each other's backs that snakes don't slip through the net. There are those who would seek to get into that line of work for all sorts of depraved reasons. I suspect your Emperor knows this by now, but has found himself entangled in a web. Until *now*, with any luck," the High Duke said with an obligatory bow, facial features still locked firmly in position. "In other words, watch your back."

"I only want to become an ambassador," Lucian defended.

"Matters not a whit. You're playing the same game. Not to discourage you. You do carry yourself the right way, somehow. I could see you as a politician."

"Good or bad, my Lord?"

"How should I know? Perhaps one day, if we meet again, you can show me."

The High Duke banged twice on the roof, and the carriage lurched forward as gracefully as it ever could, the driver speeding up almost as fast as Lucian could spur on his own horse, despite the carriage that had to be pulled. The High Duke held up a finger as a brainwave struck him, and he turned back to Lucian, looking more serious than ever.

"And stay vigilant, Mister Brodie. Trouble's afoot. Something's got the animals fevered. Watch yourself out there."

The window was shut and the High Duke's guards pushed forward into Lucian, forcing him away from the carriage, and stuck close behind him until he could roar ahead and far away. It had been an unusual sort of encounter, and Lucian was not sure what to take from it. He had been told he was politically-minded, or words to that effect, so there was that if nothing else.

A crossroads shot into view, a wonderful sight, and Lucian veered off from the Deyliath Road at the first opportunity, and on to better things.

The Frozen Wars

~

That night, when he had had enough of staring up at the sparkling stars from his inn room balcony, Isaac slept soundly, and he travelled a familiar path. Being that Balenhold refused him entry, he turned back time. Participants of a subdued scene fell in place silently in the kitchen and, at first, without his notice, as if drifting around him as smoke, and when this thought passed through him, they were indeed smoke, and did not fade into their earthly forms but appeared in them just like that, as if they had been there all along. And they had been.

"What would you know about sword fighting?" Isaac said without provocation, without having to think, without his own permission.

"Not much. Just more than you," his father said in a kindly manner.

"We're not encouraging you, of course," his mother added, and then said forcefully, "Are we, Lennord?"

"No, of course not. If you fear for such a thing happening again, you'll do well to appease yourself with some practice fighting, that's all."

It was a stressful time, the fighting with the brigands and the aftermath, and no one in the family very sure of what to say, save for Mother and Father who held everyone together admirably, as their warmth and wisdom had pulled the family together as ever before, and they moved on almost as if it had never happened, but Isaac screamed at them for not knowing better, though his words were stolen and he gurgled, drowning.

"It's highly unlikely, obviously," his father went on. "It's never happened in all my years living here."

"And yet it is proof that it can happen," Lucian, the final participant, contributed more shakily than usual.

"Indeed," Isaac said. "But it would not make me feel better to practise unless the Watch Rangers were more steadfast as well."

"Don't worry about that. I'll call a council with the Watch Patrol when they arrive and we'll sort something out. Lucian will do the same next time he's in Melphor, if only the buggers will listen. You brought this up, though."

"I know, but now I wish I hadn't."

That wasn't the end of the conversation, but he heard and saw no more of it; elsewhere, he and Father delicately swung wooden swords at one another, by Sir Martin's statue, where the ground was level and they would not disturb anyone from town. They moved in a flurry of wood beating relentlessly and dully in a peculiar fashion, as his dream plucked aspects from several training sessions over several days, and here they practised in a void, where all around them was black and the town was not visible, and only his mother and Lucian could see him, watching anxiously. Lucian had already done as much of this as he ever would, and Marcel had little interest in it at the time, later picking up a few tips from Isaac.

The Voice of Kings

His father swung high, never committing to an attack, as the wood was still thick and could do damage if it impacted. Isaac blocked, and then blocked again, this one a low stroke, and fought back, equally apprehensive, feeling the shudder through his fingers and that one dreaded *emotion* lancing through him. It was wrong: it wasn't *like* this, not here. His father was insistent that it was. He goaded him, pelted him with blows that Isaac could only block, for what felt like hours, while he cowered like a snivelling boy. *There is no truth here*, Isaac thought. The humiliation peaked, then Father's sword obscured his view, his own blocking it and racking away on it until there was a loud thud and his father's sword was flung from his hands, bouncing and rolling away. And that was the moment Isaac could be taught no more from him, for he was on fire now. He could practise alone next time, and not be punished. In truth, he had not learned much, as his father had warned him, but he felt better for it all the same, and felt better still to put his wooden sword away for good. Yet he could feel the smoothness across his palms even now, saw the artful spiralling of steel like filigree. When had he last picked it up? He was being told it was long ago, but he doubted it, and when his father came before his sight again, his sword was aloft and he carried an unsettling smile; stuck, pinned by invisible daggers to insinuate joy.

Isaac released his sparring sword, but the manner of his dream was scolding. It remained in his hand, no matter his desperation, and his father practised alone while he waited for his son's petulance to die and realisation to set hard against denial, though Isaac could not admit his need, much less explain it. So he fought his father a very last time to shut up his dream's voice, triumphed, and grounded him.

"Are you hurt?" Isaac asked, rushing to his father as his mother did.

"I'm fine," he chuckled. "No harm done."

"I'm relieved to be done with this," Isaac said, omitting his promise to practise alone. "I feel like a weight has been lifted from me. That doesn't mean I ever want to use those skills."

"Of course you don't. That means you're human," his mother said gently.

"Quite," his father agreed. "Now shall we go home?"

Isaac hid his face from their kindness, terrified, lest they see.

They did go home, and he was cheered in the memory, for in this space he was defanged.

Chapter Fifteen: The Design

The prisoner, Adrian Mortain, lay restlessly, his face pressed against the stone walls of his cell, in shame or mere reticence possibly, as he tried to sleep, his back facing the door which contained a barred window spanning the top portion. Tristan shook his head, scratching his brow, and proceeded to look up and down the hall of the dungeon as if for some inspiration. *Why? Who for? What for? What passion? What reason?* These, the questions that refracted, when touched upon the ears of Mortain, to sorrow and delusion.

"We'll not get any more from him now," Sir Pedrig supplied, his lone companion here. His helm was absent and so his greying hair was visible, much of it being a light brown. His eyes and the wrinkled skin surrounding them showed far more age than the rest of his face, and here one of them squinted in deliberation.

"Not today," Tristan agreed, hopefully.

They remained, as Tristan was still and deep in thought, and Pedrig would not leave without him or his permission. From the next cell over, separated by a thick brick wall jutting out between the two cells as they all were in the dungeon, a prisoner, who must have been previously asleep, moved to the bars on which his fingers gripped. As he opened his mouth and licked his lips in preparation to interject, Sir Pedrig, in a lightning fast movement, unsheathed his sword and banged it against the metal above the man's fingers. He quickly sheathed it again and glared. The man staggered back, almost tripping over his own feet. Pedrig let out a slightly strenuous heave, indicating to Tristan that though his technique was as sharp as his blade, his stamina was not nearly what it was in his youth. Unless he was imagining it. It paid not to jump to conclusions at the shortest provocation: too many other people did.

The man Pedrig had intimidated was one of the guards who'd been arrested from the north of the city, one who had been temporarily locked away where others had been courteously released. There had been all too many deemed unfit for duty, or under suspicion of failing to uphold the law to the best of their abilities, and those men were in cells in this passageway. This could be a further detriment to the policing of the north of the city, Tristan had thought. The Empress thought differently. She was not bothered.

Content that no one was poking their noses into his affairs, Tristan resumed his business, glancing up and down the corridor as he slowly walked in a circle, tapping his fingers together. It was a passageway with a high, vaulted roof, needlessly high really, and from the arched roof more arches jutted down, connected lengthways by wooden rafters, and above the doors at each end, a stone drakeel curled over the thick doorframe of dusty red, like the bricks, old as the castle, as were the iron double doors. Emperor Jorin liked drakeels and their menace, so it was in his prison that he had ordered fierce stone replicas to guard each door, as crude shields of their shells once guarded some of his men.

Through the middle of the wide hall ran a brick wall to prevent opposite prisoners communicating with one another, just as the columns between each cell prevented them from seeing even an outstretched hand of a prisoner situated beside them, assuming they were thin enough to fit an arm through those barred windows in the first place. It was hotter than one would expect of an airy dungeon as well, with candelabras throwing out heat from their merrily burning flames, and from old antique chandeliers which ominously cast their light down at a myriad of angles, and which would soon be replaced with any luck, as even the castle tucked snugly within a protective wall was not infallible from decay.

"What do you think he's hiding?" Tristan said. "I suspect there's a dissonance between the conspiratorial attitude he displayed at the barracks and the act of murder, and then his meek behaviour here."

"Difficult to tell. He's hiding something, for sure. He wouldn't have murdered that soldier in the manner you described without there being more to it. Could it be that you wish more pressure to be put on him?"

"No! That won't be necessary. We'll just have to look deeper into his past. We'll find his weakness that way, mark my words."

"As you wish, my Lord." He sounded relieved.

"No, not just as I wish. You're not a mindless puppet; use your head before I have to give you orders, please."

Tristan tugged, with both hands, the collar of his pristine suit, of greens and reds too ostentatious for this dark place, and nodded at Sir Pedrig to show that his reply had not been a personal attack. Pedrig already knew this and it was what impressed and surprised him the most.

"Apologies, my Lord. I heard the Empress speak very highly of you and your...intelligence, in the council chamber the other day, but still didn't heed her words. I shall have to remember how opinionated you are."

"Tell me, what *is* your opinion on torture then?" Lord Almaric asked, interested.

"In my professional life, my opinion is not usually relevant unless it is imperative to be heard," Sir Pedrig so read his script. There was something almost goading about his prosaic answer that unsettled Tristan. *He is the model of moderation,* Tristan observed, and wondered at his conclusion.

"And if I ask you to tell me your opinion anyway?" Lord Almaric went on.

"I would say... I would avoid violence until it's necessary," Pedrig said uncertainly.

"Good enough," Lord Almaric said warily. "Just as long as you understand when that time is."

The Design

Halfway down the corridor there was a turnoff point, where Tristan now stared, and through a single iron door was a set of torture chambers which made Tristan's skin crawl at the very recollection of their visage. On the way to Adrian's cell on this very day, he saw through the open door that it was as clean as a whistle, thankfully, and without the screams that had once rung up to the rafters so regularly under the reign of lesser rulers, and the instruments of destruction had been locked away in cabinets instead of on display racks, as was the norm once upon a time. This place had been used for far worse in days long past, but still it existed as a temptation, and it was still too much for him. He was aware that it wasn't the only opinion at court, and yet he had remained generally popular himself. He could view that with cynicism or optimism, really.

"The Empress said you like to pose moral questions," Sir Pedrig said to regain his attention.

"Not to be contrary, Sir." Tristan's face was awash with renewed emotion as he remembered the Emperor's words earlier that day, and he was deeply relieved as it was an excuse to leave this place. The dungeon was not a thinker's spot, at any rate. "I think we should be going now. We're going to be late if we don't make a move soon, I think."

The first window on the spiral stairs was a blessing with the fresh air it breathed onto them, strong enough to make the candle flames dance for them. Soon they emerged from the subterranean tunnels into a small but elegant hall, more elegant than it really needed to be as visitors rarely came here, but it was devoid of all stuffiness and unpleasant atmosphere, so at least it was a welcome sight after spending time underground.

"I do wonder if I'm wasting my time with that Mortain lad and all this conspiracy business. It might just end up a waste of my time. It might be something trivial."

"Or not," Sir Pedrig said mildly, with a shrug.

"Quite," Lord Almaric said, perplexed. "That's why I must see it through. Oh, and we must speak to my courier before we leave. It's imperative I have someone sent along to the upper levels, and he doesn't have the necessary pass."

"Your friend from the countryside?"

"Yes," Lord Almaric said, stopping and wiping a finger over his ring without so much as thinking about it.

"You must trust him," Pedrig replied with a curious look that might almost be called a grimace.

"Certainly I do. More than I do most."

~

Hammers fell on iron and steel with an almighty din which brought the barracks' long concourse to life around Lennord, and there was the ubiquitous clashing of weapons amidst them, carried through the wind to him as not nearby was their source, all forming a realisation within him, as it had these past few days, that they were wasting their time, as

The Voice of Kings

only an outsider would consider or comment. With the intense noises of blacksmithing, and mock battle, and whatever else mingled in with that being so consistent in their pitch and occurrence, he was already synching with this environment, which in itself was distressing but better than having them inflict headaches, having his brain throbbing against his skull in protest.

It was all being arranged to his liking. With any luck, there would be no more amateurish hammering finding its way to his ears before long, and they would be working not so independently but together, with clearly outlined goals, and hopefully only in designated areas instead of milling about where there was spare room, where efficiency had been thrown out the window. He hadn't meant to do this, having only started, as he'd predicted, when he corrected that one man on his blacksmithing; now others were coming to him of their own accord, as if he were the only man who could draw a line in the sand or was able to give advice. And from that, he couldn't help but notice and correct the poor efficiency in some areas as it was infuriating and, if he were to work here for long, he would be hurting himself in ignoring the problems of the people he was hesitant to label as colleagues. He was still an outsider and it showed. Not that he had anything particularly against them; he just didn't like the environment or the vague, puzzling military-oriented mission statement he had been presented with, to which he had done his best to act on, having fiddled with the firearms, or taken them apart piece by piece more accurately, and drawn sketchy blueprints for a lighter siege machine, mostly in a haze.

He didn't want that. He wanted to mess around with Sèhvorian steel and the like, work on some theories in peace, have casual conversations with his friend Tristan with the accompaniment of his curious beverages, and go home to his family. As he stood spinning on the spot looking for something to do before heading back to his office, the Mürathneèan captain supposedly hired by the Empress - Westrym? - walked by, wordless and refraining, this time, from giving him a sympathetic smile for his woes, yet nodded rigidly in respect for the help he'd provided thus far. And at that personal gesture, he was reminded that it was difficult not to be involved in the affairs of these people to some extent, as without trying, he had heard names and small talk from them. The man he'd mistakenly advised to correct his hammering technique, the square-jawed Gelfridus, was beneath his shelter, sweat coating his ruddy face, wreathed in smoke as he dipped a glowing hot sword in a bucket of oil. As more smoke collected beneath the roof and writhed about him and his workmates, two of whom Lennord remembered as Roderick and Yaecob, Lennord received some satisfaction at last, to see them working as a unit. Still, it was all rather pointless in the long run, if the reports he'd read were any indication. They didn't need to be making so many swords, least of all rushing them. They weren't going to war any time soon, but he assumed it was a temporary facade because they had nothing better to do.

The Design

"How's your work coming along?" Gelfridus shouted to him as he looked up and saw him staring. "You getting those materials you promised any time soon?"

"I'm working on it," Lennord replied plainly, feeling no need to go into detail.

It was apparent he felt no need to entertain anyone, for a man with a haughty bearing approached, and Lennord only wished he'd go away. His hair cut so finely and his features so practiced in their sincerity, he seemed more an official than a soldier. Wearing a doublet of eminent purple, and a chequered cloak suppressed from the wind only by the strap of a vellum satchel, it could hardly be otherwise. A sigil was emblazoned on the cloak, of red and cloth-of-gold, though damned if Lennord could make it out. Like jammed clockwork, he stopped suddenly before Lennord, expression unmoved. There was something a little jerky about the man, so that when he proffered a hand, Lennord was slightly startled.

"My name is Frederic Comnyys. I am chamberlain of His Majesty's armoury administration, and secretary for the city's funding and management of such pursuits of arms and armour, in aiding those lords who most contribute. I understand you are Mister Brodie."

"I am. Am I going to like this?" Lennord sighed.

Frederic's surety shattered. He was lost. "I couldn't say. I am here for your fitting. For your armour," he prompted. "I hope this isn't a bad time."

"No. I'd forgotten all about that. Excuse my rudeness. Let's get this done."

In truth, he'd assumed the matter would not progress, least of all for Lennord to need armour. He'd assumed, at most, that the matter would be a minor one somehow, despite all evidence to the contrary. Above all else, not one that would require acting and dishonesty. What did he need armour for?

As if the situation would be that simple, Captain Westrym, by Lennord's office, was speaking to the two bodyguards Tristan had left him, and when the captain's senses were pricked, he rounded on Lennord.

"I have changed my mind," the captain said. "I do want to speak to you after all."

"I see," Lennord replied sceptically, taking a measure of him for any clues to an ulterior motive. No such luck; he was too professional to be caught out on anything. "Alright, come on in. I can deal with you both at once. It is Westrym, by the way, isn't it?"

"That it is."

Lennord entered his office, held the door open, and promptly failed to delegate or operate, letting them stand there with him as if expecting him to be a decisive leader. He rubbed his forehead and waved a hand.

"Sit, Captain. Wherever, please. I am sorry; I've been distracted. I'm not accustomed to violence. I see that kind of brutality from time to time, just not enough to desensitise."

The Voice of Kings

"Be grateful," Westrym countered, dropping himself on a chair by the door. "Though, it's that which I wanted to talk to you about. You have a right to hear what little I know. I know it's not what you're used to, and for peace of mind you need my voice."

A voice of contempt. Captain Westrym swished his tongue around his mouth with the same painful expression as nursing a dislodged tooth. It was hard for Lennord to say he liked being near him, but with that being so, when Lennord collapsed into his chair behind his desk, Westrym didn't move any closer. There was a weight which clamped his upper jaw to the lower, his face always dour, yet frequently he managed to overcome that in light of some humanity. It seemed likely someone could touch him to reveal a full range of emotions. That person was not Lennord. Frederic neatly set his satchel on the table in the way of someone keeping a match cord from gunpowder, removing a lectern fastened with parchment and a measuring rule.

"This would be easier," Frederic advised, "if you removed your clothes."

"I..."

Naturally, there was no modesty expected of him, nor should he, as a soldier, care for it. Indeed, as Lennord shot an anxious glance to the opposite chair, the captain had not flinched. The clearer he processed Lennord's reluctance, the worse it would be. But Lennord was feigning being a warrior, at most, not a soldier. To hell with it.

"Your shirt, at least," Frederic beseeched.

So gingerly, Lennord exposed himself thus. He was not poorly built, at least, that he would be too harshly judged, no matter the reality of his fitness. The chamberlain took his arm as if he were a mannequin and set his hand on the table, measuring each digit on each finger and scrawling notes on the parchment.

"It's a fact," Captain Westrym began, "that both of those men were underachievers. They stayed out of the way. Neither had been here long. When I questioned witnesses, I had a picture drawn of two labourers hard at work, before one approaches the other, gets very close, and starts a muted argument."

"I'm not sure this is comforting."

"Well, if it makes a difference to you, I believe the murderer had an established reason. Personally, I find it easier to swallow than a man killing because he is mad. At least then he may ask for forgiveness before he goes to the block or the gallows. He may even offer condolences for your minor suffering. Whether you refuse him or not is not the point. If he does not offer, I will do so, because it is right. Do you understand?" he added sharply.

"Perfectly."

"It would be...pious. Pious," he repeated. "Pious, pious, pious, pious, pious..."

And so he went on, testing the different ways he could say it, tapping his fingers nervously on his cuisses, to the extent that even the unflappable chamberlain, after a time, flicked his eyes up to observe with restrained bemusement, before returning to his work.

The Design

Westrym eventually breathed heavily and reacquainted himself with the room, at such time Lennord was thoroughly hot around the neck. The Empress certainly knew how to pick them. Who could guess her tactics when embroiled in this kind of *eccentricity*?

"I thank you for enduring my episode," Westrym scowled.

"That's alright," Lennord replied, throat choked with phlegm. "I've heard of this affliction."

Don't ask if I can fix it, Lennord pleaded. That would be typical.

The silence was just as bad, the chamberlain's minutiae just as irritating. When he was finished with the right arm, he started on the left hand. Lennord pulled away.

"Is that really necessary?"

"Is this hand an exact mirror? *Exactly?*" Frederic pressed, void of all judgement.

"Fine." Lennord sighed and put the hand back on the desk.

In his want for something to do, Lennord scanned his paperwork, the musket spring on his desk, and more pleasingly, the two buckets of water to his left. Ice was so hard to buy in Caedor, so this was a delight. In both of them, the ice was almost gone. He submerged his hand in the empty one, then through the shimmering rainbows of the other. Parting the water warped the rays to pure white, swirling round the jewel sucking in sunlight at the bottom. Touching it, it gifted him its light, extinguishing every crease on his fingers. Lifting it, warmth flooded into his hands. The infernal things could only be predictable when fire was involved. Elsewise, where was the pattern? Lennord had assumed it would make the water colder. It did sometimes.

"You're one of those inventors, are you?" Westrym said.

"I'd like to be. It's a hard nut to crack."

Westrym was mesmerised by the Sèhvorian crystal, for as long as he allowed himself. Then he just moved on to briefing the mundanity of garrison life. After a time, the captain ended his spiel, apparently offended that he wasn't interesting enough.

"What is it?" he asked.

"You're not an easy man to talk to."

His hard face turned to stone. "You think I'm too miserable?" The whisper of a smile chased across his mouth. "I miss my home."

"Aye. That I understand."

The chamberlain, now kneeling to measure Lennord's feet, put his shoes back on and stood, brushing himself meticulously. Without a word, he packed away his effects and bowed.

"We are finished. I can't say when your armour will be commissioned, though it should only take a day or two for the imperial armoury when it is. Mister Brodie. Captain. Good grace to you."

"Go well," Lennord replied with a cursory nod.

The Voice of Kings

One more curt bow from the chamberlain, and he marched out of the office with the rigidity of a man wearing splints all over his body. Lennord rubbed his eyes, dropped the crystal in the water, and rose to leave. Some fresh air would be handsome. Westrym sprung up for courtesy; never had someone been so severe when holding a door open. When Lennord wrote of him in his next letter to Gèyll, he would have to be careful not to put him across as nervous. He felt that, somehow, it would be dangerously easy, yet untrue.

Tristan's imperial courier danced into the corner of his eye, weaving between luggage and materials being carted about, and he stopped with his hands straight beside him and his chin high before Lennord, surprised at the energy of the place.

"This is a tight operation you're running here, Mister Brodie," he said.

"I hadn't planned to run any operation," Lennord dismissed. "My thanks all the same, Marcus. What news of the investigation do you have?"

"You'll have to ask Lord Almaric that. And any other questions you have. I've been instructed to escort you to the Opera House, if you don't know the way."

"Really?" Lennord said thoughtfully, and submitted with little hesitation. "Lead the way then."

It was quite a relief that Westrym took his leave, and so politely! As they left him, Marcus Baldwin reached into a pocket of his loose robes; loose as they needed to be to accommodate his job, in which he may need to run across the city at a moment's notice. He withdrew a lump of wood smoothly rounded, of dull varnish, and with a clear inscribing of the main castle tower on it, and beneath it, "Lennord".

"You'll need this to enter the higher levels, where Lord Almaric waits for you."

Lennord turned the plate around in his hands, running his fingers over the grain to get a feel for the texture, decidedly unimpressed.

"A strange ceremony. I could make a forgery of this, no problem. What good is this for confirming my identity?"

"It will be useful for one time only, as I understand it, for the benefit of those people invited to higher levels of the Opera House today. If they are to be invited to functions in future, I expect the guards will have to remember their faces, and they will have escorts. I don't believe the personnel could be spared today."

"Do you think it's for show?" Lennord asked with a strained curiosity as he continued to align himself with the minds of those in power. "When I show this to a guard at the stairs, others may see and begin to talk about it amongst themselves. Any interest shown in government affairs is a positive sign in these times, apparently."

"Perhaps. I couldn't say one way or the other," Marcus said, himself surprised at the inventor's undue interest in the affairs of his superiors.

"Lord Almaric has been talking to me about these courtly matters," Lennord affirmed without being asked.

The Design

They saw the Opera House quite some way before they reached it, its slightly domed roof a pale tinted red, protruding from the mass of relatively short houses and shops and imperial buildings; no whorehouses, as this was a respectable area of the city. Atop the roof, Lennord noticed people scuttling about with tools and boxes of what he could only guess from here, precariously piecing the last of it together, not that that was a guarantee it would soon be completed.

"I should leave you here," Marcus said, his words drawing Lennord back, as he had leaned forward and squinted in his intrigue of the great structure, for there was always more to learn. "The route from here is obvious, I promise you, and I have much work to do before the day's end."

"You must," Lennord noted, taken aback that the courier was already raring to go. "I wish you luck if it's all of such importance."

"You needn't say so. All I need is for my legs to carry me and I'll get the job done just fine."

The courier ran nimbly and at a good pace through the crowd in the opposite direction, leaving Lennord to walk the last part of his journey alone. When he arrived at the spiral-cobble square, groups of people encompassing, curiously, the full societal class spectrum talked excitedly and seriously about matters Lennord cared not to listen in on. The opera house before him was exceptionally big, considering its purpose was primarily as a vessel for music. He guessed it was two or three storeys, taking into account that each storey would likely be taller than the average building.

At the grand arched double doors, he showed his lump of wood to one of several hardened guards, and was pointed to a stairwell to the far right of the entrance, at the end of the main corridor which ran lengthways, seemingly across the full length of the building. When he stepped inside, he was bathed in candlelight: a warm orange glow spewing from each wall mounted fixture, covered in a shade which filtered the light to make the room feel warm, combining perfectly with the startling red wallpaper and red and green carpet, which was probably thick enough for soldiers to patrol without having to worry about the pressure of their great boots. But what drew Lennord's attention most of all was the splendid wall mural directly ahead of him: an incredibly detailed painting of Aurail as imagined from a distance, and from a height advantage. It was larger than life, as the real city was not so beautiful as depicted here, and above the castle tower of Harmony, the five gods were hustled together as transparent spectres, with mighty Venlor in the middle as he always was, seemingly standing on the tower with his arms outstretched. It was rare for the gods to be drawn as ghosts, as giants too, as they seemingly were here, but it was not considered blasphemous to do so, and it nicely fit in with the image here, so no one was going to complain. Rather, their motions were so intricate and well-drawn that it was like a story was being told. Or sung. Quite what that was, he couldn't immediately guess, and he now became conscious, for the first time, of many, many voices from the main hall, echoing with fairly impressive clarity, even when straining this far.

He ignored them, as he had to, and paced down the hallway, his footsteps muffled, and as one of two guards held up a hand to ward him off, he flipped out his identity badge, feeling slightly foolish for doing so, and the guards parted.

"You are Lennord...?" one of them added with a sharp twang to his tone.

"Brodie."

"Lord Almaric is on the second floor," the guard directed.

Lennord felt safe in the tight confines of the stairwell, which lead him up 20 steps or so before forcing him to turn a right angle on a landing to continue his ascent. It had royal, or imperial, flavour, not so dissimilar from the castle interior, and indeed, he found it hard to believe it could have been constructed as such without the castle as a reference. As he neared his destination, that familiar and ever welcome pleasant voice could be heard, and sure enough, when he stepped out onto the second floor, Tristan was there, talking to a young member of the City Watch, and judging by his hand movements, was giving him instructions, only to stop upon sighting Lennord. He tapped the Watchman on the shoulder and begged him for his leave.

Now, despite having only met him again a few days ago, Lennord was more pleased to see the immutable fellow than he'd anticipated. Tristan was beaming, and stood patiently with his hands behind his back while Lennord made his way over. The balcony was carpeted but, other than that, was bland, as it had no seats installed yet, except for a line of temporary chairs pushed against one wall. It covered a fairly sizeable area, and ended with a large concave design, the edges of which sprawled along each end of the balcony where only one row of seats would likely fit. This was where Tristan stood, beside a white banister, mostly plain, but finely crafted and of decent material.

"It's good to see you, old chap," Tristan said cheerfully, as if it was the first time in ages that they had seen one another.

"And you, friend, and you."

There was a third person on the second floor with them, right the way across the opposite side of the room. Lennord's brow creased, but quickly his muscles relaxed again as Kester Irvyng's dark, unkempt hair was flung around at the turning of his head. He smiled and held up a hand to acknowledge and greet him, to which Lennord reciprocated. And then Kester was looking away once more, back to the ground floor, and in front of his face, he held his hands in different positions, as if he were a builder and was planning how to make his next move.

"What's he doing here?" Lennord questioned curiously.

"Just to imagine how his orchestra's going to look and sound, I gather. Likewise, to influence his own work when he returns home tonight."

The Design

Tristan folded his arms on the railing and looked out with casual interest to the packed room below. Most prominent were the Emperor and Empress, gliding through the crowd, pausing to talk to people with a mild-mannered and helpful attitude, while their two personal bodyguards drifted behind them, going largely unnoticed as it was in polite society, with people navigating widely around them as if they were pieces of furniture. There were lords mingling down there as well, whom Lennord would be forced to acquaint himself with eventually, but most of all there were plebeians: lots of poor or relatively disadvantaged citizens eagerly conversing with one of a number of advisors. On either side of the room there were pillars, red and white and each comprised of four smaller pillars, or so it was made to appear, curling around one another elegantly and bending at the top into arches which connected all the pillars, partly for show and partly to hold up the concave balcony above, which backed against a full three walls, unlike the balcony higher still, where Tristan and Lennord and Kester stood peering down on everyone else. Around those pillars on the ground floor, in the otherwise wide open corridor, more people crowded about, and it was strangely brighter there, even though the sun could scarcely extend its touch so far.

Because the roof was not complete, chandeliers had not yet been equipped and so candelabra lined the room, but despite that, rays of sunlight broke through the overcast sky to bath them in dull yellow streaks. Lennord gripped one of the arched pillars on the balcony as he leaned over to look directly below; arches designed much the same as those below, only much smaller. Lord Almaric waited patiently still for Lennord's appraisal to be completed.

"What do you think?" Tristan said flatly, so as not to influence Lennord's answer with his own bias. "This is how we're raising awareness of new jobs, and picking up a few ideas of our own, I'm told."

"I think most of these people won't be able to afford to come here when it finally opens. Besides that, it's a good idea to host such an event. Praiseworthy indeed, for a ruler to seek the opinions of his subjects," Lennord spoke with a stiffness that bore his lack of understanding of politics and his unease at discussing it.

"It's true, it's an unusual location to hold such an event," Tristan said edgily. "I didn't choose it myself, nor did I have any say in it for that matter." At these words, Lennord's eyes moved to focus on the Empress: graceful, beautiful, personable, and cunning, and with a wonderful grin worn with expert precision. "It seems to be working out well enough though. The Emperor's taken to it well enough, too."

"How *is* the Emperor today?" Lennord asked, for his well-being was tied to his. He understood this at least.

"He's better, thank you for asking. His illness was one of his own making. His physician told him he's well, and so he is well. The tricky part is keeping him that way. It will be a catastrophe if he slips into depression once more, as he still teeters on so dangerously."

The Voice of Kings

"You have my sympathies. It will all fall on you to make sure that doesn't happen, I suppose."

"I expect so," Tristan said slowly, followed by a snort of laughter, and he turned around to lean backwards now, resting his elbows on the railing.

Across the balcony, Kester Irvyng was getting comfortable on one of the chairs, and he rested a lectern on his lap which he was tapping with a quill thoughtfully, not yet dipped in the pot of ink beside him. Lennord remembered, from what his sons told him, that Kester would find inspiration seemingly at random times, scribbling down a note or two if it was not considered rude in the company he was with. When Lord Almaric spoke again, his interest waned at once and he turned back to Tristan, who had been following his gaze but chose not to comment on Kester further.

"I expect you're wondering why you've been summoned here," Tristan went on, cocking his head to one side to await Lennord's response. Truthfully, it hadn't taken much restraint not to ask; no use caring too early.

"Please tell me."

"The Emperor's going to be giving an address soon, to you and others who've been called upon from across the country. Him too, come to think of it," he added with a tone of wonder, as if surprised by his own memory, and nodded to Kester. "I don't quite know what it will be but I could give a good guess, and I'm sure you could too."

"Are you saying he's brought us all here just for a welcoming speech?"

"You've got the right idea, by my money. More an encouragement speech I would think, than a welcome to settle you all in. People like to know they're not being treated as tools, and an acknowledgement directly from the Emperor and Empress will do just that."

"I half expected it to be something important by the way Marcus put it."

"Well one can hope for something more substantial, but I won't be holding my breath. Never mind about that now, though," Tristan said with a strong, firm wave of a hand. "I wanted to talk to you first."

"About the murder?"

Lennord straightened impeccably in anticipation while Tristan remained relaxed; he couldn't have responded any other way. He was wise beyond his years, as he knew how best to speak with Lennord on the matter.

"In part. Yulian Eliot, his name was," Tristan pronounced delicately, scanning the inventor's face for his reaction: it was one of solemn thanks, and his brow rose and creased to indicate the name was not familiar to him. "He was quite new to the military and had done nothing to stand out from the crowd. Until now of course."

"I see."

"Why didn't you ask any of your new colleagues for his name? Marcus tells me you asked him for it, but you could have done it at any time." Lennord sighed and allowed his eyes to be distracted by the commotion on the ground floor, though his attention was fully on the conversation.

"I only asked in the spur of the moment. It wouldn't have done any good to go asking questions. They don't need a stranger poking his nose in their business, and so I keep my mouth shut lest I insult them. And, I will admit, I didn't want to involve myself with the people around me anyway. I thought it would be simpler that way." His voice betrayed a twang of guilt at this admission, if only because of the time at which he'd said it, as he remained steadfast and did not lower his head away from Tristan.

"Both viable and understandable reasons," Tristan said after allowing the words to settle. "And not without nobility."

"Have you discerned any danger yet?"

"Not yet. I will. The murderer Adrian Mortain remains oddly contrite, and yet has reservations about cooperating, so we have concluded, Sir Pedrig and I," and he nodded to the old soldier who stood by the Emperor with one hand contentedly resting on his sword hilt. "I suspect he's under oath, or gods forbid, fears for his life should he speak, even in our custody. I pray I've diffused the situation for now. Your guards will keep you safe, and yes, I know their stillness can be intimidating," he added with a smirk in pre-emptive response to Lennord's inevitable observation. "Although, from what I hear, you're not letting any of that distract you. You're making quite a mark, I hear."

"Is that so?" Lennord said, amused.

He stopped to consider this, and then walked around Lord Almaric to afford himself a slightly different view of the events down below, and just as he had seen Tristan do, took interest in the lords and ladies, though, for why, his face had not shown, and Lennord could not find much in them to be curious about, being no more important to him than the peasants they were surrounded by. Not that they would agree. A number of them appeared afeared in having to saunter by the gaping class gap, as if it wasn't there.

"All I did was arrange one area of the barracks more efficiently," he said, as if feeling prompted by Tristan's silence and patient face.

"Quite a lot better, I hear."

"Maybe. It's still work in progress, I should tell you. And I have another suggestion, which I thought to consult you with before enacting anything. It's come to my attention, having skimmed through various charters and bills and having walked around the site, that a lot of the men there are not using their time constructively. Swords get made in their masses for no particular reason, for example, and a lot of them are thrown in any containers they can find because there aren't enough designated storage units."

"So we'll have to rearrange their duties even more. It's not a big a problem."

"I still believe that's only a temporary solution. I suggest not secluding the barracks so much. Provide blacksmiths with contracts from around the city, and better training to boot.

The Voice of Kings

And hiring soldiers out as Watchmen in the north of the city where you need more enforcement."

"We do!" Tristan exclaimed suddenly and reservedly, yet showing his enjoyment all the same. "Very astute of you."

"I'm sure there's more that can be done while the workload in the barracks is evenly distributed once more. I'd be...content, to organise it myself, with your permission."

"You have it. I'll have your authority increased on the matter. I...thought you would try to avoid this kind of work, actually, though I expect the Empress wanted you to do as much."

"That's fine by me, until I have the materials and equipment I need. The task portfolio I was left with, as it turns out, was mostly nonsense. Reams of vague supposition and ill understanding of the subject matter, and a terrible idea about making a musket with a match and rope ignition. I bear nothing against the person who wrote it as such, but they shouldn't have been tasked with something they don't understand. I've already started on the appointed designs; I'm just ignoring everything else in the document anyway and drawing blueprints from scratch." Tristan laughed heartily, as most others would scarcely find the mistakes where Lennord, in Tristan's imagination, must have spotted them instantly. The lord licked his lips and tapped on the railing while he considered this revelation.

"I'll look into that. Don't worry, I'll spare you the punishment of having to read another ponderous list of manifests. Next time someone wants you to do something complicated, I'll make sure it's written plainly and leave you to the rest."

Tristan was back to observing the people below in contemplative fashion, like the lord he was, and again it was the lords and ladies of court that he was fixated on. This time, his expression was sure, and he cared not to hide his feelings. Disappointment affected his lively eyes, losing character as they glinted in the firelight, and at the same time, he played with hope. For Lord Almaric, the former could never exist without the latter to keep it in check.

"Your plan will have more benefits than I first realised. It would stamp out any rumours that Aurail prepares for war, and it would get you in the good graces of these noble folk."

"Is there any reason I should care to seek their favour?"

"None whatsoever," Lord Almaric said slyly. "Well, not from a social standpoint, let's put it that way."

"So the court is still infested with some of your least favourite people?" Lennord said without a hint of brazen attitude, for Tristan, if none other here, would not care if he spoke his mind. Now that the subject had been brought up, two or three faces in the swirling mass below shone out to him, as they were ever so vaguely familiar. And he couldn't recall a single name. But he would have to learn them all.

The Design

"Just so. It's mostly the same people, with a few additions and a few absentees, gods rest their souls. And the worst of the lot are still the worst. Still here, and still lickpennies," he proclaimed in that casual way of his that amazingly carried no malevolence. He chuckled through a grin. "We'll fix it though, somehow, eventually. The court will change its roster or they will change themselves."

Struggling to place the face of one middle-aged lord, Lennord nodded firmly but did not turn. Tristan followed his pained gaze and put him out of his misery.

"If you're looking at that thin, proud man with the long brown and burgundy coat, that's Lord Abram Carrick. You met him once or twice if my memory holds up. Though to no great outcome, I'm sure. That stoic wight with the pale hair to his left is Lord Celoden Reid. A little rough round the edges. Has a tendency to let others do his work for him, by busying himself with menial tasks, but when he does work, he does it a little too fervently. I think you met him too, but again I doubt he made much of an impression. Ah, and he took a dislike to your son, Lucian. He'll change," the lord whispered apologetically, cringing.

What on earth does he have to be sorry about?

"I think I'll soon get out of my depth if I immerse myself in politics too quickly," Lennord warned him off.

"I doubt that. You're cleverer than I, and no mistake. I can't blame you for making yourself believe that, however. Politics can be a mighty tedious affair. Your lack of experience in that world should make you immune to its corruption. You've lived a good and honest life with your family, such as some of these men and women could only dream of, or would if they could understand it. You'll do what you think is best, but these people, they've grown up in this world and grown complacent, and some of them want more and more, forever more. I've been friends with the Emperor since we were children, so my allegiance is one of trust, and hope, and the will to succeed. I fear the loyalty some of these men have pledged is not from the heart, but from an age-old discipline. Fealty alone is only a stone's throw away from greed, and cowardice, and all sorts of other unpleasant things. Don't get me wrong, they need not all become the Emperor's best friend but... well, there are right reasons and wrong reasons for a lord to pledge his services, aren't there? There are those who seem to think those aren't important."

This was a foreign concept to far-removed Lennord, yet in his heart he understood the principles of it. The basics were the same among every class of people.

"I understand what you're saying," he said dryly.

"I'm sure you do."

The Empress was whispering something in her husband's ear and grinning cheekily, but her words seemed lost on him for his face was blank at best and troubled at worst; she effortlessly took control of him with the soft touch of her hands gripping one of his arms.

The Voice of Kings

"Oh, and before I forget, I'll have Marcus collect you to have a tunic tailored in time for your knighthood," he said while watching the odd couple like a hawk. "Just for your information."

"I've already seen your chamberlain for the blessed armour. I thought you were getting me out of this; I can't tell this lie."

"Lennord, I think you've misunderstood your application as a knight. You will be a new kind of knight entirely. Or just a lord, if I can circumvent it, but forget my failings! I will have it confirmed."

That meant otherwise; Lennord saw through him, in contrast to the impassioned wisdom the lord had only just advised him with, that had seemingly bridged their age gap in a matter of seconds and had made him feel old.

"What is it?" Tristan said upon noticing Lennord's confused expression.

"You've come a long, long way since we first met, but sometimes when you speak, you sound like you haven't changed at all."

"From that silly naive boy who first marched up to your doorstep some 18 years ago? I like to think I carry a little of him around with me at all times." His lips curled on one side into the roots of a smirk, and in an instant, he was observing with a sigh, the two rulers still deep in conversation. "I should rescue the Emperor. Wait here if you please. He'll give his address soon."

~

When the lord strode across the room to the opposite stairwell, Kester was blankly staring at him with the end of his quill clamped between his teeth in frustration, the deep hole of the absence of imagination being dug deeper with every second that he failed to edit the scribbling before him. When it occurred to him that Lord Almaric was not going to ignore him, he harshly shoved the lectern to the chair to his left and made to stand for the bemused man.

"My Lord," Kester fumbled.

"Don't rise on my account. Sit." And just as hastily, he sat himself back down before he had even the time to straighten his back. "How are you faring in your search for your musicians?"

"Fine."

"That's not what I've heard," Lord Almaric corrected immediately, without hesitation. He shook his head, perhaps at Kester's poor sense of honour and the pretence which struggled to hold its weight. "There should be a singer downstairs, with experience like the Empress wanted. She's beautiful, also like the Empress wanted, oh and she's even versed in Old Mürathneèan."

"Why, my Lord?" Kester asked after failing to comprehend his meaning. "Why do that for me?"

The Design

"It's a sorry sight, watching you struggling in this world you don't understand. I suppose, to give you one less thing to worry about and let you get on with what you excel at. That's all."

"Thank you, my Lord."

With that, Lord Almaric was away, headed for the door before Kester had finished thanking him, and he was left alone with his thoughts and ill imagination which taunted him. It was true, he'd not been able to make considerable progress finding musicians, but he had no other choice than to push on with it and hope for the best, and not throw a fit over the indignation as he'd been sorely tempted. Back in Caedor, both Isaac and Lucian had provided him with advice. Isaac had given him knowledge on reforging his tongue from lead to silver, and finding strangers with minimal leads to go on, some of which had been flat out lies, becoming increasingly preposterous as he'd spoken them with a deadpan expression until Kester had told him to stop, or kept an equally straight face for as long as he could. Most of it was valuable information probably, but having forgotten most of it, those pleasant memories weren't of any practical use. Lucian had had different ideas, very diplomatic and methodical, naturally, and that advice had gone very much the same way.

Indeed, he now wished either one of them had stayed for at least a couple of days. After that length of time, Isaac would probably have returned to him with a smug look plastered on his face and a list of the best musicians in County Capital. And there would have been enough time to get drunk on ales in the respectable little tavern it had taken him ages to find, and even Lucian would attend and do the same, for his barrier shielded wondrous breadth of character.

Out of the corner of his eye, their father was staring down to the main congregation area for the crowd, appearing quite bored all of a sudden. Kester considered talking to him for want of speaking of the past and out of politeness, but he didn't look in the mood to be disturbed. It was a sense of respect for the man that stopped him intervening. Though he looked stern now, Kester knew he was a good man. That was the least he could realistically say of him, now that he was old enough to see past that facade. A good man. He'd helped him in more ways than he cared to count, come to think, in personal and general occupation, as he had so many others, and wore his pride under a thick cloak in his mind where no one could see it, when it was well within his right to let it be known. There was no reason to remain for now, then. It made him thoroughly uncomfortable to think how long that poor woman had been waiting for him downstairs.

He hesitated for a moment only, thinking when he returned for the Emperor's speech, he would find his papers gone, though he took advantage of Lennord's kind nature and assumed him as its unwitting guardian.

The curved corridor he found himself in once again was gloriously well lit, cosy even, with its ubiquitous lighting that was just short of glaring, and its colour scheme of brilliant

The Voice of Kings

red and white which made him feel as if he were treading through a royal chamber. It was all perfect, really, or would be if his ambitions ever came to a head. From the other end of the corridor to which he walked, there was an unmistakable voice, that of the Emperor, to which he couldn't help but stop and quake in excitement and fear. From his perspective, it carried a good deal of authority, but the silky tones of the woman's voice were mesmerising.

"We'll make use of every single one of them, trust me," the Empress said.

"Is Lennord Brodie still our golden citizen?" the Emperor replied wearily, though not unkindly.

"Without question. He's got the smarts and self-awareness to make him stand out without making a fool out of himself. His entire family could prove useful at some point or other, come to think of it."

"Oh?" the Emperor replied, as if he wasn't in the least surprised at her conclusion.

"You should read more."

"Why?" he went on.

"They're really quite exceptional. Such a rich tapestry of emotions and events. Read their file again, it's all there. You may be surprised. No doubt, good Lennord hammered them all into impeccable shape."

Their voices grew ever louder, at a pace Kester did not at once take into account, and accompanying the voices were a dozen or so footsteps, some ringing and clunking from the movement of sabatons, and pale shadows leapt onto the walls as they neared. Kester was away and hurrying down the stairs, still pondering the particulars of the conversation, even as he arrived before, who must have been, the singer Lord Almaric had hired for him. It was an exciting prospect, in that the Empress herself might request for Isaac and Lucian to stand before her and flatter them with important roles in court. Marcel too, of course, not that he'd spent as much time with him, but he wasn't an unlikeable man.

"Are you quite alright?" the woman said sheepishly, craning her head forward and putting on a disturbed face, as if to imply there was something physically wrong with him.

"Yes. Sorry."

They were at the rear of the Opera House, in a corridor much like the one at the entrance, only this one was deserted, save for the two of them. Of them, the woman, who was slightly shorter than he, and perhaps a few years younger, stood out the most in the candlelight with her long locks of reddish-ginger hair and symmetrical features, not that Kester paid much notice to her beauty after an initial sweeping glance. He was far away.

"Are you the vocalist that Lord Almaric hired for me?"

"To put a long story short, yes. Kimbra," she said, at once playing a curtsey and unfurling a hand for him to take. "Kimbra Lovett."

"Kester Irvyng. Are you of noble blood?" he added, noting her sleek dress.

"Not a noblewoman," she laughed. "Not quite. My father is a knight."

The Design

That must have been how Lord Almaric found her. And Isaac would have done something else entirely.

"Go then, sing a few notes," Kester said.

He looked to the ceiling as she perfectly cycled through increasingly higher notes, simultaneously musing on the Empress's motives, for she had a strong reputation for planning everything, and though he'd only met her once, he'd got that impression, as well as all the other things people said about her. She could probably hypnotise someone with a glance.

"How did I do?" Kimbra asked after the last high-pitched sound rung out and faded away.

"Good," Kester said distractedly. "No, marvellous actually." The dim voices from the hall became louder, and he paused to listen. "Excuse me for a few minutes please. I have to do something."

~

There were about 20 or 30 of them on the balcony now, men from around the country, presumably of various professions, though if any of them were inventors like him, Lennord would have been surprised. It just wasn't a job people were encouraged to take up in Burtal. They all filed into the room rather speedily and packed tightly together in rows. Lennord was in the front row, of course.

Before them, some distance away, the Emperor dominated the room. He *did* look healthier. He looked cleaner somehow and, for now at least, he showed no signs of the stoop that had plagued him last he saw the man. The Empress was at his right-hand side, every bit in control, and flanking them were their knights. Tristan was out of the way to the left, by himself, with his hands behind his back. More knights guarded the doors, and the two blocking the door in his line of sight were familiar also; they were in the throne room when he visited for his official welcome, including the young man whom the Empress had scolded for his lack of discipline and, presumably, failing to live up to his expectations. What was his name...? Sir Yanick, that was it.

And on the ground floor, Lennord could have sworn he saw a guard or two inconspicuously glancing up at them. Crowds were still milling about down here, talking to each other about the goings on over the upper level, as was the plan. A private speech, which could nonetheless be seen, was supposedly a declaration of trust, or that was the idea. The Emperor coughed loudly and, in a flash, Lennord was giving him his full attention. The ruler of Burtal swished his tunic back so as not to appear to be hiding behind it, and was confident now that he was the centre of attention.

"Greetings to you all," he began. "You've been summoned, inventors, architects, artists, and politicians, because you were deemed to possess exceptional abilities in your specialised fields, and I stand before you, here today, to tell you why. It is because our country is sick, and only the best of its people can bring it from the brink of chaos. You will act as tutors in our capital city, and in the near future, other men will learn your talents. And women too. Women have talents of their own," he said more stiffly. It must have been a pain to say it, because he knew better than anyone that his wife was more valuable than he in almost every way, and he was her plaything.

Kester hurried in as quietly as he could through the door behind Lennord, though he saw him out of the corner of his eye, fitting into a line looking flustered. No one gave him a second look, to his relief, and he could have arrived a few minutes later for all the useful information the Emperor dispensed. Maybe it warmed the hearts of the people around him, but to Lennord, the speech contained nothing he hadn't anticipated. During the speech, a tarpaulin was pinned down over the hole in the roof due to the ominous grey clouds overhead, and sure enough, it fell fast and thick, and the Emperor raised his voice to a dull roar to compensate.

"And you all will be compensated for your efforts, depending on your results, as it well should be, I'm sure you'll agree," he said after some time, showing no sign of running low on energy but hopefully rounding his message off. The Empress then spoke, less an interruption and more a helpful addition to her husband's message, though she essentially stole his fire; the whole room now fixed on her smooth authoritative tones, which could sound like wisdom even addressing the smallest of matters, so soft that they might slip by one's ears without them noticing the authority at all.

"Small grants may also be permitted on the outset, depending on your needs. Feel free to contact the castle banker through the usual channels if you're feeling duly entitled." She smiled. The Emperor flinched. "Aside from that, yes, I find my husband's words wholly agreeable, and I see that you do too. And with speak of noble men and women, I would be remiss not to mention a man who has caught my attention so recently, and in the past too, for his heart burns with fire and his mind is as sharp as any blade. His name is Lennord Brodie, a truly great inventor and creative thinker, a champion in his own right!"

She nodded to Lennord. The people beside and behind him instantly began clapping haughtily. They knew not why, but the Empress had silently endorsed it, and so it happened, and they accepted that it was appropriate, nay, necessary, to commend the efforts of this man they'd never heard of. Tristan was doing an excellent job at holding his peace, acting as if this was exactly what he'd expected, and when he turned to Lennord, he looked right through him, for fear of crumbling the illusion created by Alycia. She hadn't finished.

"Living proof that Burtal has life in it yet. And what life. From the moment I first met him, I could see something so wondrous and special in him; equal part sceptic and optimist, pious man and scientist, and to know where the two cross, as he does, is more profound than most think, as even from Mürathneè, we hear rumours of demons and magic which

The Design

would be blasphemy if it wasn't pitiable superstition first, and I remember there are uneducated men and women everywhere, just as there are geniuses in our midst. Our Lennord Brodie currently broods over projects which might seem like magic, but in reality, is just one man's vision brought to fruition through the blood and sweat of hard labour, and I know in time you will do the same," she guaranteed, though it was really an order shrewdly veiled with a motive of encouragement, and they hung onto her every word. "You will be valiant knights of commerce and artistry, and news of your efforts will blaze across Burtal on the wings of our fine messengers, and all will know of our reform. Most people doubt it to be possible, and who could blame them, but we know different."

Empress Alycia was so ethereal, it was a small wonder how her words projected over the din of the rain; her chin and cheek bones, and indeed all her face, so soft and sweet that her perceived innocence might have lessened the impact of her message, were it not for the flames she spat from her mouth, whipping round her silver tongue and engulfing her targets.

When the time came for them all to part ways, Lennord strode at a brisk pace from a few men who looked hopeful to learn why the Empress had favoured him so, and into the rain which had already died down into drizzle. Kester approached with a woman he didn't recognise in tow, and he was glad for the interruption.

"What was that all about?" Kester said, almost laughing.

"I wish I knew," Lennord replied, for it was the simplest form of the truth. "I had expected her to use me as a figurehead at some point, mind, I just...didn't expect it to happen like this."

"How *did* you expect it to happen?"

"You've got me there. I don't know. I just thought it would be less sudden, I suppose."

Silence reigned as Lennord darkly pondered Alycia's words. It was imperative to remember that she would have picked them carefully. Nothing she said was likely an accident and that went for the manner of the reveal also, not that she had revealed all that much about anything, in hindsight. She'd been very specific, however, about how he was concocting some grand inventions. If it was a bluff, it was a very risky one, and yet she must have had something in mind.

Best not to think on it too much, Lennord conceded. That road led to madness.

"My friend and I are going to a tavern to discuss business," Kester chimed in to end the awkwardness. "Would you care to come along?" Lennord looked to the pretty woman, then back to Kester.

"That's very kind of you, but I think not. There's work that needs doing and it won't finish itself."

At least, to that end, he would not be embroiled in politics for a day or two longer.

~

The Voice of Kings

Vivid was the scene in the throne room, the lords and their paravail retainers dressed in fine attire, some wearing the colours or sigils of their Houses, some reflecting the fashions of their homes more than others; those of County Flatlands were swathed in very loose robes, or finely trimmed suits and impeccable shining doublets of boiled leather, and from the mountain region, he saw men in materials they'd imported from the south, mostly dark, but bright of colour where there was some. Tristan felt like a betrayer, scanning them all in their great numbers, judging them, for a sign of allegiance to Alycia. It was for Lennord's sake, he had to remind himself, not of self-service. It could be justified. Just not too much, *not too much*. Still, he didn't have to start sweating till someone turned to one of the olive-skinned southerners and made an unfunny remark about their Mūraci heritage.

The men of Aurail were the primary targets of his reluctant judgement anyway, faces he knew from council that paid him tribute with their bows, time and again. They respected him and perplexed him, and he felt the same of them.

"Anyone else?" his friend Richard the Emperor called to the room, flinging high his hand, in elegant yet rigid fashion, as a challenge.

His form was weakening again, so soon after the physician told him of his good health. A king's duty was ever heavy, and the title of Emperor alone was burden enough for the man. Beyond his stark, stubbly face, Tristan dared peer out of the corner of one eye, where yellow fire danced at the Empress's behest, leaning forward as she was. *My liege, my friend*, Lord Tristan sadly whispered the question in his head, *what is it you think you're doing? Do you even know?*

A break in the crowd distracted him, into which a farmer representative returned and whence a smart bear of a man came, square-jawed, clean shaven, leather clothes shining, and translucent green cape billowing over his sword. He spread out his arms, spinning as he walked in courtesy for some other to relieve him, and when none other did, he strode to the foot of the dais and knelt between Pedrig and Doru.

"Sir Darith Wyman, Majesties. While you make adjustments to your city, I am yours in wisdom or defence. House Wyman prides itself on perpetuating the myths about our godly combat prowess." He smiled and turned to address the crowd, not arrogant but pleasant, and then he bowed. "Mine are the old ways. You can rely on me."

It was very like a Wyman of him. Tristan nodded but realised he didn't understand his meaning. Perhaps that didn't matter, or wasn't the point, but when Alycia grinned happily, he couldn't help but draw a connection to her veiled plans. Everything invited his suspicion now, for shame.

"Very good," the Empress congratulated. Nothing sinister, no?

When, after that introduction, the crowd at last moved to exit through the main door, Tristan hung back, deliberating the merits of each option. At the doorway, Marcus Baldwin silently slipped to his side.

The Design

"Did you see anything odd?" Tristan said.

"Nothing suspiciously odd, Lord. *Wyman* odd."

Tristan nodded gladly. That was good, he decided for the time being. Be that as it may, he was not listening to himself, not returning to his office, but following the last seen path of the knight who'd prostrated himself before the thrones, a path that led him upstairs and, catching up with him, followed him to the front of the castle, where Darith gazed glassy-eyed from the battlements. At the other end of them, Tristan looked out across what of the city could be seen, being little more than the long road stretching straight from Castle Aurail's gates. Marcus at his side, he said nothing, pretending he wasn't spying on the knight. Spying. What an ill word. He was lord paramount, not some petty fool who stalked men through the corridors on dubious grounds. Admiringly, Tristan kept the knight in his sight and all of a sudden saw no conspiracy or secrecy around him. He was a noble Wyman. There was something that bred extreme loyalty in those people at Ylden Parragor. If he was working for Alycia, he would announce it, and he would do it well, which belied the very reason he feared for the Empress's plans in the first place. Just as he wasn't a petty lord, she wasn't a petty ruler, and it would be disgusting to treat her as such. He feared only her reach, not her vision.

Eventually the knight left, Tristan leaving him be. He breathed the summer air in satisfaction.

"Marcus, that errand I asked of you before."

"Yes, Lord?"

"I'd like you to do it now, please."

Chapter Sixteen: A Long Way From Home

The 14th day of their travels in Mürathneè was the one of the greatest significance yet, if Isaac and Marcel had judged the map and its roads correctly. Honestly, they might have made it in 13 if they'd pushed themselves. But the journey, it was the most important part. Well, depending on the ending. *Think on that,* Isaac nudged himself when he felt cold.

He'd do it later, like so much else.

To prepare for the last leg of the journey, Isaac had carefully donned his new suit, much to Marcel's jest when he asked to know the price. He wore a jacket that was something like high-quality linen with a velvet inner lining, true royal blue with subtle black embroidery. If it *was* linen, it was of such class that Isaac didn't think possible with the material: durable and light and flexible all-in-one, and of reasonable thickness. Each sleeve had one button which wasn't gold, but looked close enough like it that it could be mistaken for it. The shirt beneath it was white silk and echoed the same sentiment of impeccable quality, having embroidery also, and was slightly puffed at the arms as he'd heard was a real royal trademark. Dark green breeches fit just as smartly, and above them, slick hardened leather cavalier boots ran up to his knees, as smooth, or smoother, than any he'd ever felt, and just as tough and practical, and at the top they curled over, also as a mark of higher society because most would leave it alone when it was technically functional. No one would know or guess that his roots were from Caedor.

They slowed their horses to a trot as they approached an arch over the road at the top of a hill. It was holding aloft an eagle statue of solid gold, dazzling them with glorious sunlight, that hinted at the arrival of something great and freely offered hope without consequence. Behind them, the well-paved road stretched out evenly down the hill and, in his mind, Isaac sketched the map of Mürathneè as best he could to match. It was a road which built up anticipation with its thriving shops and watchtowers which exuded power, and that anticipation came to a head as Isaac realised where he must be. If he was correct, then the road of Eagle's Flight intersecting beneath the arch at the top of the hill must have been the very spot he'd discussed with Marcel the previous night, and so he motivated his horse, so full of guile, to gallop onwards; sure enough, as he neared the top and the arch which gradually loomed over him, ever more imposing and surrounded by guards and small buildings, an expanse of water grew before his eyes, glistening like Lavellyrn's Channel but somehow containing more mystery in its blue depths, and like that moment when he'd come to the crossing, the sun was low and shivering.

When the Infinite Sea had revealed itself all it could, the ports of the city danced into view, and a moment later, all of Harth was laid bare for him to freeze in awe at. Both he and Marcel pulled off the road to stare at the city, perhaps twice the size of Aurail and infinitely more beautiful. It was larger lengthways than in its width, to keep it situated as near the coast as possible, and high walls of white brick stood stronger than any Isaac had seen. Beyond that, there was more white and, atop that, red slate roofs amidst stony sentinels rising high above them, aloof and watchful; one in particular stood out with its pale mass of thin spires and, at one end, three blocks of stone jutting upwards. If it was the cathedral, as he presumed it was, they must have housed the three bells. The other prominent sight was a collection of eerily spectacular architecture to the far north of the city, on Isaac's right-hand side, where the King's palace rested, but it was too far away to observe. The city, he now noticed, sloped very slightly upwards to the north where, from his balconies, the King could perch and take in the splendour of his land like the vigilant eagle upon House Santorellian's banner.

From his spot on the hill, Eagle View, Isaac felt a tingle run down his spine, for no feats of man or woman could have amounted to this in his imagination. His discovery at Caedor mine returned dark, vivid, and strange, and for a time, he forgot that Harth was still inhabited by human beings with flaws, and problems, and quirks, and believed that should he only reach out his hand, he could take hold of the truth and unravel it to finally lay to rest years of wonder and frustration. Marcel was clearly in agreement, discarding his doubts about the cathedral and his motives while the vista of Harth sang him a lullaby.

"What do you think?" was all Marcel could say. "Is it what you envisioned?"

"No," Isaac replied simply and smiled to let loose his true meaning.

"I agree. I hope it justifies spending 60 gold nobles on a suit."

"Sixty-five," Isaac said carelessly, as if this was an adequate way of defending his position. Marcel shook his head and sighed, though he did enjoy such replies.

"Shall we?" Marcel added after a time Isaac couldn't hope to count in hindsight. He nodded to the bottom of the hill and Isaac gave him his answer by speeding off towards the dreamscape from which golden dots soared in and out, like fireflies whizzing about a painting: the most intelligent of birds that were harnessed for courier duties.

Isaac chose the most central gate, huge like those of Aurail, and coloured in black and gold, and on the watchtowers either side, a giant flag was flown: the flag of the King, one of two variations. The High Duke carried an eagle which was still and in a shield, as he was the sworn protector of his elder brother the King, whose banner bore a Mürathneèan eagle in full flight above the Infinite Sea. Apparently the two were combined side by side in the War of the Distant Kings. The soldiers at the gate bore, on their bright armour, only an eagle ringed by argent roundels, though whether this was a decision purely of aesthetics or whether it bore some meaning of its own, Isaac did not know.

The road that carried them into the city was airy and bright with colour and purpose, holding its grip where Aurail could not when one was surrounded by its miserable offerings. As Isaac and Marcel had anticipated, the first street contained the same white brick buildings as before, and slanted slate roofs boasting sturdy gutters for the rain, and now, Isaac noticed, there were iron manholes covering the sewers, and well they did for there was no ill smell, just the lingering aroma of flowers and meat from the butcher stalls; even they were flashy, with coloured tarpaulins protecting them. And, of course, the sea air that carried a salty texture he had only previously experienced at Lavellyrn's Channel, which was nonetheless not an unpleasant feeling. At their father's advice, they stopped off at a stable because there was none by the cathedral or Rosalynn's lodging. The familiar smell of horse manure brought them back to the world of the living, for it was something not even these people could make disappear forever.

Each of them lugging their two bags over one shoulder, they stepped back onto the street. An eagle cried out overhead and the two brothers couldn't help but look towards it.

"There aren't as many as I thought there would be," Marcel observed.

"They deliberately split up the lofts all over the city to break up the noise pollution. And reduce the amount of shit in any one area. It's true."

"How thoughtful."

They allowed the city's wonders to wash over them as they walked, Isaac occasionally stopping to unfold a map against the wall of one of many smooth brick buildings, and dragging a finger over it to determine the best path; though still they got lost, detours inevitable, for the city practically goaded them to do so, as if it were a living entity. The houses and buildings, generally, were taller than those in Aurail, or what Isaac had seen of it, but because of their beauty and the wideness of the roads, they did not loom over like angry demons, and never did they feel in their shadow, even as the sun sank further and further.

At one point, an arched road led upwards into steps at its convex, up to a front garden neatly arranged with small patches of grass in rectangles and squares between thin walkways, symmetrical on both sides of the circular pond where the primary path curled around and on to the front doors; welcoming they were, and the brothers caught a glimpse of luxurious red and blue interiors. Marcel shamelessly gawped until he realised what it was, with the women dancing and whirling seductively outside.

"Have we wandered into the wrong part of the city?" Marcel asked, transfixed.

"Normally I would say yes, but... just look at it. The mere fact of being a whorehouse is not enough to determine its location as squalid, apparently. Unless all buildings in the *wrong* part of Harth are appraised with billowing gossamer curtains, and carpets, and are tended like a king's court."

"How peculiar," Marcel said for want of better words, features crinkling.

All they could do was glance at one another and raise their eyebrows before gladly moving on to whatever oddities Harth had in store next.

"I saw you looking!" a woman called after them in a cheeky voice, and ran to catch up with them, passing between them and swirling to face them. She wore a corset entirely too tight and had her black hair tied in a bunch. She grinned playfully. "I saw you both looking!"

"You did," Isaac replied plainly and politely, although he was flustered a portion. "I'm sorry to have bothered you."

"You're from Burtal?" the woman said as if taken aback, and then nodded approvingly. "You do look the type, now that I think. Don't be shy now: I can accommodate your tastes. I guarantee it. Together or one at a time."

"We're accounted for," Marcel interjected, to Isaac's pleasure.

"It's true. However, I should say you deserve far better than I," Isaac added, taking the woman gently by the hand and laying a kiss upon it; then he turned it over and slipped a single coin into her palm. Half of it would go to charity at this rate. "For your kindness."

She was genuinely shocked, and showed it now above any emotion she might otherwise have concocted for display, so much so that she appeared wary, as if it were a trick. When she realised it wasn't, she was shocked further still and smiled broadly.

"Good evening," she said as they walked on.

"And to you," Isaac replied courteously. Marcel simply waved once and nodded.

"Why did you do that?" Marcel asked.

"To get in character, I think."

Isaac spoke thoughtfully, gazing up at the clear sky as if he wasn't sure himself. It occurred to him that in exercising his silver tongue, he'd been playing the same game as her, and she probably appreciated it. He also couldn't deny, in all honesty, that he had immensely enjoyed the exchange, and if he was being more honest still, had found her to have a certain seductive flair. He could only imagine how much of it was real. Pity.

As strange as the brothel and its lavishness had been, just as strange was the cathedral, which neither of them had noticed was creeping up on them: strange for its proximity to a house of lust, but mainly for the sheer awe and respect it commanded. They carried on in silence, barely taking in the sights around them anyway, only the giant black church which appeared to grow as they approached. Finally the road opened to a plaza, vast and covered in shop stalls, which still could not make it feel any less empty, and gave the cathedral a wide berth as if cowering in its wake. The plaza was paved with white bricks placed carefully in a zigzag pattern, and the path to the grand double doors was coloured black, while the doors themselves were black and gold. Artistic markings drew their attention here, some detailed pictures, and at the top there was a circular stained glass window surrounded by five smaller ones. The roof held spires, and flying buttresses connected them all together, dozens of them, right the way to the very back where the three bells were, as Isaac had guessed. They were open for all to see, contrary to what he'd believed, and the middle bell was slightly taller than the rest, marking its highest point, perhaps 100 feet from the ground. It wasn't a patch on Castle Aurail's great tower, but then, he knew of nothing that was.

The Voice of Kings

The cathedral was, in fact, far bigger than he could have known from Eagle View, and so strong in its appearance that it could have been a military stronghold but for all the windows marking its weaknesses. It stretched back for 150 feet or so, perhaps half the length of the road in Caedor from the entrance proper to his house, and there was a whole other segment to it which was shorter than the rest but still must have been three storeys tall. It was surely where the lodging was, housing the cloisters. It was all just a taste of what was inside, he could feel it, and wished he could march through those front doors and down the nave to the famed statues of the gods, radiated with filtered light from the gigantic stained glass windows. Marcel, of course, would see it very soon.

"So," Isaac began, knowing they couldn't stand in silence forever. "How do you feel?"

"I don't think this is going to be like working for churches in the highlands or back home in Caedor," he said, half-joking.

"We're a long way from home, brother," Isaac laughed with a strain of sympathy.

"Yes, it's obvious, I know that. I just never really knew what to expect, and I still don't I suppose, but something this size must need firmer management than a hamlet church, run by a doddery old priest and attended by, well, less educated men and women than people here are, I expect."

"Are you having second thoughts?" Isaac said flatly, knowing Marcel might speak defensively if he implied that was his opinion.

"No. I still want to learn more about our gods, and healing, and whatever else they teach there. I was taken aback, that's all."

"Understandably so." In his eagerness for knowledge, he reminded Isaac of himself. He looked to the smaller wooden door on the cathedral extension, inset with an uncoloured unicorn image rearing itself in woodlands as if to imply a haven waited beyond.

"I should go now."

"You don't have to."

"But I want to," Marcel said cheerfully. "Reservations aside, I do want to."

"Good luck then," Isaac supplied, as if he was content with his brother's decision. "Not that you'll need it."

"I'll see you soon then."

Isaac nodded and remained perfectly still as he watched his brother cross the plaza to the door, where he and a guard had a brief exchange, and he disappeared inside. He was alone now. He didn't feel it. His head was spinning with everything he'd seen and everything there was to see and do, and at the same time, the plaza was eerily peaceful. The cathedral was guarded by soldiers, yes, but they were like statues and didn't take up space. A few people crossed the plaza, some lighting the lanterns to create an entirely new atmosphere, and some just passing by, though not many, and the ringing of blacksmithing wafted gently to him from one direction as the smell of fine cooked pork did from another.

Eventually he left, when the sun was so very close to descent, to find his lodging while the light of day was still of some use to him. It was perhaps a five minute walk to his destination, amusingly named The New Flatlands Inn, and fortunately it would have been difficult to miss it. Situated beside a plaza of its own that housed a quaint well, a right-angled path leading around it, it was three storeys tall and more pristine than any inn, or equivalent thereof, that he'd ever visited, though he suspected that was par for the course in this city. The roof had a balcony around its edge and must have overlooked the sea: a place of reflection for him, perhaps. The interior didn't even look like an inn, with a desk directly before him and, to his left, a corridor with doors placed sparsely along either side.

Isaac was happy to dump his belongings before the desk and was so busy stretching his arms and fantasising wisdom that he almost forgot that no one was there to greet him. Eventually a woman entered from a door behind the desk and stopped, taken aback.

"Can I help you?" she asked as if he wasn't supposed to be there.

"You can," Isaac replied joyfully, thoroughly pleased he was having an effect on people already. He thrust a hand out. "I'm Isaac Brodie. My father sent a letter. If your name's Rosalynn, you should have been expecting me. And very nice it is to meet you," he finished as if anticipating her proving him right.

"That's my name, but... Isaac? Oh, yes, Isaac!" Her face lit up and she stepped back to properly study him, clearly impressed by the quality of attire he donned, as she must not have presumed any Brodie to afford such luxuries. "I'm sorry, I mistook you for a nobleman for a moment there. Thought you'd gotten lost, coming into a place like this."

Of course, Isaac thought. A nobleman would not enter an inn of any kind, unless on the road or on business. Still, she had implied that the niceties he'd observed were fairly common place. That was good to know.

"You must be doing well for yourself to afford that," Rosalynn said.

"Actually, it was my father's money that bought me this. Expenses. He does well enough for the Emperor, it seems. He's with him again now, and his old friend Lord Almaric," he couldn't help himself saying, and she did look impressed.

"Yes, he did mention he was heading to Aurail in his letter. How is your father anyway?"

"Stressed, but well," Isaac quipped with a broad grin.

Rosalynn must have been straining to see Lennord in him, as Isaac had expected she might, and inwardly smiled at the thought. It was a fresh and bizarre experience, talking to a stranger and knowing many years ago she'd been friends with his father, as well it would be when he found that elusive Vicentei Laccona.

She had a Burtalian look about her but almost appeared to have changed to adopt a Mürathneèan visage that he couldn't quite place. Maybe it was the sun that did it. Or the salty air. Or maybe his heightened imagination was playing tricks on him, as he was sure it could, given the circumstances. She was a short woman too, at five feet or so, was about his father's age, and had long brown hair, lighter than Lucian's, freely hanging behind her back and over her shoulders. Her dress was modest, if of a higher quality than the standard for Caedor, and more creative than those his sister continued to work at: a vibrant green, it was, with artistic markings here and there, and a slightly raised collar.

"How do you know my father?" Isaac said, because he had to at some point.

"We both grew up in the same town in the flatlands, we did. A lifetime ago. Even then he was always fixing things, correcting people, much to the chagrin of his father, as I remember it." She chuckled. "I don't think he really tolerated Lennord's intellect very well, poor man. He gave his son the gift of reading and, from there, Lennord progressed beyond his understanding. He was a good man, really, though I wouldn't have admitted it back then, as children generally don't. A hard worker."

Isaac smirked and slowly nodded his head back and forth. That fit in well with what he knew and guessed of his father's youth.

"That doesn't surprise me. Didn't he leave to head south when he was 17?"

"I think that's about right, yes."

"And he's lived in the highlands ever since," Isaac recalled, half to himself, his eyes half-shut as he realised something. "How many times have you met since then?"

"Twice," she laughed. "Soon after he left, I was wed and my husband brought me here, having connections with some traders at the time. Traders who all ultimately failed, but there you have it."

"You met twice since his departure from your homeland and yet he continued writing letters to you all this time?"

"Usually once every year, yes. I get the impression he wants to see as many different angles as possible, but he prefers to hear it from people he knows, or *once knew*."

"That also fits," Isaac muttered. "He once said to me, sending letters to people in different places made the world a little smaller for him, which makes it easier to do his work. He only ever met Vicentei Laccona once, I think, and yet he still communes with him as much as possible." *And yet*, Isaac added only to himself, *he probably could write more but enjoys the isolation of Caedor*, so a balance of open mindedness and wilful ignorance.

"He's mentioned Laccona a few times as well, definitely," Rosalynn said, randomly waving a finger as she contemplated. "He's never really told me much of his opinion of him that I remember. Are you hoping to see Laccona while you stay here?" She bit her lower lip and held her head high, her dark eyebrows wide.

"As a matter of fact, I have business with him."

"To buy Sèhvorian steel?" she enquired, showing her knowledge of his supposed solitary endeavour.

"Perhaps. I'll get a batch of it eventually, for certain. I was rather hoping for a little more from him, given his reputation. A piece of knowledge to take with me back to Caedor and to uncover an age-old truth," Isaac said casually, raising his lips. "Well, it will help advance certain technologies," he added more placidly.

"Really?" Rosalynn laughed. "You are your father's son then. Just a word of advice if you're hoping to speak to Laccona: he can be difficult to find, if you can believe that of a man as sought after as he. If he wants to do something else, he'll just do it and won't necessarily tell anyone."

"He has a reputation for that, I gather."

"And of being better than Lennord."

Isaac leaned forward and folded his arms on the desk in anticipation, between a stack of parchment weighted down with a small stone statue charm of the goddess Nel and an inkpot to his other side. The desk had probably been bought, as people around here weren't so compelled to spread themselves thin, utilising as many skills as possible, as they did in some less fortunate and secluded places in Burtal.

Still Isaac did not respond, only waiting with polite interest and a mischievous smirk for Rosalynn to continue, letting her know in the process that her comment had caused no alarm.

"Sorry, I exaggerated there I suspect," she reconsidered. "But I have heard his name mentioned every so often in conjunction with Laccona's. They say Lennord is revered in his homeland but less known here, and has less to show for himself too. Without disrespect, hopefully. It is surreal to me though, hearing the name of my childhood friend mentioned by strangers in a faraway land."

"Really? That is good to know. My father will be pleased he has a reputation to build on."

Rosalynn was taken aback by how smugly and carelessly Isaac took to the news. But of course he wasn't going to be worried by what a random person on the street said, as even by his father's own admission, Laccona was likely a smarter man than he. Finally, Rosalynn smiled awkwardly, and squinted as she tried to look through him once again.

"He'll also be pleased to hear that his friend Lord Almaric has a reputation here for enforcing justice and fairness unlike any other."

"Excellent. They'll make a great pair for representing Burtal then, if the Emperor wills it."

"I'm sure, I'm sure." She paused and suddenly she looked perplexed. "Excuse me, I think I've been quite rude." She disappeared through the door without another word and when she returned, she was fiddling with a key. "I wouldn't delay to offer these to anyone else, so neither should I have to you."

"It's quite alright, I don't think I could ever accuse you of being rude."

The Voice of Kings

"Perhaps not," she said politely, and a sparkle in her eyes suggested an awareness of her excessive politeness. "But it is my job. Come, you look tired; not that you'd admit to it, on a hunch."

She handed the keys to Isaac and bustled away while he casually followed, interested. The woman was absolutely and amusingly right. He was so engrossed in holding an image that he had almost forgotten that he craved sleep. Or his body did, at least. His mind wasn't necessarily going to listen and would gladly face the consequences at a later date.

Stopping at his room at the very end of the corridor, she gestured to the door with both arms, like a showman would.

"This will do nicely," Isaac said sincerely as he opened the door.

"And for a fair rate, believe me. I've reserved the room to the left for your brother, eh..."

"Lucian."

"Yes, Lucian, sorry. If he *is* going to be staying here," she added hopefully.

"I'm certain of it. Don't worry, he's not like me."

She modestly waved the comment away, almost as if it were an insult, and let him be. Closing the door, Isaac suddenly felt invigorated: the considerable amount of candles inviting a homely warmth, the view of the Harthen square at dusk between thin silk substitute curtains billowing gently in the breeze providing peace. Beside the open window, an iron Charm of Nel hung from a thin cord of hemp, heavy enough to utterly defy the wind. Directly below the window there stood a double bed, readied for him, where most inns did not oblige, sided by a small wooden chest of drawers with a saucer of salt for his teeth. Apart from that, there was only a wardrobe in the room, yet it felt spacious, not bare. The large and crude, but respectable, rug at the door probably helped.

From there, Isaac ran his hand along the wall as he patrolled around the room's edge to another doorway. It was a stone wall, unlike most of the inns he'd ever been to which usually settled for thin wood without remorse, whereby one might hear the conversations and intimacies from the rooms either side of them. Here it must have been common enough to build lodging with more strength behind it that most everyone would have to do it, so hopefully the materials were cheaper here.

Then, the doorway at the back right-hand side of the room revealed to him another convenience, and at once he realised why kindly Rosalynn had given him a ground floor room: she surely did it out of helpfulness, or at least obligation, to Lennord's family. There was both a fixed chamber pot and a bath, of which his father was of the opinion would be a headache to pipe on anything but the ground floor, and the bath, in this case, was likely connected to a cache to be refilled at his request. Both were nothing fancy, not up to the high standards of his father's handiwork, but they were clean and more than he'd expect from any such place back home. When he tapped the chamber pot with his sword, the blade's hiss winded away, only to come back at him fine and echoic: a ghost's song. He flinched and pulled his head back, but banished that with a smile. The pot's piping must have led straight into the sewers. *My father did better than that when there was a ton of soil in the way. Knowledge is Caedor's claim to wisdom, and it shall not end.*

Satisfied that he would enjoy his stay in this room, he threw himself upon the bed and rolled onto his back, his legs spread eagle and his arms wide open, intently watching the wafer-thin curtains dancing like wraiths before the ceiling. Light of the sun still illuminated his room, and where it could not yet sleep, neither could he. Though he was tired, still he could close his eyes only to blink, as opportunity struck, again and again in his head. He'd come all this way to pull the veil from a monumental truth. Why wait till morning to start?

So he leapt from the bed, bursting with energy, and excitedly rummaged in his pocket for a map. Rosalynn had gone back inside her room but he heard her emerge once more as he reached the front door, whereupon he spun, still walking, and gave a massive shrug.

"I have work that requires my attention. I'm sure my body will wait a while longer to rest."

Despite having brought the map of the city, he barely consulted it, only vaguely pinpointing his desired location and heading in a westerly direction, where the sounds of the waves crashing back and forth against the beach grew louder and sea birds circled, awaiting the opportunity to dive and take their easy pickings from fishermen. Indeed, the smell of fish, all gathered together in heaps and carried in nets, was far stronger than he'd ever experienced, for in Caedor there was not even so many to catch in the river behind the town.

When Isaac finally caught another glance at the Infinite Sea of legend, he was filled with awe again and only hoped that he hadn't wandered off course. For his careless attitude, the sun sank from sight before he could locate the Mercenary Guild, and he would have been just as careless if given the opportunity anew. The city was not enveloped in darkness however, as lanterns lit the way on the solid stone path Isaac walked; southwards it went, a short man-made walkway which perhaps doubled as a sea defence, jutting out beside the beach. Out to sea, also, monstrous flames writhed atop two lighthouses, one crimson, the other a soft orange. To his right, he was bombarded by unfamiliar sounds of the sea and hundreds of boats moored to jetties rocking about, including, as he strained to see even further south, monolithic silhouettes which must have belonged to the navy, though he had never seen a ship of their like with his eyes before; just as he hadn't at the port on Burtal's side of Lavellyrn's Channel.

Isaac was only torn from this new world at the ever-alarming distraction of swordplay, which he knew from its rhythmic, relatively gentle pace as practice fighting, not that it stopped him from instinctively posturing himself to fight or flee for even a fleeting moment, his eyes momentarily darting to the source of the mock battle. It was to his relief that the steel sang from the place he'd been looking for, below the neat cast iron logo on the back of the building, each letter of the words Mercenary Guild carved individually. Like many other buildings in Harth, it had a roof of red slate, very steeply triangular so as to run the rain from its surface with ease. And, like the brothel he'd seen earlier, it surprised him with its efficient industry and tidiness. In his imagination, it had been far rougher.

The building appeared to be an "L" shape with the courtyard filling in the missing piece at the back, overlooked by a balcony. The interior was deserted, presumably, as only a few candles had been left to flicker quaintly in the dark, so he was down to a choice between three people: the two men fighting, or the man calmly and meticulously cleaning a longsword on a stool.

So it was him then, that Isaac approached: a tall, muscular man with long, jet black hair tied back. If he looked at Isaac, Isaac didn't see him do it, as he continued to wipe from his thin blade blood that had hardened like tree roots, curling up the length of the steel like a malicious weed, so dipping it into a bucket of stained water as he did so. It was almost as if Isaac wasn't there.

"I'm looking for the Captain of the Guild, Martello Jacart," Isaac said coolly, and yet clearly deeply invested.

The mercenary paused to inspect him, keeping eerily still, his lips puckered and his eyes narrowed, not in any threatening or suspicious manner so much as a sort of vague curiosity, as if he were simply perusing a merchant's wares. Then he smiled, if only briefly, lifting the corners of his mouth up, where one of several small scars became distorted.

"I'm Martello Jacart. What can I do you for, young man?" he said deeply, though not quite as gruffly as Isaac had imagined.

Isaac's heart pounded in his chest at the revelation, one which he could have sworn he was anticipating. He showed no signs of this of course, remaining calm with one hand behind his back. He briefly considered extending a hand for him to shake but, somehow, he knew Martello would not oblige, or at the very least would attain a poor first impression of him.

In his imagination, the man was of a distinctly different appearance from everyone else, purportedly hailing from a civilisation so very far away, but he was no different at all; maybe his skin was a little darker. His armour was black plate over boiled leather. Across the steel were blued bands, and on one of his pauldrons there was an embossed epithet of the guild's coat of arms. On his back he wore a scabbard on a sling, hung loosely, which he now swung free from himself, inserted his clean longsword into, and slung over his back once more with just as much ease. There was a whiff of sweat about him too, not surprisingly, and wet leather. What was demanding of more consideration was that, despite this picture of a warrior, it somehow gelled together, making him respectable where he should have looked scruffy.

Martello must have known Isaac was gauging a first impression and, again, showed no signs of caring. When he picked up yet another sword from beside him, to clear it of the dark red blood that was smeared stubbornly all over it, he still knew Isaac was inspecting, and Isaac knew because the Captain of the Mercenary Guild replied to a question that was not asked aloud.

"It was a tough day. Tough for round here, anyway. Don't get many serious fights in Harth, not for my like."

"That's what I've heard." Isaac paused for effect. "I'm Isaac Brodie, from the town of Caedor. I wanted to speak to you personally, if I may, about your trip across the Infinite Sea, and the contents of the ship you were on."

"Ah!" Martello exclaimed with a sharp grin, laughing as if he'd expected Isaac to say as much, sooner or later.

"Obviously I'm not so thickheaded as to assume I'm the first to ask you of this, but without meaning to sound arrogant, I consider my own case less dreary or repetitive than those you've heard before. It's not just a curiosity, see. I have a mystery of my own I wanted to unravel, as it happens, and I prayed you might be able to help me, seeing as you apparently have experienced something similar. Generally speaking," Isaac added, raising one eyebrow.

"Generally speaking?"

"Our experiences differ massively but are united in spirit by their unbelievable nature and, hopefully, a deeper, more intrinsic relationship." Isaac was careful to balance glee and a stronger, more forward tone, not that he could tell whether it was working or not, not on this man.

"So you had one strange experience and now you believe every far-fetched story you hear, no matter how many times it's been debunked? Don't you see how that makes you a hypocrite?"

"Yes, I suppose that would make me a hypocrite if it were true."

"You're still a fool to have come here. What makes you think I can help you?"

Martello laughed, mincing what might have been anger in there as well, brewing it slowly and deliberately, which unnerved Isaac only slightly.

He was unpredictable, certainly, and he was annoyingly dismissive, and yet there was something Isaac was sure he was missing in his picture of him. The way he spoke wasn't normal, almost as if the mercenary was testing him. Martello was definitely enjoying himself, and that, perhaps, was what clouded his judgement of him. He was an unusual man.

Isaac stood defiantly as Martello rose from his chair, grabbing two more clean swords from beside him and striding to a steel cabinet backed up against the wall of the building, to plant them on their appropriate racks. That it was left out here was peculiar to say the least, almost as if the guild was inviting thieves onto their premises. Somehow, Isaac suspected they didn't have a problem with them.

"You're mistaken," Isaac went on calmly but forcefully. "I neither believe nor shun the claims you made as a child, when you were first washed up on these shores. That's what I'm here to discuss. I didn't come all the way from the south of Burtal so I could just make someone believe my story and go home. And as you call me a hypocrite, I, too, could label you arrogant for assuming you're my only source. But I'm not going to."

He had Martello's attention now. The mercenary captain locked the doors of the weapon cabinet at his own pace and threw his weight around, his long, curled hair flinging up in the process. Without remorse, he appeared to be deriving some pleasure from all this somehow, though now he wore that look of puzzlement once more, as he had when Isaac had first approached him.

Now that Martello stood tall and square before him, his legs apart and his chin held high, he became suddenly more imposing. There was a part of Isaac that disliked mercenaries even though he'd never taken the time to talk to any before, for to kill only for money seemed monstrous beyond all conceivable humanity, ignoring the fact that mercenaries were not assassins. Killing one man in defence was bad enough, no? He imagined that, tonight, Martello might fuck a prostitute at the brothel of his choosing and tell his companion for the evening all about the man he'd met from Burtal, whether she wanted to hear it or not, such was the hot blood of these men.

At the same time, there was desire and ambition that drove Isaac, and tonight it was triumphant over his instinctive doubts, his blood pulsing in his veins, and he was in the thrill of the moment.

"So what were you hoping to prove, young man?" Martello asked with renewed interest.

"The truth, for now. I honestly can't say much more than that, other than I believe it to be of some importance. It relates to Sèhvorian steel, and where that is involved, there is often mystery in its wake, and so I came to you. When I was but a child, my father discovered a wall of it in his mine, but it was I, alone, that witnessed what followed, and I, alone, had to bear the weight of that truth. It revealed ancient carvings for me, and shattered itself in fire so potent it burst free from the mine, and so hot it decayed all plants in the farmland to ash."

Martello reached for his sword, revealing the steel an inch and *adjusting* it on his back, or so he would have Isaac believe, as if trying to subliminally influence him into leaving. Or just to see how he would react. Whatever his intention, he hoped to frighten Isaac, and it had worked. He wouldn't do anything, he told himself, of course he wouldn't. *He's playing a game.* He could only pray that his face had betrayed no fear before he'd gotten a hold of himself.

"That's a very nice sword," Isaac complimented hollowly, keeping his frustration on a leash.

"It's not that nice. I've been meaning to have a blacksmith fix up a new one."

"Can we get back on topic please?" Isaac sighed.

"People have believed the craziest things, some of them proven wrong over time. People believed the world was flat, and, what, that this sea was never-ending, and that stars were paintings slapped on celestial canvas by the gods. Hell, sometimes people believe things they come to regret."

The mercenary captain was starting to bother Isaac's nerves now which, he realised, probably meant he was succeeding in whatever it was he was doing. Knowing that couldn't take away the confusion, he scratched his head thoughtfully.

"I don't understand. Do you mean you no longer believe what you told King Michael's father? I won't buy into that so easily."

"Make me care, Isaac Brodie, and maybe I'll tell you," Martello said, almost devoid of emotion. Isaac was sure he was subtly dropping him a hint. He hoped he was, if nothing else, and found himself speechless to his dismay, which Martello soon took advantage of. "Goodnight to you, Isaac."

He turned on his heels and strode to the back door of the building, silently inviting Isaac not to follow him. Isaac breathed deeply, and felt at once a chill in the wind which he'd, up till now, ignored. As if to defy it, he left the fenced enclosure, turned on the sea and stared, his hands clasped behind him, listening to the clashing of waves over the clanging of swords from the two men who still would not relent.

He must have felt what men and women felt long ago, staring into what they thought was eternity, when the sky was a shape shifting painting and the gods lived in a realm directly beneath the flat planet, Mura. It sent chills down his spine, the mystery giving him hope that excited him. *I accept your challenge*, he vowed. *I will make you care, Martello Jacart. I'll do more than that.*

Chapter Seventeen: Of the Wilds

In the black of night, Lucian walked with a cool wind against him, with the intention of giving his mind exercise that it had sorely lacked. He watched anyone that passed with mild interest, and consoled himself that tomorrow, or the day after, he would reach Harth and the real work could finally begin. He would rest easier knowing Isaac was keeping himself safe and not doing anything foolish.

Harven's Watch was a small military town, technically speaking, but it accommodated many people who held no job in that industry, and had no intention of doing so either, as well as travellers, as it was directly on the road to Harth. Because of its military orientation, all the buildings, at least that he'd noticed, had roof access so archers and crossbowmen could rain down hell if need be, and indeed, right now, as he walked a narrow street, he saw two silhouettes of men above him drinking, affording him a cursory glance.

Even as he saw one of them shiver in the chill of the night, he, himself, became cold, and vaguely wished for some company to bounce ideas off of. Theoretically, he could have married one of several respectable women in the past, but always decided it was never quite the time. Maybe he would have done the same once more, given the choice all over again. At a crossroads which forked in two directions, he stopped beneath a hanging lantern to rub his hands and deliberate precisely the quickest route back to the inn, for he now knew there was nothing to gain from staying here: no slight political insight or anything else.

From the left fork of the road, a figure in hooded black robes made his presence known, though mainly through his movements as still he did not reveal himself in the light. He was proud in his posture, that much was certain, like a man of authority.

"Still wandering out and about, and at this hour?" he said with a deep, sharp tone. Lucian was listening intently for a sign of menace, but detected none. He wouldn't be mugged in a town like this, Lucian consoled himself. The man would be arrested near instantly if he called out, wouldn't he? The man sighed irritably. "Come with me," he commanded. "You look far too dour for my liking, wandering about so aimlessly, far too uncomfortable in this place, and I imagine you're of the opinion something more constructive could be holding your attention, no?"

The man turned and walked casually away, his hardened leather boots creating a racket such that Lucian wondered why he hadn't heard it previously. For a moment, he did nothing, only stood with a feeling like his organs were blocking his throat, and when he finally pushed them back down, he licked his lips and scanned the area, though for what he didn't know. Atop a building he'd so recently passed unassumingly, the two men who'd been drinking now stood with longbows and stared at Lucian intently, unmoving. If anything, this further gave ground to his suspicions, but he couldn't be sure.

He crept through the street, feeling vulnerable, as if he might now be viewed as a thief to the hooded man; a man with a very fancy sword hilt protruding from his robes, who now waited under a lamppost, despite his apparent inclination towards secrecy. As he drew his hood back, several soldiers emerged ominously in Lucian's vision, at the opposite end of the street, phantoms drifting in to protect their master.

"So we meet again, much sooner than I'd imagined."

"My Lord Highness?" Lucian replied uncertainly, cocking his head back in distrust. The King's brother wasn't indulging in the theatricality, seemingly. He was just as stoic and serious as when first they had met. "You were...following me, my Lord?"

"I do so hope you're not flattering yourself there. No, I've always preferred a more direct approach. I saw you earlier this evening, and one of my men just informed me of your persistence, though of wandering like a drunkard rather than of anything useful," he said disapprovingly. "I took our meeting as another opportunity, as it happens. What was your name again?"

"Lucian."

The High Duke nodded in recognition, scratching his dark beard. Lucian wasn't a Burtalian name, not that he expected Dorrin to overly care. Lucian eagerly wished he could ask what it was the man was doing here, but still couldn't decipher the Duke's hospitality at present. To his shame, the High Duke saw straight through him and bit his own lip irritably.

"Yes?" he said quietly.

"I heard from a crier that you're in Balenhold right now."

"I was, and will be again soon enough." He paused. "What else did you hear from the crier about me?"

"That there was an accident in your duchy; that a fire killed some people and burned some crops, and you saw to its aftermath personally, and that some sort of disease inflicts the animals, as you warned me. What was all that about, if I might ask?"

"I won't divulge the particulars of the incident that killed those villagers with you," the High Duke said firmly, commanding Lucian with a piercing gaze. He continued to speak with not a sliver of menace, surprisingly, despite his flat tone. "Be that as it may, I'm gathering as many opinions as I can, and you're the closest outsider so you'll have to do. You'd better follow me."

Lucian was led down the street, through a gate and garden, and through the door of a tall brick building standing by itself; a tall wooden door it was, and it brought him into what looked initially like a workshop but stank like death. Across the room, a physician dressed entirely in black and wearing a beaked plague mask was fussing over a dead animal of some description on a gnarled wooden workbench. Opposite to him, dozens of candles, all bunched together, gleamed so brightly they very nearly merged into one giant flame: a great light that danced on the naked brick of the walls. All things considered, Lucian could not tell the manner of building it ordinarily constituted; a butcher's perhaps, or an alchemist's workshop, though the pungent aroma of animals that must have died days ago was clouding his thoughts. He pressed a hand against his nose and every gust blowing through the open windows was like a godly blessing. The High Duke looked thoroughly appalled, crinkling his face up in disgust, but otherwise did not submit to slouching or, indeed, any compromise to his military stance.

"This is the man I came here to see," he announced. "The disease that leant the wildlife such reckless fury is a curious one indeed, and so long as it transpires in my duchy, I'll continue to investigate." He turned sharply to look at Lucian with interest. "You hail from the countryside, do you not? You must have gotten your hands dirty cutting an animal apart before."

"More times than I can count, my Lord, but to prepare them for food, not whatever it is he's doing."

"Have you not ever seen such a dissection take place before? Surely at the slightest sign of disease, someone must investigate lest the whole town fall to its evil."

The Duke led him yet closer to the source of the repulsive stench, keeping his distance at some unseen boundary, as if he knew exactly where the evil couldn't reach him; Lucian dared not cross the invisible line either. He could, however, better see the operation the plague physician was performing. It was upon a long, wolfish creature with fangs and distinctive spines on its back, probably a chupacabra, though he'd never seen one in his life, its belly surgically slit open with one leg held taut upwards while, with his other hand, the physician delicately prodded and pulled at muscle and bones with a thin silver medical instrument. Half of the creature's innards had been cut from it with the same expert precision as the slit on its belly, and more was on the way out, piece by piece, dumped haphazardly about the table and slopped into a bucket. Additionally, he was assembling fragments of bone, like a jigsaw puzzle, directly before him.

Lucian had seen thousands of dead animals in his life, without question, such that he'd stopped being squeamish towards them when he was very young, but the wide, dead eyes staring straight at him, bloodshot and bulging as if about to fling from the socket, were ever so slightly unsettling. Usually he only touched dead animals when he planned to eat them, not when they were festering with some baleful disease. The High Duke was withholding more information than he might have known, as the deep gashes on its back which, by the sight of its clogged, sodden red fur, must have been the killing blows, were not the work of any animal. They were too clean, and the skin had been ripped outwards from the killer's perspective, where another animal could not claw in such a manner, so they were probably inflicted with a weapon.

Finally, to the left of the long-battered old table, there was a crow, spread eagle with what was left of its wings, and most of its feathers plucked from it. Again, its death looked to be the work of man, as there was a messy hole through its chest and wing where perhaps an arrow had felled it.

"What are you doing with that bone there?" the High Duke enquired, suddenly stunning Lucian, making him see how obsessed he'd quickly become by the mysteries of this scene.

The physician took a step back to be safe, and emerged from his mask red-faced, wrinkling his features as he accustomed himself from one overpowering smell to another, holding a hand up to pardon for patience as he winced and swished his tongue around his mouth in disgust, as if the smell was a physical object to be purged. He fingered the sigil hanging around his neck, an ebony unicorn on a silver chain, and muttered something under his breath as he called for the guidance of Venlor.

"It's a human bone, my Lord," the physician said at last.

"So this chupacabra had fed even before it attacked my party?"

"Not so very long before, if I were to hazard a guess. I see nothing else in its system either, no trace of its usual food, though to be clear, my Lord, there is a margin of error in this work. There's very little to be exact about in this science, I'm afraid."

"Yes, yes, that goes without saying. But you theorise that this animal has been ravaging humans, and nothing or little else?"

"I do."

The High Duke frowned and stared at the ceiling for a moment, as if it would help him think not to look at the man.

"Carry on then." The physician, to his silent dismay, sank his face into the mass of spices and herbs once more and continued his work without another word. "Lucian, what say you of this? Have you ever known of animals to act with such rage? People do, of course, but I thought animals were largely exempt of that bane."

"I've known animals to eat a human in hunger, or attack in desperation or madness," Lucian said, still trying to figure out how best to speak to the lord, torn between looking him strongly in the eyes or humbly diverting him of his sight. Uncomfortably, he settled on properly facing the man at last, where his natural gaze felt like a challenge for him to back down. "Not chupacabras mind: we don't have them in the highlands. If, as your physician and the town crier implied, they attacked as a horde and have only been eating humans, I couldn't possibly comment."

"Is that what's implied? Yes, I suppose it is, isn't it? Well it's true. They attacked as a horde with wolves while a flock of crows watched nearby. Do you know if dissections are performed differently where you live, if nothing else?" he asked flatly and, again, there may or may not have been an aggressive undertone.

"I've never seen so many instruments used, my Lord, though I suspect that means we are just worse off than you."

The Voice of Kings

"Not necessarily. I would argue on behalf of my country that our techniques are likely more advanced than yours, but that being said, your people take a more simplistic approach where, just maybe, it would be easier to spot some problems than with all these tools which complicate things."

"I wouldn't know. I've never spoken to anyone about it in any depth, nor do I know anyone who could."

The High Duke let out a sigh of general disappointment, probably regretting inviting him here in the first place, Lucian woefully assumed, yet he was not dismissed. The Duke walked away and leaned on the doorframe, scratching his beard, looking ever more peaceful as he stared into the blackness. Lucian joined him outside without prompt: any excuse to leave the stench behind him.

"You really should establish contacts if you wish to become an ambassador."

"I never said I don't," Lucian defended sharply with what he thought was nerves of steel.

"My apologies, that was unprofessional of me. Do you, then?"

"I've spoken with Count Andrews at his hall of Maelphorydd on more than one occasion, and have run errands for him, helped with trading agreements, that sort of thing." The Duke nodded profusely upon hearing the Count's name spoken, beyond that, showing the smallest hint of being impressed. Lucian paused in deliberation, knowing he would mince his words should he not, nearly implying his disdain for the Count just a tongue's whip away. "I know very few people in the court, I know you'll be disappointed to hear. The Count has been a challenge for me, and I'm not so greatly in his favours to be able to speak with all his council."

"Are you married?"

"No, Lord."

The Duke showed severe disappointment, displeasure even, at the admission.

"You should. Marriage makes better of a man. But consider this: marry of your choosing now or of political convenience later, if your heart is truly set on this path." Lucian winced at the thought. It was an ugly thought, having a marriage forced upon oneself. It was something he really should have paid more heed to already. For some, it was a blessing. Lavellyrn worked in the shadows. "Is there anyone in the Count's court you would like to speak with?" the High Duke Dorrin queried further. Lucian hoped to understand whether he was now moving on from the previous conversation, such as it was, though decided not to hold up the incredibly forward Duke.

"Arlayne Thirwode... or the Count's sons..." Lucian fumbled an answer. This was a cruel question, and Lucian wasn't permitted to ignore it. "I suppose Sir Edwin Meri strikes a resonant chord with me. I can't lie that his age is a primary reason. He's a few years younger than me I think, and he holds excellent favour with the Count."

"Does he indeed? Can't say I've heard of him."

Of the Wilds

Even so, Lucian could almost see him filing the name away in a safe place, strenuously so, as if politics pained him. It may very well have done, and he might even admit it if Lucian cared to divert the conversation and ask him.

"I've seen him a few times and he was quite...eloquent," Lucian complimented sincerely. He left out from his praise that, once upon a time, he'd envied Sir Edwin for his position and power that had been handed down to him. What made him jealous in this was that Edwin was actually good at his job, so he'd been led to believe.

"I hope he's not one of these pretentious young knights who can't swing a sword without tripping himself over. I've seen enough of that sort for one lifetime."

"I couldn't say. He seemed fit enough when I saw him," to which the High Duke scoffed, as he was likely thinking of combat prowess more than anything. Lucian re-evaluated, for his sake and Sir Edwin's name. "Such things can be difficult to judge, at any rate."

"You speak from experience, I take it."

"I once killed a man, I think. In a fight," Lucian addressed hastily, feeling short of breath at his admission, and for the High Duke's hollow, discomforting expression, he might have been the one sucking the air from him.

For an awful few seconds, the Duke seemed appalled, and so Lucian could only hold his breath longer still while he waited for the verdict. It was a bloody stupid thing to say, he scolded himself. The Duke sniffed in disgust, shut the door hard and turned away from the wind.

"You think?" the High Duke asked, still motionless and blank of expression but for a twitch around his eyes.

"I was fighting another man at the time and as I parried a blow, I swung in desperation at another brigand near me and cut him deep, I know that much. It all happened so quickly, I couldn't remember what the man looked like or where he was when we analysed the aftermath. I'm not a natural fighter," he ended on, and was surprised to hear shame creeping into his words.

"Brigands, you say?"

"Three years ago, after The Purification."

"Ah. I see," the High Duke said solemnly and bowed his head. "A terrible time. I'll never know what fills men with such brazen delusions of hate, and whatever else holds men just shy of the brink of insanity as it did them. How they thought they could go around burning villages and escape the justice of Lameeri and the King, the gods only know. They must have convinced themselves they were being minimalistic. Serpents, not men," he corrected himself bitterly, snorted his disrespect again, and spat on the path. "The stragglers you fought must have been too cowardly to even fight alongside their accomplices and escaped before the battle even began, because I assure you, when the Knight of the Holy Storm commanded us through Ivden Pass, we routed them into the walls of the valley and killed every last one of them. Now that's a proper knight," he said admiringly, his eyes springing to life with a warrior's passion. "A true knight, true as one can be, who lives up to his reputation and holds the gods dear to his heart as well."

For want of something meaningful to say, Lucian instead remained silent, oblivious to how one should respond to high authority on such matters. The High Duke casually rested his hand on the hilt of his sword and scratched his beard as he appraised Lucian again.

"Where did this happen?"

"In my hometown of Caedor, Lord."

"Of course, as you told me on the Deyliath Road. Come to think of it, when I investigated the incident involving the fire, there was some mention of Caedor when we pressed the locals for information. I do believe it was Caedor," he said to himself, unconvinced. "Apparently someone was requesting documents about local mines, quite detailed documents actually, wanting to know about Sèhvorian steel, even though there was none in the area, or at least no one knew of any until... well, never mind. I don't suppose you know who it is, do you?"

"Caedor is not an especially small town, Lord. I wouldn't necessarily have even heard of it," though even as he spoke, Isaac invaded his thoughts and he prayed it was not him.

"It's almost certainly not connected, at any rate, so I wouldn't worry if I were you."

"Do you suppose one would look for that sort of information in Harth rather than a small village?" Lucian asked edgily. The High Duke huffed and shrugged.

"There are plenty of opportunities for those kinds of endeavours in Harth. It is where a considerable amount of it ends up, after all. From the Isle of Sèhvor. Why?" the High Duke snapped, raising his chin. His fingers played with the pommel of his sword.

"My father has a fascination with it, is all. He's an inventor."

Lucian was, all of a sudden, acutely conscious of his surroundings, feeling that he was being watched by hundreds of people hiding in the dark. Be it because the Duke suspected him of foul play in some unspoken illicit activity, by the paleness of his skin that betrayed a hidden thought, or simply because he sensed the discourse straining its limitations, the Duke narrowed his eyes. Then he almost smiled.

"Go on then, you're free to leave. I'm done with you anyway. Gods be with you."

Lucian knew at that moment that the High Duke was not intending to be rude, neither had he ever spoken to him maliciously. That was just his way with strangers and most everyone else probably: stern, and in this case, seemingly wanting to test Lucian's patience and mettle as if daring him to decry his manner. He was the High Duke, and yet he didn't act, Lucian suspected, with apparent rudeness just because he could.

It wasn't this that wracked his brains as he left the lord's presence in a state of unease, nor the honour of being afforded such trust at instantaneous notice by a man of such noble-blooded stature as Dorrin Santorellian. The gate creaked in a manner that was almost painful as the guard shut it behind him. He got the impression that Lord Dorrin was still watching, albeit for lack of anything else to look at, while talking to another man now.

Only when he was out of the range of their senses, and beyond what he thought was the sight of the archers, did he quicken his pace. It might turn out to be a misunderstanding, as these things often were, but as always, he took responsibility and assumed Isaac had clung to some grand ambition. He paced to the stables, and from there, rode to a carriage for hire, where he arranged for his horse to help pull it. Lucian then dozed off in the back, in the knowledge that he would rectify any mistake his brother had made.

Chapter Eighteen: Cleansing

Mists tumbled from the hills like a ghostly apparition, intrigued by the superstitious man in the roadside Watchhouse, never reading more than a paragraph of the papers laid out neatly on the desk in front of him before glancing over his shoulder for the smallest indication of death coming to greet him. In Sir Edwin's distrust, even the early morning mists could have been servants of Mūraci spies, or of the traitor Elias Olswalt come to smother him, for all the cold suspicious glares he gave to everything around him.

Forcing himself to focus once more on the records before him, Edwin saw that they spoke of events occurring at this particular Ranger stop, to help them retrace their steps when the need arose. There were so few here, as every so often they would be collected and filed away at Maelphorydd or one of the keeps. What was here showed no indication of Sergeant Denkyn and his men having visited. That could have meant any number of things, most frustratingly. It could have been that they were all illiterate, or that they considered there to be no foreseeable requirement of wasting their time with what the Count would have called nonsense, or submitting to new methods. On the other hand, he had reason to be wary of just about everyone. What he'd seen of Melphor a few days prior, and its newly invigorated state, suggested the corruption extended beyond Captain Olswalt.

The next record, on the following page, skipped five days, he noticed in a lagged response, flicking back to make sure his weary mind had not deceived him. Whether a crime worthy of note had occurred or not, someone, at some point, had to write the date and remark for nothing happening, if that was the case. Even those who were illiterate were taught to mark a cross for nothing happening if they arrived at a Watch stop in the evening and no one else had made their mark. As before, his mind tugged back and forth at every possibility, wrestling to compile his ideas in some coherent order. Perhaps they wanted to conceal incriminating information, written without such consideration or knowledge by another, but only a fool would do so without laying false records in their place, and to assume folly on the part of his enemies would be to tread a most dangerous path.

A ploy or double bluff then, to deliberately provide Edwin, or any sharp-minded individual, with a false lead; to whet the appetite while the perpetrator continued on their heinous path unhindered, to a goal that was not yet clear. Or, again, it could have carried no meaning at all. The most frightening aspect of this whole affair was that his enemies could play such tricks on him, and if it wasn't deliberate, then he was just a stupid, paranoid man fumbling around in the dark.

Sir Edwin could feel the anger rising and the bags beneath his eyes spreading - as a shadow creeps across the hills at dusk - knowing he must have been pale to the eye at riding his horse so hard. Kate's stitching held strong and, remarkably, no physical signs of infection had emerged, but it was wearing him thin. One final glance at the papers told him all he needed to know, for he knew in his heart the finality of it before he did it; rising carefully from his chair, he tucked the records neatly into their chest, as if they'd never been touched and, feeling pragmatic if little else, replaced the lock he'd beaten on with a hammer with a new, unscathed one. At the door, he hesitated and peered through the tiny window, eyes wide and breath so heavy he had to clutch at the old brick to steady his balance. After an unbearable period of time had drifted him by like a wisp of smoke, the sound of hooves rang out, as if taunting him. He knelt by the door, stolen sword in hand, and he hardened like clay, as he'd done at the Count's bidding in that dungeon time ago, ready to lash out for the truth.

The solitary Watchman ran to the door, he heard that loud enough, probably collecting something at his superior's bidding, as he would have drawn his sword had he known of an intruder in advance. It was only seeing the lock which Edwin had bent out of shape with the sword that stopped him in his paces; dread rebalanced with fortune when the Watchman, so tragically green, stepped in with only a clueless look on his face to indicate that he'd even noticed something wrong.

Edwin swung the sword, enclosed in its scabbard, to the man's face, clapping it against his jaw beneath the protection of the helm. He lunged forward to strike down again, this time upon the very top of the helm, knocking the Watchman out cold. At his own risk, he caught the man, indeed waking the demon that slept in his belly, breathing fire on his three wounds, as before. Edwin knew it would happen but caught him anyway, as if he would die if he hit the ground. It was the least he could have done, the knight consoled himself even as he cut a bag of coins from his belt, not for the lust of gold, but for fear of leaving a trail. As it now was, a band of opportunistic highwaymen might have sought to burgle the place at just the right time, and fled for fear of spoiling their good luck.

"Sorry, friend. My need is more desperate than yours," Edwin said aloud, as if it would help.

He rubbed a hand over his near bald scalp, the cold of the crisp, misty morning biting it more than it ever could when long hair had stemmed from it. As he did so, he looked left to try in vain to convince himself that he could do some good in Melphor, but it was a hollow and despondent effort at best. The judging gazes of unknowable amounts of hateful eyes would not do well to warm his heart in this dark and cold time. It was fear that kept his thoughts on the city of his birth, because through the valley, he'd passed more than one group of Watch Rangers, and he worked his memory at a sprint to recall the trail he'd left. How many had seen him? When? Where? Who of the remote villagers he'd spoken to would remember this tired face, and who among them would report him? He'd done his best to be nobody for days, but now he was a nobody who'd attacked a Watchman. There was no going back. He might have ignored the Mūraci diplomat those weeks ago and now have only his conscience in pain. Edwin wasn't raised as a darned ideologue; this could all be a less than altruistic response. If he was now playing at honour without realising, the shame would bring him too low this time.

Kate and Gèyll were his only option and he was glad of it, as Kate, in particular, spoke to the best part of him, whether in silence or otherwise, though sadly she didn't yet know it. There was to be no complication of carnality. He considered that she might like that, but it was irrelevant.

That was that, then. For once he would feel like a real knight, saving people and easing the hearts of Kate and Gèyll with his presence and sword, and to end this grand twisted plot of treachery in unison would please him like nothing else.

~

"We'll leave this very night then," Kate's mother had informed her upon Henri's return and subsequent telling that there was nothing suspicious on the road to Aurail. A decision made so suddenly that Kate knew at once that she had planned on following it through, whether it was safe or not.

With none other to share their burdens with, Kate and her mother had scarcely strayed from each other's sight during the past few days, to the extent that Mother accompanied her on her walks through the hills and by the river in the valley, saying little but providing a blanket of comfort by her sheer presence. Waiting for word from Sir Edwin had been even more arduous than expected; it felt as if summer had shifted to winter with the lack of his knightly presence, so, predictably, her mother decided he was taking far too long for her nerves to cope with. Kate remembered sighing so deeply with relief that in her distorted reflection in the window, she could have sworn that her face bloomed with colour again, like one of her flowers in the garden sucking in the sunlight with the jerky consistency of a picture story being flicked at the corners of her father's notebooks.

Her mother's pacing and constant shaking of her head had become so infuriating that, by the end of it, she'd wanted to curl into a ball and scream at the world, but had saved that for her dreams. Even last night, she'd screamed with sound that only she could hear, and it echoed through the valley of Caedor so loudly that it had shattered the tiny stars above, as the people of old had understood them, and no one heard.

That was yesterday. Today she sat by the window of an inn, wondering why she'd never tried proper mead before, the honey twang lifting her spirits, and staring into the heady dawn, recounting her steps up to now. On reflection, those days of late flashed before her as dreams as well, contrary to the aching pain that lasted almost forever.

"Entrust me with your house's keeping," Henri had offered Mother, "and I'd be honoured. Your husband did a lot for me."

The words "so long as you continue paying me" silently found their way to her, and she was unnerved. She hoped she'd imagined it because, despite everything, he sounded like he wanted someone to be loyal to and give him orders; he had polished his leather attire to as close a mirror sheen as could come of them, perhaps in the pretence that he was serving a great House of Burtal.

Her mother trusted him well enough, given the circumstances, and Kate trusted her mother, so that had been the end of it. The healer Jyric had imparted wisdom Kate had forgotten immediately, and had promised something or other, but that seemed long ago. They'd left soon after, before dark, and already she was not quite so relieved anymore, anxious at heading to the red city: as good as a foreign land to her. With any luck, her father's stories of epic detail would guard and guide her.

In her melancholy, she could only gasp when she turned to see Sir Edwin Meri standing on the threshold of the inn, holding the door. She stared into her tankard, knowing he'd spotted her, and even as she feigned ignorance, a grin crept onto her face. The knight of Melphor did not budge until she looked at him again, whereupon he beckoned with a wink and left the door to swing shut.

She found him again in the stable yard, jerking his head from side to side, scanning the landscape like a hawk, or on second thought, a mouse. His sharp gaze and strong posture lent him a predator's fearlessness; her perception shattered when she drew closer to see the alarm driving his eyes about. She'd seen it before, but in his absence, she'd forgotten, and liked it even less now.

"Tidings, Kathrynne," the knight said with elegant courtesy.

"Isn't it dangerous for you to be out here?" she said, dismissive of his greeting, unintentionally defying her instincts to greet him with pleasantries until he saw fit to put her out of her misery and speak of his business.

"There are no Watchmen staying here right now, be in no doubt. If there were, I wouldn't have walked through that door. Most of them wouldn't recognise me anyway, and not in this garb, but you can't be too careful."

"How are you feeling?" Kate said, concerned, still determined to act selflessly, barely before her tongue slipped a million questions.

"I wouldn't want to be the judge of that, so it's a good thing I met you when I did. Seeing as you ask though, I've been better. I feel sick from riding, and the worst of my wounds sometimes throbs like a second heart. I tell myself it's not all bad, and at least there is not no feeling at all: I've heard it said that numbness is a terrible sign."

"So have I," Kate replied honestly, licking her lips nervously. Confused by his sudden appearance and startling change of clothes, she remained mesmerised until such time that it was awkward to stare any longer. "Here, let me take a look."

"Behind the bird pens," Edwin suggested so quickly he might have planned it.

The Voice of Kings

Despite his eagerness, he remained in the stable yard, peering down at the sodden ground, scraping one boot around in the dirt almost ritualistically, before nodding solemnly and heading for the shed with a pained look descending from his brow to engulf his face.

"What's the matter? What happened?"

"I thought that would have been the first thing you'd ask," Edwin said questioningly.

"I took your lax attitude to mean the situation isn't so urgent that...well, you didn't seem in such a rush to me."

When they arrived behind the shed, Sir Edwin span and they faced off in silence, Kate betraying ever more interest every second as she wondered where he'd picked up his mismatched attire. He wore an arming doublet, yet no armour, and over that, a sleeveless tunic, and finally over that he wore a black riding cloak which sagged to the ground, slightly tattered and frayed but in one piece, giving him the appearance more of the rugged knight, even with the doublet being a touch too tight.

"I can't deny that I want to know, more than anything, if you discovered anything about my brother." She paused and raised one eyebrow, and looked him up and down again. "And what you've been doing."

"Quite a lot, though on reflection, very little also, if I judge my actions by their results. I have no good news for you; neither have I bad news, so take that as you will. Be that as it may, I still believe there is no immediate danger to you or your family."

The tension rolled off her shoulders, the chilly morning air now her only scorner, and so she thanked him and waited patiently for him to proceed with what she'd already alluded to in the yard, whereupon he laughed as if he'd lost clarity. He lifted his tunic and pulled open the strings of his doublet. There was a sword at his left side, she also noted: not his own. That had gone with Sergeant Denkyn. Nor Captain Olswalt's that the sergeant had left behind in his haste, as her mother was keeping that very blade beside her bed in the tavern. There was a dagger too, its hilt old and worn, at his right side, tucked up to a purse stuffed with coins.

Kneeling before him to inspect his three gashes, first she adequately unravelled the bandages such that they could be used again. She was more scared than ever that he would recoil in pain if she was not the personification of gentleness, and it would be all her fault, and so the river flowed calmly in the valley and Kate was all but immobile and breathless. When the bandage was off, a frown appeared, because she suspected, and suspected only, that while her stitching was proving her worth at that, the skin around it was stretching. Those ugly bruises needed no expert.

The skin was coarse on the sealed wounds when she ran a finger over it with the lightest of touches, and smooth elsewhere. A different tension heaved its way inside her now: one that had not risen even once when he'd been unconscious. The instant reaction was that it wasn't what it felt like, and that she wanted nothing more from him than his bravery and loyalty to justice: her very own sword of Lameeri. That he remained effortlessly, resolutely stoic and unresponsive only reinforced his image of a paragon of virtue, and the tension made her freeze for a moment as she shot the idea down. Her mother was one kind of paragon, Sir Edwin another: a personalised shield wall to protect her from the dangers she might face. He was admirable and spectacular and noble and brave: all these things she saw as if he were a perfect knight but nothing more, she agreed on, quite insistently so.

"Something vexes you?" Edwin pressed.

"Yes, your health, Sir," she fretted. "I may want to touch up on my work here and apply some more medicines. Oh, and new bandages too, if I can get ahold of any. I think you'll recover well, otherwise. In my opinion," she added apologetically, fully aware that her expertise cut short here, and would have been ashamed not to make it known. "I can't guarantee your continued health if you don't allow yourself to heal though."

"I hope I'll have the peace and the time soon enough, I really do. But I can't help the trouble that's come to pass, wish as I might," Edwin sighed and smiled.

"What do you mean?"

"*That's* why I have discovered so little. I was here the night I took my leave of you, you see. The fight I got myself into with a Watchman wasn't the worst mistake I could have made, but I can only apologise till I make it right."

"I see," Kate said distantly, wrapping him up in his bandages once more. She wondered what she was supposed to make of his confession, but was interrupted before she could begin.

"If there is one blessing that I can count my own, and there can be only one, it's that my identity remains uncompromised, and having gone straight to Melphor from there, I was then one step ahead of them, there and back. In a way," he muttered sadly.

"Meaning?"

"It was locked down when I arrived. There was an inordinate amount of guards outside the gates. I couldn't be sure they were actively acting on behalf of whatever scheme Olswalt is entangled in, but neither could I risk testing it."

"So what now?" Kate said meekly, rising to her full heart and stepping back as if too awed by his close presence. "We go to Aurail after all?"

"I can't suggest anything else."

"But what about the Count? He could hold some vital information to..."

"Forget Andrews," he snapped, or near as he could, unable to be rude to her. "Forget the Count, and forget Melphor, and Captain Olswalt, and whatever else you might think or speculate of this debacle. There are only dead ends in the highlands now, and I'm done with all this, as I'm sure you are," and Edwin raised his eyebrows half-expectedly, thus asking, in his weariness, that she would agree with all immediacy.

The Voice of Kings

"Nothing would please me more than to put all this behind me and see things return to normal," Kate replied with firm resolve. It had, in truth, taken time to arrange the decisive words in her head, and longer to say them thusly.

I'll be strong, she ordered herself. *I'll be strong, for Isaac, and Father, and Marcel, and Lucian, and let it all collapse in on me when it's all caught up. Don't let your worries bring you down for too long at a time*, she recited in silence. Family first. And she felt unendingly mature for thinking so.

Bringing Edwin's injuries to light had done the very same to the pain, and now, as he walked to the end of the shed, he took extra care not to strain anything, nodding sagely at Kate's sentiment as he did so. Upon the shed, he leaned as he examined a scene since passed from afar: just a muddy patch of lawn where horses calmly grazed in their pens. The unmistakeable cry of an eagle of Mürathneè rang in triumph from within the shed, joyous, or so it sounded, even while caged, and the poor carrier pigeons must have been scared stiff. In Edwin's ponderous moment, Kate peeked through the wooden boards of the shed and saw, through a gap in the cloth draped over its cage, the great eagle, looking at her through its brilliant eyes that inspired no fear in her whatsoever. It inspired wonder in her, with its lively, knowing face, as it waited obediently for orders, as trained ones were wont to do.

"Is that all then?" Sir Edwin said suddenly, sounding distant.

"How do you mean?"

"Well, I had an opportunity to discover our enemy's plans and affiliates, and I failed. You're not the least bit angry with me?"

She breathed in deeply and bit her lip. He almost appeared to be goading her into a confession.

"Would you like me to be?" she settled on.

"No, but I'd deserve it. If someone came to me and told me that perhaps my family was in danger and that they'd had a chance to stop it but messed it up, I'd be angry too."

"If you want me to be angry with you," Kate persisted in defiance, "I'm afraid I just don't want to be. You made a mistake, as we all do. Don't tempt me," she finished shakily, her face turned to stone in her fear of his words.

Edwin turned and stared with a pained, thoughtful expression into Kate's eyes, unblinking and sympathetic.

"Sorry," he said simply, and forced a weak chuckle. Kate breathed in relief again.

"Did the fight happen there?" she said to avoid further awkwardness, pointing to the yard outside the stables. "Is that why it bothers you so?"

"Right there, yes. I hope I'm not going to make a habit of getting into fights outside inns," he wheezed quietly through a cough. The eagle squawked its triumphant cry from its prison again. Kate remembered the eagle drawing she'd seen recently, and mused on the rest.

"Next it'll be a sea serpent," she joked, keeping to herself visions of him battling one.

"Why a serpent?" Edwin laughed.

"Oh, I saw one in a book recently," she said more clearly, remembering herself. "A picture book about the gifts of gods. It had a drakeel in it too, if I remember true, which pales before some of these foreign creatures so it wasn't given much attention. Then again, there were lots of things in it. It was a bit of a mess, in hindsight. But it showed one king with a serpent as his pet, I think, so I thought it was, not appropriate exactly, but..."

"Kate, you're excused," the young knight replied softly. "You don't have to explain yourself."

His tiredness caught up with him at that moment and, again without request, Kate helped him sit down, and then she sat beside him, her legs up and her head resting on the wooden backing. Edwin rummaged in a pocket and quickly withdrew another item he'd not left Caedor with: a small leather pouch which he'd no doubt stolen like the rest of it. From that, he took a large lump of biscuit sprinkled with sugar and cracked it in half.

"Shortbread?" he offered simply with his kindest manner.

She took it gratefully and, in eating it, felt more relaxed, not being expected to say anything. He shared fresh water too, from a hide flask. A strong gust of wind snatched at the grass and violently shook a cluster of trees on a nearby hilltop, where one particularly old and frail tree bent and creaked slightly, shimmering in the early morning light like to a stylised painting. Where normally she would be pleased to stand in the way of the wind, right now she was content with the few weak gusts that spiralled around the edges of the shed. Never mind that the wind was no threat, it made her feel safer sitting close to Edwin anyway, from even the grasp of nature.

Edwin cleared his throat only after voraciously consuming a piece of shortbread, and no wonder, for the poor man must have been starving. He scratched his scalp thoughtfully, "What did you mean when you said you *thought* he had a pet serpent?" Her face became blank. "Just now, you said in the old book that you thought one of the kings had a pet serpent."

"Just that it wasn't made clear," Kate replied with a shrug.

"Surely you don't believe it, do you?"

"Not as such," she said defensively. "We've all heard stories of the gifts for kings, never mind if they're also in a children's book or not. The book just got me thinking, that's all."

"But it wouldn't if you'd been rummaging through the attic a month ago now, would it? You wouldn't give it a second thought, but now that some madman in Mūrac has decided to fulfil the prophecy, or make his own one, suddenly you fear demons will come for you in the night."

"Am I wrong to fear them now? I mean, I don't fear that, exactly, rather...something. The unknown, I suppose."

The Voice of Kings

Edwin sighed, his eyes cheerless as he smiled.

"I know exactly what you mean. Hark, though: an image in a children's book shouldn't inspire fear, no matter the original source. Think with your brain as well. I know you've got a good one. Who knows, maybe the King was about to ride it."

"Ride it?" Kate said with the same confusion Edwin had displayed at her suggesting the relevance of the book in the first place. "I suppose if he could control it, there's no reason he couldn't attach a saddle," she laughed weakly and Edwin rubbed her hair as he too relished their moment. *Too much like Isaac.* A wretched mix of emotions came from that. It was gone again in a flash, when the fear crept back into being. "Do you believe any of those stories, Sir? Do you think the gods would bestow such gifts on men?"

There was a pause, a painfully long one while Edwin chewed on a piece of biscuit and wrestled for the right words. He knew what he meant, Kate assumed, but the foundation of believing is sometimes difficult to phrase.

"I, er...I believe," he said slowly, "that if the gods are as the holy men tell, glorious, and righteous, and understanding, they would never do such a thing while a king like Alamier yet lives. Besides, it will happen in our time of need. Have you seen any demons yet?"

"No. You're probably right." She stopped before taking another bite from her piece of biscuit and felt a smile on one side of her face. "Funny, I think my father spoke right through you then."

"Did he indeed?" Edwin mused with just the same kind of smile.

There was a glint in his eyes as he squinted at something not present, as if noticing it for the first time, and suddenly time no longer stood still for them as it had done for a few minutes. He adjusted himself to get comfortable, and Kate helped him rise to his feet at that signal alone. She'd spoken highly of her father, she thought, as had her mother. His expression was...what was that? Bleak? But more likely he was tired, and wanted to end the conversation with a compliment as that.

From her room, Kate's mother wistfully surveyed the view until the young knight of Melphor entered her vision, and she recoiled. Edwin raised a hand in greeting, but the colour retreated from his face. She was more likely to express her disdain than Kate.

"I'll be right down, Sir," Kate's mother called out, and disappeared.

"And I will take my leave of you," Edwin said to Kate.

"What?!" she blurted, more aggressively than she'd imagined.

"You'll have your opportunity to fix me up again another time, if it's so important. The next inn, or further on, even. But I feel it would be safer for me if I rode alone until we both reach the flatlands. And if we don't meet up on the road, remember this: I'll be just ahead of you, and before you reach Aurail, I'll speak with your father, and he'll ride out to embrace you."

He climbed his horse using his own strength, leaving Kate baffled below.

"Sir Edwin," she said for fear he would leave even if she didn't bid him farewell, and she gave a low curtsey.

"Fair madam." And he was gone.

Kate's mother found her in the stable yard with her neck craned back, watching the clouds drift overhead.

"Where is he?" her mother said, and her expression became one of sympathy, for she already knew.

"Gone again. We're going to Aurail and he'll meet us at the next inn, no earlier."

Kate felt an arm wrapped around her back and her mother's hand stroking her shoulder as she was led back inside. There she told her mother everything they'd discussed over a breakfast she hastened to eat with so little precaution she nearly choked, and was forced to pause and glug more mead. Ever so patiently, her mother sat beside her, hands in lap, ignoring those who stopped to study them: two women travelling alone, and not only that, huddled together like conspirators. If it looked that way, she didn't care.

Carrying their belongings to their horses a short while later, Kate's mother strode with purpose and passion, revitalised in the cold air that she so loved. Just yesterday, she'd looked older than ever: dishevelled, Kate might have even described her, and today she was as sprightly as Kate had ever seen her. If it was something she'd said at breakfast, she couldn't tell.

"There is one thing that bothers me," her mother remarked, before mounting her horse. "The next inn on the direct route to Aurail is, if I'm not mistaken, the Emperor's Crown. Does Sir Edwin know that it's a prime spot for Watchmen to stay?"

"I couldn't say," Kate despaired, tensing up at the possibilities to behold.

"He's shown survival instincts, at any rate. We'll not worry about him," her mother assured, essentially an order, for Kate was clearly lost as to what to feel. "Just whisper a little prayer, just in case."

Kate mounted her own horse next. It was a beautiful black and white mare, gentle enough for her, where her mother, who excelled at riding after all these years, had a mare with a little more temper. She exuded confidence in her plain dress, and passed it on to Kate. She didn't wear Elias's sword, although there had been some deliberation surrounding it. More than likely, it would attract unwanted attention: it was not proper for a woman to be seen armed so heavily. It waited for her elsewhere, strapped to the horse.

"You're sure Henri was the best choice?" Kate asked on the road.

"Good enough. He likes to pretend he's mysterious, but I think not. He has a certain eagerness about him. He'll do well, but even if he doesn't and he burns our house down, right now I think I wouldn't care, so long as the family is reunited."

"Me too."

The Voice of Kings

For the second time that day, Kate felt mature, for putting family first was never something she'd really had to do, and as her house crumpled to ash in her imagination, there was no regret, no dissonance in her wishes.

The mists slithered back into the hills shortly thereafter, as she galloped into territory unknown to her, where the hills grew beside the road and loomed as one last spectacle before the flatlands inevitably took command of the landscape, at which point she could not foresee. Most likely the following day, if she'd understood correctly, and if her imagination held true to life, the mists would return, especially if they were to travel via Ylden Parragor, the capital of the flatlands. She'd always thought of Ylden Parragor, surrounded on its island fortress by bogs and a moat, to encapsulate a time long past, of early sensibilities, constantly foggy and home to monsters lurking deep beneath the water.

The inhabitants would hide beyond tall stone walls, and look suspiciously on outsiders from their thatched huts. It was almost certainly nonsense of course, and her father's lessons soothed her mind, warning her not to be so quick to judge outsiders. Often such criticism was a reflection of one's own uncertainty, even if by chance it was true, he'd said, and he was probably right. Already she felt alien to these lands.

The road was winding and became thinner than usual, and but for the sky, they were hidden. Her mother slowed her horse to a canter at a sharp turning which appeared open to another wide open space, and threw up a hand for Kate's immediate cooperation.

"Steady. There's a lot of blood here. Looks like wild animals have been fighting."

Telling Kate to keep her distance only gave her a mind to move faster still, to be safe beside her mother, and if she was being honest, curiosity drove her just as much.

At the turning of the road, her mother was a picture of a ghost, and her horse huffed, and panted, and stamped its feet in futile protest. Her mother's scream was too late to prevent the scene from unravelling. Kate was by her side, and every muscle in her body twitched, her mare interpreting the movements as a signal to run at full pelt, only to have the reins violently jerked back.

All joy died, curiosity a sick caricature just as her face was, muscles pinned in place to reveal only the utmost terror. For a second that felt like a week, the wind whipped at her face and cackled. So delusional and crushed was she for that time that she almost thought she *could* hear laughter, distant and mocking, her own burbling taunting her in a cruel echo.

Not again. Not again.

Where one moment she had been frozen in time, the next she'd leapt from her horse so haphazardly she might have sprained herself, not that that was an issue. As she ran to the perversion of life, the words *not again* spoke to her a third time, only this time she could have wished to relive that day, because at least her brothers and father had emerged from the chaos of battle unscathed, and even the bandits hadn't strewn bodies like the finish of a twisted art form, where Sir Edwin's blood was the paint strewn on an earthen canvas. *Those* men hadn't butchered anyone as one would a resistive animal. And, oh, how he'd clearly resisted.

Blood was not merely leaking as from a simple stab wound, but splashed in lines and pools across the road and upon the grassy banks either side. She slipped once on a small patch, then again in a puddle, crashing to her hands and knees, fouling her green dress in the mire. Her mother was cursing in a manner she'd never heard, brandishing Elias Olswalt's sword aloft and shouting for her to come back, but she was deranged and crawling through the blood, some dried, some sticky pools, to the knight's body. She'd saved him once, and it could have looked worse than it was. *No, it couldn't.* Her eyes raced over his injuries.

An arrow to the chest, square on, a stab wound to the shoulder, shallow slashes across his upper chest, and more all the way down. Two distinct stab wounds, three, four. She counted with growing despair. No less than ten, and some, if she was not so crazed beyond reason, looked to have been inflicted from behind.

She cocked her head back. No healing proficiency or medicine could salvage him now, she admitted. The arrow couldn't have flung him from his stirrups, so what happened after? There were bloody marks beneath his feet, and strewn across the ground where he'd been dragged. There'd been more to it before that though. Had he risen to fight back after the initial fall?

It didn't matter now. He was far removed now, and her mother, who'd navigated the field of blood with more precision, was clamping her arms around Kate and dragging her to her feet.

Bastards, she screamed in her head.

"Kathrynne, we can't stay here!" she uttered clearly to make certain she would be understood. She glanced at the body, grimacing and looking, like Kate, like she might be sick at any moment. "He was shot in the chest, from northwards, where he was riding. They must have been waiting for him. The blood…it's fresh, Kate. We need to go now!"

Through tears that streamed down her cheeks and clouded her vision as she was dragged away, Kate discerned the spaces where the dagger and purse had been, and the sword. The last of him she saw was his rough, handsome face. She wished it could have been peaceful.

"Come, Kathrynne," her mother urged. "We can't go to Aurail. They know. We need to go to Melphor." Kate hoped to speak, but only a distorted gurgle erupted: a croak that censored all thoughts. The message was clear. She stared at her mother as if she were mad. "I'll explain later."

A fire burst into life inside Kate as she realised, to her horror, what her mother intended.

"We're going to leave him?" she gasped through sobs.

"We have no choice!"

"Imperial justice!" she screeched, desperately. "There's no…"

The Voice of Kings

"I know, my darling. There's nothing right to be found here."

She aided Kate in climbing her mare, now weeping like a child, so like a waterfall. She might have been crying blood for the pain that stung in her eyes. Her mother might have been crying too, but she couldn't rightly say for sure, and if at all, not necessarily solely for Edwin.

"Bastards," she now mumbled aloud in her own little world, at no one in particular. "Bastards." And she repeated it over and over, each time more desperate, her voice breaking.

There were shouts from afar, silenced by shushing and reignited in argument, and a dissenter issuing stark orders, and hooves accompanying them. Kate's mother rode beside her to slap her horse's rump, to make it start where Kate would not, and she was away, riding back the way she'd come, her mother speeding beside her. She veered ahead and signalled to turn into a road Kate could have sworn they hadn't come from, but in her tear-blinding distress, she trusted her mother's decision without argument.

The loud voices followed them. The road was cobbled and narrow, and the banks stood tall, so the beating of hooves echoed upwards and outwards. Her mother pulled in closer, her panic directed all around, diagnosing the situation. Then something clicked into place, and though she couldn't possibly be relieved, there was determination which gave Kate hope.

"Faster!" she yelled, and leaned over to strike Kate's mare again. "You need to make her go faster. Push her to her limits for just a minute, and when I tell you, before a bridge just ahead, you must stop and dismount."

The bridge soon sprang into sight: a bridge of old stone which arched over a river. Four struts, in the shape of priests wearing low-hanging hoods, helped hold aloft a curved canopy of stone over the bridge, and between the priests, on either side, identical depictions of black writhing smoke cowered in their wake: smoke where demons hid, creatures of shadow, a faceless evil. It was a reasonable assumption, in that case, that the river travelled down to the Basin of Cleansing, where men and women would once take their supposedly unclean possessions, and perform on them an old ritual.

It was no help in orienting her. She'd never paid mind to maps and roads, but now she wished she had. Her mother spoke urgently, words that were whipped away by an echo of the mob, that she all but mimed her terror.

"Slow down now, for gods' sakes," her mother shouted, and she forced her horse to a quick standstill, just before the bridge.

"What are we doing?" Kate managed, clambering dazedly from her horse to mirror her mother.

"We're both covered in blood. We can't be seen, not by Edwin's killers, and not by any Watchmen for that matter."

Cleansing

As she said this, she let go of her agitated horse and struck it hard with a "giddy up", whereupon it raced down a slope beside the bridge and continued on upstream with no sign of slowing down. Kate did the same and, at the galloping cue of horses that were not their own charging along the track, they ran down a slope across the opposite side of the bridge, sprinting as the voices clawed back into focus, both of them fixed wholly on a small waterfall that could conceal them.

Kate sprinted ahead and leapt, without consideration for her own safety, at what rocks might be waiting to break her at the bottom of the waterfall. She plunged into the river, unharmed, followed by her mother, both of them resurfacing a moment later to cling to a rock jutting from the riverbed, to fight the flow of the water and the suction of the tumbling falls. Though it was loud, directly by their heads, they heard the horses gallop over the bridge, hopefully seeing their own horses in the distance. One stopped, of this Kate was certain, and she held her breath instinctively, as if even the wind would work against her and deliver the sound of her frantic heartbeat to the enemy.

There was no indication of time in the wait for the horseman to leave them in peace. Kate was numbing to the bone in the terrible, cold water, and her thoughts were of life and death, numbing also, as if drifting into a sleep. Eventually the horseman bolted for whatever machination he'd devised, but stopped again some way ahead, where both Kate and her mother could see him, and lowered themselves further until the water level rippled a short way below their eyes. The horseman, frightful and burning against the sky, was armour-clad, wearing a covering helm, but there was nothing else that could be made out, for the glaring sun smothered their adversary from view. By mercy, he rode on again, this time never to stop while within their sight.

From the besmirched red river, they came gasping, Mother first unsurprisingly, as in Kate's opinion, she was overall more physically fit than her. Once more, they travelled the road they'd just previously arrived from, only now they walked, their clothes soaked through and hair bunched up and dripping. Kate's dress had shed much of its blood, yet only in the sense that it was glued on. Now it was just a green dress stained red, and no force of nature or mortal method could ever remove the young knight's blood. If the cost of healing people was to carry the guilt of their demise should they die, and to have to personally deal with such consequences as these if the patient happened to belong to some greater purpose, she wanted no part in it.

This isn't normal, she tried telling herself. *This is not a normal occurrence*. It could do her no good in her current state. Her own advice rolled right off her.

Shortly thereafter, two horses trotted along behind them: their own horses, to their surprise, a blessing and boon where none others could be found. How the horses escaped their hunters and located their masters was not thought upon, though it was taken for granted that, because they were siblings and had always stayed close together, they arrived at the same time.

The mane of Kate's mare was washed of much blood as it had clearly swum through the river. Kate did her best to ignore what was left and rode quickly, as if doing so could cleanse her mind of all ills.

~

"What kind of blade?" the blacksmith asked, wiping sweat from his brow and dirty beard, folding his arms tightly over his leather apron. He appeared confused at the prospect of a woman needing a sword. His guard was of high alert, such that he presumed Gèyll was in the market for a blade with the intent to murder, because no woman he knew could fight. Certainly it perplexed him, and study Gèyll he did indeed try to do, ever so hard, while she browsed a sample of his wares, which were laid upon a market stall beside his forge.

"Something like that will do me, will it not?" Gèyll suggested, pointing to a standard steel shortsword. "I've no experience, if I'm to be honest, and I'm not strong either."

"You shouldn't be using a sword at all if you don't know how to use it."

"Just a precaution. I don't like the idea of travelling with my daughter without some means of defence. We all know what kinds of men lurk some of the more tangential roads."

"Fair enough then. Can't say I blame you either. That sword there's a fine enough piece for you, I suppose. I wouldn't recommend anything bigger than that to you, not because you can't hold anything else, but because a swing with a smaller sword is easier to pull back. Good for amateurs, trust me."

"Okay, yes, very well," Gèyll said distractedly, looking all around hopelessly, as if he was simply boring her.

"Something the matter?" He leaned in conspiratorially and rested his elbows on the market stand. "Was that your daughter you came in with, back there? Everyone saw the two of you, no use pretending we didn't."

"You'd do well not to make idle suppositions!" Gèyll barked back at him, every muscle in her body tensed in rage, offended as if he'd tried to attack her. "I'll tell you what I told the innkeep. My daughter suffered a miscarriage on the road." Letting loose a few tears couldn't have been easier, and screwing up her face in fury at the injustice of it all too, because while the words rolled off her tongue, it was a different injustice that gripped her imagination. "Less than two months old, it was, when it just…bled right through her. And she was so excited to be a mother. I blame these bloody roads, I do. They need evening out already."

"I understand!" the blacksmith intervened with a rough tone. The vulgar language probably helped. "This one, was it?" he said hastily, picking up the shortsword.

Gèyll, thereafter, avoided the crowd of what must have been the entire village turning out for whatever faire she didn't care to observe, and moved inconspicuously to a deserted corner, with a poor-quality roll of parchment in one hand and the shortsword in the other. There, she shed as many tears as she could muster in as long a time as she dared, before returning to the small inn, behind which Kate sat, wearing a clean dress and her long fur coat wrapped around her, staring pensively into nothing. Traces of vomit sickened the nostrils from somewhere out of sight. With her left hand, she absentmindedly stroked her mare which kneeled behind her, while her right hovered over a large iron brazier of hearth embers: orange sparks which sprang up and were pulled away by the breeze. Gèyll followed their ascent past the sun and saw that it was still morning. Almost impossible to believe that everything had happened so very quickly, and equally so to think that a few hours prior, she'd been cautiously optimistic.

"Still feeling sick?" Gèyll said as she sat to the right of her daughter.

"Very," Kate managed, through lips as dry as bone. "I can barely keep the image out of my head."

"I know. You're no soldier; you can't hope to shrug off something like this. You shouldn't try. But you've made it through this pain before, and when the Emperor's justice meets Edwin's killers, you'll do it again. Just don't try to rush it."

"No. I need to be stronger." There was no conviction in Kate's voice: more self-deprecation than anything.

"It's not you who needs to be strong," Gèyll said softly, rubbing Kate's shoulder. "You'll be strong *enough*, I know you will. Just show your strength to the outside world and that will be enough, but you tell me everything you want, Kathrynne; you tell me everything that crosses your mind and I'll listen."

"We'll see justice done for Edwin," Kate said as if in a trance, responding with delay to words her mother had spoken a little earlier.

"Someday. For now, we look to ourselves. Here's my thinking: Count Andrews kept Sir Edwin around for a reason, and I pray he'll help us when we reach Melphor. The Watch Patrol could be out in droves looking for us at the border of County Flatlands for all we know, but it's unlikely we'll run into trouble in Melphor. How could they get away with it right in the Count's face? In killing Edwin now, they've revealed that they're not quite so well-informed as we'd feared. If Olswalt is there, we can only pray he's locked up in a dungeon."

"And if he's not?"

Gèyll waved the parchment. "I'll write to Henri, tell him everything, and I'll be clear that he should tell all our supporters the truth also, by Lameeri, the whole truth. That will be our insurance should Olswalt, or Haarjo Farelli, or whoever is involved want to play a battle of wits with us, and *if* they find us, they'll have to contend with Henri first."

"Henri won't fight the Watch. He said, didn't he?" The more Kate spoke, the more it sounded like she wanted to fester in her despair, but Gèyll was not about to let her.

"I have a feeling he will, if he's pushed to it. He likes to think he's mysterious and has so much to hide, but if we explain our story, he'll fight for us. Let us pray he will not have to when we pay the Count a visit."

Chapter Nineteen: King of Kings

On the morning following his arrival, Marcel was woken early by the three bells tolling six times, each in unison, and from there he was told by a bishop, who failed to introduce himself, to get dressed at once and proceed to a hall for breakfast; just as oblivious as he had been the previous night with no real guidance or introduction, barely so much as an acknowledgment that he was supposed to be there. At first he defied his order, sitting on his bed with hands on lap and tired eyes staring out through the archway within which there was no door, perhaps to make clear that there was to be no fornication here.

People shuffled on slowly in an orderly fashion, some silent and some mumbling to one another, at which he became increasingly perplexed, and soon wished that they would just stop it and conform to social normality. It shouldn't have been surprising; though the cathedral was more lax where many rules were concerned, it stood to reason that it would still attract the sorts of people who liked to be confined to them. He would have to pray that, if nothing else, his explicit preference towards the more charitable side of cathedral affairs would exclude him from their business.

Finally, he made a move lest anyone return to query his wanting attitude, unlikely as that seemed given the precedent. As he'd not been given directions, he found his way by following priests through the narrow, windowless, stone corridors of the inner sanctum and out into a cloister, which was cast mostly in shadow from the immensity of the cathedral proper in the dim morning light. If the sun were to bless the courtyard with its light, there would be shadows still upon the grass and bright flowers, of patterns forged in marble overhead: a dome of thin strips curling and intertwining like ivy commanded into wondrous formations, as if by Venlor himself.

The crowd was perfectly easy to follow as all but a few walked orderly, sombrely even, in the very same direction, so for a time, when none of high pious rank were to be seen, Marcel paused to admire a marble pillar, one of two of its kind holding a cloister support shortly before the double oak doors that everyone was filing through. Upon the pillar was a carving that appeared to spring to life as he touched it: a story of gods ascending from the mortal plane, the ascension here depicted literally, separated into four segments, where the five crafted the celestial plane and shot up to the sky like arrows, before vanishing completely. He withdrew his hand suddenly and with a loud, awkward cough at the realisation of a young, female priest staring with immense amusement from the shadows; a break in the orderly formation as clear as day.

When he then stepped through those doors into the elongated dining hall, he wondered if his situation had been set up precisely as such on purpose. All others were draped in various attires suited for holy men working at a cathedral, and in stark contrast, Marcel had but the clothes he'd brought with him, which in the light of roaring fires on a chandelier directly above, was cause for men and women to notice him, and observe with none too little conspicuousness that an oblivious apprentice was in their midst. Naturally, there were no bishops among their ranks, and certainly the ducevereë was nowhere to be seen, thus, at least as he queued for his breakfast, he was in no danger of being paired with anyone in particular, as he feared he might.

By the time he was presented with his tray of bread, fruit, and thickly sliced ham at the desk that fronted the kitchens, he'd already decided upon his seat: before a woman eating at the very opposite end of the hall, who, despite wearing very much the same white hoodless robes as most others who sat in lines on long wooden tables, caught his eye immediately. She was a woman, true, which was something of a rarity here, but not exactly a scarcity. What drew him in was her posture: back straight and tensed at the shoulders but relaxed in her own way, she was, and her choice of sitting alone only furthered the glare she emitted, like a beacon among duplicate dolls swaddled in dirtied cloth. If nothing else, she was alone, and if he was lucky, would provide him with answers.

His face did redden when he saw who it was, and he huffed, but she'd already seen him approach and to turn away would be to display further strangeness to her, the young woman who'd been so amused by his fascination of the pillar architecture.

"Yes, sit if it please you," she said courteously, bearing a curious but not unkind expression.

"It would, thank you," he spoke rigidly.

Mild-mannered would have been the first way he'd describe her, and beyond that, ambiguous and withdrawn, for she didn't speak again right away, only looked him up and down with excessive interest, with pale blue eyes like clear, clean water on a dull summer's day. Like the other priests, if that's what she was, she wore a hoodless, white robe of fine thick silk; a woman's variant which flowered outwards below the waist as a dress. At the collar, she wore a silver pin, a four-pointed star where each tip presumably represented four gods, and the unicorn in the centre represented Venlor. Others wore similar pieces, but not all, he gathered from risking brief glances at nearby members of the church. Theirs were less detailed and crafted with lower quality silver, if he wasn't mistaken, but judging from her rough hands, she might perhaps have made it herself, because Harth cathedral was, after all, a centre of unconventionality, if the rumours were true, and a woman as a blacksmith might be less noticed, even if quality was still out of the question. It was a concern that had festered within him on the road, ever since Isaac had brought up the possibility of Kate being inducted as well.

When he set aside his fears and looked at the woman's face, a woman of fairly short stature only a few years older than him, if he was any judge, he saw much softer features than her hands alone would have suggested. Her face showed no signs of having had makeup applied, and her long brown hair was tied back without flair, albeit with a pin that contained yet more silver.

He ceased his evaluation of the woman who was so ceaselessly interesting, and stopped his examination of the hall in general as he noticed those same men he'd looked to before further down the table; most definitely talking about him, and with what must constitute worry.

"Is it considered ill of me to sit with a woman?" Marcel asked without thinking, looking over his shoulder in hopes of proving himself wrong. And there was disappointment in his voice, which he'd not intended to reveal.

"Would you think ill of there being such a rule?" the young woman asked, without apparent bias. Marcel hesitated.

"Yes."

"Then you're one in a hundred. Stay." She patiently sipped from her tankard of water, regal in posture and movement, like a highborn lady, further muddling her already confusing image. "There is no such rule for the dining hall," she clarified when Marcel's discomfort refused to dissipate.

"What do you think they're talking of me, then?"

"Does it matter? Ignore them."

She returned to delicately sipping water, that being the end of the matter, as she was clearly not expecting a rebuke, and in the break of conversation that followed, there permeated in the air of the tall hall, a meek echo of hymn from the cathedral. He strained to listen and achieved nothing, for the reverb was such that no single word was understandable. Anyway, one might think that it was being sung in old noble Mürathneèan. His interest died and returned to him the intrigue that the woman had shown him.

"What were you smiling about when you saw me in the courtyard?"

"Oh, just at your tactile interest in that pillar. It amused me, if you'll excuse my saying so. Most wouldn't touch it. It's rather telling that you're an outsider. You have an air of the country about you."

"That's correct," he said dismissively "Is there a rule against it?" Marcel asked again.

"That all depends on who you ask," she said innocently, and looked down at her near-empty wooden plate, breaking off tiny pieces of bread and chewing them slowly.

"So you're saying it's considered peculiar?" Marcel deduced, his voice strained by her persistent lack of clarity.

"You would get a few odd looks," the mysterious woman answered.

"I *have* researched the cathedral prior to my arrival," Marcel felt the need to clarify. "I doubt I would've been granted this position if I hadn't. It would help if someone actually told me what I was doing or where anything is."

301

The Voice of Kings

"That can happen," she said plainly, smiling a sickly smile that may, or may not, have contained any joy.

"What will happen now?" Marcel asked warily. The expression she displayed was ill of its message. She shrugged.

"That depends. It could be any manner of things. I don't know what will happen to you. For what it's worth, I should tell you about the cloisters first, even if no one else will. They are linked to everything, after all. The courtyard you were in was the main cloister, Eternity, and the other three, in a clockwise fashion, are Dawn, Enlightenment, and Dusk."

At the mere mention of the word 'clockwise', Marcel couldn't help but be drawn to the clock inserted into the wall, and through his fascination of the contraption, wondered how he hadn't spotted it before. It was mesmerising, and reminded him of home, of his father crafting the parts for southern courts and constantly talking about making a clock of his own. As it happened, there was limited need for such precise timekeeping in Caedor, and so it had never been high on his list.

Again, his distractedness did not go unnoticed.

"Thank you, I'm grateful for your support," he said humbly, worried that he may have offended her. "Will the ducevereë explain these things to me in time, or some other perhaps?"

"The ducevereë?" she retorted, as if he'd just gone insane before her. "I shouldn't think you'll meet him in a hurry, nor should you be so eager to. The ducevereë is in a habit of making orders when he wants something done, which is always, and when he makes an order, he gets what he wants. Always. If you're called before him, it'll be because he wants to squeeze something from whatever skill sets his bishops have discovered in you. Don't go looking for trouble," she warned, pointing a finger at him. "Perform your priestly duties well, but not too enthusiastically."

"I see," was all Marcel could say that he was sure would be inoffensive. He wasn't entirely certain that he wasn't being tested now, so relaxed so as not to show the pressure mounting up, be it imaginary or not. "I have no intention of becoming a priest though, I should say. I'm here to tutor in more... cultural duties." She raised her eyebrows as if his use of words impressed her, and perhaps it did.

"That doesn't mean they won't ever ask you to go out and preach, or perform burials or burial rituals, or even organise knighthood ceremonies, and really anything else that needs doing," she said with a perverse excitement, for at the same time, she seemed somewhat irritated by her own words, displaying a frown around her eyes and a smile beneath them.

"I see," Marcel repeated. "Am I right in supposing you're expected not to be telling me that kind of thing?"

"Probably not," she said carelessly. She held up a hand as she chewed on more bread, begging his silence to continue before at last speaking again. "You'll be fine, I pray. You're not stupid anyway. But not confident either, and don't take that the wrong way. I would have said you're bold as brass, choosing to sit with me, but..."

The woman gently rocked her head from side to side, spying Marcel through a squint as if revaluating, before finally nodding to confirm that she'd made the correct assumption.

"I don't understand," Marcel said helplessly, glancing all about him again. "Why is this bold? Who are you?"

The woman saw that her plate was empty now, and sighed. Assuming her ladylike characteristic again, she dabbed at her mouth with a damp cloth, rose slowly in the same style, and then, just for a second, he thought she meant to leave as rudely as possible.

"Tamzin," she introduced, deliberately perpetuating, with that amused, glassy stare of hers, the same mystique that had attracted his attention to begin with. "I trust we'll meet again."

"Marcel," he replied, no less baffled as she left on such a strange note.

Alone, he ate his breakfast, until a middle-aged man approached with purpose in his gait that suggested his duties were long and many, and this was the lowliest of them all. His robes were white, as everyone's were, but were sewn also with thick gold lacing, and a white sash slung over his shoulder as with a toga.

"Marcel Brodie, come with me."

"What have I done?" Marcel rebuked wearily. The man's features were stubborn in their bemusement, and he looked slightly disgusted as he waited for Marcel to explain himself.

"I don't know. What have you done?" There was no reply. Marcel waited it out. "Come with me," the man repeated.

~

"Enter," a voice from within spoke unto Isaac before he'd finished knocking, and enter the office he did. It was a long room, of which he got the impression would be untidy if there were enough things there to strew randomly.

Swords and axes of many descriptions were hung on the walls, on wooden plaques: one thing he could be assured would never be badly looked after or left unclean. As he progressed, he noticed a dissonance in the layout where, in some places, paperwork and utensils were scattered lazily, and in others, were stacked as neatly as could be and compiled according to their purpose. So he employed a personal page, most likely.

And there, at the back of the office, beyond his desk and before the wide open doors and the balcony, Martello sat wearing the same armour Isaac had seen him in the previous evening, showing unexpected educational credentials as he read a document without much difficulty. Part of him told him to turn around and walk away, seeing Martello's ill content, and brush off any insults that flew his way. It might be safer. But no, he reasoned, Martello could not harm him. Law was law, and here in Harth it did not relax so readily.

The Voice of Kings

There could be no mistaking his disdain at Isaac's return, but he chose not to speak of it. There was no surprise to be seen upon him.

"I'm Isaac Brodie. We spoke yesterday," Isaac said coolly.

"Sit," Martello commanded. Darkness slithered into his calm voice, and though in his great unease, Isaac told himself no harm would befall him, he obeyed to make things easier for himself. "What game are we playing today?"

"One where both of us may win," Isaac replied hesitantly. "If you'll play."

"I doubt if our ideas of winning are compatible, Isaac Brodie."

"Your past may be of great significance, historically, scientifically; all you need do is recount that past to me and answer my questions. If that doesn't interest you, and I wouldn't blame you if that's the case, I'm sure something else will emerge itself to stir feelings of old."

"You know how to talk but you don't really say much, do you?" Martello chided, and as a fire sprang to life in his eyes, all the beauty of the sea, so close, and its waves, could not wash that away, becoming blurred where Isaac now focused solely upon his target. Martello added curtly, to Isaac's initial bafflement, "We don't do much actual mercenary work, as I would describe it, these days. It's mostly just hiring men out for bodyguard duty. Not that you'd see that. I may not be a talker like you, I can't see through a man like glass, but I see you looking down your nose at me."

Isaac leaned back in his chair, and carefully so, as any sudden movements could reveal that Martello's intimidation was paying him well. His legs shook beneath the desk, but as far he could tell, he'd suppressed flinching at the captain's analysis. He prayed as much, at any rate. He let his blonde hair flop back, washed impeccably and straightened, not for Martello because by now he'd been disillusioned, but for the very sake of putting the effort in and showing he cared not to smell of the previous day's sweat. In the same vein, he'd made sure that his suit was pristine and without creases. He now tugged at the bottom of his royal blue jacket, and tapped his fingers on his legs to give them something to do.

"If you were glass, you'd be rather more opaque, as you probably hoped, no doubt. I fear we're getting off topic though. Unless you've gotten bored of your own game already."

Isaac feigned a casual fling of his head, to amusedly look at the ceiling, though in reality he wanted to break eye contact for as long as was acceptable. Martello's eyes sang, or howled like a beast declaring its challenge, manipulating him into not looking anywhere else, and indeed it had been a struggle to do so; He found his own eyes bearing a stinging sensation when he finally managed to tear them away, realising that even his blinking had been disrupted. He wasn't so sure now that it was deliberate; some traits are ingrained into one's being after using them for so long.

"*My* game?" Martello asked quietly, somewhat shortly. Thank the gods, he broke the connection himself this time, returning to his ever so casual demeanour he'd first displayed in the courtyard yesterday.

"The game where you prey on people's emotions and manipulate them for the humour of it; where you play with people and their conceptions just to see how they'll react, because you're a soldier, and you have a big sword, and can safely do that without any fear. Assuming, that is, that you've lied about everything from your childhood."

He stopped breathing, in suspense to know if he'd stepped too far. There was a great host of insults floating in his head that he'd omitted from spoken word as the extent of his own fearfulness became clearer to him. Martello's black armour groaned, like the air seemed to do, stuffy and begging for a release.

"You want to know about my childhood?" Martello pondered calmly, skim-reading another document before him, as if to yield from it secrets that would guide his memory. He licked his lips and looked at once serious, though his posture was no less relaxed. "To tell you the truth, the people I knew as a child, from the land across the sea, weren't any different from anyone here. They piss like us, they shit like us, and though I was too young to be part or party to adult frivolities, I'd guess they like to fuck like you and me, too."

"You really don't care, do you?" Isaac replied, finding himself sighing deeply. "Listen, I can keep at this for a very long time, and I think you'll tire of your game before I of mine. So just be honest with me on one thing now, I implore. Did you, or did you not, wash up on these shores as a child?" The enjoyment had been sucked from the conversation, if there was any before, and now bereft of that energy, he wondered if Martello was not mad.

"Yes," the answer came plainly. "But I think you should listen to me and reconsider. I'm Captain of the Mercenary Guild. I can break your face with the scabbard of this here dagger on my desk and toss you off that balcony, break your legs and call it justice if I tell the Watch you've been harassing me."

He stood up. He wandered around the desk. Isaac stood also, frantically and defensively, his foot skimming a chair leg that, for a terrifying second, threatened to bring him to the ground, and his image with him. He'd not admit as much, unless for some improbable boon he was forced to.

"You're going to leave, through one exit or another," and here he pointed gingerly to the balcony railing. "Unless you want to hire one of my men," he joked.

"As a matter of fact, I do so wish that."

Isaac was not much less shocked than Martello. But it made perfect sense, in more ways than one. Martello did not speak.

"What say you?"

"You want a bodyguard?" Martello said sceptically.

"A guide to the city, if you'll permit me. I have to remain pragmatic, even if that means getting some other to be pragmatic for me."

"My men are bodyguards. If you want a tour of the city, you're in the wrong place."

"It shouldn't matter to you what I use them for, so long as they are willing. I wish to hire a guide," Isaac reiterated firmly.

"It *will* matter to *them*," Martello growled. Folding his arms and silencing his voice, he again proved his restraint. Unless that was another aspect of his game. "They come here to be paid for what they're good at, which is fighting, not talking, nor memory games either."

"You can't think of but one? Cast aside your prejudice of me for a moment and think as a businessman. I don't expect you to do it out of the kindness of your heart, naturally. I'll need him for, shall we say, four days? I may return at some point to renew the contract and honour you with my patronage again."

"That's it?" Martello said darkly. In the midst of negotiations, he was apparently not drawn in by Isaac's words, and perhaps remembering the time, crossed the room to his desk and scooped up his longsword with ease, strapping it to himself as before.

Isaac was agitated, save for the relief felt from distance created between them, by Martello's threat being given sharp physicality, and by the lack of impact his words were having, like an iron shortsword flailed upon plate armour. Talking was scarcely so tiresome.

Though he'd never considered himself grandly attractive or evocative in appearance, Isaac had always been given reason to believe his mother's words from years ago, when she'd said dotingly, "You have a smile anyone could trust." It was times such as this when it seemed the grandest arrogance to ever have believed he possessed any charm at all.

"I know a lost cause when I see one. Like I said yesterday, you're not my only person of interest here. I'll return when I have, or know, something to change your tune."

Martello Jacart seriously considered the proposal, while discarding Isaac's declaration of intent to return. A sign, potentially. He derived pleasure from giving off signals through his body language, as with the way he'd stroked his hilt the prior evening.

"Forty gold. That's my offer."

"That's extortionate," Isaac replied cautiously, making sure not to offend Martello. "I may be a foreigner, but I know things are generally cheaper in Harth. Twenty."

"Forty," the mercenary captain repeated, as if Isaac had simply misheard him.

"Thirty, and if I return, you can charge 50."

"Thirty-five," Martello replied unflinchingly, in a flash.

"Very well," Isaac conceded, reasonably pleased with the result on the basis of not knowing this industry or its prices in the slightest.

Martello gripped the balustrade outside his office, arms apart and eyes scanning all those below him, whereupon Isaac got the feeling he enjoyed the authority immensely, despite having no smile or typical expression of pleasure.

"Jamys," he barked. A man as tall as Martello ceased his practice session in the yard, parrying a blow from his opponent even as he turned and looked up to hear his master's order.

There was a clicking of fingers from Martello, a pointing to the office, and a snappy hiss that sounded vaguely like snake's dialogue spoken by the captain. While he waited for his man to hurry up the stairs, he glared coolly at Isaac: a challenge he was fortunate to notice only out of the corner of his eye, and made certain to keep it that way, for to look into his eyes and then away would be a show of weakness he couldn't very well afford at the present time.

The door was swung open and the mercenary named Jamys marched in, streaming with sweat that he dabbed at with a kerchief. There was a pleasing simplicity about him, as he swaggered in without a care in the world, wilfully obedient but recognising no particular seriousness in the situation or in himself. A comforting change of pace, if nothing else.

"Isaac Brodie. Jamys." Martello brushed aside the introductions and held out a hand, palm up, upon which Isaac placed a bag of money, having removed several coins, only for Martello to meticulously count through it again. "Isaac is a foreigner. He wishes you to be his guide throughout the city, and that means pointing things out and answering any and all questions. I thought you'd be more suited than most. You accept, do you?"

"I do. No reason not to." He'd barely looked at Isaac at all, and indeed was not bothered by who was paying him, or why.

"Off with you both then."

The dust truly began to settle when Isaac stepped outside, where a bitter breeze from the sea pulled him in, body and spirit, from the guild interior, and so now he felt far away from Martello already. With that, he could think more clearly, stopping to reconcile the preceding conversation, a somewhat sorry and irritating affair but for two things: two that had come to his attention, at least, but how could they not have?

Martello had protested little of Isaac's desire to hire one of his mercenaries, nor had he warned Jamys that Isaac may pester him on the very subjects he'd made such callous threats over. One might come to the conclusion that he was not as apathetic as he'd like people to believe. That was the dream Isaac clung to, for there was nothing else of worth to take from their conversation; no other moments of significance besides that restless stare, which even now gnawed at him a little.

The mercenary Jamys waited with his arms folded over his plated mail hauberk, and there upon his hardened, wide face, which bore scars low down on both cheeks, he wore a mild-mannered, thin smile. That his smile was so thin was a result of no detriment. On other men, it might very well have looked sickly, but he was full of colour and confidence, and in his own way, could be thoroughly imposing if he wanted to be. His smile remained, neither smug nor important, nor for that matter particularly happy. It was just there. His

The Voice of Kings

long, plaited hair, dark muddy brown, danced sullenly, several tendrils of it swinging before his face, yet still he waited, smiling a smile that should have been unsettling but, in truth, had minimal effect on Isaac.

"Jamys, I think I should clear something up," Isaac said because of an observation of the man. "I hired you to talk, so you mustn't feel compelled to silence as some clients may hold you to. Just so long as you've nothing rude or disparaging to say," he joked. "I'm not sure I want to hear those comments." The smile did not change, though an eyebrow was raised. "What was it you wanted to say?"

"Only wondered why you'd stopped. Where was it you wanted to go?"

"I need to locate the other guilds, if you please?"

"Most'll be city centre way. Which ones in particular, master Brodie?"

"All of them, with equal imperative."

The mercenary's eyes viewed him through slits, not judging maliciously, only curiously so.

"I have a mind to realise some big plans," Isaac explained. "The guilds are one stepping stone, the King and his men of knowledge another."

"Ambitious," Jamys said without waiting to hear a reason. Ken of his own dawned upon him. "There's something happening at the palace later, I believe: a public event. We'll go there if you think it'll help."

"I've no doubt it will, if anyone of royal importance is in attendance. Lead the way then," Isaac prompted.

The clanging of practice battle from the courtyard passed from them soon enough. The noise was replaced by all manner of men peddling all manner of goods on wide, well-kept streets that bustled but weren't clustered. Everything was arranged as in Balenhold, with the forethought of how many people would likely occupy a given area and to what end, and considerable care had been taken to see that this role was fulfilled by all, so children weaved with excitement and speed between groups queuing for butcher's fish and baker's bread.

The road Jamys led him, the quickest route possible Isaac assumed, for he seemed a very straightforward man, started to wind in a quaint manner, so that when, only for a minute, the energy of the city settled down and the crowds thinned temporarily, Isaac heard himself think with even greater fidelity. Jamys, too, was not without his considerations.

"You'd still rather I spoke openly with you?" Jamys asked. Isaac looked at the man as they walked, quietly puzzled, for he was sure now that he held many opinions and spoke of them often enough, absolutely confident enough to do so, obviously, but many of his clients must have specifically asked for the opposite in the past. So he honoured professional obligations, and mildly so.

"I'm no master of men," Isaac elaborated. "I'm a country man. I don't feel at home giving direct orders, not ones like that. You speak your mind and the mood will be lighter."

"In that case, I'd like to ask you to what Martello was so tense about just now."

"More tense than usual?" Isaac said as passively as possible.

"He's not tense at all, most times. Did you anger him about something?"

"I poked my nose in his personal business. The business of his distant past, if you must know," Isaac admitted quite deliberately, eagerly awaiting an answer of at least some consequence. Jamys reconsidered his position and response at least once.

"That's one way to get him angry I suppose, if you know what you're doing," he said flatly. "I'm surprised you do, though."

"I have a knack for it, evidently," Isaac replied vaguely. "Hear me, though. My interest in his past is not idle, or fleeting, or quaint. It matters a great deal to me, so you'll appreciate, I hope, that his lack of cooperation bothers me just as much. That will be some comfort to him, I expect, if ever he needed any from a man like me."

"I'm not judging," Jamys said in a tone just a few notes shy of apathetic, and indeed, his body language reflected this as he sauntered through the streets and carelessly swerved around a group of women carrying baskets when tightly veering into a new, straighter road. "As you do not command with natural ease, neither do I judge my clients so readily."

Isaac knew that he was being led correctly, not that he'd suspected otherwise, for there was more smoke, wispy and inoffensive, but a clear sign of industry, as he would expect from a location congregated with guild halls. And not just industry; in an alcove to his left, beneath a mesh of wooden planks held by detailed stone pillars and decorated with vines of a full spectrum of green, a painter sat. He transplanted the world before him and stylistically transported it to canvas, stroking it with his brush in minuscule increments.

Not only that, the alcove was flanked by two expensive looking businesses: overseers of trade, or tax offices, possibly. Men milled outside in expensive-looking suits with high collars and puffed sleeves, poring over large rolls of parchment without concern for the painter, who in the most squalid places of Burtal, would likely be regarded with little more respect than a prostitute; a smith if he was lucky.

"Just remember this," Jamys provided as an afterthought, when his attention was his once more. "I won't be held accountable for whatever stupid things you say and do to Martello, or worse, for what he might do to you if he decides you've become a parasite. You will go back to him, will you?"

"You're damn right. Eventually. Tell me one thing, actually. I take it from your tone he doesn't like to speak of it?"

"I don't know if like or dislike comes into it. It may just concern him so little that he's tired of men who bother him with it. The rest you say is true."

"He's *never* mentioned those days to you?"

"A few times, briefly, in all the years I've worked as a mercenary for him."

"And of those few times, would you say he was genuinely truthful when he claimed to have travelled from a land so far away, be it Alassii or, indeed, an undiscovered land?"

Jamys did not need long to decide, though he spoke with some trepidation.

"Yes."

A short while later, they turned into yet another long, wide street, with stalls lined in the middle, and men and women bustling on either side. Like the rest of the city that he'd seen, there was no homogeny to be found, but relative uniqueness; still difficult to believe for a city of such scale. A dozen banners and washing lines were hung overhead, billowing just above the smoke that drifted down the street from a forge where no less than two dozen red-faced men worked.

"This is the place," the mercenary announced. "Hope you find what you're looking for," he supplied unconvincingly.

Jamys was following Isaac when he made his declaration, and so now the pace slowed considerably. Isaac paced very deliberately, running fingers through his hair and avoiding, casually, what he assumed to be ponderous looks as to his clothes, and what business he may have here; it was surely business in such attire. He came to a halt some way ahead of the Blacksmith's Guild, which he stared at intently, consciously keeping blinking to a minimum. Jamys, as per his conditioning, said nothing, and wasn't wont to do so.

One of Harth's numerous bell towers struck suddenly: a brick tower topped with a bronze head if the glare of the sun was a true indication.

"About that event at the palace," Isaac said, unmoving. "Any idea when it is? *What* it is?"

"I don't pay attention to these things. I just hear things. It's this afternoon. I can't tell you how to plan your day; I can only advise you of what I hear."

He was silent again. Isaac rested his tongue against his cheek, eyes blank, and tapped his chin with an index finger. A sudden movement towards the guild beckoned Jamys without him having to utter a word, just as he stopped with Isaac at the wall outside the guild building. He watched, of the whitesmithing division, the forge being worked from different angles, a large piece of equipment, separated into several sections, where gems and gold were currently being wrought into jewellery. The haze from the forge melted the street and people, as if transporting him, bit by bit, into a dream; he felt as if he were gradually being moved elsewhere, with every press of the bellows, pumping new life into the machine with a heavy hiss.

It wasn't the forge that had him vexed, however, for as he worked his brain through the cloud of heat that swam around him, he focused upon the guild interior, and the well-dressed man within, who, thankfully, could not see him at present.

There he stayed, Jamys not uttering a complaint or query, though he must have thought of it, watching people come and go, straining to hear their conversations, and finally, when he thought of trying elsewhere, a scruffy, muscular man plodded by. He spoke music to Isaac's ears as he asked the well-dressed man for a position in the guild.

"We're always looking for strong new men," was the reply, and he cut straight to the chase. "The conditions will be that you work on commissions presented by the guild, based on your assigned speciality, and pay a levy for your own work. The pay will be greater than that which you currently earn, provided your skills are of suitable standard. Investments in the guild may get you further, also," he added expectantly.

They went on for a short while as the decidedly boring particulars were discussed. Isaac watched the blacksmith leave, and bided his time before marching inside, giving flattering looks to the exquisite arches and rugs hung upon the walls. Well aware that the well-dressed man had taken an interest in him, he fought instinct and pretended otherwise.

"Excuse me," Isaac said, startled in tone only. "Sorry, I'd rather not take up too much of your time." He arrived at the desk at the back of the small hall and shook hands with the man who continued to regard him with curiosity, specifically his suit, and now, Isaac presumed, his accent.

"It's fine," the man replied tiredly.

"Put simply, I'm here to join the guild. However," Isaac said loudly, holding up a finger to save the man from dispensing one of his common replies. "I have a business proposition to accompany it. Do you deal in Sèhvorian steel?"

"No," the man said irritably, standing suddenly, resting his elbows on the desk and craning forward as his interest heightened. "Telling it full, it's expressly forbidden. If you want an in to the Guild of the Zenith, you'll have to master two fields in armoury and another elsewhere, then be recognised by a palace committee."

"As it should be. I thought I'd check." Jamys's mail shuffled as he ever so subtly pivoted to peer upon Isaac. He already knew what was happening, but neither did, nor said, anything to impede its course. "My name is Isaac Brodie, and I herald from Caedor. My father, the inventor Lennord Brodie, who I'm sure you've most graciously heard of, has been friends with Vicentei Laccona for some time. You'll also have heard of his work, I hope. He works with Sèhvorian steel, that's my point. He bids you greetings, and a proposition to join me to you, and him to your guild's more esteemed cousin. I offer my services firstly, and his in advance. You will, of course, send a letter to the palace, if you accept. It's imperative to be working with the King, not against him. It's my understanding your letters are far more likely to be read than from the average man on the street."

The words ceased to flow from his tongue, and for fear of overstepping the mark, he shut his mouth, breathing a sigh inside his head as he waited for a response.

"I may have heard of your father, yes. At any rate, you make an unusual offer. But I am *not* the guild master, Mister Brodie. I'll have to consult with him first." The conversation ended, yet he appeared unfulfilled in some unclear manner. Isaac reluctantly removed a purse from his belt.

"I don't expect you to trust me on my word alone, of course. A gesture of good faith, and a preliminary investment." He shook the bag. "Would forty gold be sufficient?"

"I expect so," the man replied, somehow more suspicious than before.

He counted the coins, and Isaac did not rush him, though all the while he waited for the bell to toll and bring him a step closer to missing his mysterious appointment at the palace.

"Thank you," the man said with an air of finality about proceedings.

"Oh, one last thing," Isaac went on in a sudden burst, perhaps rudely considered by the man. "If your master happens to agree to my terms, I ask only that he specifically mentions me by name in his letter."

Isaac gave his address too, again in the spur of the moment, and left the building with the feeling of his mind being scrambled, as it gradually became in all such discourses. The smoke blasting from the forge impaired him more violently still. He waded through and allowed the sea breeze that climbed over the building tops and rushed down on him to restore him, in short order, to his former self.

One glance at Jamys made him uneasy, for it was only in seeing how visibly unimpressed he was that he'd sought congratulations at all, and so decided not to speak.

"Very good," Jamys then said unexpectedly, and quite dryly. "You know what you're doing, do you?"

"I won't know that until the results are in."

"So where now then?"

"The Guild of Couriers," Isaac decided immediately, nodding ahead to the brass sign of the building opposite. "Same again."

Blue flames struck at the sky like strange tongues of water from giant braziers containing wood and Sèhvorian crystals, and small sconces and lanterns on pillars also, doused in some alteration chemical for symbolism Isaac couldn't deduce or recall, but therein lay the crux of that day's work, between the violent blue lights, upon the cobbled stone path. It snaked upwards, to a courtyard at the top, but from the bottom, the giant clock projecting south caught his eye first, as it had done much earlier also; the great mechanical hands effortlessly jerked round, time made physical, presenting itself squarely to him as progressively one second vanished forever and another leapt to the fray. At the base of the winding path to the palace, small arable fields within stone walls were being worked at the King's pleasure, Isaac guessed, and in the paths between them, men and women walked all in the same direction at a hasty rate, funnelling into a crowd on the lead-up to the palace, where Isaac walked freely with ease, thanks to the bulky man at his side with a sword strapped to his belt.

At the top was a huge open space laid down flat and even with white stone, though the exact size was undeterminable, where two or three hundred men and women were tightly congregated, excluding the many guards, patrolling and standing stock-still, many equipped with halberds and spears, and obligingly regarding each and every citizen with distrust.

The clock was, in revelation, not a tower as such, but the strut of an arch, shadowing them as they inevitably passed beneath it. It displayed two more faces than they'd first seen, to the east and west, where the commotion was taking place, and where the palace rested. The other supporting strut displayed no clock at all, for it bore down upon the wall surrounding the palace grounds. The wall was as high as Isaac, and protruding from it was a fence twice the size again, of thick metal ending in points which, nonetheless, retained a pleasant aesthetic, for, seemingly, there was no excuse not to imbue any given architecture with beauty of some description.

Where the northern strut of the arch landed on the wall, there was a battlement wall, more a walkway really, where more guards crouched, patrolled, and stood resolute, scrutinising the events below, most brandishing crossbows. Other such battlements were interspersed throughout the length of the fence, a theme which extended to the palace also, which he now observed was not as close as he'd assumed. He saw, beyond the wall, a palace of grandness and grandeur indeed, with many a balcony and epic detail, but unusual to its design, there were battlements at the top, in addition to two stubby towers more common to a castle, though here, no less seamlessly integrated.

All this he observed, drew in, as if it were a requirement that he arrive at a conclusion of the place with due haste. The crowds were streaming past him, from the opposite end of the stone clearing, though not, he noticed, from a passageway behind him, to the east.

All his thoughts, filed so neatly, were scattered in a moment of fear when he saw the big stone execution stand. Creeping dread held his feet frozen in position. Then the elatedness birthed by reason released him from its cold grasp, as it was his opinion, his strong opinion because he'd not presume so otherwise concerning such matters, that the setup was that of ceremony, not death sentence. Banners lined the two edges of the courtyard, bearing every sigil of Harth, including four of the King's eagle sigil to drive the message home: a well-organised riot of colour, flapping all in unison in the wind, to commend the age of wisdom and its benefactors in all its glory.

The great dome of the Palace of the Sun glistened at its peak, which was a circle of gold, shadowed by an enormous flag.

And a white, metal figure glided gracefully on the stand, so bright and clean it almost blinded him.

"You think you'll find something, or someone, of use here?" Jamys said distractingly, omitting bias from his voice, for no reason other than it coming naturally to him. Isaac looked at the man, in the eyes.

The Voice of Kings

Slowly but surely, he was beginning to see his plan as an adventure to be enjoyed from a spectator's position, he was sure of it. He wouldn't speak directly of it, so it was fortunate Isaac had given him permission of freedom of speech, if nothing else. It could have been considerably worse otherwise.

"I wouldn't know until it's happened," Isaac told him.

"You won't get much from here, anyway," Jamys said with a hint of amusement.

Isaac shrugged helplessly when he saw the man continuing into the crowd, but followed him closely when he realised what trick he'd employed, which was scarcely a trick at all, but a manipulation of social perceptions.

The crowd parted for the mercenary. Of course it did. There was little else to suggest it wasn't some supernatural force sweeping them aside; a success that continued until a time of Jamys' choosing, very close to the front.

"Best stop here," he advised, nodding to the guards on the stand to illustrate his point.

Isaac took it and discarded it immediately. He was now thinking of far bigger things. For reasons he hoped would become clear, there was a thin pole at each of the four corners, upon which sat prime specimens of Mürathneèan eagles, so still that he thought at first they must be stuffed. Within their boundary, very different kinds of jewels lay, in the form of three men: extraordinary men, he was willing to bet.

To the far left, the lesser of the three men, to not make too fine or crude a point, stood out in a small crowd of guards: a middle-aged leader. The guards watched the crowd, and he watched them, contemplative stares made more real by a winged helm that implied authority. A short half-cape hung over one shoulder: a second sign of this.

The other two men ranked roughly equal to Isaac in the interest they bought. Peculiar and unprecedented, as one of them was unmistakeably the King, ascending the steps to the stand as he imagined a king should, bold and powerful with broad shoulders and clean, short hair as dark as pitch beneath a golden crown. Everything about him breathed strength, not necessarily in military fashion, but uniquely regal. His cheek bones looked as though they could have been made of steel, and even his smile, as he lifted a hand to the crowd, purveyed authority. He faced the crowd, legs apart, his thick cape rippling slightly and lapping at his feet. Beneath that was another cape, hanging down to his ankles, which, indeed, did give him more presence. Gold and platinum jewellery of novel design well reflected his status and bolstered his figure at his neck and upon his clasps. Even they could not hold Isaac's attention for long though; his eyes could not deny the glare of white metal.

There, standing alone at almost centre stage, a man, if that was not too crass a word to describe his majesty, was clad in full plate armour of the purest Sèhvorian steel. This was a feat not yet achieved anywhere to his understanding, for his father made it his business to know such things. White steel was incredible, but difficult to refine for such a specific shape, and became gradually harder to melt and mould the purer it was; there was no mistaking here that it was not shoddily made though. It was only the most perfect fit, as if the white steel, so bright and wonderful that sucked in the light of the sun and reemitted it as its own, had been birthed around his body, to his liking and to the advantage of his figure, though Isaac suspected he could have effortlessly inspired even in only battered workman's clothes.

A simple, small image of a rearing lion was emblazoned upon the two bright red clasps fastening his cape. As the wind momentarily altered its course, the white cape struck out like lightning on a hurricane, apparently immune to stains where dust sprang to life beneath him. His fingers flexed slowly in boiled leather gloves, dyed white and cut off at the second finger and thumb joints, with vambraces tapered in to encircle them at the wrists.

That was not the half of it, a truth he was almost humoured by, for his face was effortlessly grand, in some indescribable way. He was in his forties, most likely, though he was blessed with the rare quality of appearing, quite paradoxically, ageless. Time had been very kind indeed. No scars, either, for that matter, or none visible. Long red hair, brilliant red, like fire, and with as much energy, only made him more striking, and his eyes had a life of their own.

Blue eyes of deep calm, like the sea that jittered in small waves some way behind him, portraying what might have been innocence even, if Isaac didn't already know better. But there was no lie or deception that he could detect. The calm was natural, like the wind that lapped at his hair. He was bold and powerful by his very nature, that he could have been competing with his King, and been a mighty match, if he weren't also so contemplative. *He's still a killer*, a voiced whispered. *Quiet*, Isaac dismissed.

"How best to start?" the King Michael Santorellian's voice boomed over the crowd. "We all know why we're here. I, Michael Santorellian, the King, protector of Mürathneè and ruler of the realm of wisdom, will pay eternal tribute to my greatest of knights, in the last way I think I can, for his efforts and unparalleled success in everything he does."

The knight here turned at his King's signal, and dropped to one knee, bowing his head.

"Your Grace," Isaac heard him say, though many surely did not, in a voice much as he'd imagined: soft, ethereal, noble, and yet so very strong. "I am yours."

The King left him kneeling, and strode to the Watchman in the winged helm.

"Who is that?" Isaac said, curious beyond restraint, pointing discreetly to the Watchman.

"That'd be the Commander of the Watch here. His name's Cadro Leonardus, if it please you to know." Isaac chose not to humour the unspoken "why" for the time being, but Jamys replied to his next question pre-emptively. "And that man is Sir Leon Barrotti, the..."

"The Knight of the Holy Storm," Isaac finished breathlessly.

A previously unseen object was being passed along, and Isaac's attention was redirected from Sir Leon: a sword, from one man to the Commander, and finally to the King.

The Voice of Kings

"For your continued services to the realm," the King went on, "I present to you, Sir Leon Barrotti, the Knight of the Holy Storm, Supreme Commander of the Watch, and General of the Royal Legions, a sword befitting you, and only you, that you will make use of to its fullest capacity. Rise, Sir Leon."

The holy soldier did so with might and honour. The King held out the sword for him: a bastard sword as Isaac saw it, though he was no expert on weaponry and couldn't pretend as much. The scabbard was of high quality steel and there was a pale, finely cut pattern encircling it. He couldn't determine the material of the hilt but assumed it was only the finest it could be.

When Leon reached forward and wrapped his fingers around the hilt, Isaac saw that it was large enough for both hands. The eagles opened their wings to the fullest span they could manage, then returned to absolute stillness. When Leon wrenched it from its scabbard, the white steel shone as if the light had been trapped inside, glittering like a relic from an old tale of heroes as he held it aloft with one hand; so comfortable was it in his grip that it could have been an extension of his arm. And now the eagles flew from their perches, whether by this signal or some other out of sight, obeying one master or another with no more impunity than a trained dog, and they soared together as a small blanket of gold, ever upwards out of sight.

Sir Leon swung his magnificent blade around gracefully while his feet remained transfixed to the stone beneath him, audibly scything through the air, as it was far sharper than any other sword could realistically be without compromising the structure.

"This is a fine sword, Your Grace," Isaac caught Sir Leon saying to the King with all his gratitude. "I can't thank you enough."

"The finest possible," the King replied loudly. "Countless hours were spent forging and re-forging in trial and error until my best blacksmiths just knew they could not better themselves."

He handed the scabbard to Sir Leon at this point, and he attached it around his waist to his knightly plaque belt, before turning back to the crowd, brooding for a moment as he stared meaningfully at the blade, unblinking despite its mirror shine, and then addressed the crowd with noble voice.

"This is indeed finer than any blade I can think of, and so I am eternally grateful to my King. It shall be, forthwith, named Waithrydn, Lightning-Wind."

The blade found its way back inside its sheath and Sir Leon, smiling faintly at his audience, turned grimly and bowed to the King.

"Very well. Bring him out," the King commanded to unseen figures.

There was a buzz in the crowd, a strange sort, as if every participant were being repressed of their true feelings, murmurs and few cheers escaping their mouths, a tension rippling through the gathering, unnerving Isaac to the core, for he began to understand its reason. It was his understanding that such ceremonies involved a considerable deal more yelling of want for blood, and it was this lack of overblown and unfurled emotion that caused it to slowly dawn on him: a chill morning that froze him in time and space amidst the emotionally restrained rabble.

A man was hauled from a gate in the wall, he noticed, in rags that once referred to him as a good earner, possibly even noble. Isaac's eyes were opened wide, his face pale, and he bore the look of a man who was feeling too many things to be expressed all at once, but dismay was the most prominent. Nonetheless, he stood steadfast and did not cry out or avert himself.

"An execution," Isaac said plainly, quietly, for releasing his true feelings would be unwise, he thought. So it was by his design that he kept them in. "I thought this was just a ceremony."

"It can be both," Jamys answered, and for once he was not so passive, showing concern for his client's state. "We should go, if it displeases you," he said forcefully. Yet no reply came his way. Sir Leon even advised averting one's gaze, and Isaac refused.

Joy died. Adventure died. Wilfulness died. The stage was his only concern, where in some part of him, a memory played out in conjunction, so different yet so similar, and he had not the power to deny the sight of either.

The man was allowed to walk the steps to the stand himself, as best he could with him not being well, before finally stopping not far from the holy knight, who bore a mild smile and sad eyes, so calm, as if he were simply lamenting the end of summer, watching the leaves fall around him while he could seemingly never wither.

"How would you like to do this?" Isaac heard Sir Leon ask the man in a quiet, respectful voice.

"I will have my own way until the time comes. I should do that at least," the man announced weakly, yet defiantly, and at that, he did his best to stand straight in the face of his weakness. Then he pushed aside his scruffy brown hair, cleared his throat, and addressed the crowd at large, upon which note, silence ruled. "My name is Lenuzo Behnirham. I am the Baron of Mahrojv. By my own stupidity, I am brought here to attest and pay for my crimes. It's... not exactly required of me to attest, I grant you, for I was careless as well as greedy, and so there is sufficient proof that my admission could only serve to save myself some dignity before I go, and my family, who mustn't suffer my disgrace." He coughed violently and looked down at his feet, whereupon thoughts of rage or violence might have passed him by as his face became contorted. It lasted only a glimmer of a second, and he resumed as best he could. "I am guilty of embezzlement, coercion, and blackmail. I stole tax money that should have been used for the good of my barony: an act tantamount to treason. I am an accessory to the works of unlicensed mercenaries. This I do confess."

The Voice of Kings

Sir Leon moved to push him down, but the baron waved him away and lowered himself, and his head, his eyes firmly shut, his breathing monstrous. The tension in the crowd was stranger than ever. Eerie even. Not a single soul unleashed the anger that was pent up in their lungs, though Isaac saw the contempt manifested on each and every face.

When Sir Leon then removed his sword from its sheath, he felt as if time stood still but for him, and in a half-dream, its slow slicing through the air was heard with perfect clarity. The holy knight lined the tip with the baron's neck, and announced, with grandeur, another statement.

"We have our rules, and the gods have theirs. May gods have mercy, where mortals cannot."

Like lightning, he swung his arms upwards, so fantastically fast that Isaac flinched before even the blade cleaved through air and flesh and bone alike, and the body slumped while fluids spurted from its stump, and the head rolled a short way forward. Leon, conversely, was no different. A few blots of red were winding their way down his armour, but that aside, it had been a perfect sweep, and probably better than most professional executioners wielding a greatsword could do. He rested the tip of his sword on the cold brick below, still smiling mildly with that sad look in his eyes.

For Isaac, the tension was too much to bear, as the crowd appeared fit to burst from whatever force or rule was restraining them from cheering at the tops of their voices. A sigh drifted from his dry lips, as if he were merely disappointed. Already he was doggedly pushing his way through the crowd, not remotely interested in how the ceremony might go on, and in his anger and disappointment, there was confusion, which frightened him deep inside, because he would not yield the secret of that to himself.

"That was a nasty bit of business," Jamys said when they were down among the farms. "I'm sorry you chose to see it, if you're so unaccustomed to it. I'll not judge, but…"

"Supreme Commander," Isaac snapped dazedly, any excuse to move on from all that. "What does that mean? How did he get that?"

"I think it's mostly an honorary title, but it has its perks," which Isaac took to mean that he didn't know. "He can override any order the Commander gives, I know that."

"What's the point? Does that not create rivalry between them? I thought the King's court was famed for its efficiency."

"They've been friends for a long time. Sir Leon's fought in every major engagement since the War of the Distant Kings, and even then, as a teenager, he received great acclaim. If anything, Cadro holds only the highest admiration for him, from how Martello's talked of them. Listen…"

"Tomorrow," Isaac snapped more aggressively. "You'll meet me tomorrow morning outside my lodging."

Isaac stormed from the side of the mercenary, who just stood and watched. He drifted through streets not quite real, a lost wraith. He was in another place, in another time.

Chapter Twenty: Evylyn's Echo

There was already new business underway in the King's chambers when Sir Leon arrived from having cleaned his blade to a mirror shine; not in the least unusual for Michael, who was pragmatic and forward. Leon entered without knocking or providing the King with any acknowledgement whatsoever, only seating himself in a comfortable, ornate chair infused with blue cushioned padding. It was a marvellous room, full of small statues and landscape paintings, and on the wall behind the King there were four portraits of royal predecessors, including the King's father, Christopher, painted in his dignified old age, ever proudly observing his son.

The afternoon sun was still bright in the sky and, through the open doors of his large balcony, it lit the King's hard, serious features; his default expression. It illustrated an unusual strength among his few weaknesses: he was rarely satisfied, not by the greed and ignorance often associated with kingship, but by a desire to improve until such time as perfection was achieved. With Sir Leon patiently waiting for attention, should it ever come at all, only the voices of the King and Lord Theodore Hughly could be heard, lending the room a dark and sombre atmosphere. The esteemed Lord Hughly, a man of 64 years, was more serious still, and whenever the King spoke to him, he had a habit of tilting his head slightly and widening his eyes, suggesting that asking him to repeat himself even once would be a grievous dishonour and an unbearable waste of time.

Currently he wore robes, much as he always did, not dissimilar in basic design to those the King's brother wore on formal occasions where he could get away with displaying as little flash as possible, only the robes of Lord Hughly contained looser sleeves and seemingly superfluous additions hung and slung here and there, and they were mostly green rather than black. He had little hair, but what was there was of reddish brown, as it always had been. In a standing mirror tucked into one corner, Leon saw that Lord Hughly's face, which looked perpetually bemused unless, as once in a blue moon, he commanded otherwise, wore an extension of that expression: a thin, long smile of little joy as he pored over a document the King had presented him with.

"There's the matter of Lenuzo's successor, additionally," the King went on. "We'll tread carefully, to ensure a smooth transition. His son is inexperienced, and so I'll send you to his quarters to discuss this further with him. I spoke to him myself, briefly mind you, and I imagine he'll appreciate no less."

"I understand, Your Grace. You want someone serious and obsessive, someone who shan't get distracted; you'll find that in me, Your Grace."

"I did just behead his father," Leon's voice announced out of the blue. "Remember that not everyone can be so detached as you, my Lord, and you'll go far. One might easily insult a man in such a situation," he warned with only accusatory overtones. The King huffed through a laugh.

"Sir Leon has a good point. Just be sure not to stray into the realm of his emotions, if at all possible. Keep it strictly business, that's all I ask."

Sir Leon rose, his armour clanking smoothly, rhythmically, as he made his way to the balcony and looked out pleasantly upon the city. There were a number of things he could have said, and he could have done so at his leisure, for he could get away with speaking what he liked, when he liked, more so than almost any other. He waited nonetheless. It was a self-appointed style, and made it easier, he felt. His eyes met the empty arena on which he'd taken the lord's head, and he remembered the men and women shaking in anticipation. Faces he conjured, as many as he could, for always he wondered what brought anyone there. Justice little, and much of else, he feared. The stillness next to violence ever took him to dread's edge, though he never spoke it.

"How fairs you the sword, Leon?" Michael asked in the heart-warming tone that suggested he was actually pleased with it.

"Spectacular. I meant what I said on the stand, earlier. There's one irregularity, which is more a matter of personal expectancy rather than quality: it's heavier than the weight of my armour led me to expect." He delicately slid the sword out by an inch and pondered upon its shining surface, cleaned so very easily, as if the metal itself had become one with the water. The fuller only a thin, elegant groove, implemented only for style, likely contributing to its weight somewhat, yet it was still not what he'd call heavy.

"I anticipated that you'd appreciate a weapon with more weight to it, so I commissioned a sword of higher density Sèhvorian steel."

"You were considerate to do so." He paused and replayed the events of the ceremony as his eyes scanned the execution arena. "All told, I'm pleased with how everything turned out. The late baron was fortunate to have me as his executioner; most would not have cared for honour in those circumstances."

"Which is more than he deserved," Lord Hughly said blankly, free of bitterness.

"Yes, this is why I have both of you on my high council," the King mused darkly. "You disagree."

"It is why I am a knight, and you are a lord, Theodore."

"Agreed," the lord conceded without looking up.

"Oh, there was one thing," the King began, raising a finger.

Leon turned to face him fully, though he remained outside in the direct light of the sun, between two pillars, calmly looking into the room. He stood between the two of them, who were on either side of a huge desk. Directly ahead, there was the doorway into the King's bedroom, through which his four-poster bed was seen. Michael sat, relaxed on his relatively undecorated throne, waving a finger as he struggled to recollect something.

The Voice of Kings

"Before you swung the sword, you said something I've never heard you say before. It was something like, "May gods have mercy where mortals do not"."

"Essentially that. It means exactly as it sounds, really. Not a derision on your authority as King, if that's your worry, and I doubt if anyone took it as such. I'll not use that one again if you're uncomfortable with it."

"Use your own judgement," the King granted him.

When Lord Hughly made to ask the King for more documents to read, he was immediately given another, on Lenuzo's son Lenis, a fact Leon observed, as he naturally did everything that entered his vision. His instincts never let up.

"Shall I report to him at once? I may not have a reputation for jovialness, but I'm wary of how emotions interfere with people's judgement."

"No, leave him be for now," the King commanded. "Leave him be. Forget about him, in fact. Put that file away and forget about him. We don't just provide for Lenis, giving him all the guidance he needs and then holiday for the rest of the week. The Laccona man, for example."

There was a hotheadedness bubbling within the King as he grabbed for an issue to attend to without breaking the flow of the sentence. It didn't go unnoticed, but Leon, as his personal guard, thought nothing ill of it. *Even Kings aren't perfect*, and he felt neither good nor bad for being party to this.

"He'll be arriving soon, and there's much else to do. There's the Emperor's new ambitions to consider, for one." He spoke the title of Richard Llambert with an edge of amused ridicule.

"We should have the matter investigated as quickly as possible."

"I should reiterate. When I said consider, I meant only that. It was the first item that came to mind on a long list. I doubt we'll actually do much about it."

"No?" Lord Hughly enquired with mild interest.

"He can do what he likes with his sorry country, so long as he doesn't drag us down trying whatever hackneyed scheme he's come up with. I feel depressed just thinking about it. If we send a considerable amount of men over there to aid or observe, the money we put into it will never come back."

"Unless the Empress is the architect."

It was Sir Leon who'd spoken this time, and then he said nothing more. He wore a pleasingly simple look of general agreement for the King: the sort the King had come to know well, that needed no explanation.

The King chuckled heartily.

"You have a point. But 10 masterminds would have trouble making something of the mess Burtal has dug itself into." He paused and shook his head. "No, let's not discuss that. Vicentei Laccona," he said forcefully. "Do we know what he'll propose yet?"

"Does it matter?" Lord Hughly retorted. "He can't possibly fail. Even I can admit to that."

The King nodded profusely, his head now cupped in the palm of one hand. Leon withheld his opinion, though one developed in his mind. It was curious how the King spoke, as if it had been Vicentei's idea to work at the palace from the very start, when in reality, it was likely that he'd prefer to continue as a freelancer, designing and procrastinating at his infinite leisure. Then again, it was of note that the King had secretly been waiting in anticipation for his arrival, as he couldn't help raising the subject on a regular basis. It was probable that he assumed Vicentei would be motivated to conjure ideas for Mürathneè long before he'd exhausted the King's ideas, though having not yet reviewed Michael's plans for him, it was difficult to say. He found it difficult to care at present. If the appropriation arose, he could ask for the full spectrum from the King.

There was no mention of the previous inventor, and of the manner in which he was politely reassigned to somewhere far way in eastern Mürathneè, nor would there be when the genius arrived. Whatever the case, Michael was looking to re-evaluate his hold on his realm: a trait worthy of a King, for complacency was something he despised utterly.

He allowed the girl entering the room with a ladylike gait to distract him, unhindered by the guards who had presumably told her to leave, but for obvious reasons, had done nothing to enforce it. Only for family would the guards be so lax, for it was Natierlia of course, a girl of eight, and the youngest child of Michael, who was surprised to see her waltz in as if she owned all that she touched. He flashed a smile, but was otherwise impartial.

"Natierlia. It is rude of you to interrupt. I'm swamped with business. We'll sit together at dinner, I promise."

"I needed to say something," she insisted in a careless, delighted tone that couldn't have done wonders for her case.

She was about to press on when her father frowned and shook his head, but the message of grave importance danced merrily into her memories when Sir Leon approached to escort her from the King's distraction. Her face lit up, as it often did for him since being honoured so graciously with this most splendid of gifts for a knight: his suit of Sèhvorian armour. And now he was complete, with a brand new sword, as if one of her servants had just carved a new accessory for one of her dolls.

"My mother told me you were going to get a new sword today. She said it would be sparkling and marvellous, like your armour. Let me see it, Sir!"

As he drew his sword like a bolt of lightning, she briefly flinched, but was not ever afraid, for unlike some of the other knights in the palace, Sir Leon had a wholly approachable demeanour when he let it be so. He was considered an entirely safe curiosity by her, ironic considering his reputation, and even more so considering she was aware of it from her history lessons. If she was enamoured at the idea of him waging battle in a

The Voice of Kings

pointless war over religious semantics in Alassii, then her teacher was to be commended for his creativity. She playfully steeled herself side-on, in a manner roughly mimicking Leon's battle stance, but obviously lacking in that her ladylike posture was ingrained into her being and couldn't be discarded so easily. Her silk dress of soft greens and swirling patterns with a prim, tall collar only made the image more humorous, as did her pale make-up, her gold necklace encrusted with sea pearls, her hair arranged as a convoluted fashion statement, and her standing of half his height.

Leon said nothing of it. He spun his sword about until it was a blur, and could be heard slicing the air apart, as he assumed Natierlia wanted of him, and indeed, she was impressed. The King did nothing, as he knew he wouldn't, where any other knight could be looking at serious consequences for swinging a blade so close to his daughter.

"Your skills are splendid, Sir," she complimented.

"So is your vocabulary, my Princess."

"That's because she's very attentive in her lessons," the King remarked offhandedly, unsurprisingly having paid attention to the two of them despite being in serious conversation with Lord Hughly.

His words may have been of kindness, and well meant too, but he could not keep his irritation at bay, so Leon gestured to walk the young Princess to the door, and she obliged, for fear of herself or Sir Leon getting into trouble.

"Oh, silly me," she exclaimed, to Leon alone. "Would you tell my father that he has some guests waiting to receive him in the entrance hall? My mother said I have no business disturbing the King and they have no business being impatient for him, but..." she trailed off sheepishly.

"But?" Sir Leon asked softly, knowing well enough that she was all too keen to impress her father, if only because her brother was not in Harth.

"Guests?" the King said sharply. "If the Queen said not to disturb me, she's probably made other arrangements. The sentiment is appreciated, thank you very much."

"Would you like me to make sure? It won't do to keep guests waiting," Leon helpfully offered.

"I trust in the efficiency of my palace. If I have to send my Supreme Commander as a runner of errands, something is disturbingly wrong, and I shall find out soon enough at any rate."

"A fair point," Leon said, mostly to Natierlia, who, in her embarrassment, grinned. He graciously escorted her to the door.

"Men from the Watch," she whispered only for him. "Surly *Burtalians*. I decided not to keep them waiting, but oh well."

"There's work to be done," the King added confidently, gaze locked upon Leon. "If we want to better ourselves again, there's work to be done. And unlike Burtal, we'll see to it that it's done."

~

When the Empress saw to it that the renaissance should finally be enacted, due in large part to her vision, the Emperor had become rapidly more depressed and sick than even the norm; this Tristan had noticed on, he'd liked to think, the very day it kicked in, because that was one of his many self-appointed duties. It was only now that, as he willingly took on the burden of more work and tribulations, and he, himself, grew more tired, that he was fully conscious of the Emperor's mental state. Tristan was leaning upon the balcony of the tall hall that opened into the garden, and though he felt more sluggish, the force that was optimism battled pessimism without breaking a sweat, and so it was that he considered Richard's state of mind before he'd noticed his decline. He was grateful for his own health and ability to care where others would not; so he could continue to serve him where others could not.

Between his usual duties, newly appointed tasks, a stubborn murderer curled up and weeping in the dungeon, and now his interest in the Empress's secretive behaviour, there was little that should have been of comfort to him, but he saw commitment where others must have seen failure before even trying.

So when the Lord Gaoler had come to say that the stubborn murderer wished to confess, Tristan felt vindicated, which made the failure of it that much worse. He played the meeting over in his head: Adrian Mortain "confessing" to being an abomination that must be shown mercy, and yet not mentioning the murder Tristan had witnessed. "Confessing", damnably afeared, to being a sinner, before Tristan had lost his patience and sent him dithering back to his cell. What was he going to do with a confession, anyway? *Why?* is what Lord Almaric had pressed him with, thus leadening Mortain's tongue.

He tapped his small sheet of parchment with his quill as a man passed beneath him, high and mighty, and disappeared into another room. It was Lord Carrick, and beside his name on the list before him, he scratched a note faintly, to be written in ink later on.

It didn't feel good to cast suspicion upon these men, but there could be no denying the power they wielded, and the choices they made with it, and that was to say they generally opted not to make any choices at all, unless it benefited them in some way. Thinking from Alycia's perspective, she may seek to utilise such sycophants, but then again, she most commonly operated with only those she trusted and felt were worthy of her tasks. It depressed him somewhat to look down the list of suspects, but it was equally important to remind himself that Alycia was not on trial. Her intentions couldn't be questioned, nor could she, by any reasonable person, ever be accused of laziness, or lack of caring.

The Voice of Kings

Her methods were the irritant here, her vanity the birth of recklessness and self-reliance that could one day inflict some damage, and though there was the part of him that naturally tingled in shame at the thought, she was inflicted with all the quirks of humanity, because the gods didn't see fit to change that.

Footsteps echoed throughout the halls behind him, and a flustered Marcus Baldwin rushed by the door, before doubling back to meet with Tristan.

"My Lord," he said with a low bow. "I've been searching for you."

"You're back from my estate then?"

"I am. All is running smoothly as usual, my Lord."

"And Evylyn?"

"Lady Almaric misses you as much as you miss her. As she told me to relay to you, of course. Malcus is well also, and isn't slacking in his lessons or conveniently forgetting what time they are."

"Good to hear it," Tristan laughed, knowing that Marcus had not taken liberties with the wording of Evylyn, and as Marcus was fond of words, there could have been no doubt that he wouldn't.

"Lady Almaric also bids me tell you to not wear yourself out, because you work too hard, though she's grateful of that being nearly impossible anyway."

"How can I stop from getting tired without her to invigorate me?"

"She said you might respond like that. She said to please stop complaining, as you have told her before that she is best at tiring you."

"Well, that is different."

"She –"

"Wait, I know this. She told you not to read into that comment." *After all, that is rather risqué for you.*

Marcus shrugged. "Close enough. But she also said it is your fault if she slipped up."

"Hah!" Tristan clapped his hands and laughed. "Right, enough. Step to it. News…"

"She's heard nothing unusual, let alone of rumours pertaining to anyone here in court."

"It was worth asking, just in case," Tristan said unconvincingly, yet unshaken in his resolution. "You must keep an eye open for anything strange yourself, and though I don't wish my actions to reflect badly on me or appear conspiratorial, I'd ask that you do it anyway, even if it's just someone being somewhere when you'd expect them to be somewhere else."

"Of course, my Lord. To uncover the Empress's plans," he said shakily, and instinctively looked about, his eyes overwhelmed with fear.

"No!" Lord Almaric exclaimed suddenly. "I must make this very clear. I am not hatching a conspiracy, and neither is she. The fact of the matter is, the Empress is a highly independent woman, and I fear one day she may close herself in too tightly. If there's trouble afoot, I need to know about it, and yes, even if she perceives no danger, it may be there, for though she's our lady of many marvels, she is not infallible, I'm afraid. It's possible her plans for Lennord are of separate design to other clues we find."

"Lennord Brodie?" the courier asked, increasingly bewildered.

"Pay the politics of the situation no mind," Lord Almaric said fiercely, directly, to an end he hoped would make Marcus understand that it was not a trick, but a kindness, and that by the gargantuan divide in their classes, it was a mercy for someone of his status to humour him so consistently. A friendly reminder, for Tristan's mind also was wont to wander, as he spoke to so-called lesser men as equals. "It'll be simpler. You do your job, and I'll do mine. All of them," adding a faint smile.

"Without question, my Lord. I know you feel betrayed by your fellow lords, for their... you know better than I," and Marcus trailed off, and looked down to hide, with ill success, his look of horror.

"Betrayed is a serious word to use in such context," Lord Almaric settled on after a moment's hesitation, which was played with a slanted expression of mild shock. "In fact, I'd advise you to keep that to yourself, and think before you speak."

Marcus made to make a reply, but stopped at the sign of Lord Almaric's hand held up, beside a face that accepted his words that never were, and dispensed forgiveness unconditionally through a kindly reprieve.

In hallways of width and height beyond all apparent necessity, Tristan wandered without paying mind to the particulars. He could have navigated them blindfolded, even as he entered a somewhat labyrinthine section, characterised by busts and small statues on old marble pedestals along the sides, and the odd image embossed on the wooden doors, but he paid them no attention at present. These corridors on the second floor west wing, while suitably grand in their own right, or possibly beyond their rights, were not of the calibre of the halls and historical vestiges. Right now, these corridors, all straight where curves in the design were rare, stretched out, slightly warped in his drowsiness. The guards were statues and the servants that busied themselves were ghosts.

But he was otherwise clear-headed, where Richard, with whatever demons clouded his thoughts in his dark hours, would be pulled down by misery. Tristan was here for a reason, if a flimsy one: to see if, on one walkthrough, he could notice anything out of place, any lords loitering around the bedrooms where they should be elsewhere. On his way, he couldn't help but stop mottled, old Cerdic Foy, to preserve, for his own sake, some normality in routine. He questioned him, with somewhat strained interest, on his current role in creating jobs in the west of the city in particular, and his treasury expenditure therein, as had been brought up at the courtly session that very day. Lord Foy was, fortunately, of no mind for small talk, but he answered honestly, and was duly respectful toward Lord Almaric, in heart as well as image, as Tristan had come to take for granted. The wraith of suspicion hovered above, just out of sight, all the while of the short duration of their exchange, and only gave Tristan pause for thought when Lord Foy was strolling along his way with a mind to succeed in his business. Tristan waved the suspicion aside, as he was not deserving of it, and wasn't about to have his name scrawled for scrupulous assessment on that sheet of parchment any time soon, or ever.

Tristan permitted a brief moment of reflection and levelled the parchment with his eyes: a list of names, and besides them notes and times, for which there was, as of yet, no meaning to be gleaned, and perhaps none to be found. It would be a boon if he knew what, roughly, he was looking for. And he couldn't escape the sensation of having excluded vital methods of thinking from his search, or more likely, several methods. At that admission, he was wrongly amused. *Because work piling so high is an oddly hilarious sight, though I suspect I'll not think so when I'm doing it*, he conceded. Just as quickly, he became slightly sad; to gently relieve the Empress of her pride was a job that should never need to be sought out.

Neither was hunting down a screaming Guardian huscarl, yet Sir Yanick was suddenly emptying his lungs to someone in the halls, and so here he was. He and Marcus descended the great stairs in the entrance hall in time to catch the knight marching after a southern lordling and his son, into the vestibule, a congregation filtering from every door that went completely unnoticed by the screeching man. There were already more guards than usual.

It was that men and women were arriving at a steady rate from around the country, to stay at the castle and about the city, and any one of them could, potentially, be a contact of Alycia's, though by his own admission, he was physically unable to cast suspicion on all of them as a Watchman in his situation should do, propelled by an extra instinct that he lacked the stomach for. He could scarcely remember them all, but for the highborn knight representing Ylden Parragor, who'd made an impression but had kept mainly to his quarters thus far. Tristan could just imagine the Wyman, any Wyman, here. Yanick might be flat on his back by now.

As it was, the sight of Yanick following those two southerners all the way outside while they blocked him out was quite farcical.

"You're wrong, you're very wrong!" Sir Yanick was shouting. "You'll not make a slave of me. Go, run back to Sutherlend! Hang your head low and –"

"WHAT IS THIS ROW?" Lord Almaric bellowed.

All three of them jumped, Yanick in particular, frantically reaching for his sword. When he saw who'd chastised him, he let go and raised his hands. The son was probably five or six, and petrified.

"He insults me!" Yanick protested, flapping a finger in the lordling's direction.

"I asked him to take my son on as a squire," visiting Lord Aumaine, as he was, replied through clenched teeth.

"It was more than that!"

"Wait inside," Lord Almaric hissed. The young knight was shocked, but after a moment of deliberation, skulked off into the entrance hall. And when he was there, "Would you mind explaining this, my Lord?"

"As I said, I put the question to him, and yes, I pressed him on it because I could see he wasn't enthusiastic, made to approach a deal, and he got more and more fidgety. Then he snapped and jumped to his feet, and tipped his chair over. The rest is as you know."

"He followed you all the way from his chambers?" Marcus asked sharply.

"Oh, aye."

"I see," Lord Almaric answered cautiously. "Look, find Master Linch. He'll find you someone more temperate, if less skilled. Please accept my apologies."

The son stared a question at the father, who sighed, bowed, and left.

Tristan went back to his parchment. A name caught his eye on his list, reminding him of why it was there in the first place. Whatever Lennord had been thinking of that day in the Opera House, it had triggered a response in Tristan anyway. That slightly bewildered look he had shot Sir Yanick Berrhwrn was probably a reaction to his first impression of the man in the throne room, or perhaps simply Alycia's memorable rebuke. It was true that Yanick was silently developing a reputation for standing out in puzzling or annoying ways, yet Alycia kept him around regardless. The crux was that his fighting skill was absolutely irrelevant if she didn't trust him, and if he wasn't serious about his job, how was he trustworthy? The finest sellsword in Burtal wouldn't hold her interest if he wasn't deemed worthy of her trust. At best, she'd hire him, then have him sent to the mountains or somewhere remote, just to get him out of the way.

So Yanick, he refocused himself. It was pointless to cast suspicion on Marioyrne Castellon. She was almost certainly involved in some capacity, but not where the key events were happening. If Yanick, for example, was relaying information to her or Alycia, the relevance lay in how, and likewise, how Yanick or some other was being supplied. And there had to be a flow of information somewhere. Alycia likely wouldn't have decided to announce Lennord's own plans for him, based on her own judgement. She had a network, and consulted with them on a variety of matters.

The difference here was that Tristan couldn't shake the feeling of unease, where usually he would politely look the other way. Besides, it needed to stop being secret, and to do that, she would need to be given a mighty persuasive reason. And Lennord. He wasn't deserving of such treatment as tantamount to insults and mockery. Few men of outstanding quality were left dotted about Burtal, and to toss them about as ragdolls was defeating the purpose of enlisting their services in the first place. But Alycia was no idiot, and must have considered this, and so Tristan was at last left with that same feeling of emptiness again, where all sense eluded him. He would readily have pursued a hundred leads in this same manner until the only possible solution was that Alycia was just being eccentric, even if they exhausted him as much this.

Lord Almaric went to Yanick, who was shuffling at the base of the great stairs. At the lord paramount's approach, he turned on him, preparing to bombard him with a million excuses.

"He was too bold," he began. "He meant to coerce me, on my honour I avow."

"Yes, alright, alright."

Tristan frowned long and hard. The boyish knight was shivering in rage, aghast that he might be rebuked for this. Something in that stopped Tristan from carrying on. Tristan had meant to humiliate him, and yet found himself incapable. *Gods damn it, but you know how to pick them, Alycia*, he thought.

"Sir Yanick, make it up to me."

"Lord," the young knight replied quickly, suddenly grinning sharply on one side of his face. Tristan was genteel, as he was known for in his approach, and thus Yanick was none the wiser.

"I ask with little expectation of success, but do you know where Lennord Brodie, the inventor, would be in the city, if not Lameeri's Wish?"

Tristan was unsure of where exactly the conversation was taking him, because to his own admission, he was making it up as he went. His main goal, he decided, was simply to glean some small sign from his expression, while remaining as casual as possible.

"Why would I know that?" Sir Yanick replied, not seeking to hide his bewilderment. There might even have been a haughty air of deliberate overstatement about it.

"You see people come and go all day. I wasn't intending to have a long conversation about it, and I didn't mean to imply that you're my exclusive source. There's no penalty for not knowing. I'll simply move on if you don't, *Sir*," Lord Almaric enunciated quite clearly for the benefit of the knight who looked like he'd forgotten who he was talking to.

"You might try any lord who works in a barracks, or in that field generally, my Lord," and at that he was more alert, if still without discipline. "If that is where he works, Lord."

"Indeed. However, that doesn't answer my question. I was rather hoping for specifics."

Lord Almaric made a motion that implied his desire to leave in any moment, to which Sir Yanick put up a hand in pardon and physically gave the impression of thinking hard. He wandered a few feet away and fondled a candelabrum idly, leaning his elbow on the banister with his other arm. The light show that the candles afforded was a blessing that showed the nuances of his features in more detail: his mouth that was curled up on the right side, as if in perpetual smugness but for the subtle shifts that gave him away, in this case a confoundedness which he, at least, didn't attempt to cover up. What eluded Tristan was whether he truly was as smug as he appeared.

He literally looked as if he'd inherited that attitude at birth, insofar as that was possible, written all over his face, unkind observation as it was. At any rate, for as far as Tristan could surmise, he was a man born into a wealthy family, and had probably been coddled too much and was rendered delusional by the filter hung before his eyes. His hair was exceptionally clean, a muddy brown naturally, and had been grown back to the bottom of his neck. His face was too soft and clean also, and now that Tristan made effort to take him apart, this man of 19 years seemed better suited to a lordlier lifestyle, that being the lifestyle that some lords, other than himself, had taken to. And yet it was a trick, a mirror of misdirection whether Yanick was aware of it or not, because here he stood as an anointed knight, defending the halls of Castle Aurail in Guardian armour.

"I don't think I can help you, my Lord," Sir Yanick concluded. "I remember faces, not names, Lord. If I had been told to remember… but I wasn't."

"Thank you, that's all I needed," Lord Almaric said coolly, nodded, and for the sake of ironing out Sir Yanick's lax attitude, did not move until he lost the grin. He did so reluctantly, for beneath it, there was no personality. "We'll talk more about your attitude later."

Tristan turned, with his last sight of the man being what he assumed was something of an apologetic look masked by defiance, as if he was expected not to show weakness, and this would somehow make up for any rudeness. It was there that Tristan temporarily set aside his suspicions of the man, because the knight had looked little more than a boy in that moment. For the sake of professionalism, and what his weak, cynical side nudged him to do, he left his name on the list.

"I can't stay here all day," Tristan thought aloud.

"The walls are closing in," Marcus agreed.

Tristan nodded at him, and by that he was excused. The courier left slowly, at a dignified pace, as one generally would in the castle, and was hopefully mindful to remember his place before other nobles within the grounds. A glimpse was seen of Marcus's immense satisfaction as he left, the very same as when Tristan had, in a manner of speaking, pulled the lowborn man of unwavering loyalty from the pit of snakes that was the home of his past life.

Instead of consulting his list, he exited the castle through the vestibule and stopped outside to bathe in the bright rays of the sun; a heat he hadn't expected to last before autumn took over. Now he felt positively cathartic as his ambitions caught up with him again: a dream that ended with summer, leaving only the majesty of that dream as something real and beautiful. There in the great stone courtyard he stood, staring longingly out the open gates, down the long road to the barbican, and through the portcullis into the city, and he saw the dream even while wide awake, fading as he woke to an unwanted reality. Soon the two forms must be swapped, the squalor an old nightmare. So he strode on at a brisk pace, not knowing where he was going, just that wherever it was would be of some importance.

Sir Yanick had been right about one thing, and that was that anyone who recommended Lennord's abilities to the Empress would presumably already be working in a field of study that Lennord was fluent in. There was the library in the castle to consider, but it would be unlikely to be as useful to him, in the given circumstances, as the trade embassy library. It was too obvious, and the Empress wanted to remain discreet for now. It was a hunch, but he felt good about it. Certainly, making heads or tails of the situation there shouldn't be difficult, for one. Sometimes to his own disbelief, Tristan had become immensely popular, and that extended, more or less, to the insular people of the library. Most of them would be happy to point him in the direction of anything matching his queries, and if not happy, obligated nonetheless.

There were those in the streets, of course, who bore the familiar look that told him that they'd just presumed to see Lord Almaric walking alone down their road as if, for him, it was the most normal thing in the world. For once Tristan paid them little attention, as he had almost always done in the past.

With his concentration solely on completing one task at a time, he soon found himself at the square housing the trade office, so packed that here even those closest to him barely noticed him for who he was, just wanting to push through the crowds as quickly as possible. The crier was on his stand, heralding the news at the top of his voice. People were crowded round his stand, which was cause for Tristan to give consideration as he passed. He wondered, in passing, if the people found the newsreader annoying, not that there was an alternative, even if this was so, besides teaching them all to read, and that wasn't an alternative available just yet.

He allowed those natural thoughts of improvement and refinement to take a back seat the instant he stepped beneath the archway tunnel, and he was but Lord Almaric when the doors of the withered, old domed building were opened for him well in advance, as it was with the guard of the library who opened his door at the slightest inclination that the Emperor's most trusted advisor might wish to use it.

He'd never liked the musty, stuffy smell of the library. The castle archives contained many old documents also, but that was better cared for, or one would think so to smell the air, and here, above all else, it rather fitted too well with the disposition of many of the librarians and regular visitors: the poor bastards who'd become distrusting and snobbish. He thought not to mention it or show disgust. Their chance to change would come soon enough, and perhaps some even would. He spied them all, under the dim lights of the lanterns high above, which cast long shadows of them all, which in their own strange ways seemed to please them, as if one judging them would do so by the foundation of this fact, as if it helped them feel secure and enigmatic as creatures of knowledge.

In the middle of it all, as he now was, he heard a fast shuffling and a jingling of keys behind an adjacent bookcase, and as he'd closely observed the pattern of it, knew it was by his presence that it happened. A slightly hunched man in expensive linen robes emerged to greet him, bowing low, hustling as people tended to do at his unexpected visitation.

"We're honoured to have you in attendance, my Lord," the man who Tristan recognised as the master of the library said. Lord Reid was nowhere to be seen.

He was an old man of medium height and circumspective disposition. His very short hair, a pale blonde, ironically gave the impression of being bleached from protracted exposure to sunny areas, spiting the assumption that he probably spent all his time inside by the embers of a fireplace like some cave-dwelling animal. It was worth viewing the man on a blank slate then, because Tristan couldn't rightly remember his personality, or had never spoken to him enough to begin with. He might not even be in the category of the strange men who viewed outsiders with distrust; he might just have been unable to control them. Sad then, with that in mind, that he couldn't currently remember the man's name.

"Likewise, Master," Lord Almaric said warmly. "I'd appreciate if you didn't speak for the honour of others, please. Your opinion is quite enough for the time being, thank you."

"Not a problem. What was it you wanted, then? If you don't need me at all, I'll leave you be and make sure none other disturbs you, at that."

"I will definitely need some help actually, though I may be too vague for you, I warn you. I'm looking for the most recent records, or otherwise your own recollection, of activity in Lameeri's Wish barracks. I'm looking for anything unusual." The librarian breathed deeply, shook his head as if in disbelief, and looked deeply taken aback.

"I can do that for you, my Lord, but I fear you'll be overwhelmed. There have been hundreds of transactions from that barracks. I hope you know what you're looking for, but either way, I can show you if you'll not be swayed, yes."

"Do so, please. Though it's not only business transactions I'm interested in," Lord Almaric added as the librarian led him back the way he'd come. "I want to see as many records of general activity there as possible."

The librarian shook his head to himself again as they walked past the entrance and turned left, all the way to the end, where he drew a large cluster of keys and fiddled through them at a painfully slow pace, which Tristan was kind enough not to interrupt in any way. The shelves here consisted primarily of wooden drawers covered with plates of iron, firmly locked, as most of them were first edition documents with no copies in the library, not even summary notes. Quietly satisfied, the librarian set about unlocking several drawers.

"We do collect some information not of trade relevance, that's true, my Lord, but I really don't know what you expect to find here."

"If you speak from experience, can you tell me why no one would log other information from Lameeri's Wish here?"

The Voice of Kings

Tristan opened a box within a drawer and began filing through thick wads of obviously quite new parchment. The list he was studying on a whim regarded mostly food. Its thickness was startling, its contents dull, all for him to skim through at his leisure, or lack thereof, page by page.

"Because, my Lord," the librarian said tiredly, but not condescendingly, "all other data relevant to the barracks is recorded by them, and consists largely of progress reports of workers and so forth. I hope that answers your question," he said edgily, putting a finger of his lips and staring hard.

"Yes, I understand. It's obvious, I know, I just wanted your opinion. To clarify, the unusual behaviour I'm looking for will not be criminal, I suspect. Perhaps surprisingly large quantities of something were ordered, building materials and equipment most likely, for specialist builders."

"One question, if you'll permit me," the librarian said, and stepped forward with confidence into Tristan's peripheral vision. "Why are you not at the barracks? What you've told me suggests you'd have better luck there than, if I can be bold, wasting your time reading all of this", and here he held his arms out to the open drawers to illustrate his point.

"Only if one assumes the writer of the relevant document must be the man or woman I'm looking for." He paused and the light dawned on him, which made him beam a smile. Where inventing and building were concerned, Lennord had no interest in the military. "Sèhvorian steel," Lord Almaric stated boldly. "I need to see all modern records even tangentially involved with Sèhvorian steel."

"Okay, that's relatively specific. We may get somewhere at your current rate of progress, my Lord."

In Tristan's imagination, the librarian was deliberately distracting him from his present obsession, but he paid it no heed, for he was still uncomfortable with projecting guilt. Regardless, he carried on skimming through boring articles, wondering if he'd even spot an anomaly without the aid of Sir Pedrig or some other like him, while the librarian unlocked a drawer nearby. He stopped, peered through the shelves, and walked quickly round Lord Almaric to the edge of the aisle.

"Ah, ah, how forgetful of me," he said in a voice withered by his own shame. "That man leaving now has been visiting quite frequently of late." Tristan's head sprang up, but all he saw was the entrance door swinging shut. "He's not interested in industry, I don't think, but he's been looking into Sèhvorian steel quite religiously. I can't say I ever saw him here before that. Can't say I approve of people like him using our facilities like they're just for reading at a fancy, either, but..."

"Who is he? Lord...?" Tristan prompted, in hopes of extracting a more precise answer.

"No, no, he's not a lord. He's a foreign bastard from across the channel. Wears too much jewellery, but quite lordly clothes I suppose. Black hair. I don't remember his name, my Lord, I'm very sorry."

"Thank you all the same, Master."

Tristan was already marching to the door, having drawn a picture in his mind of what the wads of parchment looked like lest they be tampered with. He would forget anyhow, but he had to try. He glanced down every aisle as he passed them, crossing each of them out as bearing potential onlookers who were too keen on his business.

"Who just left the library?" Tristan demanded in a hurry to the guard on the other side of the door, a guard who was all of a sudden incredibly focused.

"A moment, my Lord, I don't remember offhand. If he ever told me."

"Never mind."

And Tristan was marching onward again, out the front doors and against the flow of a crowd where, fortunately, a few citizens, noteworthy for their generosity, stepped aside for his passage. In an alcove attached to the building at Tristan's right-hand side, there was bedding for horses to rest, and from there, a man was leaving with his steed, raising a hood over his black hair. His riding cloak was pristine, but for a thin layer of dust probably caked on that very day, and of high quality, unlikely to fray as easily as the common man's coat. He wore several rings on each finger, and a bracelet: jewellery of varying degrees of worth. One of the rings looked fairly cheap, if he was not mistaken in the heat of the moment. Most notably, there was no indication of a weapon anywhere about his person.

"You, I'd ask to speak with you, if you please," Lord Almaric called out to him as he emerged from the shadowy shelter of the pale red archway. He did not regard Tristan's presence. "You, good citizen, with the horse, I'd ask you to stop for me." The man climbed his horse, lowering his face. "I am Lord Almaric, the Emperor's aide, and you will stop, I order it."

The rider kicked his heels into the horse, head still turned away, and his horse roared through the crowd, which tore open for him, people tripping over one another to avoid being trampled. There was tenacity in the rider, but hesitation where he slowed his mount and glanced back directly at the crowd behind him. The City Watch, Tristan was glad to see, was already at his disposal, alert as they would be if a battle were about to break out in the streets.

"Guards! Follow me!" Lord Almaric shouted, feeling utterly foolish, knowing to lead them through the streets after a horse, with his only hope lying in the bad luck and incompetency of the rider.

Tristan took point by a distance which only increased as he sprinted through the opening in the crowd, to the north exit of the square where the rider had fled. It branched out into two new roads, but the crowd split open at the left fork to reveal the getaway path, and then

The Voice of Kings

again at a right turning, where from Tristan's memory, it became more narrow and darker too, with overhanging arches and clothes lines.

Whatever the case, Tristan took a gamble with barely a thought, and sprinted to the low brick wall directly ahead of him between two buildings, and vaulted over it into the small, plain garden of an upholstery store, followed by the clanging of armour, again and again and again, giving him rhythm in his sprinting, while one particularly close Watchman spurred him on, as if he were being chased. He felt full of breath, unstoppable, like years ago when he would apprehend criminals and drunkards at the Emperor's public parties. The scenery flew by, and another wall disappeared beneath him as he shot over it into another garden, where he barely swerved by the participants of a business deal and barraged through a half-open gate into a dead end street which curved sharply round to the left ahead of him.

Still he ran through the emptiness of a crowd parted, as if to his very will like a sword through paper, dozens of worried civilians backing against the walls of shops and houses for a line of soldiers streaming through in single file. Above the din of their running, Tristan could hear hooves from the road before him: a narrow corridor, just as he'd remembered it, with little room for stalls. Cries of fright bounced back and forth, and now the fear wriggled its way into Tristan as he ran, heedless of danger, into the road, where bearing over him was pungent breath and restless hooves, charging at great speed, galloping haphazardly about him as he hugged the wall; there he did not run anymore, only watching as the rider reached a crossroads, appearing indecisive as to his route, only riding left as it took his fancy.

Breathlessness warped around him, as if of physical entity, and he clutched at his stomach, bent over. His could not have been a lordly sight, it soon dawned on him, as the Watchmen all caught up in swift succession. His hair was ragged, so he slicked it back with one hand, and his clothes were ruffled, so he dealt with that too.

"What the fucking hell did we just do?" the Watchman at the very back exclaimed, careful not to say this while Lord Almaric was in his line of sight.

"Quiet!" his commanding officer snapped.

Tristan saw that six men had followed him, now gathered round him in a semicircle. He hoped they were not men recently arrested at Alycia's behest.

"We were chasing that man, that's all you need to know. I know not so much more myself, only that he disobeyed my order. Don't bother yourselves with it. No other men could have done better than you, given the circumstances, so I thank you. You may resume your watch," Lord Almaric said reluctantly.

To investigate the trade office library might be prudent. Then again, it might not. Taking the matter higher up might be wise. The castle beckoned, as often it did. On the way back, three beggars, or otherwise extremely poor women, were loitering in the shadows beneath a stone overhang before a doorway. Whether they'd been there when first he'd walked by that day, he couldn't tell.

He stopped to give each of them a coin. He knew he wasn't supposed to. It should be left to his almoner. He knew, and did it anyway. It gave him peace.

"Do you know where I might find Sir Pedrig Lannoi?" Lord Almaric asked a servant in the vestibule of the castle.

"With Her Majesty, last I saw," she replied. "Don't take my word for it though. That was a while ago."

"No, it's quite alright. It wasn't important anyway."

To wait, then, is all he would have to do. To concern himself with any number of other important matters. To his office he went, and sat behind his desk. He unfolded his list of potential affiliates and gave it one last, hard look for the day, yet nothing popped out for him. There was the option of approaching Alycia herself available to him now, if nothing else. A suspicious man had fled in the street in direct contradiction to his orders and the pursuit of armed Watchmen. A crime had taken place now.

He leaned over his shoulder and breathed more steadily as he took all that the painting on the wall offered, of Evylyn at her most ethereally brilliant. On the night before his leaving the estate, making love to her had been as heavenly as ever, her body smooth to the touch, yet electrifying, feeling not only wonderful to be so close, but overwhelmingly *right*. His hands had moved from rubbing her curved thighs, to her breasts, and finally to affectionately fondling her hair and stroking it from her eyes, where he'd seen confidence enough to drive him anywhere, and to his ecstasy, she'd seen the vision in him. In talking for an hour afterwards, she'd repeatedly told him to be careful and not rush into things. Too much, even, if that was possible, as was her way. But just as she'd advised caution, he'd pleaded with her soul to flourish.

"You'd do wonders there if they'd listen," he heard the memory of his voice.

Evylyn had licked her lips, staring at the ceiling as he did, both of them lying naked on the bed covers. The heaving of her bosom had distracted him, her thin body wet and gleaming. Raven-black hair splayed on her pillow, captured like the most artistic of paintings. She had shaken her head as she considered his words, serene as she undervalued herself.

"Tell me again how you worked that out," her dulcet voice had teased through a smirk.

"By looking at you and realising half of you is me, Evylyn, and half of me is you," he'd joked. He wasn't joking, not really. "If they welcomed you, you'd be a goddess to Aurail."

They wouldn't welcome her, not as an adviser. Tristan yawned and noticed he was tired. He sat there frowning, but smiling. He placed the list in a drawer. Confronting proud Alycia would have been ideal, but not necessarily wise at that time. Evylyn's advice might not have been welcome as it was, but that didn't mean he couldn't listen to it. She'd been right; he

The Voice of Kings

had to be patient. So he bided his time, dozing off on his chair, and unlike his dear friend Richard, his mind was still strong.

Chapter Twenty-One: Animated Shadows

One must wonder deeply, so close to the sanctuary of the gods on Mura, or rather the greatest and most holy human shrine for them, what to say, whether they will listen, and what one will feel. So Marcel now thought, having had considerable time, it felt like, with the echoes from the cathedral next door giving cause to repeatedly question what he was doing in this room, garbed in the clean white robes of his colleagues as if he belonged but, conversely, scrubbing statues, and walls, and floors like a commissioned servant. He was funnelled from place to place to do the same again with minimal explanation, shunned with the same distaste, apparently, as a criminal would receive while his masters of justice decide on his fate behind his back.

The room was purely for transitional purposes, Marcel had concluded, and he had been in there long enough to formulate a reasonable opinion on the matter. Its sole function was to be visually impressive, and that it was, with murals inscribed along the walls and even the ceiling, where the walls were forest, each containing a separate shrine, while the ceiling was the night sky: a sea of marble black punctuated by stars as bright as he'd ever seen them in reality. It was of an age Marcel didn't care to guess, for he had no experience in that field, but he knew it wasn't recent, because despite being well kept, it looked worn and decoloured by time in places. He might have been proud to step back and admire his work if it had been of his own choosing, but as it was, he was only frustrated and confused, and yet again, an echo of footsteps and voices smothered by reverb from the cathedral made him ever more enthused by the wonders within, and he contemplated peeking inside. The traffic through the room had lessened throughout the afternoon, as had the unearthly echoes behind the door.

For all the direction he'd been given, he might have been expected to stop cleaning by now and report for new duties from Bishop Eccelie, who was now irritated by his lack of presence and forethought, as if expecting him to be psychic. He dropped the rough scrap of cloth into the bucket of water, where it bobbed up and down, not affecting the colour of the fluid in any meaningful way, as nothing in the room had been more than mildly dirty at the start of it all.

The wooden door beckoned for him, the echoes creeping through the gaps around it like a choir's song soothing him, steeling his heart for the world beyond. The door, which looked new but somehow gave the impression of being ages old, pulled him closer, until he found himself opening it a crack, then halfway. From the sea of grandiose architecture, a bishop approached, to Marcel's terrible luck; he looked to be doing so anyway, and stopped only at the door to lay an inquisitive gaze on him.

The Voice of Kings

"Are you supposed to be in here?" the bishop asked rhetorically, with a twinge of uncertainty.

"I don't believe so," Marcel responded, as he supposed was the best way to answer given what circumstance betided him.

"Who is it?" the voice of another man in religious regalia echoed to the bishop from further into the cathedral, without thinking to even look at him.

"It's the latest apprentice, who arrived last night, Your Eminence, and curiosity's got the better of him. Be gone," the bishop said in a colder tone, directly to Marcel, and passively made to redirect him back into the transitional hall, gesturing that the door was to be closed also.

"I'm feeling in a curious mood myself," that same deep voice wound its way about the cathedral and through the doorway. "I shall meet him, thank you."

The bishop was wholly surprised but thought not to argue, only to silently indicate for Marcel to proceed, and do so without delay, of which he was grateful, if nervous of the man residing within. He felt, all of a sudden, very small, and in awe, as he had been when he first saw the exterior of the cathedral in all its glory. There were enough pews to seat hundreds of people, all lovingly crafted white stone with thick, leaf green cushioning fastened into them somehow, except, he glimpsed briefly, on the first two rows, where they were a royal purple. Cordoning them in were pillars as thick as tree trunks, ten on either side, each with their own vaultings, holding up a second floor which was but a fraction of the way to the ceiling looming high above him. The pillars even had their own steeples attached beside them, protruding into the dusty sky of the cathedral, past the second set of seats, and ending in finely fashioned points, like miniature watchtowers.

Every step boomed ominously, to which the man ahead of him took no notice, and so disregarding any conduct he may have had to display, Marcel looked down at his feet, and at the floor of black and white chequers, so shiny it flawlessly reflected the curved roof emblazoned with the dark fresco of black smoke: shapes of demonic apparitions burnt and forced back by men and gods alike. So real it was that a sense of surrealism would take over should he stare too intently, that reason might be supplanted by the illusion of walking on air if not for the pounding of his boots.

Only one strip differentiated itself, that being a strip of marble floor leading from the double doors directly down the nave, and to the platform where the altar stood, and on this strip was a motif of white branches climbing their way to the altar. The man who'd summoned him was upon it also, staring straight down the centre. Marcel knew him to be the duceveree from how the bishop had addressed him so formerly, but he was very real now that he was so close, and powerful also, in white robes fashioned with gold and silver inlay, and a high collar that curved and ran to his waist, blazing with a regal red all the way. His face was one of intense seriousness that looked unused to laughing, yet through it all, he showed remarkable curiosity for what he must have gazed upon 10,000 times, his eyes wide as he sucked in every detail. His hair was fair and fading, his short beard immaculately neat and braided where, on him, it was well and truly a part of him, while on another it might be gaudy or peculiar.

"Marcel Brodie," the ducevereë announced, as if bestowing him with the name. "Salutations, apprentice. Let me get a look at you."

It was a demand which struck out at Marcel and left him feeling unsure of how to commune with the man, for seemingly contrary to his own wishes, he gave Marcel a sweeping glance that lasted only as long as his head turned one way and then back to the cathedral at large, and the five timeless statues at the back that, through heavenly light distorted and distilled by stained glass windows, appeared two or three times the height of his house in Caedor.

"Your Eminence," Marcel said, mimicking the bishop.

"So I am. My name's Laryc Morzall, though 'Your Eminence' will do fine for you," he replied, as if to give him a choice. Isaac would be smirking to himself if he were here to hear that. It seemed like something he'd do.

"What have you been doing today, apprentice?"

"Cleaning here and there, as thoroughly as it's possible to, I think." The duceveree was silent. He cocked his head to one side. "I spent much of my time in the cloisters of Dawn and Dusk. I was told they needed cleaning."

"Did you disagree?" the duceveree replied sharply.

"No, Your Eminence."

"How did you take to your duty?"

"Well enough. As I said, I couldn't have done it better. Although I must confess..." Marcel went on, to speak, already to his regret, as he thought Isaac would, though not necessarily wisely. "That's not why I came here. It's a job that needs doing, you can be sure I won't argue with that, but my parents didn't pay for me to come here to be treated like a lesser citizen, and I didn't travel all this way for that, either."

The duceveree broke whatever contact he held with the five statues to regard Marcel with scrutiny, and took in a deep breath that seemed not to find its way out again. The aura of mystery was dispelled, leaving him a man who might make effort to be clearer with him, if no less fearsome.

"For both our sakes, I'll drop the act now. You were tested, as you may or may not have guessed. It gives me an overview of your personality: a social advantage, if you'll permit me to say so. You weren't treated with discrimination; you were just as everyone else in your position. Some people lose their tempers at being ignored so, some are silently contemptuous, others not only work to the best of their abilities, but look for new assignments, or work of their own accord until the sun sets and someone tells them to sleep."

"How did I fare?" Marcel asked edgily, fearful of the answer.

"It's not that kind of test," was the only answer the duceveree would tell him. Marcel tried hard to hide his confusion. *Whatever the test is for, there must be a conclusion to be had*, he thought, but didn't object. "I wasn't going to tell you so soon, but the opportunity arose, and I do tire of games."

That was that. Marcel could not hold his attention longer. He was drawn to the statues again, formed in a half-circle on a dais at the back of the cathedral, where the dome grew to the sky, higher than the rest of the roof, where in the rafters there were walkways leading from lower down, from a door into the cathedral extension, up to the bell pulls hidden from sight. Hidden, also, were a series of mirrors that somehow transfixed the sun's rays directly upon the statues, despite not being midday, as was required for the motif in Caedor's church. The intention was the same, regardless, and had nurtured in him, from a young age, the idea of the gods being one with nature, in the sunlight they so loved.

The statues were familiar, depicting from left to right, Lavellyrn of love, Nel of faith, Lameeri of justice, Saliis of souls, and Venlor of the realms. Familiar, too, were their positions: very similar to those in Caedor, only these were all naked and fully exposed. An unusual depiction, *but gods needn't follow the same rules as us*, Marcel thought as he presumed the duceveree would. What infrastructure the celestial realm operated on wasn't comparable to anything on Mura.

"So you say you're not a lowly cleaner. Why are you here?"

"To better myself, if I can speak so simply." The statues, emboldened in the natural light which they so loved during their tenure on Mura, or so it was said, inspired him to add to that, as he felt pressured to do anyway. "I'm no theologian, Your Eminence. My faith is far simpler, or I like to keep it that way. I'm no master of the faith, but it might do me well to keep learning, and I know the virtue of the gods and will always be enamoured and awed by them, I should say."

"Well, fairness be, there's a place for that kind of thinking, and you did yourself right when you expressed keenness for learning. Blessed by your father."

"I wrote my opinion on the matter in my letter," Marcel said in hopes of not having to justify himself further to the stoic, brooding man before him.

"I know. I wanted to hear it from you personally. It's fortunate you were so nervous and spoke so uncontrollably, irrefutably so. There's no danger in mistaking that for a rehearsed speech."

"I'm glad of that, at least."

"We'll make a learned man of you yet," the duceveree replied, as if having heard him speak differently, or rather, the truth of it was probably that he was speaking as he'd originally intended to, not swayed by tangents that could lead to small talk. A silence followed that caused Marcel to realise it was even less comfortable a sensation than the prospect of discussing theology with the man.

"As you say," he said, and for conversation's sake, more words came forth. "Do many people use those as a muse?" he asked of the statues.

"Men beyond counting, yes. For four hundred years. People see them as a vassal, being as they are: majestic, commanding us even in their stillness. There's no finer man-made commemoration."

"From my, admittedly limited, experience, I'd tend to agree. Although, I stopped at the old shrine of Venlor on The Wolf's Way on my journey here, and it was no less cathartic. I looked for a god there and found one crystallised in stone. It spoke to me, just not in words."

"Only the blessed are spoken to so vividly. Your response is not unusual. Although, you have an abstract understanding of the gods. I'm given to understand Burtal has less in the way of physical things to study, and you sound taken by imagination, which can be a dangerous and unruly path to tread, so I'm curious about your experience with religion."

Again, Marcel was sure he'd written an acceptable answer to the given question in his application, but spoke nothing of it this time.

"I've seen numerous churches, Your Eminence, in the county of my birth and all house scriptures true to those of ages past. There's probably truth in what you say," Marcel added when the duceveree remained unfulfilled. "I talked with my brother about it on the way here, and it got me thinking how little I know. My brother had done research on your cathedral," Marcel stressed without rebuke from the duceveree, "and he found there's a heavier sense of procedure here, but also that many things are the same. The idea of kings being given magic by the gods was brought up, and apparently it's not given much credence here either."

"Don't believe everything you hear!" the duceveree snapped. A hand was raised to silence him, and then when he was calm, he simply pointed to the ceiling with a bony hand, slow and functioning on its own time, drifting like a wraith. "Many fools believe as such, and others perpetuate the myth through indifference, even if they believe. It's true that we're unlikely ever to see it. It will happen when all the kings are pure of heart, or when all have turned to the darkness. Even a master theologian, as I am, cannot say for certain."

Marcel held his tongue, sensing the duceveree was still aggravated. He was glad to see a figure emerge from an exit at the rear of the hall on the left side: from an arched doorway, symmetrical in place and design to a door on the right. It was a woman, he now saw, and through glimpses of her between pillars, he noted her to be Tamzin, whom he'd met at the start of the day. It was beside the duceveree that she stopped, whereupon he turned and did not wait for her greeting.

The Voice of Kings

"I expected to see you at lunch, but you never showed up."

"I was busy, as you almost always are at that time. I heard you had some free time at noon, but today it was my turn," Tamzin said, standing to attention like a soldier, while her eyes worked on their own to convey a knowing caution and fierce stubbornness which she otherwise could not act out. "I wouldn't worry. You asked again, and here I am."

"Was that supposed to be a rebuke? An explanation would have been fine."

Tamzin only then noticed Marcel, whereupon she looked at once alive, and cocked her head back at her own stupidity at having not been more observant. Laryc turned and took a step back, looking back and forth between the two of them, expecting one or the other to explain all in full.

"We've been acquainted already," Tamzin said first.

"We bumped into one another at breakfast," Marcel supplied. The ducevereë became a figure of ice, chilling the air that it might freeze as a solid object and shatter upon the marble, his emotions impenetrable to Marcel's eyes, just as before.

"I'm aware of that, as it happens," Laryc said more smoothly than expected.

"Was it offensive of me?"

"To do what?" Laryc asked innocently.

"Father, be plain, I implore you," the priestess Tamzin pleaded, rolling her eyes, exhaling with an impertinence that was characteristic of her earlier self, only bereft of patience, as Marcel surmised was due to a lifetime of seeing her father act this way. The ducevereë smiled briefly, in a very sickly manner, as he relented to his daughter's wish.

"As I understand it, apprentice, that's not exactly what happened. If bumping into her is your way of describing your encounter, where you deliberately sat with her, I call your logic flawed."

"Your Eminence, you misunderstand me. Perhaps it was an error in my articulation, I don't know, but I only meant that I didn't know who she was, and did not sit before her solely because of *her*."

"You're sure there was no other masked intention? I ask tentatively of course, not accusingly. I must stress, however, that my daughter is not for sale, as it were. Her marriage will happen when it is suitable."

"Father, is this necessary? I'm sure he just sat down because there was a free seat. There was nothing ill of our conversation, I give you my word on that."

"I'm only being thorough. For all I know, you seduced him."

"Obviously, that's what I was doing."

The ducevereë's robes came alive as he spun around with speed that that was both surprising and unprecedented, but it was the cackling of the strike escaping into the air and rebounding about that made Marcel flinch, and he froze up, so as not to seem implicit or, indeed, in possession of any opinion on the matter. Tamzin's face bobbed back up, wincing, and Laryc, at the same time, lowered his pale hand which was reddened at the knuckles.

"Remember, I'm not only your father. Would that I were, you no doubt wish, but I am the duceveree, by which, holy standards are expected of me, and that's not about to change. I was being thorough."

"I understand. You should have a little more faith in me though. I was appalled by your suggestion."

"Oh, I do have faith in you, my dear. I was being thorough," Laryc said a third time. Watching him piteously examine her cheek, like a physician, was no more pleasant than moments earlier when he had slapped her in rage. When he was done, he gave Marcel his attention. "I apologise. You shouldn't have had to see that."

Marcel stood to attention, and if nothing else, the duceveree seemed to recognise his desperate attempt at detachment.

"I've taken enough of your time. You'll want to reflect on your day. There will be many more tests to come, though I daresay they'll not be of my design." Marcel looked, as he felt, mildly puzzled, to which the duceveree was kind enough to elaborate. "Ilistarty, the five days of exaltation, is next month. The week of life. I'm sure you'll have your chance to prove your usefulness then. There's no busier time, for us or for anyone else."

Marcel didn't answer, for he did not know the procedures of such an event here. Where in Caedor he spent the five days with his family, in the manner he assumed most people did, working through to Lavellyrn's day of giving thanks for the preservation of familiar aspects and people, he imagined Harth would make a grand affair of it, where huge wads of money were spent, but far more filled the banks by week's end.

The duceveree bowed to the statues, and Marcel bowed lower to him. The duceveree took it in from the corner of one eye, but stayed not till its end, for he was already heading to the exit.

"Tamzin, come. We should leave the apprentice to his thoughts. Apprentice, let yourself out the front doors when you're done."

Tamzin tagged along, but as she walked, she pivoted about, holding up an index finger to Marcel alongside a playfully commanding face, mouthing words he could not read. When they were gone, when the oak door was locked and he was alone, he felt a chill, and the statues seemed bigger somehow. So there he stood, pale and cold for time beyond his counting, with not a prayer so much as an appreciation for it all, until finally a door opened on the balcony to his right, and the strange sensation of cold joy melded into the soft tones of reality. It was Tamzin upon the balcony, whose motions above he followed on the ground, to the end of the balcony, where she unexpectedly, deftly, climbed over the railing and jumped to lower footing.

The Voice of Kings

Marcel opened his mouth to object but, instead, said nothing when his worries turned to great intrigue, as she descended a pillar with practised movements, swinging down on indents in the stone, her dress robe upturned at the bottom to aid her legs, garters maintaining modesty. Upon descending more than halfway, she stopped to study her surroundings, then jumped to a neat landing near Marcel.

"No, I shouldn't really be doing that," she muttered half to herself. She kissed the tip of her thumb and held it up to the statues. The dexterous, rebellious Tamzin vanished and she was a lady again, back straight and of form immaculate. "So you waited for me after all."

"I don't know if I waited for *you*, though I mean no offence in saying so." He paused and coughed to relieve himself. Her bruised cheek had caught his attention, at any rate. "Does it hurt much?" he asked sympathetically, and pointed.

"Not so much, no. He's not very strong."

"You might have told me of your father at breakfast, and you might have avoided that in exchange," Marcel said straightforwardly with the intent of avoiding controversy.

"True, but it was worth it to see you so confused." A delicate smile grew like a flower in soft sunlight. "I was wrong though. You met the ducevereë after all, just as you wanted. Most likely it was an opportunistic meeting."

Marcel's silence was telling. She did not break her pause, and seemed, in fact, to be encouraging response.

"It was... interesting. We spoke of several matters. His unpredictability made it all the more intriguing."

"Are we speaking of the same man?" she laughed. "That's what a church official would say, or a lord from court. Don't be so meek. Being deliberately unassertive will get you nowhere." The first thought that crossed Marcel was that of another test, but the mark on her cheek begged otherwise, and he sighed in submission as Tamzin seemingly wanted of him.

"I'll take your word for it. I shouldn't judge," he said evasively, even as Tamzin rubbed her bruise, and would likely bemoan the man next he saw Isaac, at any rate. "He did have his quirks, I'll admit."

"Oh?"

"He likes his solitude, I gather. When I spoke to him, he seemed distant: he stood by himself and spoke to me on his own time. I could have kept talking and he'd not reply if he had nothing to say. That's how I saw it."

"Not an entirely false assumption. Did he not look at you during your conversation?"

"Hardly at all."

Tamzin grinned sheepishly and shook her head.

"He does that. It's his way of reassuring himself of his authority. His wife is his holy mirror, but she's only wheeled out when he needs to remind himself that goddesses have equal power in the pantheon."

Marcel chose not to further perpetuate the hatred toward the duceveree, for he felt increasingly ill at ease, even with Tamzin's blessing, not to mention encouragement. He cleared his throat and searched for the politest way to be relieved of her presence.

"Do you have somewhere to be?" the priestess asked edgily.

"Yes."

"How inconsiderate of me. I'll walk you to the door. I was going out that way anyway."

"You're not going out the way you came in?" Marcel asked with curiosity, which had been previously dwarfed by her feud with her father.

"It's a hobby," she replied indirectly. "Walking serves me well enough most of the time. Besides, I really, really shouldn't."

It was Tamzin who opened one door a crack, and Marcel who politely waved her through first: a gesture that was quaintly pleasant for her it seemed.

"I think you're in the wrong place," she said quietly, as if half not intending for him to hear.

"Respectfully, that can't be true. I have to make something of myself here, and it was my choice to come at all, and none other's. I daresay I received nudges and encouragement in this direction, but... there you have it."

"As you wish," Tamzin said without a mind to argue. "I don't presume to order you about, and I make that clear because I sense you'd rather back away from me, for one reason or another, so I say to you now, if you think I am strange, I can live with that, as you may not be far wrong, but please don't categorise me with my father's absurdity. If it's exclusion from my friendship you want, so be it, but I ask, and ask alone, only that you don't let my father's attitude be the deciding factor."

"I see no reason to deny your friendship, if it's no danger to me. Strangeness should not necessarily be a barrier, I'm sure my brother Isaac would say."

The priestess Tamzin considered this deeply, her pale blue eyes shining in relief, though it might partly have been at Marcel's continued compliance in not praising the duceveree, whose description she lashed out like a snake's tongue when she spoke of him, and was rather too eager for Marcel's agreement. Thankfully though, that did not make her wholly unapproachable, he thought as she smiled half to herself and left him be, cathedral guards laying accusing gazes upon him.

The dark, towering presence of the place affected him even as he was faced away, in ways he couldn't describe, for better or worse, and so, for better or worse, he was grateful for the acceptance of Tamzin Morzall.

~

The Voice of Kings

Through the city gates, at afternoon's end, rode the third brother, as was his thought exactly, for finding the others was of the highest priority, if they hadn't gotten lost or sidetracked by Isaac's hedonism. By that token, the white and gold extravagance of Harth's streets was absorbed, as if for later analysis, making him vaguely aware of a culture structure he did not yet understand, as it passed him by in favour of family concern. A city, so great, that made him feel he could tackle Aurail and fix it, for the sight of it alone: something he intended to follow through on in one way or another.

Thoughts suppressed to the recess of his mind by mounting cynicisms brought from home.

The strap on his satchel dug into his shoulder as he dismounted his horse, and he felt it ever more as he marched to see an end to doubt. The sky was bright and clear, but a sea wind bit at him, snaking through the streets, and added another bad taste in his mouth.

At once, he was passing beneath the gates of the finest city ever built, then he was at the door of the inn he was to stay at, as if the journey had been skipped. Memories were rendered a blur, before everything smashed into focus, as if being built all over again. It was not for a lack of paying attention, he reminded himself, but rather a result of having realistic priorities.

So he wasted no time in entering the establishment, tall and reflective against flames of sun and candles, where a middle-aged woman sat behind a desk, her eyes darting up at him, cast with shadows of doubt and suspicion. Then she was warm and kind, as she appeared to recognise him: in Burtalian, thickly swaddled clothes of black and blue, loose at the arms and neck, and proudly displayed too, as seeing the High Duke in dark attire had given him further confidence.

"You must be the second Brodie, am I right?"

"You are, madam. And you are my father's oldest friend, I assume. Rosalynn. Tidings." And Lucian smiled and bowed, even if it wasn't really necessary. "I would love to speak with you more, but it's quite important I find Isaac. Might I find him here?"

"At another time, you will. I've no idea where he is now. Although I should warn you..."

Rosalynn trailed off and pointed down the corridor, and Lucian saw a door at the end half ajar, with shadows moving within.

"I'd better not say anymore. Any son or daughter of Lennord is worthy of favour of mine, but I have to be sensible. I don't want to get into trouble. You'll understand. You dabble in politics, don't you?"

"It's quite alright," Lucian said through gritted teeth to his father's old friend. "I'll deal with it."

He meant precisely that, for already he knew a situation had arisen and must be dealt with. His brother just couldn't leave well alone. Someone had taken to searching his room, and though Isaac was prone to riotous behaviour, Lucian found himself surprised yet again, and more so when he pushed the door open all the way to find four Watchmen scouring every last inch of the room, bed upturned, sheets strewn about, and bag emptied, and in the middle, a powerful stout man whipped around, his shoulder-slung cape flying behind him. His eyes were lead, his jaw was wide and strong. They narrowed, peering through his helm which boasted short wings on either side.

"You're not Isaac Brodie, are you?"

"I'm his brother," Lucian answered with a gasp of disappointment. "Do you have the authority to be doing this?" he asked, hardly without thinking.

"I'm Commander of the Watch. I absolutely do. And you can tell Isaac from me that word gets around fast in this city. Nothing happens that I, or the Knight of the Holy Storm, don't hear about in due course; due course being shorter a time than Burtalian Watch could ever dream of being realistic. For your own sake, don't take that as an insult. The truth can be daunting to outsiders. But it's not to me, and that's why I'm Commander, and why I can get to Isaac's own lodgings before he can."

"I take no offence, Commander," Lucian replied, secretly taken aback by his presumption. "I will only say that, on behalf of my younger brother, I offer any apology worthy of your gratitude, and say that whatever you think he may be guilty of, it's likely a misunderstanding. He's known for attracting attention and acting without thinking, but his intentions are not ill, I'll tell you that right now."

"Murderers sometimes have good intentions. Where do we draw the line here?"

"It would help if I knew where "here" was in this context, Commander," Lucian said blankly.

The Commander paused, Lucian noticed, in stark juxtaposition to when he was talking, where he seemed in a hurry, and deeply suspicious: an act which was dropped whenever his mouth shut. He was incredibly thoughtful. He scanned the corridor over Lucian's shoulder.

"You mean to say you don't know?" a Watchman to the Commander's left enquired. "What are you doing here?"

"I only just arrived in the city, literally an hour ago. I can't claim to know anything of the goings on here presently."

"How do I ascertain that?" the Commander said, lifting his head high, his teeth now firmly clamped together, and his eyebrows raised quizzically.

"If information is so freely flowing under your command, your gate guards will inform you soon enough, I pray. My cooperation is yours, know that at least."

"Your name?"

Lucian gave it. The Commander looked briefly to each of his men for a silent verdict to be reached, and it apparently was, as the Commander passed him by without another word, his Watchmen in tow. Lucian put his head in his hand and shook it from side to side. As the mature son, he desired more clarity and an explanation, but that was for later.

The Voice of Kings

"What was Isaac's crime that his right to privacy was thrown to the wolves so hastily?" Lucian called down the corridor.

"Wasting my time, so far as I can tell!" the Commander shouted back in rising anger, not bothering to turn around.

Again, Lucian was close to resignation, though more pressing questions appeared to face him down that he would be ashamed to dismiss. So he followed the four men into the orange glow of the square out the front.

"I take these things very seriously, Commander. If a crime has been done, or suspected, I will at least know its magnitude."

This time, the Commander stopped and doubled back to honour him with a response to his face. One side of his mouth formed a grin, or what looked like one, bearing some irony and conveying submission.

"I know your kind. You're obsessed with law and procedure, so I'll tell it plain and true, to the extent I think is appropriate. I was ordered to investigate your brother on account of several messages sent to the palace on his behalf, and erratic, unpredictable behaviour. The orders were vague, and the rest was left up to me, and I deemed it fit to intrude on your brother's privacy. The question hanging on the end of my tongue was quite simply, "Why?". What does he stand to gain from waking tired, old ghosts? You should ask him about it, because I've said enough. But I'll say this just for you, because I'm a family man and I'd hate to be a hypocrite: I know where you're coming from, so I'll leave you this: fear is for the wicked, so if by chance he's run away, that's very telling to a man like me. If he hasn't, you'd best convince him to stop whatever he's doing, because it leaves an impression, and he will have a reason to fear, if he continues to waste my time, if you understand my meaning."

"Clear like crystal. He won't have run away, I assure you, so I'll tell him just that."

The Commander grunted under his breath in further ironic amusement, and turned powerfully on his heel, walking no faster than before to escape Lucian, smoothly around the central well, but the message was clear that he'd not suffer being halted again. Lucian took a time to collect his thoughts and apply a caption to each one, that he might rebuke Isaac and his silver tongue.

A salesman coolly expended his last supplies, all meat, as indeed, all the stores here sold food. The salesman's voice was the loudest to be heard among a quieting square, and the salty air, too, was settling unto him with less hostility, giving him a more pleasant feeling than he had any right to. Then home was brought back to him, as he couldn't have expected.

"Lucian!" Isaac's voice called from on high. "Up here!"

He was on Rosalynn's establishment, glimpsed for a moment before disappearing. So Lucian was whirring round the spiral staircase of Rosalynn's inn, giving her an apologetic look as he went, for he did so wish to hear her story. The darkness of the narrow stairs exploded once more into orange light as he emerged at the very top, where Isaac was leaning forward, slumped even, over the balcony that captured the sea in its view. Isaac was almost white against that backdrop, yet in spite of this, it was as plain as the rising of the moon that Isaac was donned in clothes more befitting those of station and power.

Lucian's swift, sleek approach confirmed this. It was a suit of blue mostly, inarguably expensive, the imaginary price tag climbing to unrealistic heights at the notice of every fine detail and extravagant, fashionable addition. It was worth commenting on, just not now.

Isaac didn't care to alter his position greatly, even as Lucian came up beside him and stood tall, a shadow extending down his face. He did turn his head, pleased to see Lucian, and stared long and hard, his gaze occasionally passing right through him, as if he could not focus.

"What did they want?" Isaac asked, gesturing with his head to the spot where the Watchmen had lately been.

"They wanted you, and I take it you know it. They stripped your room down, but took nothing. And that man with the winged helm was the Commander of all the Watch."

"Commander Leonardus," Isaac stated simply. Lucian's eyes narrowed. He chose not to pursue it yet.

"He would not be entirely frank with me, but he was adamant of your part in something which he, himself, could not describe, yet was deemed scrupulous behaviour. In other words, you've been attracting attention in high places."

"That's the idea," Isaac replied flatly, dreamily, staring like a lost ghost into the sea. A pause. "How was your journey?"

"More eventful than I could have hoped for. Enlightening, if I dare say." Isaac appeared to grow taller, then shrank again. "What did you do?"

His tone was stern, and he meant to be even harder with him. He hesitated, and soon realised why. Isaac's smile was there, but was missing something indescribable, as if it were a caricature. His presence was minimal, and there was an uncharacteristic docility, like his persona had been sucked inside him, where it brewed and writhed under restraint. He would act quite the opposite under the heavy influence of alcohol, and at any rate, did not stink of it. With that in mind, Lucian leaned back against the balcony, where he could get a better look at his brother.

"Does it have something to do with the wall of steel again?" Lucian asked. Isaac froze. At the same time, he was not concerned, just mostly surprised. "It is, isn't it?"

"Yes."

"What is it you remember this time?"

"The same."

"The same," Lucian repeated, as if it were obvious. "You bloody fool," he said under his breath, half-heartedly.

"Are you here to stop me?"

"Don't think in such simple terms, brother, it doesn't become you or the wisdom you think you have. It's a queerer situation than that."

"It is true, though," Isaac assured him, without fanfare or riled protestation.

"I will watch where this goes then. I should also tell you to stop this mad plan of yours, whatever it is. You think you're clever, but people will just think you're a bit touched. Commander Leonardus was patient today, yes, but who can say what he'll do next time?"

"That might actually tell me something," Isaac posed thoughtfully.

The waves crashed on the shore, serenely, quietly, it seemed from here: a prominent, yet not unwelcome, intrusion on his thoughts.

"What has you vexed, Isaac?"

"Vexed might not be the right word."

"I'm not playing this game with you."

"And I'm playing a completely different game," Isaac replied as defensively as he had yet managed or bothered. Lucian waited. "I saw a baron beheaded at the Execution Arena earlier, outside the palace. It was... surreal."

"I'm sure he had it coming," Lucian assured fiercely.

"That's not the point," Isaac snapped.

"So what is? Because you have me confused here."

Lucian half gave up and turned around, to get into Isaac's mindset. Smoke drifted from chimneys all about, with a bed of red slate and white stone, and towers carrying bells, and Watchmen spaced evenly amidst them. In the north, on Kingsreach hill, a golden dome gleamed: King's Perch it was, and shortly before it, tall yellow flames sprang up, merely candles to his eyes, aided by Sèhvorian Crystals and some other catalyst. His knowledge of Harth was select, but he knew that it meant the King was to hold court for lords and ladies from across his realm. It might not happen for some time yet, but when the flames turned gold, he'd know it had begun.

He looked back to the city and wondered if any of the pillars of smoke led down to factories experimenting with Sèhvorian Steel and crystals of that ilk, and if his father had had an untold influence. He wondered if Isaac thought the same. It seemed likely, somehow. Isaac was a romantic and would be applying, in his brain, a grand connection to their father from something or other.

Soft footsteps came to interrupt them, and this time they both turned to see Marcel appear in a white, plain gown of the apprentice.

"Rosalynn said you were here," he said wearily, yet beaming.

"That suits you. Which surprises me," Isaac said to him, still morose, merely touched by liveliness.

Now they were at the balcony together, Marcel at Isaac's left.

"I had a peculiar day, and I don't know how to recount it yet," Marcel said. "I met the duceveree. Again, peculiar."

"Give it time," Lucian said, knowing Marcel was easily worn away and would wish to speak of anything else. "I can't say I'm surprised by what you say."

"Why would he call on you?" Isaac asked, as if to bend the conversation around his own curiosities, ignorant of Marcel's words and body language.

"It was opportune for him, or so he told me. I wonder if he'd planned it. I went through an odd routine today, and he claims my meeting him was the only improvisation."

A fourth set of footsteps was heard, softer and slower, belonging to Rosalynn, who then stood at the top of the stairwell, unsure of what to make of the three brothers, who were in a row, now facing her.

"Is something the matter?" Lucian said to her.

"Not at all. I came to see the three of you. I knew Isaac must be here after seeing the other two of you climb these stairs, and it makes one think, encounters like these. It's funny, I so rarely think of your father and, truth be told, I remember him vaguely as a youth and more vaguely still as an older man, but the three of you together share his features quite remarkably, even if none of you actually look like him. I must sound quite alarming to you all."

"You needn't be so apologetic of nostalgia," Lucian said stiffly, having anticipated that Isaac would speak first, but he had, ultimately, been pleasant, yet remained silent.

"No, no of course not. I shall embrace it, and maybe I shall learn Lennord anew through his sons, because he is so distant a friend at this point, if a loyal one." She stopped, perhaps sensing she was rambling, and smiled.

"What a quaint collection of men we must look," Isaac added, realising the absurdity well enough within his sullen, dreamy trappings.

"I suppose you do," she replied. "I wonder what my old friend has wrought. Oh, but I must bring you a tankard of mead each, for now," she said in distraction.

"You're too kind," Marcel thanked.

She left them be for the time being, and Isaac was whisked away back to his impenetrable thoughts, focusing on the horizon. His odd behaviour now dawned on Marcel, evidently, as he writhed in discomfort. Lucian didn't speak, thinking his face could convey a thousand words.

"I do like it here," Isaac remarked. "Mostly. It has something indescribable about it. Kate would surely love it."

"The cathedral would not suit her sensibilities," Marcel warned.

Lucian stroked the stubble of his chin.

"It's also a city of realists, Isaac. That's how it thrives. Perhaps it will wake you up."

Sadly, it became tricky to enforce this while Lucian was matching them in drinks. Luck be, Isaac would remember that Lucian fought for sobriety, and succeeded.

~

In the dead of night, at an unknowable time, Isaac dreamed vividly again, as he so often did when strongly stimulated in mind. In his house in Caedor he sat, where his sister passed him by, carrying textiles for weaving, and he felt as if he was seeing a vision of the future, though that was to say very little because her life was nothing if not predictable.

"I wouldn't go out there," she stopped to tell him, scratching her forehead.

"Why not?"

"I'd be far too scared," she admitted, shivering at the thought. "Then again, so are you, but you're silly enough to do it anyway." She shrugged, a slight nervous smile forming, which then brightened up just a little more.

His mother appeared from her room, apprehensive at best, and certainly disapproving of Isaac's decision to get up from his chair. No one else was there of course. They were all elsewhere. At the front door, he stopped to make himself look more presentable, running his fingers through his hair in exactly the same movement, with exactly the same timing, over and over again, tiring Isaac, though he did not stop.

The world grew ill of him. The door flung open and the walls warped slowly past him like gelatinous constructions, his obsessive cleanliness overlapping with his new movement of gliding through the doorway.

He was upon a public stand of white stone, and always had been. Wraiths of black mist, barely discernible as people, watched him incredulously: a whole crowd of them, at that, and very still. A sword flew from its scabbard at the hands of a knight beside him. He turned, and calm blue eyes that were so patient, and joyful, and sad stared him down.

"In your own time," Sir Leon said, holding out the blade of white light that was Waithrydn. "But do not take overly long."

Isaac did nothing. Enlightenment came quickly to the White Lord, the Knight of the Holy Storm, and in a flash, struck at the air above Isaac, violently and before he could even know what was happening. Strings seemed to snap above him and he was relieved.

"What now?"

"I would honour you with my sword, and you would honour yourself and us all to swing it and send the poor man to the gods' fancy. They're waiting on him already, so be quick."

"Why would I?"

"Get on with it," King Michael demanded of him, patience waning. He, too, seemed to have been present for all time. "Unless you have more excuses, which would not be healthy for you. Those strings weren't even there," he leered, seemingly aware he was in a dream.

Isaac made to respond, only he was interrupted by Commander Leonardus, who nodded to Sir Leon, his bearded face bearing a message of unwavering loyalty, which may or may not have happened in reality.

"It's not so very difficult," the knight reassured Isaac, ignoring the others. "You know it's not as hard as you make it out to be. Be done with it."

Isaac took Waithrydn, which weighed nothing, and swung its blade down upon the man kneeling before him, though he looked the other way, and heard no more from the sword, for his mind wandered again, to the black shades. They flickered like flames in the wind, as their ghostly way of applause or protestation, shifting their shape creepily, becoming more familiar with every second until, at the apex, it dawned that they were not so different from the tip of that fiery monstrosity that had chased him from Caedor mine, spluttering and crackling away, they were. His cheek began to sear, red-hot, as he stared, and he suddenly realised that it was no external force, but tears of his own. He sought Sir Leon's sage opinion, but too late.

"Wait!" he wailed regardless, spinning, yet finding none but the shadows. "Wait, I *need your help!*"

In a pale ray of moonlight, Isaac sat upright in his bed, very still and ponderous, ignoring the fading hallucinations leering at him from the darkest shadows, mere afterimages of a nightmare. He recounted the evening, and the drinks he'd had. Three tankards of mead, and something much stronger, but blaming that for queer dreams was irresponsible, as he felt no effects of it now whatsoever. He laughed faintly and sank his head back onto the pillow.

Chapter Twenty-two: Death to Life

"This is as fair a place to work as one could hope in a city like this, not being highborn," Kester said with extraneous admiration that only made Lennord assume he wanted something from him even more. Whatever it was, he was certain he could not supply it, and Kester was not thinking straight, him being a good man sadly not withstanding relevance now.

"A fair place if you like contributing to the war effort of a country in peace time." Lennord reconsidered, spotting hard-working men passing by the window in droves. "I'm being unkind; there are worse places. My point was that I feel I could do more elsewhere."

"I believe whatever you say. I won't argue, not with you!" Kester replied in typically adjudicatory fashion, having always been too enamoured of him. Kester had played with his sons and looked up to him from a young age, so it was no surprise.

Kester had meant to go on, building up to his quest; it was written all over him. Instead, he paused to squint at his lovely young companion, and he pressed the side of a fist to his lips, puzzled.

"Lennord might not want those disturbed," he said to her as she reached to the disassembled parts arranged at the right end of his desk.

Lennord gave the collection of parts a cursory, uninterested glance: components of a musket, ill and suitable components mixed together, with more piled on the floor against the desk. Then he glanced at his Sèhvorian crystal sitting on a platter by the window, for that was what had him fascinated and vexed. Only Captain Westrym would so much as humour him, for the progress of this science was not obvious to all. Or to Lennord himself for that matter. He'd set up a lens to focus the sun on it, and another to a less pure crystal, then again to a rock he'd found out in the yard. Saucers of water sat beneath the platters. The question was, did the pure one change the temperature and condensation more than the others? The exact answer so far was *yes, sometimes, for no reason*, and tasting the frustration again, he realised he didn't have it in him to explain. So he looked at some pieces of junk again, that young Kimbra liked the look of. Maybe they should swap places.

"They're just there to remind me that I need to do something about them at some point. Occasionally I fiddle around with them, but it's a requirement of me to assemble the musket, not a desire. It's not like I don't know what I'm doing. It's so easy that the only takeaway is that I must improve it, and you can't impede me. Handle them as you please," Lennord clarified.

Kimbra Lovett nodded politely, picked up pieces one by one and appraised them as a jeweller might; however, her ignorance on the subject was most apparent. Her dress was of vibrant greens and blues, impressively braided with gold and silver strips of cloth, and her fell of ginger hair was showier and more pedantically curled than he'd seen before, held up at the back by a jewelled brace of some kind. As she and Kester had entered the office together, he also in a smart suit of deep green, with one of his loose-fitting, expensive white shirts, he'd assumed them to have quickly taken to formal courting and thought not to probe them about it, but now he was not so sure. They were odder together than in singularity: he with his lost expression, and she with a puckered smile forged by gods, and dagger-sharp eyes. Not that the assumption was necessarily false, but they displayed none of the fervour of new love, and at any rate, it was none of his business.

"You're working on something else then?" Kester asked, postponing his own pursuit.

He was not only self-serving then. Of course he wasn't. He'd somehow remained firm friends with both Isaac and Lucian, even as the brothers had grown so very different, and had grown friendlier with Marcel too. Unlike his companion in music, he was not quite so caring of his looks; his suit creased at the edges and, still somewhat conforming to his loose style, his hair flopped doggedly as it always did, and he wore no jewellery at all, though if he'd thought it of import, he could have bought something that looked vaguely expensive to meet that end. Certainly, Lennord himself sympathised with that sentiment though.

"I'm working on lots of things, some of them my own design, others not. I've become an organiser of men and equipment, and overseer of standard forging and building. The Empress is holding her cards very close, and if I'm honest, she can keep them there as long as she likes: I'm in no rush to see."

Though it would ease me to learn of her scheme sooner rather than later, he admitted. *But Tristan will handle it.*

"You don't like playing with this?" Kimbra said with upper class elocution that yet betrayed no inkling of singing ability. She was holding a fragment of the barrel's frame to eye level, immersed in her own little world. "Kester assures me you're very forthright and will always dive into new challenges, saying it's no wonder the Emperor calls on you so."

"Lord Almaric calls on me, I should correct. And Kester overvalues me. It's just as well he's been commissioned to compose a victory symphony," Lennord said politely, scratching his chin and inadvertently hiding his lopsided grin. "I'm being pedantic, I fear. There is truth in that, I grant you, but in this case, I'm just not keen on tweaking a device to increase its probability of killing people. I've done such things before so I'm sure that makes me a hypocrite, but it's the feeling of it. It's a brand new way of ending life, and there can be no mistake what it's for."

"It could be used for hunting," Kimbra said simply, in swift response. She was probably very clever, Lennord noted, though Gèyll had also noted, long ago, that he liked to highly appraise people and work from there. Her father was a knight, he remembered, and if he'd been hunting many a time before, it was not unreasonable that she would have accompanied him.

"That it could," Lennord agreed earnestly. "And perhaps it will. I spoke only of its primary purpose. To deny that to myself in making this would be grotesquely wrong."

"I see..." she said, travelling from far away at that moment and back into her body, where she smiled shyly, and delicately placed the barrel fragment in the exact spot it had been.

"Anyway, Kester, you want something of me. I think you should ask me now because bandying favour is really not necessary. If I can help, I will."

For some reason, Kester was surprised at Lennord's deduction, and then a moment later he appeared to have known it was obvious all along.

"Me and Kimbra, we thought to present ourselves to His and Her Majesty today, with a rough design of our plans for the symphony, and it occurred to me that, yes, you are friendly with Lord Almaric, as everyone back in Caedor knows, and you might guarantee us entry to the castle, where we might otherwise have to wait days."

Lennord interlinked his fingers and rested his chin upon them. He did not sigh or protest, only sat and made sure his answer was in reasonable taste.

"Why can't you wait those days?"

"Kester wants His and Her Majesty to be aware of his connection to you," Kimbra blurted out innocently.

"I'm sure he already is."

"This would make it clear that the connection is a good one."

"Whose idea was this?" Lennord said, frowning as he tried to imagine its conception in either of these two. Kester shrugged and raised a hand.

"It was mine, but only because I've spent too much time listening to city criers. I'm politically inept, and credit all ideas outside my music to someone, or something, else."

"That's how most people think, you might find," Lennord said warmly, carrying a playful sarcasm that was yet to prove offensive to anyone. He sat back, his large desk sprawling out before him, and he looked more serious and aged as he thought. "I still think you're overreacting. Kimbra was chosen by Lord Almaric originally, which must count for something."

The door opened at the hand of Captain Westrym, whose name had positioned itself in his memory alongside all the others here, such that he felt further integrated into the society of Lameeri's Wish, if awkwardly so. Lennord's personal guards eyed him from outside, right up until the moment the door swung shut; their silent presence was proving too distracting, eerie even, for Lennord. He could not shake the feeling that they should be busying themselves, not acting like statues.

The captain strode the length of the room, clearly sparing no time, as was usual for him. He was broad of shoulders and, on his face, wore the look of a disciplined, if unintelligent, soldier, often bearing a resentful look about him. In reality, he was actually extremely professional, being the Mürathneèan man present at Adrian Mortain's arrest: an employee of the Empress's vast ambition. It was conceivable that his surname was one of ancient pedigree of a family originating from Burtal, and that they were, in fact, from the west. The Empress was very complex: that was the impression he'd gleaned from Tristan, and it was wise to assume her reasons could be bound in complexity also. Perhaps her flaw was that she assumed everyone else would see that.

"I have to run something past you," Westrym said, and Lennord felt momentarily tedious and old as he was distracted from his convoluted theories.

"If it's really something only I can do."

"I think you should see," the Captain said evasively. "Would you follow me outside?"

"As you say," Lennord said politely, stiltedly, and he did so.

The concourse seemed to grow busier each day, the barracks ever bustling with more and more recruits. Even as Lennord became increasingly involved in its operation, he remained an outsider as events unfolded without the courtesy of his permission or inclusion. Captain Westrym now talked him through the situation of recruit organisation and the need for mass-produced, decent weaponry, and there was talk of siege equipment and determining the image of the military, which was proposed to be Lennord's job as he was presumed to be a genius in all fields, it seemed. However, when the captain removed a letter from a suede aumônière on his belt, his interest was more personal.

"Oh, before I forget, a man by name of Marcus Baldwin left this with me, strictly for you."

The rolled-up letter of bleached parchment was handed to Lennord, its seal unbroken, which he snapped immediately. It was from Tristan, as expected, written somewhat informally as ever.

Lennord read the short letter, and looked casually about him. Tristan was sure someone from across the channel was relaying his activities to the Empress, and Lennord was soon ashamed at how quickly he had leapt to suspecting Captain Westrym, but how could he not? The man was right there before him, a product of the Empress's will. Besides, many Mürathneèans were indistinguishable from northern Burtalians. How might he know a spy on sight? He said nothing, glad that Tristan had asked him not to. Stranger, though, was his request for a report on Adrian Mortain and the murder victim. Heart-warming to know he was valued above all others here, but not that he, as an outsider, was trusted more than them also.

"Thank you, Captain."

"I only do my job. Will you accompany me through the new building sites then? That is a forte of yours, I gather. The men here will gladden of a real professional overseeing production."

The Voice of Kings

"Not for long, I hope. After I receive my shipment from Harth, I'll be taking on the city at large. I'd prefer peace from the hubbub of your business to work alone, but, alas, it is not to be, if the orders are from above."

"You won't order me away then?" Westrym said cautiously, a hint of resentment slipping into his voice.

"How could I?"

"I thought you held a high rank or title, or otherwise high status. I'm unclear as to what exactly."

"You must have been listening to the gossip spread by your men. I live in a town in the highlands, in a moderate house with my family, and I invent things from time to time. I'm not worthy of ranks or titles, so I have none," Lennord said, leaving out Lord Almaric's high appraisal of him, and the promise of power. "We are on the same footing, but I assumed your orders were from higher still, and even if not, I am bound by my gods-given compulsion to see things made true and proper. Alas, a second time."

The captain was relieved, overly so, to hear Lennord's correction that he was not of lower rank, and found nothing of humour in his words, but at least kept to the respect required of him, and there was no ill will. He merely nodded, as if he did not fully understand the rest of what was said.

"Lead the way," Lennord allowed.

He turned only to lament that he could not stay with the blacksmiths, where he could be more at home and would not have to involve himself in grander affairs, feeling a pang of guilt as he caught sight of Kester and Kimbra waiting for him: a mismatched couple in whatever form, or so it was to look at them.

"Go to the castle, Kester, and if you are turned away, return to me and I will help you, because my sons would never let me hear the end of it otherwise, and they'd say you deserve all you can get. No need to thank me," he ended as Kester made to do so in elaborate fashion, and nodded encouragingly.

When they had gone, he almost wished they had not, for still he was in the throes of functions that didn't suit him. In spite of that, he would open his mouth and men would take heed because of his company, at the forge, and building sites, and offices. All the while, Captain Westrym stood close by with a dour, highly concentrated expression, dark eyes flicking back and forth between participants of the conversations, often wagging a finger and looking as though he had something to say but was held back by forces unseen, as if always he reminded himself that none of it was good enough. He spoke up just enough to remind Lennord of why he was there, making the occasional snappy judgement or observation, well-thought-out, before slinking into the background, so to speak, without expecting thanks. When, after a short time, they returned to the office, having passed through various places, and having refrained from promising anything, the captain clenched his fist and scowled to himself as he remembered something he never should have forgotten.

"Ah, ah, you wanted to learn how to fight, I heard," Westrym exclaimed.

"Oh."

Someone was trying to be helpful, possibly Tristan, but not necessarily. It was likely he'd told Alycia of his musings and she'd had her renaissance captain informed. Now he was to prepare to properly look like a knight, but no matter how much training he got, it would be a hollow sculpture he'd present himself as in court. But for reasons he didn't quite understand, he allowed Westrym to lead him behind his office, leaving his bodyguards at the door, and there in a free space out of everybody's way, he donned mail and helm, and bore a wooden sword, staring gloomily at its polished surface as if he didn't know what it was.

"You're just brushing up?" the captain said expectedly.

"I suppose I am," Lennord went on with his half-lie, sighing. For what it was worth, Westrym didn't care or notice.

He stared the armoured man down. Wide of chin, he was, with deeply serious dark eyes, always striving to be more concentrated, somehow. Lennord asked that first they practise slowly, and so the captain came at him with singular strikes, hard nonetheless, not seeking to part with any information but, as they'd agreed, just brushing up, taking it low and high, blocking feints and dodging. Lennord was a man of fifty-one years who never was really versed in the trade, and Westrym must have noticed but decided not to comment. He just kept hammering away, jumping forward, jumping back, jabbing in, pulling back, not thinking but working half-dazed, as if he were doing this while deep in thought. No one was watching at least. His incompetence would be their secret, and one that Alycia would innocently deny anyway. He sighed, reconsidered, then kept on fighting anyway, somewhere else, far away, just like his combatant.

~

In the castle vestibule, Tristan stood once again, on the cusp of leaving, nervous about it as if he were eight years old again and conspiring to sneak out with Richard to explore the city because the Emperor would not allow it. In the days since the mysterious visitor had escaped his grasp, nothing of import had come to light, and so it fell on him again to personally investigate, even if that meant going to every barracks and relevant trade merchant in the city. Which was the crux of the problem. He was Lord Paramount of Burtal. He might just be wasting his time.

"My Lord Almaric!" a voice called to him, and he turned, intrigued, as it was unmistakably Sir Pedrig's. There he was, making fast across the long rug of deep reds and greens and whites, and Tristan saw, in the old knight's movements, a discipline that rebelled against his desire to rush over to him. "I heard I might find you here, but I feared I'd be too late."

"There's a problem?"

Sir Pedrig wrestled with the implications of his answer, and spoke with caution in his voice.

"I sincerely hope not. I'm not the bearer of bad news, I can say that much, but I'd urge you to step aside with me and speak in private."

Tristan could only assume Pedrig was referring to the four other guards in the vestibule to be excluded from his words of secrecy, though none of them were on his list. Tristan relented, and indicated the way to the hall from which the knight had come with a graceful wave of his hand, for Pedrig would not dare to lead the way without his permission.

So back through the hall he went, and into a straight intermediary corridor directly connected to it at the back left, behind the stairs. It was often busy, but if anyone else were to enter, they would know immediately, and sound did not echo so greatly here.

"This must be important," Lord Almaric said expectantly. "I have business outside these walls."

"It's precisely that end to which I enquire, Lord. It brings me sincere embarrassment to ask one such as yourself to halt your business and speak in hushed tones with me aside, but as an overseer of the peace here at Castle Aurail, I have no other choice. You recently chased a suspected criminal through the streets, did you not?"

Tristan did not show surprise, for he had none. He had not kept it a secret, but rather had not made it readily apparent to everyone at court.

"He was only a suspect right up until the moment he fled against my explicit commands. He was then a criminal, though he should not be treated with animosity until we know the truth," Lord Almaric went on, knowing Pedrig would go to extremes if he caught but a whiff that the honour of the crown was at stake. "And I made that report three days ago. Why are you only now enquiring?"

"Because I only read by way of my need to read all reports. You didn't bring it to my attention, or Sir Doru's, so I assumed it was for some reason. When I learned from the master of the trade library that it was your explicit intention to arrest the man, I knew you wished to interfere with the Empress's plans."

"I will interfere with nothing!" Lord Almaric protested, laughing with a great broad grin as, inside him, the knot tightened. "I seek only to bring her pride to light. Unless you know what it is she's doing? Or are you oath-sworn to secrecy?"

"I swore no oath, because there was nothing to swear to. I hear things, but I'm not a key player. If you wish it, I will swear a new oath to you, to tell the truth about this," Pedrig said, smiling grimly.

Death to Life

Tristan waved a hand, and with it Sir Pedrig's gesture was wiped away to join all the others he had let go in the past.

"Oaths between close colleagues and friends are mostly pointless, or a sad state of affairs anyway. I will believe you."

"Then I say again, I'm not involved in whatever she's planning for Lennord." It was then that Tristan assumed the knight knew of every last word exchanged between him and the librarian. "But because I am untrustworthy? I think not. I have heard her speaking of it, just not to me. Sir Doru is not a part of it either, so far as I know."

"What about Sir Yanick?" Tristan let slip, knowing Pedrig was more in the loop of his activities than any lord.

"What about him?" the old knight said with a dark frown that cast a shadow over his gaunt face. "I can't imagine what you're thinking, but he's not the material Her Majesty is looking to confide in here, I'd suppose. All I know for sure is that she was writing a list of locations regarding it, and I saw among them Emperor Jorin's Star Plaza in the east of the city, an inn beside the broken Steps of Paryn in the west, and the Manor of Blessed Voices beyond the northern wall."

Sir Pedrig stood perfectly still, showing no regret in releasing this information. Lord Almaric slung his arm over a nearby cabinet and tapped on it, slicking his oily black hair with the other hand. He, too, was very still, waiting as four lords he didn't recognise passed him by, offering him vague gestures of praise and respect.

"Why would you tell me this?" Lord Almaric said when the clamour of footsteps had died down. "Oath-sworn or not, your obligation is to the Empress."

"Then it will please you to know that I see no harm in doing this. She is hatching no treason or diabolical scheme, I'm certain, and I, in turn, do not see how I'm committing treason in revealing this. As far as I'm concerned, it's a minor operation, and so I have no qualms about aiding you, just so long as you take care not to impede her."

Day by day, Tristan was seeing why Alycia had deemed Pedrig such a valuable asset, and today was no exception, even if the same could not be said for tall, quiet Sir Doru. It was a shame he didn't know the circumstances of their acquisition, and felt especially for Richard as Alycia became more distant, cleaning her armour with such pride that she threatened to blind herself from its shining reflection.

The greying knight, fortunately, did not seek to interrupt his thoughts, so he carried on, this time to the subject of the three locations that had been mentioned. All were in pockets of lavish lifestyle among the mire, though from memory, the ruined steps that once led to King Paryn's alleged dream circus were in an area less extravagant than the other two.

"Do you think the man I tried to apprehend could be involved?" Lord Almaric asked.

"It's probable. I think if he were a spy, for one, he would not make himself so identifiable with all those rings, and if the librarian knew him to be a foreigner, then…"

Pedrig trailed off, perhaps not wishing to be facetious, or more likely did not know what more he could say. It occurred to Tristan that, with so many rings, he must be very wealthy, and then he remembered the way he had ridden through the streets like a lost newcomer.

"I will go north," Lord Almaric said firmly, standing straight again, raising his chin in finding confidence. Sir Pedrig probably wanted to ask why, but he was a man with considerable restraint. That being so, it was not out of the question that he was going to relay this conversation to Alycia. Tristan didn't care. He had nothing to hide.

"Remember, the Empress will not be pleased if you interfere," Pedrig reiterated, short of ordering Tristan not to; an impossibility.

"You're a good man," Tristan said, and meant it, even if by chance he had lied about his affiliation with Alycia's plans. "You're dismissed."

Tristan only got as far the opening to the great stairs in the main hall, opposite the vestibule door, before he was stopped once more.

"Adrian Mortain," Pedrig shouted from the corridor doorway, looking beaten by some hidden folly of his own design. "Adrian Mortain – have you seen him lately? He's very religious. I thought you ought to know."

"Most everyone here is. What of it?"

"Excuse my poor wording. He spends all his time against the wall of his cell, hunched up and praying, muttering under his breath."

"You think he's mad?"

"A little touched, yes," Sir Pedrig suggested with a strong inclination to the idea, raising his eyebrows wearily.

Tristan paused to contemplate, staring at his dark reflection on the floor tiles, and found nothing of worth.

"Many thanks, Sir."

He was already away when he spoke those words. In the courtyard, the idea of acquiring a horse barely crossed his mind, as walking at the same level as everyone else gave him the impression of feeling their plight closer to his heart. But he did so in full renaissance regalia of powerful, lively red and blue, tall boots, and black and silver family ring displayed on his right hand. He had no intention of disrupting Alycia's plans, but he would not hide and skulk about the Manor of Blessed Voices like a thief, crawling through the bushes and woodland of its perimeter, as if his cause were an unjust perversion.

As he stepped through the north gate later in the afternoon, he realised he had not walked on foot outside the city walls for some time: well before the Emperor had called him back to his place of duty. The sandy red cobbled Victory Road ran off to the horizon over the irrigated steppe, and split off at numerous intervals, like a fallen tree of stone. Houses dotted the landscape, only the one he was looking for was much further still: one of several large houses planted in clearings throughout the Wood of Jubilees. In a second realisation, at the sight of the green mass far off, he smiled to himself. That it was perhaps hollow was beside the point. Smiling was important.

He'd underestimated the distance to the manor, yet he did not turn back or hesitate. In passing intervals, he did question the purpose of his visit, as it seemed increasingly unlikely that an envoy of Mürathneè would be staying at a preoccupied house outside the city: a doubt that could mock him only in short bursts, for he shot it down. He wracked his brain, though, for who currently owned the house, and whether it was plausible that they would be asked by the crown to accommodate a stranger, or else vacate.

Minutes blew him by like the soft late summer breeze as, in bursts between his thoughts of business, he imagined walking here with Evylyn again, hazy and flickering like brief glimpses at an oil painting, and standing to stare at the dark, chilling, beautiful towers where he would reassure her of his dreams, and she as well. Now, as then, he spotted a crane-like eeligris that so favoured the flatlands: black and green, sharp and long of beak with a head near the same shape, bold enough to stand astride a drakeel, Evylyn had laughed, for she'd seen it.

He was at the edge of the wood, and he let the dream fade now, but he did glance at the decaying artwork that was the city before making towards the well-trodden track. Guards were out patrolling in the wood, who did not delay him for long upon realising who he was, and there was a child's hunting expedition, which he ignored as soon as he'd appraised the participants.

The wood was calming and let light shine down fully upon him, for the trees weren't dense. They were large in quantity, of conifer and oak, and the wide-based local variety of Merloyr, of sandy red bark like the stone of the city, and rifling up to a great peak over circular leaves of yellow tinted with reddish-brown, as summer made to bow out. The wood was so very alive, and at the same time, so very calm, and when he approached the brick wall, higher than he, surrounding the Manor's grounds at the south-eastern edge, he still was not fearful and, in truth, was more doubtful of himself than he had been in some time. There was little conceivable reason why it would be here of all places, even if it did seem the most likely of the shortlist he'd been privy to courtesy of Pedrig. The wall ran far out of sight: this he did remember. He stood at the spiked iron gate, and did not motion to enter. He contemplated walking the full perimeter so as not to disturb the goings on within. Conversely, he wondered about the impact of merely entering the grounds, to find out what it was Alycia had asked of her contact.

In his indecision, Tristan did not move at all, until an armed figure could be seen approaching across the green from the other side of the fence. It was a man lightly armoured in brown leather, and of roughly Tristan's height and age, though the latter aspect was harder to tell because he was grim and humourless, sporting scars and a bushy beard, and a nose that had been broken numerous times. Not very respectable, Tristan observed, and found himself without ease.

"Afternoon," Lord Almaric said, more cheerful than the man probably expected, which was still saying little indeed.

"If you're here on business, show me your proof."

"Proof of what? I wished only for your hospitality."

"I want proof that you're allowed to enter, or I want you to piss off."

Tristan could have said anything he'd liked, and been unequivocally entitled to. He elected to remain silent for as long as it took for the situation to unravel itself. Diplomacy in silence. He walked forward until his face was almost pressed against the gate, and stroked his family ring absentmindedly.

"What do you want?" the mercenary asked, not half as aggressively as he'd have liked.

"I'm Lord Almaric, and I am the aide at His and Her Majesty's pleasure, as you must know," Tristan announced, hoping the man had come close to reaching that conclusion already. He cringed at how self-important he perceived himself to sound, and the guard was not pleased either.

To Tristan's mild alarm, the guard unlocked the gate and nodded for him to enter. He did not bow or lower his head for him, instead looking the other way in disgust or aversion of his lordly gaze. Tristan reminded himself that not even a hardened sellsword, as this man seemed to be, would dare attack him within 50 miles of Aurail. When he entered, he was still physically unable to drop his guard completely. It just wasn't in his heart to feel safe here, not him.

"I'd have to ask if you're allowed in the house," the man warned.

"Not a problem, friend. I have no such interest at the present time."

The manor in question was a large building, made mostly of a grey stone and surrounded by gravel paths through its lush gardens, but that was no less than three or four lengths of a jousting list away. Much of the space in between was a plain, flat field, interspersed with lonely trees and beehives. More mercenaries patrolled, noticing him one by one and paying him suspicion, though not altering their courses. Tristan's head shot round to the gate guard who, thankfully, was no longer standing beside the gate as if waiting to slam it shut. He was, however, watching Tristan wearily, hoping he would not be put in a position where he would have to stop him.

Tristan was confident that he was no threat now, and relaxed to observe the grounds of the manor more thoroughly. There was nothing inherently peculiar, at least in activity. The presence of mercenaries over a loyal household guard was puzzling. From the south, the three towers of the castle could be seen to pierce the sky through an opening in the woods where trees bent and sagged apart to reveal its visage: the world imitating art, so perhaps Venlor was indeed a painter. It was an eerie sight, as if nature were suggesting that even out here in the woods, one could not hide from justice, as if the Emperor might want to stare through the gap from his tower.

On the wind, a steed's whinny was heard, and then more; trotting through the woods, there was, ever closer until the noise slowed down nearby, as riders dismounted fast and heavy. The gate guard snapped into action, marching to the open gate, wearing a grimace for them. As he made to close it, a hand clad in steel shoved it back with force, which the mercenary did not seek to reprimand or punish, and wisely so, for it was then that a knight strode past him, Sir Yanick Berrhwrn, leading four others from the castle. As the mercenary attempted to prevent any more from entering, he was treated to a hard shove from another hand.

"So you are here, my Lord!" Sir Yanick proclaimed, bearing that same smug look which may, or may not, have been an inherent deception upon his face. "Experiencing problems, my Lord?"

"No," Lord Almaric said flatly.

"I'd heard you were investigating the Manor of Blessed Voices and proposed to my fellow men at arms to see that you go unharmed."

"Investigation?" the mercenary asked with a frown, backing away.

The mercenaries drew in together from across the grounds, jogging, not greatly alarmed yet, and the castle guards fanned out as they worked to anticipate a potential enemy. When the mercenaries finally arrived, they formed a loose line, eight of them including the gate guard who was now among their ranks, and the man who might have been their leader centred, caught off guard in plate but no helm or gauntlets, and gaps where besagews should be. Plain iron rings on both hands twinkled dimly. He was not the tallest of them, but undoubtedly the most imposing, his muscles and squared, scarred face playing no small part in that.

"That man is investigating in our purview, that lot says," the gate guard announced to no one in particular, so perhaps as Tristan had suspected, there was no true leader.

It was the well-clad man who spoke nonetheless, on behalf of the other seven who were stoic and silent, and gritting their teeth behind tight lips.

"Oh?" he said. "Why would you want to do that?"

"You're addressing Lord Almaric, highest of lords. You'll pay him the proper respect!" Sir Yanick shouted back at him, and spat at the grass.

The irony did scarcely occur to the brash knight, Tristan observed, and feared that he might even be enjoying himself. Tristan had never once pegged him as a leader, and yet the other four waited on his command, as he was the only knight, and the only one of them wearing a cloak and Guardian armour, as the closest of the crown guards displayed. It was not unreasonable that the young fool was overly elated by the responsibility. Tristan stood halfway between the two groups now, as that was *his* responsibility, and he would take it seriously. It was a curious, terrifying sensation, like being 20 years old again, standing between groups of drunken spectators in the city streets, to get their attention while his men moved to tackle them if he could not succeed.

"My Lord," the mercenary representative replied simply and without humility. "I don't see what a lord would want with any of us."

"I never stated my purpose," Lord Almaric replied coldly. "Your question is valid. Why would I want anything of you? I don't have to answer to you, so I'd be more inclined if your resentment and lack of manners were not so awfully apparent."

"My current orders supersede yours," the representative said.

"Then you should learn how a hierarchy works!" Sir Yanick leered. "Learn to read so you can see how low down on that chain you are."

"Hold your tongue, Sir," Lord Almaric warned. "And your ground."

"And I will hold my ground," the representative said, plain and flat. His accomplices were not so sure. He touched the hilt of his sword.

If it was an indication of his dedication, it was not construed as one. Sir Yanick looked appalled. He clicked tongue and teeth, and the elite guard of Castle Aurail fell in beside him as his sword sprung from its scabbard. The five of them were arranged as an arrow, the tip being Yanick's sword outstretched so vainly before him, pointing at the mercenary captain. For all Tristan's despair at the knight's apparent wish to start a fight, he looked more fearsome than ever, his green cloak, emblazoned with the three tower motif, flapping triumphantly behind him, and donned in a helm, as Tristan had rarely seen him in, which, lacking a visor, pronounced his jaw, and bore a crest of wolf's fur, dyed green.

"Do not remove that sword," Yanick roared. "On pain of death, do not! Place your weapons on the ground, and let me not see any steel of them."

They did no such thing. Yanick was no longer smug. He bellowed his words, as if to compensate for an inner fear, which Tristan could only pray was not the case.

"Quiet," Lord Almaric hissed, and turned back to the opposing force, a wall that would not budge. "I demand that you surrender your weapons. The law commands it, I command it, and the Emperor would command it were he here. You have no moral high ground."

The command was surely felt, for the eight of them were hesitant. In the end, they followed their leader's example in standing firm.

"If the Emperor were here to command us, we'd obey, but he isn't, Lord."

"By what right do you defy me? Speak, I command it," Lord Almaric said to them, his voice rising as his temper drew close to losing restraint.

"I don't know if we can," the representative replied, the first true indecision on his part, and he looked to his fellow sellswords for assistance, as subtly as he could.

"If you don't, we are right to put you down," a new voice announced, that of Wylam Meyers, a rough, bold man in his thirties who was keen on codes of practice, reciting the law as he was not required to do. Too rigid was he to ever make it on Tristan's list. "The Emperor's guards have never been shamed with disobedience without cost. For our reputation, we must disarm you ourselves if you refuse."

"He speaks the truth," Sir Yanick added triumphantly.

Tristan closed his eyes in disappointment and dread, as he'd feared someone would bring that up, and if they hadn't, he would, by law, have had to order his men to charge.

"We can't," the sellsword leader said, not daring to betray emotion.

"Don't be fools! You don't stand a chance," Lord Almaric pleaded. This he believed, as not one of them was dressed in full plate, and nothing to the high standard of the armour made for the Emperor's finest.

Silence settled like the leaves that blew through the viewing gallery on the wood's edge that was the picturesque view of the castle. Judgement had to be passed. Yanick grunted, his mind made up as his thin patience was scattered to the four winds. He clicked again and four more blades materialised, singing high of voice. The five men broke into a run, arrow formation levelling out. Six of the mercenaries charged as individuals, adhering only to their own rules of battle.

Tristan felt Yanick's hand on his shoulder, pushing him hard to the ground before flying past him to engage the first enemy. Though mildly dazed by the blow to his lower jaw, he saw all that followed, the fastest of the sellswords being the unluckiest as his friends, without honour, let him charge ahead and so was caught alone, his bloodcurdling scream barely fazing the elites that he faced. Yanick swung for a high blow that was heavily parried. The same man parried a blow from Wylam, to Yanick's left, but he was swarmed, with three around him and two ahead as a shield, and Yanick slashed ear to ear, marking a trail of blood spraying from steel and fatal wound.

Barely before the body had time to hit the ground, they were on the move again, two men each branching off left and right, shadowing one another as if bound, while Yanick dashed down the middle to meet with the gate guard and the commander, who'd, ultimately, not so much as attempted to guide his men. Yanick was fearless, the likes of which came as a shock to Tristan, for his momentum did not slow even as the gate guard stepped forward and swung a blow of lightning precision which might have decapitated another man. As it was, he ducked, span, sprawled his legs and slammed his left foot down to stop him from toppling. One-handed, he deflected another blow and brought it down hard to impale the mercenary's sword in the ground.

Still gripping his sword in one hand, Yanick made to lunge effortlessly for the leader's face, only to be surprised at the destructive force of the parry imposed. His second hand gripped at the pommel tightly, and now he could but keep himself alive, desperately knocking away each blow from the two men: a fantastic talent with a blade squandered by supreme arrogance. Technical prowess had nothing to do with it. There was a reason battlefield aftermaths were so tragically packed mostly with the corpses of very young men.

Tristan was a spectator on the cusp of a dozen possibilities. As he looked about him, he saw that the other guards of Castle Aurail were faring as they should, each duo slaying their first target more or less at the same time, all four of them laying deep, quick blows without their armour being scratched. From beside the first corpse, Tristan scooped up a sword and ran to Sir Yanick's aid, wishing every step of the way that he hadn't, but not for one second delaying. Sir Yanick had taken heed of a momentary advantage; the gate guard's sword came strong and swift, but empty of skill. As it was pushed back, the young knight swept his leg to bring him to his knees, and darted behind him when he could not fall victim to a counter swipe from his other opponent. He wasted no time in slashing his sword through the back of his victim's neck, needing one quick tug to render it free from the bone, and there he waited cautiously, sense returning to him at last. In reality, he was only slightly shorter than his opponent, but he seemed dwarfed by him.

Tristan blazed past in a wide half-ring around the sellsword, hoping to make him choose to turn his back on one or the other. The sellsword saw this threat, and moved desperately, recklessly, in on Yanick, surely knowing that the knight was skilled enough to cut him down in an instant if given half a chance. It was this that gave Sir Yanick confidence. The sellsword swept his sword upwards from his right side, then his left, and cut down hard from his right side and again from the left; at that last movement, Yanick sidestepped and jabbed hard at his opponent's side. It did not pierce steel, as he must have known it wouldn't, yet it was not unfelt by the mercenary, for he wore no backplate, and the impact shook through the gambeson as the blade skipped onto it. Yanick's cry was victory come early, his steel red and baying for the final stroke. But above the clatter of steel, Tristan heard something else reaching for him, begging, and against his better judgement, he turned to where the manor was, to discover that he was right. There was a man running for them at full pelt, unarmed and dressed in a dark blue cloak, his arms frantic in the air.

"Stop!" he yelled. "Stop!" he repeated, and again he did so until, finally, the remaining mercenary raised his sword to his face as a shield and turned to his master's beckon. He was surrounded by five of the Emperor's guards now, and dropped his weapon at last. Sir Yanick only partially relented, cracking his pommel upon the man's lower jaw to disable him.

One of the men of Castle Aurail was rubbing a finger into a dent in his vambrace: fractures there, maybe. That aside, there were no injuries.

"What's the meaning of this?" the newly arrived man panted, sullen and red-faced. He wore expensive, colourful clothes of high fashion, a bronze torc and, upon both hands, rings of varying worth, containing several different jewels in all.

Lord Almaric held up a hand to silence him before he could begin blabbing.

"I am Lord Almaric. Introduce yourself?"

"Cristico Valen."

He spoke with a soft Mürathneèan accent. A man of around 35, Tristan surmised, auburn of hair and built as a warrior, yet utterly defeated he already was, as Tristan saw when he announced his own name. Tristan gathered a view of the aftermath quickly: the bloodbath in the middle of the field. It was worth remembering that mercenaries reached the age these men had by way of excelling at their job, but the guards of Castle Aurail were only blessed with their job precisely because they were superior. More fool them, one might say. It didn't matter now though, as they were all, but one of them, fighting for piety and salvation in another realm of existence altogether.

"Do you house physicians in the manor?" Lord Almaric asked.

"Of course."

"And more guards?"

"Two, not to the standards of my others," Cristico replied woefully.

"Will they surrender to my men?"

"They as much as have," Cristico said with bitterness in his voice.

"Wylam," Lord Almaric said. "Be so kind as to take two men to the manor and bring the physicians for this poor man. If you're attacked, do not kill."

"At once, Lord."

"And you, please be our lookout at the gate," Lord Almaric said to the remaining guard, so that of them, only Yanick remained.

Sir Yanick had not recovered from the near-fatal fault of his arrogance, shaking his head and holding back a barrage of profanity. A truth then dawned for him, and through his sweaty face, he looked enlightened.

"If physicians are on the way, justice can be dealt without fear of excess."

He kicked out the left arm of the remaining mercenary who'd so hassled him, and stamped on it when it struggled. All emotion was drained from the knight. To the man's wrist, Yanick lined up his sword, and was carried away in fervour as already it dug into the flesh. He stared at the blood lopsidedly, as if it were unfamiliar.

"Sir!" Lord Almaric shouted at him, that one syllable startling him so profoundly, anger he'd never witnessed in Tristan. It dissipated just as quickly to despair. "Political discussions are still ongoing. Your enthusiasm is unhelpful, appreciated as it is. Never, ever, rush into performing a deed so severe as that, particularly not so soon after a battle, when you're affected by the emotions and baggage of it all. I've read enough history to know cavalier attitudes, of soldiers and generals alike, after a battle can have catastrophic consequences. Do the words "making defeat of victory" mean anything to you? Just... think, please," he finished, filling his frustrated voice with empathy.

The Voice of Kings

Yanick retreated in shuddering rage, eyes vacant, and evasively started scrubbing off the blood that had begun crusting over his sword with a coarse square of cotton that had been tucked in a hidden pouch beneath his belt. Tristan was relieved, sorry as he felt for the knight's cluelessness, and brushed himself down of dirt from his regal attire so recently and lovingly made by the maids of the castle, weaving the smart ruggedness of Aurail with the flamboyance of Harth, as if the stone were fragile silk. When he was clean, he looked Cristico straight in his dark green, deep eyes of shielded mysteries. He'd never taken to this very well, and tapped at his chin thoughtfully: any rhythm to keep his mind sharp and flowing at a smooth pace.

"We've met before," Lord Almaric said to gauge Cristico's reaction, unable to completely remove the anger from his voice.

"My Lord, this is more complex than you think," Cristico pleaded, bowing his head to duck the inevitable singe from brimstone: one that never came.

"Why were your men so madly under the impression that fealty to you, or your benefactor, was more important than orders from the Emperor's guard, and of their lord?" Lord Almaric said, not playing into the man's vague derisions, flinching as he did so at the necessity of having to speak with his heavy lord's tongue.

"I didn't think they would be so loyal. The Empress was who they swore their vows for, and they took them at face value."

"The Empress?" Lord Almaric asked, alarmed.

"They and I. Weren't you told?" Cristico was filled with suspicion.

"I didn't know the details," Lord Almaric replied, guarding his tongue more steadfastly than he thought he would. He didn't want to. "Was the oath sworn directly to her?"

"No, no, obviously not. She contacted me through other people. It wasn't an oath as such," he corrected himself. "I took it as one, but technically it was just a promise to uphold the conditions of her request. These men took it more seriously than I could have imagined. And all because they refused to yield, you say?"

"Just so."

And on the back of a very generous payment, Tristan theorised, sadness ringing like the soft pulling of harp cords in his heart. Sellswords were not known for their honour. *Then again, there are always exceptions.*

"There was a time when I thought I was hidden from the Empress," Cristico mused, possibly to himself. "To buy myself as much time to complete my task as I pleased. What a fool I was."

"Will you answer my questions?" Lord Almaric asked.

"I fear I must disappoint you, Lord. I swore to the Empress I would be secretive. Be that as it may, I was not asked to do so. Perhaps I shouldn't have."

Tristan, in his own void, cried out in anguish at the guarded formality of it all, but even there he could call Alycia no names of spite, for he could still hear himself, after all, and that was enough to stop him.

"It pertains just to your task, yes?" Lord Almaric pressed.

Cristico Valen growled in frustration, knowing he was being backed into a corner.

"Yes."

"That manor," Lord Almaric continued, "is the Manor of Blessed Voices. It's always belonged to Burtalians, and was named as a flattery, implying House Morwnue was always meant to be of lords and ladies. It's passed to different people since then, as gifts, but why to you, now?"

"It belongs to a friend of mine. He's not here right now, having graciously vacated on my behalf as I finish my business here. I have no fear in your checking that claim."

"You faith is well placed," Lord Almaric said.

He paused to ensure, to his satisfaction, that he was being neither unfair nor unprofessional, taking in the sight of the fluffy white clouds as he liked to do when they would show themselves. From the manor, the guards were returning with two men, dressed all in unremarkable clothes. Cristico did not seek to take opportunity of the silence: a good sign indeed.

"Why did you run from me in Aurail?" Lord Almaric said abruptly. "Did you have something to hide?"

"Only what I have already... well, you can guess why. I wanted my privacy."

"That's no excuse for breaking the law," Lord Almaric continued, stone-eyed as he ever could be. "You couldn't have known what I wanted, and if you had, you only needed to recite your vow and I would have taken you to the castle to verify that."

"You can't understand!" Cristico snorted stubbornly; proud and strong he was, as his soldierly side showed through. "I am sorry, and it was a mistake and I regret it, but my running wasn't totally without reason."

"I will ask you now then, what I wanted to then. You were researching Sèhvorian steel. Why? If Lennord Brodie is unwittingly involved, then you should know he's already ordered a shipment, and when it arrives, he won't need directions from a layman. The Empress knows that too. I've told her so myself, not that she needed telling, so I have an enigma, it seems."

"Lennord... I can't talk about people I'm involved with," and Tristan suspected then that the man had not even heard of his friend from Caedor. He grimaced at the potential slight made to his friend.

"Cristico, I don't think you're being entirely honest with me, even with what you are telling me." Tristan sighed.

"There's nothing I can do for you there, Lord. So, will that be all then?"

The Voice of Kings

"All?" Lord Almaric exclaimed. "No, not even close. You're under arrest."

"Uh, I would advise against that," Cristico replied, far too surly for Tristan's liking. "I'm waiting here for one of my Mürathneèan contacts to show up. It could be any of them, at any time."

"It sounds important," Yanick said from nearby. When Tristan looked, he saw that his sword was sheathed and his face was utterly focused on the conversation. He might have been watching like that since the beginning, for how concentrated he was.

"Listen, Sir..."

"The Empress won't want you to disrupt the course of any secret meetings, now," Yanick said with a blank face, eyes wide and appearing to plead with Tristan the more he studied them. "Leave him be with the guards from the castle to keep him from hatching any funny ideas, and we'll be on our way."

Tristan stared intently at the knight and, for whatever reason, trusted him completely, on this if nothing else. He did want to. And he was so very tired.

"You may stay for now."

"Thank you! Let me be very clear," Cristico said, slimy like a conman, "if you speak to the Empress and she lets loose all the answers you want, you won't need me, and if she doesn't, what a good thing I never told you."

"Indeed," Tristan muttered.

"Yes," Yanick said impatiently. "Now give him your fastest horse, Valen."

"That won't be necessary."

"As a show of faith," Yanick added courteously, using a pocked and battered shield to hide his impudence from Tristan, inept as ever at controlling his emotions.

"Yes!" Cristico enthused, "I know you dislike me, Lord, so it's the least I can do."

Tristan sighed gently. He was tempted to make a show of his dissatisfaction, and what he thought of the envoy from Mürathneè, and how he was being played for a fool. For a time.

He allowed the man to lead him to the stables near the manor, checking his pace only to inform the guards that they were to stay until further notice. They were following the proud, or otherwise stupid, mercenary, who'd refused help and staggered to the house, flanked by the two physicians who both looked nervous beside him.

"No one leaves," Lord Almaric said. "Friends of Cristico may enter, supervised, if they have business and yield arms."

At the stables that Yanick had followed them to, Cristico presented Tristan with a grey stallion. As Tristan made to gesture it from its pen, he paused and frowned darkly again at the foreign man. He spoke slowly and deliberately.

"One more question, and answer carefully, because a wrong step might give me reason to arrest you after all. You said to me that you were waiting for one of several contacts from your own country. I know the Empress wants to base our growth on precedents set by

Mürathneè, with people from that country if needs be. From *that* country. Why are you *here*?" he said shortly.

"I'm here because, though I have no titles to boast of, I'm not powerless. Residents of Mürathneè serve King Michael, and aren't obliged to do the explicit, direct bidding of your Majesties, even as visitors in Aurail. I can change their minds."

It was a clever answer and made some sense, even if Tristan was not entirely convinced. Yanick seemed to skulk away as Tristan attached a saddle to the horse, having contributed nothing more. Whatever he hoped or expected to see never happened, and he slinked back to his own horse without a word. Grudgingly, Tristan let Cristico from his leash, staring dreamily at the clouds as he walked the horse, checking his pace only to shake his head ruefully at the corpses that were already becoming a part of the scenery.

Yanick was just mounting his own horse as Tristan left the grounds, and together they trotted directly south, carving their own path through the woods, a mass of leaves and twigs crumpling under hoof, light finding them just as often as they were plunged into darkness under the canopy.

"You should have been harder on him," Sir Yanick mused.

"You're not in a position to be judging my methods, Sir," Lord Almaric replied forwardly, not making to face the knight. He squinted, as if to make out a memory made real before him. "Tell me again who sent you?"

"I never said. My fault. But it was Sir Pedrig, of course. He asked the Empress, wise as he is, to tell him about her interest in the manor, and when she told him about the reports of ruthless sellswords, he forewarned me, ordered me actually, to come to your aid with a contingent of guards. Never imagined I'd have to actually do anything though. Sir Pedrig didn't make it sound much of an urgent affair."

Yanick trailed off, and he appeared to be reliving his combat in his mind: his smugness and elation through to his crushing shame. The shiver that followed brought Tristan to pale. It was like watching a chaste priest waking to remember his weakness of the night before.

"He told me not to let you do anything you'll come to regret," he went on, "like arresting the Empress's contact. He was very specific on that. I never meant to undermine your authority, Lord."

"Why did he send *you*?"

"I don't know. My skill with a blade?"

That, and because he assumed nothing mentally taxing would be necessary, Tristan thought to himself sadly. *Or because you wouldn't be missed from the castle. No one ever asks you to do anything, that I see.* Unless...

"What role are you playing in the Empress's plans?"

"None," Sir Yanick said, surprised at the suggestion. "I don't really know what she's doing, or what you're doing, at that."

The Voice of Kings

"Then what good does the Empress see in you? You can't follow orders without rolling your eyes, you find everything funny, and you're so green you think you can win battles with the power of your given title. I bear you no ill will and wish only for you to learn, and quickly, but I fear the Empress will grow tired of you. Perhaps she'll send you to live out your days as a checkpoint guard on the Godless Mountain if you really annoy her."

Sir Yanick became oddly reflective and sullen, and several times gestured to speak but held his tongue. *"Why?"* he must have been asking himself, genuinely in bafflement, again showing that sense of entitlement, as if coddled with too much wealth and too little of anything else. Men like that could become exceedingly dangerous, or exceedingly noble.

They emerged fully into the sunlight at last. Tristan fixed his gaze upon the knight who, along with Pedrig, had so tragically, and accidently, caused the death of seven men, signalling for him not to gallop away without uttering a single word.

"I will always be loyal to the empire," Yanick said at last, defiant. "The Empress saw that my family was having its power stripped away bit by bit, by people who have nothing better to do than leech off the fortune of others, trying to condemn us for the smallest faults, for our prestige and fortune." Tristan knew he was exaggerating, for his family was not one to show up at court often, but he did not interrupt. "The Empress saw that we were better than we were allowed to be and stood up for us, and years earlier, it was our wise Emperor who sent Sir Haldric Lovett to be my mentor, that I might follow him. I've been where few have," and he smiled crookedly, as if having trouble recalling something. "That's why I will not be sent away, though I take note of your advice."

Tristan wondered if he did. Yanick believed it, if nothing else. What he said made sense though, for Alycia was so very fond of employing people who perceived themselves to be in her debt. Likely it was her idea for Haldric to tutor young Yanick, because her arms spread far, and Haldric, Kimbra's father, had never been honoured with standing guard within the castle walls, and was as restless as Yanick, honestly.

"I wish good intentions were enough," Lord Almaric said. "Though I grant you, it's as good a starting point as any. For what it's worth, I may have underestimated you."

"I doubt it," Sir Yanick replied with a pang of shame. His emotions shifted so readily, he might have been in his early stages of manhood.

Tristan felt restless too. The three towers howled for his service, and he now had yet more to attend to, and it was not being done out here in the beautiful wilds. Ahead, he was afforded an inspiring and peaceful view of the massive red city that couldn't slow down to look at itself.

"Will you take this to the Empress?" Sir Yanick asked with the impetus of a man not expecting an answer.

"I will take it to someone," Lord Almaric replied in a voice almost reaching a growl.

Death to Life

Sir Pedrig, Tristan thought, *must hear of it first, then my dear friend Richard, and then Alycia last, because word will reach her of this and she will become inexplicably unavailable for private audience. Proud, powerful Alycia will only relent when it is convenient. Poor, proud Alycia.*

~

"It is like I said," the bored Kimbra announced suddenly, "they don't care about us right now. Why should they?"

"They've got better things to do than grant audience to the likes of us," Kester agreed. "Every one of them. Being daughter of a knight means nothing until you have something good to say, apparently."

"Art has nothing good to say," Kimbra whispered mockingly, half to herself, smirking.

Kester said nothing more, as he feared that when she did, it would be to suggest they give up for the day, and shamefully pester Lennord Brodie again the next morning. He stood leaning against the wall of the wide road leading to the second castle gate, where even the line of guards, whose only duty was to stop undesirables from entering, were not remotely keen on helping, saying they would relay a reply from within, which had yet to arrive.

He found himself adjusting his suit to look smarter for the third time, curious as only when Kimbra had strongly told him to do so had he bothered, and now on the brink of turning away, he became obsessive. The clopping of hooves sharply caught his attention, and he sighed in relief when he saw who was riding at a trot through the streets. He became hesitant just as quickly. It was kind Lord Almaric, his greased black hair scruffier than usual, his resplendent custom-fitted attire smeared lightly with grass stains, and most striking of all, his face was creased and weary, calculating and intense of gaze. A knight followed him who barely afforded him a look but was thoughtful also, and yet oddly smug and in a state of delirium, as if he'd just been blessed with a godly epiphany.

"What are you doing here?" Lord Almaric asked quizzically, before his features became soft, a wan smile appearing as he pieced together the situation. "Let them through," he commanded the gate guards. He said little more after handing his horse's reins to the knight, leading them hurriedly out of the late afternoon chill that was settling as the sun on the roofs, and through the vestibule. He told them he would trust them to find their way to the waiting room before the throne room, or to wait in the throne room itself if it was empty, and then only that they should not get their hopes up before veering from their sight at a determined pace.

Only on their way to the throne room did they see lords and knights and servants busying themselves, or otherwise milling about and making small talk, for in the waiting hall before the throne room, no one was present, as no one was expected to be directed through those old doors, one of which was open just a crack. Kimbra was content to sit herself on one of the thickly cushioned chairs positioned against a wall, energetically bouncing on it a few times to make herself comfortable, and there she sat in a mock regal posture, staring at the paintings of kings and sweeping landscapes. Kester could not resign himself to waiting, as it was, and made the last few steps to the door, pushed it open an inch further and immediately ducked back round when he saw the two figures inside.

"They're both in there," Kester said in reply to Kimbra's perturbed look, furiously gesturing to the throne room. "The Emperor, the Empress too." She peeked up, raising an eyebrow slightly and growing an amused, thin smile. Beyond that, she did nothing, waiting again for him to go on.

And so, he did again, more slowly than before, and scratched his forehead. The two of them were just standing there at the hall's end, side by side, staring up at the thrones. If they were speaking, he could not hear of it.

The Emperor was dressed in a doublet of burgundy and black, with thin gold scroll trimmings on the sleeves and sides, and dark pantaloons tucked inside his short black boots, and it was all carried with effortless style, Kester thought, though as he continued to stare, he saw that he was very stiff. The Empress, meanwhile, was infinitely more relaxed in her royal blue silk dress that shined, as her golden hair did, so straight it might have been infallible to wind. The truth of it, however, was that Kester was unnerved and enthralled by both of them.

"If I stand here long enough, I will be inspired," the Emperor said. There was sarcasm in his voice, but little effort behind it.

"You're already inspired by so little, I fear."

"You might think so," the Emperor said defiantly.

A shadow swept past the door to the left of the throne and Kester ducked back behind the door for fear of his actions being misconstrued. Footsteps came into earshot, then stopped. Kester caved in to his senses and stayed beside the door, because to hear the words at their life's end was too infuriating for the ears to bear. He didn't dare press his ear to the door, as that felt instinctively wrong, and he could not fool himself in that case, so he just stood there.

"Lord Almaric has returned to the castle, Majesties," a woman's voice supplied. "Allegedly, he was with Sir Yanick in the Wood of Jubilees, though I can't say for sure."

"And Sir Pedrig was enquiring after that just earlier today," the Empress mused. "Did you tell him to report to the throne room?"

"Not yet, Majesty."

"Good of you, Lady. We shall not hold court tonight then, as I anticipate Lord Almaric will not be in the mood, and the Emperor and I have much to give our attentions to before announcing anything new. Lord Almaric was suitably considerate about the issue of my business, I take it? Of course he was," she corrected herself, "he's a very considerate man."

"I couldn't say, not yet," the second woman replied.

"Stop, both of you," the Emperor commanded. "What are you two talking about?"

The silence that followed almost seemed to take on a voice of its own, as Kester strained to hear through it to whatever followed. Kimbra, he noticed, was watching him quizzically, not attempting to dissuade him from his sin in spite of her very clear disapproval. Footsteps retreated into the dark.

"Well?" the Emperor snapped.

"Lord Almaric was likely looking to see what I've been doing with my time, such as he is, always squinting at the fine details of the big picture. I was looking into the strange occurrences in Mürathneè. Magic, some say," she said simply.

"That's what you've been doing?" the Emperor scoffed.

"Oh, don't be so coy. I'm your wife. I see everything that goes on up there, and I know you've looked into it. Possibly before there was very much happening at all, but no one could judge you for that. I took to it later, cautious as I am, and I have it on good authority that there was an eruption of fire from a cave: such a fire it was, birthed in a cave and scarred at the tip. Just like in Caedor; just like with Isaac Brodie, only no one survived this one. There was more, I hear. More magic, some say, changing the world around it, changing people's perceptions, but the fire and the steel are the one truth we can rely on. All else is hearsay."

"You didn't tell me," the Emperor protested, his voice like a dull razor.

"We'll want Isaac here, naturally, for when we do find out. Life enjoys irony, so he may have knowledge he doesn't know is important, but the High Duke might have the same idea, because he's more religious than most and will have heeded the call, so we'll need to reach the young Brodie first. Isaac's father is known to be a genius, so we'll need him too. Maybe we'll use the whole family to promote it, depending on what we find."

The silent scream resumed, and this time Kester heard the ringing within his own head.

"You didn't tell me," the Emperor repeated more coarsely, raising his voice.

"I did tell you, in a way," the Empress said plainly. "I told you I was interested in employing the Brodies, at the Opera House you'll recall. When you didn't look into it, I assumed you weren't interested and dropped you from my plans. I meant to cause no offence."

"How dare you... you say employ? Do you mean manipulate?"

"You have shockingly little faith in me. We'll do whatever's necessary, and if ever they're manipulated, they won't know or care."

"And why do you care, anyway?" the Emperor protested.

"Because when we uncover this mystery, we might just have an edge. I'm negotiating with a man from the court of Harth, and he's negotiating with other people, and when they sell us what they know, we'll just have to find out the rest ourselves, and hide it from King Michael and his lot. We'll take what we can get, at any rate. Frankly, I'd rather not have to deal with magic as, correct me if I'm wrong, power is already complicated enough as it is. We just need to find the best way of exploiting the truth to our favour, in a way that makes us look powerful, or favoured by the gods, even."

She laughed in a light, wispy manner that sprang about the hall, playful as a child.

"I don't know what to say."

"Save your words for later, then. I'd thought to arrange a council meeting in the next few days. I mean, a proper council meeting. The table should be packed, and we will all look each other in the eye over the round table and discuss so many things. Yea, or nay?"

The Emperor did not answer, for another person entered the throne room, bearing the same voice as the previous visitor, stately and formal and very feminine.

"Majesties, pardon my intrusion. It's just, I've been informed by Lord Almaric that there are two musicians waiting to be received in the next room."

Kester sprang back, pivoting and pacing as he normally would, staring about him at the paintings, yet it felt somehow contrived. Kimbra was giving him a worried look now, and he wasn't surprised. He had no mind for politics and, even now, the words of the conversation he'd heard were slipping away forever, and he couldn't console himself with a conclusion, unsure if what was discussed was good or bad for Isaac, and Lucian, and all the rest of them. At best, it was an exciting opportunity, he knew that much, but he didn't know what the worst could be.

One of the doors to the throne room swung smoothly open, at the hand of Lady Castellon, who beckoned them in, none the wiser. The Emperor and Empress were waiting, one impatient, the other politely intrigued. Lady Castellon took her leave with a curtsey, so Kester and Kimbra were left to take a knee to the long carpet that ran from the door to the throne, and there they bowed their heads. Kester dared not raise it until commanded to and, indeed, felt somehow safer with his eyes fixed upon the lovely reds and blues of the rug. From there, he was still aware of Lady Castellon returning and standing nearby, accompanied by a member of the Emperor's Guardians.

"Rise," the Emperor stated, sounding almost bored. There was nothing particularly unkind in his manner, though no doubt he had better things to do, and again Kester feared he would be sent away.

"Musicians, in our Majesty's court," the Empress announced happily. "We don't have enough, I'm afraid. I gather this dashing young thing is someone special, Kester?"

"She's a singer: a very good one."

Kimbra introduced herself, and the Empress smiled in warm recognition at the name. The contrast between husband and wife could not be greater on this day. The Emperor was a man whose power still inspired strict obedience in Kester, yet it was muted and stale in ways he couldn't comprehend, and perhaps shouldn't try to. And he was ruggedly handsome: difficult to appreciate beneath his hard expression. That was his view though.

He needed to be a woman to understand. And the Empress relished her very being and her beauty, and she was surely beautiful, for her complexion was such that her skin seemed to shine of its own accord, and her soft eyes were so full of life. Her shape, that too. Beautiful shape.

"Do we have time for this?" the Empress asked her lord husband anxiously.

"We have much to do, I'll say that. There's always much to do. Although we asked for young Mister Irvyng to do a job for a reason." He stood tall and strong in his indecision.

"What do you think?" the Empress sprang on Kester. Surprised by the question, he drew out a long breath as he wondered what, at least, was appropriate in the presence of his rulers.

"There's always time for art, in my opinion," Kimbra offered.

"Spoken like a true purveyor of it." The Empress flashed a mischievous grin. "You must have readied a feast for the ears."

"I'm working on two songs, though only one is far enough along to be heard. Maero iymeth lavel iymeth laveth."

"Death became love became life," the Empress mused, courting a dream land, startling the other three.

"You don't speak Old-Modernist Mürathneèan," the Emperor pointed out, unable to deny his wonder now, much as he might have liked. She shook her head.

"Kimbra here chose the title of an old poem for her song. It's an awkward translation, as iymeth is a difficult word to place, but it's still a wonderful piece based on the ancient siege of Harth. Rather too saccharine for your tastes, I fear. Kimbra here is going to twist the focus on Burtal, of course."

"The idea is that new things come from, and despite, death. I thought it an appropriate influence, given how your city is to rise from the ashes, Majesty."

Even the Emperor nodded in approval. Yes, Kester's ginger-haired accomplice was very quick of wit, the Emperor had to admit.

"I should warn you," the Empress said in a more serious tone, "that it may not be easy at first. You and I know the value of music, yet the masses are to be enlightened. To some, it is a mindless diversion. When you're upon that stage, many of those men in the audience will rank you scarcely higher than the women performing their own acts in the brothels. Until you convince them otherwise." She smiled. "You already knew that. I thought to add my voice."

"Oh, I understand," Kimbra replied, slightly less confidently.

"Come then," the Emperor put in as he became bored. "Give us a sample."

"Upon the Tower of Harmony," the Empress agreed.

The Voice of Kings

There was not a person in that hall, besides the Empress, who was not taken aback by her words. Even the knight, who held a cold, blank state, craned his head out a little in anticipation.

"You have something in mind," the Emperor replied as plainly as possible, so as to not betray his interest.

"My mother would often have me sing into the wind, as she knew I would have to work hard to be heard, yet I couldn't shout, as impulse would have me, because she would recognise that also. Nowadays, I leave it to the professionals; dancing was always my love, you see, those spangled balls sharing words with enlightened men, though I still have a soft spot in me for those lessons. I've no doubt you have a voice of high calibre, Lady Lovett. So maybe I'm a fool, but I think I can wring a little more from you because... well, you'll see."

She let loose her mischief with that smile again. Kester doubted that the Empress saw herself as a fool for even a second. It was he who felt the fool for not knowing her meaning, and Kimbra was the same. The Empress was the centre of the world at that moment. Then Kester saw that they were to move, as Kimbra nodded more meekly than befitted her, and the Empress did not object, so he found himself walking to a place he never dreamed he would go, with the knight Doru leading the way on command. To the castle's south-west corner they walked, up to the fourth floor before veering into a grandly marked dark bronze door embossed with an image of that tower. The stairs spiralled round the full girth of the spire, the passageway more airy than he'd imagined, and the ceiling much the same, as it boasted impressive size that was astounding even inside. Doru led the way with a torch which, along with the few window slits, didn't give him much confidence.

Three times they passed over a landing where secrets were hidden within the centre of the spire, behind bronze doors marked with auspicious gold and silver embossments of sprawling landscapes under a clear night sky, a night shaken by storm, and a bright summer's day. Kester sensed a religious importance, as the tower's namesake was that of wisdom, inside and upon it. Small wonder the gods favoured royal lineages if they held such knowledge for worship.

The tower interior became increasingly imposing, not in what it had, but for what it promised, and as an ache pinched at the ankles, he became increasingly impatient. When Sir Doru slid the steel hatch aside at the top, the cold was felt immediately: a rush of it, not as a strong wind, but as a presence. It was only when Kester stepped onto the tower's top that the winds nipped at him, when he was too in awe to care. He span on the spot, again and again as he took it all in. There was enough room here on this circular pad for 30 people to stand and be free. When he controlled himself, he walked with none too little caution with Kimbra to the western end of the tower, and like her, gripped at the merlons that jutted up to the height of his waist, willing himself to peer down at the tiny humans below. *And small wonder kings have loved this tower so, because how could one not feel imbued with power here at the top of the world?*

His heart still thumping, he made out as much as he could of his surroundings, and mused on how strange they looked from where they were never meant to be seen: Jorin's Star Plaza to the east, surrounded by rings of water that might have a been flagon's worth for all it appeared, and in the west there was revered King Paryn's own plaza, beset, as was everything, by an orange globe of fire, and even that, as it was late afternoon, was much lower than he. The hall of commerce could just be seen hidden behind toys of red brick, and they were all around him – some whitewashed and some plain – broken into segments by the maze that was the road network, walled in from a landscape that stretched farther than the eye should ever see. There were one, two, three barracks, with Lameeri's Wish catching his eye in the north. Lennord was there, oblivious, for better or worse, of his master's machinations. He had a clever master, Kester admitted. He turned to her. Both looked equally amazed, and he wondered how often they came here, and whether the wonder could ever fade. Even the Emperor was proud and authoritative, the rugged attractiveness arising. They were both of them magnificent, their robes flapping merrily in the wind. Both gave the tower that flanked to the right fleeting, nostalgic glances.

They came to the fore as well, and all but Sir Doru looked outwards, who stood on the side of Kester and Kimbra, flexing his fingers around his scabbard.

"Don't turn away," the Empress commanded, her golden hair dancing. "Sing in your own time."

She did, and it was mesmerising. Kester would look to the Emperor and Empress, now and again, to see if they betrayed emotions that would help him determine the predicament they'd put him in, but it didn't help. The Emperor stared longingly northwards, while his wife was less obvious. They were touched by the singing, that much was clear, and for good reason. Kester imagined his music matching with it, and suddenly it seemed inadequate; the soft, drawn-out words that he could not understand climbing to heights beyond him still and riding the wind down to the streets, and he knew he must improve.

So cathartic was it that he found himself absorbed in thought, even as he and Kimbra left the castle gate, having retreated back to the real world from a song that seemed to follow them like a beautiful shade. Kimbra span as she skipped, grinning as she craned her neck up at the place where they'd just stood.

"If only everyone living here could go up there," she considered, "they might see their home city in a more optimistic light. If only because they can't see themselves in it."

"Could be right," Kester agreed, glum when he saw her lack of irony.

His and Her Majesty were impressed. Nothing else, regrettably, had escaped the Empress's lips about the family that had, to say, motivated him for so many years.

"Shall we return to my mother's house?" Kimbra suggested. "I have port to celebrate already."

"No, thank you," Kester replied forwardly, taken aback by her question.

He was truly in the raw, coarse world of Aurail again, and as he was drawn in, his dream-state faded, and it dawned on him how grossly and embarrassingly he'd misunderstood her offer.

"Actually, I shall," he said plainly. "I should escort you there, regardless. Did you hear any of their conversation in the throne room, by the way? Before we were summoned?"

"No. I wondered if I should ask you."

Kester licked his lips. "Perhaps I will tell you. Not today though, and no offence meant, Miss. It's something personal."

I will tell you after I've told Lennord, Kester resolved, *and not before. And I will do that at the first available opportunity, and leave him to his business. It's not mine.*

Chapter Twenty-three: Royal Challenge

The inventor glanced carelessly at the palace. Armed guards were approaching from there. He was damned if he was going to care until they were right before him. Other things had his attention in their grasp and he was going to savour that. Industry in motion. The shipyard. The sea. Everything beyond.

He was vaguely aware of the three guards weaving between the King's plantations, and very procedural they were too. The inventor finally turned as he was addressed; he was never rude when he could help it. The guard at the fore stepped from the ranks of the other two and held up a hand to show he came in peace.

"Vicentei Laccona," the guard said. "I'm Rayance Kemeth, first lieutenant of the Sun Guard. I've been instructed to escort you to the palace at the leisure of His Grace the King."

"It looks more like an arrest," Vicentei pointed out.

"I understand that," Rayance replied, and none too enjoyably; it must have been embarrassing for him. "With respect, you have a reputation for being unpredictable; you like to do things in your own time."

"I do," Vicentei agreed.

Rayance's tact was admirable at least. Vicentei had no breath for a fight with him, and at any rate, he'd seen men from the palace taking note of his presence in this same spot, not long ago, so had expected this, and he hadn't cared then either. The lieutenant was a patient man, as he had to be, with a reddish face and light brown hair. His armour was prettier than his followers', and there was more substance between the major components of spaulders, and gauntlets, and breastplate, and so forth. The breastplate was decorated with a bright yellow sun on a green field; the sun had ten forks, five long and five in between that were shorter and paler.

"Vicentei," Rayance said, a name he heard repeated often whenever he became engrossed in something genuinely interesting.

"I would have showed up on time," Vicentei said. "This time I would have. What the King wants, the King gets. I'm not as obstinate as some people like to think."

Rayance half grimaced, half smiled.

"Well, we're here now. If you please..." He directed Vicentei to follow with a gracious sweeping of his arm.

Vicentei left his balcony and the view that had enthralled him minutes before, satchel slung over one shoulder, to be party to the comforts of the Palace of the Sun. It was the standard guest's entrance for him, on the right of the palace face, lacking in royalty as he was. The entrance hall was long, and shined so well that everything reflected everything else:

the marble structures in semi-circular alcoves, the fountain topped with an eagle sculpture, crystal filled with a golden substance, and fantastically detailed chandeliers that hung from the black and gold ceiling. As he waited for Rayance to meet the King and return, the question of why he'd never been here before flashed only briefly before him, as he already knew the answer. "Why now?" was the prudent question, but the simplest answer was probably the right one. For now, he tried to memorise as much as he could of that grand hall, as underestimating another's work as an intrinsic stance was something he feared, and while art was beyond him, as his intellect was beyond most others, he was not averse to its pleasures. He'd never denied beauty, in all its forms.

"If you'd like to follow me," he heard Rayance say to him, now without his contingent.

"Lead the way."

The way was led up the marble staircase. Up two square landings between the two right angles. Through corridors of astounding influence. Bursting with royal blues and reds, gold and silver. Arrangement was in a manner most pleasing to the eye. Most importantly, there was sunlight streaming through tall windows: something people never failed to appreciate enough, somehow. He remained at the face of the palace as he was led to the King's office, and upon reaching it, Lieutenant Kemeth opened the door before he had a chance to do so himself and gestured onward, leaving him alone in the doorway.

For all the welcome he initially received, he might have sprung an unexpected visit upon them. Maybe that was fair. Vicentei himself was often accused of depriving people of respectable exits, so perhaps it was justice of fitting scale that he should be treated coldly at the reverse. The King sat behind his ornate desk at the far end, before the visage of his predecessor immemorial, father and son so very alike it seemed at a moment's glance: His Grace poring over immaculately arranged papers, and his father just as stern and proud, proud pride of place. And then there was the man on the balcony, who could only have been Sir Leon Barrotti. A blind person might not guess. He supposed. He was gazing wistfully over the city, cerebral and contemplative as the people said he'd always been.

Vicentei dropped to one knee at the halfway point, his eyes drawn, against his helping, to the knight, red hair glistening and white armour shimmering like a sun wrapped in water. How very fine it had turned out. A wonder they wanted him here at all, with talent of that calibre at the forge.

"Thank you, Vicentei, for the honour," the King said more amicably than expected. "Take a seat, if you please."

Vicentei sat at the only chair at the desk, directly opposite the King, letting his satchel drop to the floor. Sir Leon was standing beside His Grace now, and quietly anticipating the proceedings. Both of them were.

"I'll apologise for the way you were brought here, if such a gesture would make you feel better. Your reputation paints you as a distractible genius, so my intentions were to see that you got here before something or other took hold of you for an hour, which you'll soon have regretted. I've heard you called 'The Ghost', slipping here and there without anyone knowing where you are for weeks at a time."

"Do they say that?" Vicentei said, leaning forward. He'd truthfully never heard that nickname before. "Well that's a very theatrical moniker, and too flattering, Your Grace. It must be overblown. These things often are."

"I hope so. Though I hope the reports of your genius are as well-founded as I'm led to believe."

"But, Your Grace," Vicentei protested, sly, "my work has benefitted you for years now. I can't, in honour, admit it was all for you, but my service has always been yours regardless, through commissions and otherwise."

"True enough." The King spread an arm out over his desk, his chin balanced on the other. It was a slouch, yet miraculously one not bereft of gravitas, as he well knew, no doubt. A bear full of grace, where his regal garments and wrist jewellery did half the job, and his demeanour the other. "On the other hand, we've never met," he rested his case. "Come, show me what you've got in that satchel of yours. Assuming it's for me?"

"All for you, Your Grace."

"Impress me."

The King took that time to appraise him further, so Vicentei gladly cooperated and hid nothing of himself as he rummaged through the satchel for blueprints, drawn on parchment of his own making because he knew they would not rip, and if they did, he'd be more motivated to know why.

"Even knowing your age, you look younger than I expected," the Knight of the Holy Storm mused, with no fear of punishment from the King.

"Reputations can forge many a lie of our own making," the King admitted gruffly, nodding his head. "I admit I am in the same boat as Leon."

This was not something that surprised Vicentei. He had a short beard that made him look older than his 33 years, yet there was no short supply of people who supposed him to be a wise old sage. Perhaps he was partly to blame, what with never having sought one place to live in for long, and becoming known by one and all, as he surely would have.

He unravelled, upon the desk, one large sheet of parchment for the King to browse, and he did so with interest, Sir Leon eyeing it from his erect stance. The King had yet to request anything in particular, his methodical nature preventing him from working at another's pace when it didn't suit his wider picture. Vicentei only hoped it would not be a task of dull prospects, lacking in imagination.

"A bridge conjoining Light's End to the Isle of Sèhvor, seeing as you want to be impressed."

The King shot him a queer look, as if he were deciding whether to be amused or outraged. It was a look that challenged him.

"You say what you think, do you?" the King asked.

"I'm not arrogant, if that's what you're asking. I have, however, come to know that people are often impressed by me and, by extension, know that I am not a useless inventor. And I say what I think where it is appropriate, Your Grace. You didn't summon me for my skills at sycophancy, with all due respect."

The King snorted and reluctantly nodded before returning to the intrigues of the parchment.

"I think I'll like you."

With bated breath, Vicentei waited for what he knew was coming, resting on his enclosed fist, and curling his index finger upon the base of his nose. There had been a moustache there, but it had irritated him whenever he stroked or rested upon the skin of his upper lip, so it had gone.

"How long is the gap between those two points?" the King said at last. He made out that he knew the answer already.

"The bridge would be approximately twice the length of the Bridge of Blades at Ylden Parragor, and four feet again. There are enough islands of reasonable size on which to build struts."

"You've calculated that? And all the proportions, and the weight of the stone? Them too?"

"At least five times each, to within a negligible margin of error. Same result each time. Including the spaces left for statues, which you'll definitely want to adhere to. The gods saw fit to bless me with the knowledge of where art should go, but there is a grey void in my imagination as far as what should actually be there."

Sir Leon smiled slyly.

Knowing full well that the King would not be personally interested, Vicentei placed down a parchment with numbers scribbled all over it. The King showed more interest than he'd given him credit for, which was not to say he understood it.

"This will cost a fortune. What makes you think I'd be interested in this?"

"A fortune upwards of nine hundred thousand gold, but no more than three million if rules of efficiency are treated with decency. As for your second worry, I would say worry not. Not everyone who wants to trade with Sèhvor has the means to. Not everyone has a boat, and those who do would be better served on a good, hard road that'll be quicker and require fewer journeys for transporting heavy goods. The citizens would have no reason to be dissatisfied after that," Vicentei said with a straight face, though it might have been construed as a joke. Whatever the case, Sir Leon, who had been engrained into the island's history as a hero, did not respond. His blue eyes kept so much to themselves.

Royal Challenge

He again reached into his satchel, revealing this time a wad of parchments, all of them scrawled with calculations in far neater fashion.

"Not to mention, when the fateful day arrives, when there is no Sèhvorian ore left to mine there, residents will still have to carve their livings out on that rock, yet people might be less inclined to trade by boat if the mining that makes it famous has stopped. If you must, set up a toll booth on either end. Here..." Vicentei slapped the wad of parchment. "Twenty-three tallies based on a variety of potential socioeconomic factors: travel, the costs of food and materials, stinted crop growth, and so on. Only three of them came back to me with the message that such a venture would not be profitable for you. In theory, it shouldn't be too troublesome."

"Everything's easy in theory," Sir Leon said, and the King nodded, not looking up from the documents.

The King flicked through the sheets, let out a deep sigh at the enormity of it, and, unexpectedly, burst into a booming belly laugh, looking up at his advisor to ensure that the humour was not his alone. Sir Leon grew a genteel smile.

Over the top of everything else, Vicentei dropped a second parchment of blueprints. To strike while the iron was still hot. His grand orrery, up on the hill just north of the city, for all to see. A work of art, or it would be if he could conjure how it should look. But it would be huge, yes, and enclosed from the elements but for a mechanical roof, and not only that, it would have an observatory, to tear through the veil that mankind had once thought a two-dimensional painting of the gods. How he liked to stamp on those old misconceptions. A guilty pleasure.

"Tell me again why I would want a telescope that can see places we cannot reach?" the King said.

"Are you a simpleton, Your Grace? Complex navigation. Who knows what else? The more detail we have documented, the better. Sometimes you don't know what you're making till you step back. I'm assuming you're going to want to explore that infinite space to the west eventually, or very soon, if I were to bet."

The King couldn't help but show how impressed he was. One small victory at a time, and it would be clear sailing. He even sensed a chill go up the King's spine, unless he really was becoming arrogant.

"You're very astute, Vicentei," His Grace complimented. "You are not so very far from guessing a subject I'd like to discuss with you."

"Not here," Sir Leon added.

"Correct," the King was quick to confirm before Vicentei got too comfortable. He paused, for quite a long time, and at one point, stared out at his beloved city. "A formality as much as anything. Follow me."

The Voice of Kings

To the ground floor he was led once more, satchel kept ever close, King afore, Storm Knight behind. That was the result of no written formality, only the knight's politeness and the leader's need to lead. There was no talk along the way, and few looks were given to him but from those who would never have cause to care: servants mostly, and a court herald.

A painting of ancient Harth at one point. *Go back later*, he thought. *Remember. See if it has an ounce of accuracy.*

Music was waiting for them in the heart of the palace, in a small side room: a lute and a flute speaking excellent clarity at a slow, contemplative pace. And yet, when the King entered, he sent his minstrels on their way. The point being…?

"Do take a seat," the King suggested, waving a hand to an armchair.

The room was a small, cosy hall that one would think was for casual or minor conferences, and yet, on closer inspection, was somewhat more uniform, cloaked by its sense of style. He sat on one of two free chairs arranged around a simple, if exquisitely constructed, circular table, the other chairs having been already pushed to the sides. The chair was comfortable on the cushion beneath, and inflexibly straight at the back rest, so if someone were to slouch here, they would be all the more conspicuous.

To Vicentei's right-hand side sat an old man of average height, with hair of pale brown that snaked round the back of his head like a half crown, the rest withered away from his mildly spotted scalp. Around his neck there was a brooch consisting of three rings: one bronze, one onyx, and the last one gold, and in the central golden piece, there was a sword motif embedded. From the neck was hung a green cotton surcoat, and beneath that, a snug velvet piece that was equal parts black, as a starless night, and deep royal purple.

"Lord Laatel of House Holton," the King introduced, sitting on the chair opposite. None other could have ordered these chairs, it appeared, for he took to the shape's demand so ardently. "My Lord Justice."

"I pass the sentences that His Grace does not," Laatel said.

"Lord Theodore of House Hughly," the King announced the second man, who was to Michael's left. A man every bit as serious as Lord Holton, and swathed in robes that were mostly black save for patches and strips of gold here and there.

Sir Leon stood between Vicentei and the King, perhaps not allowed to sit here in his full plate armour as he was, though he didn't ask for an alternative, and neither did he look the least bit vexed. Lord Holton pushed a cup of wine in Vicentei's direction, under the multi-limbed candelabra.

"A toast for your arrival, of a fine reserve if I do say so."

"I don't drink when I want to use my brain," Vicentei replied dismissively. The King produced a slight, wan smile.

"To business then. The Burtalian court is getting ideas of reform and renaissance, and to put it plainly, I want you to counter every innovation they come out with. They create a revolutionary new ship design, you best it. They find a way to make reliable cannons, you find a way to mass produce them."

"That sounds awfully provocative," Vicentei said sharply, viewing the King through narrow slits as he tried to penetrate his logic.

"When discussed openly, yes," Lord Hughly agreed. "The trick is to have a passive dominance. We, as Mürathneè, create the goods, and we sell some to Burtal if they so desire, so we can't possibly be accused of anything destructive to their culture. Yet we reap the benefits of conception and production."

"We need you in particular," the King said. "You may find it hard to believe, but Burtal has some talented inventors."

Oh, they do indeed, Vicentei thought, amused. The unspoken challenge was always exhilarating.

"Has it occurred to you that productivity in Burtal is not anything to get paranoid over?" Vicentei said. "Your people aren't going to flock there and run your country into a desert wasteland. We're in no danger of becoming the lesser nation if that worries you. One country can complement the other."

"I doubt that," Lord Hughly said.

"I thought you might say something of the sort," the King said, ignoring his advisor's cynicism. "Is there any possibility such an approach could harm us?"

"Possibly," Vicentei said blankly.

"These two men don't believe it," the King said, pointing to the two advisors on his left. "A number of others don't either, and I'm not convinced direct competition will hold us back myself. It sounds simple. If you were to go to Burtal in times of doubt and investigate, that would remove all doubt. You have to consider though, they're seen as such a pathetic nation compared to us, and rightly so. One advancement ahead of us and I'll have to live with the humiliation. Imagine if they were to sail the Infinite Sea before us."

"A fruitless endeavour," Lord Hughly said sadly.

"Thus far," Vicentei pointed out. "When you look at things from a theoretical standpoint, you'll see that the impossible often becomes possible."

The King interlinked his fingers and rested his chin upon them, then stood up and marched around his chair. He grabbed the backrest of the chair with both hands and tapped his fingers.

"You might think I favour ill of Burtal," he said gravely. "It's not true. But we are the heart, and they are the lungs that simply pump a little extra breath into us."

"Then what is Mūrac?" Vicentei enquired.

"A barren womb," the King said forwardly.

"And Carlophinia?"

"Nothing. It's nothing."

The Voice of Kings

"Alassii."

"A second heart," the King said darkly, after some thought, quietened by Vicentei deconstructing his metaphor, and he looked far off for a moment. His green eyes were cold. *Mura sounds like a funny old creature*, Vicentei laughed inwardly. He carried on that way.

One could have heard a pin drop, and Vicentei was the quietest of them all, he felt, though not nearly quiet enough. Sir Leon was the stillest.

"I don't hate Burtal," the King reiterated, and Vicentei silently breathed a sigh of relief. "When it runs clear of its fundamental problems, then I will believe it can be an equal. But they have an Emperor of all things. Why would one want to openly honour their realm's darkest days? The word even comes from old Alassiien vernacular for deity."

"Changing titles can be a troublesome affair, Your Grace," Lord Holton offered. "There is the matter of how it will affect their perceived resolve, publicly speaking."

"I don't believe that for a second. Do you know what the very first act my father passed was, when he came to his throne? Anyone?"

One would have thought either of the lords would have answered near immediately, or Vicentei did anyway, as whatever else he was, he was not a master of these situations and these kinds of people: a point he was quick to remember when no answer came, and was reinforced when a voice he didn't expect to hear supplied the answer.

"King Christopher, on his coronation day, changed our city's name from Aymathneè, west's edge, to Harth, heart," Sir Leon said.

"Thank you," the King said somewhat exasperatedly, as if the delayed answer had physically pained him. "We're not just any city, we're Harth." He became contemplative momentarily. Never once, despite his theatrics, did his power wane. Vicentei would not forget that. "I think that will be enough for today. We've all got work to be doing," he finished.

They all left at that announcement, King included, and Vicentei was the first to step through the door where he found a man waiting for him, it seemed: a servant who, on the King's order, was to show him to his assigned chamber within the palace.

"You may keep him as your page for as long as you stay here," the King said, and left him be, providing no instructions in spite of his last statement in the council room. Vicentei could only assume he was being left to his own devices and, thus, found himself liking the King more for the gesture of faith.

Little further than the end of the corridor did Vicentei reach before a black-haired young girl walked from an alcove where she, also, seemed to have been waiting for him. Looked too pleased to see him. Her clothes were of remarkably high standard, and she wore an amethyst necklace, fancy and oval in its carving with fawns engraved upon the chain.

"You're the inventor," the girl said.

"I am an inventor," Vicentei said plainly.

"This is the Princess Natierlia," the page put in, and none too soon. But she was apparently unconcerned with being treated with reverence.

"My mother says you're an invaluable assent," the Princess said, delighted beyond reason.

"I doubt that, Lady Princess. Though she may see me as an invaluable asset."

"Oh," Princess Natierlia replied, slapping her forehead and grinning.

"Can I help you?"

"No, I just wanted to offer my greeting. I am a princess, so I must be fair and take interest in all affairs," she said, and Vicentei frowned, wondering where she'd gotten that apolitical idea from. "I'll let you go, if you like."

She curtseyed and Vicentei bowed, because he had no right to accept such a gesture from royalty. If someone were to see him shun that, he might be in trouble. And he was impressed, which he could very rarely say of children, all of whom he found hard to handle but this one. It reminded him of stories he'd heard of Prince Walter, half good and half bad, and unlike most of these stories, there was scarcely a way to conclude which were the most valid, yet now he assumed the prince could, at most, appear arrogant of his heritage, judging by the way his sister had turned out.

When, at last, his new page and he arrived at his new chambers, he suddenly became disinterested in the personas of the Santorellian family. It became boring just like that, and now, as he entered his room, his mind was prepared for work. He'd generously been given a room at the front corner of the palace, reasonably high it was also, affording him a view of the city and the sea. Someone must have known of his affinity for such inspiring views. Pillars separated the room from the balcony, from which ivy was entangled purposefully, and rolled up gossamer curtains hung before several of them. And between the pillars were white doors, already open. They would be replaced eventually with more secure ones, if he had the time.

He sat behind his desk, which faced the sea, and observed a large chest of steel and oak, weighted down with a slab of polished iron attached to the bottom, the key to which his page dropped on the desk. Vicentei sent him away, as his presence could only be distracting, but scarcely before he had time to unpack, there was a knock at the door and the Knight of the Holy Storm drifted in when he was permitted entry. By the desk he stopped, and briefly looked out to sea, calm as before. Like Vicentei, he seemed to see something special in these vistas, ironic considering his moniker. It seemed, when he was not in battle, the storm subsided to memory and the clouds parted. His eyes were so like the sea: powerful, even in times of ease, and ever that bright blue. It could surely make one nervous, if the knight wished it.

"I thought to see how you were settling in," Sir Leon said.

The Voice of Kings

"Very well, though I can't say I've had the time to really do that in great quantity." The knight took to his humour with a smile.

"I wanted to reassure you about the King's behaviour as well. I fear you caught him in an ill temper."

"I fear I put him in that ill temper," Vicentei countered.

"Possibly," Leon admitted. "I believe he was going to talk at some length about his reasons for asking that of you, but you rebuked it quite confidently, and went beyond, at that. Tomorrow he'll act completely differently. He'll have slept on your logic and may be willing to come to a compromise. He said he'd like to be a friend of yours, and I'll believe that over the impression he gave in the drawing room. A word of advice, Vicentei: approach him when he's with the Queen or Princess Natierlia whenever possible. The difference will be stark, I swear on the five."

Leon narrowed his eyes in mock conspiracy and looked all around, pleased to hear whatever Vicentei had to say.

"Thank you kindly, Sir. I should point out, however, that I never purported to speak unequivocal truth. I flung up an alternative to be considered."

"And so it shall. You have my word on that."

In truth, Leon was putting him at ease now, for he'd not much taken to the idea of competing so fiercely with Burtal. Competition was best served to better both parties, but he was in the service of the King of kings now. Defying authority was usually not so much a problem for him in the past, but he dared not be so direct. Leon would remove the need to be; he was known as the most loyal of friends and fearsome of enemies.

"You wouldn't say he's generally antagonising or angry?" Vicentei said with intention to provoke, tactless, as so often he found it hard not to be.

"He can be intense. Usually he's not."

"Tactful."

"An unwise thing to say, seeing as I'm of the King's high council," Sir Leon said, flashing that soft, enigmatic smile of his.

"Half of wisdom is finding out what's not wisdom," Vicentei pointed out, shrugging. "I meant no offence, though I said, for the sake of my work's effectiveness, I won't lie, and I meant that."

"Then I look forward to tracking your progress here. I find you intriguing."

"Says you of all people," Vicentei answered. "Half the fairy tales in the kingdom seem to revolve around you and your brilliance." Leon smiled at that, tongue pressed lightly in his cheek.

"Then perhaps you'll have the honour of finding out which are true."

Vicentei thought about that, and decided to take a stab at his armour.

"I was on the Isle of Sèhvor when you quelled the riots two years ago, and saw nothing of you but for the news that spread like wildfire."

The knight's expression did not change a fraction. No insult was taken, no intrigue nor surprise befallen. If the rumours were true, his conscience had every reason to be as clean as his armour. The image conjured by the rumours was a strong one indeed. Workers of Sèhvorian mines, trapped by the plague that stalled the ships at Light's End, and poor return profits on their labour besides, riled, as common folk are by a man not of their disposition; men and boys taking arms who should never have touched them, and being lain to waste by trained Watchmen, and in the middle of them, a noble knight who feared not for his life, disarming his opponents and pushing them on their way, as if in a practice session.

"It's all been said before," the knight said.

"Not to me. Not from you. People say you were as calm as the blue sky that day; some say no men died by your hand in battle, others that you struck no one with the blade's edge at all."

Sir Leon's eyes became sad, unless they had always been that way and Vicentei hadn't noticed. And he had a broad smile. Both were so convincing he wasn't sure which was real, if indeed they were not equally true somehow.

"That's a romanticism, I fear," Sir Leon said. "Men died by my hand, that I know as well as I know myself. Perhaps I inflicted no immediately fatal wounds, I don't know. There was some of that romanticism, I'd like to think, as some of those men were little more than boys swinging old swords about because someone convinced them it was a good idea. I did not want to be there at all. Were I in their place, I could be convinced to take up arms, out of burning injustice. There were men there who had more pride in their death throes than I did unscratched, and some deservedly so. No, I can't take credit for only that rumour, I'm afraid. I would shout from the rooftops if I had negotiated with leveller heads before violence broke out. Sparing lives is ideal, but if a man is impaled at the end of my sword, their life is no longer in my hands."

"You blame your sword for that?" Vicentei said dryly.

"I'm being facetious, of course," Sir Leon continued patiently. "I mean only that the heat of battle does not always afford me the kind of restraint that is often attributed to me. That restraint is not possible by mortal hands. As I own the best of them, I would know."

He was plainly amused at doubling back on his humility to perpetuate the myths of his skills, and might have been only partly joking. Mysteries aside, Vicentei could only admit to himself that the knight was as personable as the people claimed.

"Some of the soldiers got carried away," Leon went on. "That part is no exaggeration. There's no shortage of overzealous men with swords, and there have been far worse than

The Voice of Kings

that lot who fought alongside me on the Isle of Sèhvor. They weren't my men," he said fiercely.

"I've no doubt." He didn't. Leon's elites were famed for their discipline, even discounting gossip. An idea struck Vicentei and he reached into his satchel, removing a flintlock pistol. "I think we shall be friends also. Would you take this as a gift? Your feedback would be appreciated."

"I don't use guns. There's precious little reason to use them over crossbows, and I don't use them either. They won't smash plate and mail both, and if they do, they don't pierce the flesh, and they're slow to reload. They're a solution to a problem that never existed." He took the pistol anyway and held it up to the light, which glinted off its bronze surface, perfect yet uninspired. "My thanks regardless. I'm not one to refuse gifts." He frowned. "What's that tube on the top?"

"A chamber for spare bullets, Sir. The idea is that you pull the slide beneath and it will pull the whole chamber back, all but a sheet of metal with a hole in it, big enough for the lead ball to drop through. A broken idea," Vicentei admitted, shrugging again. "The bullets get stuck and you have to flick the gun to and fro just to get them to move. They fall out of the barrel if you're not quick, of course, and if you encase them in fish glue and gunpowder, as I'd planned, they often won't roll at all. I'll drop the idea if I get bored with it. It's not close to my heart."

Sir Leon nodded approvingly, at Vicentei's genius, not at the invention itself.

"Thank you Vicentei." He made to leave, elegant as any soldier could be. At one with his armour.

"Sir." Vicentei rose for the honour of the knight. He furrowed his brow as he remembered what Leon had said about the King potentially reaching a compromise. "Tell me violence was never being considered, regarding our competition with Burtal."

"It never was," Sir Leon said earnestly and marched away.

Vicentei sat. He worked for the rest of the day.

Chapter Twenty-four: There Beheld an Infinite View

Isaac battered the steel on the anvil before him: a felling axe that would never be used if he didn't bring it together soon. This fact brought a strange pleasure to him as he'd never been one for this line of work, a fiddly and exhausting business, yet he was doing it of his own free will. It was all for the dream that was so close now. If he could only see if he was on the right path. If he could unite the knowledge of the madman, the inventor, and the King, he might have a clearer picture; that, or a jumbled mess of three distinct palettes sloshed together. He reminded himself of why he'd come here in the first place: because he believed so strongly in the evidence, and that was what captured his imagination now. The constant banging of the hammer and hissing of the forge as he reheated it conformed to a rhythm that drove him on, if not for the sake of the axe.

It was his older brother who gave him cause to think with more special awareness. Lucian, who had only been told of this workshop in vague terms, had found his way here and was viewing Isaac with mild disdain, admittedly correct in his assumption that Isaac did not belong at the forge.

"You're not wearing your regalia," Lucian observed dryly.

"It must be kept clean," Isaac replied forwardly to his brother's sarcasm, as was frequently the contrary.

Fortunately, Lucian had not sought to bother him incessantly, whether because he viewed Isaac's antics with a morbid fascination, or betraying more empathy because of the incident described to him upon that rooftop. In the days that had passed since then, it had joined the growing ranks of such events that gave a bizarre sensation on recollection, of coldness and memories passing in and out of focus, as surreal as the nightmare that had plagued him that very night. For what it was worth, he was more or less his normal self again already, but for the small voice that was telling him he shouldn't be. He must have looked a sight to Lucian though, dressed in a long, leather apron, wearing simpler clothes than usual beneath, and his blonde hair must have been speckled with carbon.

"Whatever errands of my own I want to do, I still have father's job to complete," Isaac explained. "And my own will cost money besides, so it's a good job I've already signed up to the Guild of Blacksmiths."

"A good thing too that the Alchemist's Guild declined your petty attempt at coercion, or bribery, or whatever it is you're doing. You're bad enough at smithing without turning your hand to potions and volatile substances."

"True enough. Although I have my friend Thom here to guide me with my smithing."

The man pumping the bellows behind Isaac grunted. In truth, he was neither particularly friendly nor well known to Isaac due to his introverted and defensive attitude, and Lucian likely saw that also. Isaac tired of the verbal game and became suddenly conscious of the large satchel slung over one of Lucian's shoulders.

"What are you doing?" Isaac asked, furrowed of brow. "Why are you here?"

"You signed up to several guilds, remember? Responsibilities come with all of them, so I'm helping to clear up your mess; working for the Guild of Couriers as a lowly recruit, trusted only with running letters between housewives who've nothing better to do, when I should be making steps to the Emperor's court. I'll arrange for your links with the guilds to be broken as soon as I can."

"That's not going to happen," Isaac said vaguely. "Anyway, you needn't have followed, appreciated as you are. I never meant to draw you from your work."

"I'm aware of that. You're not malicious, just thoughtless." Lucian paused to reconsider his tone, looking all about the street dismissively as if embarrassed to be relenting, for one reason or another. He licked his lips. "Don't let Father down. As for your little expedition, we'll talk more about that, I promise. I want to make sure you're not insane. Oh, and I'm visiting Marcel at the cathedral later. I've an inkling he could do with some support, and I know you like to look out for him, so... you'll be there, I know that."

Lucian left him be, not running while Isaac was looking at him, understandably bitter at what he perceived to be a failing of his brother left to his own devices, and while Isaac believed his older brother sometimes enjoyed aggrandizing the responsibilities he completed on Isaac's behalf, there was little question that there was no such thing here. There had been fanciful talk of the High Duke Dorrin, and the meetings thereof, sparing, and brief, and vague, but proud, and now he was carrying letters hither and thither, being treated like a nobody.

While the heat was uncomfortable and he wanted to be away, nevertheless, Isaac waited for news, so was relieved to finally spot the gait of the mercenary Jamys against the sunlight. He was armoured as he was every day, windswept and every bit a man of the coast.

"What have you found?" Isaac asked.

"Not as you much as you'd like. I stopped by Laccona's house and it was still vacant. I stood beside it and asked passersby if they knew anything. They said he was in the city till recently and wasn't anymore. That was their view anyway. I asked for more than that, and a couple of folks said he headed northwards when he left, bags and all. Research, maybe. I don't know. Nor them."

Isaac nodded his approval, disappointment aside. The mercenary was proving to be useful for what he'd been picked for, to his astonishment. At first, he'd assumed Martello sought to insult him by pairing him with a man of limited care for socialising, or talking in general, and maybe that was true but, if so, the joke was now on him. Jamys was capable, or had become capable as his interest had grown, and his imagination about the size of Isaac's purse grew.

There Beheld an Infinite View

"We'll just have to leave it up to our friends at the guilds now then. I'm not of a mind to wear myself out searching the whole city from top to bottom for him. I've got family to attend to. After this," Isaac said tiredly, nodding to the steel. "I'm under contract."

He worked at the axe again, knowing the mercenary would not think ill of having to stand and wait; more probably he'd embrace it. To his surprise, Jamys was perplexed by what he saw and made to take the hammer into his keeping. Isaac didn't object, keen for the mercenary to reveal more of himself through what clearly was important to him, or had been once, as he wasn't the sort to speak openly of himself if he could help it. He banged at the metal viciously, skilfully even.

"In a hurry to get going?" Isaac asked.

"To see that we move on to something you're good at. You're bad at this, and it annoys me. You told me to be honest."

"I did," Isaac said plainly.

Jamys thrust the hot metal into the oil, held it as it steamed and bubbled until it did so no more, then pushed it deep into the coals and pumped hard at the bellows until Isaac could feel the heat billowing at him in the street, where the cool sea breeze had just comforted him. It was a technique he'd seen many a time in Caedor, so was unsurprised by the mercenary's next words.

"That's done," he said to Thom, who was as wary of the newcomer as he was of Isaac. "Leave it to heat up and then let it cool naturally, not in the oil."

Thom probably knew this, opting to say nothing as he was fond of doing. He might have argued for Isaac to stay, but with Isaac being only a provisional apprentice, instead asked only for a guarantee that he would return. It was Jamys's presence that influenced Thom, that was undeniable, and Isaac squirmed at the silent coercion he'd conducted. He promised he would return and promptly left with his bodyguard, bound for the cathedral. Jamys was growing more cheerful and bold, though he kept it to himself, and Isaac did not want to disturb him yet, trying to decide on his own if the man was reporting his deeds to Martello. Isaac had passed the guild hall several times in the past few days, saying nothing to Martello, who he'd made eye contact with in the courtyard but had otherwise given a wide berth, noting that neither mercenary had given anything away.

The most obvious answer was likely the truest: Martello didn't care, and if he did, he kept it from his own reach. So Isaac would have to summon the courage and put it in his hand. His tongue swished around his mouth as he considered Jamys again: a tall and surly fellow who would perhaps not look overtly threatening but for his weaponry.

"You know the way of the forge," Isaac stated.

"I worked one until I was old enough to realise that I'd like to use what I'd made. So I did. A job as a lackey got me away from my father's command in the workshop."

The Voice of Kings

So you've been the lonesome type for many years, Isaac did not say. He suspected that, to Jamys, that constituted opening up about his life. It felt strangely intrusive to muse on it for too long, and so he let himself be distracted by anything and everything else, until that great plaza came before him as he turned a corner, so huge it created an illusion of emptiness, even now when it was technically thriving with commerce and passersby. That dark monolith in the centre was quite a beast, and he couldn't help but wonder what Marcel was doing now: if he was doing something worthwhile at last, if he was standing up for the rights he paid for, not mopping the floors because someone hadn't flexed their power in a while.

Not far from the cathedral, he saw that Lucian had arrived ahead of him, and without his courier's satchel. Such was the way of time when he was gripped by thought, insistent as it was on running away with him. Marcel had come out to meet him already, still looking out of place in his apprentice robes. *Healer's robes would suit you better*, Isaac corrected himself, smiling inwardly. Accompanying his brothers was a woman of about his own age, donned in dress robes more befitting a lady; a woman Marcel had likely mentioned upon that rooftop, whose name he'd forgotten. She had a strange demeanour about her, as if stuck somewhere between being a classically raised lady and a woman of whimsical carelessness, and at times she looked about her in muted conspiracy.

"What weather!" Isaac said affably, waving his hand to order Jamys not to follow too closely. Lucian made visibly clear he disapproved of Isaac's company. "It's a fine day, brother. I hope you're spending it well."

"Acting as a servant," Marcel replied less curtly than he probably would have liked to. "Observing the work of others in the fields of alchemy and medicine."

"Being treated as an outsider," the woman put in placidly. Marcel put on an awkward smile, wincing at what have must been truer than he'd imagined to be spoken aloud. "Where are my manners? I'm Tamzin Morzall. You must be Isaac."

"That I am. Pleased to meet you Tamzin."

They shook hands, and Marcel cringed, perhaps for fear that Isaac would not show restraint and, instead, attempt to seduce the daughter of the duceveree̊. Or that Marcel, himself, was already growing fond of her. Either way, Isaac respected his unspoken wish and did nothing of the sort, nor would he, what with not being a cretin. In truth, she was quite plain but for her pale blue eyes. Albeit it, it appeared to be of her own design, akin to a Mürathneèan eagle trapping itself in a cage.

"You look very alike, you and Marcel," she said with delight, straight-backed and entirely proper in her manners. "You're not overtly similar, but there's a shared quality I can't quite place. I think I'd know you were brothers if I weren't already privy to that fact. Lucian, you have some of that quality too, don't you worry."

"If you insist, madam."

There Beheld an Infinite View

"Were you intending to meet us here?" Isaac said to Marcel, frowning as he looked over his brother's shoulder to where the cathedral main doors had opened.

"I made to wait here for you after Lucian called me out on my break, and Tamzin wanted to get acquainted. She kept us here. She likes to talk, you see." She smiled in agreement. "I never thought for us to just stand here, but then I hadn't thought much about it at all."

Isaac turned his attention back to the priestess at that, noting that a man in white and gold robes was, indeed, making for their gathering. He looked to be a slippery sort who, he'd bet, even from a first glance of the man, could only be the duceveree. He was an old man of oily disposition and shifting mannerisms, who hosted a braided beard that he must have thought made him exude power, and maybe it worked, for Isaac wasn't looking forward to speaking with him.

"Tamzin, would your father have any reason to greet us out here personally?" Isaac went on.

The three of them who had their back to the cathedral span round. Lucian made himself presentable, while Marcel merely stood straight and Tamzin sighed and rolled her eyes.

"None whatsoever. He never has, nor will he start today. My father does not greet people in earnest unless it's in his best interests, or if he's in one of his moods."

"Is he not in one of those moods?" Isaac asked pleasantly.

"No," she said simply, smiling faintly over her shoulder and explaining no more. She fell still as the grave, bracing herself for what would come next.

"A fine day to be outside," the duceveree said as he approached. "As it is indoors, where there is work to be done." He was not particularly angry, just possessing of a grating tone.

"Bishop Talihn gave me a break, Your Eminence," Marcel answered, averting his gaze to the duceveree's shoes.

"So long as I know," the duceveree replied with a wave of his hand, dropping the matter, to Isaac's surprise, where he might have harped on for all his power was worth. "There are those who would seek to shirk their duties. One wonders why they apply to vocate here in the first place. I hold no prejudice against you Apprentice Brodie, let's be clear. I merely have an interest in seeing the ship run smoothly. Tamzin, what's your reason for being here? Your public honesty, in particular, is of paramount importance."

"The same as Marcel's. Same as before, Father."

"I'm glad to hear it. Where would we be if House Morzall let its standards slip? We set the example." He raised his eyebrows to portray a stern message, his cheekbones hard and long. Without changing expression, his gaze slid in Isaac's direction, and he made eye contact at once.

Isaac placed one foot forward to advance on the duceveree's beck, stopping as he realised what he was doing. 'Challenge' was a more appropriate word to describe what the old man was doing. It was not necessarily hostile or demanding respect, but he knew it was for provocation. In response, Isaac stepped back and took care to replicate his previous posture, bowing slightly, as this was the safest option most likely.

"You're the middle brother," the ducevereë said. "Isaac. You're the inquisitive brother, set for fame by your explorative nature and silver tongue I gather, and all in the threadbare garb of a smith. Deceiving appearances can throw people off guard well enough, from time to time." Isaac considered this, almost having forgotten the state in which he was presenting himself to the ducevereë of Harth. He frowned, but held his tongue that the old man had been so forthright to compliment. "When you've explored your faith with higher priority, return to me again."

"You misunderstand. Today I'm just a humble man come to visit my brother. I never intended to win your favour. The cathedral offers no jobs for my like, I fear."

The ducevereë looked up at the sky – lips pursed, his eyes flickering here and there between quick, heavy blinks. As unpredictable as his daughter then, if his first impressions were still to be trusted. Lucian took the ducevereë's attention next. It was a wonder for Isaac if he really was systematically insulting them all, one by one, from the shades of subtlety, or whether this was just his normal bluntness. Either way, Marcel was unlucky.

"You're the eldest," Laryc said with a nod to Lucian. "You look more serious. You're Count Andrews' man, yes?"

"An ambassador in my own right soon enough," Lucian couldn't help but add. "My mind is set on diplomacy."

"So is mine. We have our own little hierarchy and systems in Harth cathedral. It's necessary to operate of our own accord if we're to do the gods' bidding."

"Do you have strong connections with the Palace of the Sun, if you're allowed such leeway?" Isaac said.

"The cathedral runs this city just as much as the King's court does, by King's permit of course, as he is the heir to the gods' gifts. So to answer your question, we have as much contact as needs be."

"What I mean is, are you privy to all the goings on and business of the court?"

"As much as we need," the ducevereë repeated harshly, suspiciously eyeing Isaac up and down. "What's your real question, Brodie?"

"You misunderstand me again. I just like to know as much as possible. Would you show me the inside of the cathedral?" Isaac said evasively. "My prayers have been lacking of late and I could benefit from the grand experience. I speak on behalf of everyone here of course."

"So could everyone, but not just any person can be allowed inside whenever they please. There are times when the common people have their chance to pray within its walls."

There Beheld an Infinite View

The duceveree ceased speaking abruptly and rolled his head from side to side, appearing to weigh the options. When he settled on his choice, he seemed to grow taller and his face was illuminated by pride, his head held high as he stood against a backdrop of thin, dark spires and stained glass windows, as if they were all his, and his alone to share with others.

"You are the brother of our new apprentice Marcel," he observed. "I'll presuppose you're as reverent as he allegedly is, you and Lucian both."

With that, he made an about turn of grand gesture and lashing gold silk, as befitting his rank, and led them towards the double doors, Jamys following some way behind, of which Isaac did not complain. His brothers glanced his way with a combination of apprehension and intrigue of varying degrees, but to his surprise, it was Tamzin alone who showed concern. She slowed her pace and, as she walked alongside Isaac, she leaned into his head, releasing an aromatic breath that smelled like the countryside, a strong scent of flowers that was warm upon his cheek, and from the corner of his eye, he saw teeth almost as white as her dress.

"What are you doing?" she whispered harshly.

"Just investigating," Isaac whispered in return. "Harth means a lot to me at the current time, so I'll wring it for all its worth. It just so happens your father is a prominent and knowledgeable figure in this city."

"He is prominent," she agreed, shrugged and pulled away from him at the slightest hint of her father looking around.

The duceveree did so as he waited for his guards to open a single door; guards who still looked out of place to Isaac outside a place of worship and perhaps always would, despite the valuable items inside. The duceveree stared through the centre of his following and winced as he saw, for the first time, the mercenary at the rear of the ranks.

"Whose dog is that? Is he coming in here?"

"He's my guide," Isaac answered. "He's rough around the edges, I grant you. Aside from that, he's just as eligible to enter, in my opinion."

"Very well. Piety can find the unlikeliest of people after all."

Jamys raised an eyebrow in contention and growled silently, eyes darting about the cathedral, which was more emotion than was usual for him, but less an outburst than justified. It was a comfort to know that no trouble would break out, so Isaac took the opportunity to leave Jamys's side. He weaved past his brothers and the priestess in as casual a fashion as he could, to draw close to the duceveree, who was in his own space of contemplation, well ahead of the others. They might as well have not been present for the attention he paid to the five marble statues standing tall and bright in the reflected sunlight. Most everything was beautiful here, yet the nave that engulfed him at such a deceptively slow pace seemed little more than empty space because of them, permeated with dust and multicoloured streams of light, wrapped in coldness that such wide spaces encased in stone seemed to draw in. When the ducevereë reached the front, he stopped and craned his head up ponderously, biting his lower lip and staring intently as if he dared not proceed to the dais.

"There you have it. Breathe it in," he said.

The other four showed up soon after, and spread out in the open space before the dais, also craning their necks and inspecting every detail they could about them. Jamys was less impressed, however, leaning on his sword pommel with his arms crossed and assessing the area more as a businessman evaluating his stock. The faint creaking of his sliding lames was the only sound, continuously so as he began playing with their straps. The duceveree didn't deign to comment, if indeed he could hear anything in his inner sanctum.

"Do you trade with the Isle of Sèhvor, Your Eminence?" Isaac asked, hoping he was being clever.

"To what end?"

"Excuse me?" Isaac said delicately, frowning.

"To what end do you think we would? We serve as a representation for the gods. We're not a business, and we're fairly unique in that, so your question is, justly, to be treated with suspicion."

"And commendable that is of you to judge one's character so thoroughly. I meant only that, seeing as you've gone to great lengths to ensure that the cathedral holds a certain aesthetic standard, I'd assume the ore they dig up would interest you."

"Items must be fit for purpose, so we trade with them when Sèhvorian steel is appropriate for a particular symbolism, which is fairly often. You know, of course, that the gods, or their forms on our mortal plane, sent the steel from Mura's core."

"I've heard that said."

"You don't believe it," the duceveree said darkly, calm and ominous, still refusing to look at him in a bloated stretch of self-importance that was beginning to aggravate Isaac.

"I haven't heard enough of it to believe it. I've just... heard of it." Isaac shrugged.

"Apprentice Brodie," Laryc called out in a voice that echoed as a dull roar about them. "Tell your brother the truth of it."

For a time, Isaac assumed Marcel would do what was asked of him, prudent as it would be, and then came the defiance that Marcel did not even recognise as such: only the truth he thought he must say, for lies would come back to him some day.

"I couldn't say, Your Eminence. I've heard the same from afar, always afar, of a gift not written in scriptures. I hear many things in Caedor. Words have a funny way of being distorted when they travel over those hills for long enough."

"You southerners breed ignorance," the duceveree muttered in disbelief, shaking his head. "We'll see to that. Remember this for now, if nothing else. The scriptures are vague, and some have been lost by careless men of ages past. You must learn to read between the lines, and I tell you now that this truth is between the lines, hidden from fools. And we all know the gods reward those kings most deserving of help. King Michael is as close to a god as we have on Mura now, so logic would dictate that is why we were given the highest quantity of this enchanted steel, no? The last of that ilk was your King Paryn, centuries ago, blessed with enchantments for those towers of his, and only gods know what else. Now Mürathneè is the great country and Burtal is a carcass rotting, ever since Jorin murdered it." He snorted in laughter that falsely reflected his lack of humour. "Who can say when the next real king will emerge there?"

Laryc was no longer speaking for anyone, and was now doing so for his own benefit, or perhaps for those five on the dais to show he would never lie by omission, their eyes never meeting his, for which he was uncaring or even grateful. Isaac paced slowly to and fro, to give momentum to his thoughts that stagnated in the musty atmosphere Laryc was moulding so effectively. Tamzin leaned into Marcel's ear, whispering something which caused Marcel to rock his head from side to side in consideration before smiling nervously, as did she. Hers was of smarm and dark satisfaction.

"You've never considered Sèhvorian steel to have hidden properties or functions though?" Isaac pressed.

"Who knows what the gods did with that steel before sending it up to us? You've started thinking now, at least, so I should be thankful of that."

Laryc swung about with theatricality that must have passed him right by, for he didn't, for a second, strike Isaac as an actor. It was just part of who he was to play everything up: a blind spot he couldn't see in the mirror. There was a flurry of robes and silk scarves and, at the end of it, still the duceveree could not bring himself to crouch down to the level of his guests and daughter. It was the fresco on the ceiling that he gazed upon now, and he squinted because it was untouched by rays of sun or gleam of torch. Lucian was bracing himself to interject if Isaac were to entrench himself in the apparent insanity of his quest, all but ignored by Isaac.

"Strange how little we know of such things. We know more about that," the duceveree said, nodding at the mural. "Living smoke and fire from the nameless realm, and gods and kings as their vassals, clashing together in the future is less ambiguous than lumps of ore it would seem." He paused and licked his lips. "That's your answer. You ask a lot of questions but you don't know a whole lot do you?"

"Enough to question my own ignorance," Isaac quipped. Laryc heaved, as if having trouble breathing.

"You can keep doing that to yourself but I doubt you'll find any answers inside your own head. You come to me now when it's convenient, yes, but where were you when your brother was first here with me? What were you doing when he was learning the way of the gods?"

405

The Voice of Kings

Say one thing and then another, anything to be contrary, Your Eminence, Isaac mused. *Hold a scroll out before you and a dagger behind your back, and swap them without irony. Never mind that you would never grant a stranger audience, even if I'd thought to meet you, Your Eminence.*

"I was watching a beheading at the palace, Your Eminence," Isaac said, stone-faced. He cocked his head on one side.

"Isaac..." Lucian said scornfully, softly, holding up a hand in warning. Beside him, Tamzin looked quizzical and reproachful, and Marcel too, but mostly her. And Laryc came down from his place on high to inspect Isaac.

"Justice needs to be done, fairness be. I wouldn't use that as a defence for how hungry I am for knowledge though. Murder is a pleasure of the rabble."

"I wasn't there for my amusement," Isaac snarled, leaning forward. Everyone else noticed his lapse before he did.

"So says the rabble too," the ducevereë rebuked icily. Isaac flinched at the insult. "If you'd applied here along with your brother, you could have a proper education instead of wandering about the city, as I deduce you have a penchant for, from Marcel's vague description."

"Indeed, that would be preferable, but as I said, I fear I'm not fit for the cathedral. Gods know I would have quite an education uncovering the nooks of your abode by washing every inch of it. Nel of fortune would grant me the opportunity to shine your shoes if I were good."

Tamzin's eyes were wide with surprise, at first abject shock and then stifled humour, whereupon she clapped a hand to her mouth and pursed her lips to stop from laughing. His words seemed, all of a sudden, quite surreal. He hadn't intended it to be a joke, so far as he could tell; more an instinctive lashing of anger. Perhaps it would have been something to laugh about if not for the duceveree's piercing gaze. He raised his head to show he was sufficiently taller, and shook it as he turned to the statues, kissed his thumb and lifted it up to them.

"What you just said could be construed as heresy."

"He's hot-headed," Lucian reinterpreted hurriedly. "He means no harm. I apologise. He likes debating."

"There's nothing to debate. We know what he said and he meant it as mockery."

"Heresy?" Isaac repeated quietly, already feeling his lips freezing shut. Silence was safer. It wasn't worth it to question his resolve further, much as he'd have liked to.

"You meant to depose the value of my methods. I am not perfect, Brodie, but my methods are time-tested and they work, and I won't have them mocked by the likes of you."

"I meant no heresy and you know it."

There Beheld an Infinite View

The ducevereë's brow creased, his lips became thin and sickly, and he looked annoyed, so perhaps he found it difficult to lie as he seemed to grudgingly accept. He licked his dry lips.

"Guards!" he shouted, and it was a harsh shout which shot about the cathedral and beyond, dragging guards through every door, no less than two from each.

It was from outside that three guards ran up the nave and stood ready for orders as Lucian protested to Isaac's harmless recklessness, and Marcel waited for some appropriate time to make protest and for the right words to materialise.

"Father!" Tamzin snapped, positively enraged. "The man had a point. Don't punish him for being right."

"Seize him," Laryc said with a nod, ignoring his daughter.

Two men grabbed Isaac's arms, strong of grip and uncaring as to the reason behind the order.

"I should let him go, if I were you," Jamys spoke, startling everyone there. He showed no signs of wanting a fight, though he was no longer quite so casual in his posture. "I can't guarantee Martello will react well to one of his clients being treated so poorly by your thugs."

"Martello would do well to keep his head down when it comes to my business. We are a force to be reckoned with."

"Martello does as he pleases," Jamys said, almost disinterested. "He doesn't take orders from you. The Mercenary's Guild is his, and when it comes down to it, he answers to the King, not you. He has no obligation to protect your preachers on the road other than the money paid to the guild."

"A dog shouldn't threaten the man holding the leash. You're wasting your time anyway," the duceveree replied more peacefully, waving a hand vaguely. "We don't keep prisoners and we don't spill blood within these walls. I'll give the order I would have given regardless."

He clicked finger and thumb, and flicked his head in the direction of the double doors. So, again, he just couldn't resist playing contrarian, Isaac thought and deigned to smile, if hollowly, as he was escorted back down the nave, catching Tamzin's sympathetic expression for a brief moment. Isaac was thrown from the cathedral, stumbling as he went but quickly regaining his balance. Bitterly, he looked about him to see dozens of people had stopped to gawk and mark him for scum, or at the very least, stare intently, curious. He'd been made a fool of for standing up for his brother, and because the duceveree hated being exposed as a fool, and he was the one with the guards.

The gawking stopped as Jamys was seen to be with him, and Isaac felt less humiliated for it. He opened his mouth, ready to question the mercenary who still bore a look of mild amusement. Another's hand upon his shoulder stopped him before he could start. He turned to see Lucian, whose eyes were dark and still processing Isaac's actions.

"For what it's worth, I'm sorry," Isaac said. "For Marcel's sake. Make sure this doesn't reflect badly on him."

"I'll say what needs to be said for him." He shook his head. "You're the last person one would expect to have fragile sensibilities. More's the pity, you had to express them here of all places."

Lucian was displeased, that much was clear, yet he relented from scolding Isaac further for precisely the reason Isaac had felt insulted by Laryc to begin with, and for knowing that he was humiliated anyway. They parted ways so that, now, Isaac called upon the beautiful personality of the city to help him think again. For that, he mellowed out quickly. Already he was growing an attachment to the clean white brick structures, the clean open spaces, and monuments down below and the bell towers above. He tried to focus on his lodging, where he would return to work and forget all about this, but there was something holding him back: one loose end. Jamys said nothing as they walked. It was plain to see this didn't reflect what was going on up in his head.

"That was a bold move you made, Jamys," Isaac noted. "Were you bluffing when you spoke on Martello's behalf?"

"Not in the slightest. Like I said, Martello does what he wants." Jamys shrugged, which he loved more than talking. "I had to do something; I have a reputation too. I will say though, being your companion should be quite something if you're going to carry on like that."

"I'm glad you're enjoying yourself," Isaac said offhandedly. "I surmise you've taken a liking to my work as well."

"We'll see about that. Money is the main motivating factor and always will be. I'm not here for your commentary on mercenaries."

They shared a knowing glance. This amused Isaac. He wondered whether to ask him now what else Martello had told him, or wait until it was completely occupying his mind again. Presumably he knew everything. With that man, one would be hard-pressed to deduce the motivations of any given action. *He does as he pleases, and what pleases him seems to be what he does.*

"Did Martello give you permission to relay my conversation in his office to me?"

"He said nothing neither this way nor that."

"So he told you of it to begin with?"

"What he told me would be consistent with the way you interrogated the duceveree." Jamys tilted his head in Isaac's direction as he swaggered, though his face didn't change beyond the calm pensiveness already present. Perhaps there was a twitch in one eye.

"Martello shouldn't have told you that if he's so disinterested in my proposal."

There Beheld an Infinite View

"He told me because I asked him. Martello doesn't give a shit what you want." The shrug, then a purse of the lips and a squint that passed for a weak protest of innocence. And Isaac was not surprised. "I asked because I was curious. As I say, guarding you will be quite something. No disrespect."

"How do you mean?"

"Your reaction at the beheading, then again in there. It's a good thing I don't care. If you gave some others in my position the opportunity to speak their mind of that, they'd tell you you country people must have gotten soft, and maybe you have but that's none of my concern."

"I see," Isaac said thoughtfully. "Appreciated."

They said nothing more, so, slowly, Isaac's ambitions returned to cheer his spirits and hopefully quash any image of sullenness he may have given off to his guide. When they arrived at the inn, Isaac made to return to his room to recollect his thoughts and decide his next move before boredom could set in, or pining for Caedor could worm its way into him. Scarcely halfway down the corridor, he was halted by Rosalynn's call.

"A moment, young Brodie. A man came for you earlier," she said, amused. "From the Blacksmith's Guild. Something about the inventor Vicentei Laccona. You're scheming something? Ambitious like your father, I hope."

"Scheming away, Madam Rosa. What was the message?"

"They say he's definitely in the city, and working at the Palace of the Sun, because resource records were ordered there with his signature attached. A good place to start, for whatever you're doing."

"Working for my father's ambitions and my own." Isaac gave a pleasant half-smile. "I'll tell you about it one day soon, assuming it doesn't all collapse before my eyes and show me up as a fool. Lucian will tell you if it does, I imagine."

"I won't ask," Rosalynn replied tiredly, then laughed. "I have a hunch that would be a lot of work."

He abandoned his workman's attire in his room for his regalia from Balenhold, pointless as it may have been. Vicentei Laccona, allegedly his father's friend, would not care what he wore or be impressed, he presumed. Isaac wasn't entirely convinced; he just felt it needed to be done, and when he stood before the mirror, resplendent beyond himself in royal blue with such exquisite linings and strong, high boots, he understood why. It felt like a suit of armour to him, though for that he still could not provide an explanation. That it felt right was enough. So then Isaac left again, leaving Rosalynn in a state unknown, as still he didn't know her at all, nor had tried to. He would have to rectify that eventually. For now he headed north, letting Jamys take the lead again. He might need him if Vicentei had turned into a ghost and left the palace again.

The Voice of Kings

It was just so. At the palace gate and in the vicinity thereof, guards, who were exceptionally well-trained not to speak but a word of the goings on within, kept silent at his questions, asking him to leave until one, perchance, per wondrous luck, recognised Jamys as a respectable guild man, and loosened up. Jamys did nothing beyond his spotless reputation speaking for him, whereupon Isaac was able to convince the guards that his intent was good and that he wanted Vicentei for business. Vicentei wasn't there. He'd been seen leaving with equipment, not for good, though they couldn't say for sure, and they laughed at his perky spirit for thinking he could make Vicentei care about any proposition he could make.

"I saw him carry a lectern and paper," that same guard who'd recognised Jamys said. "And other things I didn't care to notice. When he left the gates, he looked out to sea, and there he stood, and I wondered if he was unwell when he became dissatisfied, frustrated you could say, in his way, until he carried on and did the same at the bottom of the hill, at the balcony there. I saw him there before he was escorted to the palace for the first time. He left after that and didn't look back."

The guard laughed and shook his head as if the inventor was, to him, a strange, uncontrollable child, risible only because it wasn't his problem. Isaac and Jamys walked as far as they could in the great courtyard towards the sea, then stopped and leant on a waist-high brick wall, beyond which a very steep hill was covered in grass that led to the beach. From the palace, there was a safe path down to a dock housing three ships as large as any he'd seen, guarded vigilantly and guarded numerously. It was not in his power to visit that place, yet Vicentei surely could have and had passed on the opportunity.

"What would he be looking for out here?" Isaac said to himself, stroking the curved marble finish of the wall. The world came back into perspective and he was enjoying himself again.

"Not ships, apparently. That one at the end, Vyrmahys, has got five or six decks? Fine oak, pine as well I'd guess. And a merloyr finish? It gives the wood that shiny texture, reduces the risk of pitch sticking to it. It's an expensive ship, among the best along this stretch, you'd think. Maybe I'm wrong. Maybe Vicentei just isn't impressed by the best built ships in the King's fleet."

"It's not out of the question," Isaac mused purposefully, grinning at the memory of the mechanical bridge that the inventor had so readily abandoned.

Isaac looked to the horizon, then to his left, the south, and leaned over the wall to take in as much of the view as possible in a feeble attempt to discern where the man might have gone. At his failure, they left, a flash of gold from on high glinting as he span, near overshadowed by the block of white bricks in the centre of the plaza that was no longer surrounded by a crowd. Jamys knew it had distracted Isaac, but whatever he judged of him, he was diplomatic enough to keep it to himself, allowing him to move on with minimal trouble. They went to the balcony at the bottom of Kingsreach, where Vicentei had been that very day, and saw much the same as before, only this time, they also saw fishing boats trundling through the clear water near and far. He could see why the man might not be interested in any of that, even if it provided no clue as to what he'd seek instead.

"We'll keep following the path south, by the sea, as close we can," Isaac announced. "It's the only thing we can do."

"As you say."

They passed by farms and found themselves back in the denser streets once more, though it was not five minutes before Isaac paused to view the sea through an alcove from the streets that opened up through gaps between pillars. Then it was gone again as he carried on, obscured by the next building. Shortly thereafter, the view returned, much clearer now, of everything one could imagine could take place at, and beside, the sea, and it was seen by way of an enclosure for men of import. Again, there were thin pillars at the far end, holding up, for their part, a trellis roof interwoven with vines that enjoyed the sea breeze. In the stone enclosure, these men of import sat at their tables bridged by vast gaps, some leisurely and some discussing business, nodding their heads seriously and passing parchment about, but all impeccably dressed. Like himself.

"I wonder if you might help me," Isaac said loudly to a man by the entrance, the only way of proceeding besides jumping the waist-high wall. One of two men rose for him, and it became evident his job was to guard the way, deceptive as that purpose was as he wore no armour.

"I'll help you as I can."

"I'm looking for someone, an inventor, a friend of a friend. I understand he might be here. He's a private man so he mightn't have mentioned his name as Vicentei."

"Bearded, is he, with brown hair? About your height?"

"I believe so," Isaac answered, based solely on the way he'd imagined the man.

"He's in the alcove at the back, facing the sea. If it's the man you're looking for, he might not like having a visitor. And we're obliged to have you removed if he wishes, I take no pleasure in saying."

"Not a problem. There's no chance of him not being happy to see me."

The man at the entrance waved him through respectfully, though perhaps wouldn't have had he been wearing those smoke-sodden garments from before. The man frowned as Jamys made to follow, but said nothing all the same.

"I'll wait here," Jamys said helpfully, already adjusting to his new position.

The alcove in question was a rectangular alley, enclosed by a short brick wall, and another atop it of crisscrossed wooden planks interwoven with plants like those rustling above. The man at the end of the alcove was only interested in what was out before him. He sat with a lectern resting on the stone wall where the trellis wall stopped, and several random items around it, including a ship replica cut through the middle, and a prism that shone as if he'd captured a rainbow. He threw a blank sheet of parchment over his work and briefly examined Isaac.

"Afternoon Vicentei. You are Vicentei Laccona?"

"I am, but don't let that mean anything to you. If you want something, you had best make it quick. I've nothing against you; I just can't play architect for everyone in the city." He appeared not to be paying attention anyway.

"There's a Watchman on The Wolf's Way who'd like to be relieved of duty so he can go home to his family. I understand he wasn't pleased when you left."

"I see," Vicentei said slowly, laughing awkwardly, turning as he became invested, squinting and scratching his neck.

He was young; younger than his father. Much younger than Isaac had expected. Where was the old man of his imaginings? If he'd been told his age in the past, he'd forgotten it completely or else he would not be so wrong. His short beard was plain dark brown and bristly, lending him a sense of wisdom after all, though his eyes were wild like a child's and his hair as unkempt as Kester's often appeared, though Kester's was messy by nature and Vicentei's was ruined only by the wind, as it looked as if it had just been washed.

"Sorry, who are you?" Vicentei asked, stroking with two fingers the skin above his upper lip where there was no hair.

"Isaac, son of Lennord Brodie, hailing from Caedor."

"Lennord the cobbler, yes? Good man."

"Lennord the inventor, who lives a peaceful life in Caedor most of the time, except when he's called to Aurail, as he has been of late, and so he works there now for the Emperor. My father and you write to one another, swapping ideas, his less crazy than yours apparently."

The young inventor grinned slyly and waved a finger at Isaac, and Isaac scoffed in pleasant amusement, as he was surely confessing that he'd known the truth, yet for some reason felt the need to test his validity.

"Caedor. Yes, I was thinking you hailed from the highlands. You have a bit of a burr in your voice that gave it away. I should have known you weren't just anyone. And The Wolf's Way, you say?" Vicentei laughed and shook his head. "I already sent an envoy to disband that assembly at the bridge. It can serve its purpose as just a bridge until I, or someone else, can be bothered to finish it. I'm guessing few will try though."

"For good reason."

"That may be true. When an envoy of the King's arrives to tell you you're needed at court, however, you don't disobey. It was rude to slip away in the night, but imperative to my sanity. Gods know how many angry letters I'd be receiving now if I'd told them where I was going. Now, you didn't want just that of me."

"No, but I knew it would get your attention."

There Beheld an Infinite View

"So you have it." Vicentei stroked his scrap of skin beneath his nose again, and his boyish eyes became very still and hard. "Wise of you, considering the rumours surrounding me. Those may be true as well. The masses have the general impression that I wouldn't know if the southern half of Harth were burning if it didn't affect me. Perhaps I should afford the masses more credit, but hey-ho. Never mind about any of that though. You're still standing. Sit."

Isaac pulled up a chair beside the inventor, dressed also in plain clothing, that one might not recognise him for what he truly was, in linens and a dark blue cloak over a thin body. He looked out to sea again as Isaac was making himself comfortable, taking in every detail at an astonishing rate, or so he gave the impression of, such that he began to look deeper still, leaning in and bearing a heavy frown as if it was, all of it, just not good enough for him.

"Did your father send you here?" Vicentei said soon enough, turning on Isaac again. "Is he in the city?"

"My father's bidding is one reason I'm in the city. He's not here, unfortunately. I'm sure he would have liked to meet you again. I believe your advice was useful to improving livelihoods in Caedor."

"There is no *again*, as such," Vicentei replied at once. "I tend to attract misconceptions like flies to honey, but of course I've never heard that one."

"You didn't meet my father when he was in Harth?"

"Not when I knew who he was, or him I. That knowledge came later, when I was too busy to see him personally. I regretted that, but I sent him a letter and he was kind enough to send one back, which I'm still grateful for. It always pays to have a different perspective, and he's a cut above the rest, your father. I know what he did to your town."

"I'll tell him you said so."

The young inventor snorted, but a half-smile rose, unable to show humility without pride. When, now, Isaac could think of little else to say, he broke eye contact and stared into the waves, which still were fascinating in their majesty that repeated over and over for infinity. There was his own business to discuss of course, but now that he was here, he felt it was too soon. Vicentei would not believe him, and think him ungracious to ask so much of him.

"What brought you here?" Isaac asked to fill the void. "To this spot?"

"Everything you can see," Vicentei said enthusiastically, extending a hand to the world beyond Harth: the world beyond the world. "The boat constructions, military to our right, trade ships to the left, and then further down in the distance there are more carracks, frigates, so on and so forth. The men working on the docks and bartering on the beach, men from here, and the north. There are the lighthouses too, the prison island to the far north and, lest we forget, Nel, our lady of fortune."

The Voice of Kings

The statue of Nel was upon the beach itself, as tall as Sir Martin's timeless memory imprinted on his hill, of marble that glistened in the sun in different places at every shift of Isaac's head. Her hands were wide open to the sea, blessing all those who sailed out there, her stone cloak frozen in motion. When the tide came in at dusk, the waves would crash against it, and yet she would never lower her hands for the likes of the sea.

"Simply, I wish to be inspired, so here I am. Perhaps I'm secretly praying for something to go wrong so I can make sure it doesn't happen again. It's an inspiring view by itself though."

"An infinite view then."

"Just so!" Vicentei clasped his fingers together and rested them beneath his nose. "So, about your request. I'm not gregarious or possessive of much social insight, and yet... I sense it's not a minor favour you'd ask of me."

"It's not."

"Then it's already more attractive a prospect than most people would ask of me. The more impossible, the better. Fixing stables and houses is dull indeed."

Isaac hesitated. It was not Vicentei's manner that had him balking, as his enthusiasm had warmth, if only because of the circumstances, but this was a genius his father praised above himself. Of course he did; he praised many people above himself that didn't deserve it. Vicentei's reputation was hard to ignore, however, and he feared for what the great genius would say.

"Impossible is how you might describe it," Isaac started cheerfully. "I come for your advice. You were on a shortlist of advisors ever since I left home. When I was young, you see, at only seven, I dared to put my nose into my father's business: his mine in the hillside. It was rife with Sèhvorian ore and the like, as you probably know. In the depths, there was a wall of steel, ready-formed, that revealed itself to me; a rock wall crumbled so it could show itself, or so it seemed at the time. If I said it was coincidence, it would still not be the half of it. And it wasn't just a sheet of steel; it had carvings of creatures in it, and within an arch, I saw a texture that I'd never seen before. It looked like... water and silk."

"Wait," Vicentei said seriously, grabbing a quill of his own making, encased in smoothed wood for comfort.

He used instruments of his own to draw on the blank parchment: a length of pine and a semi-circular device of the same material. Within it was a smaller device of the same shape that could be extended or retracted to change the size of the semi-circle. And draw he did, until the arch was all but completed; all but the images between the two semi-circular line carvings.

"Creatures?" Vicentei asked haughtily when Isaac mentioned them, frowning heavily.

"Griffins, tigers, chupacabras, drakeels, serpents, eagles. There were more I can't recall, though more there surely were." Demons, Isaac thought to himself, refraining from adding a detail that was nothing more than an invention, even to him. It sounded ludicrous enough already.

Vicentei scrawled the names of the animals in tiny handwriting, adding question marks enthusiastically beneath them.

"In what order?" Vicentei said, astoundingly focused and free of judgment.

"What? No idea. That part was less clear to me on the whole. I know there was a unicorn to the right of the serpent, at the top of the ring of images; that, I've never forgotten, though I couldn't say why." Isaac shook his head and laughed cynically at himself while Vicentei scribbled on his parchment again. "It gets stranger from then on. A skeleton fell through the veil, though it neither shattered nor tore, only warped like ink. The skeleton was tall, even for myself as a child when all adults are tall: eight feet, maybe more. And I saw on the skeleton queer things: extra bones, some that were twisted or broken, and I remember thinking it looked very thin and gaunt a figure. Then I smelled something foul and pungent, and I ran, and then came what was reported by others: the flames that filled the cave. They were black at the tip, that you can ask others of, for it was seen by many, and crops far across the fields withered before the fire even spread. When I returned later, the metal had melted and the skeleton burned into nothing."

"I assumed it would end that way." Vicentei's wide eyes narrowed and he seemed to take sadistic glee in the impossibility of it all. "I'd heard of that incident, as it happens. Your father spoke of it in his letters as well, some years ago. You held onto the fire all this time?" Vicentei exclaimed.

"On and off." Vicentei seemed to approve of that answer.

"Before we go on, I must ask of you one question: a contention to be settled. This is all the truth, yes? No tricks, no hyperbole, just all the truth you know?"

"I swear it."

The inventor glared into his soul, unflinching as he was, free of whatever social normalities were needed to make him feel uncomfortable. He stroked his beard and showed a devilish grin.

"Good," Vicentei breathed in satisfaction. "That makes things complicated, but we'll see what we can do. The man you saw might have been a mutant, nothing intrinsically peculiar there with regards to explaining it. The unsavoury act of incest tends to bring about such irregularities, I find. As for the rest, the crown court uses chemicals to alter the colour of fire, but never so localised. A forge can make fire hot, but never so widespread."

"Or so hot, for that matter. I know what I saw there, because others saw it too."

"That's what I heard. A fire that can set the air alight..." Vicentei mused, looking out into the endless void of water. "I will have to consult a scholar of history to learn of who might make such a mechanism as this. It's eluded me all my life, largely. Have you considered that it was magic?"

"Not for a long time," Isaac answered sincerely. "Not for any protracted period."

"I'm sure others believe it. That's a good excuse not to investigate. Or maybe it's true. Can a griffin fly do you think?"

"What?" Isaac replied, confused.

"Can griffins fly?"

"I don't know. I shouldn't think so."

"Of course they can't! They're far too heavy and their bodies are too big compared to their wings. Yet they have wings, so surely they did once, when gods roamed Mura, yes? Well, that may be true as well. Maybe Mürathneèan eagles grew as large as horses in that old age too, as priests and the like will tell you."

"Why are you telling me this?" Isaac said blankly.

"Because I want you to understand my thought process. What you're asking of me is madness, so I'd like to make it clear that I am sane, even as I humour you and help you, insofar as that's possible. I've never denied the gods, only acts of theirs I do not see for myself, which is all of them thus far. Anything subtle or mysterious enough to be passed off as magic is intriguing in my book, and if the gods want to intervene and use real magic, they're very welcome to. Perhaps that would make my job easier. Perhaps I'd cease to be a vagabond."

He laughed at himself, then looked back to the drawing on the parchment, and he was serious again. It challenged him.

"You know what you saw then?" Vicentei asked calmly.

"Absolutely."

"Then I believe you saw it also. As I'm sure you've been told many times," Vicentei interjected pre-emptively, thrusting a hand up. "All I'm saying is, I'm keeping an open mind. I'm promising to help, and that's more than I'd do for most anyone. I can't guarantee more than that. But eagles as big as horses? There's no evidence for that. There is a precious amount of it here."

Vicentei stood, as if to show Isaac out, only to pay attention to the beach scene again. Isaac stood also, hoping to end the conversation before the promise could be retracted. Then again, he'd made a promise also.

"There's one more thing," Isaac explained. "My father needs Sèhvorian steel and crystals at Castle Aurail. Can you get me in contact with anyone?"

"I'll do better than that; I'll have it delivered there for you. Will a fifth tonne shipment be sufficient?"

"If you can get me that for a down payment of 400 Burtalian florins."

"That can be arranged. I can make people listen."

416

There Beheld an Infinite View

The shrewd inventor stuck out an arm for Isaac, and he shook it. His grip was stronger and more accommodating than expected, and he didn't let go for some time as he pondered on his next move.

"For the friend who never was a friend," Vicentei said with a sly smile. "You're a good man Isaac, and you remind me of myself, so I'm fond of you already."

"Or I remind you of my father," Isaac suggested.

"Whatever you say. I'll contact you when I'm ready. Where are you staying?"

Isaac told him, and they shook hands again. He asked for the King's approval, and Vicentei promised he'd ask of that too, *promised it*. Then the inventor sat down to tend to his work, so focused Isaac might never have been there.

Isaac felt good. One powerful enemy in exchange for one powerful friend. A fair trade.

Chapter Twenty-five: Dream Towers

From the moment the arrow smashed the knight of Melphor's chest, she could no longer keep her feet on the ground. He fell and she flew, the men whose faces she could never see hacking at his paralysed body, hauling him to his feet only to split his skin apart with their swords, splattering their twisted art on the dirt all about. All the while she was sucked into the sky until the world left her, where sound and feeling were paintings on the void.

That was Kate's dream that she now relived on the Godstone Highroad, with weary waking eyes. Sir Edwin died and, hencewith, summer shut itself away for Kate. Now the darkness came, oh how it came, accompanied by a dread chill. Before the cliffs rose up either side to draw her into the pass, she thought she saw a snow-capped mountain to the far south: a shadow figure in fog and cloud, winter incarnate. That had been hours ago, she guessed, not that she was fair of judgement, though now she was well in the confines of the steep pass, pressing her face into the mane of her mare. Henri, Henri Fealds as she now knew him, was there as protection, but he offered nothing for morale. He was large, hairy, and unaffectionate, and spoke little to her. It must have been her mother's command, for she spoke to him often, whereupon Henri strained to be very serious and appeared out of his depth, and for that service, she loved her more than ever, as she had no wish to have him as a distraction. Kate had nothing to offer in return and the guilt panged like razor wire in her heart. Her mother was undeniably weary as well, and was keeping everything together, erring on the side of fragility only once in a while when her emotions were too powerful to be contained, when she was very fragile indeed.

"Have you ever travelled this road before?" her mother asked suddenly.

"Not this one," Henri answered, as if her mother might have meant something else. His leather creaked, like a broken fence in the wind to her, and his mail rattled against the leather. "I served with sword and spear in many fiefs, Melphor's vicinity not among them."

"So you don't know if there's an escape from this ravine?" Kate asked bitterly.

"There's no escape on the map," her mother reiterated in the man's silence, though her uncertainty was surely why she asked Henri in the first place. "Don't worry about that. Hell, we'll sing our way out of a confrontation if we have to, because failure isn't an option. You have your father's smarts Kathrynne, which is more than one can say for most people. All your brothers have your father's smarts," she added with a pale smile.

"I have a sword I can't use, so my father's smarts had better do me the favour of carrying me to safety. Gods know I won't draw it before one's drawn on me. The game would be done with then."

"So you're smart enough to know that a soldier would know your sword's just decoration when they see you holding it. Leave it alone and you're a mystery. Leave it to you to acknowledge your intelligence and make it sound like a bad thing."

That was likely true. Her mother was often true in her assumptions, but this time it changed nothing. What good was intelligence when beaten to submission by brute force? *Does intelligence save a friend, riding in the wilderness alone, from a butcher's blade?* Evidently not, or else she was not smart enough anyway. Kate stared ahead, ridden with a cold despair, a dull blade on a numb wound. The walls of the pass were dark like charcoal, even in sunlight, and streaked with veins of red, stark like lightning.

"None of this changes the fact that we're going the wrong way," Kate said.

"No, it doesn't. On the other hand, we're not hiding from the world. Melphor isn't a dead end for opportunities."

"I know," Kate agreed. She'd already known. "I'm sorry."

"No!" her mother snapped sharply. "Don't be sorry about any of this, not ever. Evil men are evil of their own accord. How do good people like you or me factor into any of that?"

For that there was no answer. In a way, she wished there was. It made sense to feel guilty. For that there was no answer.

"Melphor is a good place for us," Henri said, probably out of mounting anguish and embarrassment of having to listen to two strangers talk as such. "Letters sent to Caedor by eagle go there first, and then there's Andrews. I know your mother wants to speak with him. We'll do that," Henri finished uneasily, rolling his shoulders.

"We?"

"Henri and I, and you if I think it helps," Mother said.

"That's what I thought."

Kate was not bitter or judgemental in that, rather she was relieved to be told she might not be needed: a stupid, childish reflex of hers, to leave serious talk to others out of earshot, and because she couldn't hear anything but her thoughts, all she had to do was wait for the news of triumph or settlement, and progress would be made because she wasn't there to witness the process by which the world worked. Oh what a craven she willed herself to be.

Moreover, there was no trusting Henri without him explicitly doing something admirable for the sake of the Brodies. He was a stranger, and a stranger who'd too readily agreed to come to their aid. He was more a child, riding with a hand on his hip, or sometimes his sword hilt, a look of mock sincerity and graveness upon his face, like a boy mimicking a soldier, and he was always conscious to be casual and overly attentive during conversations, as if indulging the fantasy of being in command. The only consolation was her mother's conditional trust. On the night of their meeting at an inn, she had asked many questions

The Voice of Kings

Kate could no longer recall, persistent beyond her own comfort zone that, at times, she paused, a pause meant for the input of Kate's father, or maybe she was imagining things.

"How do you know he won't put us in more danger?" Kate had asked.

"He's too desperate to prove himself to abandon us, too straightforward to betray us."

Did she claim to know what went on in his head though? Who could say if he'd be tempted to lie if the hint of a pay her family couldn't match was on the table, explicit or otherwise?

She almost drifted off to sleep during the ride, when her thoughts became too complicated, bogged like the stained dress she'd shredded and disposed of. When the scenery changed, there was no reaction she could give, for her mind did not catch up with her eyes at first, and when it did, she was halfway down the road of Melphor's lower level and she was struck speechless. The walls of the pass had not left; they guarded the city in a circular arena large enough to fit all the houses in Caedor at the ground level alone, and the same thrice again at the city proper, propped up on the cliff side. To say it was one cliff might be a falsehood; it was more like five cliffs, a giant's stairs, and occupying roughly half of it was the city. It was not on the stairs, but rather it looked as if the land had been carved, and curved, and moved to allow one to walk higher up the city. If that was possible, she didn't know how, and if it wasn't, then what a miracle it must have been, with Paryn's enchantments to thank.

It was just as Edwin had described it: dark and chillingly pretty, of rough brown rock that, from this distance, was to her like tree bark. The towers were menacing and numerous, very uniform and exact in their proportions to one another, all of them square at the tip, none remotely cylindrical. Tall and thin they were, and dotted all about the city at various levels. Henri tugged tightly at his reins and craned up to take it in, grimacing for no discernible reason.

"The Giant's Stairs: it's called that for a reason then," he said.

She winced. She'd not been so creative after all. The mind had a way of becoming muddled under such duress as this and would fool itself if it meant making itself feel anything other than pain.

"Stay close," her mother said, reaching over and gripping her arm momentarily.

This was because they were nearing the base of the cliff. The waterfall flowing from a crack in the cliff plummeted down to somewhere in the city and it was more audible now, made more so every time the wind picked up and gushed past her ears. Where had Edwin lived then? The thought was a shocking one, as it had never been considered by her till now. Was it Maelphorydd, which stood not on the cliff itself but at the highest point of the city nonetheless, as far left as it went? Would she visit if she found out for sure?

Beyond a row of villas at the city's base, a path crawled up, this way and that to the great wooden doors, again just as Sir Edwin had said. The place was strongly guarded and they were given apprehensive looks, but were not stopped, and Kate kept her head down at any rate. Once inside, they paid to have their horses tended at a stable and headed up a random street, cobbled and rough. This one, as the others were, was narrow and steep, and though the sun bore down on them, the placing of the architecture meant there were shadows everywhere, and because of that, flames flickered inside lanterns upon iron poles.

They checked in at the nearest inn: dark brick on the outside and yet supported by many wooden beams inside. The ceiling was lower than most inns and that made her long for the country, yet thankfully in her room, she felt at home, or as much as she could be while her brothers and father were hundreds of miles away and of unknown vitality. She and her mother sat by the window, of murky, warped glass, while Henri sat opposite, staring at the ceiling and twiddling a coin.

"We should decide how we're going to do this," her mother said, peering out of the window more closely, up at the city. "Where do you suppose the eagles roost? I saw some birds landing near the top of the city when we arrived. Maelphorydd?"

Kate paid more attention too and saw the silhouette of a hawk circling above; she recognised it at once.

"I saw eagles there too. They were eagles," Kate said assuredly.

Her mother nodded. She was quite pale from lack of sleep, her beautiful hair a mess, and her thin lips pronounced and dry, making her appear ill. Kate only assumed she looked much the same as she'd inherited the same hair, albeit fairer, and she'd been given those same thin lips. Henri flipped the coin, saw he was a nuisance and slammed it down on a chest of drawers.

"You might think about scouting the city before you do anything rash," he said. "Do we know where the gaolhouse is? If that Watch captain's imprisoned there, I wouldn't want to go near it."

"I won't go asking questions where I can help it," Mother rebuked.

"If you go to the Count, the Watch might know soon enough anyway."

"Only if he doesn't believe me, and if he doesn't, there's no guarantee he'll set the City Watch on me. The City Watch, not the Patrol Rangers, because my eldest son has said, more than once, that the Patrol has no business here. They're not welcome to it at all, in fact. That's why we're here. You think I'd drag my daughter into a hornet's nest on a whim?"

"Oh, I understand. I just gave an alternative. You didn't care for it; doesn't bother me."

Kate's mother peered out at the goings on of the city again, taking note of the Watchmen that marched past despite her rebuke. Then she looked up at the Count's hall on high and came to a decision.

"I shouldn't stay here," Kate said quickly.

"Why not?" her mother exclaimed, surprised.

The Voice of Kings

"No, I mean, I need something to do. I'll go mad in here."

Her mother was stern and she grimaced at the duality of the situation, so there was no mistaking her understanding. The grimace remained for a while, bound of sympathy.

"I know the feeling. I know it well because I have it too, but let's not do anything we might regret now. I think... stay close," she conceded. "And keep both eyes out for trouble. If it brews, if it forecasts in the slightest, we abandon the whole thing and we start over, as many times as we have to, until we can avoid it or it isn't possible."

Kate looked out to where her mother's eyes were fixed, here, there, all about. She wondered if the layout of the city had changed her mind. There were many side alleys and interweaving streets, almost like a maze if one were not to pay attention. Escaping suspicion, or otherwise the unthinkable, might be easily plausible.

The winding streets, dark here, light there, and often very steep, made it more ominous than it probably was. No one gave them a second glance, not even to Henri, as there was nothing special about him, nothing to suggest he wasn't a standard mercenary and, in a way, they were correct to assume that. She just kept her head down and merged into the crowds, became a grouse in snow.

Whence an eagle took to flight she finally gazed, having avoided extended eye contact with anything before then. The heights of Melphor echoed a call for her, and not without precedent. If only things weren't so bleak. *Oh well*, she thought, *there are worse places to be*, to weep, and pray, and think, and all the other things she should probably be doing. It was no Caedor, yet all the same, everything seemed simpler when considered from above. They didn't stop to be pensive though, only to be appraised at the small round plaza before the wide steps to the main plaza and the grand hall. There were an unseemly amount of guards in sight, no chances taken, as no one would dare take them on, would they? Their job was one of prevention rather than cure then, insofar as that made sense to men with swords.

"I don't think so, do you?" one said casually, stepping forward. He tugged at his cloak, a thick green rugged thing pinned to his armour: plates and mail that bore the simple falcon motif. He nodded at Henri when he received no answer. "You're not going up there with that sword unless you've got a sealed mark of consent, or if you can get someone in Maelphorydd to vouch for you. No master-less men, not with that decoration anyway."

Henri shifted uncomfortably on the spot, pressed his tongue to his cheek and looked at Kate and her mother. Kate held her breath, praying he wouldn't mess up.

"My masters are here," Henri said slowly.

"You're still a mercenary," one of the guard's companions put in from a little way back.

"This is moot," Kate's mother said. "I don't need armed escort to ascend these steps. I'll go on alone, and I'd like you, Henri, to take her somewhere you won't disturb the Watchmen in their duty, if you please."

She avoided referring to Kate by her name, she noticed. *Probably not something I'd heed until after I'd made the mistake*, Kate mused. At the best of times.

"I hope you've got a sealed letter for your behalf," the first guard said again, already resuming his previous guard post. "Good luck getting an audience with anyone in there if not."

"I'll keep a watch from some place high," Kate said when her mother made it clear she wasn't going to speak with the Watchman any longer than necessary.

It came back to the waterfall, her options did then, after her mother left. It was the perfect backdrop in her imagination, and indeed, it was the case after she'd navigated the rocky streets with mixed success and came up a narrow flight of stairs to meet the spray from the immense jet of water pounding down. The spray was stronger than she'd expected, even as it tumbled not directly into an open river but into a pit, and thus went some way below before meeting its target. From there it was carried down at great speed beyond the walls of the pit and split off into two directions: left into a dark cave and straight on into the city. Kate left it to its endless cycle, a droning roar that somehow gave her the peace she needed as she leaned, arms crossed, on a wall and looked out on the beautiful mess that was Melphor. It was high, and it was low, and everything in between, made mostly of that dark brick, yet some of it was pure black, and some a dusty reddish colour as her father had described of Aurail, and the majority of it was roofed in thatch. Just as Sir Edwin had said, she made herself remember despite its lack of any real meaning.

"Are you just going to stand there?" Kate said irritably when she noticed Henri. He was ill of her company as she was of his, and he bore a grimace of intense embarrassment, as if her mother had assigned him as a wet nurse.

"I should," was all he could say at first. "I'm here with you because I was told to be. I can't help it if that doesn't suit your preference. You know you've come to a dangerous place; it goes without saying you need an escort."

"You don't have to be so..." so *annoying* about it, she finished to herself.

He was annoying, unbearably so, though why she couldn't put her finger on. She hated that: the inability to answer and the fact that she found him perplexing at all. And she hated herself for that too. In the interests of retaining her sanity, she gazed for a plaintive meditation out to her right, between two of those tall thin towers and along that pass that would take one north. To some harbour or other? On the road, her mother had outlined a final plan, failing this, to head for the sea and see if they couldn't get to County Capital unseen by wrathful eyes.

"Are you looking for something of Edwin's?" Henri asked. This wasn't going to work. She wanted peace and he screamed out for conversation.

"Sir Edwin," Kate corrected.

"Are you looking for something of Sir Edwin's? His house, his hall? It's what I'd do if he were my master. A man honours his master after his death, if he has honour himself that is. His hall's as good a place as any. His birthplace, too. That's what people say they do."

"He wasn't my master. Why do you even care?"

"Because I should."

"No," Kate snapped back, utterly appalled. "You want to pretend to be affected by his death because you think that's what your job should be? That's insulting. Speak up if you have something to contribute, otherwise keep to yourself. Please."

That came off as a desperate plea more than intended. She couldn't help it. Perhaps she hadn't changed as much as she'd thought. Her eyes throbbed, so she swiftly turned away lest he see any tears that might roll through them. What an odd notion it was, she contemplated, to defend the honour of a man, a knight no less, who she'd known for so little time. It didn't seem so short; it seemed like she was making more progress in that time than she had over several years. When he'd been on the cusp of life and death, she'd felt like the master, then he awoke only to gently make her drop the reins, and that was all very well too. He'd been a dose of magic back then.

Knotted of stomach and throat, she couldn't help but relate things around her to the past few days. A man of short, ginger hair passed some way off, who to her could only be Olswalt. He passed from sight, and she wished she could say the same of the images of Oswalt that she had in her mind, but he was still there. She squinted and stood on one foot to lean forward over the wall as the man reappeared, escorted by four armoured men as before. The man, dressed in little more than rags, slinking through the streets, turned about this way and that. A mark on his head, a scar: identity pinned atop him for the world to recognise him. It was like polished steel in the sun for all it stood out, and it struck her like lightning. It almost seemed the case as her heart stopped and was constricted by her ribs. He was gone again, lost in the tight roads of Melphor behind a mass of buildings, while she could only stand there wide-eyed, wondering if she'd imagined the whole thing.

"You saw him, didn't you?" Kate asked urgently when her breath came back to her in a powerful rush, and she pivoted to face her protector.

"Saw who?"

Kate bit her lip and ran, for there was no time to lose. Not time enough to explain to Henri? Probably, but she'd rather not have to. At the stairs, she tugged up at her kirtle with one hand to bless her legs with room to move, and raced down with Henri calling desperately for answers as he kept pace. If only she could give answers. That wasn't going to happen because she didn't know what she was doing. The city was a blur when she sprinted through it, dodging men and women who appeared jaded by her apparent enthusiasm, jaded for her and only her: everything centred on her. Then she stopped at a crossroads to decide on the next course, and to glance back at the waterfall to gather her bearings, and everything slowed down around her as she panicked, feeling the fool she was, asking herself over and over again what she would even do if she ran into those five men.

There came a point, in a wide road where the tall buildings were sparse and the road uneven, that she knew was where Elias had been. Indeed he must have been, for the five men were further down below, at about the halfway point of the city in lateral terms, just standing at the edge of what one might loosely refer to as a square, with Elias in the middle surrounded by a cage of soldiers. Kate was on the long, curved road leading down, having bypassed the stairs that would have brought her far too close, and then she was there, at the other end of the square, peering out from behind a building at the edge. She was just there. It occurred to Kate that she must have ran, and very fast for she was hard of breathing, yet it was all a blur and she was focused on the five men, heart in her throat. There was a clear view of them, seeing as there were few people here, and to her dismay, she'd been very much correct.

Arriving a few moments later, Henri used the same caution, begrudgingly so. To him, she must have been such a nuisance. She could smell his breath over her shoulder, neither rancid nor clean, but certainly not pleasant by any stretch of the imagination. The breathing stopped. He spluttered as he transitioned from an angry scolding that never really materialised to an exclamation of pure shock.

"Is that who I think it is?"

"Him," Kate confirmed, so quiet between gritted teeth it was a wonder he heard her.

"We should go," Henri urged, putting a hand on her shoulder.

"Wait!" Kate snapped back in a shriek, and shook his hand away for her nerves were as weak as old burlap and string, and grated just as much, only these were under her skin, clawing at her bones.

Three men ascended from a wide and winding path of far more even quality and with great purpose in their stride. She could only assume they were here to speak with Elias, an observation that was, however, based mostly on their startling appearance. They were men of the far south, of Mūrac or Carlophinia they must have been. Men of dark skin were well known to Kate amongst the wealth of information her father had treated her to, and people with dark complexions lived in Caedor, for just south of the mountains the climate changed drastically, but she'd never actually seen a Mūraci. The men had skin near as dark as night, not far off black, and for that reason, they were automatically the products of her undivided attention.

The man at the fore, in particular, was overly dressed, swathed in a thick, long woollen coat, thicker than necessary for this weather, and beneath that there were glimpses of his own garb, sleek silk dress robes coloured in gold and black. When her eyes came upon his hard face, his shiny bald head, and his unflinching eyes like stone globes where light would think twice to go, she choked on her heart all over again. It was the schemer Haarjo, none other, she would bet on it. The spy and the turncoat come together to make each the other fouler still.

In her unrest, already perpetuated by a meek hunch she'd not previously been aware of, she sank to the ground, to one knee, feeling safer already if that was much to say. Her fingers ran across the cold cobblestones, collecting dirt from only the lightest of touches, running over pebbles and leaves until they found something larger made of hardened clay or brick: a small piece of a building nearby perhaps. The rock felt cold in her hands, gnarly, jagged, especially so as her flesh tightened around it, that it might have bled her dry if she'd wanted it to. Perhaps she was in fact bleeding; she didn't feel well enough to be the judge. There was only power she took from it, as it could unquestionably do damage to a man. She trembled from rage and, besides that, it was all she could do to hold back tears.

Elias was in conversation with the foreigner now, having been allowed through the wall of soldiers, although it was a conversation none too pleasant. There was no violence, and spoken words were veiled from here, but she felt tension on the wind.

"When that happens, I will not be there for it to happen," she heard the spy say smoothly with a thick accent that, nonetheless, was easy to interpret. His words slithered out, soft and stingy, about as trustworthy as a rabid snake. "When it happens, if it does, it will happen too late, so it won't happen at all, do you see? I'm a busy man."

The wind caught the following words and tossed them aside, as it did for Elias.

"This shouldn't take long," was all she heard of the man, growling his discontent and shaking his head violently. He made to step forward but backed off hesitantly, presumably hearing his escorts reaching for weapons behind him.

"You have men to vouch for you, you say," the spy responded to words unheard. "How is that enough if the evidence of a crime is written all around the criminal? I haven't any time to see if things go this way or another way."

Some more tense debate ensued, and the bald spy looked up at the sky, bitterly irritated. He said one last sentence and was off with his two men the way they'd come, pulling his thick cloak tightly in around him as a heavy pendant, of some dark yet reflective material encrusted with jewels, jangled around his neck with each step.

Elias, meanwhile, was potentially angrier than his verbal sparring partner: an attitude which was not sought to be quelled by his escorts. As he walked away to the path he'd come, one soldier grabbed him by the scruff of the neck and threw him into the midst of them. Elias shrugged off the attack and put his hands up, again bereft of a positive response. They left in the soldiers' time, not the shamed captain's.

The rock fell from Kate's hand and her heart fell with it. She stared at it, melancholy for reasons she couldn't hope to penetrate. Not in an hour would she have thrown it, not if Elias was alone and the gods guided her aim. The thought made her sick to the stomach. And for whatever ills could be labelled to his name, he couldn't have killed Edwin, and one would have a battle trying to find out who did from him, as he was surely implicated in other ways. Haarjo flickered back into the mind's eye. He might have been that rider who'd sent a deathly chill down her spine, ruthless and dark against the sky. Thinking back on it was a strange affair. She could have sworn to knowing he was a leader, but on reflection couldn't find why.

"Kathrynne," Henri said stiffly, obsessively checking the tightness of his armour straps. "We should go back before you do something you'll regret."

"I don't know if I'll regret it until I've done it," Kate said distantly, staring at the place Elias had been.

Her heart was thumping in her chest, so maybe that was her body's way of warning her that she would, yet there was reason to be confident. Elias's escorts were surely gaolers, not personal guards, as they'd shown neither love nor any desire to respect his rank, which in brighter circumstances for him might result in vengeance laid upon them. He was a pathetic creature and, for now at least, he was alone. She dashed up the stairs where he'd travelled, steep like everything here, and stood watching them walk away. Henri came to dissuade her from whatever she intended to do, which only made her heart beat faster. She breathed deeply.

"Captain!" she yelled, forcing her back into an erect posture. "Olswalt!"

The five men came to an abrupt halt and made sharp about-turns. When Olswalt seemed not to recognise her, she took the plunge and gingerly stepped forward a few paces. The hardest part was keeping her head up, for she feared his fury when he inevitably recognised her. He looked ill and lank, not as scrawny as Edwin had been at his worst, but more frightening, his face besmirched with dirt that was almost a part of his skin, his left hand still bandaged and causing him pain at every twitch. The recognition came like a flood, volatile and alarming. If there was a consolation, of which there could be only one, it was his shock at her being here at all.

"You conspired with Edwin Meri, girl. You tied me up after he ruined my hand because you wanted a way to implicate me and save his treachery."

"Conspired nothing!" Kate blurted angrily.

"His prick must have meant a lot to you."

Henri clamped a large hairy hand on her shoulder. The captain had no honour, no regret after all that he'd said before.

"Bastard!" she cried, for she could think of nothing else.

The initial confidence had faded and a haze clouded her panicked mind. She knew one thing though, and that was that she had to defend the truth however she could before these gaolers. One, who she assumed was the leader by way of how he'd coordinated the party's journey and by his controlled composure, raised his eyebrows at Elias, quietly amused.

The Voice of Kings

"Sir Edwin was trying to put a *stop* to *your* treachery," Kate said hurriedly. "To stop you conspiring with Haarjo Farelli for... for... magic rituals."

"The diplomat?" the lead gaoler asked in a tone suggesting he'd heard the allegation a thousand times, though he frowned.

"My dealings with him were well within the law and definitely didn't involve rituals, despite what insane ideas you or anyone else may harbour," Elias protested. "To arrest him you'd need actual evidence."

Elias gave the gaoler a scathing look, but the gaoler just laughed. Kate tried to use that time to compose herself. Caedor. The river. The water. The calm. It yielded not the insight she'd hoped. Why would the gaoler not be more surprised at her accusation, for one? If Elias's sergeant had told the gaoler of it, as a theory, he must have known of it to start with, for her mother had said nothing of the sort to him. He could just be that kind of man, Kate told herself of the lead gaoler; he wouldn't impart his feelings to her, much less so if he thought she was just a stupid girl. It was probable, and thus sickeningly unjust, that of now, Elias was on trial only for corruption and assault on a knight, not outright treachery or murder.

"Who killed Sir Edwin?" Kate said suddenly, not meaning to. Her reluctance to speak of her previous thoughts forced her to press on out of panic.

"Brigands apparently."

"Who really killed him? You know, I know you know."

"Prove it."

"You had a reason to fear him, that's why! He could have exposed your operations and you clearly hated him as no one else would."

"That's not proof, girl."

"Ask Patric Denkyn what happened in Caedor. Ask anyone in Caedor who saw anything of you or Sir Edwin. You know what you've done!" Kate cried in desperation.

"I know what I've done," Elias agreed. "Though if I had anything to do with his death, why would you think I'd say it in front of these men?"

"Your family?" Kate said, surprising herself with the razor sharp tone of her words and the biting sarcasm. "You do everything for them, don't you? You'd always be honest with them?"

That got to Elias, and not just because she'd hit a nerve, but because it had been her, a nobody so far as he was concerned, insulting his honour. When he stepped forward by instinct to reprimand her, his four captors went for their swords; all but the leader who flicked a shiny spiked mace, that was sheathed through three metal rings, forward at the head. He grabbed the haft, calmly eager to bludgeon the disgraced captain. It was excessively clean, though scratched, as his armour was: a blank suit bearing no sigils or motifs.

"Not a good idea, Captain," he said.

Elias grudgingly reconsidered, flashing the man another look before returning his full and uncompromising attention to Kate.

"You're very clever," Elias said, staring intently. "Very clever. When you grow into a woman, that is to say, when you've stopped fawning after men and actually marry, will you have the same innocent opinions do you think? When you have six children screaming for attention, when your husband is away bringing the gold to the table and you're sitting about staring at the same hill, won't you feel cheated of your cleverness? When, one day, an opportunity comes to make use of that cleverness, will you take a chance or will you let your family down like so many times before?"

"Is this a confession?" the lead gaoler, with malice, interjected.

"I'm tutoring the young woman about life."

So he was, and he was being very clever too. There were too halves to his speech: one for Kate and one for the others. It was a confession of sorts, and worse yet, he was not only trying to justify everything he'd done, but encourage Kate to follow in his footsteps.

"You're doing a poor job of it," the lead gaoler said snidely.

"I am a captain," Elias protested. "Prisoner or not, I won't be spoken to like that."

"Captain, yes! Technically you are. You're free to issue orders and requisitions from within your cell if you're quiet about it, or scrawl them on the wall if you find a scrap of chalk, and if you can write." Elias simply glared, genuinely shocked by his treatment. "To put it another way, your title, as of now, means about as much to the people of County Highlands as a horn of ale to a fish."

He chuckled smugly and his men laughed with him, uproarious to his temperate smugness.

"When I'm released..."

"If you're released," the gaoler corrected, "you'll do nothing to me. A man could only say I've treated you as you deserve, as a crime suspect and as a fool, because you are one. Whether you're scum or not, I leave to the judgement of Treyveurn Andrews. Now, you, girl, what's your part in this?" he asked of Kate.

"She's the Brodie daughter," Elias supplied.

Kate didn't answer, only bit her lip and tilted her head to catch Henri in her peripheral vision. He was steadfast but stiff, very stiff, and he looked oddly contemplative. His arms were crossed as if to show he meant no harm. Probably for the best, but he wasn't a beacon of confidence for her.

"Didn't Patric Denkyn order you to stay put?" the gaoler asked.

"Well I didn't flee," she answered. "Else why would I flee to here of all places?"

The gaoler was satisfied by that answer, enough to foresee no threat in Kate, and so announced his leave and made to lead the captain back to his gaol cell.

"You're not going to arrest her?" Elias asked.

The snide gaoler with his mace looked at his captive in disbelief, as if he were utterly mad, and his hearty laugh reflected that. His men laughed with him once again, leaving Captain Olswalt humbled and humiliated.

"You handled that well," Henri said when their jibes were but a whisper on the wind.

"That's why you decided not to say anything?"

"What could I say?"

"Nothing," Kate agreed with a heavy sigh. "But here you stand, claiming to protect me. I can't help but be sceptical considering you were working only for money just a few days ago. And you said you wouldn't fight the Watch so, well..."

"I worked only for money when I was only a servant. Men like me need orders, and I was proud to be a part of something greater."

Just like that? It was a hard thing to swallow. Everything about Henri told her he was trying too hard to impress; everything except his mouth. All the more reason not to listen.

On the wind, she heard sword strokes and clanging of metal. If anyone else heard, they didn't care, for it was surely just a blacksmith's work. To her, it was identical to the sword strokes imagined in her sleep, and she shuddered. All the more reason to return to Maelphorydd quickly, high above the world, and safe.

~

The bronze and wooden doors of Maelphorydd rattled and Gèyll stopped her pacing to observe, only to be disappointed when she saw they were still, and closed tightly. That was its way, she began to feel. The building was stone, created the old way with stones cemented together rather than shaped first, and it was all given added support by wooden beams as thick as the biggest trees. Though it was well maintained, it did look old; not only that, but rough and not for the likes of her to go trouncing around in asking for justice. Gods forbid the Count did his job. She hoped she was wrong, even as she noted harsh imagery on those great doors: fire, whipped by wind circled by falcons. An odd relief too; one that recurred as a fresco upon the stair railing.

Again the doors rattled, and this time they opened, to her relief if she dared call it that, as the same steward who'd so rudely suffered her plea earlier strode out. He stiffened when he reached her, as he seemingly had a habit of doing when he felt he was being prompted for more than he could give, and Gèyll sighed irritably.

"What do you have for me?" Gèyll asked more politely than she felt obliged to.

"A message, to inform you that you'll not have audience granted to you."

"What did the Count tell you? His exact words?" Gèyll urged, if only for the sake of saying she'd tried. And she would try until she dropped dead.

"I didn't say the Count told me personally," the steward said shrewdly, unflinching.

"So you, his steward, take orders from another messenger?" There was no reply, none other than the steward's flinch, a scowl if one were being cynical. The wind howled on. "There's been a murder!" Gèyll reiterated. "A knight, one of your lord's retainers, slaughtered like a pig on the road to Aurail and he doesn't care to investigate? I'll say this for you now then: Sir Edwin Meri was murdered as part of a conspiracy, and no, I'm not making this up. I'll be ready to talk when the Count is ready to listen."

"One moment," the steward said, looking alarmed.

Gèyll turned to see what his line of sight met, and instinctively made to look away but stayed steadfast, wincing and clapping a hand to her mouth. For all her breath did stink, it was not near as wretched as the body being dragged through the streets by two Watchmen, leaving red smudges here and there. The dead man was a Watchman too, and of their same order; he didn't wear the cape of the Maelphorydd Guard, nor did his armour have the special inlays and platinum theirs did.

"What did this one do?" the steward asked angrily as the body was carried up the stairs.

"He was a friend of Captain Olswalt's, presumed corrupt for a while now. He resisted arrest."

"Water!" the steward shouted at no one in particular. "Somebody clean this mess up."

Gèyll gazed up along the heights of Melphor, to skirt from the wretched sight when it was brought near, and wondered where her daughter was, for it was unlikely she'd leave except to return here. This city was fighting her wishes of it with all its might, regardless of what Sir Edwin might have loved about it. Perhaps it had died too.

In the moroseness of the moment, she'd couldn't help but wonder how things would be different if Lennord were here. Oh, he called her the strong one, yes, but he was the brilliant one, and it wasn't just her opinion. Would he have had a solution already? Would he see things she could not? Lennord would scoff at her evaluation of him naturally, but he was humble. She could be grateful that for now; at least her acquaintances were merely apathetic rather than aggressive. She'd felt a dread in her heart that this city might be something of a tawdry and dangerous place when walking its streets, or maybe that was her presently sullen imagination growing wild and cynical, viewing every dark, winding street cast in long shadows as something else come the night. Fortunately, even Lennord would have his work cut out for him bestowing wonderful accolades about her looks in her current state: bedraggled, and dirty, and pale of face, so no one else was likely to touch her. Kate, on the other hand, was a beautiful flower.

She shuddered and turned to face the steward again, who was ordering two servants carrying pails of water to the bloodstained cobbles. *So little time*, she thought to herself, *must hurry*.

"What say you?" she said. "You've just proven that you are investigating Captain Olswalt."

The Voice of Kings

"I will relay your message and make present your urgency," the steward said flatly, dead in the eyes. "That's not all though. An eagle arrived from Aurail the morning before yesterday, from the barracks of Lameeri's Wish. It's for you, I believe. It was not a priority and so hadn't been sent to Caedor yet."

The steward removed a small, thin roll of paper from his pocket, indeed emblazoned with a military seal, and held it out stiffly with all the fussy decorum that one might choose to present a king with his sword, only without the manners. Shaking at the hands, she tore off the seal, unravelled the letter and could but skim over the contents of the letter so fast that she wondered if she'd read it right. What was, at first, a welling of relief and surprise softened and filled her with joy when she calmed herself and read it again, slowly, to confirm what she thought she'd seen. She could have kissed the paper and might have done had the steward not been staring at her with those glazed eyes. *I love you too*, she thought of Lennord, smirking.

"What does it say?" he said.

"I will show the Count if he agrees to see me."

The steward huffed and looked back and forth from the letter to her face, irritated and regretful.

"The Count reserves the right to read any letters you receive or send hencewith during your stay in Melphor," he announced formally.

"Doesn't he have that right anyway? Does that mean he will do so? Why?" she snapped.

"I can't say. Now, I'd suggest you leave for the day. The Count will not hold council for you or anyone else today."

He looked as if he might stay for a moment, then his hesitation passed, he stiffened, and strode back into the void that was Maelphorydd, where gods alone could know what happened next. Gèyll was left to descend the steps in a daze and stalk the square as she waited, giving a mighty wide berth to the servants sloshing and scrubbing at the ground, of which she said nothing when her daughter did arrive shortly thereafter.

"Kate," she said exasperatedly, grabbing both her daughter's hands. "Good news at last."

"I'll take what I can. Have you spoken with him?"

"No, but it's only a matter of time. Look."

Gèyll passed the letter to Kate and waited for the same euphoric relief to unfold, while Henri watched on in futility, as he was unable to read.

"No mention of my brothers; no mention of anything in this mess. So they must be okay, yes? And... Father's to be knighted?" she exclaimed, then her eyes widened. "Or he'll be given a lordship." She smiled, and it was a real one: the first Gèyll had seen from Kate since that day on the road when the knight was still her mentor.

"Your father may have just saved us a great deal of trouble," Gèyll explained. "This is our ticket into Maelphorydd, I promise you."

"That's good but..." Kate looked to Henri for support but he looked lost. "Captain Olswalt is in the city. In gaol!" she said hurriedly.

Gèyll glanced at the Maelphorydd guards to ensure none were listening, then led her daughter away.

"Tell me everything at the inn. I wouldn't take a thing like that for granted. Just to be safe. It's difficult to feel safe in the same city as that man. Remember this then: the slightest hint of danger from him and we're gone. We'll ride to the seastrand and we won't look back, right?"

They passed into the bowels of the city again, shadows and light dancing like demons around them. Gèyll felt pressured again, and she swore she would gain entry to Maelphorydd. Sweet Lennord would get her there.

Chapter Twenty-six: Beneath the Five

Rayance, of the Sun Guard, took the lead at a thunderous pace, unconcerned with Vicentei's unpredictable penchant for taking fascination in his surroundings. A mentality to which Vicentei sympathised. He'd not, prior to now, entered the King's garden as there had not been a need, only spared it fleeting glances from the palace ramparts and vaguely noted that there might have been things of interest there. The air was cool. The sky was blue. The wind was soft in the treetops, textured with brine and seaweed, and carried the cries of hawks and eagles from the King's raptor menagerie in the garden's north wing, to his left. There was nothing special about it to whet his appetite for thought, but then that was not what gardens were for, he reminded himself curtly. Would that he could improve upon it, but it was beautiful as it was and perhaps at the peak of perfection, though he could not say either way, not being an authority on the matter. Other than that, nature occasionally felt sorry for him enough to bestow on him an epiphany, and it seemed others of his ilk in ages past had experienced the same, as naught started from nothing; nature was the oldest inspiration before the first invention. The greatest successes then stemmed from the triumphs of that which was already there, and the failures of man, rarely the other way around.

"Are you going to be my escort often?" Vicentei asked when his interest waned.

"I'll do it so long as the King asks it of me," Rayance answered.

They ducked into a wide, gravelly path lined sparsely with willows and yew trees leading, apparently, to a side entrance to the great hedge maze. To the walkway that would take him over it and to the King's reception in the centre.

"You're unpleased by the possibility?" Vicentei goaded.

"Only if it were to interfere with my duties. It won't, to be clear. The King is the King; he does as he fancies, and his fancies are usually highly pragmatic, which is fortunate for all of us."

"Am I to believe that you, in particular, escorting me to the King's reception is an act of pragmatism?" Vicentei said forwardly, as unassuming in intent as he probably sounded.

"It's not astronomy," the man sighed. "It doesn't deserve so much scrutiny." Evidently, Rayance, by way of how his life had shaped him, did not see such an innocent face on Vicentei. Instead, he saw a set of clues that would alert him to dangers, such as attempts to falsely wring a treasonous statement from him; he would mark Vicentei for who he really was without question, because the Palace of the Sun was not of a reputation of hiring the wrong men, ever. "You tempt truth, but it has nothing to give you here."

"That's all part of trial and error. Tempting truth is my life. I only wish it were more cooperative."

They came to a halt at the side of the hedge maze, whereupon Rayance put his hand on the steel gate and kept it there, unflinching, as he observed Vicentei darkly. In the shades of the weeping trees, his face still looked strikingly red, his eyebrows brown daggers above oddly dark eyes that gleamed when the light shined through the wavering leaves above. He was not amused. Which was not to say he was humourless. Vicentei was not the man to say, nor would he care to if he could.

"I guess you know what you are doing," Rayance said, pushing the gate open. "The King does, ergo you do." Rayance snorted a laugh, probably at him, though he was not deliberately cruel. "Go on then, get moving."

The lieutenant of the Sun Guard flicked his head to the bridge crossing the maze, the forks of flame on his cuirass licking at the sun as they passed from shadow momentarily. Steadfast: that was how Vicentei would describe him. He ascended the stairs which levelled with the direction of the hedge before turning inward toward the centre, and there at the turning point of the bridge he stood and watched Rayance walk the gravel path and meet with his men whom he outranked. Then he was forgotten at will and Vicentei walked the bridge, an elegant thing of pale sandstone, to the large platform at the centre, shaded by three conical roofs combined as one, engraved with nondescript patterns and tipped with gold. As he stepped inside, he jumped in surprise, as to his right was a woman who'd before been obscured by the balustrade of the platform, stark naked on a sofa and lying on her side, her body gleaming, whether from oil or naturally shiny complexion he couldn't tell.

She was beautiful: golden hair, turquoise choker around her neck inset with milk-white jewels, thin. Before her sat a painter, and there she was on the canvas, though she was in a field, and surrounded by a ring of roses, white and red. As the real woman did, the canvas goddess also held an open palm betwixt her breasts and smiled radiantly. Lavellyrn, born again in paint, it seemed. The King did know where to find women most luscious then, yet when Vicentei turned, he saw that Michael was poring over his work at a desk. Disquieting to see, and Vicentei felt uneasy now at having been stirred by her brilliance. Sir Leon stood behind the King, against a balcony, also reading from parchment, his eyes flashing in Vicentei's direction as he approached, as if to capture that one image and examine it in his own time.

"Harth does not shy from beauty," the King assured him, looking up.

Vicentei's attention had waned as he'd spotted the Queen beside him also, facing slightly away with a book in hand, forming, for her part, a ring of ladies, real ladies, the rest of whom were sewing. His attention was fully on the King once more as soon as his liege had spoken, unable in a split second to define his deep tones as either commanding or simply speaking as himself.

"Sit," the King said.

The Voice of Kings

"Your Grace..." Vicentei acknowledged, as he sat opposite the King. Today he wore a tight-fitting satin doublet, embroidered with gold patterns on a field of royal green. Appropriately kingly. "This is all very elaborate."

"We're making the most of summer. I can feel its grip slipping, I feel it in the air. All should appreciate it for all its worth."

"I appreciate winter just the same, Your Grace. Winter brings hardship, and hardship is a better motivator for men like me."

Queen Helen looked over her shoulder at him, lips puckered and quizzical.

"Whose hardship?" she enquired, soft of voice. In quiet dignity.

"Mine or anyone's. I don't push it on anyone, my Queen. I observe it and see if it can't be avoided."

"Inventors are painters, and they paint the worst of the world as it should be," the King said to his wife, reaching out and touching her hand briefly but fondly. "Lord Hughly said that once, though I think he read it in a book."

"As he would have, Your Grace," the Queen replied simply.

"Vicentei," the King said in a deeper voice after some thought, looking away from the Queen to arrange his paperwork.

He coughed loudly. Ensuring that Vicentei knew the conversation was moving along. The Queen knew it already. She was buried in her book again. The Queen was pretty but wouldn't be so desirable, perhaps, without her status. It suited her well, that and her dress and heavy implementation of jewellery, so she made a good Queen. Or maybe those things made her a good Queen. Maybe it was the same thing either way.

Vicentei became unconcerned with the subject and allowed the King to fill his thoughts: the King who was immensely focused on being a king again. The inventor's eyes could not help but reach out to the beautiful thing on his right, serene of smile and baring breasts that needed to be seen again. The King's eyes followed his gaze then flashed back to Vicentei, entirely unfazed by her.

"I'll be hosting ceremony for grand council within the week," the King said forwardly. "Lords, and Barons, and Dukes will be in attendance. While your presence might be a boon to us, it might also be dangerous. I think it unlikely that you'll be among those lords and ladies, such as it is. There are delicate matters that might be discussed."

"Confidential matters?"

The King seriously considered this.

"No, I don't think so. Delicate matters is the right of it," the King reaffirmed. "You could uneven the balance I need to oversee. Some of those lords and ladies may not be fond of one another, and it's my job to see that these animosities are deconstructed. That's part of the point of all this. So I have enough to worry about without the risk of you blabbing at the wrong time, at the wrong place."

"Yet His Grace is talking to me of it," Vicentei said curiously.

"You will be on hand for as long as it lasts, as an advisor to anyone who needs you," the King said dismissively, before looking more serious. "And my brother will be here. He sent a letter. Do you know what it said?"

"Should I?"

"You should extrapolate."

"I've heard nothing of the High Duke for many months, Your Grace. Not as I recall."

"You're just as narrow as they say then. Or focused, if it please. To summarise, he's concerned about an instance of chaos within his Duchy but won't tell me more than the common folk could hear from any herald on the street, not until we meet in person. You're the genius, you work it out. What would motivate a duke to be coy about wildfire or a vicious disease amongst his wildlife?"

"Panic control," Vicentei suggested at once.

"Why hide it from *me*?" the King pressed. "His own blood, his King."

"Perhaps he, too, is afraid? I presume you want a scientific explanation, yes? There are diseases I've seen in the south, and farther south still, that I've not seen here, in animals and in men. The far south is where the real oddities are. Perhaps you should look to your records of those lands. But I'm sorry, I am not an expert in this area. If I have the time…" Vicentei pondered in all sincerity.

The King let out that same deep, short chuckle from their previous meeting. A sort of cough and belly laugh.

"I hope your enthusiasm's contagious," the King said.

The Queen craned over her shoulder again, smiling in her highborn way at Vicentei. Pleased, with an air of superiority, she was impeccably prim, short, thin, with straightened dark brown hair that was dull from some angles and glistened from others, even appearing jet black in direct sun. There was a wildness to it at the tips. She was quite pretty. Vicentei ignored her.

"Very well, I'll have it checked with expedition records, and those of King Kristofel Tallastan. I trust his discoveries at least as much as I trust the knowledge of Carlophinian locals, destitute nation that it is. They can't claim to have mastery over their own land so very well if they've allowed half their forts to crumble and their people to scatter and die in the cold and the wild."

King Michael was bitter, as before. Of course he was. Kings of his ambition would always dream of such things, but he had the pragmatism and restraint not to compromise his own country in favour of some faraway land. If Burtal was a lost cause in his eyes, Carlophinia truly was nothing, just as he'd said.

"Is that all, Your Grace?"

The Voice of Kings

"The man you were with at the docks," the King went on at speed, ignoring his question and, in doing so, answering it, such as a king could do. "A foreigner playing lord, I'm to understand, a sheep in wolf's clothing." The King stared intently, unblinking. Terrible wan smile grown once more. "What did he want?"

"He wants many things, Your Grace," Vicentei answered, puzzled. "Most of which I can't provide for him, because he's out of control and doesn't know what he really wants; he is me with a different life."

"Everyone is someone else by that criterion."

The King stared pensively into the distance, only for Vicentei to then discover it was old Lord Hughly he was scrutinising, who was waiting his turn to be received, looking cynical and unimpressed as Michael likely wanted of him. He, too, averted his gaze from the naked woman.

"That will be all," the King said after some thought.

Vicentei rose slowly, confused at the King's lack of interest in Isaac. If it was trust that cut the interrogation short, then the King was confident indeed. His stern features gave nothing away. Or there was nothing at all to hide. The King slapped his hand gently on the table and Vicentei turned sharply.

"My brother is not an easy man to scare," the King said. "He's as tough as they come. However, he's pious and puts much stock in benisons, more than most men can. If the purpose of a benison was to be feared, he would fear it."

"Are you answering your own question, Your Grace?"

"I'm offering solutions," the King said quietly. "My brother might fear for his people if it was beyond his helping, though how that would come to be, I know not," he then mused. "Never you mind though. That'll be all. Keep your mind sharp."

The inventor left wondering why he'd gone in the first place, and wondered soon thereafter if he was slow of mind that day, as he became suddenly conscious of a rolled up piece of parchment in his pocket that he might have mentioned. Might have, he corrected, if he'd been a fool. He was probably a fool himself to pursue the young Brodie's work at all, but he'd been so startlingly sincere, and it was simply so absurd that he couldn't, in all honesty, say he wasn't entertained by the idea.

Only on the gravel path did he think again to ask, as the living reminder of the brilliance of white steel approached. At first he was lost in his own thoughts, and was then startled to hear armour upon stones and saw behind him the storm knight, subtler still as he stalked the shadows of the yews and willows, shining as a beacon in the bastions of sunlight.

"I'd speak with you, painter," Sir Leon said softly with a thin, sly smile, and Vicentei stopped at once, for he was as interesting a project as any others he had. "I sense the King was too vague for your tastes."

"Will you make it your duty to apologise on behalf of His Grace after every meeting?"

"I offer no apology," Sir Leon said coolly. Not offended in the slightest was he, not even surprised, just silently calculating in his mild-mannered way. That was either a relief for him or a stark warning sign. "Isaac Brodie of the Burtalian Highlands, I sense, was a topic you wish His Grace would have expounded on more. You mustn't be alarmed. He trusts you, he just wanted to lure a reaction from you. That, and you weren't enthusiastic enough."

"If that's so, why follow me and pursue the conversation again?"

"I have no opinion on the conversation so I'd like you to help me form one. I like to think my reputation for caution is well earned, master Laccona. This young man, Isaac, is he a friend of yours?"

"An acquaintance of an acquaintance; a near friend," Vicentei answered. He was aware that this may have been a test, but he had nothing to hide.

"He was brought up during council, labelled as a precaution for being, shall we say, too clever for his own good, getting the court's attention in any way he could, though the court reacted half-heartedly, honestly. Not one man in that room cared enough to press the issue, not one man who wasn't out of steam when they tried to explain his actions past the obvious; Commander Leonardus finds him an irritating distraction, Rayance said something unsavoury and ranted for the sake of ranting, I recall, and Lord Hughly played the advocate of grave concern, but they had little to argue with."

A man doing anything to be seen. The precise opposite of Vicentei in that regard then. Indeed he was again, Vicentei realised as a chord struck him. The young man had relayed a message from a man on The Wolf's Way, in humour as it may have been, and he'd already forgotten his promise. Forgotten but remembered, he corrected. Not that it was unusual.

"I promised I'd humour his request to meet the King," Vicentei said. "He wants to talk about forgotten history."

"I would wait if I were you," Sir Leon advised. Vicentei's mind raced.

"Was he suspected of being a spy?"

Leon came alive, shockingly so, as one would not expect from him. He laughed loudly, grinning wryly, more animated than Vicentei ever thought he'd see him, yet he reminded himself the man was renowned for his speed. Already the knight's natural subtlety and stillness had made him forget that. That must have been one part of the danger of him.

"Briefly," Leon conceded. "Very briefly. But listen, there are spies in Harth almost all the time, but most are nothing to worry about. Burtal sends spies as information gatherers when envoys will do, you see. It goes to the trouble to send Sutherlenders to masquerade as those paravails of the eastern lords that like to marry into southern families, but despite that effort, they achieve little. Sadly, Burtal lacks subtlety, and the result is lots of insects scrabbling about doing precious little good or bad. We don't have to worry about them unless they worm their way up the Kingsreach."

The Voice of Kings

The Knight of the Holy Storm paused for rumination, sad in the eyes and smiling as if ironically amused. He was a strange and secretive creature, adrift in shadows. An eagle screamed as it flew overhead.

"What did he want?" Leon asked, barely changing his expression.

Whether it was truly Leon speaking, or the King speaking through him, Vicentei couldn't hope to tell, though the sight of the storm knight alone, in shining white steel, roused his hopes.

"This," Vicentei said, removing the parchment from his pocket and placing it in the knight's hand, waiting politely with palm up. "He wanted me to discover what this is."

Sir Leon's soft blue eyes scanned the contents of the paper, seemingly unperturbed as they flitted from corner to corner. Finally he let his guard down as he realised he could make neither head nor tail of it.

"What am I looking at?" the knight asked, shrugging.

"I was hoping you'd be able to tell me that. You're a man who knows his way around the world. You've been from the Isle of Sèhvor to Dormalii, from Aurail to Castle Türith, and everywhere in between. Have you seen nothing of the sort on your travels? A construct of white steel it would be, not necessarily this I'd say, because hell if I know what it is."

"And it would be old?" Sir Leon deduced. "When I fought the war in Alassii, I was only 18, and I was learning just how gifted I am at violence and testing how deep that ran. That was the half of it, and the other half was making sure that that's not all there was. With some success. But war demands violence, as it happens." He smiled grimly at the memories. "I wasn't paying attention to miners or treasure of that kind. All I remember of it is how what I saw was not all the same as the white steel here, and I remember men talking of the formations they found the steel in. In some places it was aligned in wondrous interconnected formations, in others it was blotted about in fragments."

"Many years have passed since that war," Vicentei reminded him, looking him straight in the eyes, fascinated. "You must have seen more of white steel since, and Sèhvorian jewels, lest we forget."

"I've seen nothing since then that another couldn't comment on more accurately. I only brought up Alassii because you did, and because men were not so aware of the uses of this steel and these jewels back then, so all were free to speculate."

He rolled up the sheet and respectfully returned it to Vicentei. He tucked it in his pocket for another day, another person.

"You're the expert, you think outside the box," Sir Leon said. "Did you blueprint this armour of mine?"

"I devised the method of its making most likely. Let me take a look then. In the sun."

They walked to a spot beside the gravel path where the sun shone down, near unblocked by leaves save for a great swaying when a gust blew down to stretch the branches here and there. Sir Leon thought nothing of being inspected, but looked up into the top of the yew tree nearby, away from the glint of his armour that would be painful to look at on the brightest of days. Pure, Vicentei had heard it described as, and pure was right. It was art. In its brilliance, the plackart melted into the curiass, and its acid etchings fazed in and out of being. There were even lames beneath the armpits, a dozen thin as parchment, that his movement would not be restricted, impossible with other metals.

"Your sword, Sir," Vicentei said, not thinking to actually request it.

The knight obliged, unsheathing Waithrydn to half its length, which was a weapon in and of itself, a beam of white light that glowed thicker and less distinguishable the more he stared. Along its flat side, Vicentei ran a finger to ascertain its perfection, then he moved it to the edge and felt a nasty tang, a sticky metallic texture that warned him that his finger would be cut to the bone should he so much as nudge it. Even carefully pulling it away, he caught a glimpse of its malice as it seemed to cling to him and would not leave without drawing blood, whereupon he shook his finger and wiped it away.

"Very impressive," Vicentei said, though he seemed not to sound it as he heard himself speak. He blinked rapidly to cast away the blotches on his sight. "Soft and hard white steel are wonders alone, and malleable too, but combining them for sword smithing, that's a painfully difficult task, in purity even more so. The window of success becomes increasingly slim over time. It's not just the heat needed, it's like the steel is *fighting* you. Fail but once, and it will run from you and ruin your forge should you not act quickly. It's no wonder some men call it a test from the gods. To craft it this well, and make it that sharp as well... you have a sword worthy to you at last."

"If I am perfect then so it is, you're right."

Sir Leon put out the light.

"Perfection shouldn't be debased for executions," Vicentei scorned.

Leon stared at Vicentei, impenetrable, long enough to make Vicentei question himself. The knight blinked heavily and looked away. "No," he said slowly. "It was either that, or let Janis do it, the first nomination. I couldn't allow it. I only knew him from afar, but meeting him was enough to set my decision, no matter how much I might loathe it. He's the Behnirham family executioner. He requires his victims to wear the cowl at the best of times. Do you take my meaning?"

"That is not uncommon, Sir."

"Unfortunately. That has no bearing on the depth of my melancholy."

Vicentei pulled an expression that could be interpreted either way. Just for a moment, a twitch sliced up the side of the knight's face, his eye responding badly, as if he were physically pained. Worse, the rest of the face stayed serene. Vicentei knew exactly what Leon had meant until that, now he was adrift. Best not push it. He wasn't that socially ignorant.

The Voice of Kings

"Do we have a problem?" Vicentei asked.

"It's quite alright," Leon answered, one half of a warm smile appearing but not chasing away the eternal tranquillity. He sighed peaceably.

As good a note as any to end on, for with the highest courtesy, the white knight made to take his leave.

"Enjoy the woman in His Grace's keeping, Sir."

Sir Leon stopped only briefly to turn, and Vicentei thought, for one chilling moment, the knight had interpreted him as meaning the Queen. Sir Leon's face betrayed nothing but the slightest hint of disapproval. Leon smiled amicably and walked on.

To the palace the inventor returned, setting his mind on other things. He detoured as he went to his chamber and observed the efficient workings of the palace. Contentment flourished in its inhabitants. Only where cynicism was needed was it found, in Rayance who had nothing to do but was contentedly bored, and in visiting lords who had much to do before meeting the King in his garden, and before more lords inevitably piled in and the flames sparked gold on the Kingsreach, assuming that was still practised.

Janis.

The name prodded him. Anxiety in his step, Vicentei searched for the executioner, asked about, got some directions, went to the wrong places. Eventually, he went to the palace guard's mess hall. Asked the barman. There, Janis, at the back, alone, drinking in his warped reflection from a pewter mug. Vicentei's approach didn't do much; Janis was tiring of his reflection and slurping of it. Only as Vicentei remained fixed did he attract attention, Janis darting out of his chair in what might have been panic but was intended to frighten. Vicentei stared blankly at the sweaty, wrecked, floaty, drooping wight across the table. *I believe I understand, Sir*, Vicentei finally replied, with a smile that evidently didn't go down well, for there was much abuse thrown his way, even as he took his leave. *How very astute of you*, Vicentei marvelled of Leon.

A short time after working in his chamber, he grew restless and stalked the corridors again until, half by chance, he found himself upon the palace ramparts beside the dome which looked just as those on a castle. There he stood and looked out over the garden as if he were the lord of it, for that was the mentality he wished to take for it to yield some secret of science. To his left, a field of blue tumbled up and over itself, the infinite view, and ahead there was a flash of light which, at first, he hoped to be some strange and unique phenomenon. It was Sir Leon exercising, running, at the back of the garden on a circuit unseen, as he'd seen of him the previous day. His sword was drawn and, as before, in his left hand he proudly bore the escutcheon of Harth which surely must have been a heavy piece. It looked it.

Beneath the Five

Vicentei dreamed by day and waking life of what he wanted. Or dreamed of the dream. He felt the parchment in his pocket. It would set him straight and narrow for the time being.

~

Again Isaac passed the Mercenary Guild as a spectator, and again he saw Martello from a distance, working his daily business with nary a care for the next day, just as he'd expected, as Jamys told him. His mercenary was beside him, quietly amused at the whole situation, to be sure. For all Isaac took unkindly to such men, Jamys was helpful enough and tactful enough to not be a nuisance, to the point where he might be sad to let him go within the next few days as his need for him dwindled, unless he could come to listen to his advice on smithing which would pass through his ears like smoke. Oddly, Jamys felt this more strongly than he, for he became increasingly brazen and asked questions about his work with guarded interest.

"You need him to open up," Jamys said plainly, not a suggestion but of intention to point out the obvious.

"I need him to care."

"Like the King cares for the Emperor. That's your lot."

"Stranger things have happened. A wall of steel breathing fire is a lot stranger."

"And here I thought you were giving up."

"Did you? When I am proved wrong, when I see at last that I'm a madman and that my memories are false, constructs of a frightened child in a dark cave, then I will give up. And I will slink away and no one in Harth will ever hear of me again, I promise that."

"I don't need you to promise anything," the mercenary grunted in jest. "Doesn't bother me what you do. But I'd like to see where this is going, mind. Would be good if it's true. I've been wanting something interesting to happen lately."

Arriving at the boarding house a short time later, he greeted Rosalynn briefly, guessing the truth of the matter when he saw her face.

"No inventor's come by here," she responded when he asked of Vicentei, "nor a runner on his behalf. Give it time; the man's in a world of his own. Well, you know him a little better than I do," she added when he raised an eyebrow theatrically.

So he returned to his room and slumped into a chair beside the bed, deep in thought, racking his head for ideas to pass the time, or otherwise move the mountain by the seastrand, the stubborn ignorance of the mercenary captain. Mountains did move, at least, piece by piece. He'd see soon enough if the comparison was apt.

"If you're concerned about promises, you might want to get back to the smithy," Jamys suggested, sounding bored, and shrugged.

"Your contribution should count for three of me," Isaac said distantly.

The Voice of Kings

He looked at the mercenary, who leaned over the bed into the window, gently pushing aside a gossamer curtain, not caring if he appeared conspicuous as he glared out. Isaac remembered again why he was so worth the money, should a reminder be needed. Here was a mercenary who was not in the least thrilled with the standing about in silence that his job generally entailed, content as he was with it, and was more than eager enough to step in and take half the workload away at the smithy without a word or threatening glance to rip more money from his pockets. He could even have him help Lucian, who was noble in his discontent, delivering letters as if it were his sworn duty. If his older brother had a sworn duty, there would be none more loyal, Isaac admitted, and was surprised to find himself smiling at the thought.

Jamys was a reliable pair of hands, true enough, he thought to refocus himself. Moving the mountain would be far worse the struggle without him. A thump sounded from the wooden door: a rapping that was a hollow roar because the wood was so strong and the hinges so tight.

"Tamzin Morzall here," a voice said, all silk and proper form. "Just a moment of your time, if you please."

Isaac found himself launching from the chair and striding to the door, throwing his filthy leather apron into one corner and ruffling his hair, not for the first time, of any remaining soot from the furnace. The priestess Tamzin waited innocently with hands clasped together behind her, unmoving without the appropriate gesture from him but for a minor rocking motion.

"I'm glad to see you again, Lady Tamzin. I was sorry not to speak with you more when we first met."

"As am I. You're not sorry for the fuss you caused?"

"If it causes offence then I'll apologise, and I'll do it sincerely because I meant none, but I don't think you care."

"Fair observation," Tamzin agreed firmly. "For me to care for my father's honour being questioned? I think not. No, I came only to warn you not to return to the cathedral without an apology prepared, or intent to avoid my father or any of his men who might recognise you."

"I'm guessing that wouldn't be healthy for me. Is the duceveree afraid I'll show him up again?"

"He won't say as much. Although insulted would be a better word because he doesn't find any logic in your words, only the power to make it sound logical. I think he saw your interest in the cathedral and was afraid you'd be off to the crypts next, actually."

"Go on," Isaac said pleasantly.

He was keener to hear of the duceveree's opinion than he thought. No doubt Laryc counted his insult as one to Venlor also, but he couldn't imagine the god paying attention to his exploits until he drew his sword again, and even then he'd only ever used it justly, his own foolish emotions aside. Then again, the word heresy was used, not blasphemy as he recalled. Maybe they were the same thing where a duceveree was concerned.

"Go on how?" Tamzin asked reproachfully. "You want to know about the crypts? They're old, older than the cathedral. There's nothing of secret there, though he'd beg to differ. He doesn't want people like you interpreting the hieroglyphs and disgracing the tombs with your presence."

"What hieroglyphs?" Isaac went on with eagerness.

"All sorts, nothing too unambiguous." She sniffed and folded her arms. "I don't have time to speak at length, anyway. I know you want to talk about your childhood and your purpose in Harth, but I can't listen right now. I'm not supposed to be here at all."

Isaac hardened, putting on a smile in courtesy. That Marcel would tell her of it wasn't surprising, the only question being how much.

"My brother already counts you as a friend," he said instead of pushing the matter, trusting that Marcel would feel the idiot for telling her too much. "I'd like to do the same."

"You have a deal, Isaac of Caedor."

"Fair day to you," Isaac added before she left.

For the sake of politeness, he stood in the doorway to see her off, listening only to the sounds of men and women bustling around the well and the markets outside, from where smoked fish of various varieties blessed him with their smell until Tamzin took a right turn at the end of the corridor and disappeared, waving steadily to Rosalynn as she did so.

"You won't be lying with her anytime soon," Jamys imparted.

Isaac shut the door and made his way back to the chair where he sat and tousled his blonde hair, made darker still by labour not suited to him, then ran it through his fingers to neaten it once more, all the while sizing up the similarly dirty mercenary by the window. He studied the outside world unexcitedly.

"You take after Martello, do you know that?" Isaac said. "Tamzin's a priestess, and while she's a nice enough person, she doesn't stand out to me aside from being a little odd."

"If you say so. I say what I see. You should remember there are places you can go if lying's what you want."

"Where one pays in gold and soul," Isaac rebuked scathingly. "In Caedor you'd have to use your imagination, or walk a mile out of town to the nearest brothel."

"The wrong kind of brothel at a guess."

"We're not having this discussion," Isaac said with a sigh. He rested his elbows on his lap and steepled his fingers as he thought. Possibly it was best to return to the forge already.

"There were Watchmen outside but they're leaving now," Jamys said calmly, already forgetting his previous point, for as Isaac guessed, he hadn't much cared for it to begin with.

The Voice of Kings

Isaac stood up in alarm and ran to the window, peering out to find that, indeed, there were two guards of the City Watch leaving the square.

"They were watching this building," Jamys said. "Showed no signs of conspiracy I'd say, not that they weren't taking in the view of it a bit too much to just be coincidence."

"They were here long?" Isaac asked, annoyed.

"A short time. It was best not to disturb you, they weren't actually doing anything."

Jamys froze for a rare instance of quiet contemplation. He turned to Isaac, licked his lips, and his face turned to cold stone, a gargoyle pasted with a worn smile.

"Stop provoking them, that's my advice. Men might get the wrong idea."

"Fine," Isaac relented. "I leave the task in Vicentei's keeping for now, then I think very carefully if he doesn't produce results. I can always pick Martello's brains out while I'm waiting."

"Wait before you do that too," Jamys suggested. "Trust me. Leave him. Wait."

There was something about the mercenary's manner that made Isaac trust him instantly. To be deadpan and conceal his motives was not within Jamys's capabilities, because to say he had motives would be a discredit to his hedonism. Outside, a group of Watchmen walked by without glancing in his direction, though Isaac watched them all the way to the point of their disappearance, and then watched some more. Harth was less mysterious already, he observed. Not less fantastic, just more real. The most intricate secrets were secrets by way of there being something hidden, for good or bad. It likely didn't matter, not yet. Reality would be a godsend enough.

~

Returning to the cathedral, a shadow smothered Tamzin as she recalled tales of the fires of Caedor, and of Marcel's guarded explanation when he spoke on his brother's behalf. A wall of steel engraved with ancient hieroglyphs was all the peculiarity Marcel Brodie would impart and not in any context, and so she couldn't help but mention the crypt when speaking with Isaac. It was a testament to her father's confusing, endless droning over the years that she found herself, at first, jumping to the conclusion of magic and hastily backed away from the idea immediately thereafter. Her father said a lot of things, so if she assumed all of it was nonsense, she'd have to believe the world was not real, but even so, gods were real, not random acts of magic. Magic of the gods was far more subtle; that she believed of her own accord from study.

At the cathedral main entrance, she arched her back before forcing it into a perfect erect position. With her head held high, lips flat and hair mundane, though she let her priestess skirts flow as she walked as that was acceptable, she felt a greater warmth than she expected upon entering the mouth of the dark stone beast, for the sun was bright through the stained glass windows and the candles burned strongly. Unlike her father, she did not stare gormlessly at them, but for a moment she did pause for thought. With a forced cough and a sniff, she walked through the cold cathedral corridors, speaking to no one, making eye contact with no one. At length she drifted before finding Marcel in a study wing; drab this one was: colourless, conformist with its rows of bookcases that carried no character, unlike the cathedral proper which was truer to Venlor's vision, for he loved beautiful things.

Before Marcel noticed her, she had sent a man to him to inform him of his new duty, to abandon his unreasoned reading of a baffling tome and to meet her in the cathedral. There she moved with all swiftness for her presence in that area was not looked upon too kindly. Marcel arrived shortly thereafter, very conscious as always, nervous even. He did not speak at first, not until he reached her. She smiled.

"Your runner said you have work for me?" Marcel said sceptically,

His eyes darted about, half enthralled by the hall as before and half paranoid, as if her father would crawl from the woodwork, and no one could blame him. He did look very much a brother of Isaac, come to think of it, though the differences were greater still. It was just an intangible quality she couldn't help but smile at, tilting her head to one side as she did so.

"We're making sure the flames are well lit in the crypt. This is a task I've set," she said when he looked set to protest. "It needs doing anyway. I want you to see something."

The foreign apprentice sighed and, after a moment's hesitation, followed her, tugging at his robes as he seemed wont to do, sore thumb that he was, as all apprentices did. To the back room she led him, where her father dressed and met important figures and performed his own ceremonies prior to leading them for the men and women waiting in their seats, as if that one was not good enough for him, what with all the men who weren't duceverëes in the pews.

Banners hung from the ceiling, of religious imagery and Mürathneèan House banners alike, a sea of silk sewn with animal sigils and interpretations of the five, a sea of colour surrounding the room in a circular shape that Marcel was all too quick to slow down for, glancing about before he remembered himself and looked anxious.

"No trouble will befall you for this," she assured him. "As I said, it needs doing. We'll just do it before anyone else gets there."

Then through the stone door they passed, old, but not as old as the stairs, which were not as old as the crypt. They each took a pyrite lighter and brand from their sconces, well-aged and free from the weathering of the world's elements but for greying, as even men did. As she began to wave her torch about and reignite struggling flames here and there, Marcel once again slowed to a crawl, sombre and respectful for the sarcophaguses that lined the tremendous corridor in their lunette alcoves, where there were cages of tinder and straw, and flanking the coffins, the hearth pits with which to fill them.

"What are we doing here again?" Marcel asked bleakly, straining to see through the blackness, or otherwise grimacing from the new brightness of the world beneath the world

The Voice of Kings

that gods hid from mortal men. "Bloody hell," he muttered to himself, fumbling for bearing.

"Look at the walls," Tamzin prompted, giving off a strange smile in the fierce glow of the fires.

He did, and looked very closely, waving his torch above his head to illuminate the grey stone walls, marked black with soot here and there, ingrained into the very bricks themselves. But those patches that flashed darkness at him, like curses above the dead, were few and far between, and so the apprentice was none the worse for it.

"Old markings, like your steel wall," she said.

"Maybe," Marcel said reproachfully. "I never saw it before it was... destroyed. Melted. I got the impression that those were older than this. Much older. I don't know, might just be my imagination, or Isaac's."

"Well there were the fledglings of a city here when this was made," she admitted. "I don't know much about the countryside, not your countryside anyway. I don't know how you date these discoveries you find in the wilderness."

Tamzin found herself studying the markings herself, not of random creatures though, but of war, where the gods were difficult to make out from the humans, and the creatures of shadow faded, for they were not clear to begin with apparently. She spotted a demon with a twin-pronged spear, held aloft like a bolt of lightning, ready to strike someone down. The foreign apprentice found some other image to his evocation: a swirl of blackness that fired the carved men with fear. A smirk beset her face in the soft light as furrows appeared on Marcel, like so many others she'd seen down here.

"What am I looking at?" he said slowly, gawping, shrugging in mild unrest.

"Shadow, they say, of hell or the nameless realm, or whatever you want to call it. Not all demons need take form to mirror ours. Or any. This one decided not to."

"Shadow, Tamzin, or smoke? To me it looks adrift, thick and restless."

"Most people say shadow. Once again, I find you in the minority. Don't change, you amuse me," she quipped offhandedly.

"And this is prophecy, like the cathedral ceiling?"

His brow and mouth seemed jagged in the flickering light, tense, as if any gesture she might make on the matter might actually satisfy. She swished her tongue about, the eccentric waving of her own hand crawling across the fresco distracting her.

"Let's call it speculation," she replied vaguely. "Already it's an interpretation of older drawings. Some of this writing's probably taken from different places too. I take care not to see it too lightly, mind. It's one thing where I'm on the level with my father." When he didn't answer, she licked her lips. "I remember a funny thing he read me here that I always thought he got right. He read that everyone is defined by the shadow they stand in, be it god, or king, or man, and the larger the shadow you stand in, the heavier your responsibility.

Beneath the Five

But at the same time, gods cast the largest shadows while demons cast none at all, because that's all they are, you know? Evil has no shadow because it hides in everyone else's, I think the point was. I saw it on an old shrine transcription too, come to think of it."

"Evocative," Marcel murmured, holding still his torch at last. It occurred to Tamzin she must have sounded positively passionate. "If demons aren't metaphors though, I don't see why it can't be smoke."

"Oh, don't think I'm rebuking you. He also separated men from kings, and said most men can't tell the difference between gods and kings anyway, so he's not too reliable, you see!"

They went forth again, where beyond the war of light and dark were inscribed more static images, some metaphorical like the ring of blackened petals with a spear thrust through the middle, and writing she couldn't read and couldn't care to remember from her father's lessons. The important thing was that Marcel was getting some joy from it, lack of recognition put aside. Then the story of the carvings ended.

"They just finish here?" Marcel exclaimed.

"It wasn't supposed to go any further. The rest is much newer, where our forebears lie."

Marcel looked over his shoulder and saw, as she did, little more than an orange hue, a glare that obscured the end of the tunnel. He bit his lip and looked at her, more sorry than he had any reason to be.

"Anyone you care about?" he asked.

"Only important men of the cathedral are found here, or revered scholars of the faith. My mother is in a field somewhere. My real mother, not that reclusive woman married to my father." She shrugged. "Are you happy you came here?"

"To this crypt?" Marcel answered after a telling pause.

"Here."

"We'll see," the man predictably replied. "I don't know yet. It's a good city."

"You might be better off here than Aurail at least. It's going to get worse, my father says. I don't know if he's right on this theory. He's about as reliable as a coin toss I'm afraid. He's confident though, I'll tell you that. He says Burtal will rip itself apart and Mürathneè will assimilate it piece by piece as is convenient, or just leave it if their court makes such a terrible job of it all."

"Hmm," was all Marcel could say. "I haven't thought about it. There's nothing wrong in Caedor."

They reached the end of the crypt, a hard flat wall, unmarked and white, as forbidding as could be, and she was stuck down here with the man she'd invited but felt at once embarrassed, for he was distant with her.

"Your brother told me you're proud to count yourself a friend of mine," she said, and the flames seemed to grow crueller, then his face softened and he was completely surprised.

The Voice of Kings

"I think so," he said. "I think so. I have none other here so you've done me a kindness."

The crypt was silent.

"There's more work to be done," Tamzin supplied, and smiled broadly, gesturing to the hue of flames at the other end of the crypt. Again Marcel treated the gesture distantly, but smiled back at her.

Chapter Twenty-seven: Trials of Court

"How long do we try this charitable approach?" Lord Celoden Reid put to the council, looking left and right about the packed table, but his gaze kept returning to Richard. "If the people begin to play on our charity, what then? It's all very well, organising seminars and holding the people's hands and allowing them to browse apprenticeships at their own leisure, it must be very therapeutic for them, but when all's said and done, people need to do jobs they can do well, not ones they fancy having a go at."

"First you have to be charitable," Lord Almaric said pleasantly to the lord, who sat just four chairs to his left. Tristan held his hands up as if they were scales, shaking them up and down. "Your sense of balance is lacking, Lord Reid, for one who deals in information. Your proposal of funnelling the people to preset destinations doesn't work, not here."

Lord Reid opened his mouth to object but Tristan cut him off, smiling empathetically.

"It's never worked in these circumstances, not particularly well. The crux is that this freedom isn't usually given so liberally, so there's not much to go on and, thus, we assume, by history, that it must be the only way. Just trust me my Lord, happy men are hard-working men."

The room bustled in a quiet, reserved manner, every man in the council chamber, all 40 of them, adjusting themselves in their seats as if this was a radical new idea, yet it had been brought up enough times for regulars of court to have no excuse. There were many who'd not been in the room, or even this city, in some time however. And some in the city who'd spurned council. One would think Lord Aumaine had been scared off by Yanick, but he simply avoided the castle, and, indeed, few had even had a good look at him or his son. It wasn't a great image for the crown.

Two places to his right, Tristan could feel Alycia's presence, proud, and strong, and fully in control, as this was her doing, nothing special on the surface perhaps, but he would assume she had something planned. He leaned back and looked over Richard who was bent forward like a great, tired bear, resting his chin on one hand. Empress Alycia sat bolt upright, striking in a green dress laced with silver thread, blonde hair hanging loose over her back, unsmiling but not miserable. In muted enjoyment, she surveyed the room, not making contact with Tristan's eyes just yet, keeping him waiting as she did, blessed Alycia, on how much she knew of the incident at the manor, though there was no chance any detail had eluded her at this point. Yanick and Pedrig, and sharp-eyed Wylam especially, must have told her everything. In that hall of Emperors, beneath a giant chandelier that bestowed light that swam over her smooth skin, she held her cards hidden for reasons he hoped not to have to question.

The Voice of Kings

He could show her up and tell the council everything he knew to portray Alycia as a villain, but at length he'd considered it in his bedchamber and decided that it would not only be cruel but pointless, and humiliating for himself more than her. No, he chastised himself, her arrogance was not deserving of vilification beyond her misuse of Lennord. Boldness yes, and hard truths hard told. Boldness and truths with all respect.

"Hear, hear!" Lord Abram Carrick said loudly and confidently when he was sure His and Her Majesty agreed wholeheartedly, and other lords nodded also, hearing him with perfect clarity in the specially designed chamber that sprung voices from one end to the other and sucked echoes into the ceiling and the walls. Alycia had much to say but needed not, and so left the lords to their imaginations.

One man did not nod for he saw no desperate need, nor did he seem to disagree however. Sir Darith Wyman sat at the other end of the round table, directly opposite Tristan, scrawling notes while various facial expressions crossed him, all of them carrying an admirable calmness and comfort that was lacking in those surrounding him. He would listen intently, scribble something down, raising his eyebrows in tandem or puckering his lips in concentration before interlinking his fingers and listening in silence again, silence unbroken in 10 minutes of council. Tristan wished dearly for his input out of grand curiosity, but there were others he knew needed his attention more.

"Lord Paramount," Lord Reid so ignored other dissenters, "you have me mistaken. Whether I condone my suggestion is frankly irrelevant if it needs doing, which is not me passing judgement on your flock that you love so much, just a hypothetical scenario to consider. Well consider this then: since Her Majesty had some two dozen Watchmen retained in the dungeons, the people feel safer."

"Which says nothing for their guilt even if what you say is true. Or for *actual* safety."

"It speaks for the mindset of the people," Lord Reid rebuked sharply, holding up a finger, pale like his face, like his hair. His eyes were a lively green in contrast, full of a warning; he was a sad person to believe in. "They want a show of force, ever a show of force for resolution, and that includes other citizens..."

"Yet you propose that they all be abused so their sadistic joy you speak of will be outweighed," Lord Almaric said, stroking his jet black hair. He tapped the fingers of one hand on the stone, which rang through the silence of the chamber like a drumbeat. When Lord Reid made to object, Tristan spoke up once more to intercept him. "They're afraid, Lord! Of course they want tactile evidence of change, but violence is what they see anyway, so naturally they see it as a solution. As a highborn man privy to great halls and servants, I would think you'd promote peace as I do. You know it, they do not. It's the prerogative of every man in this room to pass this life on to the common folk."

"Gold and all?" Lord Haemon Searl laughed, a wealthy fief resident of the flatlands come to attend court at beckon.

Trials of Court

One couldn't fault him for actually arriving, unlike some others. Then again, those others might not have been at fault. Tristan couldn't tell yet and was loath to assume the worst. Evylyn was right: kindness was easier given when received, though of course she cited him as the exception.

"Philosophers have linked greed with jealousy and, in my experience, that's quite true," the Empress mused very deliberately. "Counter me your own philosophy, Lord Searl, I beg it."

He didn't. The hall at large deliberated and, as often happened in these instances, Tristan felt as if time slowed for him and his body tingled with an implacable feeling, such as power did to him. It was strange after all these years and he didn't much like it, so he became further conscious of his own thoughts. Across from him, the scrabbling of a quill pinged softly about and a similar sound came from the corner behind him, where Lady Castellon was ceaselessly writing minutes, no doubt as a reminder of who did what and how to deal with them, each and every one.

"Lord Paramount has spoken," Richard put in at long last, rising from his slump and reclining, attempting to look as imperial as possible in his long, velvet robes lined with wool, and heavy jewellery that now rattled. He needn't have been so worried, he never should have been, yet he was, still not the ruler he had in him. If only he would be more open. Even when Tristan had told him in anger of his experience at the manor, he never challenged Alycia. Not much longer now though, not so very much longer. "He's right as well: we work with the people, not use them as tools."

Out of the corner of his eye, he saw the Empress nod slightly, wispy hair flapping ghostlike. Richard peeked in her direction, as if hoping not to risk her wrath, but she would never rebuke him at such a time: that he should have known.

"Tools break," she said simply to nods of approval. The rest she left to the imagination.

"I'll back that view," Lord Foy said in his hoarse voice. Good and reliable old Cerdic. "As a treasurer, I see the effects money has, and our good Majesties have the right of it so far as I can see."

"I foresee complications," Lord Reid persisted. "I've noticed advisors from across the channel in the trade embassy, all over the city actually. I can't see it ending well if more are recruited. We're Burtal, not Mürathneè, so we shouldn't act like them; too many of these people here could make us look weak, enough to attract the attention of the King's court and destabilise our position."

"Our position is destabilised by default," Lord Foy scoffed.

"The people will protest! They don't want to see men from abroad thieving of their country, especially when those foreigners are more accomplished, for why would they then try at all? Majesties, such tolerance could have catastrophic consequences in the long run.

The Voice of Kings

We need to spurn some of these embassies, publicly, and learn what we may through espionage. Spies will be more useful to you, though I fear to say it."

"There are no guarded secrets to Mürathneè's success," Lord Almaric laughed in disbelief, shaking his head defiantly, though his heart weighed heavy and he fought to stay proud and upright. If Richard, in fact, bore the same affliction, his heart must have been too heavy to hold. "The lessons are in its society, not locked in vaults. No, my Lord, no, superstition will be the weapon to take our own heads with, belligerence the excuse to let King Michael do it for us. The best spies in the country will do us no good and I wouldn't condone the act if they could. A dire and antiquated way of thinking won't revive a dire and antiquated country."

Tristan withheld a sigh as best he could and scanned the faces that stared blankly at him, all looking in to that one point at the table where he sat. Many were nodding profusely and wearing serious faces, and there was some purposeful muttering too between lords and their paravail retainers. These were the most minor lords of Burtal, most of whom would not voice their opinions to the court, rarely if they agreed with their masters unless to shamelessly repeat, not ever if otherwise. Oh, but something would have to be done about that also.

"Would you not condone it if it were the only way?" Lord Reid asked heavily, not remotely enjoying presenting the falsehood that he so tragically believed in.

"My Lords, please," the Empress said coolly, gently waving a hand in a half-circle like a leaf swaying in the breeze. Tristan knew the real power lay in her voice but, predictably, people were taken with her simple gestures. "Celoden, what you say is consequence of thorough consideration, everyone in this hall knows it. In thinking so little of mine and my husband's idea, what have you done in its stead?"

Richard perked up as all the warning signs of a covert insult began to ring in deafening unison. Alycia, straight of face, leaned back in her chair and, still keeping both eyes on Lord Reid, held up a finger for Lady Castellon to tell her to observe most astutely.

"I meant to cause no offence, I must stress first of all. To Lord Almaric also. As for your question, I've been focusing on seeing that information flow is not stilted, Your Majesty."

"Lord Almaric's view was perfectly respectable," Alycia agreed. "To disrespect it would be to disrespect him. Although, you have me misunderstood. In thinking so little of the plan already in motion, what have you done in its stead?" she repeated.

"I'm attempting to keep tabs on how information is interpreted by the people so to..."

"Just answer the bloody question!" a new voice spurted in anger.

Imyll Lyrdred, a younger cousin of Alycia hailing from the Grey Rose, was rubbing his forehead with one hand and rolling his eyes as if Celoden had physically impaired him with his short-sightedness. Lord Reid made to try a third time but Alycia's stare cut him short, showing now how unimpressed she'd been since he'd started speaking, and his blood fizzled and burned to ash in his veins. He held eye contact for moments uncountable before lowering his head in apology. Tristan wished he could stop himself, but a smile of relief surfaced, despite himself, and Richard's was more satisfied still. The joke was shared only by them, if not Tristan's sentiment of the Empress. For all she frustrated him, he loved her at times as these.

"That's what I feared to accuse of you," the Empress said in sadness. "I won't heed advice given in malice or whimsy. Lord Tristan is right, spies won't help us for such matters. If we look to our own borders, we see at once that we've acted selfishly for too long. What times are these when honoured knights are ambushed and butchered for their steed and a few scraps of gold?"

No one could answer.

"Her Majesty is talking about the tragic death of Sir Edwin Meri," Lord Almaric clarified.

"A good man," Sir Darith Wyman spoke up. "He came to Ylden Parragor a couple of times and seemed a man of principle. I don't... I don't remember anything specific he said to me right now, but we did speak more than once. It wasn't what he said, I suppose, though I remember he was eloquent. I just remember him being very conscious of every little thing around him; yes, an honoured knight as the Empress said. So, I say farewell Sir Edwin, I say I hope he'll be avenged one way or another by all of us, gods will it. Lord Almaric, you have my support."

There were more nods of approval and murmurs, stronger and more impassioned than previously. The knight's supreme confidence struck such a positive cord that Darith himself nodded with them, strong and serious as he suddenly acquired the taste for publicity. He puffed out his huge chest, around which he wore a doublet of boiled leather, a smooth high quality sort that shined in the light of a hundred candles and was emblazoned with two standards. On the left side there was the black swan of Wyman, and on the right a ring of fog enshrouded swords, of his mother's noble House.

"Why does Ylden Parragor send a knight to do a lord's job?" Richard asked when the commotion died down.

"The lords of Ylden Parragor will come when they're not needed there anymore. There's much talk of money, I know that, and they're not allowed to leave until it's dealt with. My uncle, the Count himself, gave me his blessing when I offered to represent his city."

"Very well."

"Welcome to the council then," Alycia said warmly.

"How's Lady Bethen?" Tristan asked, for he had fond memories of her visits when they were both children, she a teenager when he was small, and then again when they were both fully grown, when she was bolder than he.

As a child, he'd always been compelled to make peace with other noble children as soon as possible, a part of him which had stuck with him in some form all those years, to his frequent amazement. Bethen had found it highly amusing. One might say that Richard should have been adjudicator, for that was his destiny, but it was not so, and Tristan would have been the worse for watching failure after failure.

"Tenacious as ever, my Lord," Sir Darith answered enthusiastically.

"We have a country to run," Imyll Lyrdred interjected.

"Calm down, Cousin," Alycia said lightly. He would likely not call Alycia "cousin" however, not here. "But fair enough. There are critical matters to discuss."

Tristan sharply looked the way of his enchanting Empress but found nothing had been given away, so turned as much as he could without drawing attention to himself to see if the knights Pedrig or Doru could give him the slightest hint. From what he saw of them, they gave nothing away. She began to talk of the image Burtal should be giving the rest of the world, letting him down again in her elegant way. Only a knock at the door cut her short, and at Richard's beckon, it opened, whereupon Marcus Baldwin came to save Tristan, it seemed, as his personal runner looked across the table at him in particular, with apprehension at having interrupted the meeting.

Not that he needed saving, Tristan thought. Some of these others though...

"My Lord Almaric," Marcus announced. "You have a visit from a friend. An urgent visit. He was quite insistent on that point."

Richard gave him leave, thankfully not seeking his wife's consent, though more to his own detriment than hers, most assuredly. At any rate, she would not risk weakening his position in such an obvious manner. At the door, Tristan briefly took in a wide view of the meeting which carried on as if he'd never been there, all eyes meeting those of another within the ring, as if, to them, there was no world outside of it. Lord Reid was less forceful, he noted, only for Lord Searl to take his place as an advocate for misguided ideas. At that, he left them to it, tired and frustrated, to be welled with joy at the sight of Lennord in the hall. He was not his usual self, his 51 years weighing on him as his cautious optimism would not permit any other time. His age showed because it was his eyes where his love for life was instantly seen, and now wrinkles enclosed them over dark skin.

"Urgent business?" Tristan said when he was right before his old friend. Over Lennord's shoulder, he saw to his further surprise that the musician Kester Irvyng waited some way back, looking most paranoid. Tristan took Lennord gently by the arm and led him away from the guards and Marcus at the door.

"My sons' friend here has told me a disturbing report." Lennord checked on the oddball gravely. "I had a hard time convincing him to come at all because he feared punishment for his eavesdropping. He shouldn't have heard it, but he did, and it was worrying, so here I am."

"Eavesdropping where?"

"Outside the throne room. You told him to wait there."

"Ah. I did. I won't say I regret that." Tristan grimaced. The young were often fools, but then so were the old, and it was never an indicator of a bad person in and of itself. "What did he hear?"

"The Empress wants to use me and my family for some sort of publicity, so he says. Possibly more, but she wouldn't even be clear with Richard apparently. She was very clear on encouraging Isaac on playing up his memories of that day you came to Caedor, and myself, also, in particular, all for, what, second-hand superstition of magic from Mürathneè? There was talk of a similar phenomenon, Kester says: whispers from Alycia's men, fire from a mine hot enough to turn men to ash."

As Lennord's face hardened and he ceased to speak, Tristan wondered if he was recalling his recent mention of it, of hoping to one day discover its method. When he spoke of it then, it was a curious dream to laugh about, though no doubt he hoped not to see it resurface in this way, not with Isaac pulled back into something he'd long since gotten past, and not with more deaths. And once again, Alycia just couldn't resist making plans with impunity, and keeping secrets where they weren't needed. The poor woman was too smart for her own good.

"It won't come to fruition," Tristan said sternly, angrily even, patting Lennord on the arm. He shook his head. "I'll confront her. I should have done it earlier, when I suspected her of wanting too much from you. Everyone needs to hear opinions other than their own."

"That's not all. The Empress heeds reports that the High Duke has men searching day and night for the answers, tenacious as they say he is. That one I can believe; any man in his position would feel helpless, and men like him don't like being helpless."

"You want Alycia to send you there?" Tristan replied at once, alarmed. "Alycia might approve, but I can't speak for Dorrin Santorellian."

"I want to see that Isaac hurries up his business and gets right back here when he's done!" Lennord snapped, whiplike. "If he gets wind of this, he'll run head long into it, assuming the High Duke's men don't find him first."

"You said yourself he's a capable young man," Tristan pointed out.

"It's a dangerous phenomenon, this. Even Vicentei Laccona wouldn't be safe, genius as he is, if he can't work out what it is. Though I worry that Isaac might become obsessed again, just as much as I fear for his safety. More, probably. I must go to Harth!" he blurted out.

"You mustn't," Tristan said sharply, and smiled pleadingly.

Tristan checked on the guards at the door of the council chamber as he said this, suddenly aware of how loudly they were speaking. They were elite Guardians, wearers of the green cloaks and impossibly disciplined, unwavering and unflinching. If they'd heard their conversation, they showed no sign of it, and would do nothing with the information if it were so. Yet, anxious he was, and was ashamed of that fact. He shouldn't have been; he was going to tell Alycia anyway.

"I'll see to it that Dorrin's men don't find Isaac. I don't think they will, and I think you worry too much, but I'll do it anyway, I swear it. But you can't leave! Alycia would never agree to you wasting valuable time like that, not publicly."

"Implying she'll not stop me if I don't seek her agreement?" Lennord rethought this in an instant. "Convince her, if the situation becomes worrying, and come with me to Harth. You're the only one who can help me if Dorrin's men act with impunity and place Isaac under guard."

"It won't happen," Tristan assured him calmly. "If it does, there are plenty of men up to the job."

"No others who are you." Lennord paused to show on his face a grim determination and sincerity, lest his words not convey his meaning well enough, as if that could happen. There was wisdom also, such as men like him were bound to develop in later years, even if they were too humble to recognise it. "Friends come and go like a summer's breeze, true and loyal ones are rare anyway, but you're something else, my Lord. Men as incorruptible you come by once in a generation. If I was permitted to go, I'd ask no accompaniment but you. You've said it yourself, the game of politics is not one you expect I'd enjoy."

"Some of the lords need hard lessons," Tristan admitted. He sighed and laughed bitterly. "If you were to say fuck them, I couldn't blame you. As for myself, I serve Richard: I've sworn to, *especially* when he's sickly and sullen. You can't ask me to leave court."

"If the time comes when I need to go," Lennord repeated more severely, more deliberately, "ask him. Consider that at least. I'll think no worse of you if you don't abide, but consider it. Anything to get away from court duties. I don't want to have to pretend to be a knight any more than they want to endure it." He smiled grimly.

"My friend!" Tristan laughed. "Forget about that, forget the knighthood. I'll have Alycia grant you lordship like I originally suggested. Caedor will need one as it grows and I can't think of a better man for the job. Knighthood was a bad idea on her part, and I should have put my foot down harder, respectful as I am to her, and always will be."

Lennord's humility never failed to amaze him. Again he was quietly taken aback beyond belief, despite him hearing nothing new.

The doors to the council chamber creaked open and there was a bustling of lords pacing and muttering to one another in a cerebral manner, stopped by the Empress's beckon, to what end he cared not to hear at this time. In haste, he approached Kester, conscious not to miss Alycia, as there was no guarantee when he could next see her if she was still intent on keeping herself from him.

"You'll receive no punishment from me," Lord Almaric said. "I don't know what exactly you were doing, but you can't be held accountable for words that reach your ears."

"My Lord," was all Kester said.

There was nothing about him that screamed fear, though it had to be noted that he'd been listening to the prior conversation. He was plain of face at present. He hid himself well. Men were filing out of the hall once again and Tristan looked back worriedly.

"There's work to be done," Lennord said rather perceptively.

"I'd better do it then."

Lennord squinted and, for a moment, he was fully alive again: snide and playful, as too few men of his age were, and he left with the composer at the implicit understanding that Tristan had given him leave. At the door of the council chamber, Tristan bumped into Sir Darith. He looked stronger up close, and had a sense about him of a will to get things done. His lack of sword by his side was to his detriment as, in the throne hall, it had seemed very much a part of him.

"My mother and father both had kind words to say about you and our Majesties. If ever you need a job done without delay or fuss, name it."

The other lords were just as polite, even Lord Reid, as if their conversation at the round table had indeed been nothing but banter, and Lord Carrick made his blessings abundantly clear, as he generally did. Then at last came Richard and Alycia followed by Pedrig and Doru, and young Lady Castellon who was ever too serious for her age and didn't choose this moment to change that. The cloaked guards at the door joined the group and walked at a purposeful pace, much to Richard's chagrin.

"The voice of reason," Alycia said softly, with a slight bow.

"I don't appreciate being treated like a fool, Your Majesty," Lord Almaric said forwardly, choosing to ignore her comment, and not lightly. "How can I serve if you're so compelled to deceive me?"

"This is about what happened at the Manor of Blessed Voices," she informed him.

"I fear so. I've just been told what you intend to do with the Brodies."

"You must have heard wrongly if you're offended by it. I'd say what I propose is nothing less than flattery, but you're more stubborn than you know. If nothing else, keep an open mind."

"Lennord isn't looking for flattery. Nor does he want his family put up on display in court to be badgered by lords and knights from here to the Renorrmyn Shore."

"I don't agree with your hyperbole, my Lord, although your passion is already noted. To be clear, their uses will vary depending on what we find in Mürathneè. We might not even find a political use for your Brodies, if comfort is what you want." She lifted an eyebrow and cocked her head to one side in question.

"Yes, Lennord told me about that. A friend of his overheard a private conversation you had in the throne room. Everything he heard I now know. Do you want Lennord to investigate that mine?" Lord Almaric asked scathingly.

The Voice of Kings

Tristan strode to keep up alongside Alycia, whose regal dress swayed in time with her movements as if it were part of her, and in stark contrast, the tired Richard swaggered along her left flank, his pride and style sapped by her. A look of pain shot across her face and she sighed.

"You've misunderstood me entirely," she said. "You think my foreign contact at the manor was researching Sèhvorian mines for Lennord, don't you? You're confused, my friend. He's just a mediator for getting in contact with the men we really want to talk to: men from Harth, Lord Tristan, who know things that may help us. Whatever secrets Sèhvorian mines hold, we'd best get there before anyone else, and these insiders are going to help us."

"This is even worse!" Lord Almaric cried angrily. "Your Majesty, think what you do. I know it sounds inane to play politics the honest way, but the more honest we can be in political affairs, the more we can be with the world. This game is a dangerous one."

"Our sources are the ones being dishonest," Alycia said with a shrug.

"Unfortunately, I have to agree with the Empress," Richard said irritably.

He bowed his head when Tristan looked his way. Clearly Alycia had already told him all she knew, likely not with his consideration. And she'd been convincing enough for him to yield to her wishes.

"What do you propose?" Lord Almaric said more calmly.

"Wait, for now. When we learn more about our insider, we'll arrange a meeting. I suspect they'll not want to come here, and that I fear. Someone will have to entreat for information wherever they wish it."

"You must send me," Lord Almaric said urgently. "If it's to be done, I'll go and see that it's done right."

"I could think of none more suited," the Empress said.

There was no lie in her voice or jest of any kind, but a tender approval, at once sweet and powerful in a way that made Tristan's heart pang with regret, for she could have been like this more often, yet chose instead to revel in secrets and deception. They reached a stairwell and it occurred to Tristan that she was likely heading for her chambers. Whether Richard would accompany her he couldn't tell, but somehow he doubted it. His heart panged again as he remembered the shower of blood for the grass at the manor.

"The deaths of those mercenaries could have been avoided," Lord Almaric said.

"That wasn't your fault," Richard said fiercely, coming to an abrupt and clumsy halt. Alycia met her husband's dead stop, seemingly to the very moment, and looked Tristan sternly in the eyes.

"Sir Yanick told me how you rushed in to protect him when you garnered the impression he was in danger. I always knew you were better than other men."

"I did what I had to do. I *shouldn't* have had to."

"I hear you," the Empress said sombrely. "I don't like keeping secrets. It is the price I pay for choosing to be involved in politics."

"There are other options, Your Majesty. I've sworn my loyalty a hundred times, and I'll do it a hundred more if I have to. You can trust me. So if it please, if Lennord's involvement in this was an afterthought, then that means you've yet to tell me what you had in mind for him."

"Trust had nothing to do with it."

Alycia frowned and looked all around the room before returning her bold stare to meet his, as if the answers he sought had been with him the whole time. Sympathy was her gift at that moment.

"Sometimes you think too much," she said plainly, squeezing his hand, and she whisked herself away.

Tristan did not move. He bit his lip and watched them slowly shrink.

"Pedrig, Doru, with me please," he called out almost before he knew what he was doing. Alycia merely shot a tired glance at the two knights breaking off from the formation, as if she'd never cared for them being there in the first place, and disappeared around a corner.

"My Lord?" Sir Pedrig said quizzically, while Doru said the same with his face.

"Sir Pedrig, you told me about the manor because you didn't fear being a mediator. Would you do the same for me again?"

"Would I or will I?" the aging knight answered thickly.

He was not being rude, Tristan was sure, in spite of his low tone. His loyalty was unwavering, in service and in respectfulness. Tristan only wished he knew why, and more so yearned to learn the same from Doru, who he didn't know at all, though he followed Richard more so than Alycia. Pedrig was grizzled, and yet retained a huge amount of grace, always keen to do the proper thing, whatever it was in the world at the current time. Sir Doru, dark of complexion and hair, and dull of mood, must have been of similar accord or else Alycia wouldn't have brought him so close to her affairs.

Only Tristan cared to ponder the basis of their loyalty, and as when he first received lordship and a thousand times again, he felt a sensation of being beyond the bounds of his body, as if he were in a dream all this time, and his lack of cohesion with the state of things served to tug him part way out of the dream. Though for as unheard of a consideration as it was, he didn't feel mad for questioning why such men would be so loyal if they had no ambitions. Whatever the case, Tristan held admiration for them, even as he didn't understand it fully: surely such loyalty was to be loved in return.

The two knights waited for his reply, Pedrig icy cold and Doru wary as he often looked; one would think him the one to be scared of most, but Tristan was very conscious not to judge him.

"Either now or in the future," Lord Almaric replied to Pedrig, "will you tell me of the Empress's affairs? I need help. I need to know what she wants with the Brodies so I can rest easy, or stop it before they're hounded by lords familiar and foreign alike. I don't see it ending well when they prove not to be helpful. Unless..." Lord Almaric trailed off and looked strained for an answer.

"I haven't heard anything," Sir Pedrig said.

"I spend most of my time with the Emperor," Sir Doru added.

"You don't take orders from the Empress? She hired you. I thought she might have tasks for you seeing as she brought you into her inner sanctum at such short notice."

"Technically I take orders from the Emperor. He's an easy man to work for; he doesn't demand much of me. The Empress gives me most of my orders, you know that, yes, only I would have to take his orders over hers if it came to it. And his over yours. If the Empress told me anything about whatever this is you're talking about, I would probably tell you, Lord Paramount. Probably. Maybe not. I don't know what it is now, do I, so I can't say."

Doru frowned, showcasing many deep lines cut into his face like scars, and shrugged apologetically. Tristan took a step backwards and stroked his hair back idly. Even his hair felt younger when he was with these two, not because they were old, wicked and world-weary, but because they were made wise by the way of a soldier's life, a kind of wisdom he was grateful never to learn.

"Has it occurred to you that you know only what the Empress knows?" Pedrig suggested. "There might not be a grand plan, not now, maybe never."

"In passing, I suppose. I'd rather know for certain."

"And you're suggesting what?" Sir Doru said darkly.

"Suggesting nothing," Lord Almaric replied tiredly, feeling a sense that he'd been in this situation before. "I mean exactly what I'm saying, Sir. Lots of men would jump to the same conclusion though. That's what happens when we treat each other like mouthpieces for ideas in council; we forget the mouth has a mind connected to it and it was spoken for a reason. I wish I knew every reason, every lord, the thinking behind every prejudice and folly." Tristan tapped a finger on his chin as he thought in silence. Pedrig shifted where he stood.

"I think the Empress wishes something similar," the old knight dared to say. "She goes about it in a very different way than you, of course."

Pedrig's social perception was highly impressive for a man of his line of work, and his resolve was strong to boot.

"Forgive me, Sir. Why are you here?" Lord Almaric said to his own surprise. His curiosity got the better of him. If nothing else, he hoped it would help. "Here in Castle Aurail that is, as an imperial Guardian."

"I was approached to be known as one of the most trusted knights in Burtal; doesn't that, in itself, answer it?" Sir Pedrig answered.

"Quite," Sir Doru agreed, furrowing his brow.

"Everyone has different reasons for doing things, good Sirs. I'm not questioning the worth of your decisions, only the reasons for them. Nothing sinister, nothing judgemental."

"This is the pinnacle of anything I could ever hope to achieve," Sir Pedrig said proudly. "I've no mind to be a knight errant as I once was, and I was already on guard duty in Aurail when Lady Castellon approached me, so this is just a step up from that. A grand step."

"Furthermore..." Sir Doru said gruffly. "You may not know this, from where you come from, but when you are born as I was, you might make mistakes and assume you must continue to do so. Discipline is hard to come by. As a Guardian, gods Tristan, I'm made right at last. It compels of me the discipline I failed to achieve on my own. Where once I was only my mistakes, now I must rise up to my potential. It's as simple as it sounds, my Lord, though I have to say I'm flattered by you making it complicated. I was a captain in the army and I can't lie, I'd always wanted to work in the castle. I knew I needed a direction. I didn't ask for this, mind, the honour was given to me because I deserved it. So the honour was greater still, you could say. How many other places can I serve such revered people?"

"Do you ever wonder about honour? To serve because it's honourable is beyond me, I'm afraid. Isn't honour an attribute, not a reason unto itself? I hear it used as the latter far more often, and it frightens me. It can be used as a strong shield without much effort."

The knights were both puzzled at this simple statement, Pedrig cerebral as he pursed his lips, and Doru more anxious. One might say that was the correct response. Perhaps it was.

At almost the exact same time, they seemed to come to a suitable conclusion, for they both loosened and realisation crossed them in a flash.

"I know you're talking about these unhelpful lords who play with power just because they have it. If I can be that bold," Sir Doru said without the smallest hint of anxiety or regret.

"You're forgetting," Sir Pedrig put in, "that we provide counsel as well as our steel. As I said, nowhere else could I be trusted like this. I won't try to convince you, I'll take it you know what you're talking about."

Doru nodded profusely, stern and serious as could be.

"Not because I'm a lord," Tristan said matter-of-factly, half-joking.

"A reputation precedes you," Sir Doru told him, playing with his scabbard like a beast grooming its paws, utterly inoffensive. And he was a beast of a sort with that wild, dangerous look, if such a beast there was that could be so disciplined in everything else. "This honour, it's more than I could have asked for, to have my mind valued as my sword. But I know my limits, Lord. They stop short of ruling the country."

The Voice of Kings

Tristan couldn't help but smile at that. That was quite a sharp answer in all fairness. He raised a hand to put a stop to it, and just like that, the knights stood down, the conversation dropped.

"I'm tired, I meant no offence," Lord Almaric said, and in their silence, they told him how unnecessary his apology was. "Sirs."

He bowed, and they bowed lower, and though he walked quickly, he didn't get far before the greying knight called out to him, standing in the precise spot Tristan had left him like a dog waiting for orders. Sir Doru was almost out of sight already, striding away gripping his scabbard tightly, bolt upright, cold and forceful like a winter's wind whipping through the stone corridor. The other knight was shining as he stood by a candelabra.

"I've heard it said you take a lot of advice from your wife," Sir Pedrig stated, voice blank like his face but for a tinge of his slyness. "I've heard it said she always acts from the heart. Maybe that's your problem."

"If my reputation is so legendary as a result of what you rightly heard, I call that a result. What would court be like if more men listened to Lady Almaric?"

Pedrig's expression shifted to exaggerated consideration, and in what Tristan could only assume to be a moment of mutual humorous understanding, Pedrig raised his brow and left him be, alone in the cold corridor to process another conversation to as profound a degree as possible. The candles made the corridor quite warm, considering.

It all came back to Alycia's words though. To entreat potential enemies was something he'd never done, not in this way, not to this extent, and as Lennord said, for what? He would do it regardless. He had to. Who else?

To treat for ancient knowledge then, like superstitious men of old. At the Wood of Riches, as like it would be.

Chapter Twenty-eight: Blinded in the Rain

The rain in Melphor was like fog this day, especially light to look at as if it was swimming through the air, thick and slow. Oh, how thick, and from the sound of it alone, one would hear it for what it was, fast and unrelenting. It was upon a battlement that Kate stood in this storm, underneath a near hollow watch tower within which no men of the Watch currently stood their duty, though if one did come along, she would move. The tower protected her from the worst of the weather, yet even as she looked up at the distraction of footsteps on floorboards, she saw that the stone interior was lined with wooden beams, as much of the city was, as if none of the stone was trusted not to crumble.

She looked out upon the circular valley again; she stood there at the edge of the ramparts squinting like a hawk that had lost its way and didn't know what it was doing anymore, the vague shapes drifting through the foggy rain equally likely to be friends or the hunters. She listened to the rain in dreariness: she listened to its pattering on thatch and in the gutters, and its war beat on stone, in the hundreds of alleys that jutted at random from the main streets and went forth into the fog or circled back around into sight. She listened to its ringing on armour, its music made upon dozens of Watchmen who wandered about or stood stiffly on the walls like statues. It was better than listening to Henri Fealds, or rather waiting for him to speak. Like a creature preparing itself for winter, she tugged tightly at the collar of her woollen coat, long and coloured black.

Henri sat on a wooden chair at the back reserved for Watchmen, perpetually aware that he may have to rise at any moment, always keeping his hands far from his sword.

"You could have gone with my mother," Kate said.

"No, I couldn't. Not when I have orders to stay with you. What sort of reputation would I have if I disobeyed orders?"

"I'll just be standing here for a very long time. How is this dangerous? Elias is locked up in gaol. Hopefully he'll rot there."

"Elias didn't kill your friend, Kathrynne," Henri answered with an awkward cough, grim and intense and frightening as he stared straight ahead like a beast with one set purpose. "It was more than one person, and Elias wasn't there. Who knows where those men are now? On the road you'd think, but like I said, who knows? Do you know?"

"My mother is at the palace!" Kate rebuked bitterly, refusing now to close her eyes in disgust, as the temptation was, for fear of what she might see there. "Those bastards could be there."

"Elias recognises you because he's seen you recently; he might not remember your mother's face. She believes she'll be fine."

The Voice of Kings

Henri did not dare look at her. What was wrong with him? Was he scared to look at her? He seemed so. Kate was not at ease looking at him, but she hoped for something that inspired confidence at least.

"Don't you believe it?" Kate challenged him.

"I believe it."

"That's it?" Kate pressed, mouth agape, eyes searching without real hope of finding anything profound.

"What do you want from me? I have a sword; that's all I have. I don't know what you expect me to say. I'm no philosopher, I'm not a quick thinker. I came because I had to. I didn't know it would be like this. I..." he trailed off.

His voice was like two razors grating on one another. Something would snap or shatter soon. Here was a strong and brooding man admitting to a woman like Kate that he didn't know what he was doing. He had no idea how to inspire confidence or what that meant, but his muscles were plain beneath his mail and boiled leather, and he was serious enough. Some of the Watchmen she'd seen didn't look so strong, so that would seem an advantage for Henri, but she knew nothing of fighting. One thing she did know from her father was that his sword wasn't going to cut through plate armour, no matter how persistently he sought to make it shine, or how often he adjusted the strap or flicked up the sword from its scabbard with his thumb.

Some soldiers, even experienced ones, had little ticks where their weapons were concerned. Maybe these were Henri's. Nothing for her to worry about, that. She wanted to see no violence here. No violence. None.

"Why did you have to come?" Kate asked in very real curiosity, taking pressure off her legs as she slumped somewhat against the wall of the watchtower.

"Debts have to be repaid at some point. I learned that as a vagabond: debts beyond the promised price. Respect is hard to come by for mercenaries and there comes a time when a man needs respect. I did, anyway. Money's all well and good, Kathrynne, just not enough, not for me. I know the truth of it; I see people who serve and I see them happy or content or whatever you want to call it. The higher the master, the more content the servant, that's what I see. Your father is kind to me; he's different to other people. I'd guess he's worth more than most people, so here I am... testing the worth of service. Being loyal."

His words were of no consequence to Kate. Ask as she did for his answer, he was just rambling now. Her head ached and she slowly mulled his response over in her personal space, the banging of the rain acting as a shield wherein she could pretend she was alone. When the words finally caught up with her, she winced and sent Henri a look of disbelief, taking her gaze quickly away before returning it in defiance, feeling both shy and confident at once.

"A test?" Kate spat. "Why not go test your loyalty on someone else, where people aren't being murdered?"

"I didn't mean that," Henri exclaimed in defence, face flushed red as if to show his pain by way of blood. "I'm serious about this; this isn't just some experiment to me. You have my service. I can't guarantee I'll say the right things all the time. I wish I could, but I can't."

Just as swiftly as her temper had bubbled to rage, Kate deflated back to sorry contemplation. Henri Fealds was not as he should have been given his shined leather armour and unfriendly appearance, though neither was he the man she'd hope to have around watching her back.

"My brother Lucian knew what you were?" Kate asked pensively. "He knew who you are?"

"He knows I've travelled about a bit, mostly in the highlands, mind. I don't know much else. He knows your father's done work for me too, when I stopped travelling. I don't know that he cared; he's a sharp one, your brother, didn't let up his intentions. I remember not being able to work out if he was just asking questions for the sake of it or not, but he did ask about my mercenary work quite a bit. I said I was done with that and it seemed to please him, I think. A life of service is the best for me."

"I don't want to serve," Kate said without thinking.

Henri swished his tongue around his mouth, more conscious about what might spill out if he wasn't careful. When he opened his mouth to speak, he was cut short by Kate's mother entering, none more welcome a sight at such a time. On second thought, she was just happy to have her around at any time now, a tired and ailed representation of a god if she could be so bold. She was thoughtful and reserved beneath a woollen cloak much akin to Kate's.

"You're still here then," her mother said.

"Better out here than being cooped up at the inn."

"No cage for you," her mother said with a pale laugh.

"Did something happen at Maelphorydd?"

"Nothing happened. Nothing happened," her mother repeated disappointedly. "I've been standing outside that hall day after day and hardly anyone ever seems to come or go, just tight-lipped guards and that steward who won't grant me audience with Andrews. I meant to send a letter to your father, and he took it and just said he'd think about sending it. I should have worried more when he told me the hall would reserve the right to read letters sent to us. I have a theory I'd like to test sooner rather than later."

"Is it dangerous?"

"I hope not," her mother said, biting her lip. "I have a feeling we're not allowed to leave this city."

"Wouldn't Andrews just arrest us if he was suspicious? The way Edwin... the way Edwin described him makes me think so."

"Could be. If I'm right about this, Andrews might have had sentries at the gate memorise our appearance, which means people are watching us, or the gate guards already know what we look like."

"Sergeant Denkyn?" Henri suggested, back to his gruff self.

Kate wandered to the doorway, running her fingers on the dark, coarse stone, and looked up towards Maelphorydd, the great beacon of the city as it now was, fronted by half a dozen pyres so strong and bright they swallowed the rain like a drakeel does a rat, so inconsequential one wouldn't even notice a difference in its behaviour. She wondered what secrets were held there, not that wondering would do her any good, and she remembered then that the prison was hidden up near there too, or so she'd heard.

"Why wouldn't Sergeant Denkyn be locked up with his captain?" she asked aloud, for which her mother had no answer. Kate knew that, most likely, he wasn't even in the city. She hoped so; the further away Olswalt's men were from her, the safer she'd feel.

"We'll just have to see for ourselves what the situation is," her mother explained. "We have to go to the gate."

The rain painted misery. She enjoyed rain usually, only today it just personified something in the world she wanted to shut her eyes from. It may well have been a farce to think as such, she understood that, but thought it anyway. In that light, an illness was illuminated, by which she would have to trust her mother on this to err on caution, whatever she chose to do. Crazy as it sounded, she trusted that the idea was a valid one and could help them assess their situation.

"The weather isn't so kind today, but it won't kill us," her mother said encouragingly, and added, for good measure, "we'll take it step by step. Neither of us is putting the other in danger here."

Kate nodded her obligated agreement and was the first to step outside, throwing her own hood as far over her face as it would go, and now the rain hammered on it and echoed inside it. Lowering her head in paranoid instinct, she ironically felt like a spy herself, peering from beneath her woollen shield like a hare from its hole, working her way through the rain from shadow to shadow insofar as that made sense, as this whole little world was cast in it.

At the stables where she knew their horses were kept, she searched with eyes alone for her beautiful piebald mare, noticing soon enough that she was the only one to do so. Her mother had just chosen to stop here because the exit, the wooden double doors of the city, wide open, could be examined in certainty from here.

"Do you recognise anyone here?" Kate asked anxiously, shaking her head ponderously as she failed to recognise any faces, for better or worse.

"None," the reply came in firmness. "What do you think, Henri?"

"See what happens? I wouldn't risk recommending any of my own advice without proper thought. I think I shouldn't go through with you, not right away, that's all I'll say."

"Do that," Kate's mother agreed. "Follow after a few seconds."

Her mother tugged at her arm more sharply than she'd expect from her, reminding her in stark fashion that both of them were scared of what was or wasn't to come, serving only to heighten her awareness even more. Her steps felt plodding and loud, an error which she was alarmed to discover when she strode right past her mother, so forced herself to slow down and steel her nerves. But it didn't change how she felt, how there seemed only one path left in the world, or how every inflection of every guard was like a sword being drawn on her. One shuffled in his spot, and another passing by touched his pommel and she nearly jumped. One at the gate took note of them.

Her shuffle at last brought her to that exit, the archway passing overhead like a blessed gate of the gods, though she dared not check if it had paid off, speeding up to meet with the wall. There she stood for a while, looking down upon the outer city, then suddenly it dawned: it dawned in glorious light that no suits of armour could be heard clanging beyond the music of the rain, no shouts of "halt" nor shadows of soldiers bearing over from behind.

And so it was to the eyes when she turned to face the city. There was no interest in her from the Watchmen on the wall, and the gate guards had stayed put. A relief washed her clean but something still gnawed at her, because in the recesses of her brain, she was told that it didn't make sense. Henri walked through the gates unmolested and stopped dead before the two of them, working the joints in his shoulders as activity to calm his heightened awareness.

"This doesn't make any sense, does it?" her mother muttered. "Why would they make a point of reading and withholding my letter if I'm allowed to just leave the city and send another?"

"Could the steward be acting with impunity?" Kate suggested.

"Or taking a bribe from someone not acting in the Count's interests," Henri added. "What was in the letter?"

"Nothing incriminating, I assure you. I'm not so stupid as to spell out our situation. I was vague, although maybe not vague enough on reflection. I wasn't stupid enough to sign it at least. Lennord would recognise my handwriting from two arms' length away, so don't worry about that."

Much seemed to happen in the following time, yet nothing really did. Illusions sprang up in all corners of the brain that came to nothing: trying to imagine where Patric Denkyn would spy on her from below; what he would do if far away; what Martin Caedor had done when he'd passed here. She frowned at her own thoughts. It was odd, but it was all her imagination would allow, two armies cramped in what was once a field while they planned their next move. And if Patric Denkyn wanted to know the same as her, where would he stand to observe that imagining? Kate's mother distracted her, taking dread with her every step as she made to return to the city. Then she stopped, beckoned for the two of them and shed fear as they returned together.

"Where're you from?" Kate heard an unfamiliar voice say once she was inside, cold enough to freeze her.

"Highlands, same as you I should think," Henri answered.

Kate made herself turn, trying to keep her face in the shadow of her hood. It was a Watchman who'd halted him, one by the gates, but it wasn't him alone that worried her. Others congregated around the area in no real formation, casually watching the situation unfold.

"We're on the lookout for suspicious men and I don't know that your like isn't a bit suspicious," the guard said. "I don't like the way you're patrolling about."

"I'm just walking."

"And your friends?"

"Same."

The guard scoffed at this. He licked his lips, looking around to make sure he was not alone in the enquiry, and reached for Henri's sword, pulling it out halfway, and there he looked very closely at it, running his fingers on it as if working out its length and width in his head.

"Quite nice," the Watchman admitted. "Very shiny. New, is it? Doesn't look like it's been used to me."

The Watchman simply loosened his fingers and the sword fell back into its scabbard, though the man kept his hand as if to provoke Henri, and perhaps that was his intention, as that wasn't all. He was giving Henri a quizzical look, then all of a sudden, he stepped back, and in a slow, wide arc drew his own blade and waved it in Henri's direction like a toy, before holding it out still to catch the rain, for it to run from the tip like a waterfall.

"Show me how you fight," the Watchman challenged, to the mild chagrin of some of his fellow soldiers, and the pleasant surprise of others. However, none of them lifted a finger to stop it, nor the civilians mingling in the area, and certainly not Kate who dared not make her presence known beyond what was absolutely necessary, as if the slightest movement would cause all her secrets to come spilling out.

"Why?" Henri said to him haplessly, shrugging defensively.

"Because I've told you to. Because I need to know who you are, and what better way to do that?"

"You can learn about me from my decline, can't you?"

"No, come on, draw sword," the Watchman goaded, still to the ambivalence of all.

"I used to be in the County Watch Patrol: I was a respected member and still have that respect."

"I don't give a shit what you were. Let's all see what you are now."

The Watchman jabbed his sword forward, quick and precise, precise enough to slit Henri's throat, she presumed, right up to the moment his hand fell limp when his will to care faded. In an instant, his dignity returned to him, and he resumed his post as if he could regain his respect as a public servant just like that. The servant Henri didn't wait for the leave of any one of those men, taking care to maintain his own dignity, or what was left of it, as he did so. It was the urgent obligation of Kate's mother to pull her from the scene: something Kate had forgotten to do while she tried her hardest to place that Watchman's face, in the hope that it would help her or, gods be merciful, save her life. She was sure she could recall the gaoler's face well enough, why not this man's?

"Thank you for not losing your temper," her mother said, spelling her appreciation in every syllable. "It's best you don't give people like that what they want. We have no idea if he was acting on a whim or not. If he was, he won't bother us again if he's smart. If not... at least we know not to trust the City Watch."

Henri was positively intrigued by this, so much so one might think it hadn't crossed his mind before. Kate couldn't analyse a man at a glance like Isaac could, but realistically, she was probably correct in her first assumption here. In spite of her father's lessons of never underestimating people, she couldn't help judging Henri now, for the implications of his ignorance unnerved her.

"Did I hear you say you were in the Watch Patrol?" Kate said. "Was that a lie?"

"It wasn't. I was, for a time, just like I was a mercenary. I don't know that I was respected: that part was a lie."

The admission made him immediately exasperated, and his face flushed red again: in shame as well as embarrassment? His teeth grated together and, in general, it didn't take a master of the silver tongue, like her brother, to see he wasn't feeling well.

"Why wouldn't you be respected?" her mother asked.

When he failed to answer, floundering in his torment, her mother led the way, without notice, down one of the many side streets in the city, a narrow thing lit by candles swinging gently in the wind, shielded from above with leather canopies.

"Have you got something to say?" her mother pushed when they were all there. He hesitated, but it was plain he wanted to speak.

"There's a reason I was stuck doing what I could back in Caedor. I'm not gifted with a sword, as it happens. I'm not skilled enough for the Watch Patrol, not vicious enough for a mercenary's life, not clever enough to go my own way, nor much of a survivalist for that matter. Why would they respect someone they feel they have to drag through the hills and the towns on a lead?"

"But look at you!" Kate cried. "You're strong! Anyone can see that. That must count for something."

"It counts a great deal, but it's not what the Watch Patrol want. They want men of discipline and resource who can fight in formation, and that's not me; I've tried long enough to know it's not. I could join a town guard somewhere but... no, not now, not anymore."

"So that's it, you can't fight?"

"I never said I couldn't fight," Henri said, pushing the corners of his lips up. "I said I haven't fared in skilled combat. My fingers can't get the hang of it."

"It's really a good thing you didn't draw your sword then, all considered," her mother sighed, rubbing her wrinkled forehead. "Best you keep it that way. You're menacing enough without having to do anything; better let that be enough, I say."

"No argument here."

Kate kept to herself, nodding in place of doing anything meaningful, though she felt more melancholy at the whole business and many words were said to herself of what would happen now, ever trying to develop a mind for a strategy; an uphill struggle to do it alone. As they went out into what passed for natural light, Henri's dark features were lit to again express vulnerability, however miniscule, that no man seemed infallible to. When she met eyes with her mother, more ghostly words were thrown back and forth. All she received from that was a message of trust. Certainly she felt the need to trust Henri less, but obviously that wasn't it.

Later on, she sat in her bedchamber, just with her mother. By the window she was again, as a cynical old woman might be when judging the world. She was with someone who wasn't cynical, to hold her back at least, and no, she wasn't old either.

"I wish we could know for sure whether we'll be stopped if we leave," her mother said very suddenly. "Maybe we should leave if we can, head for the nearest harbour, get far away from the highlands. Justice can wait as long as needs be if we're truly in danger."

"There's no one to trust here," Kate replied agreeably.

"What about Sir Edwin's parents?"

"If we can find them without having to trust anyone else."

Anything more Kate had to say vanished as, like a startled cat, she sprang from her chair and peered out the window as the thunder of hooves echoed up the street followed by the horses themselves, slower now by fault of the steepness, yet still speedy. Upon the back of one was slung a large bag, and all of the reckless riders appeared to have dried blood smeared on their armour. Everyone was on edge for reasons most veiled, and it was only a matter of time before the violence reached her. Condemning Elias for his crimes could not be avoided now, and to do so would oppose whatever fledgling ideals took flight without her permission whenever something threatened to go awry. After seeing Edwin's death a thousand times in her mind's eye, she was beginning to understand why. Fear begot fear. It was only surprising that a part of her seemed to already understand that.

If the play of her father's new status was to work at all, it would need to be pushed, and soon. *It failed already, miss*, she heard, and, as quickly, wondered if that was right. The Count had denied its existence outright, nothing more. *Serve*, she thought wearily. Whatever move they played, they would have to make it in all haste, she felt in her bones. Before anyone had the chance to perform real magic.

Chapter Twenty-nine: The Mirror

The magic of having Harth as a playground faded further. Quaint new aspects became familiarities to Isaac: he saw Tamzin Morzall, the daughter of a prominent figure, in the streets and stopped to exchange pleasantries and coy observations of each other's jobs, he received word from Vicentei in formal fashion stating the reality to acquiesce to his most realistic of needs, and baited interest in the others. And Harth was like a second home.

It was Lucian's quarters he visited for enlightenment; an odd way to humour his situation, that he must have truly been starving for momentum for his personal venture. Either that, or it was a mildly funny joke planted in his brain by a bored god. Either way, he was going to follow the instinct and see what came of it. His dreams were cerebral enough to make him pause for thought more when he was awake, so he was going to exhaust that method for all it was worth. Then he would rush back into the fray. It couldn't keep waiting for him.

"Have you come to ask for help?" Lucian said, looking up from a mess of papers that he was exploring with admirable aplomb, considering how half of them were petty and irrelevant pieces, gleaned from Isaac's prior skimming of them. "When I'm not doing work to clean up your mess, I'm trying to find the best way of working for myself. Although, actually, if there's a chance I can prove you wrong, I'll help you if I can, when I can."

"You presume much, seeing as I haven't said anything yet. And of such a touchy subject too."

"I don't think I'm overreaching in my presumption, little brother. Am I wrong?" Lucian put to him bluntly, showing an inkling of uncertainty.

"Though your help would be appreciated, that's not why I'm here. If I'm honest, I'm hoping you could start by telling me why I'm here," Isaac mused in jest, half to himself, then he waved a hand to wipe the slate clean on consideration of what Lucian might have to say about that. "What are you doing?"

Lucian, quill in hand for marking interesting sections of whatever dull papers he was building enthusiasm for, made to answer that question by referring to the documents, only to sharply snap his head back up. He inspected Isaac in graveness until a truth clicked into place for him, and what Isaac would hesitate to label as satisfaction set in. He'd adopted some local clothing, as flamboyant as he would ever wear, which wasn't saying much, and thus looked at least a little relaxed.

"I'm attempting to discern the most relevant and interesting data for my own benefit, before I go out and seek the people most implicated with such areas of ruling," Lucian settled on, deliberately stilted though perhaps more so than he was aware of. "What are you doing?"

The Mirror

"I've been doing much the same as you, for my part."

"Sadly your charade is based on memories of your child ghost and nothing else; I'm working based on empirical truths. Don't take it personally, it's just how it is."

"We'll see," Isaac said affably. *Today*, he whispered to himself. *Get back to work today. Waiting far from home is no more productive than waiting at home itself.* "Tell me about the High Duke."

"What?" Lucian said bluntly. "If this is part of a riddle or trick, then I'm sorry I offended you. I'm sorry I riled you up. Only, at some point you'll have to accept the illusion for what it is." Isaac's brother took to his feet suddenly, fire burning in his eyes, but only at the right angle was it visible. His passion was subtle and dark, yet there it was, masked by his frustration. "I thought you *had* given up. And I was relieved. We were all relieved. What will Father say when he finds out what you've been doing? Or when you tell him. You'll tell him I expect, because you're cocksure enough to think he'll approve. Think what you've become. Just hurry up and finish this for good... I don't want to see you go mad."

"If I've always been wrong, perhaps I've always been mad. I don't believe that, but I don't presume to know what it was I saw in that mine. I've been objective. I know because I've thought about it for long enough. Tell me about the High Duke. Tell me what he told you, I know you've wanted to."

"You want to believe what he saw was magic too?"

"I want to believe nothing of the sort. I'll believe what I see, then I'll decide whether I care. But I've heard intriguing rumours about the incident in the High Duke's duchy. They say creatures sprang out from the woods and attacked his men as one; they say they cared not for their own lives."

"Who are they, pray tell? I know you're not talking about the criers."

"It's a rumour. I haven't heard it from the criers, but you'll be surprised what you pick up when you're as bored as I am, when you overhear a conversation and pursue the subject matter with anyone you can. I don't believe anything yet, but you can't deny something strange happened on the High Duke's land. I haven't a clue what it is, but no one will until it's investigated. That's how the world works. That's why I asked you the question; there's really nothing else to it. Knowledge doesn't just drop into one's lap."

"And so it doesn't, but that doesn't make just any speculation viable. I won't fault your intention, but I can't agree with that. Don't trick yourself into believing what suits you. You're smarter than that."

Isaac frowned. His brother wasn't going to tell him of the Hugh Duke's story. Of course he wasn't; Lucian feared what Isaac would do with the information. The ironic truth was that, now the subject had been dropped, he'd lost interest in it entirely. Isaac sensed he was no longer welcome and turned for the door, only to feel a hand grab his arm tightly, and there Lucian stood, clutching it with unnecessary strength. Isaac looked him up and down as if he were mad, putting on a smile in the confusion. Then his brother spoke in the tongue of grave warning, eyes locked open.

"Don't let this control you. I don't want to see you go mad over this. Stupid thing to lose your head over..."

"I'll bear that in mind," Isaac replied, his fire fizzled out.

Outside he then went, without delay, breathing in the crisp, salty air, cool in the evening light. It wasn't highland air but it did its job: it helped one think. His attire was a great comfort: high class for the highlands. Today he wore the same clothes he'd worn upon setting out for Harth: a standard doublet over a more elaborate white shirt, though he wore the boots he'd bought just recently.

Jamys arrived after not too long a time, typically pleased, in an understated sort of way, at having been given a task other than standing upon the spot, and still covered in soot from their day at the forge.

"Martello said nothing of you, try as I did to make him think of you," he said, shrugging. Isaac mulled this over, though in truth had already made his mind up. "Is that all? May I go?"

"You don't want to see me coerce your master first?"

"I advised you to wait."

"So you did. It's been two days since you said that; what am I waiting for?"

"For long enough to make it seem like you've forgotten about him. To make it look like you had many other important things to do."

"I have, and that's true, and I don't have the money I did last week to bribe the Cooper's Guild, and the Bigamist's Guild, and Vicentei's Guild of Licensed Dithering, and whatever other obscure institutions you have tucked away. I'll not delay anymore."

"Well, your call. Just remember not to sound too fascinated by him."

"I'll muster all my strength... I never thought of you to lecture anyone," Isaac joked.

"Why? Because I've killed people?" Jamys said mildly.

The mercenary's intelligence and wit seemed to grow every day. If he'd just met the man, he'd think he was hiding something, but no, he was thusly astute and smarmy in oddly situational ways. Already he knew what drove Isaac in the most basic sense, and this latest comment didn't fail to impress him. And make him smile, shockingly: a sort of sad, ironic smile, yet a smile it was, and he enjoyed it, despite himself.

"We're going to see him," Isaac decided firmly.

"As you say. It should be good to watch."

The mercenary wasted no time now that his order had been given: a purpose assigned and taken gladly, for the perverse thrill of watching a verbal battle between his two masters was an idea he could put his weight behind.

The Mirror

To the coast they went, taking a different route this time, to the south of the city where the closest thing Harth had to a slum was nestled: a thriving community of its own that still put much of Aurail to shame from what he'd seen of it. The streets were far narrower, there was less vibrancy in the clothes and less brightness in the wooden buildings, and more grime on the whole, really, yet it was well enough to deceive. To this, Isaac couldn't give much thought however, and when the roads leading, in his estimation, to the guild hall came and went, he had to question his guide's intentions.

"Martello isn't at the guild hall," Jamys said. "He's out on business. I could take you to the hall if you really want. You're just not in the mood for waiting, I'm guessing."

"You're right, only I have an inherent wish to have no part in his business that isn't directly tied to my own."

"So you shouldn't. Just relax and trust I'm not leading you into a blood orgy."

Isaac had to trust him, he decided, and argued no more. Westward, Jamys now guided him, to where the relatively flat coastline of Harth finally jumped up into a small cliff, upon which cramped farms were tended to and took in the sea air with great appreciation as it was apparently good for these kinds of crops. It was only when the two of them neared those cliffs that all turned to ash around him in the flames of rage, and his blood was petrified in his veins upon hearing that most odious of songs: that of swords.

"You promised this wouldn't happen," Isaac confronted Jamys.

"Not *this*," Jamys protested calmly in a semantic correction that was so rare of him. "Martello is probably there, but it's not what you think. Just trust that I understand how steel speaks. So does Martello. The man he's fighting doesn't. There'll be no blood orgy, Isaac. Like I said."

Reluctantly, Isaac followed, though in his heart he couldn't deny the intrigue of it. Fairness be, he was quick to turn the last corner before the road opened up through a dilapidated marble arch to the cliff top, where a crowd had gathered to watch a display of violence: the mercenary captain fighting a man half a head shorter than he, who was flailing a sword in what he prayed to be competent fashion. Martello, in his stunning blue armour, jumped back from a slash aimed at his head, more dexterous than he should have been, only to then hold his longsword out for his opponent's weapon to meet, letting it slam into his own blade and barely flinching. There the steel of their weapons grinded, Martello overcome by a fierce concentration now, death written on his face, while his opponent's was strained and had life scrawled on it, for now.

Suddenly, the impasse ended with little strength, Martello flipping his sword skilfully and, in half-swording his blade, clobbered the now stumbling man away such that he almost tripped over his own feet. Martello span on the spot to naturally control the exertion of his powerful blow, dark blade flashing in the sunlight momentarily, plain and undecorated, the opposite of how he portrayed himself now. Then, in an upward motion, he struck his enemy's retaliatory blow, driving it high before, with much the same brute force, circling it round and, like a puppet, dragging the poor man from his battle stance, finally trapping the weapon between the grass and his own longsword. Once there, the expected happened. The mystery man attempted to cling onto his hilt for dear life, but in half a second, it was ripped from his fingers and, clutching at nothing, he staggered and yelped.

"I yield!" the man screamed near incoherently, throwing his hands up.

Martello was quietly smug about this. What he was expecting from this as he glanced carelessly around at his audience was anyone's guess. If it was appreciation he sought, he'd have to try a lot better than beating on obviously weaker opponents. And he could stop enjoying it, the bloody-minded fool. To start with, he could cooperate, and end with learning a semblance of decency.

Martello gripped his longsword in just his right hand, then tossed it to his left, grabbing it from the air as though it were a dagger. Then he held out his free hand for his defeated opponent, who was reluctant to take it but felt he had no other choice. When their palms met, Martello clenched tightly and pulled him in to get a closer look at the pain-stricken face.

"Good show," Martello imparted with a sound of utter boredom, blank of face and all the more menacing for it. "To the City Watch with him," he ordered loudly.

Four men of the guild stepped forward to take up his offer: a mismatched group of warriors in no matching armour. Some wore more plate than others, and they shared no visual motif. And as they came forward to relieve their captain of the supposed criminal, Martello was once again a tad more respectable, emitting an aura of professionalism. He looked about him in sternness with an eye for jobs that needed doing, though when in one dark moment his eyes met with Isaac's across the field, he rolled his eyes and threw his sword down on the grass, beside where his scabbard and sling both lay.

The daydream ended with that stark stare, Isaac remembering his place and realising that, in his throat his heart had been lodged, and where before he'd shown no attempt to withhold his nervous contempt, he raised his eyebrows and put on a mild face. Such as it was, he knew he did well of it. To face a nightmare vision of oneself with waking eyes was no trifling thing, for it was already bad enough when a mirror in a dream showed an unfamiliar face when looked upon.

"Funny to see you here. I heard you get sick at the first drop of blood," Martello said when he approached.

"Rather predictably, you've misunderstood me entirely."

"It's a good job there wasn't a real fight," Martello rambled on, acting oblivious to Isaac's response. "When he challenged me for the right to go free, I guessed he didn't have a clue what he was doing, but, well, I didn't think he'd be so stupid. He'll have a long time to regret that now on a prison island somewhere."

The Mirror

"You wouldn't have let him go if he'd forced you to yield," Jamys pointed out, carrying the smallest hint of a question.

"No. I wouldn't. More fool him for thinking I'd do that. Funny really. He was a good thief and stealthy enough to evade the City Watch until now. Do you know how many counts of thievery he has on his belt?"

"We'll not talk about this," Isaac said.

It was obvious the captain was playing his game again, though not even Jamys found it amusing, or no more amusing than most other things. But Isaac could play too, and he was far better at it. Jamys folded his arms in declaration of his independence, allowing Martello to be the centre of attention.

"I've been thinking, actually, about your arrival to Harth. There's a damning oversight I should have asked before you lost your temper last we met. If you sailed here all the way from a land yet unmapped, you must have spoken another language, yes? Why would no one believe your story then, assuming they could work out what you were saying?"

"You probably know the answer to that. If you don't, hearing the answer from me won't give meaning to your life."

"I want to have a real conversation with you, and decide a few things on my own after that."

"I told you what might happen to you if you wouldn't shut your mouth," Martello interrupted matter-of-factly, then resorted to his trick of physical intimidation as he pretended to adjust the strap of his bastard sword. If this was all he could offer, he was a sad man indeed. Isaac chimed in swiftly thereafter.

"And for the record, I don't appreciate being talked down to by men who use threats as a substitute for proper discourse. One might even get the impression you're not the man you like people to think you are when you're out there putting on a show with your sword, or when you're behind your desk piling parchment. Maybe, *maybe*, you care about your past more than you think it's acceptable for a real man such as yourself to admit, and you get offended whenever people bring it up."

Isaac waited again to see if he'd been as much a fool as his brother would have him believe, praying that Jamys would play the part of advocate if Martello lost control. The captain was tough to figure out at times like this, when his real face was swapped out for an identical mask that was stone hard and bore reluctance as its unflinching bugbear. Unless that was the true face.

"What do you want, Brodie?" Martello put to him, surprising him with his seriousness. "You wouldn't believe how many people have asked me about my life across the sea. They come in droves and think to take away a token story, but I doubt if many of them think at all. Most of them take their leave in a hurry after they remember who I am. You, though... what is this, the third, fourth time you've hassled me?"

"Third."

"I can't decide if you're a smart man or an idiot. What do you really think you'll gain from all this?"

"Help me and we can find out what happened to your ship and its contents together, and in turn we'll find out if it has the connection to my experience that I think it does. Or, you can go back to repressing those memories and I'll find another way to finish what I started."

In the tension, Isaac was sorry to experience a heightening of his senses, as Martello's stench became all too apparent. He couldn't have broken a sweat fighting that purported thief, yet the whiff of it came and went in conjunction with the sea wind that jittered about on the cliff top.

"My old tongue was too similar, I was told, to Old Mürathneèan, with bits of an old Alassiien language. They worked out what I was saying after a bit of effort, and when I described my home country to them, they told me it must have been Alassii, that I'd sailed all the way round the world. That's what you wanted to hear, right?"

"It's what I expected: it's what I've heard, and what a story it is," Isaac replied, guard high. There was no possibility, this time, that he was going to look the fool, so he kept his emotions to himself and waited for the captain to impart some ridiculous claim to insult his intelligence.

"It's the truth. I can't say how that happened because I don't have a clue. I can tell you I believed I came from what they called Alassii for a long time. Until I realised it was nothing like what I remember. I never went as far east as the capital, but I was in the country to fight the last war there. What I saw was all wrong, and what I heard of the east didn't match up either. It was about then I decided I wanted nothing to do with it. Lot of young men found their calling in that war, and I was no different. I get to do what I'm good at. No amount of caring about my past will change that."

"If you're so sure you're not from Alassii, you must have a good memory of it."

"I remember enough."

"The ship you were on, the Salet Antonia," Isaac pressed, forgetting his reservations that he might draw the most from Martello. "Were your parents there with you?"

"Only my father."

"Where was your mother?"

"Not aboard. I remember she expected me to be gone a long time and wanted to come." Martello fell to silence.

"Your mother might still be alive and you haven't bothered to find her?"

"Were you born yesterday, Brodie? There's a thousand reasons that would never work. If I got back to my home country, I might not even recognise it."

"Tell me about your father then."

The Mirror

Isaac checked his tone. He'd been very forward, but there was no need to tread carefully with this man about family matters. Whatever affection he may have had was a crust of a memory, his dependence that all children have forgotten. Martello expressed no regret. Again, Isaac thought, maybe this would lead nowhere, but he was here now and he'd do all he could.

"My father was captain of the ship," Martello said deliberately, as if his recollection was in doubt. "It was the best ship ever built, or at least he told me so. It needed to be good because we were sailing as far as east goes. We had Sèhvorian steel with us, since you wanted to know. Serolem'hir I think we called it. And those bloody crystals, and more I bet. Don't think I ever knew what the point was, try as I did. I wasn't told. I was just the son of the captain: a midshipman who didn't pull his weight as far as the others were concerned."

"That wasn't the worst of it," Isaac prompted, stroking his hair into presentable fashion as he stared intently, nodding in barely contained intrigue.

"The storm was the worst of it," Martello spat, causing Isaac to flinch. Suddenly he was a dangerous man again, smelling of old sweat and utterly unpredictable: his eyes racketed in Jamys's direction, then back to Isaac with all the might of his sword swing. "It just happened one day, came out of fucking nowhere, and it's not just my memory playing tricks on me. On that trip, I forgot much; I slept half the day sometimes when I was too tired. Later, when the water ran dry, I felt dazed when I was awake, and only felt alive in my dreams. Time had no meaning, but even now I can see that storm as clear as you are to me right now. You've never seen a clear day turn to hell that quickly, not even in your highlands. Hell, I bet you've never seen a storm like that, never so many lightning bolts in so short a time. Salet wasn't so pretty after that."

His mood darkened, enthusiasm setting slow and eerie like the sun. As if on that cue, Isaac realised he felt hot, right before a gust of wind caught him, whipping up his hair in a flurry, and he was at once very cool, cold even. He feared for Martello's temper, but was too fascinated to let it affect him.

"That wasn't the worst part either, come to it," Martello continued. "The worst part was the aftermath. Weeks or months might have passed, I couldn't tell. It was okay at first, until one by one the crew decided they didn't want to share the food anymore. I bet you've never seen men so desperate and violent, have you? If you can't take the sight of a lopped off head, you'd probably have jumped overboard just to avoid seeing this unfold. Started off subtle, you understand, then escalated. Poison was ditched for daggers to the sleeping, and that for a battle on deck until I was the last man standing. Well, boy. I remember I waited inside like my father said, and he led me to a rowing boat and dumped me in. Irony was, we were nearing Harth by that point, not that the ship could be saved then. Our shoddy repairs were crumbling even as I was dumped into that boat, and my father, he was already bleeding out. That's about it. I hope you're happy now," Martello said mildly, rubbing his hands together.

"No one would be happy to hear that," Isaac murmured flatly. He sighed, for now he felt ill to ask anything of him. Not that Martello was badly affected by telling his story. "Do you know where it sank, forgive me for asking?"

"Roughly."

"Let's go there," Isaac insisted.

"And do what exactly?"

"Anything we can. Does the Alchemist's Guild have anything to help one hold their breath underwater?"

"What you're asking for is magic. That guild doesn't do magic, as much as they'd like to believe."

"Drop anchor then, see if you can drag anything up with rigs, shine lights down there, swim as deep you can. Anything we can think of! Subtlety is not in our best interests, so to hell with that. We are not the crown. If it wasn't well explored back in the day because you weren't believed, or what have you, we have it mostly to ourselves."

Martello looked away and out to sea. For a time, Isaac wondered if the mercenary captain was hoping he'd leave out of boredom, yet there he waited, and waited, for a reply.

"Tomorrow," Martello Jacart decided, "meet me outside my guild hall soon after first light. Don't oversleep; I might have changed my mind by midday. I'll need to hire a couple salvage hulks, which I can't do by tomorrow, but I'll action it. And you, Jamys, you're coming too. That's an order. I need someone like you who's had a lot of contact with this man."

And so it was that arrogant Martello had no more words, and in this state sauntered away to collect his longsword, likely wondering if he, too, was an idiot as he so claimed Isaac was. In truth, he didn't feel it himself, only a chill and a sense that he had a very small window of opportunity before his luck ran out. He was grim, too, as he took in the sea's majesty.

Jamys nodded approvingly, and that was high praise from him.

"Good luck," the mercenary said. "I can't wait to see how this ends."

"Oh, I can understand that," Isaac agreed solemnly.

"Having second thoughts?"

"None. I was just thinking about something else, for what it's worth. The first time I met Martello, I said he was very much like me, and in a way I suppose that to be quite right. I likened him to a mirror actually."

"What do you see in him then?"

"Horror."

The Mirror

Eagles came in to roost at their lofts in clouds of green and gold, ever an unearthly sight that no one else seemed to notice. A butcher chopped meat on a street corner, fish was cooked in someone's house, long shadows were cast by clothes hung to dry overhead, far longer shadows swallowed the light courtesy of the monolithic watchtowers ever on duty with their human silhouettes circling the great bronze bells, and Isaac Brodie walked the streets, alert. He took it all in, all his surroundings telling stories to him, and he gave them all some thought in between his personal contemplations.

Finding his way back from southern Harth wasn't troubling. There were enough landmarks to guide him, only, as he walked, his direction changed along with his mindset, Lucian being too disinterested to satiate him while Rosalynn was too much a stranger. The dozens of spires of the cathedral protruding into the sky were the beacon of his beckon. Laryc would have something to say about that. Then again, it was apparently his devout mission to have something to say about everything in as negative a way as possible, regardless of trivial factors such as making sense, so perhaps he wasn't as offended as he'd appeared to be.

Isaac stopped short in the square before the cathedral, as he had when he first arrived in the city. Even the shadows seemed to be in the same place, and the markets in the same state of clean-up. There, Isaac planned his next move to reach Marcel in the least offensive manner possible, tapping his foot as he did so and scanning the building. The gulls were out now from their nests in the alcoves and under the buttresses, for now the skies were free of danger and the shores were awash with the day's catches.

"Hello again," a womanly voice greeted him.

Tamzin Morzall had her head tilted on one side quizzically, though otherwise was a figure of proper form, pleasant with a quirky element about her, especially in her blue eyes where it swam unchecked. She was in her white priestess robes, and very modest she was in them. Isaac took little notice of her beyond that, as he was searching around for his brother in case he was following some way behind. When he saw Marcel wasn't there, he smiled warmly and unassumingly at Tamzin.

"Why did you come to greet me?" Isaac asked.

"I saw you from on high," Tamzin answered, nodding to the heights of the cathedral, "and you looked like you wanted a friend. I can't imagine you came to beg for forgiveness. Your brother won't be able to see you; my father has him working late."

"And not yourself?"

"There's less work for women."

"One prejudice is saved by another?" Isaac chuckled.

"If you want to be optimistic about it."

A fine idea. Isaac had ideas of his own and they involved being clear on a few things, for he lacked clarity.

483

"I should take my leave, Tamzin," he said, careful not to sound rude. "At the first opportunity, I'll buy you and Marcel each a drink."

"You're having trouble with something?" Tamzin astutely remarked. "Something to do with this mission you're on?"

"Not exactly."

"I don't believe that. That's the reason you're here. You could pretend you're running an errand for your father, but then again, it strikes me that you have no intention of pretending that hard."

"So?" Isaac countered, sly of face despite his lethargy.

"I want to hear your side of it. It's a good enough story to be heard more than once. Come on, tell it to me and see if it doesn't help. How will you know until you try?"

The point was a poignant one for certain, as he'd made just the same one to Martello an hour earlier. So reminiscent was it in its wording that Isaac was made suddenly self-conscious, in wondering whether he'd driven the point into Marcel's head so many times that even he quoted it without thinking, only for Tamzin to use it as a needle to touch his nerves. Manipulative or not, she was right, and showed genuine interest. It wouldn't be such a crime to allow her to have her way on this occasion, Isaac decided. There were worse ways to spend an evening. She spoke softness again, to that notion.

"Come," Tamzin hearkened when she seemed to sense his decision, and clicked her fingers at the cathedral. "We should go near the top."

"What's near the top? Are we going through the main doors?"

Tamzin gave no straight answer, coyly telling him to be patient and trust that no harm would come of him, which was fairly reasonable when the gods should be present, but not altogether expected. She did guide him through the double doors at the front, and the guards did take note of him, though whether they were the same men as before, he couldn't honestly say. She didn't care at any rate, and she took him to the back of the cold hall to a spiral staircase, up to its peak to a level unseen from the ground floor, as it was not exposed by a balcony. It was a small enough place as it was: a slim corridor that led them the direction they entered the cathedral by, and when confronted with the option to either continue down that path or enter the room that made the corridor even slimmer, she took him through the door and made sure it was shut behind them.

The room was cramped, or cosy if one were inclined to it: just big enough for both of them. Tamzin gestured to the chair on the opposite side, and there he sat without question for now, in spite of the growing strangeness. Between them was a table of highly polished wood that grew from the ground as a stem and opened out into a circle, and as part of it there was a wooden disc lying flat, covered entirely by a circular layer of stone save for a rectangular slot directly before him. An image of a sword was carved in the wood there, and

The Mirror

painted silver. Tamzin, meanwhile, adjusted herself in the opposite chair, interlinking her fingers. Then she was pale and jittery, and the atmosphere was frigid.

"You don't want to talk about your mission here, do you?" she said.

"Excuse me?"

"You even said it wasn't on your mind. Is it about the other scar you have? You saw a beheading on your second day here, didn't you?"

"How much have you been told?" Isaac replied, a rattle of misgiving at her question. That confirmed her suspicion.

"Enough to know you're thinking about it a lot. You told Lucian, and he told Marcel, and he gave me a good idea as to why you might think about it."

Tamzin pulled a cord beside her and the shutters turned around, revealing the city, and beyond that the sea, spraying sunlight into the tiny room, and then she pulled down a mirror grafted onto the wall above the window, and adjusted it until the sunlight burst onto the table in a focused beam. *Gods like the sun ever so much*, he thought. Every speck of dust floating between them, and there was much of it, was revealed in detail. Through the dust and light, Tamzin's face had regained some colour as she busied herself with a lever on her side of the table.

"Would you want Lameeri's attention?" she enquired. "Is justice what you need? Is it something specific or is it too difficult to categorise? Do we appeal to any god? We might also employ a sigil of some other kind."

She pulled at the lever and the wooden disc span until the rectangular hole in the stone showed a symbol of each of the pantheon's five, all painted silver.

"You have me at a loss. I don't understand the point of this."

"Your brother obviously worries about you. There's only one solution to this. If time hasn't softened your anger, only reason will."

Isaac was still at a loss, for he was looking for some deeper meaning in her actions. Then he remembered her anxiety and how she'd appeared uncomfortable with the whole affair, and it dawned on him that she was truly affecting no subterfuge. Confessing, by the rules of this formality, was no price to pay; presumably it wouldn't do any harm, yet to speak to a near stranger on the matter wasn't an idea he was fond of, if there was anything to confess at all.

"I was right at least," Tamzin said, and after a moment's hesitation, turned the disc back to the image of the sword. Perhaps that was right of her. "Your brother tells me you clam up at death. Sorry, killing. The reason he gave made no sense to me. You killed a man in self-defence, and felt guilty forever after."

"Not a man," Isaac found himself correcting in fluster. "Not much of one. He was 16 or so. I don't know, he was young, and what an idiot he was, associating himself with that lot of brigands."

The Voice of Kings

"Sixteen is old enough to be a scoundrel," Tamzin pointed out. "So a man who happened to be young came at you with a sword, and you killed him first. How does anyone ration that to be a bad thing? Tragic, oh, mightily, but villainous?"

"That's not the point!" Isaac snapped.

"What is?"

Isaac sighed and looked away, out through the shutters. There was an urge to be honest, whatever that would entail.

"It's easy to say it was the right thing when you weren't there. The action was right, but it's not the action one should take issue with. When I engaged that man in combat, I know what I felt. I was scared of course; I had no idea what I was doing in the heat of the moment. Then I saw his eyes. I still remember those eyes, and I was angry. Not just angry, enraged! I think that's why I won in the end, because hell if I'd used a sword before then. I just swung it at him again. We blocked each other's blows clumsily again and again, and as I got angrier, I became a better fighter, or he fell to fear. But that's not even the worst of it, oh, no! I know what I felt then: I wanted him to die, I felt more alive, I felt the blood in my veins. I didn't understand it at the time but... I've heard it said that one soldier in a hundred gets a true battle rush. I'm not even a soldier. How did I become so terrible that I can enjoy ending a man's life? And the way it ends... you wouldn't believe how strong a man is. When I impaled him, my sword got stuck halfway through, so I pushed it again, and then when I tried to pull it out, his whole body worked to stop me. I remember the sound it made, his blood sucking at the blade."

Tamzin was oddly quaint after Isaac's breath ran out and his words ran their course. She was unnerved, yes, but she was still in the strange world inhabited only by her that allowed her to emote as others were wont to try to understand. In shame, Isaac silently took his anger out on the contraption before him, wondering what the thing really was.

"If you feel so guilty, shouldn't that tell you something? You can't be evil. Even if you did get a kick out of it, which I find hard to believe, you must have exaggerated it. We are here, inciting the gods in their hidden place to listen, and I believe they are with me now to reason. There's no way anyone can be so different from one minute to the next, not unless they're not being themself to start with. That's just it. The man you just described doesn't sound like the person I'm looking at now."

"That's logical," Isaac agreed. The truth was plain. And remote. He let everything sink in, then tapped his fingers on the table, unable to reignite the conversation. Tamzin was lost in herself. "Shall we swaps places? You could tell me about your father."

Where, at first, she wore a ladylike smile, she now looked very serious, and dreaded what he was asking of her. When it became clear to her that he had need of a vested interest in her, she nodded slowly.

"Not here," she whispered.

The Mirror

There was no discussion on the matter. Whether by paranoia, or just the need to leave that cramped space for somewhere she could feel free, she took him back downstairs, outside, to freedom, and they walked together with the cool breeze to make everything better.

"You're not going to talk about it, are you?" Isaac said after some time. "Unsurprising."

"I think there's too much to say about him. My father is hateful. He's not just selfish, he takes any opportunity to make anyone else look bad, and I don't think he fully realises what that means. Maybe some other time I will tell more." A pause gave way to more, however. "My mother is not dead, as you'd think. She is put aside."

Then it was done. True to her wishes, Isaac said no more of it, and nor did she, obsessed as she otherwise was with the subject.

"I would see your plans sometime," Tamzin changed the subject awkwardly, squinting at a cloud of gulls.

"They're all up here," Isaac said, tapping his skull. "What I have on parchment is other people's writings, and would mean nothing to anyone else. But I could talk you through them. Isn't it true your woman's conclave discuss all things mad and hopeless?"

"We do, Isaac. I like to think it's not for naught."

Then that was done, also. They walked without talking, the clacking of their shoes on the cobbles pleasingly visceral.

It was only when they reached the boarding house that Tamzin perked up again in a mixture of quirky movements and ladylike formality. When Isaac invited her inside, he had no real desire to do anything with her, and she said nothing either way.

They merely stood in his rented room and stared outside. That was until they sat on the bed and did the same again, and then they did the same some more, only they sat closer to one another now. It was one of those times that Isaac had nothing to say, despite his intentions, and the face he pulled must have communicated that fact, for Tamzin nodded sagely. Eventually Isaac had to be the one to make sure there was more to it than that, studying her face and looking her in the eyes with warmest kindness. When she smirked at him, all the layers about her crumbled away and she was a new person, all gone in less than a second, though perhaps she didn't even notice. Isaac put his hand on hers and rubbed it.

"Forget the cathedral for one night, Tamzin. Forget your worries: they don't exist in this room."

She grinned from ear to ear and put a hand on his knee. Tamzin was instantly more appealing then, more attractive even. He removed the clips in her hair, and as it fell down in curls, he was correctly assured. Her hand stroked his leg, upwards until it reached the top and lightly closed in on his manhood, slowly working it in a way that suggested she was very quickly learning it again. There wasn't a chance she hadn't done it before, Isaac thought, the only question being how long ago. They kissed. But who'd initiated it?

The Voice of Kings

Quickly, he took off his shirts, and she in turn slid his boots off and threw them aside, and more rapidly still did the same with his breeches as she grew ever farther from her other self. Breathlessly, she snuggled out of her boots and then unlaced her robes until she could let them drop at her feet. In the faint moonlight she glistened, body kept in check by a corset, and it was a wonder he'd ever thought her unremarkable. She gripped his shoulders firmly and pushed him back, falling with him and giggling, feeling her way up his legs again with tickling fingers. The new Tamzin grew bolder every second.

Isaac worked his fingers through the threads of her corset, and when he reached the last one, tossed it aside, and wrapping his hands round her, rolled them both over. In the dim moonlight, her face lit up, her small breasts gleamed, and again she giggled uncontrollably, throwing her arms out, grabbing the pillows tightly. She set him off laughing too, for nothing but the fun of it and sheer disbelief at the change in her. When he was inside her, the giggling only grew louder and more insane, and soon enough, she was back to groping him, wherever she could, whenever she felt like it, sweat building up between their skin, and more so when Isaac's thrusting became more urgent.

It was with both of them breathing heavily when the giggling and the frantic scrabbling reached their greatest points, when Isaac rolled onto his back, splayed without a care, and stared intently up at the ceiling, chest rising and falling as fast as the blood rushed through him. He didn't normally play with such franticness, not even with strangers, not that this could be considered an issue in spite of its peculiarity.

"Will you be missed?" Isaac asked.

"Probably not."

He laughed. He shut his eyes.

When he dreamed, he dreamt of the endless waters, of everything and nothing, of answers with no meaning and questions with no answers, hope and joy, and tomorrow and every day after that, and a void to be filled.

Chapter Thirty: A Man Unburdened

The hour was late and the world was restless. Thunder crackled as a low echo through the halls of Castle Aurail, lending a certain atmosphere to a late dinner that was otherwise bereft of much feeling. Tristan watched the lords of Burtal eat their fill of spiced game and golden-brown potatoes that were arranged on their plates with precision that they took care to appreciate. They would reach across the table, delicately so as not to catch the sleeves of their velvet and silk jackets on the food or bronze candelabra, and they would take a jar of wine sauce or pluck up a handful of fruit or vegetable and proceed to eat in proper form, all while stabbing one another with suspicious glances and debating about where money should or shouldn't go. At least the lords who tended to their own land were especially passionate. Still, it was a surreal sight that spoke of a country made ill by subjects brought about to care too little of the wider picture, and worse, of liars who honed their skills for a cover in court. What use was such a position to anyone?

They couldn't be faulted for at least being here. If things were to progress, they needed a bigger picture of events. House Morwnue, House Surelrn, and most affiliates of the south were conspicuously absent on account of the distance in part, House Blackwel was still shut up in Silverwyck presumably, and thus far presented no enduring reason for doing so, although others vouched for them with assurance, while House Andrews gave no specific excuse at all and required a second summons of urgency.

Tristan ate his pheasant breast and sipped his chalice of red wine, and for now chose to listen, as that seemed to be the best way to gauge the sensibilities of the guests. He sat at the corner of the long table, and to his right Richard sat, at the end, looking straight ahead, down at his retainers in hateful boredom, chin resting on his hands that were interlinked at the fingers. To his right, the Empress sat back, almost without presence except for the light prodding sensation in everyone's brains that told them she was still there and that they were to watch what they said. One needed only to catch, in the corner of the eye, a flash of her taffeta dress of royal purple and silver strips to be made conscious of her, or the twinkling turquoise choker at her neck, or a dozen other details to be drawn to her and see that her face bore a look of intrigue, that her bright eyes missed precisely nothing. She and Richard both were backed by the fireplace, nearly big enough to fit a man of average height at its tallest point, and though the fire was relatively small this night, it cast a strong light around the two hosts, at the end where only they sat.

Opposite Tristan, young Lady Castellon squinted and curled her lips up slyly like a snake slithering across her, as if in coded thanks that they were among the sane people at the table. Instead of relaying the gesture back to her, he returned to studying the other guests; now their plates were gradually emptied and the table was filled with patches of shining silver, well revealing the faces of those men and perhaps making the performances more difficult to play. No doubt they would have to keep returning for court at dinner, even though, as seen tonight, not all lords could be in attendance without the prospect of adding another table while they waited for the marble round table's construction to be completed. It was an odd choice of priorities on Alycia's part, but there was nothing to be done now.

Tristan's line of thought was brought back to the conversation as Sir Darith made himself known to his sight, leaning forward as he was, in the same manner as Tristan, not participating in the debate so he could be cool and objective. When he saw Tristan, he raised his head in friendly acknowledgement and rolled his eyes.

"I've personally been very upfront about my spending," Lord Haemon Searl said to the men around him, employing a boisterous tone that was cause for alarm. It was obvious the discourse would escalate to defensive boasts eventually, and so it was, and so the lord continued. "Copies of my records have been handed to the crown for examination, though I can't say the same for everyone just yet, so I won't be called out for saying I'm hiding money from the cause."

"Who are you implicating?" the dull voice of Lord Reid spoke.

"I'm merely explaining my position."

"Not of mere," Lord Carrick said, fast to take a swig of wine before hurrying to swoop in. "As far as the Emperor knows, your records might be false."

Some of the lords nodded and murmured for the sake of unity in the presence of Richard and Alycia where they otherwise wouldn't have cared.

"Are you making an accusation also?" Lord Almaric asked. Abram shook his head and the lords around him lowered theirs, as if to leave him alone with Tristan without impediment. "It seems to me that there's no less effort in promoting your Houses than actually talking productively."

"No, I agree. If I've wronged my fellow lords, I apologise," Lord Carrick said.

"You can keep doing that," Sir Darith interjected, "but remember it's by the grace of our guests that you can. My mother would tell you what you are, so too my father for that matter, and my uncle the Count wouldn't have the courtesy to take you aside before telling you to shut up. I don't think you'd do well in Ylden Parragor, come to think of it. Now, I was trained to speak with my sword, so with you knowing that, I must say I'm only stating facts when I say my family isn't one to suffer fools."

Some of the men at that table instinctively turned to the Empress, for they feared to be too bold in replying, and they found her unfazed by the proceedings, the definition of objective, yet upon her, there was noticeable enough captivation that she surely wanted to be seen. Lord Carrick must have expected her or the Emperor to intervene, and looked embarrassed when they didn't, but at the same time, had done nothing to discourage him.

As he made to rebuke, Sir Darith paused in motion to interrupt, holding the rim of his chalice to his lower lip before he could drink.

"Fools," he repeated in the same deeply noble tone, and he drank, thinking hard as he swished the wine around his mouth. "Do yourself a favour and prove you're not one."

"I fear I caused all this by not being clear to start with," Lord Searl wisely said before the haranguing could go on. "I never meant to imply I won't give more money, only that we have considerations of our own. As it stands, I would happily have some of my soldiers sent north if my Emperor would say the word, and as it will stand when House Aldrich presents itself beyond good Sir Darith, I'll gladly submit to them."

"We could do with more soldiers up here," Lord Reid agreed. "Inevitably the people will get restless when change happens, and we're going to make a lot of change happen. From the Grey Rose to the Renorrmyn Shore, patrols should be doubled in strength to accommodate for the increased brashness of the people and the unwanted attention of Mürathneè."

"I think not, my Lord," Sir Darith put in. "How do you propose hundreds more soldiers patrolling the north coast will make us less conspicuous? You think they're going to see them, get scared, and forget they ever saw it? You don't think the King will come down, wondering what's going on?"

"We had a very similar conversation just recently," Alycia's tongue of thorns whipped out. For certain, they were hard to see because they were dug in Celoden's neck, but he felt them all too well as she looked at him with disdain: a fleeting shot that told him she would lose interest after a time, as perhaps he wasn't worth bothering with.

"Alright, I think that's quite enough," the Emperor announced to the room at large, and everyone lost their fire at once.

Richard rubbed his eyes, and Tristan was close enough to see his intense frustration brewing that he might have unleashed in a rant if he wasn't also tired and ambivalent. A sword in his hand would give him power, but that was ill-advised, and so there was only this until Tristan could teach him of patience, as he'd apparently forgotten. He hadn't always been so crushed with disappointment, had he?

"This isn't at all momentous," the Emperor said. "If there's nothing else..."

"That depends on whether you'd like me to tell them about the embassy tomorrow," Alycia inserted.

"By all means," the Emperor said, failing to hide his cluelessness, at least to Tristan.

"As you wish. My Lord Tristan, you offered to entreat Cristico Valen and his contacts from Mürathneè, and so you shall. For those of you unaware," *which is all of them*, Tristan thought, "we have a situation with regards to the strange occurrences in Mürathneè that the court is so keen to hide: of the rabid creatures, and wildfire, and other such things. To explain mine and the Emperor's decision to pursue information would be pointless

The Voice of Kings

unfortunately, for now at least, but I'm compelled to tell you of it because of the massive operation surrounding it. When you see soldiers gathering in force in the courtyard tomorrow morning, do not disrupt them, in fact do not expect them to get out of their way for you, and please, resist the temptation to spread rumours."

"Your Majesty, tomorrow?" Lord Almaric asked in alarm after waiting for her to finish.

"Sorry for not giving more notice, but Valen gave me no time. Frankly, I'm not of a mind to make many demands; I want to let him have a reasonable amount of power and see where this goes. The power he has will be short-lived, and at my expense, and if he fails to play by my rules tonight, he will not leave the Manor of Blessed Voices come the morn."

"Name the place then," Lord Almaric replied, straightening up and turning very serious. The other lords didn't matter at that time; this was a folly for him to fix.

"The Bryndton Isles."

The lords in that dining hall were interested now. They put down their cutlery and chalices quietly as they strained to hear more. Even Richard had perked up, bearing a look that mixed disgust with intrigue. It was an understandable reaction, for there seemed little reason for a planned treaty to take place amongst fishing villages and old ruins.

"Which one?" Lord Almaric asked.

"We don't know yet. He didn't specify."

"Treaties rely on a bond of mutual trust. I'm not put at ease by being in the dark."

"So you shouldn't. You shouldn't trust these men for a second. You're there for information and you won't be alone. Cristico and his contact are trying to ensure their safety in being so vague, and they won't be alone either, you can count on that. But if they show up with a fleet of carracks, you turn right around and we wait until they're serious. The housings of Castle Aurail won't be seen as ashes of greatness. We are greatness again. We won't be trifled with."

"But why Bryndton?" Richard said loudly. "Do they want somewhere to ambush us?"

"I wouldn't count it out," Alycia replied.

"Then they will go for the Eye of Sand," Richard said assertively, waving a finger accusingly. "It's deserted and there're a thousand places to hide."

"There's space enough on the beach that we should be able to avoid that," Lord Almaric pointed out. "If that's their plan, they won't stop there though."

"You're smart enough to avoid a plot, my Lord. You'll have 50 pairs of eyes with you just to make sure: 50 good, disciplined soldiers who wouldn't let the sight of a fish in the water pass you if there was even the smallest chance it mattered."

"Fifty?" Lord Almaric exclaimed.

Alycia put her left hand, all smooth and healthy in the candlelight, upon Richard's right, highlighting his more wrinkled skin and veins that protruded like worms under his skin. As if to transfer her power, she squeezed his hand and looked to him with admiration flaring in her eyes.

"That could be excessive, couldn't it?" Richard put to her, scratching the back of his head.

Her smile flickered, and Tristan did the honourable thing to respond before he did.

"I don't doubt the need for 50 elites," Lord Almaric clarified, "only the need for the need. There are always peaceful solutions to these problems. The irony is that both parties usually assume the other can't see them."

"It can't be avoided this time. Cristico hails from Harth. His contact, whom he was keen not to name, attends court there on occasion, and this much I know because Lady Castellon and other servants of His Majesty's household wrung it from him. He came to us and told us this man works close to the King and so is privy to information other men aren't, but forgot to tell us he worked in Harth too."

"How much more did he forget?" Lord Reid chided. "These men often have bad memories."

Most of the lords laughed raucously at that; considerably less found it funny, most likely. Alycia raised an eyebrow as if playing teacher, presiding over a fun little children's game.

"Perhaps he really did forget," she suggested mildly. "You're probably correct, but making those accusations, in your position, is dangerous. Were you there, my Lord? To my own regret, you don't fully know what we're discussing, so it would seem premature to conjure crass jokes."

"True," Lord Searl admitted. "It is a solid plan, Your Majesty; I doubt anyone here means to question that, such as we are."

The two sides of the table were lined with nodding men. Unseemly as it was, Tristan knew the time was fast approaching when such councils would be filled with more deliberate, honest faces. Whether they would be on the same bodies, he didn't know. He prayed for that. There was hope representing their ranks, as some lords already put thought into this at least. Alycia's cousin Imyll had no part in it, still eating his dinner in his own world, and there were more besides. For now though, Tristan had his elbows pinned to the table, fingers combing through his hair as he tried to understand the logic of the conversation, forfeiting his own food and drink until it was done.

"Forgive me, but is there something you're all seeing that I'm not?" Lord Almaric said. "The men I'm to meet tomorrow, who I'm to buy delicate information from, in private, are known as men who kneel before the seat of power in Mürathneè and have sworn fealty therein. What could there be for us to gain from this embassy? If they're working for King Michael directly, they won't have anything to say to us, or worse, will trick us. If they're turncoats, they're more dangerous still."

The Voice of Kings

"We allow them to have their way, to the extent we determine," Alycia explained, "and they will trust us."

"I don't see it. There is no *trickery* we can do on them. Being aware of theirs doesn't change the fact that they will employ it and it will work. This is a bad idea, Your Majesty!"

"They will trust us," Alycia said patiently, "because I have reason to believe these men are neither true traitors nor real loyalists. They'll continue to work for King Michael, only they'll have more money, and whatever else you choose to give them. Is there any other way I can put you at ease?"

"I am afraid not. I have my fears and I will keep them close until this is all finished."

"I'll aid him," Imyll Lyrdred proclaimed for all to hear. "I can take two dozen men of mine, no problem. He'll be at ease with a Lyrdred around."

"Numbers isn't the problem, Cousin," the Empress replied to that. "On the contrary, too many men will spook them. And a Lyrdred's presence might not speak much to these people unless he actually *speaks*, which you've said isn't what you want."

"I'm but one man, but I'm worth a lot more," Sir Darith said confidently. "If it's personal protection he needs, who better than a Wyman? If it's a second pair of ears and another tongue, mine work fine, and I'm clever enough to know when to shut up. Name me his guardian, Majesties, and leader of the 50 men."

"Majesty?" the Empress said admiringly to her husband.

He studied the knight long and hard, then his eyes flicked up to the right, as if catching sight of something extraordinary in his peripheral, and there they stayed, looking thoughtfully up at the ceiling. Something wistful passed him by at the core of his being: some strength founded on times past, shining dark in his eyes and pushing his mouth up at the edges. It was peculiar to behold, like a warm breeze making its way through the land in the midst of winter. Only, there was some machination working away and it was probably bad: recalling his imagined days as a fighter most likely, as he was surely conjuring an idea. After a time, he turned to Alycia, restraining from voicing his ideas, and nodded slowly. In return, she nodded back at him with clearer pronunciation, weariness leaping across her face momentarily before he gave the court his answer.

"Granted," the Emperor declared.

"Him, not me?" Imyll said.

"You're needed here, with respect," the Empress rebuked. "He's the natural choice; he's defended his city and everything around it from brigands for years and he's been training for far longer. Ylden Parragor has a good reputation where fighters are concerned, to the point of hyperbole in some places. From listening to only the more lively examples, you'd think Ylden Parragor's in a state of constant mock battle and tournaments with Houses Wyman and Aldrich as the unbeatable victors, stopping only to do some ruling on the side." The lords laughed at this, and Darith most of all. "That's fine by me; the more imposing one man can be by Lord Tristan's side, the better. I think that's what Sir Darith was trying to say."

"Very good," the Emperor said. "I'll trust you in my friend's keeping for whatever tasks are necessary. Now if that's all, I'll speak with my wife and lord paramount in private."

The Empress didn't try to make him change his mind, only gave her tidings to various men from her chair, almost as elegant sitting down at the dinner table as she was on her throne. Lord Foy took Tristan's notice as he'd not attempted to refocus the discussion at all. He looked more than tired enough for sleep but sharpened momentarily to bow to Tristan as he walked. The other door, leading to the kitchens, opened and servants entered expectedly at the sound of commotion, only to be waved away.

"Leave us," Richard said gruffly, then waved a finger as he remembered something apparently vital. "That wine I asked for, bring it now please."

When the shuffling of boots faded, the hall was truly quiet. The ceiling was such that sound echoed quite well without losing quality, and yet it was very quiet now. The lords had seemed not to be making much noise at the end, but it seemed so in hindsight. Perhaps it was the stillness of it all, the long table full of abandoned seats tucked neatly beneath it and the mostly empty plates bereft of the little clangs of cutlery, while they, the four of them, were bunched up at the end. Lady Castellon had remained, not for a second assuming she was included in the order for all to leave, and it was Alycia who told her to go before long. When it was just the three of them at last, the mood was more relaxed; better to confront Alycia in personal conversation than with a wide audience.

"I want something made clear, please," Tristan said. "Is there anything else I should know that you have withheld? I don't want to have to improvise because I haven't been given the full picture."

"Nothing," Alycia vowed. "What would I stand to gain from hiding anything?"

"What did you stand to gain when you did it before?"

"Sorry about that," she laughed softly. "It was just easier. Hiding anything about the meeting from you now would make things decidedly complicated. You'll have to trust me on that."

"I do," Tristan sighed.

"It only made it easier for you though," Richard said and immediately wished he hadn't, as evidenced by a painful grimace.

He hadn't told Tristan either, though she may have told him little enough. He was right, however. Alycia was organising according to personal ease, and in a saddening way he could see why, as she hurtled along this path by which she was the most important person she could meet.

"I can tell we're not going to have a productive talk tonight. It's quite late," she reconciled, as if to not hurt Richard's feelings.

The Voice of Kings

Then she gently clanged the rim of her chalice against Richard's, which Tristan now noticed was empty again. How much the Emperor had had to drink during that dinner he didn't know, but he suspected it was more than should be consumed for a council meeting. Alycia leaned across the table and echoed the same sentiment with her glass against Tristan's.

"Enjoy the wine. Goodnight."

And at that she took her leave, at her own pace, leaving enough time for either of them to call her back, which they didn't. Richard shook his head.

"That woman kills me sometimes," he said bitterly.

Tristan said nothing. A servant arrived cradling a bottle of wine, its glass thick and murky, its label obscured by the man's hands. He could, however, make out the thin, red liquid swirling within the confines of the glass, and a strong, defined smell of fruit from the open top.

"Leave it; I can pour it myself," Richard said, and so they were left alone again in the large hall.

"I shouldn't drink more wine," Tristan protested when Richard made to pour into his chalice. "It won't be good for my temperament tomorrow, much as I'd like it now."

"One glass," Richard said, and poured to no protestation, reluctant as Tristan remained.

The aroma was sweet when he brought it up to his nose, and cool on his tongue from its time spent in the cellar when he sipped it, and he did only sip it. Its flavour was luscious but he paid it no more tribute than his circumstances allowed. Richard was less concerned, taking sips, but regularly so, and soon he would refill. Tristan fingered the rim of his chalice absentmindedly, and studied his friend in pity.

"What's this for anyway?" he asked.

"Nothing. We're friends: we sit and drink wine together, and say to hell with our titles, and talk and be honest with one another, because we're friends, yes? Not nearly enough, I know; I have to suffer these idiots fawning over me every day to get anything done, and there's not much time for anything else."

Richard gestured grandly to the table at large, as if spirits of the lords remained seated and were to take their scolding without putting in a word one way or another for once. Richard would have liked to do that, and perhaps he thought about that now.

"Not a good excuse you might say," Richard continued. "You manage without them, and Alycia navigates their nonsense like a ghost, no matter if they're with her or not. I swear I'll go mad if I have to endure them much longer."

"Good times change people," Tristan offered sensitively. "Just don't wait for them to catch up, that's my advice. That'll drive you mad."

"That's the truth of it, I think!" Richard agreed, with a pale laugh that echoed through the hearth, and the silver, and the high ceiling in hollow triumph. "Never mind me, I'm just speaking my mind. Drink to your victory tomorrow."

"If you want to call it that. Sounds a tad too dramatic. Depressing, actually." Tristan considered this and a twisted smile grew as he settled on a toast. "To not dying at Bryndton."

"Aye, good enough for me."

"And what a silly thing to die for it would be."

"To die for..." Richard echoed in agreement. "Who's to say if it'll be worth it? Much as I hate to admit it, my wife probably knows what she's doing here. You can't deny the facts. The things I've heard from Mürathneè, they can't be explained by logic. Animals don't unite for suicide runs, events don't just transpire because the world forgot to give them a cause, fires don't start by themselves! Fire isn't black, Tristan."

He looked expectantly at Tristan. It wasn't an opinion he was asking for, but a mirror, and Tristan was loath to give it to him. He didn't need reassurance right now, he needed the truth. Often the truth wasn't so bad anyway, art in itself, and certainly the dark places Richard's mind took him to weren't worse than the injustices ever cycling in on themselves within Aurail's walls.

"I don't know how to explain those things, and I don't try. Even Lennord Brodie's sceptical too, and he's a genius, my friend. He suggested a gas that could catch fire may have been released from something in Caedor mine, so perhaps the same could be said here. As for those crazed animals, I haven't a clue, but magic is a serious word."

And this proves it, Tristan thought. Suddenly everyone's willing to believe. Maybe even he'd believe too if people kept talking about it. He couldn't deny it was fascinating, and yet there were good ways and bad ways to go about these things, and this could be a very bad way. He knew if there was magic, it would be gods' magic, for he knew of no other kind ever to exist in this earthly realm. If it was returning, or believed to be so, one would surely think to look to the old shrines in the wilderness for activity, for a sign of any sort. On the next day, things would be clearer. Just knowing how Mürathneè was thinking about it would help, assuming these men he was to meet were cooperative; help to put to a stop to the whole situation, hopefully. He knew these were strange times, only this wasn't what he had in mind. Men and women should be helping one another as people do, he told himself, not slithering about looking for magic tricks. Still, Alycia had spoken.

"Serious situation if the rumours are true," Richard predictably said. "People from across the channel believe it's serious at any rate, and they're better to say than I. My wife obviously does, so we should probably listen to the rumours. Listen, I like it no more than you do. Just be grateful you won't have to put up with this lot at Bryndton," and again Richard waved his hand to indicate the phantom lords.

The Voice of Kings

"A Lyrdred would be useful to have along though," Tristan reconciled in an attempt to ease Richard's mass prejudice. "Everyone knows how much influence they have, and that might be appealing for Valen and his men to know."

"You wouldn't want Imyll with you. I find him too unpredictable. Maybe he'd keep his mouth shut, maybe not. Still, whatever else you might say about the Lyrdreds, they preside over vineyards bloody well."

"This is from the Grey Rose?"

Richard nodded and smiled slyly, as if to imply he should be shocked by such a revelation. If he hadn't already known of their fondness of fine drink, he would also have to hold some grudge, or otherwise maintain a pretty low opinion of them to elicit the kind of surprise Richard was expecting. Either his friend was becoming too inebriated for his own good, or his melancholy was greater than had been apparent.

The Emperor was not outwardly sick, not that he could see, not as he recently was, but his health teetered on a knife's edge, where the point was his mind, upset at the slightest perceived rupture to his dignity or insult to his intelligence. He was angry, Tristan felt this in his bones, though if he asked him to express this so, his reaction was not rightly predictable. Richard poured wine into his own empty chalice under Tristan's circumspect observation, to the accompaniment of a dull tapping of fingers on wood. The chalice was filled to its brim quickly as Richard steadily tipped the bottle furthermore, his grip on it steady enough, now at least. The incessant sipping started again.

"I don't have much in the way of scorn for the Lyrdreds," Tristan said, for he saw a need to make Richard reconsider.

"Of course you don't. You wouldn't," Richard laughed. He mulled this in dark amusement as he sipped his drink. "Consider this then: you remember a few years ago, the last time we held court at full capacity? I remember the castle was packed then, like you wouldn't believe if you didn't see it yourself, like you couldn't imagine a castle this big being. This tawdry little hall wasn't even considered for hosting dinner in! You'd have to be touched to think it would work! But anyway, I remember, in the great dining hall, everyone was at their best, and every House had brought the best gifts they could afford to give away, laying them at the back and before my table. Then at some point, Imyll's father stepped forward, Alycia's uncle, what's his name? Kornel?"

"Kornel."

"Right. He came forward with a crate of about half a dozen bottles of his finest wine, and this here was one of them. Imyll carried two chalices, solid gold, and put them on the crate, and who came next but the most honoured guest, King Michael himself, with his wife and his storm knight, arms filled with all sorts of gifts. A painting of Harth in a gold frame and other art pieces besides; from the knight, a jewelled necklace for Alycia I think, and cloaks and the like for me; and from the King, lots of things made of expensive metals and a bejewelled dagger. But then..." Richard paused to laugh, shaking his head. He drew his chalice to his mouth, taking it back as he laughed again. It was sure not to be so humorous for Tristan. He knew what Richard was going to say; he'd been there at the time and hadn't made anything of it then either. "Then, Kornel, who's still standing, comes back to the table after feeling in his pocket and puts two rings on the table. Obviously he was just trying to outdo the royal visitors because he thought he'd been shown up, but honestly, he would have been better off sitting down like any other normal person would. I don't know what he was thinking."

"We know the Lyrdreds had saved more gifts to give you later on," Tristan reminded him.

"We know that. We don't know that he meant to give me those! Even if he did, what a stupid time to do it. Why did he think I'd care? Charity's all well and good, but why did he think I'd be impressed by a couple of rings? Alycia's got rings beyond counting. So must the Lyrdreds for that matter. Do they think I want so much flattery because I'm the Emperor? Would they want that themselves?"

"Is that the point you were making?" Tristan said plainly, and Richard screwed up his face in puzzlement. "Tell me how this conversation started."

"That was the point I was making, I should think. I'll trust you if it wasn't," he said wryly, and shrugged. Sipping the last of his current chalice of wine, he appeared deep in thought. "Funny actually. That was the last time Aurail was worth a damn. It's like he mocks me, that King, even without knowing it. He was the last thing that brought this city to life, and now it dies again."

"We're not talking about the Lyrdreds anymore?" Tristan said just as flatly as before.

"You think I'm drunk? You might be right, but I know what I'm saying."

"The people are the city, Richard," Tristan sighed. "The people are not all dead, nor all lost. There are men with power who care, though some of them are yet absent, and there are women with less power who care just the same or more. Evylyn could be here at short notice if there was only a demand."

"Evylyn?" Richard exclaimed. His brow furrowed and wrinkles emerged. He looked older than he should. Tristan's heart was in his throat. This seemed more important than anything else, like the country was resting on the outcome. "She's welcome to come to court. People would value her opinion, I'm sure."

"I wish I was."

"Lady Almaric is Lord Paramount's wife!" Richard laughed.

"She is my wife," Tristan echoed. "These lords respect me; I know this despite how it might seem with this bloody show they insist on putting on. They may not necessarily appreciate me, but I know I have their respect, which is a privilege. Evylyn though? I think not. She is Lord Paramount's wife."

The Voice of Kings

"They'll respect her as much as I tell them to!" Richard boasted angrily.

Tristan could only wonder to what extent the Emperor comprehended his own meaning. He was seen as a beast of paper that could fake a roar well enough, yet could be blown over by a breeze.

"We have enough problems without having to worry about the people with the best ideas being shunned for one reason or another," Richard went on. "Imagine Evylyn as Lady Paramount. I'd like to see the looks on their faces then! We wouldn't need them at all with half as many people like you two. Being diplomatic about it is another thing entirely, of course."

From the manner of nervous anticipation clogging his throat, it was to guilt clutching at his heart as he remembered his promise to Lennord. He'd offered him nothing more than a consideration, for what else could he have done? He'd wanted to promise more, but was obliged not to, for the sake of everyone else, the good of the realm over a friend, though it didn't feel at all good. Now he was reminded of it, at first puzzled as it sprang to his attention in such violent fashion, then the reason dawned and he fidgeted uncomfortably.

"To see your halls bustling with passionate people would be a dream come alive. If we could make that happen soon, would my presence here be such a necessity? If I were to leave for a time..."

"You can't leave," Richard interrupted. "You hold everything together. The people on the street love you. If you miss Evylyn and Malcus, just summon them here, everyone else be damned."

"If I was *needed* elsewhere," Tristan clarified, "if Isaac Brodie was suspected in Mürathneè of knowing more than he let on and was sought for that knowledge, would I be permitted to leave with Lennord, even if it meant leaving Evylyn in my place?"

"If it came to it. I would send 50 soldiers before you, or a hundred, or two hundred. I would send you as a last resort."

Richard reached for the wine bottle, but was stalled by Tristan's hand; Tristan, who slowly made him lower it before sliding it out of his reach. There was an acceptance in Richard, because of what he'd been given to think about, one would hope. He was serious enough; it was just how much he was absorbing of the conversation that was in question. While Tristan could think of nothing else, Richard's brooding seemed more strained, as if he couldn't keep up with himself. If there was anything to be thankful of, it was that he wasn't pining for the wine any longer. With any luck, he'd remember the details of the conversation the next morning.

"Go to bed," Tristan ordered, to the blunt tone of which Richard chuckled heartily.

"The wine is best drunk on its first serving."

"I'll make sure that happens."

Richard's meagre stubbornness had reached its limits now and he gladly lifted himself, standing tall and proud in the firelight, as he always should. After patting Tristan on the shoulder, he strode away. If anything, it proved the innate strength Tristan valued in him but never seemed to come forth.

"I'll get this business done at Bryndton to the best of my ability," Tristan said. "The sooner we put this to rest, the better."

"You say it as it is."

It was only now that he was alone and there was no one and nothing to appease that Tristan indulged in the wine, though the shadow of the next day loomed dark before his eyes and he couldn't stomach it without his wits about him. When he tried his pheasant, it was cold, and he realised he wasn't hungry. Dropping his knife and fork suddenly onto the plate, he was nonetheless not angry, merely frustrated at his narrow path and, for some reason, was hesitant to lay blame on anyone yet. These thoughts were given no time to truly fester however, as the door to the hall was opened and one man alone became three: an odd little group. Marcus Baldwin sat opposite Tristan with but a look to him to confirm he was permitted, and there he made himself comfortable. He wasn't dressed for an occasion as had just passed, but then again, he knew Tristan wasn't of a mind to care.

To Marcus's right, Sir Darith seated himself heavily, like the courier seeking permission through a stare's words, in his case a rise of the eyebrows and a polite bow when he saw he was allowed to do so.

"You have me taken aback," Tristan said mildly. "And you have my attention."

"I searched for your trusted courier first thing after dinner," Sir Darith explained. "I've learned quickly how you rely on him so. I knew of none other to take my enquiry to, so to Marcus I went, and here we are."

"He came asking questions about Bryndton, and I was reserved to keeping what thoughts I had to myself," Marcus clarified. "I could only speculate as to what he meant."

And you entered the dining hall without asking, Tristan thought to himself, amused. The knight of Ylden Parragor shifted his stocky frame to his comfort in his chair, gripping the armrests as if he were sitting on a throne. Even his slouch seemed to carry discipline in its stride: straight of back like an alerted predator, and uncaring like a tired cat curled up on the floor. What Tristan noticed most was the smell of him: an implacable aroma, harsh and strong born of the unusual soaps they made from whatever they could find in the swamps, woods, lakes, and mudflats, honed over hundreds of years into something courtly: odd, but bearable. Then there was his demeanour, which couldn't be ignored. Only now, when Tristan evaluated the knight to the best of his abilities, did he see the fierceness in him: a rage somewhere in his harmless wolfish grin, and sardonic pleasure in his eyes that grew ever more intense with the passing seconds: a demon looking out through a kind man.

The Voice of Kings

That was what it came down to. It was just there, and perhaps Darith didn't know it was there, but it had become ingrained in his face from spending so many years looking down sharp objects coloured silver and red. It epitomised the soldier everyone wanted: a beast of chaos on the battlefield, and a more than reasonable man when sat down in a dashing suit with a high-class meal steaming before him. Which was probably how House Wyman as a whole wanted to be seen. On the contrary to the popular image of the people of Ylden Parragor, however, Darith had no facial hair beyond a day's dark, bristled stubble, that suggested he'd have no trouble growing a full beard should he desire it.

The muscled knight grew his wolfish grin further, and again he separated himself from the vision of the people. It was of loyalty to Tristan, who he'd thrown his lot in with so quickly, for some reason.

"Marcus neglected to mention that he feared to tell me what he presumed I was talking about," Sir Darith said. "Rightly so, I'd imagine. A loyal one you've got here. But now that we're here, I'll get to the point. Are you going to tell me what we're doing tomorrow? What's got our Majesties so vexed?"

"Magic," Tristan said at once.

"Truly?" Darith exclaimed.

"Truly. A lot more people are vexed, at that. By the sounds of it, whatever people think has been going on in Mürathneè was intended to be kept a secret, and so may remain for a while, until more than agents of the crown start picking up rumours. Before you know it, the country will know one thing or another. Whether they'll know a truth or not could depend on what happens at Bryndton. If all it accomplishes is acquiring the knowledge that it was all in vain, then I will sleep easy tomorrow night. What greater result I could wish for, I don't know. Anything else would be too profound, I fear."

"I'd drink to that," Darith agreed broodingly. "People's blood ignites at the promise of magic, and when I say promise, I mostly mean lies, by the by."

When he let the hall engulf them in all but silence that none would take up the mantle to destroy, Tristan took the bottle of Lyrdred vintage wine and held it up for their perusal. They both took up empty chalices and he poured to fill them completely. Darith drank it more like ale, finishing half of it in a mouthful. Marcus, of course, was proper: the peasant who drank wine like a lord. The gods had their way of reminding one that there was life to be found for those who were dead inside; enough for a city of the undead even.

"To hell with magic," Darith said. Marcus shrugged and Tristan did the same, and they knocked their glasses together. It felt good, and that alone amused Tristan further. "There was magic in Ylden Parragor once upon a time; anyone who's spent a significant amount of time living there knows this. There are signs everywhere, but it's all faded now. That doesn't stop people trying to use it, in one way or another. Pray that this affair doesn't become so bloated that paranoia wins the favour of violence over reason. When swords are drawn, there will be a set of winners on one side and a field of ghosts on the other."

"For a man who hails from a city of soldiers, you're very keen not to fight," Marcus pointed out.

"A true knight knows when to fight, and when to talk, and when to shut up and draw his sword. Which is more than I can say for the indecisive members of this council. They say that lords have the wisdom and the courage, for what I can only assume is our other natural asset, and yet my lady has more of both those aspects, and last I checked she had something decidedly womanly between her legs."

Darith spoke so matter-of-factly he might have been commenting on the texture of his drink. The crass humour of soldiers wasn't entirely lost on him then, though he saved the laughter for anyone else, if indeed he was joking, for he was very quiet now.

"I thought your mother was the one you compared them to," Tristan ventured.

"Her too. That's not really fair though; she's tough by standards of men and women alike."

That was the truth of it, Tristan supposed, as he'd guessed in the past. She was deceptively dainty but had something of a hardness about her, not so apparent to just anyone. Darith swigged his wine and wiped a drip from his chin, whiplike, with a single finger. He was already perplexed by something of more pressing value, in his view.

"Will you wear armour?" Sir Darith asked. Tristan sighed, a heavy thing it was, for he dearly wished to proclaim that was the proper thing to do, to walk the beaches of Bryndton's isles all clad in plate and to peer out at the world as a helm would allow.

"If every attendant expects a battle so readily, one can only conclude that there will be a battle, no? I won't allow that kind of rampant paranoia to rule negotiations. Logic and amicability will decide a peaceful resolution, not fear. Fear stinks when it's rooted deep enough. Imagine that smell on a hundred men."

"Did you ever smell it?"

"As a knight, yes."

"How many lives did you claim in that career?"

Tristan stuttered, surprised by the intrusion. He shook his head, squinting. "None. I can honestly say it never occurred to me at the time. After the fact, aye, but when I had the opportunity? No."

"That right?" Darith said mildly, attacking a piece of meat lodged between two back teeth.

"Is that so surprising? Your own uncle only killed once, and he was in several nasty encounters. And I was in glorified squabbles only. Men who have never battled think that for those who have, killing is obvious, but I can only wonder and fear at where the idea has come from. The only obvious truth for me was to maintain order in violence until I could restore it in peace, and I wasn't alone in that thinking. Though, I never talked of it to the men beside me."

"This is true," Darith answered easily. "It takes discipline to do it: a certain forced consciousness throughout the battle. Or something else," he said darkly, leaning forward and raising an eyebrow.

"Or that," Tristan agreed, setting his mouth to a thin line. "That is why we avoid it altogether when we can. I will wear no sword and don no armour. I would like to *solve* this problem." Tristan sniffed, glaring into his glass, wondering whether to drink. "Hitting words with swords will not kill them. They will live, and the swords will be used again."

"As you say. If nothing else though, wear something you're comfortable running in."

Tristan could agree to that at least. Against his judgement, he drank with them now, and it calmed his nerves, allowing him to focus on the basics of his task, that humoured him in a sick way: to speak of magic and reality on the morrow, at sand and ruins, at Bryndton.

~

So while Tristan brooded alone in the dining hall, Richard, alone, walked the halls of the castle to his bedchamber, not caring to make for there at first, but to detour as he pleased, to watch the rain through the windows as he passed the battlements, where it pounded on stone, strangely loud like war drums, and lightning struck somewhere far off: a thin fork of pale blue light. Then when he arrived at the door of his bedchamber, he was truly tired. Not too tired for the detail of the ghost guarding his room to come to his attention, mind. There were guards in the corridor, just not in his antechamber. He let the matter go at once, as he wasn't of a mind to care.

When inside, he had more pressing issues to worry about. It was at the far end, on the left side of his four-poster bed, that Alycia sat in more than modest comfort, her legs hanging off while her feet tapped the rug in a slow gait, her right forearm resting on a plump pillow that was propped up on the headboard while her body was slouched sideways. It was startling, to say the least, to see her there, and it was stranger to be strangeness at all. For him to see his wife upon his own bed shouldn't have been the subject of scrutiny or suspicion, or the awakening of emotions long betrayed to the past. In her left hand she held up a book lit by candles on the wall, reading at her own pace until finishing a sentence or passage, whereupon she snapped it shut with her fingers and thumb and respectfully placed it on the desk beside his bed.

"Let's get this over with," Richard said. "What have I done wrong now?"

"Perhaps you'd like to start with what you're doing right, and I shall follow?" she put to him, sliding smoothly from the bed and gracefully making her way towards him. Her dress was loose around the arms and legs, and flapped serenely around her body; what a perfect body it was, purple and silver, shimmering ghostlike. It was her face that really caught his attention, for it was serious indeed.

A Man Unburdened

"Be plain, for gods' sakes," he protested. "What does either of us stand to gain from this elaborate word play?"

"You think me wicked," she told him after an intrusive glare into his soul. "The poor Emperor, who wields more power than almost every living soul in this world, who inherits money beyond his capability to spend on personal things, is brought down by his wicked wife who pulls his strings and connives behind his back with dagger and bribes."

"What have I done wrong?" Richard repeated, temper rising.

"You're destroying the reputation of your House, of yourself, and you're destabilising your power in Aurail with your flamboyant show of weakness. No matter how I try to empower you, you can't handle it. You show the both of us up in front of crowds of people, lords and knights, and so I'm left to deal with both our jobs. I'm manoeuvring your limbs as best I can, and trying to move my own without appearing stilted, and in my opinion, I do an astounding job, but how long can it last? How long can it last, Richard? Burtal needs its true leader to step forward. Try as I might, no one believes you're worthy of your birthright; they all believe I'm some witch who does all the work for you, and sadly they're not far off the mark."

"Then you have your wish, my dear."

"Oh, that's my wish?!" she exclaimed sarcastically.

She grinned at how preposterous it all was to her. In spite of what he knew she was, her smile gave nothing away. It was more than beautiful; it was alive with mischief that came so naturally to her, and few could see through it: only two. If he dared to be honest, he pined for that smile as it was, but for now it was just a shell, its natural warmth nowhere to be found. If fires could freeze...

"How could you think that would be my wish?" she continued, seriously again. "How could I possibly benefit? I can do much without your permission, but right now the world needs to see the Emperor of Burtal make choices, be strong and kind, and defiant to whatever crimes his ancestors, whose skeletons rot in the ground, once committed. I can't replicate that, for the love of the five, I just can't."

"And I can't satisfy what you're asking of me. I work when the sun rises until sunset, and it's never good enough apparently. I *do* work, and I do care, much as you'd like to demonise me."

"That's not what the people think. They don't know, and they won't until the day you die, because it's your weariness that you wear upon your face."

"I am weary. I'm burdened by duty most people will never understand."

"They don't see it!" she repeated in a hoarse whisper, as shrill as she could ever be. She stepped in closer to him, commanding his attention with hypnotic eyes. "They will say you were burdened sure enough, but not as you say. He was burdened at times, they will say, but scarcely much at all, if that is a credit to say. He was a rare ruler free of burden: he was unburdened by his name, unburdened by the squalor of his realm, unburdened by the hardships of duty, unburdened by the cries of his people. For how can any man feel the burden of something he does not carry?"

"A lie," Richard protested, though his voice was cracked and carried no strength, only anger.

"That's it?" Alycia responded. "You know it's the truth then, and what a sorry truth it'll be if you don't change it. So you have to start trusting me. I am not a conspirator of wicked deeds, you must admit that for a start. I am a conspirator of great ones. You must think I'm sending men to Bryndton to die, but I had spies follow Valen about long enough to determine his intent can't be destructive, even if he doesn't want to treat us with the respect we deserve. I didn't tell you about that, just like I didn't tell you about the plan, just like I didn't tell you about spies in Harth."

"Harth?" Richard spat out. Alycia blinked in bemusement and delicately wiped the spittle from her face. "To what end?"

"To see how they do things on more than a superficial level, my love. I did not tell you because you're not to be trusted. You're rash; you make mistakes very openly."

"You didn't tell Tristan either. Is he not to be trusted?"

Richard felt his anger rise as he felt his friend being insulted, far more so than Richard himself being abused by her in this humiliating fashion.

"Lord Tristan!" she crowed. "The only reason not to tell him is because he'd go straight to you about it. His hard work puts everyone else to shame. He and I are the only ones doing anything monumental in this castle. Our lord of change has his work cut out for him! If we left for a week, we'd probably return to find Castle Aurail as a pile of rubble."

"He'd be a better Emperor, I don't deny."

"Neither will I then. I daresay if he was Emperor and I was still Empress, I would have no reason to keep from this bedchamber."

It was abject shock that struck Richard now, as hard as the lightning carved the landscape in the distance. All the while Alycia smiled, yet for all her cruelty, it was one pained, deeply so.

"What did you say?" she said, tilting her head, putting a hand to her ear. "You've nothing to say? I have just confessed a desire to adulterate and to see Tristan take your bed and throne: two counts of treason in one and you have nothing to say."

"What shall I say?" Richard answered in disgust, mouth agape in shock beyond words.

Alycia sighed and shook her head. If it was anger she wanted, she could be sure it was there, only as of now, he couldn't express it in words. It bubbled and seethed as he attempted to comprehend her. In a strange way, he knew quite soon he would explode.

"You really are tired," she said.

A Man Unburdened

"And I was the one who tired you, once upon a time," Richard joked to his immediate regret, knowing he'd been absurd, not clever.

"Once."

She had nothing more scathing to say though, unlike him, shaking with rage, eyes wild and bloodshot; she couldn't have expressed herself more differently. She moved in closer and put a soft palm flat on his upper chest and kept it there as she circled him, wrapping her arm beneath his. For a moment, she bore him in her arms, tender but not sensual. From there she ran her hand smoothly over his tunic, all the way down his chest at a painfully slow rate that made him restless. He did nothing to stop it. He loved her and hated her, and could reach no resolve to throw her aside as was well within his rights. In a strange way, he wanted it and waited to see what she would do; 99 men in a hundred would take her if she offered herself freely, yet until now, he'd told himself he was of the exception.

For all Alycia's splendour and self-control, she couldn't hold back her bosom from rising and falling rapidly, though less than his heavy heaving, made only worse by his attempts to trap his feelings within. When her hand reached down between his legs, her fingers sprawled open and curled inwards, and all the while Richard stood stock-still, gawping at the opposite wall. Alycia leaned in close over his shoulder so he could see her; enough to see her expression of mild interest and sly smile.

"So there is something down there," she said in mock surprise. She stepped back and instinctively he spun about to face her, wearied by her manners of testing him. She was neither pleased nor smug, tempering her own lust better than he his own. "You're not just anyone; you are the Emperor of Burtal. You inherited that through blood right bestowed thousands of years ago. Be the man you were born to be and you shall have the favour of the people, and mine. You'll need time alone," she finished, seemingly as an afterthought.

Like an early autumn's wind, she'd come to warn him of the fall of summer and flitted away, leaving him to his warm weather for all it was worth. He collapsed into a chair and could again hear rain and thunder rumbling through his halls as all else fell to quiet. His head rang, and through the countless glasses of wine that slowed him, he cursed himself for his drunkenness and focused with all his will on Alycia's words. By the second, they sobered him ever more so, such was her influence, and a stony vision, whether of his own design or hers, came to the fore: be the Emperor.

"I will," he slurred.

Chapter Thirty-one: Of Loyalty and Ambition

Before the world awoke, life stirred within the castle walls. The sun peeked over the horizon to flood Tristan's bedchamber with a soft orange glow. It was too faint to wake anyone up; Tristan noticed it because he was already awake.

A hard rapping came at his door, rapid too and full of purpose. Tristan leapt from his bed and threw a robe over himself. Wylam Meyers was the one who'd knocked on his door, dull in the face but utterly awake, probably embarrassed that he of all people was to wake up a lord, and so early as well, thus any stiltedness was understandable. He was buckled from head to toe in his armour, including his helm that sat neatly over his head and gave ample room for his vision, all of it shined to mirror sheen.

"I've been informed to relay the message that we're to leave the castle within three hours," he announced.

"Based on what?" Lord Almaric answered.

"On giving time for the men to eat their fill, suit up, and on the basis of arriving at Bryndton early enough to sweep it thoroughly before nightfall, if it comes to it. And on orders. If you want to overrule that, it's none of my business, but that's what I planned for until Sir Darith Wyman took up my duty, and he's made no alterations, not at this early stage at any rate."

Tristan thanked Wylam, to which he bowed sincerely and took his leave. It was happening then, Tristan told himself, whatever the hell *it* was. He dressed himself as he knew would be appreciated by members of the Harthen court: in a loose-fitting white shirt and tight, patterned doublet of black and dark blue lined with gold, the same for his sleeves, plain breeches that matched, and a thin royal green and silver cape that wouldn't fight with the sea winds, bearing his pentangle and mullets, and finally, high boots that were sturdy, hard on the soles and flexible enough to run in, much as he'd like to have ignored Darith's advice.

The halls of the castle seemed of towering height and exhausting length as he walked through them that early morning, not a soul to be seen or heard, not an echo save for soft-footed maids and servants every now and again, endless dark passages of red brick hued by orange through tall windows. Before he even descended to the ground floor for breakfast, he went to the battlements that overlooked the garden and found the world at large to be of little difference: still slumbering, it was. The world within the garden, however, was a different matter entirely. He heard the racket before he stepped onto the battlements and he gazed up to its source at their edge, hands taking a loose hold of the coarse merlons either side of him as leaned forward. Dozens of horses were being filed through the garden, greaves and hooves like thunder on cobbles even as they marched in slow procession, overseen by the watchful eyes of Sir Darith, and Wylam at his side. As of yet, Tristan's horse was not present as there was but one horse for every man there, and his would be caparisoned in a royal sheet to differentiate him from the rest.

The air was very cool this morning, as if the heat had been sucked away by the storm of which there was now no evidence, and the view of the sleeping city he was afforded was refreshing and, above all, peaceful. *Fifty soldiers and one diplomat*, Tristan mused. *Let's see how this works out.*

During his breakfast, eaten alone, he called for a servant to bring Marcus to him as he pondered his situation. It was a large breakfast in which he alternated between cramming food into his mouth and willing himself to eat at a more sluggish pace, accompanied by water, only water, to drink in copious dosage.

Armoury chamberlain Frederic Comnyys appeared unbidden, to assure him of how smoothly the operation was going, while Tristan merely sat and listened.

"Valen has not yet been released, so that he may not arrive ahead of you with much advance, if at all," Comnyys spoke stiffly, looking straight past Tristan into the ether. "I do not know if he wishes to attend at all. I am given to understand it is important that the situation is controlled verily. There are many here that would cheer to see Mürathneè wearing the pauper's shoes at last, and begging for alms from the lords of Burtal. And I am given to understand that you may result this from your deeds today."

Nodding, perturbed at this man being so presumptuous, Tristan rose, his breakfast done, and the chamberlain left hastily. And just like that, he was finished and moving again, striding through the vestibule already as if time was truly merciful today that it would allow him to skip it so. Emerging into the calm morning of the outside world, he, at last, took a moment to slow down, to feel the breeze on his face, and to watch the soldiers gather in the plaza. Still they were not all here; some men were on the path between the castle and the wall, and few, by sound alone, he surmised, were with their horses in the garden. Furthermore, each man had at least two swains riding on attendance, *far too many* to take ashore. No chances were being taken, he could see, and the point was driven home further, if there was an inch of his brain that needed waking up, to fully take control of the situation at Bryndton and resolve everything with his armed men standing as far back as possible. They were all of them armed with swords, and most had pollaxes. Most, if not all, had shields at the ready or slung over their backs. A select few, perhaps ten in total, were additionally equipped with crossbows and longbows also, fine yew creations half a head taller than a man, and those few individuals strong and skilled enough to wield them had slung upon their backs a quiver stuffed with arrows. That they would be opportune to fire at that many targets was nothing short of absurd. If he were a member of the embassy from Harth, it would not go unnoticed then either.

The Voice of Kings

As if that wasn't protection enough, some had spears of the ranseur variety, piercing the sky, white sunlight skewered upon their points. The second blade of the cruciform design was at the base of the rod's steel front end, a crescent moon as sharp as any dagger if he were to guess. Presumably at Darith's orders, the soldiers wore exchange garnitures that forewent mail and full plate, wearing buff leather to fill the gaps between pieces, for that might make it easier for men to haul them out of the water should they fall in.

Sir Darith came through the crowd wearing a dry smile, fresh-faced and generally looking as alive and awake as could be, proud to be in his armour as Tristan hadn't seen him otherwise. It was plate armour deliberately made dark grey, as if scorched by fire hotter than any furnace could create, intricate silver whorls dancing all about it in spectacular fashion. In his right hand he carried a tall heater shield bearing a striking image of a jet black swan taking flight on a silver field, while his left hand was settled on his sword's hilt as if he were about to let it free any second: a hilt wrapped in crosshatched black leather that would have been supremely comfortable to wear if it were in clothing.

"My Lord!" Sir Darith said, so joyously one might be excused from wondering if he'd just returned from claiming victory at a great battle. He removed his helm and shook his head, that his hair could fly, and stuffed it under an elbow.

"Morning Sir. When will these men be ready to go?"

"They're ready for your word to move. I'm surprised to see you so eager. Invested, yes, but I'd thought not to call you eager."

"I'm eager to see what the fuss is all about. Don't worry, I'll do my duty at Bryndton, just as you'll do yours," Tristan said sincerely. Certainly the knight would stand out, and that was half of what he wanted. As for the other half, he was ready to be impressed. "You know, this reminds me of my days as a knight. I would organise soldiers too, at least as many as this, and often more. Looking back on that is like remembering a past life really. I don't know if that makes you a younger me though. I was never such a good fighter."

Darith grinned, showing his teeth. The same grin could be forewarning of a blade across the throat in different circumstances, but here it was perfectly innocent. Before either could say another word, Marcus slowed to an abrupt stop; Marcus, who didn't know anything but running.

"You called, my Lord?"

"You're not doing anything important today, Marcus."

"I'm not, my Lord?"

"Not here. Not if you'd like to come with me. I could use another pair of ears when I'm negotiating. As someone who runs around with words all day, you've come to understand them quite well, I'd say. If you'd come to Bryndton and listen as best you could, I'd be eternally grateful for your opinion afterwards."

"It would be my honour."

"That's what I thought. It's not much of an honour really, but thank you. Saddle up."

Tristan left both of them be. He reconsidered. They were all very busy and dedicated to their jobs, these soldiers, and such an attitude would also not go unnoticed were he to be of the Mürathneèan group. His endless reconsiderations were short-lived however, put down by the sound of yet another suit of armour, sabatons echoing on the smooth floor of the vestibule and then the cobbled courtyard, and so Tristan turned to greet them.

"You too Sir?" Lord Almaric said in surprise as Sir Pedrig approached with purpose in his heart. Sir Pedrig's face only hinted at haggardness from being awake so early, as indeed was the most that could be said for any of the soldiers here. The sight of them gave him energy.

"Sadly no, I'm needed here, though I know what it is you're doing. I came only to give you a warning, if I dare call it that, my Lord."

"Regarding?"

"Our little enigma moping in his cell in the dungeon. You may have lost interest amidst your other duties, and I can't blame you, but a man needs a hobby. I walk the dungeons from time to time; I did so just now and saw Mortain sleeping soundly, though I can't say he looked well." Sir Pedrig paused to reflect on his purpose, showing a first sign of tiredness as he rolled his shoulders back. "I've been doing some digging on him and his deceased friend Yulian Eliot, who he so casually murdered."

"They were friends?" Lord Almaric said sharply to make sure the knight wasn't being hyperbolic.

"Apparently so. They worked together for some time, it turns out, and men have reported seeing them drinking together at barracks outside of working hours. No one noticed anything suspicious about them, but then again, I can't squeeze any anecdotes out of anyone, so whether they were really friends is up for debate. As for their activities outside of work, they've both been known to send letters north and south."

"That's not exactly damning."

"It's a consideration concerning a known murderer, my Lord. I should add that neither of them has been known to receive replies from Mürathneè and wherever they were sending letters in the south. Here lies the interesting part: apparently they would check the eagle lofts anyway, so they must have been expecting replies, and the last one by Eliot was sent not to Mürathneè, but within County Capital."

"Not to the same people then," Lord Almaric replied, resting his hands on his hips as if to support his tired body.

"That would seem the most sensible assumption." Pedrig's well-aged face became a mass of creases as he became severe of mood. "If it was to the same people, the same people who never return his messages, one can only assume he spoke to an envoy personally. Whatever the case, I fear you were never wrong. If Adrian hated Yulian, that was almost certainly not the reason he killed him. The wiser thing would be to assume it all comes down to Lennord Brodie, or you, my Lord."

"When wilful paranoia is wisdom, there is something wrong. I'll take you for your word on this. You came to me now of all times though. You're thinking Mortain's collaborators and Valen's are one and the same?"

"I see no reason to believe that in particular," the knight said, dropping his guard to express a hint of humour upon his face, sly as a fox across his lips. "I've correlated records from Lameeri's Wish to those of the Empress concerning Valen, and I saw crossover in where letters were being sent. I pressed Adrian on it last night, and lo, he had nothing to say. Perhaps he has gone mad, as you say. If he hasn't just yet, there are other ways to make him talk as a last resort."

"A pointless exercise, Sir," Lord Almaric said scathingly. "I won't authorise torture; it doesn't work."

Sir Pedrig raised his eyebrows as if he was learning this for the first time. It wasn't sarcasm that bore it, merely a mild acceptance, indifference if anything, backed by agitation at not being able to end the affair so easily. So the aging knight did have honour, definitely. He wouldn't dream of torturing Adrian without permission, though whether he would seek Alycia's was another matter. Tristan would have to trust him not to, and her to deny it. Terror might dictate he assume she wouldn't, but there was an objection, a fierce one, telling him she was better than that.

"My Lord," Sir Pedrig went on, changing tack. "Have you seen anyone you suspect, or been given any reason to look over your shoulder?"

"I don't think there's anyone I know who'd harm me or Lennord."

"Then you should be careful where you place your trust, if I may be bold to say. I wouldn't trust anyone. If it's you that's wanted for some reason or other, their only shot at you would be outside these walls."

"Who would be so brazen to ambush me with an escort such as this?" Lord Almaric said with a wave of his hand to the dozens of riders forming as one unit in the courtyard, feeling a sense of pride creep into him. "For that matter, what contingent would be capable of taking down 50 guards of Castle Aurail without attracting a great deal of attention before it got within but five leagues?"

"Indeed," Sir Pedrig said simply, craning his head to the sky, his posture growing prouder still if anything. There was no answer he could give, or rather his grave silence was answer enough. The knight showed his years through his face in whatever way was needed at the time.

"I'll trust who's trustworthy," Lord Almaric told him firmly.

"Caution's your prerogative, my Lord. You employ it as you see fit."

Of Loyalty and Ambition

Sir Pedrig had more to say, Tristan saw it, only he refrained from speaking it. It was just his thoughts painted on his face right now and he had no intention of voicing them. Tristan thanked the knight for his help, for he knew of nothing else to say, and Pedrig bowed low and swept his being away in his aged grace. Tristan watched the knight intently as if hypnotised by the rippling of his green cape, though as he admitted when Pedrig had gone from the vestibule, he was just distracting himself from the real issue.

At that time, Darith came forward with Tristan's horse that was draped in a green cloth bearing the device of three red towers on either side. Tristan hopped upon the saddle energetically, feeling the tension return to haunt his heart, and Wylam and Marcus came up on his left side. Gears churned, and wood and iron creaked as, before him now, the great gates were opened, lumbering and ominous as they never were, as if this morning the world chose to act in drama for him. The long, wide street outside the wall lay in wait, not a soul in sight, hues of the rising sun creeping down the buildings either side, striking through the barbican's gate. Sir Darith was saddled now too, and he settled on Tristan's right side, shield slung over his back. He rested his elbows casually on his horse's neck, reins loose between his fingers.

Behind Tristan, for he had to look behind, the company was assembled on horses steady, some grating their hooves on the cobbles. The courtyard was filled with them, and their riders, all in the shadow of the castle, looked to him, the trainer Havdan Linch among them to Tristan's surprise, perky and inquisitive with scars stretched on his face, and he eyed the others as if he held some position of power here.

"They wait for your command," Sir Darith supplied. "I'm not needed yet. This company is yours."

"Away then," Lord Almaric spoke. And then, more loudly, "Follow."

~

It took a few seconds for Isaac to compose himself. He lay there as he processed the previous night and then, with a grin, turned his head as it all came together. Only a creased imprint in the bed sheets remained of Tamzin there. He sat bolt upright. She was gone. Off home no doubt. On the bright side, she would have joy in her heart for a good while now. If her euphoric behaviour under the moon's rays was any indication, she'd have as good a memory as any to switch off to while her father spewed his nonsense. It did Isaac well to be appreciated. He exhaled contentedly and rolled out of bed, whereupon the cold breeze sweeping through the window nipped at his naked body. Instinctively he went for his clothes: his regal suit of royal colour and exquisite fabric, of blue and clean white, and pleasantly dark trousers, and his cavalier boots. Then he arranged his hair with a comb only shortly, for the sea winds would do away with any effort at being presentable, and he felt overdressed as it was, but felt, for his part, the need to play the nobleman to the capacity his peasant blood would permit.

The Voice of Kings

He wasted no time; he certainly didn't disturb Lucian and, to his regret, neither Rosalynn nor any other was at the front desk, though later he would hope to tell of success and be content once again. So he stepped into the outside world and headed to the Mercenary's Guild, to the sea. When he arrived at the large, square yard nestled besides the L-shaped building, he found it near empty save for a few men in armour warming up with their swords at the far side, perhaps as it was still early. Not as early as he'd have liked, and not as early as the unpredictable man with the longsword would have liked, he remembered out of necessity.

Martello Jacart was there indeed, inside the walled yard. Isaac spotted him instantly through the fence upon the wall, sitting at a bench at the side. He was not of pleasant temperament, Isaac noted as he approached, as his face was dark and highly bemused. It was worth remembering he'd felt a fool for accepting Isaac's offer the previous evening, and probably felt more so now. *Don't play into his darkness*, Isaac told himself, *he'll not respond well.*

"Sorry I'm late," Isaac said as not to bandy words. "Where's Jamys?"

Martello looked up from twiddling his coarse fingers together and squinted into Isaac's face. His eyes made for the balcony, and then the door to the building, and then the sea. His head travelled around his shoulders, searching all around before his eyes returned, sharp and black as night, to Isaac, then straight onwards with Isaac just out of the corner of his sight.

"Not here, obviously," Martello replied. His voice was that of mocking, though whether he took humour in it... probably not.

"You have me confused. Shall we be plain?"

"Let's. We'll start by waiting for the City Watch. From there, you're a dead man. So to speak."

Isaac shuffled backwards an inch or two, and he swayed slowly like a thick branch in the wind.

"You're having me arrested?" Isaac said guardedly. Less so than he'd hoped, as fear had crept into him.

The enthusiasm in him waned, that he might now snap like a twig. Panic ran through his body telling him to drop the conversation and bolt, but before that came curiosity, and before that a part of him died inside as everything crumbled to dust, his joy sapped by the disturbing calmness that masked whatever horrors were loose in that man's head.

"I will not be made a cretin of by the likes of you," Martello answered. He rose suddenly, and he was taller than Isaac remembered. "I misjudged you; you're even smarter than you come off as. Course, other men are smarter than you. Tell me, after you retrieved what you wanted from the seabed and had a good look at it, what were you planning to do with me?"

"What are you talking about?" Isaac spat in disgust and bewilderment.

Of Loyalty and Ambition

Martello had been swaggering in Isaac's direction. He checked his approach and examined Isaac hard, though Isaac didn't cease to back away…until he reached the wall of the guild centre: then he would run, where didn't matter, he would just run.

"Are you an assassin as well as a spy?" Martello asked, to his own doubt. "Are you a spy?" he repeated firmly, and this time it was a real question.

"If I were a spy, do you really think I'd enquire for information from the person with a reputation for being volatile? If I wanted you in particular, don't you think I'd ask for something only you would know? I bet there are dozens of ways a spy could find out the exact location of that ship wreckage in this city."

"You know what I'm talking about then," Martello pointed out. A shiver ran down Isaac's spine as, like a sword swing, enjoyment flashed across the mercenary's face: a twisted sort born of not knowing whether he should be truly amused or whether to bare his steel.

"What the fuck else would you be talking about?" Isaac despaired.

He couldn't hear confidence in himself anymore. It was more a whine now, if anything. Martello took his time to approach Isaac, intentionally so, and though Isaac was beside the exit, he did not yet move.

"If you're innocent, you can explain that to the City Watch."

"Why can't the City Watch arrest me at my boarding lodge? They know where I'm staying; they've known for a while now."

Martello did consider this, though Isaac feared he already had a conclusion in mind that he was going to meet with one way or another. Isaac sagged at the shoulders, the fight gone from him, and so that day was all else. The hopes of the day had been dashed, and now they were fading into fantasy with only the aftermath burned into his vision to taunt him. Whatever wound had been dealt behind his back was damage done without a hope of repair. Not here. Not with him.

The mercenary captain stared so long and so still in his contempt that he appeared to be a statue now, so much so that Isaac half-wondered if the gaze would not falter if he stepped from it. He would do that, he decided. He lifted his shoulders rigidly and made to leave, and with that, he came to an acceptance that Martello was lost to him. The armoured man stirred. A thumb reached under the strap at his shoulder, his left arm was a blur reaching behind his back, and so too was his sword thereafter. Its song was a dull hum and, beyond that, a high-pitched scream as it howled by Isaac's ears. He crouched from its bite haphazardly, the wind whizzing as it was cut open above his head.

Isaac staggered backwards as he did, his left foot catching on his right, causing him to tumble. It was his left foot to save him, landing hard and flat, and now his body was low again, his arms outstretched either side for balance. All the while, Martello stood there in the gateway, longsword in hand still with scabbard and strap both. There was only him, there was nothing else: Isaac's eyes were wide, yet his peripheral vision was meaningless. He was holding his breath, he realised, so he exhaled, only to go too far with that to the point where his skin grew hot and red and he was wrought with dizziness. *Breathe in*, Isaac commanded. *Breathe out, breathe in.*

Martello said nothing. He drove the chape of his weapon to the ground before him at an angle and, releasing his hold on the scabbard, took a tremendous step back. With his right hand alone, he freed his dark steel from its cage and swung it out to the side. There he held it outstretched, as he had done the previous night, and as Isaac had seen last night, Martello expressed not a hint of fear or even concentration, as if goading Isaac to attack. There was something to be seen in him, and it wasn't fear: it was calm, it was joyous, it inspired fear, it was a black pit in his eyes.

"Wait!" Isaac shouted when he saw that intensity, throwing his arms out in surrender. "You're being made a fool of by someone, but not by me. I've been only plain with you; my words last night were mine. I couldn't have said or been as such as a liar."

Martello listened; Martello disregarded. He sprinted forward, face reservedly malicious. And it was the face Isaac was drawn to, horrified as he stared unblinking. The huge mercenary's sabatons beat on the stone and, just like that, he was bearing upon his ally made foe, swinging his sword out before him, strengthening his blow with his left hand mid strike. Isaac ducked again, wheezing in terror as the air did above him. The long blade was still moving. It slashed back at him, Martello using its momentum to his advantage rather than try to stop it, and with that he made a gigantic stride, more of leap than run. Isaac jumped back, avoiding the longsword by a great margin, though again Martello's back foot was sprung out and he made for an uppercut that Isaac turned to avoid, so speedily and carelessly he fell back into a locker pressed against the wall.

Pleasure was in Martello's eyes. He was lost to it; that, or wilful stupidity. Isaac had had the right of it; he'd noticed his selective intelligence, and for ignoring it, he paid a cruel price behest by manipulators. The steel cabinet was cold on his back, cold and crying for attention.

Behind him he reached with his right hand and it clamped upon a leather hilt, bringing its blade to the light. Martello had stopped, before even he'd made for the sword's company. Isaac breathed in, breathed out, each halation strenuous and controlled while his body tried to sabotage it all. Before his waking eyes was the scene at Caedor, the young brigand's face transplanted pale upon Martello's. Isaac brought his sword up and held it out diagonally to match his own ghost form, but it was treacherous, it was wrong, and he knew it. One sword fight was not another. What was old was not new; only he was the common link, and he was not the same.

Desperately, he dared look beyond Martello to no comforting sight. Jamys wasn't there; he'd been sent away, or arrested, or been shortened at the shoulders even, and no one else cared to intervene; they weren't surprised to see this fight transpire. Martello's head tilted to one side, another goad, then he lunged, arching his sword high and bringing it down hard. There was strength to it, yet it was strangely clumsy, and Isaac dodged to hear its ring deafening on the stone plaza.

Isaac was already running, hearing death's call a short way behind. So he sprinted head on so he wouldn't be slowed, straight for the wall of the yard, and jumped with precision he prayed to be true. One foot landed on the wall's edge, then the other, and he kicked off in the direction of the exit. The man in blued armour was already lumbering before him, and his weapon slashed at Isaac's chest again. Again Isaac dodged it by the skin of his teeth, only to see it was nowhere near him. If Martello was playing with him for time, he had a sick sense of humour indeed. Nonetheless, to assume that was the case could be a mistake he wouldn't live to see. He held out the sword.

Not like that! You're already liability enough. Hold it right at least, or you die.

Then Isaac brought it high, holding it steady alongside his head with the blade pointed straight forward. Once more Martello lunged, for his neck now, and by impulse, Isaac sidestepped and scraped his sword edge against the longsword, sliding it round in an arch before jabbing at Martello's face. Shock crossed the mercenary captain's face. It turned to a grin, as if now he truly knew what Isaac could do. The next strike came faster than before, clashing against Isaac's sword so hard there was nothing he could do, no amount of skill in him enough to change it. His fingers stung from top to bottom. They were empty. His sword clattered far, far from his reach, but worse, Martello came again for his chest, and it would hit this time. Amidst the blur, Isaac saw the hilt twirl in the mercenary's fingers.

Isaac's stomach was whipped by steel, the flat of the longsword it was, and it hit so hard his organs seemed all to be forced to his throat because at once he couldn't breathe. He screamed in pain as he was flung from his feet, and tripping over them again, he whirled and landed on his face. His eyes were bloodshot, terror was their message. With his face upon the ground, he wheezed to no avail. He breathed in again and again, and each time his stomach constricted farther. To drown, then, out of water, upon himself.

"What's the meaning of this?!" someone yelled, the voice unfamiliar to him.

Sabatons resounded on the white stone ground, several pairs of them.

"I was preparing him for arrest," Martello replied edgily.

"This is how you question people, is it?" the voice bellowed. A pause, and then footsteps drawing closer. When the man spoke again, he was quiet, but the anger hadn't died down. "I don't even want to hear your excuse. Anything you say will show you for the lover of violence you are."

"He had a sword."

"For gods' sakes, help that man up," the other voice said, casually ignoring Martello.

There were tears in Isaac's eyes from the pain, so by now he could see nothing at all. He felt a hand tug at his waist and clap him across the back. His insides burst, from his mouth

The Voice of Kings

venting, copious vomit. On his lips he felt a more metallic texture too, and he could have sworn he saw red on the ground. The tears were passing now as he was pulled around to see Commander Leonardus of the Watch. He'd have recognised that half-cape and winged helm anywhere. Whether Isaac was pleased or not, he couldn't himself yet tell.

"Isaac Brodie," the Commander said. "I'm placing you under arrest for charges of conspiracy against the royal crown."

The Commander waved a hand and a second Watchman from his group came forward after handing his halberd to another, and he helped support Isaac, though his head still sagged and his legs were sand. Leonardus returned his gaze to Martello, fearless and enraged.

"If you ever pull a stunt like that again, I'll throw you in the dungeons myself." As Isaac was pulled away, he heard the Commander mutter to himself, "Imbecile."

Consciousness seemed to come and go at its leisure, or at least memory did. The sights of the city were not beautiful then, nor were they ugly or even bland. They were there, they were white, were tall, were short. Terror washed over him anew as another vision begot itself to him, that of a boat that rocked so violently it made him want to vomit a second time, and of a lonely prison tower off the coast where he would rot, or be put on a pike alive like the Mürathneèan traitors of old. It took him a time to come to his senses. By the time he could become startled by being dragged up the Kingsreach, he was atop it. Through a gate he went, through a grand door and halls that were even grander. Warm light turned to dinginess at the top of a flight of stairs that he would have fallen down if not for his helpers, and at the end of the corridor, a thick iron door loomed closer and closer. It opened, it was slammed behind him, and Isaac was a prisoner below the Palace of the Sun.

Chapter Thirty-two: A Kiss in Summer

"Take us through, slow as you can," Lord Almaric told the captain of Tormyr Sorenys. It meant something like 'Noble Serpent', an unusual name for a modern ship, and put Tristan in mind of the Wyman choosing it because of that. "The afternoon is young; we can afford not to rush, and we need to be slow enough for the men to spot any signs of our informants."

The captain barked orders to his sailors and they scrambled to open the sails out to their fullest, as the wind was partly against them. The sails were of the finest cloth a ship could ever need for its canopies, having something of a shiny texture. Translucent they were also, in the day's bright light, unimpeded by clouds; the motif of the three red towers upon a green field could be seen through the cloth from his spot close to the captain and his wheel upon the sterncastle. The carrack, as it was, now skirted between two of the six main isles of Bryndton, and on both, no more than a few hundred people lived. Both isles specialised in the fishing trade, as any man with eyes could pick up on, seeing the dozens of fishing boats trawling around their respective bays, and nets sprawled out from small piers in the harbours.

Both were some distance either side, it had to be noted, and both were hilly where their only grass grew, blocking any potential informants from sight. Sand rimmed the islands in great width: beaches that were covered in weathered grey rocks here and there, some as big as this very ship, and amidst those rocks were slabs of rock red and grey: pieces of history left as reminders, fragments of towers and keeps shattered by the huge trebuchets of the Mürathneèan navy in Jorin's War of the Chosen, not so many years ago. Those were the visual scars for all to see, but there were subtler ones that ran deeper. Tristan paid the scars no tribute, for they were just that: demons of the past brought to life to harass the reputation of Burtal. It was true the war's aftermath had caused resounding damage to the country's development and been of boon to Mürathneè, but it was for him as lord paramount to be the voice of reason; Richard was haunted by the ghost of his ancestor, unduly so, though one day in the coming years, when Aurail thrived, he would lay the past to rest.

Then again, history almost aligned itself here, on these harsh stony islands. Here they were again, squabbling over magic. *So it would seem*, he corrected. The Battle of Bryndton was then, the Embassy of Bryndton was now.

The marvellous black and silver armour of Sir Darith caught his attention suddenly, glinting where his back-slung shield would allow, as he stirred his calm, controlled being, while upon the very prow he stood tall and gazed into the distance. Here he looked even more at home than when Tristan had met him that morning, gleeful in his suit of steel and standard-bearing shield. After half an hour spent at the prow, Darith was making his way back along the deck, weaving around all the busy sailors without slowing, and around one of the iron cannons, of which there were three on either side. Tristan had protested to their presence and so they were pulled back from the gunwales to make them harder to spot for outsiders. Below, there was a deck where port and starboard both were lined with ballistae: that he couldn't change, but it put him at ease.

Sir Darith joined Tristan on the sterncastle. He breathed the salt air viscerally. Indeed, it was pleasing to the lungs, and the wind was gentle, yet in light of the shadow waiting to fall, the knight's attitude surprised him. It was probably for the best, him being the military leader in his company. He had to admire him for it.

"No news for me or you to give, then," Sir Darith supposed in confidence when they met eye to eye. "They won't be on either of these two islands; we both know that, I think."

"Why would they be at any of them, Sir? If they were smarter, they might have asked us to attend at a spit of land off the Mürathneèan coast, unless I've become paranoid."

"I wouldn't go that far, my Lord. I disagree, but it's wise to watch your footing among these grounds of politics; it's brambles and hornets' nests all over the place." Tristan gave him permission, with a look, to continue, and Sir Darith was cheerful to do so. "It's as the Emperor said, they will be at the Eye of Sand, or the Eye of Crow for that matter. Both are reverently left uninhabited, and have plenty of places to hide."

"The Emperor was right. I've been on both. Not only is the Eye of Sand the biggest, but the King's fleet never bombarded either of them, having not reached that far before Jorin's navy intercepted it. The Eye of Sand, as I go back to, is derelict, but the roofs and walls aren't strewn on the seabed, they're just collapsed, and one could veil himself in the rubble. Good for those inclined to treachery, not so much for us on the receiving end if we're going to be cynical."

"Have you considered that it's, let's say the Eye of Sand itself, that's of import?"

"Oh, I have. It was a sacred place once. If they have something to show me, I'll be relieved, for it would put my fears to rest, and we'll at least have an idea where they're coming from in this matter. That's what I'd like to believe, as trust will make the discourse easier. You can be my advocate opposition if it really please you."

"Not at all," Sir Darith answered earnestly.

The Tormyr Sorenys scythed through the sea, passing beyond the two isles though their hilltop ruins were still to be seen for some time yet, and now they entered open water. Ahead, the two last isles waited, the ones Tristan knew they would visit over any feeble conjecture he could contribute regarding the other four. There was another isle also, ahead and to the left some way before the last two, but while it was a very rocky affair, people lived there too. That was what it came down to. From the centre of the deck, Wylam hurried up the staircase from the depths and immediately began searching of his own accord, even as he made to join him and Darith, gazing all about as if in desperate need to orient himself. When he reached Tristan, he bowed, though his eyes fell on him only shortly. He squinted as he looked up, hand shielding his face from the sun.

"What's he doing up there, my Lord?" Wylam asked, more quizzically than he'd probably intended.

Tristan smiled, knowing Wylam's meaning at once. It was Marcus he spoke of, standing atop the crow's nest of the main mast. He was happy there, Tristan saw, just as Darith had been posing in his soldier's way on the prow. Well, it was good to see people were getting something out of the trip, and to see that Marcus could willingly trap himself in one place without jogging on the spot. He would joke about it too, come to think of it, as he knew what people's reactions were to his rushing about all the time all too well.

"He's searching, just as we are," Lord Almaric answered patiently. "His eyesight's proficient, I'll have you know. Captain, take us between the isles of Sand and Crow and circle around them."

"My Lord..." the captain grunted in acknowledgement.

It was the third island to the left that Tristan suddenly had an urge to explore for signs of a foreign party, though he'd just put down the suggestion personally, and for good reason. To the very stern of the ship he walked, to appease his nerves by looking out through the gap between the previous two isles, and there he saw fishing boats again, for what else? Sir Pedrig himself had admitted the reservations in his warning. If there was a third party willing to do battle with this ship, it would be intercepted before it could cross the horizon. Tristan allowed himself to be composed by the hypnotic swirling of the water behind the ship, staring deep into its white frothing, churning motion until such time that Sir Darith bid him pay attention to what was ahead. As Tristan did so, he tugged at his cloak and wrapped it tightly around his chest, folding his arms over it. He gave this some thought. He dropped the cloak from his hands and let it flap merrily around his ankles. It was only wind; it wasn't going to kill him. It was scarcely cold; he felt exposed in other ways.

"What do you see, Marcus?" Tristan called to the courier in his nest.

"Soldiers," the call was returned. "On the Eye of Sand. As many as we have."

The Tormyr Sorenys was sailed halfway between the eyes of Bryndton, just as Tristan had commanded, and now they all could see the soldiers on the island, some of whom were donned in expensive plate armour with insignias upon their cuirasses, all of them milling about under archways and in broken buildings near the centre of the isle, staring beadily at the carrack. Then there was light, flashing at Tristan in glory, for striding amidst them, unnoticed as a ghost, was a figure dressed in treasure it seemed: a display of wealth and grace that unseated Tristan. It passed beyond sight, and the world was dimmer, though no worse for it.

The Voice of Kings

The isle was long, with a concourse road running right through the middle as long as that of Lameeri's Wish, and that was up to the crumbled temple at the rear, and the natural stacks of rocks extending behind. The buildings here were much older than on all but the other eye, perhaps six hundred years old. The remains were all of stone, but made mostly in the old way with rocks conjoined with great volumes of cement, an old kind that nonetheless stood the test of time and weather well enough that he could live to see them. And not only were they red, but white also, exactly like the city of Harth.

Tristan recalled his last visit, when Richard and Alycia had come together in mutual bond to walk its old halls under blue skies to decide upon its fate, and he remembered how Richard, like his forebears, had put his foot down and forbade that anything be done with it. Jorin had had many of its inhabitants executed besides the value of it being invaluable, and so Richard, with writ of pain upon his features, declared it off limits to contractors again. Tristan tried to think back with more scrutiny, to recall its layout when he walked amongst the ruins with sweet Evylyn before even Malcus was a thought in her womb.

On the starboard side, the Eye of Crow was a barren and dusty set of ruins, red and black turned grey: a temple dedicated to death and the life thereafter, where carrion birds would circle in their swarms when dead men were brought for burial on request, out here away from the mainland. There was no one there now but the skeletons under the hard-dug reinforced tombs, with no birds to sing their praises save for a few gulls gliding high above, unbeknownst of them.

"Captain, turn us about," Lord Almaric ordered. "We know where they are; to carry on lapping them like a pack of wolves would appear incredulous of us, disingenuous even."

"About!" the captain bellowed, and followed with various instructions.

"How many other lords would have commanded the same, I wonder?" Sir Darith said. "I think back to our council sessions and I wonder if you're the only one."

"That's not for you to say," Wylam snapped scathingly.

"No, no, it is," Sir Darith replied, half-mockingly. "Our Lord Almaric's words, not mine. No reprimand for telling the truth, at least from him. Lord Almaric said as much late last night, and very kind of him it was too, because gods if that's not a truth in your eyes, then you've obviously never seen the lords of Burtal sitting round a table holding knives behind their backs."

"It's true," Lord Almaric intervened as an attempt at tact. "I said it and meant it, Wylam; don't let it bother you."

"As you say." Wylam surveyed his surroundings for want of some important deed to oversee meticulously. "Should we not prepare for landing, my Lord?"

"Of course. See to it."

A Kiss in Summer

"I'll gather the men from below deck," Sir Darith said, gently clapping a gauntleted hand on Wylam's shoulder at the top of the stairs, as gentle as a big man like he could be in such exhilarated animation.

They both took their leave and Tristan composed himself at the fore of the sterncastle beside the captain and his wheel, tapping his fingers on the wooden railing as his confidence grew, watching eagle-eyed Wylam and the boatswain commanding the sailors to prepare boats for winching, and soon thereafter, Sir Darith boldly leading his 50 men from the darkness of the ship's bowel, leaving squires and pages below. They arranged themselves in formation before him, covering the whole deck with the sailors at the forecastle as the ship cruised slowly through clear open waters. Marcus clambered down the rigging and joined them in looking to him for their orders, broody Havdan Linch again giving the impression of authority, but if he had any, it was minimal. Tristan could only smile in amusement despite himself, as they looked ready to hear a speech from him, and certainly he'd likely given that impression. Well, a word or two couldn't hurt, he thought.

"Gentlemen, it's come to my attention you may not be fully aware of your function in all this," Tristan called out to the silent men, armour bearing smiles of light where the great canopies would permit. "I fear some of you may overestimate the chances of a battle at Bryndton here today. They are low at default, and they'll be consigned to the ether once I, and my compatriots, step up there and get this farce over with."

The men began to laugh in good spirits and nod their heads. To speak a declaration of peacefully resolving a silly dispute like a heroic battle herald was a curious thing, but it amused all involved. A victory then, as Tristan privately allowed himself the joke.

"Right then, to the boats. To be done with this. Blessings of five on you."

"And remember," Darith added, "anyone falls in, that's why you sacrificed your mail. Do walk out. We will wait for you."

Sir Darith ushered Tristan into a boat first, where he sat at the back looking to where his men would be rowing. For a moment he considered offering to help row, only there was a line between being helpful and stupidity, and that would cross it, as it would serve only to disrupt the exact pattern of their rowing and tire him before the meeting could begin. Sir Darith sat opposite him, lowering one of the two chests of money between them while soldiers took their positions in this and three other boats. Three would have been enough in total, but the weight, Darith and Wylam had advised, of fully armoured men would best be distributed over four, even ones with high draught as these. And so it was. Sailors lowered his boat first, rocking dizzyingly even before it hit the waves. Tristan aligned the crashing and rocking with a rhythm in his head, and a tapping on the side where water splashed on his hand over and over again, and the whole thing became strangely pleasant. Before him, Sir Darith rowed as a Wyman was expected, jamming his oar into the sea like a knife

The Voice of Kings

through butter. Technically his timing was the same as everyone else, yet he appeared ten times fiercer.

With their strength, the Eye of Sand beat closer and closer, and informants and their soldiers with it, though they stayed put in the centre of the island still, the man in extravagant armour at the fore with his arms crossed. His face could not be made out, even as the boat was beached. Tristan leapt over the edge, casting ceremony aside.

On either side of the road before them, Tristan noted two walls more than twice the height of a man, mostly red though there were patches of faded, dirtied white brick organised in neat patterns, and the broken arch overhead was white too, and cleaner than the rest. Halfway down the isle's road, the soldiers still did not flinch. Tristan sighed. It was his prerogative to orchestrate a truce while they hung back warily; he was right to take such precautions of sensitivity, for quite predictably, they were too in fear.

"Sir Darith, Marcus, Wylam," he said when they'd gathered around him. "You'd best accompany me now. The longer we delay, the more this becomes a contest of suspicion."

"You heard him," Sir Darith said to his newfound followers, all of whom straightened in alarm at his call. "We'll be negotiating out there; you lot will stay put. Very simple. Havdan, I leave them in your keeping."

Tristan led the way, *visibly* led the way, while on his left, Wylam marched and Marcus strolled, and on his right side, Sir Darith Wyman was a noble weapon coursing down the road with all his pride laid bare, only accentuated by that skin of steel. He noted this, as he noted the moods of his other two compatriots to his left, and the stone road unseen beneath his feet, long since blown with sand and never cleared, and all the details of the labyrinthine ruins around him, crumbled as burnt wooden houses, only these were wounds of time. Ahead there was movement at last from the group: two men walking out to meet them, one of them in armour most extravagant, the other dressed in robes wrapped all around him. *It's Valen*, Tristan told himself at once.

The next distraction to pierce the scene was of sharp steel unsheathed, held aloft for all to see as Tristan had hoped never to see it. He looked to Sir Darith as if he was mad, though Darith was clearly not of such disposition.

"Your sword!" he bellowed to the two men approaching them, his voice a raw, booming thing that could not have gone unheard. "Put your sword in the ground!"

He spun his own blade in his hand and rammed it into sand beside the path, where it quivered as if in fright, the vibrating sound resounding as music in itself. He removed his helm and tucked it beneath his arm. There was reluctance in the armoured man ahead, who stopped suddenly and raised his arms as if ready to decry the whole thing and leave in a fuss. He did not. He echoed Darith's sentiment, much as he hated it. It made Darith smile.

"He might have damaged his sword, not checking the ground before he did that," Darith observed. Tristan was too nervous for humour.

A Kiss in Summer

"Wylam," Lord Almaric said to the soldier now drawing his sword also. "I think it's best if you stay back. One soldier is enough."

He obeyed without question. Good. Sir Darith was a presence to behold but not unduly threatening when he wanted. Wylam, for all his fervour, possessed a stiltedness he was wont to display even as he would obey every order of Tristan's. He was a stickler for proper form and it would show, just like two guards would make Tristan out to be the vulnerable one if they were looking for excuses to push their thoughts onto someone else.

They met at last. There at the centre of the road, sand blowing at their feet, all five of them risking as long as they dared to survey the others, which for Tristan was little time indeed. He held out an open hand, to which the armoured man winced, for a time seeming to pretend he hadn't seen it, then when it was clear he couldn't ignore it, he frowned.

"Observe a gesture of good faith," Lord Almaric treated. "I've done my part in initiating it. I ask only that you accept it. If you cannot, then you have no faith in me, and without faith in one another, we have no reason here."

The armoured man was pained by the experience for whatever reason he seemed to have no intention of divulging, but he took Tristan's hand firmly and shook it hard. It was this time that Tristan took to examine the man further, as best he could understand any man within three seconds. His armour was highest quality steel of exorbitant value, fire-gilded all over to the splendour of the sun, with exceptional engravings of white antler and silver snaking outwards from the cuirass to his arms and legs. His empty scabbard bore the same motif, though that struck a different chord altogether. On his left shoulder he wore a large pauldron that, burnished in enamel, was embossed with a star wreathed in what looked like dead petals. His presence was one no one could deny, for his armour was godly, its patterns bordering on gaudy for Tristan's tastes, though there was not a crest or banner of any kind to be seen on it; that star was no device Tristan could name. On the whole, it was not modest, nor had he skimped on sheening it. Yet, sand had attacked him these past minutes and the man had not noticed those small particles. How ashamed would he feel if he knew?

As the man continued to shake his hand, obsessively so, as if he were apologising for his rudeness, Tristan turned attention to his face. He wore no helm, exposing his short, black hair on hard head and heavy stubble everywhere else. Not black like Tristan's, mind, which was naturally oily, or Evylyn's locks, curly and soft, dark black like the clear sky on a midsummer's night; his was dirtier, more a very dark brown, and reflected in its grubbiness was the state of his face. His jaw was wide like Darith's, and unlike Darith's, was so sharp at its corners it might have been capable of slicing parchment. Although, in spite of the hardness of his overly severe face, it gave Tristan the impression of a man who'd recently lost a lot of weight, even as his physique was still something striking. There was a sickliness in his face, in his all too apparent discomfort that distorted it, and in his eyes, almost too dark to make anything of that remained, still as black stones on the beach. It was a wonder why the man came at all if he was so averse to it. Whether to pity or respect was something he would know in its proper course.

"My name is Lord Almaric," Tristan said after too long a delay.

"I know," the man replied, nodding to his associate, Valen. Valen had a bruise on his right cheek that hadn't been there before, but Tristan didn't stare.

The two hands were released from each other's grasps, and there left behind a creeping sensation in Tristan's blood. He squinted.

"Forgive me, you look familiar."

"Is that right?" the man replied, near smiling at the recognition. So many emotions tore him apart. "It must be true you recognise me. This morning I was Captain Westrym at Lameeri's Wish; this afternoon I am Jacopo Beriddian again. That's what I really am, my Lord, the blood of Beriddian."

"You'll have to explain yourself better than that."

"I have 54 men. Fifty-five were counted with you. If this goes sour, no one's getting out unscathed."

"I appreciate that, however that's not my concern."

"I was voicing mine," Jacopo rebuked airily. "I was there at the behest of your Empress. She wanted someone with experience and ended up with Westrym. She didn't know I was going to be here, but neither did I till recently."

"If you've been in Lameeri's Wish for weeks, how is it that you're my contact today? Why aren't I speaking to someone with first-hand knowledge?"

"I know more than you think. This business with magic in Mürathneè isn't as new as you think. My contacts have told me the rest. But there it is, your answer," and he shrugged.

"If you think that makes you trustworthy, you're mistaken, I'm afraid," Lord Almaric now spoke his mind. "I've made the effort and now that I'm here, I find myself pushed into a difficult place. Now that I mention that, I must mention your relationship with the King."

"I serve the King in my way, more so by and by," Jacopo was quick to say. "If I report the contents of our meeting here today, I will not reveal the source."

"And your men...?" Lord Almaric went on, now noticing the eagle crests on some of his soldiers' armour.

"They'll do as they're told. They know exactly as much as they need to about this, nothing more, nothing less."

"Well," Lord Almaric said, coming to the only conclusion he was really allowed to, "I shall have to take your word on that for now, and all of yours this day, my Lord."

"Do not call me that," Jacopo scowled. "I am no lord until I deserve it. Primogeniture would have made me one, but there is more in my country that decides a man's worth now."

A Kiss in Summer

Cristico Valen rolled his eyes at Jacopo's aggression, a repeat bemusement if guesses were to be made. Whatever Jacopo wanted, this had been important enough to bring up to him alone.

"Either you have a claim or you don't," Sir Darith pointed out in the mock tone of one who knew no humour.

"I should be a lord. The Beriddians are nobles, it's as simple as that. The transgressions of my family have caused it to fall into what some might call obscurity... I should be a lord. My Lord."

"I'm sorry, but I will not dwell on that," Lord Almaric clarified. "I won't have this jeopardised by affairs so personal to you. When you earn your title, I will name you by it. Until then, I am no less happy to do business with you, unless my apathy makes you uncomfortable."

"Shall we move on?" Valen said. Jacopo nodded, then paused.

"Who's this creature?" he said of Marcus.

"This *man* is Marcus Baldwin, my assistant in this matter. And my knightly companion is Sir Darith Wyman of Ylden Parragor. May we proceed?"

"Yes, fine. Fine, fine, fine, fine." Cristico Valen leaned over, focusing him with rhythmic taps on the shoulder and clicks of the fingers, that Jacopo made effort to process. Jacopo forced his tongue to still.

"Name your price," Lord Almaric said. "I must have perspective."

"Very wise," Valen put in diplomatically.

How he'd become the mediator all of a sudden was startling given what Tristan had learned of him, and entirely welcomed it all the same if Jacopo was going to be difficult to contend with. Cristico had apparently made an effort to stand out as an arbitrator from the start, unless, like the last time, he was just being flamboyant in his own quaint way. Today it was a patterned, yellowed robe wrapped around clothing befitting one of Harth which came into view whenever a gust tore at the robe around his collar or legs.

"Wisdom, maybe," Jacopo said. "But really, how can I name a price without knowing how much information you want? It will have to do to know you have it with you."

"We have money with us," Lord Almaric confirmed. "It's just money you want?" he went on, unsure whether to be disgusted at their pettiness so early on. Jacopo screwed up his face and rocked his head side to side, his indecision all the answer he'd give. It was just as well, it was all that was needed. "We'll take all the information you'll give us, if you please."

"It would help me to know what you've already picked up."

"So it would," Lord Almaric said, remaining polite. "I know men under the direct or indirect command of the High Duke were attacked, killed I'm hesitant in saying with any certainty, as it's only one of many rumours I've heard and they can't all be true. None of

The Voice of Kings

them might be true, one would be forgiven for believing. My reports claim they were attacked by creatures from the wilderness in force, wolves and the like, and even crows some say. A great murder of crows was spotted flying from the area at around that time, this I have confirmation of. And all while investigating the loss of a number of lives, gods give them rest, at the investigation of some phenomenon... fire hotter than any other, its source unseen, maddeningly."

"Like the other incident in your highlands years ago, correct?"

"I couldn't comment," Lord Almaric said, permitting himself the lie. If he wasn't going to allow Alycia, of all people, to have the Brodies be used, he wasn't going to give a stranger the opportunity. "I've heard of it, but the facts surrounding that have become too lost to legend already. I could as well speculate on the west winds."

"What do you mean?" Jacopo said sharply.

"One hears rumours about things that come from beyond the sea, like that ship. Nothing may have come of it, but as Lord Paramount, I have access to facts not available to the common man. And still, could I say more of that than of Caedor? Not in certainty."

"Well..." Jacopo said, then trailed off as his train of thought ran cold, or else he locked it away. He was gripped, positively *gripped*, by discomfort. "Almaric. My Lord. Your spies are misinformed."

"All the information we've acquired, we've acquired through legitimate channels, and if that makes it unreliable, then so be it. We're here now for that very reason, because we refuse to partake in that kind of paranoia-driven behaviour. Our country practised that as an indulgence and it dug us into the ground."

We will treat with possible traitors, though, Tristan said only to himself. He checked the faces of Cristico and Jacopo for signs of distress, thankfully seeing none. And so he'd kept his disgust to himself. Marcus was probably pointing out the hypocrisy in his head too for that matter.

"You're mistaken either way," Jacopo replied carelessly. "It was wolves and chupacabras," he corrected pedantically, as if Tristan had been so very far from the mark. "Some men were killed, some survived. What you missed entirely was the detail of what happened before then. Men were investigating the cave that spat fire, and I know this because I met them, if my sources haven't failed me."

"Again, I'm sorry to say you've not done well to make yourself sound trustworthy. These men, whose orders were they under?"

"The King's, they said, though I question that. I didn't know what they were doing at the time. I haven't strictly taken orders from Harth for some time, you see, so I was just a captain looking for means to prove myself to the King."

"You were a wandering captain with no real power, yet some of your men have royal devices upon their armour," Sir Darith said.

A Kiss in Summer

"The men I had with me then, and more," Jacopo explained as patiently as he seemed able to muster.

"One more question, Captain: is it normal for a captain to be wandering as a vagabond in Mürathneè? Were you not sworn by oath to a barony, if not a city, or town, or important individual?"

"My House is all but disbanded from liege service, as it's almost disbanded as a House. I have permission to show my quality, though not from the King directly here. When I'm seen as lordly, I will be a lord."

"Wouldn't this be high incentive to report the entire contents and context of this meeting to the King?" Sir Darith pushed unrelentingly.

"I've explained why I won't. I do this for gold and curiosity; the King knows the truth anyway and you have nothing to give him that he doesn't have. May I continue, *Sir*, my Lord."

"I am done," Sir Darith said smoothly.

"Uh," Cristico Valen interjected, coughing. "This is where I come in to exonerate Jacopo of being a turncoat. I liken myself to a merchant of information as well as all else, you see, and that is no crime. This man is a patron to me as His Grace is not, and in that way, my information is worth more to him. Meaning, he trusts me, and when I advise that Aurail will do no harm to our land by this meeting, he listens. In this case, he agrees. What His Grace will not tell you personally is not necessarily worth secrecy. That is my belief."

Tristan nodded and received something short of a curt expression from Jacopo. It was short of it, that was the important thing. He could work with that. Cristico was much the same and had made a habit, Tristan was noticing, of pulling, in growing irritation, at his robes around the shoulder and neck increasingly often as the wind denied him the comfort of it.

"To return to the point, my Lord..." Captain Beriddian said exasperatedly. "You've missed the point. I don't know for certain what those men were doing in that cave, but I have an idea. Whatever magic dwells there isn't native to these lands; it comes from far away, or else it travelled far afield from Mürathneè. I heard of it in Harth first, years ago. It came from the west, I know, and it won't stop here. It may scorch the earth barren, or worse, and we will be the ones to make it happen, all of us. It is arrogance and pride that feeds it. We cannot help but encourage it, and there'll be not a god to stop it."

"You could stand to be less vague, Captain."

"I couldn't, not yet," Jacopo said. He frowned and now had shadows carved through his face between deep lines. "Have you really not heard any of this?"

"None of it."

"Not from this legend of yours? At the mine?" Jacopo pressed forth with a true hardness. "Tell me of it, legend or not."

529

"I honestly don't know where to start... the fire was tipped with black, they say, that much is commonly spoken."

"Did anyone start it?" Jacopo said intensely. "Was there anyone to start it? Was there anyone to start it?"

"I heard you the first time, Captain," Lord Almaric answered softly. He had a touch of madness about him to be sure. Though... perhaps not. Jacopo frowned again and shook his head in disappointment at his apparent insanity. "I don't know if anyone started it. But I will find out what I can of all these threads, and make to connect them."

"Captain," Cristico Valen interrupted just as delicately. "Haven't you forgotten something?"

"Perhaps. My Lord Almaric, I have been vague. I shall try to be less so. If you'd like to show me how much money you've brought, we'll continue negotiations. It would give me time to think. I bless you, so I do."

Reluctantly Tristan agreed, met by more reluctance from Jacopo when he bowed, though he did not bow low. He was preoccupied in his thoughts before even Tristan had taken leave, wearing puzzlement heavy on his face. Sir Darith was the last of them to turn away, taking several steps backwards before spinning and pacing alongside Tristan. Shortly thereafter, Wylam joined them, so as four again they went on.

"Where do we even start?" Sir Darith said brashly. He laughed deeply, straight from the belly, and shook his head as if in grief. He licked his lips and tried again with almost mocking delicateness. "He has a fey quality about him. You'd be mad to trust him."

"I agree. It might be wise to call it off," Marcus suggested. He scratched the back of his head, clearly uncomfortable at giving advice on so critical a matter; humility a boon that couldn't prevent him voicing his opinion when it clawed at him.

"I've half a mind to," Tristan admitted sadly. "What does it mean if I do? That I can't trust him? That he's not ready to part his true intentions? I knew that at the start, so does calling an abrupt end to this reflect badly on my judgement and suggest I'm prone to panic, or is it just that much more real now that we're here? I don't know the answer to that yet..."

"You saw him as well as I did, Lord. He couldn't even help himself at the end there! He as good as admitted an interest in your knowledge, not just money. It could be a feint. He may try to trick you into telling him something else entirely."

"Noted, Marcus. I was prepared for that too, fairness be, so..."

Tristan stopped. Something terrible had happened very fast and he was still catching up. There was a whizzing sound and a thud, and though there was a flash of self-preservation telling him to check his own body, it was to his right that he pivoted, to where Marcus stumbled forward drunkenly, quarrel in neck. Tristan dashed to catch him, his own look of shock trifle compared to that of Marcus, whose eyes were wide and red on pale flesh. His blood was flushed away to run circles round his bane, splintered, marked with death.

Armoured hands clamped Tristan's arms and he found Wylam pulling him free. When Tristan released Marcus, he was overwhelmed with horror, as if he'd caused this. His friend staggered again, unsupported, and collapsed to where stone could yell its dull cry in place of he, and sand be drowned in a crimson river. Beyond him, as Tristan turned to sprint as far away as he could, he saw Jacopo's small company mobilising as one.

His feet took him down the road, he did not command them. They whirred, it seemed to him, though never fast enough, the pounding of his boots a mantra for his survival, to the archway where, from the refuge of the two walls, his men were pouring like starved wolves freed from a cage, and there in the open, they glowed the sky above them alight with pollaxes and spears lowered, and there was the sound of steel that chilled through blood and bone. Sword and spear both were ready for their duties, and shields kept close for theirs.

"Back!" Sir Darith shouted at them. He donned his helm as he ran and retrieved his sword thereafter. "Back, get back behind the walls!"

They were only charging because of loyalty for their lord paramount, Tristan knew, and so with logic permitted, they retreated fast. Tristan was there now, near colliding with the right side wall as he made to take its cover as quickly as humanly possible. His men made a gap for him at its very centre, and there he slammed hard against the brick, back first, and resisted the urge to slump and rest his head upon his knees. Sir Darith and Wylam came in swiftly either side of him, less exhausted than him but equally outraged, as it was so painted on them. Their gazes were drawn to the four rowing boats, as were those of a great many others whose thoughts raced like the wind to hide from death's shadow.

"We can't use the boats," Wylam said. "If we try, we drown, if we're lucky."

"I wasn't born yesterday," Sir Darith growled. His eyes flicked all about, gathering information for the solution. He grimaced, baring his teeth like a cornered lion. "We can't stay here either. You need to be taken to safety, my Lord."

"You can't break your numbers for my sake!" Lord Almaric cried, finding himself laughing at the absurdity of it, if it could be labelled that when bereft of all joy. "One thing at a time."

"Oh, we'll put them to the sword," Sir Darith assured him with fervour that was frightening to behold, and here he raised his voice. "The whole fucking lot of those treasonous dogs will be food for the gulls."

He froze, they all froze, perking up as the thunder approached along the causeway: the unmistakable shaking of armour. How it shook, as they ran, and Darith and Wylam in unison were ready to make their orders as it grew louder, then it broke down to an abrupt halt and they frowned. Instead of men charging at them, an attack more subtle crept on them, first heard humming some way off, then streaking overhead in a high arc, sacks spinning against counterweights on rope lines, followed by torches that burst them of their powder and oil. It streaked upon the sand, on the boats, cracking and popping into fervour. Tristan ducked instinctively, though how that would help he didn't think of. A sudden clatter of shields resounded, every man in his company swinging theirs overhead. It was Darith's shield that Tristan was now beneath after the knight had slung it from his back with great speed and near uncontained energy, as by consequence of his speed, he struck the wall hard with it.

Tristan looked out from the shadows, despair heightening as his breathing returned to as close to normal as could be and the cloud parted in his head. Fires extinguished as they buried themselves in the sand all before him, and struggled for breath on the water.

An itch irritated Tristan's skin, salt water on his face: tears were in his eyes that he couldn't bring himself to wipe away. *Marcus*, he screamed at himself as his sanity returned. He was alive last they saw. He shouldn't suffer like that, out there alone. Tristan prayed for his friend's death to come swiftly and silently if it hadn't already: prayer muttered aloud, he slowly realised.

"We must call for help," Wylam said, tapping the wall with his fist at every annunciation. "Assume no one on the ship can see us, for one reason or other, and assume there are more ships waiting to run aground carrying more foes. I will swim, to the ship or shore if needs be."

"I need you here," Darith bit back.

"Who here can swim better than I?" Wylam challenged. "I need such a man now."

Whatever the truth, no offer was spoken to be considered. Already Wylam's shield was abandoned and his sword point jammed beneath the joints in his armour at the shoulder, cutting the straps without a care for his own safety while he fiddled them with his free hand best he could, seemingly crushing his own fingers in the tiny gap, though again he cared not. Sir Darith bit his lip, eyes full of anger. He sighed and ignored Wylam.

"You, Havdan," he shouted hurriedly, pointing to the man on the other side of the wall. By expert planning or intuition, Tristan couldn't tell. "Those men, that half with you, they're yours. That side, it's yours, do you hear me well?"

"I understand," was the staunch reply, scars stretching as his lips crawled up his face in grimace.

"We form a block of shields in the clearing at my signal, we don't even let an ant through our defences, do you understand me? You're Aurailian elites, not green boys: you fight, you fucking win. Bowmen, you follow behind, you hide your bows as you run, you cover us when the phalanx breaks."

"They'll not break us," Havdan said with a grimace, "no matter their numbers. Good places to wedge ourselves in. Bad for them. Didn't think that one through, did they?"

Darith slapped Tristan on the shoulder and he jumped. He'd been listening, keen as a cat, but he'd been hypnotised by the boats, by the thick black liquid splashing here and there, even in the water where it spread with the malice of a rapacious weed. Sir Darith's face softened just a tad, and, bizarrely, it appeared that his anger had never been entirely an uncontrollable emotion welling from his soul but something he manipulated to his desires.

"Follow last, but close."

"Whatever you say, Sir," Tristan replied weakly.

"With me!" Sir Darith yelled straight from the belly, a guttural battle cry that none were left unshaken by, echoed shriller by Havdan.

Darith charged with his shield held close, and like the swan emblazoned upon it, he seemed to take flight. With his left hand, he struck the sky with his sword as a challenge, and with their spirits lifted, his men followed, roaring. They ran together, quickly moving into formation, and isolation, freezing it was, enwrapping Tristan as the last of them disappeared. He steeled himself and spurred on, tears now becoming one with the sweat that made him cold where it trickled.

"Gods save you, my Lord," Wylam said, retaining all formality.

Already components of his armour were strewn about him, and there was a cut through his leather garments at his shoulder that he deigned to not pay heed. Then he was gone, as madness overtook all, as Tristan ran his fullest with the rest of them, to a dark place he never dreamed to be. Although for the surreal madness of it, he saw none of Jacopo's men jeering at him to make his blood run cold, for all he could see were his own men: they blocked his vision completely, his gigantic shield from the horrors ahead.

"Shield carapace!" the command came from the front rank.

At once, the block of men came to a frighteningly abrupt halt, all skidding to one knee, falling together as one but not clashing, and their shields were brought overhead as a vertical wall, on all sides but the back, where Tristan ducked behind. Two of his crossbowmen grabbed him and dragged him inside the formation, pushed beyond the last row into dimness. His men shifted their tight formation to allow just enough room for him, so there he knelt on one knee, his arms crammed into his sides and his neck craned painfully forward on his knee.

Behind him, a man's bow dug into his back, the smell of sweat grew hot and foul, the air thick and dizzying, and he was cold from the steel pressed on him. The strumming of the enemy's bows was dreaded music dulled by the steel above him, and much the same way, their impacts were without punch, all bar none, rattling upon the metal carapace they were never designed to pierce; they must have been ensuring the company would not move as they closed in. Tristan shut his eyes as tight as he could while he regained concentration.

True enough, the music permeated the air around him; arrows bounced and rolled upon the steel surface and must have been piling up there, for they didn't break beneath. The gaps in the carapace were few and tiny, providing the only source of light in thin strips, and some were further blocked by spears propped up between shields. It all paled in insignificance to the fact that, even if there was a hearth pit burning sombrely for them, it wouldn't have made the damndest bit of difference, because it was the mayhem outside their little box that was the true unknown. In all honesty, the darkness made him feel safer, primal and childlike it may have been, as a child shuts his eyes at night to avoid views of imagined monsters, but he didn't care.

He jolted as now he began to differentiate the hammering on the shield wall at the fore, harder and more brutal: crossbow bolts they must have been, though they caused no more harm. If only the first had missed and hit Darith's shield instead of supple flesh. *It did miss, bloody fool,* he swore at himself. *The bolt was aimed at you.* He breathed heavily as he pushed the image from his head, feeling the heat from it radiating before him. Tristan tensed yet again, stopping his breathing entirely just as quickly. The shooting was less frequent, he wasn't imagining it.

"Break formation!" Sir Darith shouted from the front, vaguely confirming his suspicions.

The formation cracked open at the exact middle, running as two units in separate directions, and terrible sunlight flooded him, just as he was falling in love with blackness. Arrows fell limp by the dozens all around, while a very real threat gathered ahead. He felt a hand on his back, pushing him to the left, and several more did the same until he was free of the back row which strafed at a snail's pace. Crossbow bolts were unleashed, striking no less than two men in the face without so much as scraping their helms, and those two men collapsed accompanied by a single spray of blood.

Tristan watched. He watched as he sprinted for his life to the relative safety of the ruins; he just couldn't help himself. His vision was blurred, but he thought he caught a good enough glimpse of the enemy and saw why Darith had led them away at such a time. The bowmen had moved to the sidelines, to make room for the incoming shield wall, and in their vulnerability, were now being picked off. Aurailian archers strummed their bows at lightning speed, unconcerned with actually hitting targets, or so Tristan saw it. They shot to the edges of the ruins where the enemy shield wall had split in desperation to match, slowing them down by making them cover one another with their shields.

He was in the ruins. The image passed, and he was focused with all his self on the roughly 30 men before him, still running they were, and so was he for he wouldn't feel safe if they couldn't. Sir Darith urged them on with another battle cry, and his sword could be seen by all, held above him to rally them, rouse them. Even Tristan felt spurred on by the knight's bravado, not that it did much to sooth the knot in his stomach. With every aspect of his run, his organs bobbed inside him, vomit was caught in his throat, and he fought his own battle to keep his fear in check. If he'd wanted to relieve himself, the best opportunity had already gone and now he would have to bottle it up. *Just keep running. Don't think.*

Through a low doorway he rushed, leaping a pile of bricks as his company had done, and he ran into what once would have been a much larger building. Not now, now it was derelict, though the white patterns could still be seen in the red like a mosaic artwork. Ahead, Darith was preparing to draw first blood; a startling sight it was, as he charged for the unlucky ones not yet integrated into a shield wall, perhaps thanks to the miracles of the bowmen. He screamed and put all his weight into his shield, barraging into his first opponent before pushing his shield out wide, breaking the man's defence as if it were butter, causing him to spin and stagger, and Darith moved in hard with a slash to the neck. That was where carnage was unleashed, and so it was, spraying blood as he span and fell. Darith's first line was with him, closing in on two more like flies devoured in a web, bashing them back and forth like rag dolls without casualty to the Aurailian sheltron before they cut the two men to ribbons.

"Shield wall!" Sir Darith commanded, and they instantly fell back in line. The knight searched all around frantically, the first he'd been so, from his static place at the fore, quickly coming to a decision. "To the wall, men."

They moved as one into the great wall to their right for cover, though one line was level with a doorway, and the man unlucky enough to be there in the third row turned, stood firm and locked his shield against it. Tristan ran into the back and, as with last time, his loyal men pulled him in to that last row, and he was amidst their ranks as if one of their kind. It felt wrong to be there, and it was about to get worse, but he was locked there and was safe. There was nothing to complain about, yet. The rage would come later, a thought ticked at the back of his brain. For now, he tried to integrate himself into the wall as a layman like him could, mirroring those around him. He put one foot forward and grabbed, to the best of his ability, the armour of the man before him at the neck. The men around him backed their shields into the man in front, but short of that equipment, his way would have to do.

"Spearmen, behind," Sir Darith snapped suddenly, speaking now on audacious whims, Tristan would think if he didn't know better; he had to trust the logic was sound.

The pieces of the shield wall moved like a puzzle, no one ever once stepping from its boundaries for more than a second, and though it was a messy affair in principle, the elites handled it like a ballet, albeit, in this one, every movement was met with a scraping or banging of metal, each of which stabbed Tristan's heart anew, a thing that was already so fragile and begged for peace. Of course, peace was something unlikely to happen until one phalanx had flattened the other. Tristan tried to keep himself occupied, on the lookout for the enemy just as his new comrades were, and again he was reminded by their fearlessness of how distant he was. Through the old doorway of the building Tristan strained to see, for the causeway was where Jacopo's lot had been, even if, most likely, they'd moved into cover by now. As the soldier in the door moved, Tristan caught a glimpse of Marcus upon the ground, lying as peacefully as a sleeping man, but painted in the red river. Sooner or later it would begin to dry, and like weeds strangling the other plants and pulling them down, he would be one with Bryndton, life becoming art along with so many others soon. Aurailian victory was the only just victory. There was no other choice.

Again he was startled by a loud noise and gripped the armour ahead of him, his fingers scrabbling uselessly without proper holds. Armour made music, sand sprang up; a small force marched through the ruins from where they'd retreated. They too had split in half, which only showed Jacopo had the intelligence to make a decision a child could make.

Tristan craned his neck around, feeling suddenly vulnerable of the gap behind him. He longed for the tortoise formation again, much as he gawped in disbelief just to think it. But it was true. To his relief, just then his bowmen came running and, at the very back of the wall, peered round the corner, longbows and crossbows at the ready, searching to no avail as was written plain as day on their faces. The quivers of the archers were half empty. It hadn't been in vain, Tristan told himself. He wasn't a strategist, but staying positive was surely one factor of victory. And now he had a reason to be positive, if he dared call it that, while Marcus's cadaver was still warm. They slung their bows behind them and retrieved their shields, and their swords too; Tristan shuddered as they cut the air, and they formed tightly behind him. Now they were six along by four back, plus four bowmen swapping their faces to men-at-arms to reinforce the sheltron at the rear.

The enemy marched towards them at a steady pace, reluctantly having now to fight on Sir Darith's terms, though whether Jacopo had devised a plan was open to interpretation. Tristan was sure of many things, so sure they burned as fires within him, but this was not one of them. Certainly Jacopo had had the advantage of surprise, and had apparently squandered it... unless they'd been aiming for Darith with that bolt: a blow to shatter the leadership of the group. Something shot down Tristan's spine: less a tingling and more a pin being drawn through his skin.

He shuddered as if to shake off the dark thoughts and focused ahead as stoic as a man like him could be, which was very little, something he never thought to be sad of. The faces of the enemy were becoming clearer now, and that made matters worse, if only for him.

"Second row, third, you will be ready," Sir Darith ordered gruffly. "First row, stay focused and follow my lead."

Darith lifted his right foot and stamped it down defiantly in front of him, whereby he held firm with his shield, proudly toting his Wyman standard for the enemy's viewing terror. He brought his sword up as if ready to stab, and his first rank followed him exactly, only to opposite sides. Though Tristan couldn't rightly see, Darith appeared to raise his back foot up onto his toes and bounce gently, ready to run it looked like, and his first rank did exactly the same. The enemy marched closer, breaking formation only to hop over rubble and skirt around pillars and ancient walls. As Tristan strained his senses like string stretched to tautness, all so adept, he felt capable of differentiating every wave in the sea to his near left; he made out the same happening to the south of the road. A battle was about to begin.

Tension washed over his men like a curse, its influence undeniable. Despite it, they did not falter. And Tristan raised an eyebrow in confusion as a heavy, forced sigh erupted from the knight.

"Oh, come on!" Sir Darith jeered, exasperatedly. His arms sprung limply up, his discipline evaporated. His was the frustration of a man who'd just lost a bet on a tourney joust. "My men were ready minutes ago; they're prepared to kill. This is going to be a battle, not a stroll round the barracks; start treating it with respect. Or did you think assassinating my Lord would make you warriors?! You curs started this, now you don't even have the fucking guts to finish it! Let the sea take you if you don't; it'll be less painful."

They were only a few paces from the shield wall as he said this, or rather yelled it, laughing in disbelief as he sized up their ranks. They were afraid, some more than others true enough, though for whatever reason, none responded to his challenge. They stopped just shy of attacking range, and there was the plunge, the breath sucked from the 50 men or so, as if their small battlefield was submerged under water.

"Your commander's nowhere to be seen, I notice," Darith pointed out. And so he wasn't. Such wonder that Tristan hadn't noticed before. His nerves were doing him no kindness, then. He had to focus.

Darith resumed his posture, tapping his sword lightly on his shield's side: a tinny drumbeat, a taunt the enemy did not yet take up. As Darith's rank eyed their leader for a signal, the opposite rank teetered back and forth as if considering whether to take the knight's offer to flee, or to charge in a blaze of stupidity or glory, whichever that would be. Their second rank dug their shields into their backs hard, into a first rank oddly consisting not of the soldiers in eagle motif armour as one would think. They lunged as one and their backup moved with them.

"Drop!" Darith commanded.

His front foot slid back and he very much looked to slip, but he came down hard on one knee without faltering and his shield was pointed up. His rank followed suit and all but disappeared from view. What Tristan did see was an opposing force, pushed just far enough by momentum of their own making, lowering their shields, and with that there was a crashing sound resounding from out of sight. Spear tips eagerly warped into Tristan's focus, clamped beneath the shoulders of the second rank, and at once they sprang forward. The gleam of spear tips vanished instantly beyond the dark recess of flesh and bone, whence blood splashed and trickled upon their armour. Four of the six men were struck in the face in tandem; four shrieks of lightning fast metal piled four times loud, four faces caved of bone and shattered when steel twisted and withdrew, with each a sickening crunch to call their own, and bright and red as evening sun they were, if the sun were so volatile as to spit its contents across the sky.

The Voice of Kings

Tristan caught something vile worming up his throat before it could work its deed, and swallowed it as he grimaced. It burned his insides, but his lips were sealed and they wouldn't open for that. They wouldn't. He stared shakily ahead, against the inner temptation to shut his eyes too, and saw that the two spears that had failed to meet their targets were now jammed between two shields before the crescent moon blades, and with at least one sword were held there; to grab the shaft would be risky indeed given how sharp those blades looked. The spearmen of the second rank twisted their poles to break them free, and regardless of whether it would have worked, they stumbled and cried out from attacks unseen.

Darith pounced from his crouching position, ramming his direct opponents aside as he breathed a mighty grunt, met his enemy's sword and scraped his own down to its hilt, around the cruciform guard and sliced the man's fingers off. The pain of the screeching steel was suffering enough to the ears, but this man screeched harder as his fingers were lopped off and, like a spinning hammer, Darith's sword came down onto his shoulder; his armour looked good enough to Tristan's eyes, yet the gaps between the joints were half an inch thick, that being half an inch too much when faced with this knight's precision, and thus it sliced through gambeson and skin alike.

Darith's shield went in again, hitting the man hard in the chest to get him out of the way and hasten his descent. Still Darith wouldn't settle for that; he stepped out of line and, with the aid of two spears, brought down the shield of the last man in the original vanguard before he slashed at his throat. A new vanguard of fresh faces was already in place for the most part but for where Darith stood. No less than two men with eagles emblazoned on their cuirasses set on his shield with their hammers, seemingly uncaring as to how much it would damage them so long as the barrage was enough to drive him back, and so it did. He slotted himself back into the line before anyone could forge a path from his absence. The enemy shield wall had had its morale taken down a notch, yet that served only to make them more cautious. Every shield at the vanguard smashed together and thunder echoed upwards, high into the sky. Little wonder how some soldiers complained of their hearing after a battle, a true battle scarcely imaginable where the vanguard stretched four hundred feet across. Yet this company had helms to protect them, and Tristan had nothing but strands of hair to blow over his ears. He braced himself for the next impact, another shudder to reverberate through the sheltron, but it never came.

He tilted his head to one side to get a better view and it was as he'd thought: the fighting was at a standstill, the shields grinded on each other as their wielders waited for one good opportunity to strike, or parry a hurried attack. The world was eerily calm in that moment: a false peace in which one could hear the sea lapping at the beach and the wind whirling cerebral around them.

A Kiss in Summer

"Push, my Lord," the man to his right said through gritted teeth. "You've done this before, right? Let's split open that wall of theirs."

Tristan put his weight into the man before him, readjusting his grip yet again, and this time his fingers slid uselessly. They ached. To get a good hold on anything would be painful at this stage. It wasn't going to work, he despaired. He formed fists with both hands and the fingers creaked at every joint, so instead he put one arm round the man's waist and pushed on his back with his right forearm. As he inched forward, a shield dug into his back. Comfort was not an option, he knew that, he just... needed more time to adjust to pain. But here he was, not affordable of that either, so he breathed deeply, slaving on to an end, whatever that was.

The peace ended. It was sudden and took Tristan by surprise, his mental preparation counting for nothing. The shield to Darith's left was circumvented and, in a flash, the same was attempted upon Darith himself. The entire enemy shield wall was focused in on that gap between the two men, taking the assumption that the knight's left-handedness could be a weakness, but it was his since birth, and now their bane. As if to refute that claim in the most insulting way possible, Sir Darith roared and pushed his opponent's shield aside, spat in his eyes, and hacked diagonally across that man's face. The helm laughed off the blow, but it didn't stop the sword. Concussion reeled him, allowing Darith to flip the lock on his visor and cut deep through the nose. It sucked the blood from him, that he must have been white beneath the scarlet.

More blood sprayed, closer to Tristan this time, so close some splashed on his fine cloak, and before he knew what he was doing, he was shielding his face. The man in the doorway had been killed somehow, and a Mürathneèan soldier dashed into the gap, backed by at least one more; more than that he couldn't hope to see. A shortsword was shoved in his direction from his left now, then waved frantically as if he wouldn't have noticed it. Gingerly it was traded from the hand of its original owner to Tristan, who crushed the leather-covered hilt till his knuckles turned white. It was soft, comfortable even, at a time when he presumed was not possible. In the near flawless steel, his pale reflection glowered, fearing for what he would do with it. He'd held a sword so many times when he was younger and always made sure to be terrified of that warped face looking back.

Another man dropped to his right, to his knees alone but incapacitated nonetheless, and a second's victory could toll victory for longer still. The Mürathneèan soldier fending his corner like a demon in the doorway had eyes of fire. Yes, it struck Tristan just then, he could see the eyes, and that was just another burden of a man-at-arms, to look into the fire before extinguishing it. Another man fell by his sword and now he was dangerously close, and his friend had forced his way into the sheltron to make matters that much more dire. *Do it*, he told himself. *Do it and live with it.*

The Voice of Kings

Tristan lunged over the shoulder of a man in a pure defensive stance, nearly toppling through him. The shortsword hit the man's helm and Lord Tristan felt the force behind it as he felt it bite his heart. The soldier's expression was one of utter shock. Tristan jabbed again, finding his blade drawn from serious harm. He stared at his blade, seeing his frown in its clean surface.

Somehow, it was distraction enough; the soldier's concentration wavered for just one second and three pollaxes hammered him. A bloodcurdling scream was heard, two in fact, the second as heavy as lead.

"Jacopo!" Sir Darith yelled at the top of his lungs, snapping Tristan out of his current predicament in the highest alarm. It was with Darith shoving another man back that he shouted this, though the remnants of the opposing wall were avoiding him now. And there beyond the cluster of soldiers and strewn ruins was the gaudy gold and silver armour glowing some way off; bright it was as to reflect the personality of its wearer who slowed down from his sprint. He stopped entirely. He glared at Darith. "That's it, Jacopo, run! Honour to the craven who leaves his men to die! Go cower over there and restore the glory of your House!"

The craven did not flee, nor did he attack. His hand slithered to the hilt of his sword, and though it was impossible to make out anything in particular, Tristan imagined his finger bones crushed close to breaking point in rage, for he doubled back a few paces and glared, it must have been a glare, from black pits, regardless of whatever danger he'd perceived himself to be in. He would have stared a hole right through Darith but for the knight's loss of motivation to continue such a charade, reverting to what he was best at. And still Jacopo watched his men being cut down in a battle they would surely run from, given a second's chance. Calm or vengeful, it didn't matter, he did not move either way. If his House was disgraced by his own doing, then he'd do well not to be insulted when he never restored it, as he never could. In the end, it was Cristico Valen who tried to lead him away, to which action Jacopo waved away agitatedly, then proceeded to follow him soon after.

Valen, Tristan despaired even as he held firm the line, joints aching from metal digging into his ribs and back, and his arms burning like fire from the rattling they took at every shudder of the shield wall. His shortsword was pointed to the sky, supporting a comrade's back, as it dawned on him truly now, the blood of his once solemn enemy dripping down the hilt and already smothering his hand. Hypocrisy to feel guilt from its cold tingle perhaps, when a hundred times its quantity ran at his feet, but it was Valen's visage in his mind that disturbed him so at that time.

The sheltron shook, and he most of all: a last defiance from a foe about to be crushed, so in a position where running would be suicide, they took their chances here, and took them hard, roaring as they pushed through the doorway and against the vanguard.

A Kiss in Summer

"We don't need a shield wall for a few green boys, no matter the creatures on their armour," Sir Darith shouted triumphantly.

At that instant, the sheltron was smashed at the doorway again, and three Mürathneèan men, once inside, formed a half ring against it so they could back out if they needed to, only to be trapped by the bowmen turned men-at-arms rushing them from behind. And so a ring was formed around them, at the back of which Tristan was caught, and though he was likely safe, he felt their dread well up inside him as he joined the death march inwards, shortsword held aloft above the shoulders of two men before him. Around him, the sheltron had disbanded and charged the remnants of Jacopo's men, surrounding them and beating them about with their shields. They all resisted, though whether bravery was a factor was difficult to tell for many without much courage would do anything to survive with their minds in such a scrambled mess, their essence about to be plucked right from them. Some men called the almighty hacking and slashing of flesh and bone so freely 'sweet music for the soul'. It was nothing short of haunting. All the while, the ring advanced on the three men, and Tristan could almost smell their fear.

"We will take them as prisoners," Lord Almaric said authoritatively.

"We can't," Sir Darith replied despite his seeming lack of involvement. "We can't afford to hold hostages if we have to fight again."

The three men took their sentences as well as could be expected. They lunged as one small wall and the ring tightened like a fist. Their shields were knocked and twisted like string, and as their fingers must have broken in the holds, the pain began. A man was beaten down, armour was hacked, and though it was to little avail by vision alone, the remainders were winded deeply by the bombardment. A face was robbed of individuality, breath stolen by constant bombardment.

Those last two bodies dropped with a thud incomparable with any others, and for a time, Tristan only gawped. All three were alive, surprisingly, and though the Aurailians noticed, they merely watched them wearily. The pain had stopped, but for Tristan it was not over. He staggered back, bleary at the eyes, attempting to bring order to his impenetrable thoughts. There was a clang upon the sand-covered stone that resulted from the shortsword slipping from his hand; fingers that, in his daze, didn't care for such things.

Everywhere he looked, he saw the dead, and horrific as it was, he was wont to pay his respects, for when he looked up at the bright blue sky, it provided no comfort, only a message to give his attention to the fallen again.

"Advance!" Sir Darith's loud order made him jolt, then as the company noisily assembled, he put a finger to his mouth to hush them and showed them his palm to halt them. "My Lord, with me if you please."

Tristan pulled himself together and gingerly made his way through the field of dead men, choosing his path carefully, even when it dawned on him that avoiding the red river wasn't

The Voice of Kings

possible. To be reverent in not wishing to step in it made him feel marginally better. He counted the dead to quell his screaming conscience: five Aurailian men by his counting, and judging from the repressed grunts, more were injured who weren't going to complain about it. There were more than half Jacopo's men at peace here though, weren't there? He'd given them his greatest yield. Tristan stopped beside Darith, then he winced at a strange whiff, and almost as if washed in by the sea breeze, a ghastly stench made itself known to him, bitter and hateful, utterly overpowering that it seemed a miracle he hadn't picked up on it before.

"That smell never gets any nicer," Darith said.

For all his glorious passion of battle, he gave Tristan no reason to disbelieve him. In fact, as he stood close to the knight now, something very different emerged. His facial features were strained as if in great pain, and his teeth were gritted. His joy crumbled as his battle shell did, and he gazed mournfully on the dead, a potent mix of anger and sorrow held just at bay; mostly anger. He transformed and his posture became tall and regal. If he'd put on an act before, it was a highly convincing one.

"My Lord," he went on, huffing slowly, his tongue searching for moisture in his mouth. "Did you see Jacopo? Did you see what he was doing?"

"I saw you taunt him and then he just... watched you for a while."

"That's what I feared. I saw the same but wasn't sure. That man doesn't strike me as a leader, but that wasn't cowardice, his running away, not entirely. I think he's not done yet, if you want my opinion."

"Your opinion's worth more than mine, Sir. Lords don't inherit knowledge or wisdom with their privileges, as you well know." Tristan hesitated, licking his lips. It was for naught, as his tongue was as dry as a bone just the same. "I must question the logic anyway. Why wouldn't Jacopo have his reserve attack with the rest? One army is stronger than two separated."

"Now that, my Lord, is a very good question." Darith sighed and rubbed his forehead. "No one can be that idiotic. I won't give him the benefit of the doubt though. We've got one way to find out, and we're going to whether we like it or not. I haven't heard battle from the south of the island for a while, so for our safety, we'll assume they're dead and meet up down the line if they're not."

Before Tristan could answer, a boom rippled through the air from the water and instinctively everyone dropped to the ground. Tristan, for his lack of protection, took it harder than anyone else. Already pain itself was becoming numbness, and to that he had nothing to say other than presumptions of his mental state. More pressingly, the implacable pain of being thrown so far from his comfort zone did not cease to take its due tolls. The boom was a punch in the gut to him.

"Cannon fire?" Sir Darith spat, uncertain.

A Kiss in Summer

He hauled his heavy frame from the ground with ease and ran to the shore. Tristan haphazardly did the same. He would have spat the sand from his mouth if he had saliva left in him to carry it, so the best he could do was brush his tongue and face with his hand. At the shore's edge, where the oblivious blue ocean lapped at his stained boots and the wind stroked his cloak, he followed Darith's westerly gaze, and there, crawling from behind the craggy island they'd thought not to investigate, was another ship. A flash of gunpowder erupted, barely visible from its deck, and the whole ship rocked violently in its wake. And no wonder...

"Is that a converted merchant vessel?" Tristan ventured.

"Looks to be. It wouldn't stand a bloody chance against the Sorenys on paper. If it's already hit her, that's damnable. If it's armoured out of sight, that's another matter entirely. Come, we've no more time to waste," he said scornfully, as if implying they could have finished the battle sooner.

At the sorrowful scene of the battle's aftermath, Darith stabbed his sword into the ground and scooped up a shield, and although it was a decision made in haste, there was surely a stroke of uncertainty as his eyes probed the mess of ruined humans for something appropriate. A wan smile flickered across his face as he found his target: an Aurailian shield bearing the three towers clear as day, spattered with blood, but along with its deep white scratches, was more a wound to be shaken proudly off, and proud it was to Darith so long as the standard could be seen, and by way of being seen, feared. Even the sword he kicked up into the same hand was an Aurailian sword, need be damned. He stuck them out for Tristan to take while his men watched, like some kind of initiation ceremony. Tristan grabbed them both, and then he paused as he saw into the knight's soul. His fervour and, really, everything about him, were the only anchors to the world away from the Eye of Sand, to a woman he barely knew and would be frightened of, were she an enemy. Indeed, he was Bethen's son through and through. If she had the physicality to be a soldier, she probably would be. She even had something of a masculine face.

That would have to do until he could recover the likeness of Evylyn and Malcus to the fore of his scrambled mind. He flinched as an Aurailian helm was flung his way against his expectations, trailing blood in its wake, and Tristan just caught it in his shield hand, hugging it to his chest to stop it falling.

"Lord Tristan," Sir Darith snapped. "Concentrate. And worry not. You're my liege regent in all but name. I'm your second sword, and second shield, and a suit of armour in the stead of your attire." He poked Tristan's shield with his stunning blade, every silver twirl on his armour shimmering as he twisted. He was stern now, and deep of voice. "Three towers will never fall."

"Three towers will never fall," Tristan repeated, wringing all the enthusiasm he could into those words.

The Voice of Kings

"And today, a black swan circles them," Darith added with a sickly smile.

A few of the men chuckled at that. The more solace the better, no matter how small. Then the talk was over. Sir Darith pointed his sword and began to jog east, and Tristan followed with the rest, donning a dead man's helm as he did so. He kept all his senses in check and, for his own sanity, had to turn his attention right for a glimpse of the other half of the company. There was no trace of them, not that he would have spotted any if there was. With the exception of the gap where the road carved its mark, the ruins were thick like a forest. Better to not think of it, Tristan decided. He nearly tripped while his attention was drawn from the path, so now he looked there once again. The ruins were becoming more varied now in their design and shape. This is where the sandstone buildings were, he remembered, intermingled with red and white still.

Beyond, out of sight, there was a sound like thunder, only instead of fading, it grew louder, and shortly afterwards more soldiers could be seen, again some in Harthen armour while most were a mismatched bunch of mercenaries most likely, and this time there was a great mass of them, pelting onwards, screaming. Tristan's blood turned cold and he nearly froze there and then but for what he knew would happen if he did. Darith's furious energy drove him on with yet more determination, despite the knight's all too apparent shock.

"Faster!" Sir Darith shouted. "Under the bridge!"

The bridge he spoke of was some 20 or 30 feet ahead. Beyond it was a clearing, though that was surely not what Darith had in mind. The breadth of the bridge was such that perhaps the entire small company could wedge itself underneath and withstand a monstrous attack from a force that outnumbered them. They rearranged themselves so that the freshest were at the fore.

"Bowmen, with me!"

As the four bowmen caught up, still playing men-at-arms, Darith pulled Tristan by the scruff of his cloak and he was forced to run faster lest he fall. The bridge was ahead, then it loomed over him, then just like that, its shadow had passed and, in the sunlight, the opposing force charged him. He skidded to a halt at Darith's behest, as did the bowmen to his left, and there he cowered behind his shield, every muscle in him tensed. The enemy wall collided with his. Pain rattled up his arm, a sensation like all his bones being compressed and shattered. He staggered back, was caught by a soldier of Castle Aurail, and pushed forward again. Already the sheltron was formed and back in action. Responsibility fell on him to keep it that way. He took a strike on his shield and wildly returned the favour, meeting his opponent's war hammer mid-swing. That man, whoever he was, brown bearded and thin of nose, was far stronger than him, so Tristan's arm slowly retracted under the weight. The man behind Tristan tugged him back and the bearded man stumbled, courtesy of his own strength. Tristan slashed at a gap in the armour at the elbow. Blade clanged against armour, then slid between the gap and cut right through the joint, and he spiralled back. Darith, almost as if it was no bother to him, eviscerated the man's neck and carried on fighting.

"We need to move!" the knight shouted in his ear when he was back in line.

They sidled to the right, playing defensive, and the bowmen followed suit. Perhaps realising what was going on, to Tristan's mournful ignorance, the enemy pushed harder, and Tristan was crushed against the wall of the bridge. With all his might, he rammed forward, then again, and again, using his strength to beat at the shield pinning him down for all its worth, but he did it, and now he let out a scream like the rest. Darith was at a dead end, it seemed. The knight of Ylden Parragor had other ideas. He hopped the half-crumbled banister of the stairs and jabbed at a man who dared to come for him, striking him in the eye, then held his arms out for Tristan's. It was pure madness, but he did it anyway. The knight knew what he was doing.

Short of being able to hold Tristan with more than two fingers, he instead interlinked their arms and hauled him up. The man's strength surprised him again, and like that, he was on the bridge stairs, blocking the way up at Sir Darith's left. The bowmen followed soon after and formed a line four men across with two behind.

"Go," Sir Darith said fiercely, shaking his head back. "You're needed up there."

So they did, and so there were two left, Tristan guarding the way with one of the renowned warriors of Burtal as if he, himself, actually had combat prowess. Maybe it *would* give him what he needed. He just needed to use what he had first.

He leaned back as a sword was swung at him, and swatted it away, hurt him as it still did in its shock. Darith chopped down on the man's shield to help him, and with that blow he almost fell to his knees. Tristan jabbed. Against his will, it became a slash, cutting deep at the face, so deep he could feel it dislodging teeth. Tristan's shield connected with his opponent's face and he tumbled back, knocking down the man behind him.

"Sir! My Lord!" came the cry from above.

Both of them ran a few steps back and risked a glance round. The four bowmen had thrown down their shields and swords and were crouching at the top of the stairs. There, between them, was a lump of stone, near enough round to roll with enough force, and by the gods they did give it that. Tristan and Darith used the banisters to support them and jumped it, while below, the men seeing it for the first time were too late. It barrelled through one soldier's legs, tripping him clean from his feet onto his face and so smashing the formation in an instant. Sir Darith charged back down to slay the man next to him, Tristan at his side as a defensive aide, then the knight kicked off the helm of the man who was rising, and like a mighty hammer, drew his gleaming sword down upon scalp, rending bone. When he wrenched it free, they retreated higher once more. The sight from on high was not comforting.

The Voice of Kings

The enemy must have numbered 50 again, even after how many had died already: a wall six men deep. Most probably, if the other company existed yet in this world, they would have an easier ride, for a Wyman and lord paramount together would be top priority. *Yes*, a voice called within him. Every now and then, in the quieter moments of the battle, the wind carried new music of steel from the south, like ethereal music of the dead.

Presently he was overwhelmed, but it wasn't impossible, not while these men fought to the last breath, which he prayed wouldn't be necessary. Below the bridge, all he could see was ranseur spears poking out, jabbing manically, their crescent moon guards being obliterated even as he watched. At the front, pollaxes flashed up and bore down, over and over. Upon the bridge, behind him to his left, the four bowmen, two archers and two arbalists, knelt behind a barrier and chose their shots wisely with dwindling ammunition. The enemy was wise to them. Those not at the vanguard bowed their heads to let their helms take the brunt, though still reeled or worse, but here and there they could not hide, and the bowmen would lease only when fortune was skill's guide. At every strum of the bow, arrows would strike deep at the neck, and bolts deeper. The Mürathneèan archers who'd put away their bows took them up again and moved to the back. And in retaliation to this, Tristan's four men propped up their shields against the low barrier of the bridge.

That was where hope lay, and from the back of the enemy shield wall, it was cut down again, for Tristan at least. To the rest, he was just another mercenary, but Tristan strained to recognise him, and a moment later he did. The man, tall, brown of hair, and scarred across the cheek from a sword hilt's blow, saw Tristan and recognised him. Hencewith, his blood turned cold again. *Why was he released?* The mercenary looked all about, as if checking for someone who would stop him. He should have been arrested at the manor. Why wasn't he arrested at the manor...?

"I promised to take you back to Beriddian," the man yelled. "And I'll take the head of your friend in the fancy armour, thank you."

Tristan's eyes flicked to Darith instinctively, yet his unique armour, cloaked in blood but still recognisable for its scorched grey texture and intricate silver patterns, meant nothing to him, for he stood on his toes and searched the ranks of the Aurailian company. Truth dawned on Tristan and he was surprised. Sir Yanick could rip him to shreds were he here and he should have known it, were that knight to shed vanity.

"You are very welcome to try!" Sir Darith challenged in misunderstanding as he killed the next man to run up the stairs, shoving him back into his comrades.

All about, Tristan glanced for options. He saw that the bridge once stood longer the other side of the stairs, where it was crumbled, and the area where the bowmen loosed their arrows may, in fact, have been a platform for very different announcements to people below. There was nothing of help to him, ever and anon nothing.

A Kiss in Summer

The mercenary leader, if that's what he was, predictably took Darith's words to challenge as only someone who devoted his life as such would do. It was a grimace and a smile combined that he returned to Darith, bearing all the courage of himself and Jacopo, for he was still nowhere to be seen. Tristan ignored him for now, holding strong at the peak of the stairs with Sir Darith, seeking only to defend, bashing his shield at any blow that came at him, jabbing speedily to make the enemy stand their ground, jumping back as he liked to think only he could do without armour, for he needed some personal strength to take hope in.

He caught only glimpses of the battle proper every now and then as his attention wavered for a fraction of a second, and he saw Aurailian spears being rended from their wielders hands and stabbed back at the butt before clanging off armour to the ground. He saw bowmen down to their last two arrows and bolts, and Aurailian soldiers about to be pinned from escape as Mürathneèans, a larger group this time, made their way to the rear.

He took all the brunt of another strike on his shield for want of something better to do, and desperately trawling through memories of old training sessions, came to the conclusion that he should let it pass him, like one of his soldiers had done for him in the shield wall. He took a step back to try, but the sword of the man, who was weathered and middle-aged, stuck with his shield like glue. Frustrated, Tristan used brute force, chopping the enemy sword down with his own and catching the man on the gorget with his shield. Panic drove him; he knew it well enough and went through with it anyway. He wanted to be alone in his own space within his helm which cut out distractions of both sound and sight of the rest of the battle, but he couldn't help checking on it now and again.

"Bowmen, finish up if it please," Sir Darith shouted. "You're needed down below. We need to cut off their flanking manoeuvre immediately."

Two longbows were dropped at their owners' feet, and two crossbows were flung into the mob as they knew they wouldn't need them again, and all four together recovered their weapons and shields and charged with all haste to the stairs. Tristan was pushed behind again but he felt very much a part of that living wall yet, keeping balance to the men in front as they shoved and hacked their way down the stairs at an alarming rate. Through two men's shoulders, he saw the calamity that was being inflicted, how the enemy was tumbling and crashing into one another, how they slipped on blood and entrails which painted the whole stairway, as Tristan constantly worked to refrain from doing, stamping his boots down, not sidling forwards as cautious instinct would have him do. Very soon he was given no chance but to tread on the bodies for there was no room between them, and through his disgust, hope shined, if only until he glimpsed the Aurailian shield wall. Whatever its number now, which he couldn't make out, Mürathneèans had pushed through and were beneath the bridge as well.

The Voice of Kings

The flanking force stopped in its tracks to take down Tristan and his five companions before they tore Jacopo's company apart from the inside out. They came with malice. Great wonder Tristan could still hold a shield when the wall was barraged again at the foot of the stairs. No doubt he would feel that agony later, and the guilty pain of inflicting it on others now.

Would that he could forfeit that. Before him, one of the archers was batted away. Tristan made to fill the gap but the enemy was blocking his path with swords, prodding again and again. Sir Darith roared and pushed hard, as if exhibiting such raw emotions actually restored strength to him. Tristan ran in behind him, and swiftly the other three followed. The knight of Ylden Parragor hacked a path furiously, not aiming to kill this time but to drive for freedom, as even he was too swamped to risk any killing blows. And so it was that the five of them pushed through, shoving with shield and sword either side of them for mere survival, if indeed that could be mere in place of ending human life.

Darith broke through, and Tristan dashed after him while there was still time. It wasn't over, he reminded himself, to his own heavy exhaustion. They had to check if any flankers had made it round, and merge with the sheltron either way. The three former bowmen burst through after them now, pivoting on the spot and backing away until they lodged themselves between two pillars. The opposing force may have been dwindling once more, but to underestimate would be to submit, so they made no effort to attack.

Then it grew worse. The survivor of the Manor of Blessed Voices charged by himself, as he was used to, longsword in hand. If he couldn't kill Sir Yanick, he wasn't going to take down Sir Darith. Then again, maybe. Darith was tired from battle; the mercenary hadn't killed a single man so far as could be told.

Sir Darith took the challenge gladly, leaving the three others to fend off the encroaching foes as best they could. He started off in defence, taking the first blow on the edge of his weathered sword, then shifting his position sideways and directing the man away. Despite his bulk, he quickly recovered, spinning around and running in, only this time Darith was on the offensive also, setting about parrying one heavy blow after another, jabbing between them, not to kill but to make him dodge, to wear him down. The mercenary, tired of this, in his own way and in a rage, ducked one blow, parrying it on the forte, and quick as a snake, swung his sword overhead. Metal rang all around; it seemed like it had done for an eternity, yet that blow rang like a bell ushering in a silent dawn and tore Tristan's eyes open. It was well placed, not sliding off the smooth, curved surface of Darith's helm, but rather denting it.

The bold knight staggered, almost dropping his weapon, face a blur of muddled thoughts as the concussion rippled through his head. The mercenary moved in for the kill, and at that moment, Tristan felt he'd been here before. He moved in fast to distract from the killing strike, jumping back when he was swung at, an attack which chipped his shield: another white notch in the three red towers. Darith swung himself bolt upright. His eyes were burning with rage. Looking over his shoulder, he saw the losing battle his men were fighting but showed no despair. If it welled inside him, he was even stronger than he looked for holding it at bay.

"Run," Sir Darith ordered bluntly. Hesitantly Tristan made to be off, slowly now, and for that, the knight scolded him. "East, my Lord, or south, not back to the shield wall. Don't die here with me." A poignant pause. "My mother told me it would be you," he laughed.

Loyalty. For one reason or another he was talking about loyalty. House Wyman was founded on it.

Darith shook his head as if to get comfortable, and when there was no avail, he ran two fingers up into his helm and, with them, tossed it aside, scowling while his eyes stared unblinking. Tristan ran. It wounded him, but he ran, eastwards so if nothing else he might catch up with Jacopo, and if he could best him, hold him hostage. Tristan slowed to a jog and turned, hiding behind a piece of broken wall. Sir Darith, sweat-laden and hair sagging free, attacked the mercenary again, tougher than he'd ever been by Tristan's eye, parrying a sword blow, and his black swan ducked behind the mercenary's shield, hammering his hand. Then again, on his foot, and up he brought it, the top rim colliding with jawbone. From the mercenary's mouth, blood spewed, and teeth with it probably. From the rear, three Mürathneèan soldiers ran at him, and clumsily he pivoted to them, blocking one attack and taking more on his armour before being rammed with a shield. He span like a rag doll, as he'd done to others that same day. There the mercenary rose up like some beast, clean sword shining, driving it clean into the knight's mouth. His blood glinted brightly in the late afternoon sun on the other side. Tristan shut his eyes and shook his head.

"Don't cry here," he whispered aloud, though he had a feeling he already was.

Tristan ran again, and in proportion to his leaving the field of battle, its music died, not just to his ears he was sure, but to the world, to time. The key to Aurailian bias and to the truth rested within only him now it seemed, and what a lonely thought that was.

The remains of the yellow sandstone temple flashed before his eyes between broken walls, where Jacopo surely was. Before he reached it, he threw himself against a wall, hoping to pounce on anyone out there in the open, yet that was impossible. He was a haggard creature now, breathing like a wounded ox; to these cruel people, he was lord paramount only by the vague refineries of his regal attire and expensive green cloak, none of which the colour they once were. It sagged, the burden of death made material, and he would carry it for as long he wore it, as if being punished. *No.* Tristan shook his head and slipped around the corner, sword held high.

Gold and silver obstructed him. His sword arm took a punch to the elbow from a gauntlet, from which his arm could take no more, and at that, the sword flew from him and covered itself in sand. Jacopo emerged in full, punching him again, at the shoulder now.

The Voice of Kings

Tristan was helpless to resist. He felt himself swung round, his arm locked up behind his back, and his helm joined his sword too after a hand wrenched it from him. Next it was his shield, and Jacopo showed no courtesy in alleviating the pain from rending it free. Tristan gritted his teeth, for he knew the pain would come out like a flood if he let it. Then the commander, the lord as he dreamed himself to be, dragged Tristan to the foot of the great steps leading to the temple, where Cristico Valen solemnly stared at the ground and two bodyguards were statues waiting for whatever heinous order to bring them to life. Tristan heard something very different again, of metal being drawn, but not a sword; it was cold against his head, the bronze barrel of a flintlock pistol. The flint was clicked into place.

The remnants of Jacopo's men returned, that mercenary among them, throwing prisoners down. Whether to be glad there were so few enemies, at least, he didn't know. He was a mess all over; he couldn't quite think.

"Hold!" Jacopo shouted to his men. His breath on the back of Tristan's neck was like a venomous spider, though oddly it didn't stink as he expected it to. "We're not done yet. There." He pointed to a wall to the left, where, for a moment, a figure was seen poking out before ducking behind it. Tristan's heart skipped a beat. "Come out! We have your lord at gunpoint."

"Don't," Lord Almaric ordered. "Not until I've negotiated your safety."

"Sorry?" Jacopo snapped, genuinely surprised. "What makes you think you have the power to do that? I'm holding the power right this second. It doesn't need your permission to kill you."

"Jacopo Beriddian," Lord Almaric panted. *Focus.* He had to ignore that he wasn't even sweating anymore and focus on surviving the next minute. "If you kill me, the Emperor will have every single soldier in County Capital, bar none, out looking for you, and he won't stop there. He'll summon all his bannermen to court and demand they bring great hosts of their own. Tens of thousands of people will be scouring the lands for you. I don't know that I'd be so rash but... there you have it. That's what Richard will do. You must know he and I have always been friends. Take me hostage, let these men go to tell about it, and you won't have that pressure. You can negotiate my release later or... well, that'd be best," Lord Almaric settled on.

Jacopo sighed. He knew it was the truth. Tristan heard him licking his lips, could almost hear his brain whirring for that matter. And his own thoughts came into focus. It must have been the view down the causeway that set him off. He could see the beautiful blue sea at the other end of it, where it had all started... half an hour ago? He'd come a long way, or no way at all depending on the view. Less than no way.

All was quiet with only the wind to keep him company, whipping up sand and dust throughout the lonely ruins. He found tears again, hidden behind bloodshot eyes, and freed like a dam. They flowed freely down his dirtied cheeks, accompanied by no sound.

A Kiss in Summer

So many dead. What to tell poor Bethen Wyman and so many others? She had expected... what, of him? Their anguish filled him already: echoes from the future. Marcus too, Tristan remembered. His courier, his friend, lying on the road, but a dot to his vision. He felt Jacopo's head brush past his sodden black hair, training his eyes to the same spot along the road. He looked back and forth.

"Ah, him," Jacopo said carelessly, taking neither joy nor guilt from it. There might have been a twang of regret; an emotion of some description at any rate.

"Marcus Baldwin," Lord Almaric replied.

"Well he's gone now, there's nothing that can be done. You must let him go. Do you hear me?" he pressed, shaking Tristan slightly. "You have to forget about him. You have to forget about him, Lord. He's not for the likes of you to go worrying about. You're not obliged to."

"What's obligation got to do with it?" Lord Almaric answered, confused at the man's sudden change in attitude. He seemed, to Tristan, a lost boy in a man's body, talking and acting on whims. Those hard eyes had deceived him.

"My Lord, you've not understood me." His mouth flapped open and closed, tongue slapping his lips while he deliberated his bizarre monologue. "Now you, Lord, you're worth much more. I suspect that Mortain boy saved your life, and too right, yes? My Lord Tristan, are you listening to me?" he snapped angrily.

"Jacopo, we need to get moving," Cristico told him from behind. "There's not time for whatever the hell you think you're doing."

"Yes, fine, fine," Jacopo sighed. "I was getting to negotiations anyway. You're willing to be a hostage, Lord? Answer me this, then. Wouldn't negotiating your freedom later still come back to haunt me?"

"I know your name and your likeness, nothing else. You've hidden your true self before, you can do it again. You even deceived the Empress."

"So I did..." Jacopo said sternly. Tristan detected pride in him, which vanished like it was never there. Maybe it wasn't. This man struck Tristan as thoroughly joyless.

"Where would you take me? Think carefully before you answer, please. If it's somewhere secret, keep it to yourself."

"I don't know, the Kingsreach maybe," Jacopo said offhandedly.

"Will that impress the King?"

"What? Perhaps it... quiet please, my Lord, while I think," Jacopo replied distractedly, annoyance seeping into his voice more than before. "How to get rid of your soldiers... This hasn't gone well."

"I don't know why you risked it in the first place," Tristan blurted angrily. "We didn't bring anywhere near enough gold to justify this kind of stunt, even for someone with no morals. And unless you already knew every possible thing we might tell you, I don't understand why..."

Silence smothered the island as Tristan trailed off. He was under the impression there was already no sound from Jacopo, but apparently he was wrong. His breath could not be heard or felt, and he was stock still, as if petrified. It was so quiet Tristan thought he could hear the creaking of Jacopo's neck as he turned to Cristico. The gun was lowered but he was not released.

Puzzlement clawed at every pore, every joint. Tristan lowered his head and turned it ever so slightly to risk a shot of Cristico. He was frowning. Tristan's head fell forward and he huffed in laughter, just one beat of it, but he wasn't amused. Tears welled up again, only this time he kept them there. His thoughts raced frantically as he stared out at the nothingness of the road, for now his time was up.

Evylyn, Malcus, Evylyn, Malcus... then it came to him like a shooting star, white and beautiful in the darkness: Evylyn's face. Years ago he'd embraced her in his arms not 20 paces from this very spot. Warm she was, elegant; she always was, always would be. There was little wonder the romance had never died. Tristan would have become as such too, with her by his side. She was him, or a part of him. He'd followed that shining star all his life, so obviously he'd never strayed from the right course. Her visage smiled at him now, stroked his face, was not afraid as he was.

It had been warm that day too, he remembered. It was all he wanted to know: a sweet, pure kiss in summer long past, not kisses of steel or bronze. His hair was yanked back. The bronze was at his skull.

~

"Wait!" was the plea Havdan Linch, pitiful leader of the tiny Aurailian force, heard from a voice unfamiliar.

A bang rang out for all to hear, laughing. Havdan looked out in horror and he could take no more. In rage, he rallied his four men and the prisoners to charge with him, to avenge their fallen lord, splayed upon the yellow stone with blood pouring from his scalp. Looming over him, a treacherous whore in gold armour staggered back in abject shock, blood covering his face. His men gawped and, as if in fear of what they would think, he cowered away, hunched up, rubbing his eyes so hard he might bury his thumbs in them.

"Kill them!" he yelled in agony. And so it went on, the music to battle's end, his rally cry as he stalked away, repeated over and over in madness as if he knew no other words, each time shouted differently than the last, *"Kill them, kill them, kill them, kill them, kill them, kill them, kill them, kill them..."*

<u>Chapter Thirty-three: The Lord of Change</u>

Penned by Yoclenn Wailyn when he was feeling particularly humanistic and sentimental after the siege of Aymathneè (Harth), when the King's son, suddenly and emotionally, declared an end to war in his lifetime, as his mother was carried through the streets. Your Majesty may wish to note that this proved as true as realistically he could have hoped for, as well becoming intensely religious. By tradition, sung by females of high voice in Mürathneèan courts.

'Twixt the hills and estuary
East of nothing, west of me
There thrives that city, white and free
Ill fires begged to sleep, consigned to sea

Here where one year knew an eon's strife,
Where death 'came love, then to life

A grey did grip the sullen night
By day there loomed a shadow's might
"Be gone!" the King did there beset his right
But on his throne his eyes caught in light

His love and life to bear
A regal wife, so black of hair
Pale as milk, without a care
'Fore death 'came love, or life

Beyond the walls an army slept
And in their holding sorrow kept
While in the streets the widows wept;
The plague, cold bodies left

"Bleed, for the ocean," declared the shadow
Or so heard the folk, despaired, crazed, beaten, tallow
House and manor turned to barrow
White of city, painted red, bereft of hallow, bereft of hallow...

In devils' grip the land did shiver;

The Voice of Kings

The King alone a'fear, aquiver
Till one morning light did sliver
Death saw love, alight of silver

Silver water, silver light
Silver robes that sighed by night

On litter white was she carried from there
Amongst the dead did folk stop and stare
When Venlor breathed upon her hair
To open hearts for their queen, so fair
When death was lost to love

The King mourned coldly for his dead
His son touched a petal to her head
Said he: "tarry not for death and dread
Take heart as her and follow stead"

Here where one year knew an eon's strife,
Where death 'came love, then of life

In their prayers they breathe a song
The suffer'd folk who did no wrong
They pray for health, understanding long
Ere is drawn a blade in wrong;
Gods preserve us;
Passing through the mourning throng,
To view the tomb and know where thou belong

On shores of gold and heights of white
Here to pray for love and life

"Trust holds nations together, when all's said and done. Which is not to trivialise money, you understand, and pragmatists who spend it, nor intelligence and passion that idealists spread around, and soldiers with more than half a brain to guard it. You know it all, I needn't presume ignorance, though I might do it anyway because it helps me think to have an advocate, and because it amuses me."

The Lord of Change

Alycia looked up from the poem on the desk, paled in the years since she'd asked for it, tucking it below her work piled neatly, and smiled serenely. She had no mirror to inform her so, but there it was, and she knew what it was down to the tiniest inflection. She'd had no intention of being so precise; it had come naturally, and Marioyrne, in her coolness, had worked that out long ago, and didn't presume, by some hilarious logic, that every movement of her face was the dynamism of a sort of elaborate puppet show as her very husband believed, the poor thing. By now he should have picked up a knack for when the play was in motion and when Alycia Llambert was being Alycia Llambert, if she could so differentiate between the two; it was always good to throw some acting into a discourse to manipulate the tides. He did know, once, she courted certainty, and forgot because he wasn't feeling depressed enough for his liking, or some other such self-deprecating nonsense. Giving him security by way of arms was an evening stroll in the woods in comparison to saving him from himself. Ah, and again she was proven right, of mind ruling strength, even in the worst of ways, and how hollow a victory it was.

"So you have candidates lining up to be renaissance men at court who fulfil all or some categories but the first?" Marioyrne astutely inferred, back from the conversation's dawn.

"Mmm," Alycia murmured. "Many. And many more already here as our good lord paramount so pointed out in his kindly way. I shan't name them now, I think, for their sake. These other men and women though..." Alycia said, soothing the names on the paper before her like a conqueror to the lands on his map. "I'll give them some noble occupation to do in the lands they came from, to milk them dry. It would be a waste to deny them completely. Still, Marioyrne, they'd thank me if I made them understand. It's probably just as well they don't interfere with Aurail, isn't it? Those with selfish ambitions won't find a whole lot to be cheerful about here."

"Very well, who's on that list then?" Marioyrne asked, steepling her fingers and resting her chin upon the dainty structure.

Her dark purple gown sagged at the arms at this gesture, if 'sagged' wasn't too unkind a description. It occurred to Alycia again that the young lady still didn't appreciate her own elegance that had become integrated into her being over the years, as a white budded tree in spring has no eyes to see its beauty. It wasn't necessary to make her more amiable of course, but then again, some would say it wasn't necessary to stop the city outside the castle becoming a stone-guarded cesspit either.

"You don't need me blunting your brilliant mind by feeding you reams of useless information," Alycia settled upon to boost the young lady's pride to its due. "And it is useless to you. If you must know, read it later when I've exhausted its purpose. Keep an ear open if you will, actually, as I'll take your council gladly."

"I may guess them all anyway," Marioyrne said.

The Voice of Kings

"Really?" Alycia laughed. Her slender finger and thumb took hold of only air, instead of the quill that tempted her to work. She nestled into the chair, warping the velvet cushioning to her will, and crossed one leg over the other. "How many names on this list do I count as undesirable?"

"I couldn't guess without a moment's notice, Majesty."

"You're free to count very, very quietly. It's rather cynical though, no? I don't doubt your ability to spot philanderers from honest men, I only wonder about the sourness of doing it as a hobby."

"Your Majesty, I protest that accusation. That I enjoy it doesn't denote a lack of sincerity. You'd like as not be a jester if that logic were always true."

"Ah!" Alycia laughed, short and sweet. Marioyrne's laugh was more a subdued thing, longer by way of strain on its fibre, like fine string tugged too hard. "Perhaps I was too rash to voice concern then. I must seem to you rather too motherly at times. I should stay to being Empress. The concern I have is one I make sure to keep close to myself, you understand. I know who I think are enemies and who are merely petty criminals, but voicing it in my shoes makes it so in the eyes of many. Don't worry, anyone not fit to be here will be dealt with in proportion to their offences, but not before they're real. I suspect we'll hear of some very soon, when the men return from Bryndton."

Alycia's eyes whisked off a gaze in Marioyrne's direction, insightful in its silence, full of possibilities, and stern, which generally had the very successful effect of holding one's tongue down. If the young lady were to probe about magic again, she'd feel compelled to answer despite her right not to, so better to prevent it entirely rather than having to put an unpleasant gag of silence upon herself.

After a short time, she turned herself to the left, vaguely keeping eye contact before blinking and taking in what sights of the city she could from her seat. It was a trivial thing really, but trivial or not, she was glad to have moved her desk close to the edge of the room, where the silk curtains between the open balcony doors fluttered to and fro. Out there, of the south, she was obsessed at that moment, taking in what she could see over the balcony wall and through its embrasures, and processing it for a very special kind of scrutiny. The red buildings and city walls seemed to melt in the evening sun, which said its farewells gradually earlier with the passing days. Aurail let orange light wash its grime away. On the morrow, it would return, but one day it would not; this old relic would see use again, and not just as a cautionary tale. *Death to love, to life*, I suppose, she mused. *And tarry not for death and dread, but take heart as her and follow stead*. Seeing it as poetry was one way to be positive. If Aurail was art, worthy art, then it was timeless.

To that she sighed, as to a hot bath. How to make others see was something else. Something that could be interpreted as magic might help, or not, or actual magic, depending on how it could really be classed. What people would want to see was the kind of magic alleged to hold Castle Aurail up however, not whatever vicious thing sprang from the depths of a dark cave somewhere. To make matters worse, men would be vicious in return, one way or another. If it came to that, anyone from Burtal with any bright ideas about that would be punished and made an example of for would-be ne'er-do-wells to have a little something to consider. She sighed again, this time by her own command, for the darkness of her thoughts didn't do her well, necessity born as they may have been.

Laughter prayed for her attention to fall on her chamber again. Two of her serving ladies were finding great mirth in something as they sewed, sitting upon chairs across the other side of the wide, open room. Even in the dim light, she could see their faces warmed, discussing something they deemed cheeky as they whispered excitedly to one another. Their eyes were wide awake and mischievous, as if hoping to catch every inflection with them. So bawdiness was the subject, and to finish work in all haste their desire, as in dissonance they switched between twiddling their fingers and sewing faster than ever.

The soft, light colours of her room provided the tools for her scrutiny, making sure to harness all available light that wisped through the tall, wide windows, and throw it back out with a splendid aura: ocean blues and grass greens from the floor and from paintings of romantic landscapes, while others shining with paint of silver and royal colours on the walls meant her chamber was assured to stay in such form. For obviously, if she couldn't keep this space of hers a piece of poetry, in stillness and motion, she wasn't going to inspire much hope elsewhere, nor punish others for dryness without hypocrisy biting at her heels.

For comparison, Alycia turned to her right, where through a wide archway lined with fresh yew, another serving lady attended to the refineries and neatness of her four-poster bed without fuss, and another was manoeuvring about with much the same aplomb to light the candles.

"Suffer your labour a little longer, good ladies," the Empress said half-joking to the two women sewing, the dresses they embroidered drooping upon the small, ornate oak table before them. "One can sometimes talk without compromising work."

"Majesty," they replied in tandem, smiling politely as they bowed just a fraction.

"We shall drink when our work is done," the one called Guenn affirmed casually, respectful as she was. "Me, I shall have mead as these ladies still don't understand."

"Is that a lady's drink?" the Empress asked. "Wine is more for nobles."

"Well yes, you are right. Perhaps I shall have wine instead."

"I've just decided I hate wine."

"Mead it is then," the lady replied with a coy smile as she caught on to Alycia's game, her face flushing red.

Alycia fingered a small bejewelled amulet at her neck as she watched their hands work the silver threads once more, her other arm residing at a right angle position on the armrest, stiff but not tense. If she appeared to be sitting as if on her throne, that was not arrogance, only an indication that she was a slave to duty as much as she controlled it. Her head span hawklike at the sound of dullness and dread sullying the sky, rising up through red to streak through clouds of orange and grey. Its gait was long and hollow.

"What horn is that?" Lady Castellon said, rising from the work she'd returned to on the opposite side of the desk.

"Whalebone?" Alycia ventured doubtfully, hearing piqued. She shook her head slowly, unblinking as she stared into the distance. "No, I shouldn't venture to guess at all."

She rose, and with a swish of her dress was at the balcony, where she glided to its edge and there stood with the fingers of one hand lightly pressed upon a merlon as, in grace, she leaned out slightly.

Her bedchamber being at the south-eastern corner of the castle, she was able to turn left for a fair panorama of the city's eastern stretch without compromise or effort. Over buildings big and small, arranged neatly and jumbled like children's building blocks, and over the water-rimmed Jorin's Plaza, and on dark horizon beyond the walls, no horn sounded. In the barracks of Woenyls against the southern wall there was peace, and likewise in that of Imperial to the east, in which the imperial armoury resided, the smoke of its industry wafting against the angry sky. Startled, she looked down as like a heavy thud it rang again, this time much closer, from the south. It was the same as before: drawn out, piercing, and now between exact, short increments of silence it carried on, not jaunty enough to be triumphant, too booming to be lamentation. It was a stark warning that she took with fear, while her serving ladies gathered about her. A single rider came into view, galloping firmly from the east and turning hard to get closer to the castle, where he was obscured from sight by the outer wall.

"Something is very wrong," the Empress said clearly, catching herself out before she had time to mumble the words. "I'd best see to it myself."

She was gone from her chamber at speed, and when was from all sight, sped up again, delicately bunching up her dress with one hand as she marched, almost breaking into a run, trying to drown out the clopping of her boots with her thoughts which manifested too many possibilities of equal standing for any to be of use. She finally settled on meditating for the unexpected. When men and women alike stopped to nod in the hallways and stairwells she traversed, she presented glances of acknowledgement to belie troubled conjecture on her part. At the vestibule, she saw, through one open door, a man in the courtyard leaping from his horse clumsily, nearly collapsing but urgently shrugging off his ailment, all while guards flocked to him like ravens. Her presence rippled at once when but one guard saw her, and they flew away, leaving the rider alone with his frightened, wearied horse.

"Majesty," the man said as she came to him. He was in worse shape than his horse. Suddenly she realised that it was not a stranger but Wylam Meyers, not kitted in armour as he must have been when he left that morning, but wearing fatigues to be worn beneath, creased like screwed up paper and damp all over. His face was no better, white as a sheet not because of his news, or solely because of it, but of genuine illness that might make him sick were he not so stubborn to hold it down till he was in a private chamber.

"Did you not go with Lord Almaric this morning?" the Empress asked, dreading the answer.

"I did. Bryndton, Majesty: it was a trap." He dropped to one knee and his head dropped with him. "I don't know what they wanted, but they got it now…"

"Where are the rest, Wylam?" she said urgently.

"They killed Marcus Baldwin first, with a crossbow. I, alone, swam from the Eye of Sand for help and made it to the ship to find its crew fretting whether to risk a cannon run on the enemy. Before I could convince them it would be enough to scare and scatter them, another ship attacked and I abandoned them as I had to, to…"

"*Where are the rest?*" Alycia asked for the second time, and oh she would not ask again. Her voice trembled as she parted the words, her tongue lodged in her throat.

"Dead," he snapped quickly, shaking his head in shame. "All of them dead."

"You cannot be sure if…"

"A Watch Commander, your Majesty, watched from his boat with his telescope. These prisms aren't clear of course, but he was certain when boats picked up the Mürathneèan traitors, that only they boarded, and much less of them than earlier on. He said they were bloodied and took no prisoners."

There was no movement from Alycia. She gawped, rage and sorrow filling her in ways she couldn't fully understand yet, eyes wide as they stared at nothing. They fell into slits and, trembling, she returned attention to Wylam.

"Rise!" she barked. The loyal soldier was brave to look her in the eyes, for she knew they were a maelstrom of anger now. "Who was it, Wylam? Who was the informant?"

"Jacopo," was the reply, rightfully shameful again as he obviously couldn't recall the surname. "Jacopo. I was not right by so didn't hear everything, though I don't want to excuse myself in saying so. I know I heard that he was working on behalf of the King. I wouldn't have believed it, but some of his men wore armour with eagle standards."

"We won't be insulted like this," Alycia snapped. "Gather as many men as you can, and a captain for them. Send word to the three main garrisons to be ready before nightfall, and to ride through the darkness to the shore. And have the Manor of Blessed Voices surrounded. Meet me in the throne room when you're done."

"What should…"

"You have all the information you need right now," she wheezed, spinning to stride from him, head held high while men still watched.

The Voice of Kings

When entering the vestibule, already her head weighed like a slab of stone, and still she strained to keep it high, for she was the Empress of Burtal and would not break down here. To be sad, the people would understand, in theory at least, for they would not differentiate as well as they presumed to. At the vestibule's exit, her head was a mountain's weight bearing on her, and on a whim, she detoured in the main hall to a corridor to her left. Once inside, her head sagged and her legs shook so much from the tension she'd pent up that she nearly fell over. It was the base of a wall mounted candelabra that her hands clutched onto for all her might, because just then, a week's worth of sleepless nights was piled on her and her cheeks itched to behold tears streaming down them. She squinted and tensed to avoid sobbing, but one came through in defiance, louder than it should have been, and here and there more escaped her grasp to wail down that corridor, all for the dreams crumbling with those men at Bryndton, cheeks reddening from what felt like poison searing down them.

After a short time, the tears stopped, and with maniacal pupils, she searched the blank, cold stone, as if for profundity in its indifference. She'd dared to joke about what would happen if she and Tristan were to disappear from Aurail, and now one of them was truly gone, not for a week, but never to return, and she was all alone to refashion Aurail's every last brick without a lord of lords at her back. How did one justify putting out such a light that brought music right into people's souls? Oh, he was naive, but that one quality was a thousandfold the worth of all the fibre of a cowardly assassin. At that, tears flowed freely again, stinging her face, and she couldn't help but sniff and wheeze.

Her fingers tightened on the iron between them, as if to rip it from the wall, and she pulled herself up, wiping her face clean as best she could, trying to grant prominence to anger instead. Returning thusly to the main hall, head lighter than a feather, she looked about wildly for a harbinger. "Send my Guardians to the throne room," she told the first servant capable of finding them in swift course. "Any who are in the castle and not with the Emperor; I'll disturb him myself when I must. And bring ample writing equipment." So in the centre of the throne room she waited, the great emptiness of which seemed to play with her mind, as it was not just empty but soulless then, empty through all time. She might have been naked for the chill that settled there, piling and rotting as with a bog. The tall thrones were her comfort, though she sat on neither, only observing, as the thought of it empowered her not at present. She would stand and defy the strain, for she would need much strength for what would soon follow.

Sir Pedrig entered first, her loyal servant whose years were each a lesson, not burdens heaped upon him. Proud he was to be the first, she surmised, and he didn't wait for her to turn, but walked a wide path around her to save her the trouble. Then it was Sir Doru, and men of lesser intelligence but powerful battle stature, Sir Balis and Sir Jerroyl, and lastly Sir Yanick, rushing in what he presumed a very knightly manner, joining Pedrig at the far right, where now five half-circled her, and that would do. Now that the five swords stood there before her, fine green capes still around their ankles, refineries glittering in the candlelight, her inherent power was felt like a hurricane. Would that she could just point them at the enemy and have justice done with.

"We're listening, Your Majesty," Sir Yanick said, betraying a hint of impatience. Hopefully he would become wise in the future, that being the near future.

"I should hope so," she said distantly, looking straight past him where words manifested as wisps that she spoke softly in sadness. "Our lord of change has been taken from us, Sirs. There are vile creatures out there who'll do anything to undermine and hinder us, and one such creature took the life of our lord on the Eye of Sand this very day."

The knights were motionless as they calculated this information and wondered whether to speak their surmise.

"Lord Almaric?" Sir Pedrig said at last, leaning forward in anxiety that reflected his tone.

"Yes, Lord Tristan is dead," the Empress answered, firm now. "And all that were with him were put to death just the same. For Harth cannot handle the thought of what we'll become of our own volition and charge. They paint their own city in silver and white but won't suffer others to do the same. See how their subjects so liberally pour sorrow onto us."

"I spoke to him just this morning," Sir Pedrig said. He, like the others, had become melancholy at her words, as she'd hoped to inflict, heads half-bowed and bearing frowns that knew not how to truly articulate how they should feel. "I spoke to him in private several times actually. Every time I did, he always had something to say and knew how to say it. Maybe it'd be disingenuous to guess what his loss means, but I know I feel there'll be something missing."

"Absolutely," Sir Yanick added loudly for misplaced need of relevance, clearing his throat. "I spoke to him not long ago. Not a word was wasted from him."

Through the sorrow that lanced her and the nobility that fought it back, Alycia raised an eyebrow at Yanick Berrhwrn, not overtly mocking in nature. Rather, she let it speak for itself. At that moment, they were joined by more men and women, who would be party to the lamentations. The servant Alycia had ordered to send the knights was first of the group made four on her travels, carrying a lectern with her, and Marioyrne, who simply couldn't stay away, was at her side, also with a lectern. Her initiative was keen, by which Alycia's predecessors would have used as excuse to lock her in a maid's gown. Behind the women, swiftly overtaking, Wylam and a captain came for counsel.

"Your Majesty," the captain started uncertainly. "I've been told to assemble a company to take back the Eye of Sand?"

"It's not occupied, Captain; it's an open tomb. Find those responsible for the crimes perpetrated there, recover them alive, and bring our dead back with all decorum. Leave the enemy dead as you find them," she added on a whim, one she knew she wouldn't regret.

The Voice of Kings

"Wylam tells me they went by merchant vessel. How will I find them?"

"Stop every merchant vessel you find on our side of the channel, question every inhabitant of the islands, and every fisherman and sailor, and find out where it went if you can't catch it. Take as many men as you need. Take five hundred men if you can assemble them quickly enough, recruit more at the harbours and let it be plainly known by what offence you've been driven to this. Don't let the night stop you, Captain. My husband will be counting on you."

"It'll happen, Majesty," the captain promised, bowing to avoid eye contact as much as anything.

"Wylam, stay a while. Lady Castellon, I'm glad you're here. Send a summon for my son immediately, and another for Lady Evylyn Almaric and her son, the heir of Almaric Keep. They may be in danger."

Marioyrne took her lectern, with paper and inkpot nestled in a circular hole, to a chair at the hall's edge abreast a candle stand, making sure not to be encumbered by a pillar blocking her sight from the meeting. Alycia smiled weakly and the bold knights were in her view again, running her hot blood like a waterfall. She continued before the pace was lost.

"It's just as well. A man who'll, for one petty justification or another, murder one of abject peace like Lord Tristan might not differentiate the innocence of women and children. King Michael may try to trivialise its impact. He's free to. But have we not been insulted enough? We'll accept justice, not one piece of gold or drop of blood less than we deserve. Miss..." the Empress then said to the servant, unfurling her fingers to take the lectern. She paused as it was held out for her, tongue in cheek. "Sir Pedrig, would you do the honours?"

Pedrig took it instead, and for the sake of the servant not spreading false rumours, she was allowed to stay and see the whole thing through. And Alycia paced slowly, flailing her arms like a painter, conductor, and oarsman all in one, and just as disciplined in their wispy, chaotic way. Pedrig hugged the lectern to his armour, quill poised over ink.

"We'll be addressing King Michael personally. Write as I speak, Sir: It is with great regret that this letter is written to you. You might sigh as you read it, but I assure you my grievance is a hundred times the pain of your inconvenience."

Widows' cries will fill these halls soon enough, she thought. *If there is grieving in your kingly halls for the instigators at Bryndton, then you are indeed war criminals.*

"We demand to know how, not half a day before the writing of this letter, men serving under you on a mission of treaty came to see it appropriate to slaughter our noble lord paramount, and 50 other men whose names accompany this letter; a deed which they accomplished." Alycia wagged a finger as she pondered, and Pedrig stalled. "Pedrig, we know the first name of their leader, but we won't name him here. And leave out Valen, for that matter. Write again: Within ten days of arrival, we expect a return letter with the names of those responsible, for that's as long as I'd have my people bear it in form of rumour, or if that is impossible, a detailed reason as to why not within the same time period."

Of which we will judge as satisfactory or not, she kept to herself.

"Whatever your first action, we desire," *we command*, "that you hand over all participants of the atrocity for whatever justice we choose. If you cannot, we will make for Harth ourselves with a royal caravan."

Or an army.

"The people of Burtal will rightly demand it of us to see it happen soon, so you can understand why you must respond thusly, to clear yourself of guilt. You must do what's right."

You must pay the price.

Alycia was trembling once again, in the immense heat of that moment, and perhaps if one of the people around were to catch her in the right light, they could notice it. To quell it, she made to finalise this first stage. She sent Lady Castellon to fetch her imperial seal and took the quill from Pedrig to scribble her signature beneath the letter, leaving plenty of room for Richard's own mark above it. She froze at an angry call, and in dread, her eyes shut to escape from it all.

"Would you mind telling me what's going on?" Richard's voice cried out as he stormed the throne room, and no wonder, for if the horn hadn't disturbed him, then the frantic gathering of soldiers to be heard from the courtyard certainly did.

He was dressed in a thick cloak around his regal clothes that were fitted to him so well that day, and by the same token, he made an effort to be the Emperor he was as he passed through into the hall: forthright, strong, and patient. His gaze was cast all about and the strangeness of it all built up plainly on him, unbeknownst to the worst of it. It was Wylam that at last grabbed his attention: a man bedraggled and sodden by a day of burdens.

"Who are you?" Richard said dryly. The Emperor squinted and the rusty gears began to move in him. "Wylam, is it? What the hell have you been doing?"

"He went to Bryndton this morning," Alycia answered.

She bridged their gap to find him more cleanly than usual. Even his breath was scented, which must have been a scorn for his absurd fanaticism for the warrior in him, the hero that never was. Her husband looked back and forth from Alycia to Wylam, and for the fool, her heart broke, as in his green eyes, something died: fear, then anger on top of that, then the pleading of a desperate man, all before he knew what conclusion he'd reached. She took his hands, not nearly warm enough as they were, and clasped them betwixt her breasts.

"Richard. My love..."

Chapter Thirty-four: Below Golden Wings

The morning came to wake Isaac from his uneasy slumber, though when his body obliged, he didn't know it, for the sunlight in his cell was minimal and, at first, he thought not to leap from bed to check. Nor, as his distant wont had been, did he pace with glee in preparation of the coming day, an open book for his writing, or cheekily recall a night of pleasure with the duceveree̊'s daughter and, surprisingly more strangely, the words exchanged prior. These things, they flashed before him, but he paid them no heed but for a guilt that panged for the woman he may have endangered. Maybe Lucian was right; maybe he treated life itself like a joke, maybe he couldn't see, but for the past, ahead. Lucian was often right. Isaac lay on his back, unmoving, on the bunk, eyes half-closed that he might slip back into sleep if he wasn't careful. His brain was slow to start and he didn't want to shatter that fragility with a flood of pain. He felt aches ripple through his chest with every breath, so to move beyond that would surely yield yet more unpleasantness.

The white ceiling, he noticed from his endless watch, was scrubbed clean save for a cobweb in one corner. If he was to take that as a sign, he would be looked after for as long as he was imprisoned; that was not greatly comforting, as despite his relief at not being thrown into a prison tower out to sea, the hospitality of his captors was the least of his concerns. That alone was depressing, and at least if he'd been taken to one such tower, he might take relief in knowing his appeal was as good as any other, but Isaac, the humble traveller from afar, was below a palace of kings, unless, in fever, he'd dreamed the whole thing. What was it Martello had accused him of? He'd spat the word 'spy' at him and, insane as he'd turned out, it didn't add up that he'd reached that conclusion alone.

He wasn't going to learn any more about his situation lying there, he decided, so in pre-emption of his bane's awakening, he clamped his teeth together and proceeded to lift his upper body up, slow and jerky like an ineptly animated puppet, outstretching his arms behind him in aid of balance. At the peak of his rise, a jolt struck his lower chest and, akin to a snake, slithered about under his skin. He winced, for it was not only painful, but the sensation was deeply sickening. Pulling back the folds of his clothes, his noble clothes speckled with dabs of red and generally lacking in nobility, he saw a spot of black and violent purple where the flat of Martello's longsword had struck him. All he could do was try not to think about it.

He made himself fully aware of his surroundings in line with that expression. A heavy iron door blocked his passage directly in his sight, not far from the foot of his bed, containing a sliding hatch at eye level with which to speak through; closed, naturally. If they knew so much about him, they must have known that he wouldn't stop talking so long as he saw fit, or else spy on any passing person with only the highest scrutiny. Alas, it was shut.

Below Golden Wings

To his right there was a basic wooden table against the opposite wall, the shape of a tankard pronounced in the gloom atop it. He recognised the cell now, though not in any fondness. He'd been thrown in here the previous day, he assumed, laid on the bed at length, was taken by sleep at some point, and woke at some unknown hour of the night when the silver moon was mirrored as token favour around the bars of his window like slivers of shining water out in the cold wilderness. He'd fallen asleep a second time and woken to find the sun had ousted the moon, and its gift was less of mercy and more of rude awakening, dim as it was.

Isaac shuffled to that window at the back, one arm wrapped around his waist. The window was slim; big enough for a five-year-old to crawl through if the four bars were removed. As it was, he was stuck in this dingy cell. Indeed, he would stay there if escape was an option, as that would prove only that he was a buffoon, not pragmatic. He took the bars with both hands and carefully pressed one boot against the wall, then the other, and hauled himself up the few inches necessary to get a level view of the outside world. It was a grassy knoll he was beneath, steep and overlooking the infinite waters, and there to his right was a dock that housed two great war ships, at which there was a bustling, ringing of bells, and wordless voices that calmed him. The sun beat down on blue waters from its place of hanging unseen. And it must have been the hill he'd looked out over with Jamys.

"Jamys..." Isaac sighed.

He dropped, grunting in pain. He wondered if Jamys was alive. He could handle himself no doubt, but against how many? There were many reasons to believe he was not dead, Isaac conceded. If he'd been cast under the shadow of this same ludicrous plot, he might be just a few feet away where brick could not avail. Iron slid over grease, which startled Isaac. A gaoler was peeking through the newly created hole in the door. Enough of his face was visible to make it clear to Isaac that he was going to give him trouble. There was nothing in the cell of suspicious nature, unless he was intent on throwing it on the bloody tankard, and yet his bright eyes were keen for danger, his lips puckered in dissatisfaction, chosen before he'd opened the hatch.

"I thought I heard you scrabbling at the wall," the gaoler said. "You weren't trying to escape, were you?"

"Does it matter to you how I answer?" Isaac sighed bitterly.

"Maybe, maybe not. Explain yourself all the same."

"I wasn't trying to escape, I assure you. I was looking out the window to get my bearings while I wait for justice."

"You're a spy, I hear. What justice do you expect to find?"

"I am not a spy," Isaac said, making sure not to sound defensive. He wouldn't give the gaoler that pleasure. "There's been a misunderstanding."

"You better pray they'll see it that way. I stay out of politics, but if you're found guilty, you won't be leaving Mürathneè with your head."

The Voice of Kings

"If you're inclined to stay out of politics, then I'd ask that you actually do it. Until I'm called to present the proof of my innocence, then I'd like to be left in peace without the sneering judgements, please."

"You'll be called soon," the gaoler said flatly, and disappeared.

Isaac wiled his time sitting on the bed, watching specks of dust dance in the pools of light reflected from outside, there cradling his tankard. He submerged one finger in the water and sucked it dry to find it lukewarm but otherwise fresh, reflecting its clearness in the tankard. He denied the urge to guzzle it down, opting instead to ease his barren throat with regulated sips, a pragmatism that comforted him and told him he wasn't mad after one forgetful night in a cell. Eventually a metal door opened from afar, at the end of a long corridor judging by its echo, and soon his door was flung open at the command of two tall, lean guards of the palace, on whose armour the sun shone and forked out ten rays each that struck light around the place.

"Come with us," one of them said forwardly.

"Am I permitted to ask why?" Isaac said courteously, rising to appease any sense of entitlement they might have, or likewise quash judgements of insolence.

"You go to stand trial for your alleged crimes. It's best you don't ask more questions; I will answer few."

The corridor outside the cell was more generously lit, but there were no windows and most of the light was concentrated on the desk the gaoler sat behind in the alcove at the edge of a turn in the corridor. The gaoler sat slouched, bored to the point that chastising all who passed him, outwardly or otherwise, was the only thing he could derive entertainment from. His face rested on a palm and he stared at them from his ball of light. Isaac ignored him. Immediately to his right was a wall, and to his left, rows of cells twisting away from sight. It was onward they took him, down a narrow road beneath the earth and up a flight of steps to the civilised world.

"May we go at my own pace?" Isaac implored as they took the arduous task of climbing the steps. "Your Commander Leonardus will confirm that my treatment by the sword of Martello Jacart was unjust and violent, and I heard him say I should be given every courtesy because of it, unless I dreamed it," he lied, risking the repercussions, for he thought them miniscule enough.

"We serve Sir Leon and Rayance of the Sun Guard, but do as you like," the same guard said, only a tad begrudgingly.

So Isaac, still in their strict keeping nonetheless, made his way up the steps at what slow pace his body would allow without waking the demon in his chest. Colour greeted him when, at last, he left that underground world behind, making him squint for a short time as he adjusted to the reflective marble floor of the thin corridor he found himself in, laid down the centre with a rug of distinct blues, greens, and silvers, and round the edge there was a motif of trees with white bloom all interlinked. Even the skirting boards were carven. Beyond the corridor there was a hall barely visible where sunlight bathed freely, but he was not taken there, nor directly past any windows or doors to the outside world. He was afforded only fleeting glimpses of rooms of real meaning, guided away from the residents of the palace in general, and those smart servants who did pass by dared not to look at him for long. He was not overtly frightened for what it was worth, though he knew he should have been. The feeling was that he'd been spirited away from one bizarre scenario to the next, first to a sword fight, now to someone's palace which packed all the majesty of the renaissance into one building: warm, vainglorious, and above all, nuanced. That was the King's intention, no doubt.

Before long, he was fed into a room at what he assumed was still the western wing of the palace, and there, marched up the aisle of a hall, not great in size, with obsessively polished wood which even the stone walls were suffocated by, and marble flooring. It was presided over by a timeless creature upon an aft dais, of green and golden wings outspread, carved from marble, and painted to grant it life. Down its noble beak it glared at him, as two men did sitting at a desk before it, of equally noble quality, on the face of which was carved, in horn, a script of some old Mürathneèan language. More looks searched and violated him from the sidelines beyond a wooden barrier either side. They were not so very different from him in a way, or rather Isaac could have said as much when he'd set out to meet a more amicable destiny the previous morning. They were clad in richly woven surcoats of various designs, some merely fashionable, others apparently with House sigils, and there were men wearing puffed velvet doublets and striped hose, showcased by heads knightly and lordly, though presumably none were of highest importance or consequence here. His guards nudged him along until he was made to stand upon a circular pad, pure white and protruding from the floor.

Isaac deliberately noted the man at the far left of the dais who ordered the two guards to stay close by: certainly not Leon, as without that armour he still remembered that face. This thin man was reddish, as if possessing a natural sunburn, dark of lips, and about Isaac's height. More pressingly, Rayance, as Isaac would label him until given reason not to, was curiously displeased, examining Isaac with a plain face. Plain was good; it meant he'd dealt no stroke of absolution and was prone to a little push onto his side.

"Don't look at him," one deep voice spoke, clear and crisp like carving its mark through the windless air. "He's here to coordinate his men, nothing more. You will speak only to myself, being Lord Hughly, and to Lord Justice Holton. To the rest of you, you swear confidentiality on all that occurs in this room."

They did so as one.

The first man was more a bird hunting for prey than anything. His inspections missed nothing, and his demeanour dripped with cynicism that he failed to hide with the erect posture and interlinking fingers reflecting his noble birth, his *fair quality*. The second man was perhaps a little older, somewhat spotty with a crown of hair round a bald head, and seemed to wield the power here if his sparkling livery plaque collar was any indication. Isaac might use him as his shield, for Lord Hughly was more dangerous, so a hunch told him.

"I stand accused of a crime I didn't commit," Isaac said.

"Of spying on Mürathneè for Burtal," Lord Holton replied. "For something you thought Martello Jacart had."

"Have you reached out to the Burtalian court? If you think I'm a spy, it makes sense to destroy the root of the problem, not the branches that will continue to grow, even in a preposterous dream."

"We will ask the questions, I think," Lord Hughly said, bemused.

"Why was it not a relevant question?"

"The point is, we are interrogating you, Isaac," Lord Hughly bit back, raising his eyebrows.

"It will be a very one-sided interrogation if you continue to enforce this arbitrary rule, my Lord."

"Reasonable questions may be asked," Lord Holton declared, straightening himself as if to match his fellow lord. "But you are in a foreign land by which you must follow the laws as if a citizen, and so under suspicion of treason, you must not expect a reply immediately."

"We have a disturbing amount of evidence that points towards your guilt, for that matter," Lord Hughly spoke.

"I should like to hear it, my Lord," Isaac answered heavily to that, checking every syllable before uttered to ensure no sarcasm could be interpreted, as his inflection might have yet more damage than making him cough every now and then.

"You should be patient. We will scrutinise all of it in turn."

"Consider this, then," Isaac posed. "This is important. Just how exactly do you suppose that I'm a spy having lived in a highland town all my life? I can have half the residents attest to my constant presence up to the time I left for Mürathneè, I'll swear by the five."

"Neither of us accused you of working on the Emperor's behalf in particular," Lord Holton droned on in his gravelly tone. "There are other far more likely candidates who'd hatch treason."

"I've had no part in anything of the sort," Isaac defended, temper rising already. He clutched his chest, and with his free hand, swiped back at his dirty hair, which swung lazily about as he rubbed it vigorously. He had to treat it like a battle, he conceded, and that way would take it seriously. His life was on the line, he knew, although as of then, it was still a fact kept low in those men's stomachs before and behind him.

"Anger betrays guilt more oft than not," Lord Hughly pointed out calmly, looking to the watching men in turn, as if to tell them what to think if they'd dared to display a semblance of free will. "Your guilt piles so high I can barely see what you are beneath it. Consider *this*, Isaac Brodie: you were seen to be partaking in suspicious behaviour throughout the city, interacting with as many prominent figures as you could find in your mission."

"Indeed, that much is true. You know I know. The Commander of the City Watch came to warn me, Watchmen have spied on me. They should have found some more sturdy argument to base this ridicule on by now, given the effectiveness of your Watch, assuming I was stupid enough to go on with my treason with knowledge of their eyes on every street corner and in every doorway."

"You did what you thought you could get away with, a man would wager, and you judged poorly. Tell me, if you're so innocent, why did you come to this city? Again, I bring up the matter of your behaviour, as reliable sources inform us that you've acted without the consistency of any ordinary merchant or businessman. Hindsight lets us know that this is the hallmark of a spy who hasn't grasped the particulars of human behaviour, who'll trot around from place to place doing random deeds, which as we know, only sweetens the scent and draws attention to the criminal."

"Am I that stupid?" Isaac said, for he was dubious.

His true emotion was astonishment, for his verbal sparring partner certainly seemed to be projecting his own sorry state of mind unto him. Whether this was plain on his face, he couldn't know, as he was tired, and the reality of the situation had yet to sting him deep. At present, he floated all around the room, through the all but purposeless flying buttresses arranged on the sides for style's sake, and before the faces of every man there, down the aisle and upon the eagle's head, as if soaring aloft the palace skies, as if he wasn't so low. Responsibility dropped like a lead weight and he fought to keep his back stiff. He wasn't going to be bullied to the gallows; he was no sheep and Hughly was no shepherd, he reconciled, just an old man with a dagger tongue, to be frozen as hot metal from the forge.

"I came to Harth for my father's sake, Lord," Isaac proceeded. "I assume you know who he is, though I've assumed too much already. I came for Sèhvorian steel. I even approached a guest of this palace regarding it."

"To what end?" Lord Holton asked unassumingly, holding a quill over his notes.

"To whatever end my father chooses for it. You do know who he is, don't you? Your research is somewhat lacking if not, which makes your other argument look weak."

"We know who he is; that was as easy to find out as most other things about you," Lord Hughly rebuked. "Pointedly, that isn't all you've done in all your time in Harth, is it?"

"That also is true. For personal reasons dating to my childhood, I took it upon myself to research events related to Sèhvorian steel and peculiarities surrounding them. No one assigned me that task, as again residents of Caedor will attest to, if you choose to pursue the correct channels."

"No one would hang onto superstition for that long."

The Voice of Kings

"You would if you'd lived my life, my Lord. Although, you used the word superstition; not me."

"You can't put the blame on me for whatever deeds you're responsible of," Lord Hughly said, supplemented by a sickly smile that had nothing to say of joy.

"But I made no mention of blame either."

"I can see you think to wear my patience," Lord Hughly brayed. Patience was exactly one thing he had in great supply. The man was old but it was a deception, if the reasonable assumption by it was weakness.

"That's quite enough," Lord Holton barked, on whose behalf wasn't clear. Isaac was too disillusioned to be certain either way, and his stomach bore two screams: one for his illness, one for the body of his that withered away on the podium.

"Thank you, my Lord Justice," Lord Hughly said. "As for you Isaac, I feel I should stop playing games with you now," though in truth, men of numerous counting were playing with him, whether they would admit it or not. "Let's see. If you won't admit outright your purpose here, I'll bring the people's attention to your transgressions on The Wolf's Way, shall I? Thanks to your breakdown in intelligence in giving your name so freely, some rather disturbing claims come to light to back up your illegal actions. It was reported that, in your hurry to reach Harth, you attempted to bribe a Watchman to pass a bridge under maintenance..."

Isaac shut his eyes, sucking in air. "Riding quickly is not a crime," Isaac growled, losing his temper. "I saw others doing the same, only they didn't give charity to Watchmen. If the punishment for my crime is beheading, they should be rounded up and quartered."

"You're defending the wrong point once again," Lord Hughly said calmly, resting his chin on his open palm and descending deep into thought. Descending ever deeper.

"I'm defending my right to be treated with common sense," Isaac objected, an ache crawling its way up his innards, digging its claws into his throat. "What I saw on The Wolf's Way, and in every town, and in Harth itself, was the evidence of your country's greatness. Its foundations are clear, not the wondrous magic of invisible gods balancing them on giant hands. What I'm seeing now is the cataclysm of that foundation pulled down by someone who doesn't understand cause and effect." In vain, he made the jury his audience and looked as many directly in the eye as he could. "If you blindly side with this line of questioning, you condone the flawed logic that was cast out by your King and his father."

"You speak with a very mild poison," Lord Hughly remarked, to which Holton only rolled his eyes. "And you will face us, on pain of beating."

"What am I accused of, Lord?" Isaac tried again, frustrated. His plinth was a cage where he was gawked at. None came to his aid. The bird behind the two lords was still.

"You are a spy and a manipulator. You may be smart, but you can't elude us forever."

"You very much implied I was a halfwit several times already, and now I'm a master manipulator?"

"Jamys Flint," Lord Hughly declared in deliberate ignorance of his statement, raising his voice as the palm of his free hand met the table, echoing a dull thud around the chamber. "Martello Jacart has told us he's been assigned on a new mission. It's worth suspecting, since he was seen with you, by multiple witnesses, stalking the city together, that he is a part of your plans. Was his current assignment orchestrated prior to Martello giving it to him? What is it?"

"I've no idea!" Isaac pleaded to his utmost defiance. "I should like him to defend my innocence when he's available. And, if it's all the same, I humbly request Martello Jacart and Commander Leonardus to give their stories here in this hall of trial."

"You'd risk a man who arrested you and a man who hates you to give favourable accounts. Why?" Lord Holton asked with bated breath, one emotion of many poised to drop over his face at the answer.

"I know they would give the truth, and that's exactly what I want to hear. Martello, for one, is confused, and attacked me out of misunderstanding."

"A fabrication," Lord Hughly predictably interrupted, to Isaac's growing despair. To say he didn't know when to shut up was an unfortunate miscalculation, as he spewed acidic lies across the hall of trial with little in the way of men reading between the lines, as if his mind had decided to give up and plunge into madness for real now, out of pity for itself. Here was an imbecile who was under the impression every word he spoke would be taken as fact, to the point where he'd convinced himself of it, a gibbering creature with a designation for stupidity, or something considerably worse. Perhaps the eagle would help him. He could rely on that about as much as anyone else at present. And Lord Hughly's glory was to be heard again. "You drew a sword on Martello Jacart, and tellingly, multiple witnesses again can attest. It was made clear you were to remain in his custody until the City Watch arrived, ergo you declared war on the Watch when you picked up that sword, and in doing so, defied the law whether spy or not. But only a guilty man would do so. Guilty of what I've declined to guess, Lord Justice, and will continue to do so until the ice beneath him sufficiently cracks to his own breaking point."

"His longsword was drawn!" Isaac shouted, holding out his arms in disbelief. "It's almost as tall as me; it demands attention. When Martello is with sword, the world will behold it. He drew it, he took swings at me, he tried to kill me; people had to have seen it. Bring me my chosen defendants, or I'll call you a liar, Lord! Three is all I ask. Three's all I need to throw your claims off course."

"A liar," Lord Holton noted unceremoniously, his brow furrowing as he jotted it down.

Meanwhile, Lord Hughly's voracity for Isaac's pain became no less bloated, though for now he was silenced by his fingers digging into his bony cheek, staring fixedly with eyes half-closed: a fitting visual representation of the malice and plain contempt that vied for control. In that quiet interim, the sea could just be heard whispering along the wooden boards, licking the buttresses and meeting the air with a sweet hiss, overlapping and swirling together as the waves. Isaac listened and tried to let it calm him. Kate's tack would not be so abstract, but rather to imagine swimming in it, and it would work somehow, nature's lady as she loved to be. Well, maybe not here. Anything she stood to lose was of far less consequence than her own life, and if here, would show herself as distressingly vulnerable. As he imagined all too vividly. There was no comfort to take from imagining his sister tormented in his place, nor for that matter, the workings of her imagination, yet here he was with both in hand. Lord Holton interlinked his fingers and frowned.

"This is going nowhere. Your cooperation, or lack thereof, will have to be evaluated. In the meantime, loosen your tongue in the dungeons. To one end or another, you'll need to be more helpful than that."

"I wouldn't say we've gotten nothing out of it," Lord Hughly reconciled. "I've learned valuable insights about Isaac from this meeting. That aside, you have the right of it: we should adjourn for now. Next we meet, Isaac, I can only imagine you'll be more cooperative."

The lord's eyes seemed hollow and curious in that instant, and gleamed pale in the light of candles. Isaac was seen to shudder. If in their ineffectual, vague manner, they were too cowardly to utter the word, ordering his torture...

"I have answered all questions to the best of my ability," Isaac pleaded, holding his voice in line, attempting to produce a proud, booming voice. "Scarcely my best given the dire opportunities I've been afforded by Lord Hughly, but for that, I can't be held responsible. Don't treat my honesty with depravity on the basis that I *might* be lying. How then can I know if my word will ever mean its true worth to you, and like as much, how will yours be anything but air to me?"

Lord Hughly nodded to the guards either side of Isaac without deliberation, and they made to tow him out. Happily enough, he did as was needed of him without the encouragement of armed men, as the lords might call it. Then again, he recalled, they were kind enough to him before. When he was at the steps to his dingy cage, he would humbly request their aid when Hughly was nowhere close, and until then he would suffer the beating of his chest, the animal writhing up his black bruise. *The trial*, he said in his head as distraction, so consumed himself with the workings of those machinations. What a bizarre affair it was, disjointed and meandering without apparent purpose or structure, yet appearances could deceive and Lord Hughly had all but admitted as much, assuming that in itself was not an act. He concentrated harder. It wasn't worth being so paranoid. He wasn't going to be certain of many things for now, that much was obvious, and repeating that point till his brain hurt wasn't going to enlighten him. And perhaps he was about to have a lot more to worry about.

"Hold fast," someone commanded.

He obeyed, and the guards also. It was Rayance, as Isaac would still call him, who was no less perplexed now than in the hall of trial. As he drew to a halt, his hand passed over a keenly carved bust of a woman at his side, as if blessing it, or in reality, was more likely looking for something to lean on and assert authority. His hand found his sword pommel on the same side of him, there resting while the fingers drummed on the hilt. His stance was bent to his other side, so his sword took not the strain of his weight, and his body oddly relaxed in that way, while his face was dexter to it. In the reverse manner of the Knight of the Holy Storm being of around five and 40 years and having a face so timeless it could have been made anew every day, this man was probably younger than Isaac had judged him when up on the dais, yet had a wizened look about him. Surprisingly so. He couldn't have been in a position of power here long.

"You put us all between a rock and a hard place back there. It's not for you to issue ultimatums, but that can't be taken back: the damage is done. I'll give you some advice then, as proceedings will become stale and eventually very unpleasant if I don't intervene. No, don't speak, just keep your silver tongue where it is and listen. I imagine by now you've come to the conclusion you're damned whatever you do, but I promise you that's not true, for whatever that's worth to you. Admitting you're a spy won't necessarily net you a death sentence, depending on the severity of the associated crimes and the intent behind it. My guess, my highly well-founded guess, is that the King's court would ransom you to Burtal for all but the most heinous applications of a spy but, no, no I don't look at you and see a murderer. If you're not a spy, then you'd better rethink your strategy regardless; I know you're not short on time."

"But I won't waste a minute of it," Isaac replied, not knowing how he would occupy himself for even an hour.

"See that you don't. Whatever you do, remember that Lord Hughly is doing his job. He's cynical, that's who he is, that's what people want him to be when he's on business. Don't condemn yourself to a world of pain just by misunderstanding that."

If Lord Hughly's role was to treat Isaac as dirt, they might do well to have someone filling an opposite role. Isaac kept that to himself. He wasn't about to torch the last bridge that shrank into the mist at his feet. Rayance was already embarrassed enough, stiffly staring into his soul with very raw displeasure, as if even as he'd talked, he'd changed his mind and had decided to judge Isaac.

"You've done me an unlooked-for kindness in this foreign place," Isaac said. "I should thank you in kind."

"No need," Rayance snapped. He drew himself up and, all of a sudden, emitted a more high-class aura. Then he turned and left. "It would make me feel unclean if you were then judged as a spy."

Not you half as much as me, Isaac muttered with silent tongue.

He would have plenty of time to debate back and forth now, at any rate. The vibrant colours of the world were taken from him; he was swallowed by his cage in the darkness, and there he paced as he went over his time in the hall of trial in meticulous detail, such that he wondered if he was making things up. That was a vicious worm, and he paid it no heed whenever he could. It was already trouble enough to decipher Lord Hughly's blither.

He decided early on that, to make the day go quicker, he would, whenever coming to a remotely satisfying conclusion or when he noticed a change in the light, go to the desk and take a sip from the tankard that had been refilled, lick his lips and carry on. Sometimes he would afford himself a look across the bay, and every time it was sweet, and bright, and blue. They couldn't take that away from him just like that, the principles of the mind that made beautiful better still when rationed with such starkness, and so appreciate that great sea whenever he chose to look out on it or taste the clear water on his lips. Slowly he became disillusioned and lost track of time through boredom but for the sun that rolled across the sky. Occasionally the gaoler would open the hatch with intent to intimidate, but Isaac never spoke to him, in the hope he would get bored of whatever problem plagued him. When the pain in his stomach threatened to overcome him, Isaac lay down abed, to which the gaoler would respond by rattling the hatch to make sure he hadn't fallen asleep.

Morning became afternoon, and that turned to evening, and Isaac, in his lethargy, could scarcely recall how he'd spent the day. At some point or other, sleep took him out of pity, and there he saw the shadow men that had surrounded him on the stone podium outside the palace when Sir Leon Barrotti had handed over his sword. That, too, had been a dream, he surmised. Now, as then, these shadows were wreathed in flame, or were flame, and through them ripped that same shadow as their being, from the mouth of something: a cave it seemed. And as with the impossible way of dreams, he could see the shapes of the men outlined in the shadow breath, despite them occupying just the same shade of black, if it could be said to be a shade at all. Lord Hughly was with him even, and smiling Tristan, as last seen at that inn on the road last year, on whose tongue was wisdom, though he spoke too quietly. It all meant so much, then nothing at all, for it was only a dream.

Chapter Thirty-five: Fierce of Dark

From being left to study alone, or to clean the walls and the floor, alone, or any other random jobs Marcel was given, he learned only to think of the duceveree as a pest, though he felt terrible for that. It was Tamzin's energy that had kept him alive the whole time, and her discreet admission that her father was still testing him for his character, or until he'd decided watching him flail about was no longer making him feel powerful. Those were her words. Although for the absurdity of it, he would have perhaps left already but for her, and thus she was allowed, at her insistence, to accompany him to meet Lucian, regardless of her not having a stake in such a deeply personal family matter. She took the lead through the quickest route she knew, quiet for once. There was something sluggish about her, as if she hadn't slept in days and was finding the world overwhelming. Her energy subdued, her quirks repressed by forces unseen, she was rather more affected by Isaac's disappearance than he had any right to expect. Tamzin probably needed a friend a lot more than he did, that in mind.

As she walked on, she covertly tilted her head at him, and when he looked back at her, her eyes flicked away as if embarrassed. Then she stared intently at everything but him, deep in thought. When they came into one of the much wider roads, she seemed relieved, and by extension so was he. The mingling aromas were stronger out in the open, and all those smells were part of what leant the city its welcoming atmosphere. At present, the street was occupied by two dozen people, but there was no bustle, even with women cradling large baskets of clothes, and men hanging great joints of meat to their stalls, and hanging fish on others, all while two Watchmen trotted through the crowd on brown horses that parted the people like a stone rippling water. Casually they made a sign to another of their ilk performing his watch upon a shop's roof, leaning on a low merlon, his sharp sight piercing all that could be seen unhindered by the horizon or taller buildings. Beside him, a woman of no affiliation to him hung wet clothes to dry on a thin railing connecting to a building across the opposite side of the street. And all of it was without hurry or urgency on that late summer evening.

It was a wonder, given the apparent easy disposition of these people, that they weren't immediately drawn to and suspicious of him with his air of desperation about him, blowing erratically like a ship in a storm through the crowd. The two Watchmen probed him severely as they passed. They were tall and important on their horses, and paid him no mind after brief inspection. But that was not how Marcel had presumed it. Isaac had told Lucian that Watchmen were loitering around his boarding house, and then there was this mercenary companion of his to consider, also scourged from the face of the planet.

The Voice of Kings

Lavellyrn, Nel, Lameeri, Saliis, Venlor. To pray against all injustice could do no harm, and indeed, he couldn't help himself.

Soon enough he was in familiar territory, and the prayers were cast away where he hoped they would be caught. He turned into the plaza of the lodge, where Lucian waited with a dark mood hanging over him, leaning back against the central well.

"Tamzin..." Marcel began.

"I am here already; I'd look silly and petty to leave now. You don't have many people to trust; don't send me away for the sake of family formality, or whatever basis you think you have for it."

"I don't want you to leave," Marcel relented, shrugging.

She smiled momentarily and patted him hard on the back, then erected the invisible barrier around herself once more. Lucian was ill in the face, but it was a bitterness that he brought to heel with ferocity rarely seen in him. Lucian would not be seen helpless. His eyes gleamed, even as the rest of him was as still as a graveyard. He was planning on taking action, Marcel knew it already; action that would suit him best of all. The elder Brodie brother searched around him inconspicuously, then rose bolt upright as Marcel and Tamzin arrived.

"I know where he is," he said. "It's as I'd picked up from hearsay: he's been arrested. I spoke to Martello Jacart and he did not mince his words. He told me Isaac was taken to the Palace of the Sun on the day of his disappearance, and according to him, would likely stand trial yesterday, given that his *injury* might impede him on the day of his arrest." Lucian spat the words in utter contempt. "He was exceptionally clear on the fact that he'd disabled Isaac personally. The damn oaf. If I had the power of a true ambassador, I'd appeal to have him stripped of his leadership, to teach him where wearing smug insolence like a badge of honour falls alongside justice."

"Isaac's been hurt badly?" Marcel replied with alarm.

"Not that I could work out, after I pressed Martello about it. He wouldn't tell me where his man Jamys was. So be it then. I don't think we'll get any more out of him. We must take this to those who really know what's happening."

Lucian led Marcel and Tamzin inside, appearing apprehensive to speak out in the open, despite his urges. He would have liked the option to proceed without sneaking around, Marcel was sure, though he took it in his stride. Rosalynn, scrawling something at the front desk, looked up sharply at their passing.

"Lucian," the short woman said. "A man came for you just a few minutes ago, left this letter. He said it was urgent, though I can only hope it bears good news."

Lucian frowned as he took the rolled-up scrap of parchment, ripping off its band hurriedly and dropping it carelessly on the desk. Marcel was on his right side, Tamzin the left, peering over his shoulders to read the letter, which, without delay or ceremony, was unfurled so fast it might have torn. As if to read it out like a herald, Marcel's brother held it up and cleared his throat. Three words sat upon the parchment, bold and splattered like blood on canvas. They all were frowning, Lucian most of all, as if the words physically wounded him. *Neath your cloak*, it declared, a mighty boast it seemed to Marcel, but it was only his imagination running away with him, for now. Half of Lucian's mouth dropped open, and he was suddenly fixated, disgusted even. Disgusted and dumbstruck, for his free hand rose near his chest only to deliberate what his yield would implicate. Then he took the plunge, frisking his chest until, upon the third pat, it froze, on his upper chest beside the opening of his black Mürathneèan surcoat.

"Rosalynn, my dear father's friend," Lucian said formally, hurriedly, waving the letter sternly, "who gave you this?"

"He didn't say. I don't remember what he looked like; he was very ordinary."

"You must tell me if you remember. This pertains to Isaac I daresay, so I entrust you not to speak of it to anyone. We'll be in my room, and we mustn't be disturbed if possible. If it isn't, you must give us all the warning you can."

"Is there anything I can do to help?" she asked, biting her lip.

"Listen, I think it best you claim ignorance for the time being. It might not be wise to throw yourself into this. You can help by giving us peace. And the rest, you leave to me."

Me, Marcel repeated in his mind, taken aback. Was he planning on solving the situation himself? Certainly he was more likely to know a way out of the predicament, but so long as Marcel was here, he couldn't be expected to merely sit back and accept everything as duty. That was Lucian's absurd expectation, that everything here was his responsibility. He went now ahead of them with that very ideal dictating his stride, and even the way he pulled protectively at his surcoat and was as tall as could be.

"I warned him," Lucian muttered angrily. "I warned him not to meddle in this business, to not let that ghost from his past go on pushing him around 18 years later, but no, he couldn't stay away, even with the Watch Commander's order. I swear by the five, if this is a ransom demand..."

Marcel's eldest brother had nothing to say on that. Really, Lucian didn't know what he would do. Not go on raging, at least. His rage was what he threw about like a warhammer right now, but it wasn't at Isaac as most would discern. His face was weary, Marcel saw at the door of his room, ever searching for a peaceful restoration. Once inside, they split up: Marcel sitting on the bed, Tamzin sitting on a chair in the corner with one leg over the other and arms tight across her chest, and Lucian standing before the window, wearing an orange hue around him. Quite different from Marcel than even Isaac was he; nonetheless, a Brodie as his actions would currently attest, as would his hair comprising blonde and brown from Father and Mother both. As if to make up for that lost time gazing out on the plaza, he very suddenly turned on his heel and whipped another rolled-up sheet through a fitchet in his cloak, casting aside the band upon the bed, causing it to unravel itself.

Marcel found himself with hands on knees and neck outstretched, where before he'd been straight upright. Lucian scanned the page ruefully until, finally, he stared away from it, at a wall, though not at him or Tamzin, or not at first. Lucian frowned at Marcel and, through that, forced a brief smile before he scanned the page again. It couldn't be dreadful news, whatever it was, or Lucian would not be in so tolerant a mood.

"The alleged crime," Lucian started after clearing his throat and raising both eyebrows evocatively, "is spying with intent to compromise security, or steal information guarded by Mürathneè. The trial is underway. His danger may be greater than even that would make it appear. Destroy this letter; wait for word."

Respectfully he handed the letter to Marcel, thereupon stepping back, adjusting his clothes as if they moved to constrict him, and in the evening light that made to obscure him, he stroked his chin thoughtfully. The letter was as Lucian had read it, word for word, not accompanied with greeting or signature of any kind. Helplessly he turned it round in his hands, as if to make it reveal its secrets, before passing it on to Tamzin.

"At least it's not a ransom," she contributed weakly.

"At least," Lucian repeated. He paced, and his facial features strained as he thought. "Have you ever known there to be any vigilante groups operating in this city, Tamzin?"

"Uh, no. That wouldn't happen. They'd probably just join the mercenaries."

"As I thought," Lucian said grimly, though he sagged with some relief. He was probably right to feel so. Such people were the last thing they needed interfering. "I can't obey this stranger's demand and wait for word as the letter says. Its contents are no more helpful than a ransom letter would be. We've no reason to trust our mysterious assistant besides that. If I'm to free Isaac, I must do so through all the legal channels. We *cannot* sit around and wait for... this man's illicit activities to take effect, nor do I look for his permission to do so myself. The law is our ally."

"Man?" was all Marcel could say.

"Doesn't it look like a man's writing to you?"

"I suppose so," Tamzin agreed half-heartedly. "I wouldn't put money on it; if anything, it looks rather bland." She dropped the letter over the table to her side and watched as it drifted downward like a leaf without wind. "Allow me to draw whatever I can from my father; he likes to poke his nose in court business. There's a chance he'll know something."

"You really think that's a good idea?" Marcel said, dubious, astonished at her audacity alone.

"I won't be direct, Marcel; I'm not stupid. It makes sense to me. He's your brother and you're my friend, so I have a vested interest, you could say."

It mattered not when a rapping came at the door, and Marcel's soul was at once steeled for trouble. Lucian opened it to see that Rosalynn had been true to her word, for she was alone but glanced fleetingly out of sight to her left.

"Isaac's mercenary companion is here to see you; not with Isaac I'm sorry to say."

"Isaac is in a dungeon, though you needn't worry," Lucian said bitterly. "There's been a colossal mistake. What does Jamys want with us?"

"He came to see you about Isaac; wasn't specific."

"Captain Martello must teach obstinacy to all his men. Fine, send him in."

Rosalynn motioned with her hand and the mercenary swaggered in. He had the good grace to wait until bidden at least, but the air was made stale by his presence, degraded at his very entrance. There was an edge on proceedings, not abated by him slicing swiftly and silently through that thick air covered in plated mail, in about the same state of mild dirtiness as before, with a sword winking like a backstreet peddler after dark. No blood was to be seen, but there was some dried mud. He rolled his shoulders back as he leaned against a wall. When he noticed the stern looks he was getting, he laughed gruffly and put his hands up before folding them away from the immediate reach of his sword.

"Explain yourself, please," Lucian implored.

"If I was here because someone told me to be, do you really think I wouldn't just get on with what I was told? The palace has already arrested one Brodie on vague suspicions, they can do it again if they feel like it; don't need me to help arrest two random foreigners who probably can't fight back."

"Your logic holds up well enough for me," Lucian said, not totally open-armed about it. Well *enough* was the right sentiment. He paused as he went to continue and pivoted to Rosalynn – still with them and not of a mind to go. "It's best, for your sake, if you don't stay. This could get complicated. But I will update you, I promise, since my father's friendship demands it."

She smiled weakly, looking at all the faces before her, and finally curtseyed without demand. Lucian had not been overly rude, but was stern and a little discomforted. It's true that Rosalynn's investment was unusual, given how long ago she'd known his father. Then again, three of his children had shown up under her roof and acted familiarly with her, and now one had been arrested. If Lucian's worry was that she may have been driven by false obligation, then perhaps he should rethink. But she was gone now with a sense of disheartenment, taken with pride, and shut the door behind her. Though not before Tamzin glanced over at her as she'd done to him on the way here, and she returned that same sentiment with the same amount of words.

When the door shut, the mercenary made it a point to notice her, and was mildly surprised in recognising her as the duceveree's daughter. For a moment, he appeared ready to launch a barrage of questions; a moment that came to naught when he sniffed and focused, if he wasn't too casual for that word to be applicable, on Lucian, who'd taken his place in the sun once more.

"I would have come earlier, you know," Jamys said. "I did come earlier, rather. I was waylaid when I saw a man slip a note into your coat and I chose to follow him. I didn't go for long, mind; I lost him quickly and I don't even know if he noticed me."

"If it wasn't you, then who was it?" Marcel asked as agitation scratched him deeper, the mystery not solved after all.

"Not a clue. Did you find the note yet?"

"We found it alright," Lucian said. "It was no help whatsoever. A note from a stranger, telling us to wait for instructions. I have no intention of following his order, but I'll have to destroy it, that's for sure. Do you want to tell me what you're doing here?"

"To see what you knew about Isaac's arrest. I didn't even know about it until I got back from an amateur's mission on the edge of the city; didn't realise it was just to get me out of the way for a bit. Whether it was Martello's idea... well, I don't know, but someone thought I'd cause trouble if I was there with Isaac. Frankly, I'm flattered to be rated so highly."

"Was that assumption of you *correct*?"

"I fear so. Your brother was entertaining me greatly before he got his sun blocked out. For the very same reason, no doubt. I was with him a lot; I can't imagine what else it could have been. Seriously, I don't know how the bloody hell this happened; the Palace of the Sun makes mistakes like this when the tide comes in bright green."

"Go on," Lucian said. He wasn't of want for something to say, Marcel was sure, and that made him clam up also, but neither of the brothers were readily displaying it, he hoped.

"So I figure, if I've been insulted, I'd like an apology. I was quite looking forward to going on a wild goose chase across the ocean for Martello's ship."

"I'd ask for a little more respect than that," Marcel snapped at that. "My brother's not a fool, paying you to watch him do parlour tricks."

Jamys grunted and shrugged to yield to that. Tamzin smiled gingerly, but then her gaze wavered. No one was looking at anyone else; the mood had truly dried up. They had the help of one more man, him bringing no help or hope at all. Marcel swirled his tongue in his dry mouth and looked down at himself, white-robed and resplendent, for all the good it did. He was not entirely comfortable in his attire still and it showed, for his body frequently nudged and twisted, his resolve somewhere else entirely. Wisdom it did not reflect, though none should wear it that didn't have it. He would have to use Lucian as a crutch.

~

The sun rested its laurels on the sea and set it ablaze with forks like the arms of some great creature. Just with the grand tradition introduced the previous night, Isaac did not allow himself the privilege of staring too long. He wondered if this was the path to madness, not longingly looking out on that personification of freedom, as if he really had done something wrong. Thinking about falling to madness all day probably helped that decline, fairness be. So he tried to reminisce to pass the time. His memories would not come to the fore so easily, even now in his hour of utter need. Perhaps he should welcome the battle for the right to view them as an old friend, just as the actual memories.

A few weeks past, he'd streamed through a body of water that seemed to him no less endless than this, and he'd laughed with Marcel on the deck despite, or partially because, his bowels bobbed violently inside him. Then incorruptible, infallible Mürathneè had swept him up and, for a time, ridden him in a place high and mighty. Little wonder, he thought still of the waters, that this sea inspired such wonder when it was explored, to indeed find no end at all. His father had been enchanted in the same way, and he'd been a free man to let it inspire him at any point along the coast, so perhaps it wasn't half as strong a feeling for him as for Isaac locked up in a little box. Nor had he claimed any personal connection with the land beyond those billions of waves either, or deigned to throw in his lot with a volatile swordsman who was more than a little touched in the brain.

Isaac dropped from the bars and thudded heavily. The hanging was not so bad when he found a reasonable position and hooked his arms round the bars, but the landing shook him, shivering through him like a hundred pins tapped upon his flesh. The light that waned on sky and clouds would warm him enough now then. He was as stiff on the spot as his joints were, his jaw tightly clamped, light eyes fixed half open within sockets of a dirtied face. His clothes were the same way, though if nothing else, he was grateful of them, for even dirty they were exquisite and comforting. He'd worn them as his armour when he was free, now they were merely battle-scarred. He should have been more grateful of the water and fresh bread given in generous amounts, but his stomach whined for more. He put that away and, in his mind, placed himself on Lavellyrn's Channel like a chess piece, and rolled back time to his arrival in the red city, trotting through the threshold into a surreal new world with music in his heart. His father was at his side there. He was turning scrap wood into a ship right now, Isaac imagined, or dining with that lord in the castle whose special quality whispered to his soul, his mother working by the fire, while Kate sat on the stony shore or lay upon the tallest tor, by herself until she could admit she was a bit lonely.

The shutter scraped open. His eyes slammed to a close and he sighed, letting the cathartic thoughts flutter out into the open air. If he was to face his situation head on again, so be it.

"Dreaming of that other world?" the gaoler said. It was the rude one, not his amiable replacement.

"Find another way to entertain yourself; you'll find me very dry I'm afraid."

A key clanging in the keyhole was cause for his full attention, and he saw that the gaoler was being pushed aside, replaced by the same two Sun Guards who'd escorted him the previous morning. He gave as much politeness as was appropriate, being his only friends in this place along with Rayance, or as close as he would get.

"Isaac," Lord Holton said when he was on that white podium, being judged by the lords and whoever else was at the sidelines behind him. "You've had plenty of time to gather your thoughts peaceably, more so to you it must have felt than to any of us. Have you anything you'd like to say before we begin?"

"Thank you, Lord, but no, nothing new. I will answer your questions, given ample convenience to answer them."

"Honestly," Lord Hughly supplied as if it wasn't obvious. "Here's a riddle that's plagued us: where were your brothers when you went to meet Martello?"

"My brothers don't believe in my quest," Isaac laughed weakly. True enough, if not strictly correct. It couldn't be proven against him. "I wanted Martello to help me prove myself right, about what I saw as a child. They don't believe me; I intend to change that. I always have."

"It must have been quite something for them not to believe you. We've been doing some digging, as it happens, and we fully understand why you would choose to follow that path wherever it led you, if what we know is correct. It was brave of you to push yourself through the years with that burden, and braver to seek out the answers. Intuitive was the word that was thrown up, in spite of truth or fallacy. But you go too far. You should've been content to tough it out on your own, not consort with spies and the like in your greed to fast track the road to knowledge, which is long and arduous for those who play by the rules. We don't need your side of the story, as it happens. Our accounts cover that, and our witness testimonies connect it with what's going on here. Everyone in your audience has seen the evidence, Isaac."

"You imply a lack of certainty on my past, then pass your speculation off as fact?" Isaac spat, remembering in a flash of pain why he'd so hated him in so little time. "How can you truly... if I'm to be honest, I need you to..." He trailed off and composed himself. The man had blinded himself with lies; anger wasn't going to change that. He patted down his jacket, signalling a very obvious and intelligent change. His head was high and he lengthened the chord of silence for effect. "My Lord, have you my chosen defenders on call?"

"Sadly for you, no, though we considered it at length. The evidence is too overwhelming. How, if you'll humour me, will it help to bring in these three men when so many people will speak against you? There is no doubt in my mind that they could disprove a number of more petty observations we've made, but beyond that, you are flailing in deep water and cannot swim."

Fierce of Dark

"*My Lord*," Isaac argued, stressing both words in his fury. "How do you propose I answer that question when the very explicit purpose of summoning those men to my trial was to give evidence I cannot?!"

"I have no further questions, Lord Justice," Hughly answered, every bit as foolish as Martello, if not more so. How could Mürathneè strive so thoroughly, so utterly, when its forerunners were buffoons of the highest degree? "Lord Holton, proceed as planned, if you wish."

Lord Holton winced and stroked his fingers over his shining, pocked head, fingers apart as if tousling the hair that had long since left him. He touched his necklace with finger and thumb, and was hard and stubborn in the face, wavering now and then until at last he was bereft of his morsel of goodwill. The paper before him was his instrument of dread.

"Isaac Brodie, we can't know everything about you, or what you're doing, not from you at least. It's been concluded that to try would be folly, if not dangerous. We, all of us, have seen the incriminating evidence that would put our relationship with Burtal at risk, as your antagonism would yield if successful. We conclude you dangerous to the extreme, that a long trial would fulfil. In shortest form, on the morn two days from now, at 11 o'clock, you will hang by the neck until dead. Pray for your soul while you can."

Nothing could be heard in that hall, nothing but the void laughing. Isaac's ears rang in its grip, his eyes flickered open and shut as he recalled those words, searching the dead air for answers. He called for breath; already there was none, his throat starved for air like a man underwater, yet dry as bone. His cracked lips, like barren earth, in an instant flapped open.

"No," he spoke his fear quietly. The guards grabbed him at someone's order, he didn't care who; the gallows flashed before him, the noose around his neck. "No!" his voice cried, stinging the silence with terror. "You have to present me to the Emperor; this must be a treaty violation. The *Emperor*, my Lord, or anyone from Aurail... I call you a liar, Lord!" Isaac screamed desperately as the doors were flung open for him, his last chance ebbing away into the darkness, as his life did. The bastard sat below the eagle's head, uncompromising in his violent stupidity; embarrassed if anything. So Isaac went on, and on, and on, in his tirade that couldn't hurt him any deeper regardless. "You're a liar, Lord Hughly! Lord Hughly is a liar. The evidence is false and this trial's a fucking sham!"

The two guards he'd hoped to call friends tugged at him in his disarray, and he was out of the room of trial, being spun around to face away from it all, his last glimpse of the hall being Rayance in startled form following close behind, ordering for a gag that someone had refrained from bringing as a courtesy. Isaac called for help to any who'd heed him in these royal halls, but no hero came for him, and the tremendous carvings, and plating, and cloths of white, gold, and silver were at once tacky and hollow to him. One of the guards shut him up with a hand pressed over his mouth, thereby forcing that he breathe slowly and heavily out of the side. Then he was wrenched from the spot again.

The Voice of Kings

"Halt," a voice commanded, just like the last time he'd been whisked away to his cell, only this was not the ordinary voice of Rayance. He recognised it, booming and sharp in its assertiveness like the killer flick of a sword, not to mention hope's harbinger, or maybe that was Isaac's poor interpretation in his delirium. "We were walking through the palace nearby when suddenly we heard a fell shout. When it persisted, which is to say someone failed to make it cease, we had to investigate. I'd like an excuse, for the record at least, or a reason, if one exists."

Isaac was guided away, and with his cooperation this time, the guards were not rough with him. Back he went, and off into a much wider corridor that appeared to open out into a grand hall with a high ceiling, barred by King Michael at the head of his little entourage of nobles, bold and tall with a soldier's iron will, though he bore no weapon of any kind. His gaze shot from a face covered in half with short, black hair, a cause for godly thanks only for one in utter despair, Isaac's mind nudged him somewhere at the back, which he promptly ignored. One hand was relaxed on his hip and belt, embroidered velvet surcoat flowing under it to his ankles, his other hand disappearing beneath it behind his back. He looked ready for a portrait to be drawn of him. His storm knight flew up alongside him, just as ethereally calm as when he cut that baron's head off, abstaining from passing any and all judgement, only watching through blue pools. His right hand was reached across him to his sword, but he was so relaxed he surely didn't expect to use it. Feeling no immediate threat from him, Isaac's attention was drawn between him and the King, past the nobles, to Vicentei Laccona's contorted face.

He was wary, heart in his throat, and expressing a mix of surprise and horror. Isaac pleaded with his eyes, for what he didn't even know, to which the inventor considered with all seriousness presumably, but his face did not change in the slightest. Lord Hughly hurried between Isaac and the King, who immediately spoke verily of the situation.

"Lord Hughly, some mistake has been made here. I would know what it was."

"We didn't have a gag for him, Your Grace. It happened on my watch; I have no excuse."

"Is this the Burtalian prisoner? Not what one would expect of a man so accused. It's a reminder of how our senses can fool us, though I'd be interested to know which way this swings."

"Your Grace, I've been sentenced to death on a whim," Isaac said when the guard's hand relaxed at his mouth. "The trial's been a sham from the beginning, no attention to detail, no..."

Isaac was not feeling his best. He searched for the means to *eloquently* portray the injustice. The King listened carefully, his eyes slanted. And Lord Hughly had more to say.

"It was a carefully calculated decision, not close to a whim. I've already had one report sent to your office, and another will make its way there before his execution. He started raving with madness when Lord Holton read the sentence."

"That's a human reaction; you could never hope to control his emotions. Perhaps you shouldn't have done it here. As you, in fairness, admitted, a gag should have been on hand whether you expected to use it or not. Imagine if my daughter had been running about upstairs and heard that. No girl of that age should be subjected to that."

"I can only apologise. It won't happen again. If I dare risk to say, we didn't expect him to display such madness."

"Was he trialled as insane?" the King asked in sudden alarm, holding up a finger.

"He's not literally mad, that I can tell. I used the word lightly."

"That's what I thought you meant. I'm a King; I can't be too careful, not ever. I've read your first report, and I shall read it again, and study your second with a toothcomb."

The King inspected Isaac, so hard and fierce of gaze that it became painful to be at its mercy. Then it broke away like a taut rope being cut, and his hope was but a sliver again, based solely on King Michael hopefully noticing an appallingly written document, or Vicentei stealing a look himself and working his genius in ways too complex for Isaac to imagine. That was a comfort, of a sort, that his comprehension was too pathetic to anticipate what the inventor might do.

But shortly thereafter, he was alone again, in darkness again; complete darkness soon enough unless Refeer or the stars would grace him. He collapsed on the bed, too tired to weep, fading between worlds. Or maybe he did cry. Yes, at points he could feel it on his cheeks, and his pillow was wet. He didn't try to stop it.

Chapter Thirty-six: The Royal Tomb

"I'll kill him myself!"

He'd declared that more than once, at tremendous volume, and it might have shook the castle for all the power he'd delivered it with, and now it shook only him when he listened on it in hindsight. He was fearful, embarrassed, hateful, apologetic, and he wasn't quite sure where to place all of these emotions. He still remembered, clear as day, how his hands at Alycia's chest had taken on a mind of their own, tossed her hands aside and slammed a palm into her shoulder. It was not pain he'd caused, but his wife's majesty had shattered like brittle glass, and the worried scepticism, nay, fear, which came over her face like a storm was not something he'd taken pleasure in. Now she was at his side again without asking for apology, so he was infuriated beyond words, thus he bottled it up, didn't try to speak it. It was through the same tall hall, where he'd greeted his friend to Aurail not so long ago, that they passed as one deadly force, Richard and Alycia, surrounded by Guardians on high alert, and out they went into a day as forlorn as he, the sun struggling to be noticed through grey clouds.

To his far left, along the path between the castle and the wall of the castle compound, he heard many a sullen voice, as well they should be, then when he progressed through the garden, he saw better that guards were posted in a straight line, blocking the passage of a small crowd who wanted justice. The word must have been out across the city by now, and by tomorrow, any fallacy of rumour should have been quashed and all would know it as cold hard fact. In particular though, there was a man at the front of the crowd who he knew, quite ordinary save for looking very sprightly for his age, no doubt all to his own credit. Regret panged as he wished he knew what his late friend had been so fond of in that inventor. He had a feeling he was going to find out in swift course. Not now though, Richard scolded himself, forcing himself through to the chapel. He caught sight of the knights behind him as he turned, and Sir Yanick Berrhwrn most of all irritated him, now oddly contemplative since that historic scene in the throne room, yet still putting on that annoying smile occasionally. Richard could face away from him, but that scene's horror caught up to him again. Never did he try to outrun it.

"I'll stick a knife in his throat and watch him die!" he had screamed along with so much else he couldn't remember, parading about and raving. "And I'll have a thousand spectators watch him bleed and they'll jeer, and they'll sober and realise justice hasn't brought their lord back to life. That man will hang from a post at the very north coast, and when his corpse is picked clean and black with rot, it will be a shadow of what's to come for the rest of his kind."

The Royal Tomb

Some of it was probably nonsense, he reflected. After a time, when his adrenaline had wilted, his will to rage was rained on by sorrow; his raving had stopped and it dawned on him that he'd been shouting at the walls and the ceiling, for none had replied to any of it. But when that letter had been drawn up before him, he couldn't sign it soon enough. It was high in the sky on its rendezvous with destiny now, for which he gave prayers for its speedy arrival. Already it was too little, thus he brought himself before the doors of his chapel where the great lord's mortal body lay in eternal rest. He hesitated, with fingertips smoothing the bronze handles, as if half expecting to be confronted by Tristan's wraith. Then again, if that were to happen, he'd deserve all the scorn that Tristan would be too polite not to pile on him.

The doors swung with a dull, quiet creak and he was met with sobbing and sniffling from his left. His heart sank when he saw it was Evylyn, in mourning gown much the same as Alycia's, whom he'd not met on her arrival to the castle, as if his imperial majesty wasn't already in question enough. She teetered on the end of the back pew, eyes wild like a rabbit about to be gutted, before resuming her solemn service. He wished she would stop, for soon she would set him off. Richard patted her shoulder but did nothing else to comfort her. He was still figuring the particulars of that awful task. Instead, it was to the front row he went with only Alycia beside him, and he sat on the right side, fixated now on the marble sarcophagus resting upon a hollow stone plinth. The thought of Tristan in there churned his stomach, and it all came back to the machinations of Jacopo, whoever the hell he was. The bastard had ensured they couldn't even have his face exposed at his funeral, as any true noble should. He'd lost his mind and control of his tongue again when he was told how little of it there was left.

Alycia was not so approving of the choice of sarcophagus, the only one in the castle patterned with gold and silver engravings, though she was indeed respectful.

"It was admirable to give up your own coffin for your friend," she said, brushing against him as she sat to his immediate left.

"I don't need one of those things yet."

The flames mesmerised him, five strong, held aloft by candle stands carved in the shape of humans, or gods rather. Only at Alycia's touch was the connection snapped.

"Richard," she said. "We have to start thinking about how we're going to win justice for Burtal. We have to prepare for the possibility that this grievous wound won't heal by King Michael's hand. You know as well as I that countless pitfalls stand between us and justice. Michael may not be able to find this individual we seek, he may give asylum, he may have condoned his actions, or ordered them at worst."

"We'll find him."

"It was an acutely coordinated trap," she whipped up a fury, raising her voice in a way that made him jump. "I did all the research I could on this meeting; I had those I trust doing the same, and we were all played for fools. We're not dealing with a common assassin here. He had *help*."

"I'm sure he did," Richard scowled. "I'll do what I can to find him."

"That is not going to cut it and you know it. We'll work together and we'll be seen doing it. If diplomacy fails, we have to be braced for the storm that comes after, too."

"You can't be talking about this," Richard responded in disbelief. He was so tired from lack of sleep that everything in him had slowed save his heart, yet here he managed to frown to adequately shocked degree. "If we start a war with Mürathneè, we'll be pounded into oblivion; there won't be quarter given this time. They'll sweep across the country instating new lords in every major stronghold, and smashing the ones that resist."

"What if they want us to start it?" she whispered harshly in his ear. There was no fervour or twisted joy to be detected in her: things that would have fuelled his argument. He had nothing to say. "You must realise how many men are receiving military training for our little renaissance, and how many highly capable leaders we have. There are even those who can inspire and help who don't know how to fight. If it came down to it, Aurail is one of the greatest siege cities the world has ever known. Castle Türith might outmatch it, something that hasn't been tested you'll note, and if they want to flee all the way up there, well good, it'll mean we've been doing something right. If we play our cards right, Alassii won't arrive to their aid in time. So what happens if we refuse war? If Mürathneè wants it, they'll whip up a fabulous excuse to do so. I can't imagine why they would: that's the riddle."

"I can't let my people down," Richard mumbled as if this was the first time he'd been made aware of this. He rubbed his head in his hands and groaned. "Tristan's isn't the only death we need to avenge."

"Mm. We wanted House Wyman's attention, and we have it now. It couldn't have happened in a worse way. The same goes for Count Aldrich. You are the Emperor though; technically you don't have to answer to them."

"Technically."

Alycia smiled faintly, for that was what she'd hinted at, he saw when looking up, maintained perfectly as he couldn't hope to replicate. He didn't especially wish to know what she was thinking, considering what she'd told him so far, but her points were valid, as they too often were.

"I know you'll appease them," Alycia continued. "You won't exercise power to scare your own people. Burtal doesn't do that anymore; it's not how countries become great. Yes, like Mürathneè."

"Doesn't that involve *not* going to war?"

"Definitely. Preferably. It's early days yet, Your Majesty," she said sadly, yet encouragingly, as if some good could be taken from this. "We have a long journey ahead of us, I think. So to speak."

The Royal Tomb

She patted his knee and spirited herself away. With her presence removed, Evylyn became immediately apparent, sobbing at the back. How she could keep it up so consistently, with such energy in her sorrow, was beyond comprehension, but there it was, and there was nothing he could do about it. A tinny echo filling the chapel with grief: sobbing, sniffling, back to sobbing. *Gods, make it stop*, he begged.

But she deserved this just as much as he deserved his silent prayer, if he could even muster it, if not more so. Who the hell was he to complain Tristan's widow was mourning too loudly? The Emperor, yes, but it would take a monster like Jorin to issue a gag order. Richard turned, spreading one arm out over the pew's backrest, and gave the woman a pitying look. It was peculiar what thought came to him first, as it was of her dishevelled look, and how Tristan would be able see right through the tears and pained, reddened eyes, and call her the most precious beauty there was. She was quite beautiful to be sure, or usually, but Tristan had never stopped seeing her as a goddess.

"Evylyn," Richard called out, deep of voice because he wanted to sound strong enough to comfort her. Her crying subsided for now. "Your husband, my friend, will have a funeral service as soon as possible, and when that's done, there will be a procession through the streets of Aurail for all to show their appreciation. As I must do," he finished half to himself.

"Thank you," she sniffed, wiping her nose with a kerchief, and with that simple motion, an air of elegance came over her despite the sadness. "I'd like to be at the front if I can."

"You shall. Try as they might, no one will stop you, not with the amount of security I plan on bringing. What of Malcus?"

"Ah," she said sadly, head shaking profusely. "I can't speak for what he'll want, but I'll make him come whether he wants to or not. It would haunt me knowing he'd regret his absence later in life. As for right now, he refuses to leave his room, not even to see his father's coffin. He's frightened, I think; it's the finality of it."

"I know I was frightened," Richard answered to that, attempting to sound both wise and humble. For an Emperor to be afraid, of all things! "Tell him that, my Lady. No, I'd better speak to him myself."

"Thank you," she repeated, frowning momentarily.

It was likely she thought him a little queer to be so gentlemanly, and he wondered now what had given her that lasting impression, last they'd met. He considered this as he rose, stretching his aching limbs in the stale light projected upon him from the world outside. Like Tristan, she was impossibly optimistic, inspiring cynics like him to smile and revel in fantastical dreams, to rejoice at blank canvas before ever a drop of paint touched it. Much the same as Tristan, she would view him with a veil that prevented too much scrutiny to pass.

The Voice of Kings

Ignoring her for now, he went to the sarcophagus and put his hands upon its cold surface. Tristan was a contorted mess beneath it, the surgeons said, where a lead ball had been shot through him with incredible force: execution, they'd suggested, or some deadly new musket. His fingers twitched. Morbidly he wished to push the lid from the coffin, to have it crash like thunder to the floor, and in that boorish spontaneity, observe what had been wrought. He thought he would, his fingers were ready and he was tensed, but it was a farcical fantasy. He'd never sleep soundly again, and it was misleading besides, as that wasn't the true Lord Almaric in there; the true Tristan wore mirth and kindness on his face, and that was the one whose tribute would be paid by thousands. What a ridiculous fool he was, to consider it in front of Evylyn.

"What were his last words to you?" her echoic voice sang in monotone, though far more passionate it was at its source. Surprised at the question, he turned on his heel, to which response she rose sluggishly and made for the coffin.

"I don't remember," Richard answered, screwing up his face. His illness was returning, thus sacrificing his memory for its own longevity. "It was nothing so final, my Lady, nor did he say farewell or smile fondly as if he knew his time was nigh and he was to leave this world in dignity. Though that's what we'd all like to believe he did."

"He did," she rebuked simply, quietly, utterly resolved in her dismissal. "However, I'd be lying if I told myself it was a good way to die, because for that to hold sway in any form, no injustice could have been left in his wake. The best I can say is that he died the hero he always was, and his work was not finished, only because it never could be." She shrugged. A smile grew in reminiscence, her pale eyes distorted by still tears. "He took my heart in his hands and carried it everywhere. It was a weapon to him."

"Was it indeed?" Richard said in wonderment as it all came flooding back. He remembered now, so, so clearly, and he spoke as if in a daze. "I was with him the night before he died, Evylyn. We had a council meeting at dinner and it was all very dry, and it matters not half as much as what we were eating, I imagine, but I remember what your Tristan said to me afterwards. His thoughts were all for you, fittingly: he spoke of you as his equal, but lamented the world's different perspective, and I fed him some drivel about how he was overreacting, how I could click my fingers and you would be lady paramount of Burtal, and all the land would rejoice of your wisdom. I fear I have to tell you the same thing, but I'll... I don't know, I'll seek Alycia's help," he sighed, wincing, spluttering before regaining composure. "I promise you, my Lady, you will not fade into irrelevance."

Richard had his hand on her arm, clasping it tightly, though for all she noticed, it might have passed straight through her. She closed the gap between herself and the coffin in a flurry of black silk and black hair, so that, when she swung her head, the back spread out madly, like a raven's feathers: a creature of death spreading its wings. Her thin face, thin like her body, was remiss of his statement as if it no longer mattered, wanting to be optimistic, yet despairing all the same. Now she repeated his gesture, placing a hand flat on the stone.

"Did he tell you his last words to me?" she asked, contemplative.

"I don't believe so, my Lady."

To that she murmured softly, gave it more thought than it deserved, and kissed the sarcophagus at the point beneath which Tristan's head lay. For all the effort she'd expended to drag herself this far up the chapel, her courage now settled and her lips remained stuck to the stone. After a time, she sagged to her knees, and pressed her ear upon the coffin as if hoping to commune with Tristan's spirit. And there she knelt with eyes shut, so peaceful she could have been asleep, rendering Richard uncomfortable as nothing more than a spectator. Now made suddenly self-conscious, he felt his aches return and he coughed violently, suppressing it to his own detriment so as not to disturb Lady Evylyn, nearly choking on his own phlegm. He collapsed back into a pew, clutching his throat and clearing it with a single cough. There he sat, there he agonised, there he plotted, there he dreamed of taking victory against his enemies on horseback with his countrymen at his beck. His eyelids fell shut like hammers on anvils. The injustice, the grind to reach its gods-directed resolution, it physically hurt him, fumed across his chest like wildfire. The Emperor let it fester.

~

"Beautiful," Lady Lovett observed of the flowers flooding the castle courtyard, with delight bordering on tone-deaf.

How right, Lennord kept to himself. The great and the good outdid their peers in showing reverence, laying brighter and livelier displays by the hour, so that there was a whole new garden sprouting from the stone.

When Lennord Brodie watched the sullen procession of the imperial couple netted in a cobweb of bodyguards, over shoulders of spear-keen soldiers, he knew terror was soon to be unleashed on a scale that would dwarf the battle on the Eye of Sand. Or that was what his gut told him in his misery. He'd no experience with politics, as he'd made clear, and war less so, and he had no intention of letting anyone change that now.

"What do we do now?" Kester said not for the first time, for he was nervous, and needed an answer more than he wanted one.

A good young man. He had a fair head on his shoulders, if a little unstable at times, now being a fine example of that. Lennord wondered if he'd even been worried by the prospect of his vocation seeing a tumble into the ether, whether it had crossed his mind at all that was to say, or if it really came down to an admirable devotion to the father of his friends. But Kimbra Lovett was at his side, so that devotion might stretch on without cause, roping in a cluster of men and women with no stance in proceedings, not just for him but for so many others in so many places. He decided to believe in her good spirit, because despite her rash, inappropriate donning of a stunning green dress when Kester called her out without describing the occasion, she'd vehemently stuck by his side. And believing in people had served Tristan like magic, until the very last time.

"*We* don't have to do anything," Lennord explained, scratching his chin. "I have a connection to Lord Almaric; I have to stay close to proceedings. You'd do well to keep well away from me until the Emperor declares his justice before his city, for your own safety and for Kimbra."

"What would you have me do?" Kester responded meekly, shrugging.

"Keep your head down. Work. Find some inspiration, you and your friend. As for me, I shall bid my sons return and do what I can here in the meantime, then I'll resign myself to Caedor for a while, if I may. I want my family to be one again. I want to sit about the fire in winter and talk of Lord Tristan's life, to heal myself of his death."

"I'll stay with you, if it please," stubbornly oblivious Kester insisted. He rubbed one arm defensively, and his attention darted to Kimbra.

"My father is a knight. If there's trouble ahead, he'll come for me. Besides, I've nowhere else to go right now, and I would sooner witness this executioner's demise than hear its song. If your loyalty lies here, then so does mine."

Lennord's disturbed frown was short-lived.

"Are you three in the middle of something important?" a feminine voice of high nobility posed. "I hope not to interrupt."

Lennord found himself bowing before he'd even completed his pivot, as the Empress's voice was one of the most distinctive he'd ever heard. It perked the ears and took your attention, whether you would give it or not. All in black, she nodded sombrely, as did her greying knight, whoever he was, vaguely familiar to Lennord. The knight searched for something in Lennord that could not be known.

But it was between only the Empress and him that the conversation took place, for the small crowd behind gave a wide berth, and the nine soldiers blocking the way from wall to wall were stricter in their duty than ever.

"Your Majesty, you have my condolences," Lennord said.

"That's very humble of you," the Empress laughed. "He was your friend too, so you may have my condolences if that means anything to you. As his friend, people will be looking to you now for advice."

Because you've told them to? It was a cynical observation, yes, only he was rightfully afraid of her meaning and so he could be no other way. Disputing this before its time would only be a show of his hand, so he was content to let her go on and discover it for herself. There was no way to overrule her anyway.

"You're a smart man," she said to voice her high expectations, "tell me what the situation is at Lameeri's Wish."

The Royal Tomb

"Diverse, Your Majesty. I won't claim to speak as the voice of those men, but I've noticed some have taken their work more seriously, to the point of fanaticism if I dare accuse, while others are just confused or trying to not be influenced. There's a buzz in the air, I can say that much, and I don't like it."

"It sounds like these men are preparing for war," she laughed sourly. "We have to put a stop to that, don't we? Image matters more than you may credit it for, you'll consider. Don't allow a levy to be organised, whatever you do; that will pin the nail in the coffin as far as they're concerned. It's the last proof they need that war is coming, and we don't want them to be proven right, even if they're still wrong. Rumour carries on the wind, and rumour has an annoying tendency of becoming fact of its own accord, nay? If war occurs, it won't be our fault."

Not our fault, Lennord wondered, *but she doesn't deny Burtal would start it*. She was a smart woman, so naturally he had to wonder about the deliberation of that choice of words. Or all of them, for that matter.

"You know I don't have that kind of power," Lennord replied.

"Respect is its own power. Tristan knew that. Do what you can with what you have. I eagerly await the results."

"This is inappropriate," Lennord defended, biding his time be damned. "I know what you'd have me do, and you won't get what you want out of it, Majesty. I can't give you a magic trick and lead those men."

"I sympathise, believe me," she responded straight from the heart, hitting him hard in the chest with that surprise. "I understand better than most, so perhaps that makes us friends, in a way?" She pivoted and scanned the garden sadly for a second or two before returning to him. "Gods bless you."

"And you, Majesty."

He bowed low to avoid eye contact, and didn't rise until her black-cloaked visage had been whisked from sight, her knight rattling quietly beside her. Kester patted his arm nervously.

"What do we do now?"

"*You* shall wait and hope this all goes away; I shall do as I'm commanded."

So he would. And he'd pray for orders that suited him. But his sons would not be left in Mürathneè.

Chapter Thirty-seven: The Blood Dance

Leon watched from the King's balcony until the King himself appeared from his bedchamber in his livery of various shades of royal blue and green, twin surcoats black on the outside and heavy purple within, and an understated silver and ruby ring on his right hand. Even his short beard had been combed, for all the good it did. Most wouldn't notice, but there it was, the effort that never died. Predictably, he wore no cloak that could drag along the ground, his hatred still too strong for the wretched things that he wouldn't so have servants scurry along behind him to make him look so pompous unless it was worthwhile in some other obscure ceremonial manner.

"I shall see you there," the King said.

That was all that was needed, there being an understanding between them. *Long may it endure*, Leon mused, for endurance it would ever need. Received by more bodyguards, the King left Sir Leon to his watch. None who passed escaped his gaze, those from beyond Harth who were milling and joining with friends from separate chambers elsewhere in the palace, and others who were just now entering the palace gates, all flinching and looking up when they caught a glimpse of evening sunlight skimming off his armour. It was quaintly cathartic knowing he was still the inimitable figure of peace and justice. He didn't even have to do anything. All the while, they were objects of his study, and like shooting at a loophole, they couldn't hope to see him doing it. He never expected to notice anything out of the ordinary, yet it was worthwhile, he felt in his bones, for if everything he'd seen and heard was any indication, the next few days would be peculiar to say the least.

The great hemisphere braziers cupped golden flames that lapped up at the air like serpents' tongues around the Kingsreach hill and alongside all three paths leading up it. They glistened in his eyes for a few moments, then he swirled away to join his King.

King Michael was in the antechamber behind the throne room, as expected, further enhancing his presentation before a gold-framed mirror taller than he. With his Queen Helen at his side, he stood before it, rocking his head from side to side until an attendant brought two crowns: Helen's band embedded with pearls, and his more decorative piece that sucked in all light and spat it out as a rainbow. The years had strengthened their bonds so now they looked an extension of themselves when sat around the head. If the King was at all anxious, it was because he wished to see his brother, to which Leon sympathised with on this occasion. A second servant marched through the back door of that cosy little room, slightly perplexed.

"Your Grace, Laryc Morzall is here after all."

"Morzall," the King grunted, rolling his eyes. "Cunt..."

"You'll be politer than that once we're out there," Helen said curtly.

The Blood Dance

"Obviously," he replied, running a hand lightly over her dress. "But if he's here, he wants something."

"Not money," Sir Leon speculated.

Leon smiled wryly at the King, who nodded in agreement without altering his expression. That was all the consideration Michael was going to give, hell if he was going to let that man hold him up. He interlinked his left arm with Helen's and indicated for Sir Leon to fall in. The throne room was so alive on the other side of the door; the volume of merriment from lords and their retainers communing at dinner was a fine accompaniment for their entrance. So in they went without any fretting, and all fell silent but for the scraping of chairs as they rose; three hundred of them spread over four long tables, two on either side of the throne room, leaving the centre free for dancing later, and for men and women to make entrances and exits where they could be well seen. Though there was one door on either side, it was the double doors at the back that would be used by the guests, for they lead directly into the plaza fronting the palace. Two rugs, more decorative than usual, had been unfurled at the double doors and before the King's table, leaving the central passageway free to shine its crystal blue, with the dying light from outside streaming through the eight gaunt windows, just the same as candlelight, drawing towards that marvel embedded in the floor: a great strip, soft blue yet regal also, and shimmering lightly, not so different from the awesome silver glass structures of Dormalii.

Leon smiled mildly as he strolled behind King and Queen, arms peaceably crossed at his back, well away from his sword. Overall he was but an imposing and apparently attractive supplement to those figures marching ahead, waving around the room at specific individuals, not just to the room at large, as Leon had advised on his first year as royal bodyguard when he saw how no one was paying as much attention as they should to Michael's general gestures. It wasn't smart of him, he maintained, just an observation more easily made by someone not currently playing up being the most important person in the country. Right now he tried to continue that job as observer, noting specific individuals and their moods if they were close enough. There was the newly appointed Baron of House Behnirham at one close end of a table, whose father Leon had prayed for after he'd taken his head. At least the crowd had been respectful. He couldn't abide barbarity in spectators; they weren't even a bloody jury, and all present that day had remembered that, knowing Leon would dismiss them like children if they misbehaved. Sir Leon nodded to the young baron, who returned the greeting amiably. One suspected he may have been vaguely aware of his father's transgressions and was unhappy with them.

After a drawn-out period, the King and Queen stood behind their table, situated at the foot of the dais where the thrones sat, and the King indicated all to be seated, then cleared his throat. His gaze passed over those three hundred men and women broken in two by

The Voice of Kings

that representation of the sea in the hall's centre, and the golden clouds embossed high above, high and golden like a mysterious bird surviving the old world.

"My friends," the King began, voice carrying dramatically across the hall, "and those I wish to be my friends. I always fear to be redundant giving such speeches at our annual gathering, but my Queen advises me not to fear so long as it is truth and not formality. She is right of course, and so again I am grateful to rely on the counsel of others to depose any desires to misuse my powers. And so again I will give the same greeting, because it remains true. You are most welcome in my hall, for you've all earned the right, and as we further approach the five days of enlightenment, I hope to see your own examples of noble spirituality. We all strive to make Mürathneè worthy of eternal remembrance here in Harth. Just recently we brought the genius Vicentei Laccona under our wing, and may soon sail that infinite sea. In such men we will believe, not rumour."

He surprised some with that statement, but put up a hand as if to apologise for any insult caused. His gaze wavered then fixed on his stern brother nearby, as he already planned to dispel those rumours entirely. High Duke Dorrin subtly raised an eyebrow and, in doing so, became a little more unsettling: a simple gesture that materialised almost as a challenge. Michael deliberated silently.

"Enough of that," the King said. "Tonight we shall reacquaint ourselves with one another, and tomorrow begin talks. Music!" he called loudly after a pause, inputting a certain little vocal flourish.

The lute players, flute players, and drummers came forth, near unnoticed amongst all the royalty at the hall's edge, and they strummed and sang with their instruments in an upbeat manner, quaint and quiet yet reaching every ear as if riding currents within the throne room. The King hesitated in giving a new order though it was plainly on his mind, for with his tongue in his cheek, his glare was fixed on the minstrels. Whatever was on his mind, he let it drop and sat himself at the centre of his table facing his many subjects, Helen at his right, and beyond her, sweet, young Natierlia being decidedly ladylike and thoroughly enjoying it as usual. To her right were two cousins, and then to the King's left, four seats were left empty as was a modern custom so he could invite people to sit with him when he desired. And, of course, Sir Leon stood behind King and Queen, the highest man in the room at that time.

"Sir Leon Barrotti," inquisitive Princess Natierlia started already, hands in her lap as she turned. "You won't take a seat, even for a meal?"

"I've already eaten, dear Princess," Leon replied mildly. "I'll eat whatever scraps are left at the end if it please you."

"You jest, I think," the bright young thing giggled.

"I'm sure he wants to be left to his watch," the Queen chided her.

The Blood Dance

"Not at all," Sir Leon replied with a tiny bow. "Let the young lady sharpen her mind, and we may amuse ourselves by it."

"Thank you, Sir," she went on more cautiously, embarrassed at her mother's comment. She stared at the ceiling as she thought. "Must you stand watch when we already have guards around the room?"

"It's not danger I'm watching for, you'll be pleased to hear," Leon replied with a smile, slight but warm. "I want to see who's talking with whom and who they're avoiding, though of course that shouldn't happen because we're reasonable people here. Suffice it to say, it's a fine way of getting an overview of proceedings, especially if I compare to last year. Well, if I can remember."

He smiled softly again and winked, and she seemed to find his answer acceptable, as she nodded approvingly. From there he stood in silence as he was designated to do, and calmly eyed the men and women at the four tables, knowing full well, and it was not arrogance to think so, that his eyes were soft and unimposing when he demanded them be so, giving nothing away. Even the servants he watched, marching in and out, aspiring to be ghosts, making themselves as seamless accessories of the hall as could be, and he measured the attention spans of the other guards too. At the end of one table, all the guild heads were collected, still turning heads as not all were lords. All, to correct, but Jacart. Leon understood there had been a bet in the Sun Guard common over whether he would show or not, which made for uncomfortable listening as it made Leon believe he'd missed something. The music went on, quaint and merry.

"Minstrels," the King called. "Something new, something with more pace."

He flung a kingly arm upwards enthusiastically to illustrate his meaning. So they played with vigour, louder, quicker: quick and joyous enough to dance to. Michael nodded, chin cupped in a huge hand, biding his time for something, and like a flower in summer, Natierlia grew bright and happy when the room was alive with such music. From Leon, she drew fascination again.

"I hear you dance, Sir," the Princess said.

"My dance is not fit for splendid halls. It's not a real tarantella, and if that's what you've heard, you've been sadly misinformed."

"No, a real dance," she insisted, surprising him with her manner of dismissing his ambiguity that suggested she knew of what blood dance he referenced. "I've heard you dance, like a noble knight should."

"I'll admit I've been known to dance. When I dance publicly, I dance well, but I've not done so for a few years now." He contemplated this, trying to remember the exact date of his last public dance, betraying something fussy and compulsive to himself, and so gave up quickly. But he thought he knew the time and place all too well. "I'm sure it would greatly amuse you to see me faltering a tarantella in front of everyone, but I have to weigh that against the desire to not acquire a new derogatory title alongside my nice clean ones."

"I must refresh your memory," she laughed, finding ample humour in every word. "No?"

"He's far too tall, sweet," the Queen sighed, "whatever you might like. Go to Sallrhys or Eduard; I'm sure your uncle would permit a dance."

"Please do," the King interjected. "And have your uncle come see me, that's a good girl."

The Princess skipped across the throne room, clasping a masque that no one could have asked her to wear; she must have had her mother commission its forging explicitly for her, not by her father's permission who would likely have dismissed it in an instant. He did nothing to stop her now if nothing else, as she twisted and turned between the few people who'd taken to dancing already, wearing their own masques that obscured their eyes, flaunting the colours of their House. One danced with the House, not the person, in such functions as these, in theory at least. It certainly made for an interesting show. Leon looked forward to having his men influence the dancers later with a little subtle persuasion. They were going to find themselves dancing before a House masque not in their graces, whether they liked it or not. In the meantime, Natierlia waved her Santorellian masque around her waist, speaking with the young Lady Sallrhys and Eduard, both of whom were about her age. Finally, Sallrhys came out with her, for seven-year-old Eduard was likely not so excited by the idea. Natierlia, of course, would prefer a knight, but she also probably wished for Leon or her beloved brother to swagger to rescue her from a tower of evil soldiers, who presumably, in her fantasy, didn't spray arterial fluids or have names; a memorable jape. Better that than seeing his sword dance, Leon conceded.

The King snapped at his attention when he rose to meet his brother, rather than wait as he otherwise would, reuniting with the High Duke at the table's end where they firmly wrapped their fingers and thumbs around each other's arms, staring each other in the eyes as if duelling with minds before embracing. Dorrin patted him hard on the back and withdrew, immensely casual, inhibiting the staunch, soldierly persona that had become so ingrained in him. He was so very like his brother in many ways. They sported near identical beards, though Dorrin wore it on a long face, and he was lean yet somehow stronger than Michael. And unlike Michael, tight black robes akin to a toga of high quality were swathed over his more decorative attire, enough for it to be admired, yet expressing something very different as a sum of the parts, the Santorellian way. Not to mention his black boots that were more for riding than royal functions... For all of it, he was the High Duke; he looked the High Duke.

"Your Grace," he said.

"Brother."

The Blood Dance

Leon closed in on the duo, close enough to catch every word they spoke, an act which did not go unnoticed by the King, who didn't care.

"You should have asked for me sooner," Dorrin humbly pointed out. "Lady Amelia was worried by your avoidance, as she wondered of it, thinking perhaps you'd been disturbed by something."

"Nothing of the sort. I'll apologise to her myself shortly."

"No Walter tonight?" Dorrin changed the subject, noting the Prince's distinct lack of presence at the table.

"He's playing regent up at Castle Türith," the King said reprovingly.

"Oh?" Dorrin answered grimly. "How does one *play* at regent?"

"By overspending, whoring, and drinking oneself half to death while his name is writ on a deed. I hope to see him matured next we meet, but his letters insinuate it's made him vainer. I'll see to that," King Michael added as if there was ever any doubt.

The King's posture changed subtly, and he looked out on the courtiers, engaging in conversation across every table, and dancing between them in the middle.

"Your letter," the King spoke without attempt to ease into the conversion. "We need to discuss it."

"We do." Dorrin breathed deeply as he gathered his thoughts. "I didn't dare articulate my experiences in full in the letter in case I ever gave the wrong impression, and I tell you, it's especially important I don't. I've seen some peculiar things."

The High Duke looked somewhat tired. He explained his story of which rumour was the demon, of the flames that had sent every last speck of dust from men's bodies into the afterlife, of fending off creatures from the wilds, and of crows that waited for death on dry leafless branches.

"They haunt me," Dorrin said. "When I see a raven now, I wonder if it's following me."

"You can't be serious," the King replied fiercely, refusing to inject humour to lighten the mood. "Ravens do not spy on people. If they did, who would they do it for?"

The High Duke plainly put stock into this question, which again surprised the King. Gods, obviously, Leon mused with little conviction.

"It wasn't an isolated incident, Michael. I heard of it again, in my duchy but further west this time: birds from the treetops that eyed a man being killed by a sabre cat."

"The black fire?"

"None apparently," Dorrin admitted. "It had no mouth from which to breathe, you might surmise."

"I will surmise nothing," the King said flatly, his voice grating somewhat, though only because the magnitude of his brother's claims was sinking in now. Dorrin didn't lie. "What did you do with the carcasses?"

The Voice of Kings

"I brought a couple with me, and had them studied day and night until the hair and feathers moulted away. The skin was black and men could smell them from a hundred paces upwind, then I burned it all off and have carried the scorched bones with me ever since. I don't know for why. All we found was evidence that the chupacabra had devoured men before us, and the crow we took was well fed. I should throw those bones into the sea for the tide to take them far away," the High Duke added darkly.

"I'm to believe there was no evidence of their madness anywhere about them?"

"None that we could find. If there was anything, it was beyond our understanding, just as this whole grim affair is. I dare not say it's magic before anyone but you and your storm knight for fear of how it might be taken, but the truth is, I believe it. Everyone knows gods' magic isn't the only sorcery this world has seen."

Dorrin's eyes were wide and shot a chilling glance at Michael that he meant no ill will by, and was not taken as such, but he was serious as he ever was. Leon was tempted to label this as fear, yet it was so difficult to tell as the High Duke had never let that demon persuade him to alter his course, no matter how monstrous.

"We will keep the bones," the King declared firmly, utterly unflinching. "Cursed or not, I'll risk their wrath soundly enough. The day suspicion clouds my judgement so thickly that I cower before a creature's blackened remains is the day I hope someone will rip this crown from my head and melt it down."

Dorrin made a noise halfway between a growl and a murmur, nodding his head in gladly relenting to his King's demand. A moment's thought garnered new words that were never spoken, as Dorrin allowed them to be stolen by a bird's cry from outside, that of golden wings, not black. And such a call would go unnoticed on any other day, in any other conversation. He took longer still to compose himself, unembarrassed by the extreme caution he exercised. He sniffed with a heavy nasal sound and tried again. The eagle's screech sounded clear and melancholy, riding the air as it always did, like a stone skimming water. Then it was a chorus. They sang in unison, a dozen noble birds letting out but a single beautiful note each that stretched on like a sigh of relief across the sea and up to the stars. Beautiful and dreadful. Where, before, Leon's hand was relaxed at his side, now it was on Waithrydn's hilt. Others in the throne room were startled to be sure: an odd fancy for them to discuss offhandedly when it had faded away, while Sir Leon watched the windows with prejudice as if expecting the glass to shatter before creatures robbed of their self-preservation. The brothers Santorellian were cloaked in an eerie presence that stalled them dead, and the knight wondered if they were in touch with something indescribable, theirs alone to dread.

Leon relinquished his hilt's touch for the sake of everyone in that hall who might fear trouble ahead, and so speculate on and on until it was out of hand. The King turned sternly, though not tensely, to his brother who was of the same frame of mind, at once accusing in his manner as if to say *you've brought it with you*, and indifferent in knowing it couldn't have been helped.

"There's nothing we can do," the High Duke said after a while.

"So we wait. We'll do it without incident."

"Your Grace," the Duke then said slowly as a light dawned on him, none too pleased by its brightness. "The people who died in the cave were miners sent from Harth at the behest of the court, so the locals said."

The King's serious face screwed up, revealing all he needed to by that, eyes containing fury as he searched for the answers. *I don't remember doing that* was the sentiment, and his brother growled beneath his breath in disappointment and dread.

"I'll wait for you at my seat."

"I'll meet you there soon. Good to see you Dorrin," Michael added earnestly, and Dorrin actually smiled.

The High Duke had to shake Leon's hand which came as no shock, knowing what great esteem he was held in by the Lord of Valicato, for what he knew of him, what he'd seen of him, and what he believed of him, which may or may not have been strictly true. All the same, Leon bowed. Michael brooded as an onlooker to the frivolities unfolding everywhere except where he stood. With arms folded, he turned and perched on the table's edge.

"What do you think, Leon?"

"Mürathneèan eagles don't do that," Leon answered honestly.

That was all, that was enough. The King wouldn't push for rampant speculation. As if nothing had happened, the King summoned for the duceveree who, tonight, had refrained from wearing his robes, instead opting for something more practical and of less pomp even if it retained many of the same motifs. Michael wouldn't share the previous conversation with him, Leon assumed, nay, knew.

"Your Grace," the old man flattered him.

"Eminence. You have something you'd like to discuss, I gather, so don't be coy, come out with it."

"I've heard some disturbing rumours, my King. If dark magic is being practised, I should be present when it's put down..."

"How does this involve me?"

"I require license for my Astuciants to perform exorcisms. If rooms could be set aside in some of the guild halls for emergencies, it would ease our minds. If you could speak with Commander Leonardus..."

The King guided the duceveree away, perhaps because he needed a walk and nothing more. It didn't matter now. Leon was by himself; he was the storm sheathed in calm summer clouds that stood to strike down traitors without warning. He stood his watch, and he watched all: the guests, the Watchmen, the servants. Only most of them went without standing out in the wrong way. The northern lords tried to keep to themselves, even the ones who he'd presumed knew each other little, entrenching themselves in the myths of being sad, being *otherly*. The lowly Marneffes stuck as a unit, representatives of Prince Walter from Türith who never wanted to be caught alone to handle accusations of the braggart's misconduct. Amidst it all, Holton and Hughly did the rounds: Holton becoming more unprofessional the more he drank, Hughly currently lecturing the rudderless Baron Behnirham inappropriately and growing exasperated. Ultimately, this was all the norm. It was overwhelming now, per usual. Hopefully it would make sense later.

But, there was one servant who'd been scurrying around all evening thus far, waiting at the sides, disappearing for periods of time seemingly without cause, and so the process repeated. His nervousness spoke to Leon; it was like a knife in his heart. Through his sadness, he steeled himself; outwardly he was no different for it. A conspiracy was afoot in the palace of kings, that much he knew, and already he was doing his part to find its roots. Now he may have a chance to put a torch to them, he thought, expressionless but for a slight pleasant smile.

~

Lucian breathed deeply. The night was cool and still. Golden pyres crackled behind him that he must have been illuminated in full for the Watchmen on the palace fence walkways to see, not that he cared, for tonight he was an ambassador. It was probable he'd end the night with an act tantamount to treason, or so the corrupt folk who would hang Isaac for gull food would say, but until then he was Lucian of the law.

"You should go now," Lucian told Marcel. "Taking you this far was risk enough; you don't need to put yourself in any more danger."

"I'll put myself in as much danger as I need to," Marcel protested. Lucian was proud of him, even if it was all words. He looked cold despite the mild weather.

"You can't offer any more!" Lucian snapped. "Only one person need do this."

"What of our mystery helper? Will you search for him at least?"

"I wouldn't know where to start, Marcel; I wouldn't have a clue," and Lucian sighed. "Clearly our man has intimate knowledge of the palace, but how are we to know if he's even present tonight?"

"Or she."

His brother's persistence surprised him still. His logic was sound enough, Lucian supposed for the sake of open-mindedness. Stranger things had already happened, and would indeed happen soon.

"I'd ask you to leave the city, you know, take your horse and gallop east through the night, only that would not be... politically sound." Lucian winced. "I don't suppose it would do you any favours where impartiality is concerned, running away. Just stay at the cathedral then, and you'll be protected. In fact, I think it's best you do it now."

The Blood Dance

His youngest brother looked ridiculously young in that bright gold light. Vulnerable: that was the word he was really looking for. He was more sensible than bloody Isaac at least; his initiative would get him far if Lucian didn't return for him. It was a pessimistic thought, pessimistic but necessary, for it bred caution. Lucian was the one to initiate an embrace on that fateful night, under dim cover of stars and blankets of cloud, and Refeer that was a half-disc, pale silver, scarred red and blue. It was awkward for Lucian, who was never tactile enough, on heavy reflection, for one who claimed keenness in politics, for one who hoped to appeal his good nature to others, and lead and draw attention.

"Go on, go," he said. "I'll see you when I see you, I suppose."

He shrugged. There was nothing else to say without being depressing. Marcel said his farewell, and beyond the pyres ever gold and bright on Sèhvorian jewels, he at last vanished into darkness at the foot of Kingsreach. Lucian was fixed as if helpless until even his brother's shape was swallowed up and reality pressed down on him. *Where the blackness ends, the light will blind you,* he recalled from the letter, and for the thousandth time it all came back to him.

"I'm here to see the King," Lucian said to a guard at the gate.

"Oh?" the guard answered sceptically. "I've heard nothing about him giving audience to citizens tonight."

"He wouldn't at this hour, besides," another put in.

"I have no appointment with him, but he'll see me if you tell him trade ambassador Lucian Brodie is at his gate for reasons I shouldn't discuss here, and he'll be decidedly displeased if you neglect to inform him until tomorrow morning. And I, meanwhile, will have credited the displeasure of my father's friend Lord Tristan Almaric."

"Well played," the first guard said as if suspecting a lie but not willing to risk ignoring it, yet bored at the same time. "You'd best be telling the truth, I tell you."

A guard on the walkway was sent away, and a few minutes later he returned to collect Lucian. The palace was a beacon on that night, and across the plaza from the throne room that glowed through the tall windows, he heard echoes of conversation, of mirth that failed to uplift him, and music not so different from the foreign tunes played in Caedor from time to time. He put that out of his mind as he was searched for weapons so that all he could think of when he was marched through those double doors was the execution of the next stage. The great hall was packed with people dancing, drinking, and loitering around the tables, overall creating the quintessential atmosphere of high society at its very warmest. He was moody in the midst of it all, frowning and glaring as a mother does to shame a disobedient child, then in a second he turned pale as he spotted Laryc Morzall making himself extremely well known amongst the guests. There were few people he wished to see less at present.

The Voice of Kings

"You threaten to offset the mood of my party," the King chided him, revealing himself suddenly with royal tunic clapping around his ankles as he marched toward Lucian, gleaming crown set upon him. The King's face softened and, in doing so, only then seemed to focus on him: strangely vexed at their meeting, but reasonable from there. "However, I understand your passion, for I know why you've come. You can't be blamed for the timing of this."

Lucian bowed, sidestepping around the King as he did so to block any eye contact from the duceveree̊.

"Your Grace, I must urgently request you stall your investigation into my brother's activities until it can be done properly, with defenders from my country and lords to entreat with."

"Rather forceful for a foreign commoner," the King noted, raising an eyebrow. Lucian said nothing. Again the King's face softened as he ceased to care.

"I stand as an ambassador of Caedor, Your Grace, so yes, I've learned to be forceful. I mean no disrespect by it, and I shall alter my tone if you wish it."

"You're not an ambassador, you're a glorified messenger. Yes, Mister Brodie, word gets around quickly in Harth."

"So I'm learning," Lucian muttered. "I am a politician nevertheless."

"I thought you said you were an ambassador? That would make you a diplomat."

"Begging pardon, Your Grace?"

"Politics is about preserving the day from the march of the future; diplomacy is stopping the future from regressing to the past. Only a King can do both. You might observe that nuance when you presume to meddle in royal affairs.

"Listen, I sympathise with your plight, as it happens," the King admitted. "I partly agree with you. The trial was not done to our standards: it was amateurish, embarrassing, a damn mess!" he said angrily. "The witnesses were not brought in to attest, so in the end I had to speak with them myself, me of all people, as if I'm not busy enough! I have some words to share with those lords. Though..."

He looked grim, so Lucian prepared himself for the inevitable punch to the gut, preparing to switch faces.

"Have you been told your brother is to be executed tomorrow?"

"No!" Lucian lied, feigning abject shock that drew more than a little unwanted attention. "He's guilty of no crimes, none; my brother wouldn't hurt a fly."

"But for all the misdemeanours of the trial, the evidence is overwhelming. I see no alternative. I must conclude that he is a spy."

"That, Your Grace, is not possible," Lucian growled. "If it were, wouldn't it be more prudent to ransom him to Burtal? Just let me talk to him, and then with your lords at my leisure, and I will bring you the proof you need."

"Do it," the King said immediately, strong of resolve. "Bring me a shred of proof as to his innocence and I give you my royal word that no execution will take place tomorrow morning. If you cannot, then I commend my prayers, for all deserve to be judged by gods on their own terms when this world has crumbled to dust around them."

The King clicked his fingers and ordered a servant to bring him paper, on which he wrote a short note, signing it and stamping it with his seal, which would allow access to the dungeons and ambassadorial immunity to return to the throne room on his own terms. It was a bold gesture, assuming he was not in league with Isaac, and so the evidence that had apparently been arranged, forged, and bought must have been specific indeed, and very convincing such that only Isaac was implicated. That marked all but the end of Lucian's opportunities for a peaceful resolution, he concluded glumly. Someone was forcing their hand from the shadows, thus the frame of whatever legal means he might try for would be shattered at the base from out of sight.

He was bid good luck in earnest by King Michael, and was led away by the servant to his left. He checked his pace as another familiar face came into view, standing out gaunt and proud along with everyone else, that of Lord Dorrin, and like last time, he had no idea whether to be pleased, guarded, or terrified. The High Duke caught him staring and recognition came instantly, whereby he cocked his head back and his brow furrowed. Lucian saw no more of him, the throne room left behind. He could always appeal for his help on his return by the sliver of hope that he'd developed some sort of positive bond with the royal lord. It wasn't to be trusted, nothing was, not even common sense, or so the world would have him believe presently. The possibility that Isaac's folly might itself be deception indeed... it didn't bear consideration, surely. His brother was not mad, just unpredictable and lacking focus, all but for this bloody affair that should have been buried and was thought to have been. *And there is the crux I suppose*, Lucian thought, angry in his confusion, that it possessed his brother and was real enough for men to wish his death for it.

Well, that was beyond his helping. He was the eldest son and he would act it. If anyone ever doubted his love for Isaac, they would be proven wrong to see him now, himself included. There were worse ways to do it, and better ways to die than the punishment of failure.

~

Isaac's stomach growled at him; it rumbled so hard it hurt. It was more like a creature trying to devour him from the inside out actually. His food plate was empty, still. He actually took stock of that fact as if he hadn't been aware of it for hours. They'd promised him food and none had ever arrived. He laughed at that: a cackle, it sounded to him. On the morrow, his neck would be snapped before a crowd, a respectful one if he was lucky, or if they were told to be, or however the hell it worked here. So in the face of that, his desire to live was stronger than ever. He would have clawed at the bars if he'd thought it would help.

The Voice of Kings

All of a sudden, voices. Quiet, then loud. He leapt from his bed, agape. He blinked furiously in disbelief and strained to hear. Gods be praised, he thought, he wasn't mad! Never had he been more pleased to hear the iron hinges scrape together.

"Lucian! You're here for me?" Isaac asked.

His brother's mouth opened then shut again, for he never expected to see Isaac so raggedy and poorly. Lucian was pained at the sight, and it warmed his heart.

"Don't get excited, I haven't had your reprieve authorised just yet. I came to assure you help is on the way. No need to thank me. Do it when you're breathing fresh air and the sun warms your face."

"How can you do it before tomorrow?" Isaac said in amazement. "It feels like everyone's baying for my blood."

The cur of a gaoler scowled silently, as if he actually had an argument with which to refute that statement, but he went ignored by Isaac. Lucian, however, was completely mindful of him.

"Whatever happens, Isaac, whatever doubt you may have in me, just remember what our House has accomplished in the past. Remember our words." Here he grabbed Isaac's sleeve and spoke slowly and clearly, and Isaac followed his lead just a few words behind: "Where the blackness ends, the light may blind us; when madness begets that stone becomes wood and wood becomes steel; when fear rings out from the heart, we will remember our blood of the hills, that we don't die like normal men."

"What the hell does that mean?" the gaoler enquired, screwing his face up so hard he might have been preparing to vomit.

"It's our words," Isaac said. "An ancestor wrote them, a poet."

"What do they *mean*?"

"They remind us, in times of plight, that we've had it at least as bad as this before. When you understand that someone else from your family has been in the same pain as you, it can help to work through it. I wouldn't expect you to comprehend its context; that's why they're the words of House Brodie, not whatever shithole you come from."

"Keep talking," the gaoler growled.

Isaac coughed as he tried to reply, nearly throwing up whatever contents of his stomach remained. It burnt him like demon fire, so hot his eyes were just shy of watering again. That was good, he laughed inwardly. Hopefully. It gave more credibility to his lie, and substance to the distraction from the nonsense of it all, that and the insult. Just as well, he consoled his paranoia, just as well. The lie was poorly delivered.

"Forgive him," Lucian intervened. "He's not his normal self, as you can imagine. I'll be back soon," he then told Isaac, huffing as if wounded in the chest, his tongue writhing in his closed mouth as if he'd been physically sick.

The Blood Dance

Lucian left, Isaac stayed. Isaac paced and shut away despair, for though it tempted him, he had more to be hopeful about now than ever before in this dingy little hole in the ground. It was also frustrating; the words of the riddle rolled silently off his tongue as he mouthed them while every distant strumming of an instrument or loud voice from the King's party hammered in his ears. The hatch had been left open because the gaoler had turned suspicious in his boredom. As he was so sad a person, it occurred to Isaac that all his taunts were the bidding of that. Isaac dared not finger the hatch closed personally, for fear of fuelling his suspicion.

"Where's my supper?" Isaac asked, giving the gaoler something else to balk at.

"How should I know?" He frowned. "Don't look at me like that."

"Would you mind closing the hatch then?" Isaac said to him. "My head aches and you don't really want to listen to my groans."

"I could make them stop," the gaoler said casually.

"Do you fancy explaining to Sir Leon Barrotti how you failed to restrain a half-starved, unarmed prisoner?"

The hatch was slammed shut. It rang like sword on sword and Isaac waited, very still, for it to die down. Then he fretted over a riddle that might save or damn him, and at length he realised he was no longer deciphering its meaning as his brother intended it, but allowing himself to be swept away by the hidden gears churning dead air behind it. How would Lucian have organised such a thing? A thing. Such an empty word. He breathed deeply, concentrated, lost concentration, concentrated.

After time uncounted, the shutter slid open, so distracting that, angrily, Isaac spun and prepared to chide the man however his tongue dictated. The face was different: it belonged to his other keeper who was as kindly as could be, considering the circumstances.

"Has Marckon told you of Rayance's order?" the gaoler said, speaking of his impetuous shift replacement.

"He's told me nothing that doesn't amuse him."

The new gaoler winced.

"The execution method has been alleviated from hanging to beheading. The long drop setup devised for you was deliberately not enough to snap a man's neck, so you'd be in pain for a while. Beheading gives you a clean death, easy as going to sleep."

"Though most people wake up eventually." Isaac produced a wan smile, wan like the moonlight that shone around him. "Thank you all the same, however I won't be losing my life tomorrow."

Now he had to convince himself that was true.

~

Truth brought Leon hither and thither through the palace, but he was yet to catch up, unsuited as he was to social stealth. Conceptually, his role was the absolute opposite, so to

The Voice of Kings

avoid being noticed by the servant, he rarely kept him in sight, instead following his trail by way of asking of him from anyone else he met. Whenever the knight did spy him from across a hall's length, the servant did nothing to quell his doubts, with behaviour both erratic and suspicious. Rayance and inimitable Cadro would have the throne room under control, so thought of a protracted absence didn't bother him, and at least it was to the east of the palace, not so very far from the King's party, chance had it. He'd half expected the man to leave the building entirely, but he never did, nor did he ascend any stairs. Where he did go was not comforting, though neither was Leon fazed by the idea of following through the door before him, into one of the armouries.

It was at a corridor's end, intersecting with another corridor that ran off to his left, where a second door led to another part of the armoury, where the weapons were mostly kept, while ahead of him was a hall of mostly paperwork. He would go through there then, not because he had a plan, but because it was nearest and he anticipated ending this charade in twenty seconds flat, excluding escorting him below ground for questioning. He strolled through the door, muscles twitching of their own accord, preparing to become lightning at the first sign of a poorly conceived attempt to take his life. What he found was puzzling, little else. The wide-open space originally made for wooden weapon practice, floored with shined stones, was indeed open and spacious; moonlight crept in from the east and candles flickered quietly all about. To his left, it was also quiet save for gloved fingers flicking through paper and men browsing a small collection of swords. Five men, there were, all pretending to mind their own business, for he'd seen them all flinch in exact unison, some more than others. Some had been here longer than others, he assessed, looking over their faces. They'd all been here a while, he judged, two of them more than a year, all but the Watchman who brooded over a desk facing the open space, looking bored by the papers before him. He was a Watchman of the city, not of the palace, and Leon had no way of knowing from memory alone how long he'd been employed in that job.

"Sir," the Watchman said gruffly, about 30 years old.

It was clever of them, and that was what worried Leon. They'd picked a good night for it; the description of "it" about to be unveiled, because hundreds of important people needed protecting elsewhere. Guards would walk by this room but likely not think to check it.

"This is an unusual sight," Sir Leon said, of pure calm.

"Unusual how?" the Watchman asked sharply.

Leon nodded to the servant he'd followed.

"You were assigned to tend to the needs of the lords and ladies at our King's gathering. Yet I find you here."

"I was relieved, Sir."

"As I saw it, you were not."

"Begging your pardon Sir, but allow me to explain."

"In a moment you shall have your time. You, I would enquire to you," he said pleasantly to the Watchman. "What are you doing?"

"Reading requisition orders. It helps some men to have a view of the bigger picture, my captain says, so here I am, reading about what's become of our new weapons."

"You have a perfectly serviceable one at your belt," Sir Leon pointed out. "What business do these men have?" he went on without leaving time for a reply.

"I employed their services, though I confess I didn't check with any lord for their availability. If any man is here out of insolence or has disobeyed direct orders, take him at your leisure; I had no part in any of it."

Leon said nothing, merely strolled to the desk, holding a sad smile in place as he scanned it. He knew he stood out as a symbol of poetic violence to them, and if he left them to their imagination, they wouldn't dare test its limits. He went to sift through the documents, then paused, checking the Watchman for signs of stupidity, before pushing the papers aside, beneath which there were more like it, only they were definitely not requisitions. They would be nothing of revelation or of shocking nature, but the man had lied, obviously, because a Watchman and four servants don't mill around the armoury at night when no one's about.

"I think it best you come with me," Sir Leon said flatly. "I trust my decision to come alone was not in error," he tried, hoping they would betray an inkling that they might yet escape.

He put up a hand in protest to their defences. He would hear them later, when they were in separate rooms, and when he had someone like Vicentei Laccona with him to interpret every blink and inflection like numbers on parchment, if he was as ingenious at deciphering people as he was at crafting and planning. They assembled before him, the storm knight of Kingsreach, without fuss, five breaking before the implied might of one. The Watchman was first, passing downtrodden at his left to wait by the door while his accomplices followed a short way off. They were stupid for coming here, for there was nothing incriminating or valuable here, only paperwork as boring as it looked. And the Watchman, sadly, was the stupidest of them all. He was quick, that man, yet not so quick that a head start to his hilt favoured him victory. His blade was naked at Leon's left and so was Waithrydn: perfection bolted from its scabbard in the manner of his namesake. Sir Leon skidded back an inch or two, ducking and canting to the right to strike hard on his opponent's sword, slicing a clean chunk from it. *Gods below, this blade is sharp. Best ease up; we can avoid a massacre.* His left greave skidded fast at the Watchman's right boot, knocking him a fraction off balance, at which juncture, Leon pushed forward, sliding Waithrydn along his enemy's blade, and in the manner of his martial skills, used that man's own strength against him as it came, allowing the opposing sword to reach forward. Then he skipped around to his right, feet barely leaving the ground, drawing both their swords round in a high arc. Waithrydn's white glow scraped sharp and swift at the guard of the hilt, and so the Watchman flailed at his very mercy until, when that enemy sword was low in the arc, Leon flicked his own sword down and cracked its pommel upon the Watchman's knuckles.

The storm knight flicked his greave forward again, and this time went deep against the man's left foot, pushing back, and tripped him flat onto his back. Only then were the four other swords drawn into the light, and by that he measured how quick he'd really been, and suddenly hapless servants became something entirely different. They were four, he was one, but they were unarmoured, and thunder would rattle the nerves from them. Still, they didn't seem unacquainted with swords, for their postures were adept, and they fanned out to pincer him. He sprinted, faster than ever he could in other armour, as did they in the hope to surround him, as if he hadn't trained specifically for that circumstance. Feigning a high strike on the first man, he instead ducked, still moving onward, spinning as he did so and sweeping the man clean off his feet. A sword came down on his red head, but he never lost his orientation; his left arm was already scything through the air and a clang sounded as the vambrace hit its flat side. Still he was oriented. That was the key to fighting with such blinding speed; instinctively he saw in his mind's eye his very self, fighting on the battlefield with all its nuances, to calculate his spins as he kept his momentum. Sir Leon rose from his sweeping manoeuvre, face clear and peaceful, his hair like fire, and like a viper, his arm was intertwined with his opponent's, and his hand locked the nerves at the elbow joint: a technique that might have been magic for how little he knew of its working. Leon's new puppet bent double at his whim, sword clattering at his feet.

And Waithrydn played a high-pitched tune on the steel of his two standing opponents, whizzing back and forth, forcing them nearer with each twist; once, twice, thrice, and on the fourth strike, slipped like a bee sting, slashing one of their wrists open like butter. To the rising man at his left, Leon flung his captive puppet, meeting pommel on skull as he did so, and lunged for the man before him. Again the knight's speed was too great, as Sèhvorian steel sliced the flesh at his waist and Leon tripped the servant up, flinging him over his back into a flash of armour: the Watchman who'd rejoined the fray. The Watchman found the knight bearing before him, and he, too, clutched his sword hand as his wrist sprayed blood.

One was left, and Leon made to incapacitate him just the same as he stumbled to his feet: the servant from the throne room, by happenstance. His balance was knocked out at the feet, and he slipped on blood as Leon spun his sword up, cutting deep into his back, rending through flesh right the way up to the neck. Then there was a shower, and white became red. He was twitching on the floor, and Leon stood with a pained expression, for he knew the man was dead. Just as he'd hoped to believe the mythology surrounding him, of being able to refrain from killing any man in battle, there it happened to the contrary. So many things could happen, all he could do was control himself; a promise he could not make for any who dared to challenge him.

The knight just stood there, staring at the twitching man, listening to the moans of the other four, though looked oblivious to them. When palace guards rushed to his aid, perhaps 20 or 30 seconds from the time the Watchman had drawn steel, Leon did not move, almost as if he hadn't noticed their arrival.

"Fetch the King," Sir Leon ordered. "Rayance can stay in the throne room; I'll concern him with this later."

So the King came at his request, hurrying with a look of burden on his serious face. He slowed, of course, when he saw the carnage, and sighed wearily. Others were with him, seemingly hoping for spectacle. Leon was leaning against a wall, letting the blood trickle down his sword, for he knew how easy to clean it would be. He watched apothecaries tend to the wounded. His face gave nothing away, he hoped.

"He left them alive, you see," the King declared triumphantly. "Gods be praised for that. We need them to talk."

"He's not alive," Sir Leon answered, nodding to the servant who he'd decided not to touch. It was voiced as disappointment, and even he was surprised, because to believe the rumours was beyond folly.

"It happens," the King said. "Not very often in your case. What happened?"

"They were infiltrators, I'd hazard. Spies. I already suspected trouble afoot."

There was a conspiracy afoot, he meant, and he would root it out.

Chapter Thirty-eight: Stone, Wood, and Steel

The morn came pale through the blackness. Isaac was aware of this by way of being awake when it came, not bursting with energy but kept from sleep by a perpetual dread, until at last, fear alone could not hold true against weariness and he was sucked into a deep slumber, or so he thought. It was hard to tell, lying in a daze repeating the same words over and over again. Over, and over, and over. It didn't matter how many times he did it; meaning was not forthcoming. At some point, he noticed the sun was brighter from his bunk, and assumed he'd drifted into sleep, wasting valuable time. Sleep yielded wisdom deconstructed from trials of the day before, that was true enough he'd felt in the past, only now his mind was blank. At first he jolted upright as if all was lost, as he frantically tried to remember the words that had seemingly slipped from him forever. Then they returned without fanfare, foreboding, unhelpful.

So whatever happened, he would be blinded by light and presented with stone, wood, and steel, and fear would be in his very heart. He had food at least, to stop him collapsing; double the amount to make up for its absence the previous night, with ham beside his bread which he scoffed down just slow enough not to choke himself to death. Despite the generosity, his thoughts were still morbid. People had a tendency to shit themselves upon death, he recalled, so him being given so much food made precious little sense for any sensible gaoler. Sensible or loyal.

He wasn't going to die, that was the line he drew, so he contented himself with food and water, and when the door creaked open, he rose willingly, already dead around the eyes as it felt, black like the stains spotted across his clothes, but he made no fuss, which only meant it probably hadn't sunk in yet. No matter, for now he would pretend to be noble, and perhaps it was realer now that he had no aid from his attire, and he would pretend to retain the intelligence of his former self too. The gaoler Marckon took him by the arm, and yanked him away to shatter any semblance of dignified flow to his movements, flanked by two guards of the palace. Left he was taken this time, along that corridor that would lead somewhere new. Ominous in its dull light, never did it end, until almost as a shock, it did, round a bend and up a flight of stairs into the blinding light of the sun. It was warm on him, and the wind was cool. The stone was white and beautiful.

Where the blackness ends, the light may blind us. It did, though Isaac searched for his next task to no avail. He was within the palace grounds, emerging, blinking, beside the outer wall that overlooked the sea. Once he was there, then he was at its front, as if he'd been taken to sleep, or the gods were hasty in snatching him away before his time. There, waiting, was a monstrous crowd that sang a roar of murmurs like the first time he'd been here, eerie as the shadows of his nightmares. In a way, he wished they would scream at him, but then, to have his final seconds to think stolen by a rabble had no appeal either.

"This is not appealing," Isaac muttered to himself, trying to keep from despair.

The gaoler shot him a hateful glance, saying nothing. Isaac would have laughed that, finally, he had nothing to say, though on reflection, he'd never been talkative, just quietly aggravated. But now, at last, he was brought through the plaza where men and women stared mutedly between open gates. Ghostlike he passed through the crowd, instinctively bunching up and tensing as a thousand faces drifted by, all hard and perplexed. It was such that the open air at its finish was a blessing he whispered praises for, where steps guided him to his place of death. Starkly, to his left, from the arch upon whose great face shone its clock's hands, there tolled a bong for the first strike of 11. Isaac, on the stone platform, dirtied blonde hair and regal clothes fluttering slightly in the salty wind, stared with eyes pulsing hard, over a crowd of hundreds that waited nonchalantly for his head to roll. Looking up, bell still droning, he saw, upon the arch, golden light in the shapes of men stalking back and forth as they did all around, among them the man Isaac deduced to be Rayance, unless his blinded eyes deceived him. So he was blinded again, and no vision was carried in the hue.

His heart skipped a beat. There was a platform extended from this one of cold stone, that of wood that had been wheeled out for him and left there. A wooden pole craned up and speared the sun, bereft of the rope that gave it its purpose. *Stone, wood,* he shouted at himself within his head. Now all he needed was...

The bell tolled again, beyond his counting. He winced. It hurt.

All he needed was steel. His twisted gut took no heart at this news for it knew now that Lucian had arranged no safe passage from this place. The tolling ceased, and wind rattled the banners around him in replacement as a man stepped forth and read from a scroll the horrors of his crimes to a public who didn't even know. A burly man was donned in a black cowl in the corner of his left eye: a little demon. In his right eye, three armoured men wore suns upon their breastplates, two watching him like a hawk while the last looked far off into the distance, into the south of the city.

"Your last words," he heard a man say. "Do you have any last words?"

Isaac nodded, the man stepped back, and the executioner let the axe slide between his fingers from its ready position so that its wooden base cracked on stone. Isaac paused; he gawped at the man, as he otherwise wouldn't dream of doing. He hadn't imagined it: the man was shaking, his eyes bloodshot. Isaac breathed. He made to be at the front of the stage, his feet aching in his boots but keeping him proud and tall, or as tall as he could be.

"The charges..." he began quietly, phlegm catching in his throat. He was angry at himself for this, the slightest fault of speaking poorly to the hundreds who judged him. "The charges," he threw his voice out to stream across the Kingsreach arena, "are entirely false. I

The Voice of Kings

shall deny all of them for the scandalous lies they are, and I thank each and every one of you for listening to my true confession. You will forget me, of that I've no doubt, then one fateful day you will be made to remember. Whether you care or not, I cannot say, and will not think to judge, but you will remember, because that particular day will be the day that lords of the Palace of the Sun are proven guilty of corruption."

The words stopped coming. For a moment he heard their aftershocks ripple. At their death, he was truly speechless. There was only so much nonsense he could repurpose as brave nobility, even if in a way he pined for them to come true. *Better they don't forget me at all,* he thought on reflection, though he dared not flaunt the possibility of his escape. But when he cleared this throat to delay the execution further, he was stalled by white robes flapping elegantly at the rear of the crowd, atop the winding path that ran down to the farms: fair green farms that men toiled even as he stood here. He shook himself from the stupor. His brother was going to watch him die.

Marcel was not going to watch him die. Nor Lucian, though he was nowhere to be seen.

"To the gods, I pray for protection," Isaac carried on, waving the executioner away as he edged forward, to the wood that bore no steel. "Not for my alleged sins, but for all those I've committed over the years and not atoned for, trivial as they may be."

"Stop wasting time!" a brash yell came from the audience.

"Shut your mouth," a guard shouted back at him, and crossbowmen on the walkway behind the fence trained their sights on the general area of its source. "When you are standing on that stage, you'll be free to say as you like."

That time of diverted attention was valuable: time Isaac did not waste. He scanned the wooden platform as he edged ever onward, but nothing shined or winked at him, with only the lever given to tactile feedback. He gawped at it. He shrugged. He was going to die if he didn't resist. Risking a more horrific end was a trifling matter to him now. So he lifted one foot to walk forward and dug its point into the stone. His balance was destroyed, and like an age-old statue having taken a beating from one wind too many, he toppled, half expecting to shatter as he smashed down upon the wood: wood that came to greet him like a lightning bolt, giving the desired effect of surprise despite the planning behind it, and though instinctively he drew his head to one side, he couldn't stop it colliding with the solid boards that rattled as his head did. Indeed, he wasn't so sure he hadn't shattered upon impact, his bruised innards writhing again. A shadow swept over him bearing a sharp, curved blade. Its flat edge was frozen malice seeping through his clothes, shuddering against his back. The executioner's free hand drove hard upon his elbow, to grab him and tear him back to the stage, back to the block, fingers jittering and teeth chattering, shames to which the man would not admit.

"No," Isaac snapped. "I would keep my pride, if you please. You needn't go to lengths for the comfort of your victims. Your job is far simpler than that."

Stone, Wood and Steel

The executioner backed off, affording him a second chance. Isaac crawled, as if more pained than he really was, at eye level with the crowd. It was too much; he looked away, just staggering to his feet, clasping the smooth lever as his balance aid, for more aid than that he prayed, and down flung the hatch. And there flung something else from the other side, underneath: a hinged board of wood that presented him a sword as if by magic: a god's gift to a warrior king. He was on his chest again, hilt firm in his right hand, rolling now to his feet, to a wave of gasps echoing out around him. He found a slew of swords breathing bright into the open air, and a flurry of shining plate metal charging his way from left and right. There the first blood was shed, not by his hand, but by that of a traitor, and just the same way, gasps rippled outwards, seemingly forever. The Sun Guard who'd so pensively stared into the distance was red with the blood of a friend, face hard and fearless. The slaughtered guard had turned his back, and from the back of his neck, a river ran red to stain his white death bed. Before the other could rightly respond, his fate was matched in kind, this one pushed into the crowd of spectators.

Screams punctuated the air such as had nary been heard on this hill since before it was the home of kings. Mindless terror supplanted the enforced calm for reign of the hill, the screams grew louder and more numerous. Chaos erupted on all sides. The unarmed populace ran one way, Watchmen and palace guards another, fighting against the surf of panicking men and women, beating people aside to close in on the stage with all haste. People tumbled around them and rippled in their wake, halberds bobbing like the fins of some curious sea monsters streaking towards their prey. But they were not his concern, not yet. The executioner lunged with his axe, Isaac skipping back just out of reach. Already his mysterious ally was engaged in combat with another soldier, this one of the City Watch, who was at the bottom of the steps when the fear had taken hold of everyone, and so escaped the stampede that way.

So Isaac was alone with the executioner, who he danced around to avoid the deadly aims of the crossbowmen that he was all too aware of, quarrels taut against the strings of their devices, waiting for the opportune time to be unleashed. The axe shrieked, cutting down clumsily. The executioner was dragged along after it, merely its wielder, not its master. Isaac jumped from the blow, knuckles white with sword in hand that begged to steal the man's life, while the rest of Isaac decried its bloodlust. The battle rush came to him like an old enemy, blood pumping through him, but there was no joy, only dread at what he would do. He swung his sword, meeting the axe's haft head on, embedding it in the wood. He wrenched it free and the same happened again. His bones shuddered at the impact, but it was nothing to him right now. He flinched. He saw the executioner's eyes, the raw fierceness they possessed despite his waning energy. Surely only a soldier could withstand staring down an opponent in battle.

The Voice of Kings

With that, Isaac was driven back, but he was quicker than the dazed man and came back, knocking the axe down for a moment, and driving his sword to wherever it took him. Its course was straight and bloody. It was stuck in the man's shoulder as if his very body was repelling it. Isaac was in a daze now. His attention shifted back and forth: one moment he'd be deadly focused, the next anything and everything would distract him. The golden dome of the great palace glared him; the soldiers on the ramparts surrounding it just the same. Isaac bellowed from his gut, for why he didn't know, his muscles freezing as he thought to drive his sword through the shoulder, instead heaving it free, almost tripping as he did so. And the madness went on, ever spiralling into absurdity. A dagger was drawn in the crowd, seemingly by a random spectator; its blade was in a Watchman's throat. The perpetrator had darted away. Two more men tried the same elsewhere, and suddenly in a great whirlwind, everyone around the Watchmen dived low as halberds were drawn to sweep all about, and again and again, prodding and beating people far away as their owners screamed for cooperation.

A hoard of soldiers poured from the palace gates as one impenetrable entity, fearsome as the elites they very much were, spears and pollaxes drawn back as if on springs, ready to snap and stab at anyone who so much as mildly disturbed them. And there outside the palace grounds, they came to a halt.

"Close the gates!" one man ordered from the walkway, neither quivering nor hesitating. "Close them and remain steadfast. Trust me to do the rest."

It was Rayance indeed. Isaac ignored him so much as that was possible. Two men charged up the steps at him: one a palace guard brandishing a halberd, the other a familiar man in dull padding, unadorned save for an eagle sigil emblazoned on one upper corner, and his name was Marckon, an unruly gaoler who most assuredly wanted to see him bleed. Isaac, keeping up a constant movement to avoid crossbowmen who might deem him too dangerous, beat down on the halberd that prodded him, while in the same way, the traitor, if he was ever a palace guard at all that was, fended off Marckon defensively. Of the four, none took any chances. All the while, dozens of soldiers swarmed like hounds, and they would pick Isaac Brodie clean, his time running out. His ally, in desperation, lunged at Marckon, who countered without conviction, for in the end he was a prison guard, not a warrior, it seemed. His snarl turned sour, and for his trouble, his throat was slit, though it wasn't so deep that blood sprayed like a fountain, and so he passed with jaunted stagger from sight, falling from the stage with hands over mouth. Isaac's ally, as he was for now, was stung upon the cheek at the same time, and like a rod of lighting, the halberd of Isaac's foe struck him across the face.

Isaac's blood was cold. He knew he would lose a fight, and wished only to be free of eye contact with the man who would end him. At his feet, the executioner crawled away. That was comforting. Perhaps it was twisted of him to think so, but his mind was so wrought with the instinct of survival, the essence of violence that wanted to break free to make it so, that he had no idea. But suddenly it was of no concern to Isaac. Isaac turned; Isaac fled, just as he was expected to. Wood then pounded underfoot, and he leapt from the stage and ran faster than he or any other man had run before, so it felt. Several men around him did the same as they saw him make his escape, including no less than two Sun Guards who sought to get a shot in on the real guards as they turned tail and sprinted for safety. They were his now, perhaps, to do as he willed with. Probably not.

He didn't bother to follow the winding path, instead bounding down the steep slope, almost tripping and slipping more than once, but to conform to the path would be to lie down and die. His blood pumped ferociously now, so energetically it might have burst from him there and then, and for every second he continued his sprint, that felt like it should have been physically impossible. A bell rang from behind; it wouldn't have bothered him anymore, but he discerned it as different from that which tolled his execution. Stark it was, painfully high-pitched that it echoed in waves that stung his ears. And oh how it rang, furious, without stopping: a warning signal that all were to know and fear. Soon after, a nearby bell tower played the same agonising tune, then another far away, and so it went on until the air was thick with the awful sound. All who ran alongside him seemed to wince at its sting. So loud was it that he could scarcely hear his boots beating on stone, but his heart, that he heard loudest of all. That and the gargled splutter that expended the last of his phlegm.

Beside him ran one of the men who'd helped him: a lean, haggard man with long hair, dressed in civilian clothing. With him, Isaac thought to stick close, as a mother and baby, against his better judgement. The man's head span round, alarmed, gawping at him like he was mad.

"Get away from me," the man growled in frustration, shoving him away.

There was no time to think on the particulars of this bizarre behaviour, nor the energy to spare for it. He just carried on past the farms, along the straight and narrow road, on the assumption that his body could work forever, dropping his sword to beat his arms faster. Harth loomed beyond: all white structures of the most excellent workmanship and efficient roadways, intricate archways and bright flags fluttering in the sea breeze, and countless towers that played the dreadful music. Sometimes it was clearer than ever; other times it was a blur through eyes straining as he struggled for consciousness. The city was upon him, the shadows engulfed him, but still it was too light, and the breeze cast no blessing as he made for the tightest road he could find. Men, women and children already scattered before the terrified mob. Two smartly dressed men were on horses draped with finery, which were snorting and panicking in the commotion, as Isaac heard before he witnessed with his own eyes when he darted from one road randomly into another. One collided with a market stall,

The Voice of Kings

and the proud beast nearly fell, but galloped away haphazardly with its rider clinging on, very pale.

Swords clattered not so far behind him, combatants he could only speculate on at this time of confusion. Still he was running with no idea as to a destination, the city being ill and nondescript to him now. A bluish-green cloak that must have been trodden on, and as such ripped from its wearer in the commotion, lay sorry upon the paved road. Sorry no longer, Isaac stooped and whipped the sheet of clothing from its resting place, to swathe himself in it with such fervour as if it would make him vanish from the world. So one blessing was taken gladly while a curse hit him hard, for the break in stride had wounded him, the pain he'd ignored catching up to him so that he couldn't so much as jog to safety. The mob had dispersed, the blood-driven energy passed, the fatigue digging its claws in. All that was left was for the truth to be uncovered and scrutinised. That at least was good. Probably. Isaac slinked away into what he could scarcely call an alleyway. He was lucky even to find a road so thin that only three people could walk abreast in it in these parts, because some king or other, who'd long since died, had decided that such small compartments in his city attracted criminals in the darkest recesses of the night, as moths are drawn to flames, and all kings since then had been taken by the logic.

He collapsed against a wall and gazed slack-jawed up at the puffy clouds drifting merrily across a bright blue sky. His chest heaved, his clouded mind not making it easy to assemble a plan of action. If he could only do that, he might yet escape the city with his brothers. That was the key, he decided. To motivate himself. If he could get out of the city, he could get to the highway; if he could reach the highway, he could get to The Wolf's Way, and from there sail the channel to sweet home. No doubt Marcel would rise to the occasion and eventually cast off his lamentations for what could have been, and Lucian would be actually personable. And when he arrived at Caedor, he would tousle his sister's hair till it was merely a big, scruffy mess, like a dog that's just shaken itself dry after a rainstorm. His parents would be pleased too; he would be remiss to forget them. Of course it would be a marvellous heart-warming reunion, but first he had to be shot of this cess. He laughed hoarsely, though not for long. Such a shame, he brooded bitterly as he stared around at the astonishing architecture of the perfect city.

It was a sigh he breathed out next, as he remembered the second wispy figure beside Marcel at the back of the crowd, who must have been privy to the madness breaking out on the execution stage in advance of the sun's rise that morning, or else Marcel wouldn't have brought her. What to do with her, the cheeky daughter of the duceveree turned traitor, or close enough to warrant concern?

If the bells stopped flooding the streets with their insufferable ringing, he thought, he might be able to piece together a plan. He jolted at a memory that corresponded to it. He'd completely forgotten about Lucian's riddle, and ironically the alarm bells handed it back to him. *Fear will ring from the heart*, it went, and it was certainly an apt description, but not exactly sterling advice. From the heart of Harth then, that was only logical. That meant getting an overhead view and discerning which tower was most central, by which the only means he knew of was to climb Rosalynn's inn, which he dared not even approach.

But over the din, footsteps could be distinguished by their hastiness and metallic echo. Isaac roused his unwilling body, and was gone.

It was rarer than a blue moon to see the city in such a state, Isaac wagered, where half its inhabitants withdrew inside, and those who didn't pressed themselves up against the sides of streets, leaving much of them unfittingly empty, conducting their business like paranoid criminals, throwing uneasy glances here and there. Running would be no help, for the City Watch would easily hunt Isaac down by that suspicious action alone. The cloaked figure that was Isaac thus strolled at a brisk pace, trying not to betray a limp or heavy breathing, and when he passed guards hurrying from the south, or east, or west, he stopped breathing entirely until their footsteps were but memories. At some point, he found a building around which stairs spiralled to its very top, mostly flat but for a sloped roof at one end to siphon rain away. Meant for soldiers, as he saw by its battlements, he dared not stay long, so rushed to stare out from an embrasure, at all the city that was grinding to a halt, taking on a new, twisted function as guards on edge swarmed hither and thither. The bay, he noticed, had never been so bereft of ships: just a shimmering, blue mass that now had few objects with which to measure its distance, save for a few dots, although for that matter, the harbour was not in view at this height, so his judgement of that situation was limited.

None of that mattered. The watchtowers, of which there were many, were his focus. Isaac became immediately frustrated, and reprehended himself for his poor choice of lookout, for the view was not ideal. Despite that, he forced concentration to overcome petty, inner squabbles, and so was able to determine roughly where he should look, bracing himself precariously against the merlons as he searched. There was a tower that might have marked the city centre, of cylindrical design upon a square base, of which there were few of its kind. He had no better ideas.

No Watchmen harangued him on his journey, because most wouldn't even know what precisely the bells were supposed to be telling them, and if they knew they were on the hunt for someone, they wouldn't know what that person looked like. So, he had to keep on at his brisk pace, ahead of the ominous force he imagined trailing behind him, that of the news of his escape spreading like wildfire.

At the central tower's base, he stayed in the shadow of a nearby building, so the men gazing from its lookout high above would be blind to him and his questionable presence there. There were five roads shooting off from that round plaza, forming a star shape, again all but empty of civilians, and there was no clue as to his next destination. Only now, someone strolled up from behind and Isaac jerked around, hands high as if he could actually defend himself. Jamys gritted his teeth half in smile, half in grimace, as if the situation was merely an awkward inconvenience, then he shrugged and carried on walking, left hand on sword scabbard until he was a few feet away. He'd never been so pleased to see the man, and likely never would again.

"D'you do all this?" the mercenary gestured vaguely around him.

"It was done on my behalf," Isaac answered painfully, bent double, using his knees for support. "What now?"

"Your brother went looking for you; he'll be back soon, and when he is, that will be all of us. Then we go to the sea."

"And what's at the sea?"

"Water." Jamys sniffed and his brow furrowed as he tried to remember. "I'll be your escort. You're not staying in Harth, you're going south."

"That's more than a passing kindness, Jamys."

"It is, considering how much I was paid."

"You implied you're not coming with us," Isaac redirected the conversation, ignoring the mercenary's comment as he was ever aware of his time running low. "What's your chosen leisure?"

"To stay here?" Jamys replied dubiously. He shook his head as he weighed his options. "To come with you might be interesting, and by extension, guarding you will as well. I assume your obsession with the land beyond the sea's off the cards for now: a shame, but not a deal breaker."

"Your mild but obsessive intrigue in my affairs entitles you as the most trustworthy person I've met in Harth, as it stands, friend. Rather depressing, but I'll take who I can get, and I could do far, far worse."

Jamys laughed sourly in thankful recognition, and half-rolled his eyes. It was then that Isaac thought he saw doubt spoil the senseless but inspiring bravado, and whether it had happened or not, doubt festered in Isaac now. His skin crawled as he waited for his brother to return. Only one of them, he recalled the mercenary say...

Then there were alarmed voices heard over the harsh bell tolls: not ones he recognised. Jamys waved Isaac away to a deeply inset doorway, and in turn went out to meet the owners of the voices in the plaza.

"I told you," one of the voices said in the tone of one expecting to be complimented.

"Your friend from the guild says he spotted you heading this way, and so you are here," a second voice conceded, this one much thicker and more formal.

"We're not friends," the first voice corrected. "But not enemies either."

"The bells are tolling for terror, and you're stalking me through the streets. I wanted to stay alert for when the fights break out, however that will occur. Shouldn't you be on your watch doing the same?"

"You've been known to affiliate with that foreign bastard who should be getting executed right about now, and his brothers too," the second voice said.

"And you haven't shown up at headquarters despite Martello's request," the first voice eagerly pointed out.

"Captain Martello owes me an apology. He hears one rumour of my client's unproven illegal activities and sends me to do a layman's job, because he fears I'll use common sense to convince him to stop his little game."

"I wouldn't think that'd matter to you," the first man said, so taken aback he sounded somewhat sickened.

"It doesn't. But it puts a strain on business when the captain treats me like a child, and I should expect an apology of him for that reason, no?"

"Now?" the second man suggested gruffly. Less a suggestion, more a nudge with a sword point.

"Aren't you going to arrest me?"

"We'll straighten this with your captain first. Then I may arrest you depending on what this is all about." Isaac imagined the man gesturing to the tower beside him. Even he sounded annoyed by it, teeth grating at the mention of it.

"So be it," Jamys agreed freely.

Three pairs of footsteps were heard, and from the doorway, Isaac saw Jamys accompanied by a mercenary and a Watchman. If it was indeed the mercenary's idea to confront Jamys, as it sounded, then it must have been only money that drove him, and so he was dangerous. The Watchman pivoted on the spot, and Isaac retreated into his alcove, pressing his back hard against the wall. The Watchman approached. His shadow could be seen faintly overlaid with that of the building: standing, watching. A sigh was drowned out by the bells at its conception, and the Watchman turned quickly away.

Now Isaac had no staunch ally to defend him. It was just him and himself, and after a time he decided he must search for his brother. When he stepped from the alcove, he heard a gasp, and from the end of the street his older brother ran, dark cloak tucked tightly around his body but for a flailing at his knees where it loosened.

"You made it," Lucian exclaimed, actually laughing in disbelief, almost choking up; odd coming from him when his sternness might actually be warranted if he hoped to lead, but it was understandable and strangely moving. Indeed, he was rightly shocked at Isaac even being alive, though Isaac looked scarcely healthier than a pale corpse in his grave, he presumed by Lucian's pained expression.

"You thought me dead," Isaac replied, nodding. "As did I."

"We're not safe yet," Lucian reminded him, darkness overcoming him, and he spoke hurriedly. That was Lucian. *I wondered where he was*, Isaac laughed inwardly. "Harth is a very efficient machine. Whatever you started up at the palace, it's going to hound us wherever we hide, for as long as we stay here. Every gate will have been shut and barred by now, and defended by walls of elites; every trader and fishing boat recalled to the harbour for inspection, or else running the risk of being boarded by one of the King's warships."

"So?" Isaac prompted.

"We're going to the bay," Lucian repeated Jamys's intent. The stupidity of it made Lucian flinch as he said it aloud. "Don't ask. Later."

"Marcel..."

"Later!" Lucian barked. He pressed a leather flask into Isaac's chest, water sloshing within. "And drink this. Before you die."

Acerbic as he was, he was completely serious, and for good reason. Isaac felt ready to collapse, and guzzled the clear fluid greedily. There and then it was tastier than any water, mead, or ale he'd ever had. Lucian was not feeling so blessed. He bit his lip and stared scathingly all around, as if the architecture had wronged him.

"Jamys was waylaid," Isaac said pre-emptively.

The eldest Brodie brother said nothing. He grimaced, tugged at Isaac's arm, and they were both gone. No one recognised either of them. They might not have been there at all. The Mercenary's Guild was given a wide berth as they otherwise followed the coastline before eventually looping back round to it in the south of the city, overlooking the sea and shingle beach with their backs to a length of wall, where the sheer cliffs rose up on their left. As if signalling their arrival, the bells, one by one, were silenced, until only far off jingling shook through the wind, then a true calm enveloped the city where they were, and it was like being unshackled at last.

"That doesn't mean we're safe," Lucian said. "If anything, it means they're fast getting organised and no longer need the bells, so we need to disappear shortly."

He sounded unconvinced. He obviously wanted to wait for Jamys, and Isaac, too, wished for that rough bravo at his side, but more strikingly was Marcel's distinct absence from his sight.

"Did Jamys say he'd be gone long?" Lucian pressed.

"He just followed the Watchman and his friend... acquaintance, rather, and said no more that I heard. Where's Marcel?"

"Not coming," Lucian confirmed his fear, though he was none too happy, as if already he was regretting it. "He'll be safe at the cathedral. Laryc Morzall may be abrasive and condescending as he pleases, but fortunately he's also a hypocrite, and will defend the people he insults if they're in his service. On principle. Tamzin guaranteed it."

Hearing her name out loud made Isaac's eyes pop open, the most animated he'd been in a while, and when that was done, weariness sank through him like lead. To have made an impression so positive that she'd throw herself into this affair was humbling but distressing. Though perhaps it was arrogance on Isaac's part, and she was doing it for Marcel.

"I'm confused," Isaac replied. He might have been angry if he'd had the stomach for it. "That he'd *probably* be safe here doesn't denote it being a good idea to leave him under the duceveree's protection."

"It's better than being a fugitive," Lucian said scathingly. "When the time is right, he'll walk out those front gates without anyone thinking to stop him, and they won't think to stop him because he'll be an innocent man and a respected member of the community. I have no idea how long we'll be away from home or where we're even going, hence why I'd like your armed friend with us. I just do what my anonymous friend tells me to do. He leads, I follow. If I could ask questions, I would, but he's just ink on parchment to me: a guiding spirit if you like," he said hopelessly, seemingly trying to emulate Isaac's hyperbole. He tapped his upper chest to indicate something beneath it. "He sent me letters telling me how to help you, and here we are."

"And they were scant on details?" Isaac said bitterly, though really he was intrigued, and if he lived past this day, he would wake up with a burning desire to know the truth. That had served him ill of late, but it wasn't going to stop him wondering.

"Details enough to be thankful for, and we shall repay our friend if ever we can." Lucian paused with his mouth open before he could utter another word. "Finally."

Isaac span about to see that his loyally hedonistic mercenary had emerged with as much swagger as could be expected from him to exhibit in the face of a dangerous situation, which apparently bore a strong resemblance to most other situations. His armour was spattered red. Where it had come from was not clear, but his sword bled from its scabbard also, as perhaps he hadn't bothered to wipe it clean at all.

"The embassy went very badly?" Isaac asked while he approached, hoping Jamys would interpret that as what he would consider problematic, not being the average man.

"There was no embassy with Captain Martello. Bastards tried to kill me before we got halfway there," he grunted, and winced in pain. "They knew I'd been consorting with your like. Seems I've got to thank the duceveree for that: told Martello I'd been causing trouble at the cathedral and that I bear watching. There's money in trouble."

He nodded at Lucian and coughed.

"They'd already seen me, and gave me a chance to explain myself. I suppose not speaking enough got me into trouble this time." He shrugged and coughed again, violently this time. Isaac saw now that though not all the blood was his, there were rents on his armour, and from the mail he pulsed dark red through scraps of cloth wrapped round him, and another light, long cut was on his face. "We'd best assume they told someone their discovery before they died, to err on the side of caution."

"Are you going to be okay?" Isaac asked gormlessly when no one else spoke, and the words sounded ridiculous as they entered the air.

"The Watchman's sword was sharp," Jamys answered evasively, smiling all the same.

The Voice of Kings

The smile was disturbing. The whole situation had a fey, surreal aspect to it. Isaac had collapsed and vomited at the punch of Martello's sword, and had staggered through the streets with two men supporting him; Jamys took sword bites at the steel's edge, not the flat, and he must have been in agony, for his face twitched, and one leg or the other would flinch now and then as if his strength had finally crumbled. Only he was still standing, and maybe the wounds were not fatal, but Isaac couldn't rightly see them to be sure of that.

"I'd like to take to your advice," Lucian interrupted the silence. "We've stayed too long already."

The ceasing of the bells' alarm had sapped some of the urgency, or Isaac blamed his lack of action on that, and Lucian had reminded him of reality, though he didn't need telling twice. Jamys stopped at the threshold of the shingle beach, and such was the wonder he exhibited through the pain that he might have had an epiphany.

"I'll rest here for a while," he grunted. "I need to catch my breath."

"If you sit down here..." Isaac protested.

"Then I shall follow you in my own time, yes," the mercenary responded scathingly, dignified even as he slumped back against the wall. "I'll only slow you down right now."

Lucian hesitated.

"Remember: the Port of Vilchentah," he said, and Isaac stood dumbstruck as he watched, wondering if in his illness he'd missed something; it was stranger still to watch him speak to the man as if he were merely about to nap, here at the shore with blood seeping from him.

"I know. I know where it is."

"We shall wait for you there," Isaac put in. "To die for me might not be your proudest moment."

Jamys tossed a bag of gold that Lucian fumbled to catch, but catch it he did, and he said no more to the mercenary. Grounded, canted on the shore, was a small fishing boat, and on its deck was a blue rowing boat that they hauled into the water, Isaac merely following Lucian's lead, who himself was not filled with certainty. Along the coastline, Watchmen patrolled in their droves, and though there was a patch here currently free of them, he wouldn't count out them swarming upon it in short course, so he moved with all haste. The boat was cluttered with several items that Isaac was not of a mind to examine, not yet, but Lucian slung two pairs of iron shackles from beneath a bench and proceeded to fix them upon Isaac, who, though stunned, didn't complain.

His older brother grunted as he slid them away with an oar, because he was not a strong man. Isaac watched the pale mercenary until he, himself, slumped sideways onto the bench and gazed up at the cloudy sky, listening to the uneven heaving of the oar as he left Harth.

Chapter Thirty-nine: The Knight of Old and New

Gulls screeched noisily, circling overhead, hoping for more corpses to harangue. There would be none today, not for a while, not on Sir Leon's watch. His prediction had come to fruition, the day's nurturing peculiarities abound with each as they passed.

He strode past all the lords queuing outside the throne room, who didn't question why a knight was permitted to the King's sanctum while they were not. In all likelihood, they were grateful of having to wait and have him as their fodder to test the waters and calm the King, and he was eager to oblige. Commander Leonardus, still maintaining the pace at his left, flicked his shoulder cape over his back, which meant he was irritable at the lack of results and wasn't looking forward to presenting himself to Michael with nothing to show but his fancy armour, as if the King would accuse him of slacking off to shine it; not that anyone else noticed.

"I hope you've got something clever hanging on the tip of your tongue," Cadro muttered as they marched into the hall, and he was entirely serious, for to Leon, he was never condescending.

Afternoon light streaked through the tall windows, the sea was alive and shimmering in the hall's centre, and Michael's face was dark in contemplation. On the steps of the dais, he sat with chin resting heavy on interlinked fingers, while Helen perched precariously on his throne as if she'd just usurped it from him. At first Michael betrayed no movement at all, then he sprang to his feet in a burst of energy, majestic and furious, though his lips were pursed and he knew better than to start raving.

"Your Grace," Leon and Cadro said in time.

"You can call me that when I bring some grace to this damn catastrophe."

The King had exerted some effort in saying that, as he must have believed he deserved to publicly forfeit formalities for the duration of the meeting as a standout ruler, yet as royal lord, he was very attached to his status, and so his words had clung to the inside of his mouth. But he forced the humility into the open; that was the important thing. The truth was that his kingly power was a chained up beast, and he controlled it himself as much as he demanded others keep a beady eye on it.

Lord Theodore was next to arrive, holding the door open for Lieutenant Rayance, as if to save face from the idiocy he'd indulged. They took their places at Michael's right; they were now all here, the four who'd been summoned for the private session.

"I'm listening," the King proclaimed loudly, as if to a wider audience.

"Fatalities have proven few," Lord Hughly announced. "Thanks to your physicians. Your executioner is going to live, miraculously, though he will, I fear, be seeking a new profession."

The Voice of Kings

"That was fine work Isaac inflicted on him," the King said dryly, face unchanging. "I won't hear medical reports, however, not now. You're my best men; update me on the wider picture, and if you've been running blind for over 24 hours, throw me some speculation as to how, precisely, investigative elites have been fooled so terribly."

"It had to be a job conducted from within the palace gates," Commander Leonardus supplied. "There was just too little time for anyone else to have reigned in an operation of this magnitude to such a high standard."

"There are few times of year it could have struck worse," Rayance said. "So many people have had access to the palace recently. But we'll get through everyone eventually. Main trouble is not offending all your guests."

"Spies," Lord Hughly spat, rather predictably hypocritical. "If I were to assume the worst, and I shall for it's not my job to dismiss things as coincidence, I'd say there were more spies from Mürathneè we didn't know about, brewing something up for Isaac the moment his arrest warrant was signed."

"That's a very serious accusation," Sir Leon said. "One for which you have substantial evidence, no doubt."

"The evidence is right before you, Sir!"

"Leon is right," the King growled. "We can't go making accusations like that until we know more. It can be exceedingly dangerous simply to open one's mouth at times as these. By all means, continue with that train of thought, my Lord, but under no circumstances speak of it to anyone not in this room."

"Be that as it may, coincidence is a word I find hard to swallow," Rayance added.

"We won't know until we've anything to show for it," Cadro came to Leon's staunch defence, raising his arms as he shrugged. "And I see no one with a shred of evidence. Which is precisely why we *do not* treat anything of trifling concern."

"The prisoners…" Lord Hughly started.

"…did nothing more than scrounge around for anything someone happened to leave out, which is nothing," Leon finished calmly. "Moreover, I'm of the opinion the Watchman instigated the others, seeing as he may have been the man Natierlia greeted. Any connection to this business is speculation. We'd do just as well to accuse the hounds of treachery, because they were incompetent."

"That's the only reason we didn't know they were spies sooner, Sir. We mustn't count out the possibility of more accomplished members of the Aurailian court skulking in our midst."

Which was true, Leon conceded. If palace security wasn't so impossible for a servant to break through, they would have taken whatever they wanted. But they couldn't. And they didn't. And no spy could hope to attain a higher purpose in the palace than that of a servant.

The Knight of Old and New

"I shall play the advocate once more," Lord Hughly so generously offered. "Within our meetings if nowhere else, we must consider the possibility that Aurail's resentment towards us has become bloated and wicked, of the kind that may persuade them to declare war, or else try to incite it."

"No, we can't consider that, not yet," the King said harshly. "Not because of this, anyway."

His strong chest heaved outwards as he sighed, removing two rolled up pieces of paper from his doublet and holding them up as if to awe them by their presence, and have the four of them cower and prostrate themselves, for his face flickered from bitterness to deep contemplation and back again. He waved the papers. When he spoke, the words came out in bursts, heavy and furious.

"I received these not ten minutes ago: a letter from Castle Aurail demanding how it came to be that Lord Tristan Almaric and imperial consorts were deceived, brutalised, and murdered in cold blood while holding embassy with men under *my* banner."

For a time no one replied, because there was nothing to say. If this was true, then Waithrydn's Sèhvorian edge would soon be rending through a new foe. Leon thought wistfully of his last visit to Castle Aurail with the royal caravan; wistfully because such occasions got him away from Harth and were always interesting to observe, and better still, it was one of the few places where, on rare, special occasions, he was invited to have an opinion. A cathartic experience in many ways, he nonetheless could reach no conclusion as to how his experience would stop a war if it was to be. Perhaps he was the only one there thinking it.

Queen Helen's shy elegance caught his attention, biting her lower lip as she was, balanced still on the edge of Michael's throne, having heard the letter already presumably, but rightfully fearing its contents. Often she was allowed to sit in on her husband's meetings, eager to do so despite her silence and poor understanding of politics. Yet here Michael's decision to permit it was surprising. Her involvement, Leon suspected, was often more a mutual arrangement to stop her acting on rumours.

"Do we have confirmation of these claims?" Cadro said warily.

"There were upwards of 150 men under my command, supposedly. Those who died on the island are being guarded by Aurailian soldiers who scare away the carrion birds when they draw near, so their faces might be recognised, and they've alerted various authorities to have them examined. That does not sound like a bluff, gentlemen."

"The letter mentions your banner in particular?" Lord Hughly enquired.

"They were wearing high class Mürathneèan armour!" the King despaired. "Eagles were emblazoned on their breastplates. How does this happen?!"

The Voice of Kings

It sounded rhetorical, but it was not. King Michael found such questions tiresome; he genuinely invited an explanation. The King glared at the sky through the tall windows, musing upon it. It brought him the right words to say.

"Believe in coincidences. That we captured foreign spies doesn't denote that all who would play Harth to their whims are of the same allegiance."

"Vicentei Laccona is one such individual who seems exempt from criticism, yet might be cast with scrutiny. A man who we shan't forget did recently indulge mirth and business with Isaac Brodie," Leon declared mildly. He smiled, raising a finger. "But, neither should we condemn him yet. To become obsessed with a single idea is to lose sight of what we are trying to accomplish."

"Well spoke," the King grunted. "On that note, Leon, Cadro, Rayance, you will conduct separate investigations: you will not share evidence until appropriate, or take counsel from each other. I'll be waiting. As for myself... I shall go into the city, I think; the people need my guidance. I would have you at the palace gates in an hour, Leon."

Leon bowed, as did his companions on each side, and they took their leave with him, three soldiers in their exquisite armour scrabbling after a ghost: a fugitive who was no longer in the city, if the gods had taken even a passing interest in him. If Isaac's older brother wasn't to return to his lodging, and he wouldn't, then he had indeed left with Isaac.

"It should be you and I," Cadro interrupted his thoughts. "We'd cover more ground if we pooled our resources."

"We will. Eventually. Rayance, my young friend, you too."

So, Leon split from the two men and went higher, where the sea wind would catch his hair, upon a balcony where he stroked the railing with two fingers absentmindedly, walking proud at his own pace, for it was hard not to look proud in such armour that inspired men's and women's imaginations of heroic deeds, of great nobility. He smiled wryly at that. He hoped to reflect that belief. Gods below, he tried. But expectations were too bright to make out, and they dulled the mind. Every action was less heroic than the last to him now.

Stopping now, three floors from the ground, he leaned out and stared at nothing in particular, except gods painted in the clouds in his mind. The wind would help him think, and he did need to think. It was to be war soon, his instincts said, only in some ways he saw distinct parallels with his experiences fighting in the War of Distant Kings already. The war flooded back to him, and everything it meant with it, because without it there was only bloodshed, from men with no names, no less. At that final confrontation, the Battle of Ei Dukar, rammed into a shield wall at the far left flank, long out of sight of the rest of the army, he stood as a brazen young fool who happened to be quite skilled with a blade.

In the morning, it was, with the sun to his right, streaming across a row of a hundred shields in the vanguard on both sides, like fire from the celestial realm. 'Fiery' described the battle well: immense and hot it burned. Although these days, people were prone to say his

The Knight of Old and New

sword was like a bolt of lightning. He was a good soldier, fighting for dreams that drew out like a dramatic play between that and every other battle. Revered Sir Belfiris Walten, commanding the vanguard at his right side, was struck down; his blood blocked the sun as it sprayed, before ever it could break free of the horizon. Captain Marrigno Albero took his place, until a battleaxe stripped his soul from his body before the morning was late. They all fell. To his left, wary Miguel, who he'd never really known, whose surname had gone from his memory, tumbled, half-dead, at the strike of midday and never rose. The sun washed bright over the dead as the enemy advanced, until that swarm had fallen like so many others, and another wall of Alassiien soldiers waited not far off for slaughter. Ominous, blessed by gods, their visage did deceive, as Mürathneè was feeble then and they were many: they were confident.

Whenever, on the rare occasion, that he dreamed of this, the young man of square jaw who came up on his right side wore the winged helm he did now. Leon was no knight, but a boy of 18. But a boy of 18 who'd survived his elders all morning and beyond. Whatever crossed his mind had been inspired by that, as it dawned on him how he'd so survived, and a young ego did the rest, for he took command of the disarrayed vanguard and when, at first, they doubted him, he charged, charged alone like a man who wanted to die. *Never, never.*

Afterwards he recalled being in a daze of it, as if taken by madness, yet now no such strangeness shook him, which he liked to believe was a sign of maturity. Not that he didn't have his doubts, but he took risks then and he took them now, so it must have been too late to turn back on that: far too late.

It was the threat of war that vexed him most. The War of Distant Kings left memories of some of the very best times of his life, and some of the most utterly miserable in equally vivid context, and some moments that still couldn't be captured properly by words, unfathomable in that sense. Leon grimaced, for a new conflict with Burtal could never bring that elation, but the misery was certain. That war had been vengeance for the gods, as if they needed it, and all they stood for, then it had turned out to be pointless. Now he would fight over a dead man. He wondered if its conclusion would be the same.

Leon remembered himself and saw that he'd been too wistful. Perhaps he was turning doddery already, he joked inwardly. And then he remembered why his exploits in the war had come back to him at all, seeing what now he must do. To Vicentei he must go, and so he did.

He burst through the inventor's door, shutting it behind him, and immediately began upturning the man's desks and pulling drawers out, removing every item, all to the bemusement of Vicentei who sat at his desk. At first he just sat, hands in his lap as if it was all a quaint interference that would soon blow over.

"What are you doing, Sir?" Vicentei said flatly when Leon did not stop.

The Voice of Kings

"Searching for evidence of treachery. An incident like at yesterday's execution won't go overlooked, and you are not immune to scrutiny."

The knight's blue eyes sparkled, giving little enough away as he needed to. Vicentei swigged water and sighed quietly, still not moving to intervene.

"Speak your mind," Sir Leon said.

"If you're doing this now, I can expect this to happen when more men come to inspect me, I presume."

Leon had to smile at the man's lack of urgency. Through it all, Vicentei was nervous. He fidgeted, and his normally distractible gaze centred on the knight, thoughtful and, more importantly, focused.

"Speak freely if you wish," Leon repeated.

"If you're here by choice, I take it we're not going to be put on spikes before the day's end."

"I'm the Knight of the Holy Storm, Vicentei; it's my word against most others', even if anything discriminating could be charged against us."

"It's very unlikely anyone here will have outsmarted me," Vicentei said in honesty. "I was merely making sure. The magnitude of your operation surprised me. The repercussions, they'll be enormous I imagine, but I'll have as little to do with them as I can."

"You shouldn't be surprised. You put in half the work at the least."

"From a distance," Vicentei retorted. "Anyway, it's the nasty view from my window of which I refer to mostly. That was what made me consider the enormity of my work in very real terms. Organising the intricacies of so many correlating events, and keeping it secret, can be no more alarming than organising a fayre for me, a complex fayre I grant you, but the point is, I tried to detach myself from it emotionally, and succeeded better than I'd anticipated."

"You're feeling the guilt of it now?" Sir Leon asked respectfully, rising from the mess he'd created, swishing his white cape behind him. "Heap it upon me if you can; I can take it."

"Oh don't mistake me, Sir; I was happy in aiding Mister Brodie. But I'm speaking my mind. As you asked me to. I only hope it was worth it."

"I wish for that all the more," Leon said with a wry smile. He paused, listening for signs of compromise from outside the door, just as outwardly calm when he was satisfied. "I shall take Lord Hughly's head, and all in Harth will know why, but first I'll expose every last degenerate snake slithering behind at his bidding. I was never especially fond of Theodore. That's something the King's valued, only he's gone too far now. The traitor will die for this."

Vicentei sat back, mouth crooked as he considered something that displeased him. Leon paced slowly back and forth before the desk, pivoting when he reached his gait's end, happy to glimpse the bright world beyond the inventor's balcony. He imagined the turmoil in the hearts of the City Watch as they scattered all about, searching for the men who must have presently been far from Harth if they had any sense. Vicentei glared all the while, a mild glare but it was displeased all the same, and he would speak in his own time, so Leon did not press him.

"You're a traitor too," Vicentei pointed out forwardly.

"Technically."

"Shun it all you like; the world will keep spinning, the tides will come and go, and you've committed treason. As have I. How would you convince the King otherwise?"

"He's approved of my disobeying him numerous times before. It's always been for the best. It's what I'm for, in part."

"Will he approve of this?"

"Perhaps not," Leon admitted. *Probably not*, as he'd acknowledged to himself already. "However, what's done is done, and I didn't do it lightly. I didn't tell you, Lord Hughly tried to have a prison cook poison Isaac's food. That cook is holed up in a prison tower now, on false charges. When the time is right, I'll bring him back and line him up alongside the other conspirators. The question remains, why would Theodore so ardently want a stranger murdered that he'd mock up fake charges, and pay or coerce men to be his witnesses?"

Vicentei, the great genius, had no answer to that. The crowing of the eagles returned to Leon's consciousness just then. He'd forgotten about them entirely in the pandemonium that eclipsed their magic, though that was strange, for at the time he'd reached for his sword and had pondered on every word Lord Dorrin had spoken in uncharacteristic tenseness. There were some parallels with this and what he knew of Isaac Brodie's mission, whether appointed or taken personally. By that logic, whatever Lord Hughly knew, or thought he knew, he was protecting with extreme methods. *Yet, best to keep it to myself*, he thought. Vicentei would dismiss it without evidence.

"Do as you will," Vicentei said, knowing full well that he was still of use. "If this goes sour, it'll be from your actions more than mine. There's the fact that you're the only man Rayance told the contents of Isaac's first trial to in early course to consider, and I hope you know where your hired swords have run off to."

"Have some faith," Leon said pleasantly. Vicentei grinned toothily and bowed, suddenly amused in a sickly kind of way. "I'm not at all pleased with the violent approach some of them took against my orders, but all the more reason for their silence. I have experience; I'm not taking unnecessary chances, and I know how to do basic research at least. I know you've been entertained by men as well as women, for one."

"Once," Vicentei corrected, unconcerned by the weight of the revelation. "Not in Harth. It was... interesting."

The Voice of Kings

His features were screwed up in distaste, and suddenly he was far away, attention snatched from the matter that actually meant something to visit a dream world, unpleasantness notwithstanding.

"Speaking of doing research, those thugs could not have been hired if they were not already in the King's books. No doubt they thought they were doing royal work, but I imagine they'll figure they've been duped soon enough and disappear. Likewise, our friends at Vilchentah."

Something caught in Leon's throat. If Vicentei was suggesting his helpers at Isaac's trial were not strictly... *yes, well*. It was all he could do not to spit on the floor.

"This is not a game," Leon warned.

"I know."

Vicentei deflated, saddened by having to accept that. He truly wanted to believe it could be a game, no matter how futile the effort. The knight's experience told him differently. There was no backing out of this now that he'd stuck his head in. To its end he would go, for he was the Knight of the Holy Storm, an entity that could allow no such compromise. He smiled sadly. He'd never lost a battle.

Chapter Forty: Judgement from the Height

"...And who will argue that a town the size of Caedor should not have its own shrievalty?" Patric Denkyn challenged, to a roar of approval from his side of the forum. "Lobby the Count. Get Blackwel to do his job. The Watch Patrol is ostracised enough without having to take people's money. Leave tallage to the tithers, damn you!"

At the next roar of approval, Kate slunk back a few steps from the archway. Now seemed a funny time to press this point, when the sergeant was already in hot water. The forum, walled and pokey, but public, was an even worse place for Kate to be, even if she loitered outside. Patric, dressed quite finely, was well backed by his fellows, while lords mesne opposed them; all standing, for there was no seating, and they didn't look like they wanted it. Arbitrating, Haarjo Farelli was still stony, arms crossed, flanked by his ilk in thick, bright cloaks. Sleet attacked them, through the stone trellis roof, leaving none fazed.

Kate found herself slinking farther back. Served her right for going outside.

Beside the window of her room at the inn, Kate sat not quite awake, not quite asleep, staring out like some manner of miserly fellow guarding his money, or an old crone, that all she needed was sewing equipment and a hunched back. That was the more pertinent of the two. She felt rather ill, sitting here for uncounted hours over days that were like weeks, certainly imprisoned though the door was unlocked for her to leave at any time; the doors of the city, now that was up for debate.

Apparently Lord Almaric's name meant nothing around here, or else the three of them would have met the Count by now and left this morbid place beyond a horizon's horizon. In a flash of genius, she'd concocted the idea of having a letter sent to Aurail, the contents of which would be made publicly known so as to force Count Andrews' hand; it was very sly and cunning and made her feel a little profane, only as her mother had patiently pointed out, that would require a means to send it on its way in the first place. That in mind, she didn't count on any more flashes of inspiration, but secretly hoped.

Again, Kate reflected on events of late, to put them in perspective, build up the empty framework of days squandered. The bard, regular to the inn, played a funny tune on his lute directly beneath her very chamber: it wafted between the boards, slow and warm. He was a handsome young man whom she'd first taken notice of recently, three days ago to be precise as she liked, with a short beard and prominent cheekbones, who comforted her at dinner, though he didn't know it. But he wasn't singing right now with that jolly voice of his.

Last night, after his voice had faded away, contrary to her silent begging, she was restless in her bed, and when rain petered down, she snuck downstairs to the front door, which was no further than she dared at such a time, and listened to the beat of the water echo around the long, narrow street. There she imagined, just imagined, as the thoughts came to her. If the night was pitch, then she worked miracles to slide through it, if the rain was from the gods, then she was blessed. If the inky pools that gathered at the gutters showed visions of the future, then their blankness ensured she could change it as she liked. In Melphor's black reaches, she swam in nothingness, for the buildings here were dark, unreflective things, and the fires seemed to float in a void, high and low. Her enemies could dwell in those voids, their evil told her. But if Patric Denkyn was there, why wait? What was anyone here waiting for? Either way, that was how she would recognise the previous day, not by achievements. Ah, and the bard, if she could remember his songs. Today would be marked by wishing to contact Edwin's – Sir Edwin's – parents, and fearing their wrath. It surprised her when self-confessed incompetent Henri Fealds volunteered to locate them, and when she awoke an hour ago, she'd heard his loud voice from below, so perhaps he was asking about, and thus she might meet them whether she liked it or not.

Her mother entered a short while later, from whatever errand she'd been on; she couldn't have gone far, as agreed, because whenever it could be helped, Henri would guard the two of them together, or persuade people he was defending them with his sword firmly sheathed.

"You've been crying," her mother said.

"I think I have, yes, now that you mention it. Only a little. Quietly," she mewed dazedly.

"Save your justifications for people who'd care," her mother replied. She was incredibly tired, yet amazingly perky. "Our friend has located Sir Edwin's parents, or near enough. We sent a runner to their home and asked them to meet us at Maelphorydd. Whether they'll show up... that's another matter, Kate. If they do, the father may help us if we sing Edwin's praises."

"That shouldn't be difficult."

If we have our friend with us, Kate mused, still wondering on her mother's choice of accolade. If she was honest, Henri was not a friend. She wouldn't be honest though, so perhaps it was best not to preach it to herself either. A lack of conviction might kill her at this rate.

"Good," Kate exclaimed, springing from the chair, a crafted piece of wood, her bane of all things. She nodded profusely, blinking rapidly as if the sun was actually beaming on Melphor. "We'll go to Maelphorydd, Mother."

With her long woollen coat draped round her, she marched with her mother and the poor failure, dressed pleasingly as something grander, with his sword strapped nicely at his waist. She almost wished to make up an excuse not to go up to that ghostly hall upon Melphor's highest point. Almost. The heights called to her, the fresh air sang in her lungs, and if this was the only way she would feel it, so be it. In spite of her confidence, her doubts still gnawed within, magnified by the dark, winding roads which didn't sit well with her. Someone might have been watching from the shadows of an alley: foe, but not likely friend. It was with great relief to her, more so her mother, less so the fraud Henri, to arrive at the foot of Maelphorydd, where the cobbles inset beneath her feet were large and jagged at their edges, yet smooth on top. But to be here in this square was no achievement. To be just a short way ahead at the top of the two dozen steps, with the doors open for them, that was the challenge.

"What now?" Kate said, trying to recognise Edwin's parents by their son's likeness among the other people milling about: most of high stature, easily discerned. Melphorian noble clothes were mostly dark, subtle, elemental, with choice frills and flashes of jewellery on buckles and around necks.

"I don't know what they look like," Henri admitted.

His voice was wrought with apology through its gruffness, at least. How tenacious. Regardless, they had to search for Edwin's parents now, and it was easier than she'd made it out to be, considering their place at the Count's court.

"Excuse me," she said to a Watchman at the foot of the stairs. "Have you seen Lord Meri today?"

It occurred to her that he might not be a lord and prepared herself for a scathing look. Instead, the Watchman lifted a finger and slowly pointed over her shoulder. She span, gripping her coat as if to cower behind it. There, deep in conversation just beyond the reach of her hearing, was a man and a woman of middle age. The man was bitter and quietly furious, the woman bleakly despondent. He was tall with greying auburn hair and wrinkles; she possessed Edwin's blonde hair, with pale eyes. Kate saw the knight's strictness in posture in the father, and the nobility that flowed thence. Either that or she was dreaming it. Edwin had implied there was little of himself in the man, if she rightly recalled. At that she turned away, shivering.

"How should we do this?" her mother said half to herself. "No use in fretting about it anyway. I'll lead, you follow."

"Yes," Kate agreed, only to contradict herself. "I'll lead."

She regretted it already. Her mother didn't object, and Henri respectfully stayed clear, so the decision was hers to live with: one that she enacted with, hopefully, admirable reverence.

"Begging your pardon," she said with a bow. "Lord and Lady Meri."

"Are you going to tell me why someone's so interested in meeting my wife and me?" Lord Meri asked, hostile in his surety that she had summoned them.

"I came to offer you the truth about your son's death," Kate pleaded her case, to their immediate cooperation. "More than that I can't promise. I'm just Kate Brodie: I can't

The Voice of Kings

compensate you or give grand gestures. I can say that when Sir Edwin came to us, my mother and me, he was no traitor. I'd like to have known him better."

"Thank you, but to the point please," Lord Meri insisted, frustrated.

Kate's presently fragile internal structure shuddered at the blow. It was understandable though, she forced herself to believe. The lord and lady looked at her as if she were just a silly young woman. Well, the silly young woman was not so far from concurring currently. *Be steadfast*, she told herself, *and as for Lord Meri, take heart in Edwin's quality.*

"Take heart, Sir Edwin risked his life and reputation for my family out of pure selflessness. My brother's activities were taken interest in and misunderstood, and men thought to manipulate the situation for their own ends. Your son wasn't killed by bandits, I'm sure of it."

"This is what I've been saying," Lord Meri fervently agreed, then he was puzzled as the emotion passed and he wondered how she'd come to this conclusion.

"Who is responsible?" Lady Meri said quietly.

Kate hesitated. For her, as a nobody, to accuse someone of treason without proof wasn't necessarily wise. Then again, she wasn't going to be allowed to leave before Edwin's parents were satisfied.

"Elias Olswalt: that was the name that was most frequently used. Edwin told him so to his face. And the ambassador, Haarjo Farelli."

They considered this in awe: of her courage or of the revelation, she wasn't certain. They must have heard of Elias's imprisonment, unless Melphor was truly lost to itself. Tears clouded Lady Meri's eyes and she sniffed noisily, because she adhered to the laws of her ladyship which might have told her it was inappropriate to cry in public, while her husband's furrowed brow betrayed little more than he demanded of himself. Kate, mightily awkward before them, withdrew her neck into her body and rubbed her hands together, as if somehow everything would be made better by it. Her mother's presence was felt like a cool gust of wind blowing alongside her.

"He persevered until the end; he never considered just saving himself," Kate supplied. This was not undeniable truth, it dawned on her like the bright, fiery sun on a cloudless morn. It didn't matter now; she dismissed the notion. "He was my friend. I was his. For my part."

"He was a knight," Lady Meri said, nodding.

The tears did not stop rolling, singular as they were, as if she composed herself when each one fell and broke apart again the second after. Worse, they were born of anger. Kate said no more, at least recognising when any words she could conjure would do no good. Instead, quite randomly, her hand patted Lady Meri's arm. When her consciousness caught up with her instincts, she cursed herself for the idea, right before Lady Meri placed an opposite hand on Kate's; she now marvelled at the sensitivity in her spontaneity. Kate comforted the woman with her other hand. Lady Meri must have thought her worthy, to be a part of a knight's legacy, so for the flattery, she suddenly leaned in and hugged the lady tightly, and this time didn't doubt the fairness in her judgement so long as she kept her mouth shut. Lord Meri stared through a squint, pretending to be bemused so as not to be set off by his wife's weeping, if she were to guess. To avoid it herself and let Lady Meri have her moment, Kate gripped tighter, rested her chin on the lady's shoulder, and gazed well away, up at the fissure from which poured an endless supply of water. She listened to its booming, carried quietly on the wind, and was content.

"Gèyll, Kathrynne, come with me please," a voice spoke.

Kate glanced round, at first sluggish, then more speedily as her interest was piqued by the man standing erect and emotionless there for them. Recognition passed her mother's face, and after a few worried heartbeats, it occurred to her that the man was the steward of the Count. Lord Meri joined the fray to the careless waving of a hand.

"Not you," the steward said. Lord Meri growled quietly, but apparently knew better than to argue.

Kate, as she pulled away, drew a deep breath and sighed. Blood flowed coolly and smoothly in her veins, her head light as a feather that she might drift off. When her mother gave her sincerest condolences to Lord and Lady Meri, she strode up alongside Kate and gently put a hand on her back; smiling she was, her face genteel and approving in the morning rays. Kate ran her hand on the railing as she ascended the steps, fingers bouncing over the grooves of the fire motif. Despite it, she was cool, for now at least. She found herself before Maelphorydd, with one heavy oak and bronze door being slowly opened. The steward looked over his guests and frowned, as if having missed Henri before.

"Not you either," he said. "It's not a matter of security. You are not invited."

That sunk Kate's spirits, though in reality, no single man could fancy his chances against an entire household guard anyway, as she with her limited knowledge could work out. Following her mother, she crossed the threshold and was within the silent hall: the great structure of wood and stone that few ever seemed to enter or leave. The door was shut from the outside, the sun blocked but for windows high around the hall. Now she felt the heat. Hearth pits stretched more than half the length of the hall, one on either side, tumultuous from their rivers of fire snapping up at the air, billowing smoke into the high rafters and chimneys.

There was more to be seen of stone than wood on the inside. Kate's boots echoed on a hard stone floor, the pillars, rectangular like the watch towers, were just the same, though part of her wondered if they, and the rest of it, were built over wooden frames. It wouldn't have been the first she'd seen.

It all paled when she saw the skeletal creature sitting upon the throne at the rear: ornate and heavy wood it so appeared. The Count slouched, cheek caving in on his fist, brooding.

The Voice of Kings

On her left side, beyond her mother, the steward speedily went and passed through a door on the left side of the hall, leaving them alone with the ill-tempered man. For a time, there was nothing save the whistling of the wind to hear, then at once, the Count stirred and spoke, raspy yet booming all the same, words pointedly pronounced, like his bony cheekbones.

"You've disturbed me," Treyveurn Andrews informed them, a hint of amusement breaking through his bored tone.

"You summoned us, Lord," Kate's mother reminded him.

"Before that. When you entered my city, you disturbed me, when you and my defected knight frolicked in the countryside together and had a captain of the Watch Patrol arrested."

"He didn't defect," Kate was quick to correct.

"He helped us, Lord, for the sake of..."

"I know what he was doing, vaguely, and why Olswalt is sitting in a cell."

The Count, with surprising quickness, rose and presented his full self, unfurling his long frame. He was as tall a man as Kate had ever seen, or taller: seven foot she wagered, if she wasn't too influenced by his now imposing nature. His doublet and robes were rich with quality fabrics, mostly dark with stretches of silver and red, but dull like his surroundings which contained precious little Kate expected from a grand hall, with only a few trinkets and shiny things sparkling here and there, and banners hanging limp from the pillars. Andrews motioned forward a few steps with his long, spidery legs that somehow sustained him with a certain nobility.

"With respect, Lord," Kate's mother reasoned again, "you haven't heard everything we came to tell you. Sir Edwin believed Haarjo Farelli and Captain Olswalt to be planning dark magic, and when he was suspected of knowing too much, fled to operate freely without molestation. And it was us, because they believed my son Isaac to be in possession of information they wanted." The Count perked up at that, clearly enough that Kate's mother checked her plea momentarily – simply no response was given, so she had to continue. "The two of them were working on behalf of someone abroad: Sir Edwin made him confess. Olswalt sounded like he was in it for himself though."

"And this Isaac, where is he?"

"In Harth, Lord."

The Count nodded ponderously, yet his eyelids didn't move. He just stared through a perpetual squint, until suddenly, they sprung wide open to reveal something fierce that disturbed Kate.

"So why are you here?" he asked. "In my city."

"For justice, and for protection. We feared to head north because we didn't know how many men Olswalt had paid off. We didn't count on him being here of all places, but we were glad to find him locked up."

Judgement from the Height

"There you go too, saying the same thing Edwin's father's been filling my head with: murdered by Watchmen! You have proof, do you?"

"Common sense, Lord."

"Common sense... your son might be in danger, and you did nothing," the Count exclaimed mildly, as if completely unsurprised at her perceived negligence. "And you, for your brother, Kathrynne."

"Not so," Kate retorted unthinkingly.

"That's what I thought," the Count scoffed. He ran a hand over his scalp, lined with grey hair, now looking up at the ceiling for inspiration, as if for answers to be revealed as images in the smoke.

"We did all we could," Kate's mother said calmly. "We were impeded by rules from this very hall. I would have thought you'd want Lord Almaric's help, Lord, and from my husband, who's soon to be honoured as a knight at the least."

"I can handle the law within my own city, madam. No matter, though, no matter. The situation has become dire in other ways, I must inform you. You would have found it rather difficult to be assisted by Lord Almaric, seeing as he's dead. Murdered, actually. A foreign assassin fired a lead ball through his brain."

Just like that, Kate felt the wind taken from her, as she gasped and her shoulders fell dead, in time with her mother's. There was no shortage of misery to go around then. The more Kate considered it and remembered her father's stories, the more Tristan was real, raven black of hair and grinning mischievously. Her father loved that man. Her mother was affected too, for she was thinking of her Lennord.

"Now you begin to understand why I summoned you: when I tell you that the very same nonsense infecting my subjects is playing with men's minds up north; when I say men are so desperate for something which sounds suspiciously similar to the rumours from my county that foreigners will risk killing Lord Almaric and a consort of a small army. I'm just waiting for a reason to put Olswalt's head on a spike. I swear to the five, if the root of this is the folk tale of your son, I'll have the good captain quartered for his bloody-minded stupidity, as well as everything else. You begin to see now, yes?"

Kate was silent. What was she supposed to say? Was that even an actual question? Count Andrews was both loud and clear, and had the crude voice of a snake's hiss to make her re-evaluate any response for fear of his wrath. Given what Edwin had warned, she wasn't in a hurry to test him, though all the same, her mind raced to understand the Count, at which she failed miserably. Lucian may understand him, but he was ever reluctant to voice his affairs before her. Was Andrews thus among all other company, or just random women whose opinions he knew he'd never have to entertain again?

The Voice of Kings

"Tell me what I need to hear," Kate's mother said cautiously. "But please, tell me what I want to hear at the end of it. I couldn't bear being away from my husband now, and I would like your leave and trusted company to reach Aurail safely."

"I can guarantee you won't enjoy what you need to hear, Madam Brodie." The Count coughed, slithering his tongue about his mouth in ponderous preparation. "Which is to say, I would have told you whether you had asked or not. Lord Almaric's death drew the curtains that blinded me; your son's involvement in Harth was the call to arms. I shall have words with Haarjo Farelli and see if he hasn't been pulling the strings of the madness taking flight over Mürathneè, because a little bird told me, this very day, that your son has been arrested for attempting to steal information, or for spying or something of the sort."

"Isaac?" Kate snapped, to be sure of the Count's meaning through his wall of self-indulgent babble.

"Indeed."

"What's being done about it?" her mother said, a stopped heart giving way to words slogging through the air like bricks through water.

"I wish I knew. Like as not, it's all done with by now, one way or another, or else he's being detained until Castle Aurail gets involved, if it cares to. If Edwin was around, I'd have him take up the cause and clear the matter, but alas, if he were alive, the three of us wouldn't be having this conversation."

"We must know one way or another," her mother said, caring less and less for polite courtly procedure as the panic rose in her.

"Can you spare any other knights?" Kate pressed with the same urgency.

"It's not a knight I need, miss, just someone competent to investigate and relay the facts in the shortest possible time. If it's honour you think is called for here, you're mistaken, and if you think that's a requisite of knighthood, again you are sadly mistaken."

"If I'm wrong, I'm sorry to be so," Kate answered, just about audible. "Sir Edwin set an example that should be followed."

"You knew him well?" the Count enquired. "Think as you like, but I warn you, I'm sensing a fey, hazy sensibility from you that you might want to check. Many people living in the country have the same ideas, mind. Sir Martin Caedor: one of the most honourable knights of his generation, they say. If only those people knew he commissioned his own statue scarcely soon after he began to settle there."

"He had an enchanted greatsword of stone," Kate added, dubious of it herself, though all the same, suspected the Count was making a point on his own terms and wouldn't stop until it was done, so she played along with heart throbbing in her throat.

"That may well be true, just as well as it mightn't. Though these days, I'd be more inclined to believe it," the Count muttered. "But why would wise King Paryn pass an enchanted sword to a vain man? Now Lord Brandon, it's more feasible that he had a flaming sword, if only because he was worthwhile in rebuilding Melphor. The point stands: a flaming sword held aloft in the dark, snowy mountains is very evocative imagery, so men would be wont to spread it at the first rumour, and a length of stone around a haft beside it in the blizzard, better yet. Them freezing to death, not so much." *Not so long after Martin stood staring from that tor*, Kate remembered.

"Is this relevant to my son's imprisonment, Lord?" Kate's mother said icily. Kate would have smiled if she dared.

Treyveurn Andrews sighed. He looked down his long, straight nose at her. Looking down on people was all he could do, fairness be. That fact did nothing to alleviate her discontent.

"I was merely educating your daughter as to the dangers of presumptions. Which I thought pertinent, I might add, because I sense you'd presume incompetence or uncaring of me, as couldn't be more wrong. I take great concern in lawlessness in my county and my city."

"I'm sure, Lord," Kate's mother said. "I just don't care for your education right now."

Nervous Kate took that as a cue that discussion of her brothers was open once more.

"What chance does Isaac stand, with both my brothers in Harth with him?" she asked, subconsciously cocking her head forward and biting her lip.

"In Harth, arrests are rarely made mistakenly, or at the very least, the palace would have people believe it. For spying, or seeking to use dark magic? The man is likely dead already."

"Enough, enough!" Kate's mother cried out; just as soon as Kate had been ready to collapse, she was startled into upright form as a fury awoke in her mother such as was never seen in the gentle woman. She looked not just insulted, but disgusted, face contorted in utter shock. "Is this what you have to offer? You lecture my daughter to the end of her understanding your wisdom, and this is how you exert your authority? Does it please you to frighten young women?"

"You forget your place," the Count replied sternly, so very still, his face dark in the wan light of the hall's centre.

"My place! Don't presume that I didn't catch your tone because I am lowborn. You weren't just telling the truth; you chose to twist a possibility into that, and in the most harmful way possible. Because you can, Lord."

"I require silence of you," Count Andrews' voice scythed through the air, loud and harsh, that a bird in the rafters would take flight from its chillness, if one were there.

Kate's mother strode forward several steps, hitting an invisible wall erected by her own semblance of common sense that remained, for that was all that could stop her. Kate flinched at the force with which she took flight, like a fire driving out the darkness of a starless night. Neither could completely withhold the tears that welled up.

"I will not be chastised for my passion!" her mother screamed, laughing ill at the absurdity of it. "Will you gag me and shut me from the world because I didn't curtsey or shed a silent tear at your prediction of my son's execution? When I met my Lennord, I was exactly what you want of me, but he raised me up, taught me to read, taught me to live. Am I now to be brought so low by a high lord?"

"Steady," the Count ordered, causing Kate to spin, because his gaze was between the two women. She jumped. By the front doors, a heavily armoured warrior with broad shoulders had guarded all along, half cast by firelight, hand gripping the hilt of his sword. "Bitches bark, even when they've been trained. Never should you forget, even when others will. As for your question, madam, the gossip's bridle has been driven from this city by my eldest son's moralising, but I'm sure I can dig up two from the storerooms."

The Count, who'd so quickly earned the hate of his guests, drew in closer, anger rippling across his face. In no hurry to see it unleashed, Kate kept to herself and prayed it would regress whither it came.

"The lowborn are becoming more brazen every year," Andrews lamented to himself, then sloshed his tongue across his lips as if wiping away an overly salty flavour, and his evil turn passed, as begrudgingly he appeared to realise the sense in his opponent's words. "You make fair points, madam, though I'd ask you to be civil in future, or our relationship will be bitter. I have every intention of following through on..."

A heavy creaking could be heard roaring through the chamber: a Watchman heaving at the front door, to burst through in an instant.

"Lord!" came the cry.

"What's he doing here?" Count Andrews questioned his bodyguard.

He sounded almost bored and clearly didn't care for an answer, as the bodyguard correctly construed his meaning without hesitation, driving himself from the hall with the Watchman in tow.

"As I was saying, madams, I have every intention of seeing justice done. If Isaac needs saving, I can have no part in it. You can appeal to someone else, because you're going north to tell your story to the Emperor. I will do what's necessary here."

Two pairs of footsteps resounded again from the hall's entrance, and Kate, daring to look away, saw it was the Watchman from before, let in by the bodyguard who stepped aside for him and did nothing more. The Count gave an ill-favoured glance to the bodyguard before realising something was very wrong. The Watchman dropped to one knee.

"Lord, Patric Denkyn has freed Captain Olswalt from gaol."

"Freed?" Andrews spat. "You mean, broke him out?"

The Count was already marching to the door, clicking his fingers at the Watchman to rise and follow, who had to work hard to keep up with Andrews' giant strides. Kate and her

Judgement from the Height

mother closed in, and walked side by side at a safe distance, yet close enough to hear the heated conversation clearly.

"They can't have gone far," Count Andrews stated, angry in suspecting this was false.

"They've already left the city, Lord. We didn't know until they took the road north, and when men tried to follow them, they were stopped by a wall of fire. Burned out quick enough, course, but they'd already had a head start."

"No one saw two fugitives running through the streets?"

"More than two, Lord, but Patric had men killed at the gaol and gate, and no one noticed that at the time, so they slipped away."

"Worms will do that," the Count scowled. "So they head north to escape the canyons quicker. As smart a move as they could make, but it doesn't matter: we'll catch them. Was rather well planned though, no?" The Count's head swivelled, perturbed, and he regarded them flatly, but even as such, Kate knew what he meant in blaming her.

Into the outdoors he entered, and when Kate stepped out there with him, she saw his skin was quite pale, as if he wasn't used to natural light. That, and the wrinkles of a face over 60 years old, and his spindly form, should have made him frail to behold, yet in stark contradiction, he stood upright, eyes flitting here and there as one overlooking an army must do, for power resided there, as it did in his unbreakable posture. To the edge of Maelphorydd's pad he strode, and clasped the stone balustrade upon the wall, gaze protruding through the soft mist to the lands below. So vigorously did he search that Kate wondered if he could truly make out what was going on in the lowest level of the city, in the field. Whatever the case, he came away unhappy and dissatisfied. His face became brighter, and sombrely he came to a revelation, muttering it aloud in quiet awe.

"I can't give him a merciful death. Not now. The people deserve better than that. But I've got my own house to keep in order."

Through gritted teeth, he made a sharp sound like a hiss, clicking his fingers at his bodyguard and painting an invisible line upon the bottom of the steps with a finger, by which command, the bodyguard hurried down to where more guards than usual stood.

"Shield wall!" he bellowed, and brought order to their frantic motion, summoning Watchmen into the block of soldiers also, until there was a wall two men deep at the foot of Maelphorydd's steps, facing outwards: tense, twitchy.

"There's no time to spare," Count Andrews went on. "I'll have you taken to Aurail at once, and with no minor escort. You can take your friend too. I've heard he's got a good head on his shoulders."

Before Kate could work out what the lord meant, Henri stepped forward, having been nearby, and the Count studied him briefly. When he was bored or impressed enough, Kate didn't presume to know the workings of his mind, nor did she want to, he ordered his bodyguard inside to fetch able, *loyal* men at arms, stressing it in guttural tone for an effect

The Voice of Kings

harsh on the ears that wouldn't be soon forgotten. He returned with six men of the Maelphorydd household guard, whom the Count silently approved of, if only for now, because he made clear that it wasn't nearly enough.

"Locate everyone in the city affiliated with Patric or Elias: family, Watch Rangers, the lot, and flush them out," the Count ordered of his bodyguard. Then he turned on Kate and her mother, and indeed their new accomplices. "As for you, you're out of my hands now. Go to Castle Aurail, by whatever means you require to avoid the Watch Patrol or destroy any rebels, seek audience with the Emperor, and tell him all you've seen and heard. It shouldn't be too difficult. Now you have your chance to save Isaac, and I have mine to find out where the next war is being started."

"I'll do everything I should," Kate answered. Perplexed, Count Andrews glared, likely bemused that her definition of 'should' was not as extreme as his. *I'll do all I should*, Kate resolved quickly enough that she didn't have to think about it.

"I suppose you have no desire to see me ever again," the Count said. "That, you are very welcome to fulfil at your leisure. Go."

He jerked his head in the direction of his city sprawling out before him. Kate's mother said nothing, she noted, expended of all words, or showing her gratitude for the escort by withholding her opinions of the man. Away they were taken regardless, in haste down the steps with Henri adhering to his appointed role of paper beast, staunchly protective at her side, and she only hoped no one blew him over. At once her attention was captured by the man jogging up the steps in plain plate armour, bloodied spiked mace at his side, face positively ill compared to how she'd seen him escorting Elias, and rightly so, for he was about to run into the Count and presumably have to excuse his failure with considerable eloquence. In her curiosity, she looked over her shoulder, at just the same time as the gaoler's head spun violently around, as he processed her identity. She refused to make eye contact, and so, still proceeding down the stairs, shying away from the gaoler, caught sight of the Count one last time, firm and bold as the near tempestuous winds scoured his hall, hacked useless across the battlements of the city walls. He relented no more than they did: the stick figure made of stone that looked prepared to stand there for quite some time, and that was what she would take away of the man, who indeed she wished never to see again.

The enforcements of his bodyguard were enacted swiftly and noisily, moving along behind Kate and her accomplices like a flood, extending itself far and wide with more and more soldiers joining the cause to arrest every last acquaintance of the two traitors. At one point, some five or six men formed a line at an exit to the road they took, holding their shields up to the nothingness that currently faced them along that steep, dim pathway that would soon erupt into something very different, she could only imagine. Then she stopped imagining it, because it was unseemly.

Judgement from the Height

More men joined Kate's party as they went, as word got out to the supposed loyal guards of Melphor, snowballing down to the foot of the city: them with their dust-scarred armour ringing all around, she with her woollen coat tucked close. Her scant belongings were fetched too, before she reached the inn. If there was anything Melphor was good at besides being a darkly beautiful monument, it was military efficiency, which was reason enough to not wish to return any time soon.

"What do I do?" Henri said when they were given a free moment at the stables.

"The same as you've been doing," Kate's mother replied. "The threat of violence is more comforting anyway. I don't want to see any fights."

"It's possible there will be?"

"It's possible my sons are in danger," her mother answered edgily, and shrugged. "I don't know what's going to happen, but we're going to bring them back. I ask that you do what you're good at."

"I will. I'll do what I need to."

He sounded a little disappointed, probably that he had no chance to practise with his sword, as he'd grown attached to it as if he was being drawn in by his lie. But he said no more, gladly, and rode with them down the winding slopes beyond the city gates. Guilt seethed through her when she looked at him, but for why she couldn't say.

"Well done," Kate heard herself say aloud to her mother.

"For what?" was the justly surprised answer.

"You pulled that off very well, opposing him."

"I didn't pull anything off, but thank you. Pat yourself on the back too, Kate."

She was far away when she said that, for obvious reasons. If Kate was going to harass her mother for her thoughts, she didn't have time anyway, because when they reached flat ground, they sped up to match with their guardians, turning due north between the houses. On their right side, a line of horses galloped by, of a party who would hunt down Patric and Elias. They were soon well ahead; their legacy was dust floating thick in the morning air, then between the high walls of the northern canyon, the riders disappeared.

Fingers clawing at the mane of her black and white mare, Kate flung a last look at Melphor. It would have been nice to see if Edwin had been laid to rest yet, probably in a special tomb, and to marvel his effigy if one was being carved; of course it was. How people remembered him was out of her hands now. It always was, really. Even including his time unconscious, she was less than three weeks in his 26 years. At that she sighed, but was no less tense for it. At any rate, she had a new task pressing down on her. She could only put the living before the dead, or the dead would drag her with them. With a rush, she was enveloped in the canyon, and Sir Edwin was a spirit flying behind. It threatened to strangle her: the denseness, the darkness.

Cold water in Caedor, cold water in the stream...

645

Chapter Forty-one: The Silver Star

The manacles jingled as Lucian held them up. Not for the first time, he considered keeping them. It was a farcical idea; no one would believe Isaac was his prisoner anymore. Once was luck, and that was manufactured by very specific circumstances, created by individuals well-versed in this sort of thing. He flung the manacles into a thick bush, and they landed with a dull thud and a last jingle. They were smothered now. Even if they were shiny enough to reflect the light, there was little enough to be had in there.

Through the woods, he returned the way he'd come, not by way of a path, but by a distinctly random journey. Isaac was where he'd left him, sitting against a tree, now with his right leg pulled into his chest rather than his left; sitting where the yellow twilight could reach him through the leaves, and where the inn and thin winding road could be seen just a short walk away. Seeing him now, Lucian couldn't bring himself to seek out the next inn, as he'd considered walking through the woods, for Isaac's skin was black around the eyes, as if he'd been beaten, and his legs were horrendously worn when he'd seen them: red with veins taut against the skin. And there was his fevered suggestion to consider, not befitting his intelligence: the over-engineered plan of leaving the manacles outside a Watch House or blacksmith's, in the manner of making them appear lost.

At least he'd had the sense to recognise Lucian's urgency in buying new clothes; it had been suicidal to stagger around in his previous attire: bloodied and dirty, drawing looks at the best of times.

"We're not waiting for Jamys, are we?" Isaac said suddenly.

"No."

Truly he was thoughtful enough, just not in the wild, unpredictable way that was the norm; not for the first time, since arriving in Harth, Lucian noted. This wasn't the way it should happen. Still, he had to acknowledge that his brother had been very brave, even if he'd just done what his body had told him to, and had to stop berating him into revealing his emotions.

"You need to sleep in a bed," Lucian informed him.

"Yes," Isaac agreed.

That was the day of their escape.

He would have let Isaac sleep longer if he could. All the same, Isaac was more alive than he had any right to expect after the experiences of the previous day: still solemn, yet taking everything in, filing his findings away after appropriate dealing. They set out southwest, back towards the sea which they'd sought to steer clear of ever since leaving that blue boat behind the jagged rocks that were crashed upon relentlessly by the waves beyond Harth; where Isaac regretted what could have been as he gazed on its outer wall and towers, and where Lucian had just thought about what to do next. Only now, as his cheap, stubborn horse trudged along a long road, well-used but out of the way, did Lucian think the same, and in weariness didn't know what to believe just then.

Most shocking of all was how, momentarily, he thought of what could have been, if he'd moved his career forward quicker, if he'd married one of the lovely young women he'd played with in Caedor. Which was to say, fornicated with; there was no use acting pretentious to himself, now of all times. Caedor was irrelevant now, though. When he got back, he'd be back; it was as simple as that. For now, survival was the priority, by his leash and no other's, not to forget.

When the road flattened out and the wind could be felt more, his horse was happier to gallop, as close as could be said of it, and the landscape opened up. All they had to do was follow the signs at the crossroads, so that quite early in the afternoon, having seldom stopped for food or drink, they rode over a ridge, where below them the Port of Vilchentah stretched some hundreds of feet. The town bustled at every jetty, and dock, and everything in between, making the air rich with the sound of hundreds of conversations overlapping, and bells, and large ships tearing through the water with masts creaking, with sails of many different colours, and even House banners flapping, flapping in the gusts that brought all those sounds up the hill: all clear, all inconsequential. It was quite a scene, yes, but Mürathneè wasn't short on them, and it was micro-details that mattered. He reined his horse in hard to lead it to the highest point of the hill, aware that he was taking his frustrations out on the inanimate cords of leather pre-emptively for what he expected not to see. And indeed, that which was not seen. They'd have to get into the middle of it to find their captain: their means of escape. If they were lucky, it was to be the very man who'd saved their skins already, and if they were unlucky, it was a stranger who didn't much care for their safety.

"Do we have plain instructions for our next move?" Isaac said, mind's eye as keen as a hawk's in that instant.

"Plain, but vague for men like us who don't know the area. And here the instructions end. Our lives may be in our own hands after this."

"I'll try not to comment on that," Isaac replied flatly with a hint of sarcasm that might have escaped accidentally.

Of the buildings lined up at the water's edge and further inland, the dockyards, the offices, warehouses, and sailor's lodgings, one stood above the rest: a great square office made with the same bright white brick as Harth, and it was notched all over, or so it first appeared from this distance. They were alcoves, all filled with statues, while on the roof were two domes, each with a flag atop and flaunting dark blue strips between wide intervals, held up by dozens of pillars. The largest dome had the largest flag: a huge thing. A wonder it didn't tear as the wind dragged it out from its pole like a whiff of smoke. Upon the flag

The Voice of Kings

was the Santorellian eagle, and on the smaller flag there was a convoluted motif of a tree on a sea blue field, the tree extending at the top into a sail upon which was emblazoned a pile of coins. Its purpose was of more pressing concern than the architecture though, and Lucian decided it was perhaps there that they needed to go: a mastermind or just plain dishonest man waiting for them where no one would look, right in the middle of a place of legal commerce.

So, with Lucian slinging their bag of precisely two pairs of clothes over his shoulder, they went down and saddled their horses in a stable, where later he would sell them if they were really to leave this country on a ship, for meagre takings, mind. As they walked through the bustling crowds, perfectly integrating into port industry life, including Isaac in his modest clothes and with his lively yet reserved persona, Lucian's mind wandered despite his efforts, half expecting the revered High Duke Dorrin Santorellian to call him from behind a work shed, all lordly and with seemingly well-rehearsed primness. That was the most realistic scenario he could conjure, and it was utter nonsense. His father had the smarts to pull off something of that magnitude, Lucian knew, but not on such short notice, and there was no reason for him to even be in Mürathneè, so it was back to the void with his speculation. He couldn't let that stop him searching over the crowd though, and it was to Jamys that his thoughts turned, if only briefly. The man was obviously dead. It was perplexing to look back on their last conversation, unable to infer just what the mercenary wanted, but if that's how he wanted to go, that was his right and his business. Gods gave him peace, and such reverence did his corpse deserve that was for the diction of those in robes who knew what they were talking about.

There was no one walking with him anymore. He'd raced ahead of Isaac, or perhaps his brother had lagged behind, though for all the torment of the previous day, wasn't so paranoid that he felt the need to hobble frantically on without heed to his current state. That was Isaac, really, it just never manifested itself properly. Again, it didn't matter now, as Lucian reminded himself with surly resolve. At the entrance to the building with the two domes, Lucian stood with hands on hips and head high as if he was perusing it for purchase, Isaac deeply studying it, bereft of charm or jaunty spirit.

"I'll keep watch, and I'll do it well," Isaac announced before Lucian spoke.

"You're not a watchman, Isaac."

"For a few minutes today I am, evidently," and there came a brief, yet distinct smile before darkness crashed down.

It was very astute of Isaac, knowing he contemplated going in alone, so Lucian had few reservations as he marched in a replication of royalty through the open doors, trying to look appropriately serious. He should have been in his element, only presently he couldn't get into the moment; he couldn't align with the situation, and so he was left cold as he strode to the necessary desk, fighting his way through the crowd. If he was lucky, his stiffness would be a positive sign to an onlooker. If he was lucky.

"Ah," Lucian feigned surprise inexplicably to the suited man standing behind his desk. It had been proper, possibly. It had sounded like an afterthought in his busy day. "I'm waiting for my ship and it's not where I was informed it would be."

"I'll need more than that," the bearded man said, briefly looking up from his mass of paperwork sprawled before him.

"I was told to wait opposite this building if troubles arose, thus I shall, but I'll learn what I'm waiting for, if you please."

"That's it?" the man replied, confused. "What's the name of your ship and captain?"

"I only recognise my ship by her visage; they keep changing the name, as they do my captain."

Reluctantly the man sifted through his papers, and when he found nothing in the mess, he left his desk, just holding up a finger to keep Lucian put, as if he needed instructions. On the outside, he was a mirthless businessman, on the inside, he writhed at his choice of social approach, readying to run should the man return with Watchmen at his flanks. Technically, he hadn't completely lied, for what it was worth, in that he was supposed to wait opposite this building this afternoon. To Lucian's invisible relief, the man returned with no armed escorts, and his advice was that he simply do as told for a short while, specifically within a small dockyard where a fishing boat was waiting for repairs.

At the water's edge rested a boat shaped like a crescent moon, big enough for maybe ten people at most, cupping a weathered mast precariously on its single deck that looked liable to snap if it went out with anything less than a blue, cloudless sky as far as the eye could see. Indeed, that may have been accurate for this sorry thing, because a hole gaped in its hull, and there were oars all across it for this inevitable occurrence. It elicited no friendly looks from Lucian and his brother, who was rightly dubious, though as if to confirm its pathetic nature, Isaac got close to the hole and peered inside, and banged on the wood at various points. He didn't know the first thing about boats, yet he was trying to learn very, very quickly.

"Is this our saviour?" Isaac said, unpresumptuous.

"I've no idea."

"Allow me to make a suggestion for the scenario in which it is: we forget this entirely, because we're not imbeciles who'll wait for a piece of junk of this calibre to see repairs, we sell our nags for a rouncey, and by and by our lives will be our own, not left down to some old boards."

"Agreed. Our company will consist of unpleasant individuals either way."

"So pirates?" Isaac deduced immediately.

"Probably," Lucian conceded.

The Voice of Kings

Isaac took a hard look beyond the boat, down the slipway, into the sea. His face didn't change as he turned away and sat on a makeshift bench before the boat, free from the bite of the wind, though it rattled the wooden roof at random intervals and so shook the light that peeked through. Lucian sat beside his brother. And he waited.

"Yesterday you told me Marcel would be protected," Isaac started, "and I detected no lie, but I have to ask again now that the storm has passed: is he safe?"

"As I said. My opinion hasn't changed. It wasn't my opinion to begin with. *As I said.* Tamzin Morzall advised me."

"What did Tamzin have to say for her own safety?"

"She's the duceveree's daughter, Isaac," Lucian replied almost chidingly, rubbing his forehead with his hand. "For the same reason that he wouldn't hand Marcel over to the King without a fight, he wouldn't do the same for his own bloody daughter of all people, even if he doesn't love her, and I won't presume to know that."

"You've only confirmed my speculation, Lucian," Isaac said mildly, brightening somewhat at the news. "I have the muffled screams of the executioner I stabbed fading in and out of consciousness, and I see my death before me a hundred times new, but I've not lost my mind. My concern wasn't that Tamzin's direct part in my escape would come back to haunt, or else Marcel would be meeting the same fate. However, if I didn't know better, I'd have said I was inexorably tied to her. In more ways than one..."

Isaac put a lot of thought into that, ruffling his dirtied blonde hair as confusion, pain, and reminiscent cheerfulness crossed him, with Lucian unable to fill in their gaps. After regressing into stupor, presenting a glazed expression to the crowd that swished as if in liquid state, Lucian saw the conclusion materialise without even working it out. He'd lain with her, hadn't he?

"Tamzin Morzall," Lucian said aloud. He didn't shake his head, didn't collapse his head into his hands, just showed his concern for Isaac. "Did anyone see you with her?"

"I don't believe so. If she made no reference to me, explicit or otherwise, I see no reason to fret. I'm glad," he added.

So he was. Isaac was running his fingers through his tangled hair now, straightening it down either side of his head where he could. It was like he was preparing to return to normal just like that, the last necessity of casting off life as a fugitive being the adjustment of his hair. Or it just made him feel more secure among some of these prim men walking by: lining himself more with them, less with the seafarers. Lucian sighed, repositioning himself on the uncomfortable board.

"I have letters from our helper with me that you could go some way to explaining, and you haven't asked for them. Why?"

"Sometimes my interest is strong, then it wanes again for some time.... I wanted to guess for myself before consulting the letters." He paused and decided to relent. "Come on then, put me out of my misery."

Lucian took out the two pieces of paper that were so oddly mismatched in colour and material, and handed them to his brother. First Isaac read the riddle and its accompanying explanation which confirmed what he'd already worked out, then the letter with the list of instructions, and they were compiled as a list, even if in the impeccably neat structure of proper paragraphs. Isaac stopped reading for a time, craning his head back and blinking wildly as his gaze met the sun. Then he read it again.

"Interesting," Isaac announced. "Clever, too, changing his writing style between paragraphs like that. Looks like he switched to his left hand for at least one of them. I have to say, it ends rather too abruptly considering the heavy detail he implements elsewhere."

"One would think he didn't have our ship ready for us at the time of writing."

"Nor access to respectable men, unfortunately. If masterless mercenaries were his trump at the Palace of the Sun, we can expect no better here." Silence fell, but only over them, for around them men kept working, the world kept on spinning. Isaac, mightily inquisitive all of a sudden, read the letter a third time. "This is all rather familiar, actually: the cryptic nature of random portions, the short sentences. If I had many more reasonable explanations, I might not jump to the conclusion, but here we are."

Isaac rolled up the letters with loving care and returned them to Lucian.

"I believe they may have been written by Vicentei Laccona."

"The inventor?" Lucian blurted out.

"None other."

"You have been busy."

That told him a great deal, yet at the same time nothing at all, for the worth of it, unless Vicentei Laccona was to meet them here, in which case they were in the hands of a genius. However, if he wasn't, they at least knew who to thank if the opportunity, by unlikely chance, arose, or who to pray luck for. If that would help. Otherworldly justice dictated it would. He'd been given plenty of time to think on it too, as the "soon" the clerk spoke of came and went, or else the captain was running a crushingly unfunny joke of a schedule.

Time could be seen to have moved on while they wasted away without it; the shadows elongated into warped creatures across the sand, in that two hours might have passed into the ether before a slender silhouette barred their view, such as it was until, as it stepped forward, it was seen to possess a plain brown beard, thick and wagging gently in the wind over the neck, ending just below it. It was of a man who could have been anywhere from 30 to 50 years old, attributed partly by that and partly by eyes that betrayed few secrets. When the man had brought attention to himself in the form of the lean, dark figure, Lucian had leapt to his feet, reminded of the High Duke: his build was almost exactly the same, perhaps sparing more meat on his bones, thin but by his own fitness regimen. His posture, too, was cut from the same cloth: one arm leaning on nothing, as if so used to wearing a sword that when, as now, he was bereft of it, he pretended it was still there. If only he cared as much about his hygiene as Dorrin, Lucian's first impression would have been more complimentary.

"Can we help you?" Lucian said.

"I thought I was helping you," the man replied quizzically, not coarse, but smooth of voice with an odd accent, owing mostly to Mürathneè with something else mixed in. "You're the ones I'm taking with me, yes?"

"We have a criminal record we'd rather not pay tribute to," Isaac said.

"I've been told you're looking to escape the law, yes. Captain Aventtari, or just Captain to you." The captain nodded.

"Lucian and Isaac," Lucian said, holding back from cringing as he spoke their real names. The daft thought was that honesty now would help them later, and he stuck with it.

"I'd better show you my ship," Aventtari said. "Or the ship I colour mine, if you care for pedantry. No, it's not that rickety bloody disgrace," he laughed, guttural like a cough, one side of his mouth shooting up in the very definition of slyness.

He rubbed his hands on his dirty brown shirt that was cut into a slight V-shape at the neck, exposing the top of his hairy chest. Beckoning them to follow, he then broke forth into fast, calculated strides. His boots were clean only by way of being submerged in water recently, was Lucian's guess, as it was again, because he took them close beyond the ever-changing threshold between beach and ocean. He had an amber cloak that flittered behind him, catching the spray: something which the captain was quite comfortable with.

"We're leaving the smaller boats behind," Lucian observed.

"That's because mine is not a small boat."

They were mostly larger fishing boats, merchant vessels, and warships docked hereafter, the small boats appearing cramped and unwelcome.

"What was the promised price of my accepting you aboard?" the captain queried almost jovially, leading them up and over a large slipway.

"That should have been paid," Lucian insisted, aware he was treading on thin ice in resorting to lies already. So much for being honest. It wasn't a terribly convincing lie at that, or rather he wasn't, for it stood to reason that Vicentei Laccona would have paid this man off. "I was only told to pay a surplus," Lucian said to play it safe.

"Show me," the captain demanded, frostily at the tip of a pleasant request, and now he swaggered about and walked backwards.

Lucian's brain stopped in a frozen panic, his hands clasped on a jangling leather pouch, and so produced the bag Jamys had given him, quite heavy and not something he wished to part with.

The Silver Star

"That?" Aventtari said, not judgmental nor insulted, nor anything at all actually.

"It's all we were told was needed," Isaac provided, neatly slotting his lie into the gap of time where Lucian was thinking, trivialising the bag of coins as he did so. The sly bastard.

The captain held up a hand without a word, prompting Lucian to throw it without any objection of his own, yet he faltered at the last moment, the gold tight between his fingers. He shook his head.

"I should like to see your ship before any of that. I reserve the right to decline your offer."

That one-sided smile unfurled broadly on the captain's face, thoroughly unpleasant given the situation. One might find it charming in more innocent circumstances. If anything good could be found, it was that, paradoxically, his beard and short hair were clean and not clogged with dirt, as the impression would have been from looking at the rest of him. Aventtari whipped himself round to move on quickly, taking them away from the shore when it became impossible to navigate for all the boats blocking their way. By that intrusion, they looped around where the ships, by and large, grew greater still, where the forest of masts thickened into a clutter of various woods gleaming polished in the bright sunshine, bearing a vast number of motifs and every colour the world had summoned into being on their sails, in several stages of furl. Their captain was keener by the second, such that he could have broken into a run and Lucian wouldn't have been shocked. But no, he kept his jitters confined within that wolfish body of his, all wrapped up in a controlled coolness, unchanging as once more he swaggered to face them, nodding to his left. There a warship as big as most others lurched in its shallow confines, blank sails one quarter unfurled, blank yet not white: translucent they were, catching the sun as it came, and wreathing it around the cloth in a sheen of pale silver.

On the rear of the sterncastle, the words *Serestt Javiss* were emblazoned in colourless writing. Aventtari, Lucian just noticed, was nodding faintly to himself, as if congratulating himself all over again for stealing such a fine vessel.

"It's called the Silver Star, to you."

"Why isn't it a she?" Isaac asked. "I thought you were supposed to refer to ships as to a woman."

"I'm not so taken by that concept," Aventtari replied. "If it had a woman's name, now that might be different, but it doesn't, so I won't."

"When can you be ready?" Lucian said.

"Soon. Very soon. Whether it suits you or not, actually, though I know it does. There's only so long you can blatantly commandeer a royal carrack in its own harbour before you're fucked, never mind if you've got some vaguely official documentation to back you up, as we do."

The Voice of Kings

"How are your crew? Have you briefed them on us?" From what he could see from here, they weren't to be taken lightly by outsiders.

"They'll not bother you," Aventtari promised; possibly promised, sensing Lucian's unease. "They're a rough lot, I'm sure, but I'll discover that soon enough. I only bought them recently."

"Slaves?" Isaac said reproachfully.

Captain Aventtari shook his head, brow furrowing along with it.

"I don't keep slaves. Too risky, for one thing. You've reminded me though: what exactly are you going to be doing on my ship?"

"Whatever we please, within respectable limits, or so I would implore," Isaac said.

Lucian said nothing of it, however annoyed he might have been at his brother's interruption. Bold-facedly requesting permission to lounge on this man's ship was not what he'd had in mind, but it was something he would have to live with lest Aventtari notice the disparity in their opinions and try to pry them apart.

"Why should I allow that?" Aventtari answered.

"You should *encourage* it because it makes you out as a very fair captain who pays his dues," Isaac went on. "Your men expect money for their labour, whereas we do the opposite for the right to mind our own business."

"They'll resent you for it," Aventtari said flatly.

"They may resent you for putting two men to work who aren't up to it and aren't trained. But give us a cabin of our own if that be the case, enclosed and with a key to keep them out. We don't require great amounts of living space."

"You're forgetting," Aventtari took relish to point out, "you're fugitives; you'll be losing your heads if I leave you here. Well, that's the impression I got."

"I've forgotten nothing, Captain. Regardless, you may chide me, but I know pirates have reputations too, if only with other pirates, unless you have the firepower and skills to hide from the whole world. There are pirates out there I know I wouldn't want to be on the wrong side of, I'm sure."

"It might be wise if we put in some hard work," Lucian intervened, nodding in profound agreement, as if he were passionate about the idea. "A cabin of our own might be in order."

"You drive a hard bargain," Captain Aventtari said, taking a step back to properly study the pair of them. "Granted. The surplus charge, if you please."

Lucian tossed it to his new captain, who snatched it out of the air easily despite the bad throw, half turning once he realised he was going to catch it, disquieted for some reason by the stolen ship.

"We leave soon," he repeated. "Within the hour if I have my way, against the tide. If you have any last deeds, do them now."

The Silver Star

"Captain," Lucian said harshly to Aventtari who was already making for the jetty. "Where will you take us?"

"Where I'm going." He shrugged, the beginnings of a grin forming with that. "I don't know precisely where that is yet. You won't be working with my men and I inland though, which is probably for the best. I'm taking you away from here: that was the deal."

It was a sketchy deal at best, with loopholes and ambiguous, exploitable elements, and an untrustworthy figure given complete control of its execution if they stepped aboard that vessel. In the meantime, Lucian and Isaac went to sell their horses and returned shortly, checking their pace at the foot of the long jetty.

"We can still go back," Lucian suggested. It was good to get the option out into the open air. It met the fresh air well, being quite appealing.

"We may as well stick our heads into this now; we're already up to our necks."

"Fair enough. We may as well let the wind guide us if we go it alone."

"Wind guide us," Isaac echoed, smiling faintly because he'd said it with the pretence of seriousness.

That remark decided it then. They boarded the ship, observed by many men of varying sizes, though all were burly to some degree, and most of the men older than 30 were weathered; some deigned to guard their looks, others not so much. That was until Captain Aventtari, who compared to these people viewed the whole affair of piracy as something a little queer or quaint, called from his place on the sterncastle that they were work-shy, accusing them of being susceptible to distractions so readily that he might have to throw some of them overboard before they even left, to get their attention. One or two wouldn't completely drop the matter, even as they hurriedly prepared to sail free of this place, for they shot daring glances here and there. The captain missed nothing.

"If you're looking for some company from a man," Aventtari declared loudly, "you're very welcome to wait in the bilge after your duties are done and see if any of these fine colleagues of yours will join you."

There were laughs all around on the main deck, except from those who'd been insulted, and Isaac and Lucian, who slipped away, casually, to the sterncastle, where they were henceforth ignored, even by Aventtari. Lucian listened to every order, thinking perhaps he could learn something important that would save his life later, unless paranoia was seeping in before they were even shot of the dock. Yet soon they were, and nothing could be done for them contrarily. The Silver Star lurched, cumbersome as only a ship of this size could be at first, until in open water where it streaked through the ocean, its prow like a sword cleaving butter, the visage of the ethereal sails now flapping strikingly as if they controlled the wind. Those sails drove them on, the Port of Vilchentah drove back: a great land of opportunities wrenched from them. Though he was tempted to blame Isaac over and over again, every time he remembered the faceless menace that lurked at the back of his mind that commanded ills aplenty in the palace of kings, threatening to rape its reputation if more disasters like that occurred.

All that was merely the inhibition of a creature dwelling in the past, and a shadow of events to come, but not for them. The port was at first too large to comprehend, then the boats sank into a single conglomerate, then a dot in the blueness, then nothing. The crew was in contrast to the quiet reveries of Isaac and Lucian, their voices boisterous, their actions weighty. Merrily, Captain Aventtari went into his cabin and procured his sword at last, which he tossed from his right hand to his left before attaching its belt around his waist. It was a thin sword with a one-sided sharpness on the blade and a short, black crosshatched leather hilt. His merriment was writ on his face clear enough, even if he didn't flaunt it; it was a smug superiority that seemed stretched onto his face.

Lucian had seen enough of him for one day. At his request, the captain showed them to their cabin, one deck beneath his own, which unsettled Lucian, who wished for privacy as much as Isaac did, for the time being. He said nothing, not churlish enough to truly expect his demand would, or could, be met. It was bigger than he'd hoped, at least, with two hammocks along with a table and two chairs, with a comfortable space between each. No lock was on the door, unfortunately: the first strike against the captain's honesty.

The table was moved beside the single window when they decided they needed to see what was causing the rocking of the boat lest they fall to seasickness quickly. With a lantern hanging nearby, swinging rhythmically, stretching the shadows to and fro, Lucian and Isaac sat opposite one another to eat. The food they were offered was more fulfilling than expected, consisting of salted ham and biscuits, and ale that was just a tad too strong. Isaac lapped it up, while Lucian's stomach could not agree with the notion.

"Should we say a vigil for Jamys?" Lucian suggested after a length of quiet. He wasn't joking, pleasant as he said it.

"Do you even know how to perform a vigil?" Isaac shrugged and raised his eyebrows.

"Just pray for his soul like any other person. Not that we can affect where it goes now, but I suspect the gods will hold sway on it based on his last deeds alone." Lucian hesitated. "Pray anyway: it'll help you at least. I don't know how to do a vigil..."

Candlelight flashed across Isaac's face, back and forth, and it seemed to Lucian that with each new cast of brightness, a new emotion was layered on him, starting with his kind naivety that was innate to him, and adding everything else bit by bit. Lucian, growing sick, cast his gaze onto the darkening waters of infinity. His strength returned.

When tiredness overcame Isaac and he fell asleep, Lucian went to breathe fresh air on deck. In the endless dimness lit by partial starlight, the lanterns were the brightest thing for miles, for they'd sailed from the land, perhaps for fear of being caught. The sails were not silver tonight, just blank rolls of canvas. Only the four cannons on the main deck trickled any hint of yellow flame down their iron surfaces, firepower enough to make Lucian grimace in the hands of this rabble. At that, he proceeded to lean upon the railing on the captain's cabin, not seeking to speak with the three men on main deck: just being seen was enough. To be known and not regarded was all well and good in theory, but he'd decided the crew would be burdened with suspicion if he wasn't spotted outside.

His train of thought came to an abrupt end as a hand shot into his peripheral vision. The hand had caught a drinking container thrown into the sea: a hand belonging to Aventtari.

"Not one scrap of waste gets thrown off this ship without my permission," Aventtari scorned the half-drunk man, breathing down his neck.

Saying no more, he joined Lucian on the sterncastle. His expression was sincere on a face with very pronounced bones, and Lucian had a strange feeling he was about to be lectured too, proven wrong immediately when the captain strolled past. Lucian had had enough of the outside too.

That was the day after their escape from Harth.

More days passed with not nearly as much consequence, lengthy as they were lived, inconsequential fragments of time in hindsight. Aventtari was an interesting individual, such were Lucian's limited passions now. He was either there in full force, a presence to be reckoned with, or gone for hours at a time, leaving his first mate, Maevich, in command. The Isle of Sèhvor was of minor intrigue, then it was gone and it was not. They, he and Isaac, were provided with just enough work to ensure that they were never in peak condition, yet like a puzzle with its pieces fitted into place by a ponderous individual, Isaac's mind began to heal; he saw it come together with his very eyes, though it was not quite the same.

But for now, all of this paled before the truth that, one after another, the sun and Refeer the moon took turns to glitter in the sky over endless waters: first yellow, then silver, and so it repeated. Yet that paled before the conclusion that Lucian had to be more resolute than ever, and prove with heart in throat that his years of sauntering around as a political advocate, as a strong elder brother, were not for nothing, for the waters grew ever distant, and wherever their destination, they were not going to Burtal.

Chapter Forty-two: Beyond Control

From the battlements of Lameeri's Wish, golden brown leaves could be seen to take flight, their trees bereft of them. They came not in vast groups but in twos and threes, riding the invisible currents ever cooling. The heralds of autumn flew far from sight, leaving Lennord Brodie to stare instead at the steppe below. Outside the city, business carried on as usual, he knew, and to a stranger it would appear so inside also, yet even being here for a short time, he could feel the tension strung between every resident when he walked the streets, so thick he could almost cut it open and watch their fears spill out. Lameeri's Wish was arguably worse. He turned to it as if this needed confirming. Beyond tensions being high, there was a sense of urgency that had spread like a plague and got into men's heads: that they were expected to train, and grind, and hammer as hard as possible for the war. There would be no war, the Empress had tried to convince him, and if it broke out, it would be her responsibility, not her fault. It was already happening as she predicted, despite his efforts to cut back the festering weeds: a layman with a blunt knife before a veritable forest of unwanted vegetation.

Something had to be done. Someone had to do it. *Why couldn't it be a professional?* Lennord mulled again, suddenly quaking in fury at the Empress: a woman so marvellously bright with such a blind spot where he was concerned, apparently. She'd implied she wanted him to be at the forefront of the pacification of Lameeri's Wish, and for the first time, truly believed it. Beseeched in subtlety, no less, which he strived meekly to understand. It might go some lengths to explaining why no courier had come to confirm or deny the rumours about Isaac's imprisonment that had suddenly sprouted. Before he had the chance to decide what he was going to do with this mad portrait before him, a stout man in a leather apron approached him, wiping beads of sweat from his bald head. Lennord was taken aback. Gelfridus, the overseer of his forge, had never sought him thusly before, in the manner of checking even the battlements.

"Troubled, Gelfridus?" Lennord said, injecting as much enthusiasm as possible into his voice.

"You've had people knocking on your office door for about half an hour. They resorted to asking your bodyguards."

"Asking them what?"

"Don't really know. Lots of things probably."

"Who do you think told them I could help them, Gelfridus? If one person gets the idea, that's a passing fancy, two could be coincidence. When they come as such..." Lennord said thoughtfully, gesturing to his office, a little thing floating atop a sea of red, "...that's less easy to explain."

"If you didn't want people to look up to you, you shouldn't have started giving out advice, maybe?" Gelfridus suggested, completely serious.

"Indeed, but I've given out enough advice to make it clear that my experience with their professions is extremely limited."

"You're a genius, they say," Gelfridus said with a shrug. "If that's not true, then it's gotten around nicely anyway. Besides, you've got friends in high places."

"Oh?" Lennord exclaimed. *Oh*, the light dawned, *of course*. "The late Lord Tristan…"

"It's well known, yes. Lots of people saw you two talking, and I don't mean like lord to subject."

That was a flattering yet sorry presumption to make. If people were warming to the idea of him following Tristan's legacy, they were sorely mistaken in their judgement. Genius or not, he didn't possess the spark to ignite people's hearts anew at the flash of a smile, nor did he wish to try. If Captain Westrym hadn't vanished, this might not have happened: the renaissance bringer who'd been driven from the city by a mob, so confirmed reports. That Lennord had taken a detachment and put a stop to this behaviour at the other garrisons hadn't helped him remain incognito. A champion for Mürathneèans and a friend of Tristan made for a powerful symbol, like it not. Lennord assumed, for the benefit of his section of Lameeri's Wish, that the captain wasn't coming back, same for the other victims driven from their homes needlessly. People were pretending it hadn't happened.

"Walk with me," Lennord said. "I'll return to work. Oh, and thank you. You've done me a kindness, going out of your way to alert me of the situation."

"I was just wanting to get those people to stop asking after you. Like I'd know what you do with your time."

"Now, no need to devalue your own initiative. You could have just put up with all those requests and took out your frustration on your steel, like I found you doing when we first met, but you didn't: you made a decision to seek me out. Again, thank you."

Gelfridus, true to being an introverted blacksmith, was modest and took the compliment lightly, at least not protesting anymore. They walked down the spiral stairs of the nearest watchtower and along the centre of the great causeway, where frameworks were being smothered in red bricks on both sides, by Lennord's design, whilst old buildings were much darker in colour. Around them, young men were training with shield and sword, the dangerous weight of responsibility hanging overhead like a knife from a string.

Rarely did Lennord experience being old as some others did at his age, so it had chosen a decidedly ill opportunity to drag at his feet, now of all times when he needed the rush of youth to fit in with these soldiers, for what purpose Alycia Llambert contrived. He wanted to be sprightly, not Lennord the wizened. If he had a sign…

None would come, he assumed, not until it was his time to be manipulated. It was easier that way. Outside his office, he postured himself broadly and stroked his chin, scratching

The Voice of Kings

his palm with prickly stubble. Yes, he decided, he would allow himself to be manipulated now, at the time of his choosing. He requested Gelfridus wait some way from the office, along with his protégés, Roderick and Yaecob. At his behest, his bodyguards spread out, clapping their hands violently for attention, ordering passersby into Lennord's vicinity; anyone would do, so long as one or two captains were witnesses to what was to unfold. There was the distasteful possibility that it would suck him deeper into the goings on here; a risk he would have to take. For better or worse, he needed to properly show himself to these people. About 40 people had gathered when Lennord returned from acquiring a wooden box, which he dropped before them and, upon it, felt their prying looks. He trusted the group had enough power in numbers to draw others in.

"Gentlemen," he started loudly, coughing to clear his throat; public speaking was not a natural gift of his. "It's come to my attention that I've become rather a valued asset at Lameeri's Wish, to one cog of this complex machine at least. Such is my reputation already. I can assure you that most of what you've heard is probably steeped in hyperbole. If I'm honest, and I must be, I've never worked in a barracks before; I never even wanted to be assigned here."

"If this is a resignation, it didn't need to be public," one armoured man pointed out, bearing all the hallmarks of someone with authority. More men gathered round, no less demanding.

"Begging your pardon, this isn't a resignation," regrettably omitting the part about his inability to submit one.. "I'm just being honest. It will be easier for all of us if you understand that I'm an inventor and engineer by trade, but I'm new to the military. I have no cure-all or device of all trades. What I do have is a sharp mind and a fondness for the late Lord Almaric, who I knew well as a kind and personable man, none other to his credit. I can tell you he wouldn't approve of some of the things I've heard slip from men's tongues here. There's been a lot of talk of war."

"On his behalf," the same man replied forcefully, certainty wavering even so.

"If there is a war, it will be on his behalf, yes, I've no doubt," Lennord spat out quickly. He licked his lips, quiet as if making up for the speed of his outburst. "However, the Empress herself said the same as I. She knew Lord Almaric better than I, but we had that to agree on. We are not at war yet, gentlemen, and it's both dangerous to speak of it in any protracted capacity, and disrespectful to wantonly anticipate violence."

"Words don't kill people," someone shouted.

"Words have as much power as any of your steel. We don't know how our rampant speculation will reach foreign shores. If enough soldiers talk about war approaching, civilians will say the same, and when everyone is saying it, one might wonder, in King Michael's court, if some information has been leaked. This isn't the first you've been told of this!" Lennord said fervently. "I know you were ordered not to raise the levy, and yet I hear much talk of making weapons for an increased levy of amateurs. I've heard *serious* considerations to appeal for it," Lennord added. "If lords encourage it, ignore them. If the Aurailian court decrees that we are at peace, then we are at peace. There's no middle ground between the calm and the storm for any of you."

That was true. He didn't necessarily believe the hearts that were broken were strong enough to resist waging war, but it wasn't for the likes of these people to worry about. They were thinking about it, he saw; he couldn't ask for more than that. If only he could end with something poignant.

"As a friend of Lord Almaric, I say this: I notice I've been judged as his advocate, and in light of Captain Westrym's... absence... have become your revolutionary. I have no explicit desire to be so, but if this reputation persists, there's little I can do about it. Just remember that I am not the same man as he, my friend Tristan; never would I dare to accept that honour. I do the best with what I have and honour him any way I can." He paused, realising his lips were dry. "Thank you," he finished hurriedly, stepping from the box and so ending the speech, at which point the crowd stirred, mumbling all as one.

Obviously some would follow him. He'd not done much to quench the rumours, nor denied the limits of his power, contrarily implying he'd spoken with the Empress. But it was said now.

There. He'd done right by his conscience, even if he wasn't sure what precisely it was saying. Alycia Llambert could decide if that was good enough. Now, if he could reconcile contact with his family, some cheer might yet be brought to this sombre place, though still he'd rather be elsewhere. Whether Tristan's deeds would hencewith echo as strongly as he prayed, that he would have to wait to find out.

~

Lord Theodore Hughly's every aspect was driven to power his contemplation, to the extent that, in his chair, he could have been construed as dead, save for the odd blink here and there, fast like lightning. His hands were each clasping a knee. A grim, resenting expression was set upon him, his brow was furrowed into thick creases, and he wondered with increasing fury at Jacopo's failure to arrive in acceptable time. The reports couldn't have been wrong; he was in Harth, and he'd been ordered to return home.

One more time, Theodore scanned the drab room which might have been an office, or was when Jacopo was last here. The long oak table, directly to his left, amazingly collected more dust particles as he sat there, disturbed at the puniest of breaths that saw them erupt into the light streaming through the window of the wall it was pressed against, cascading down once more in grey rain. It might have been an office. Knowing Jacopo, he could change it into something entirely different now without explanation. Theodore noted the row of inkpots pressed neatly against the back wall on the desk. Only the piece of leather slumped at the edge of it ruined the obsessive neatness; leather that Theodore nursed as he

The Voice of Kings

stared across the room like a parent in his dead child's home, for it was bare of colour except for the fine rug on the floor, and Jacopo Beriddian was as a son, for better or worse.

Downstairs, a door opened, and whoever entered checked their hasty approach, running into Theodore's guard before resuming just the same, thundering up the spiral staircase, as such making out that he was in his needlessly showy armour, but while Jacopo did show himself, he had the decency to wear something decidedly ordinary. He stood in the doorway, bemused as ever. He frowned, which meant he was not expecting to see Theodore for some reason, unless he just couldn't rid himself of it this morrow.

"Lord," Jacopo said humbly, bowing low and long as he walked.

"Welcome back," Theodore issued solemnly, a bite to his words. "Is it true what I've heard from your men? What you did at Bryndton?"

"Lord," Jacopo breathed, instinctively bolting upright, humourless smile creaking into being. Of all his deeds big and small, this was what filled him with pride? Was there something *wrong* with him? "Yes, Lord, yes. It was I who slew Lord Tristan Almaric."

"Oh don't be so smug. You didn't fell a great warrior; he was a lord of peace, for gods' sakes. Do you expect an ovation for your stupidity?"

Jacopo's smile was already gone, contorted by anguish bubbling inside that he withheld, though for his stony gaze, he knew not the extent of his mistake. The sole heir to Beriddian took a step forward. When Theodore, not quick by any measure, reached across to take up the leather flail with his right hand, Jacopo must have known what was coming long enough to remove himself from harm's way, instead opting to stay put as he deserved. It screeched as Theodore whipped it outwards, clapping hard on the right side of Jacopo's face, who grunted at its sting. Theodore rose and brought the flail back for another swing, putting all his limited strength into whipping Jacopo's left side this time.

"You stupid oaf!" he heard himself cry out, all his anger flowing freely, imbuing his arm with new strength, leather cracking loudly on flesh on the second strike.

Two wasn't enough to give him a lesson he'd remember, and so, enraged, the flail came down on Jacopo's left cheek a second time, staggering him on the third strike. It brought him to his knees on the fourth, the sound resonating a different texture this time, and with little wonder, for below his left eye, the skin split open like a flower blooming in sped-up motion. Theodore was heaving as much as his victim. He fell back into his chair and slapped the flail onto the desk.

He shouldn't have done it, not to that extent. He shouldn't have. He was a lord. Unfortunately, Jacopo did deserve it, and he'd taken it without lifting his hands or screaming. It was remarkable actually, now that Theodore gave it thought with a clear head. That was a man with strength, more so than it appeared given how he'd lost some of his muscle. It was a shame he'd been so weak of mind. Now he sat on a chair opposite, refusing to scream, and in turn, grunting and coughing without opening his mouth, twitching like a crazed animal. Blood trickled at a painful crawl, going ignored by Jacopo who was staunch before his injuries, staring widely from the two pits in his head.

"I shall have to spell out your woes," Theodore said, rapidly calming down. "You murdered the most popular man in Burtal on a whim."

"It wasn't on a whim," Jacopo protested.

"It looks like it!" Theodore snapped hoarsely. "What chance does a hidden truth have against an angry mob of millions when it can't even justify the heinous act?"

"With respect, Lord, he worked out that my purpose was to find out what Burtal knows of the gods' magic."

"How did he work that out?" It was a rhetorical question to which Jacopo was wise not to answer. Cristico Valen had already told him. He'd had the sense to keep most others out of earshot of the conversation. Theodore also knew that he'd waged battle before Lord Almaric even knew. "Are you at all aware that this incriminates Mürathneè?"

"*Obviously*. But it was an internecine victory: I sent the first 50 men to deal with them, to wear them down, and it had the effect of giving us a more heroic look when all was said and done."

"That will not suffice," Lord Hughly said dryly. "Burtal doesn't care how many men you lost. Their only regret there is that more didn't die."

"I understand that, I was simply..."

"I've heard enough, *sirrah*, I've heard enough."

Theodore groaned, actually physically pained. Jacopo, as if realising his own pain because of this statement, flinched and swatted at his face, smearing blood onto his hand, and he spat more onto the floor which he then eyed conspiratorially.

"In contrast, when I had a similar incident," Lord Hughly went on, "I didn't try to kill my subject without care, and he wasn't even a lord, let alone one loved by all."

"Although, Lord, you did fail," Jacopo pointed out.

"Extraneous circumstances," Theodore replied half-heartedly, knowing he couldn't hope to praise his own actions. "I suspect war is on the not so distant horizon. If I were a naive man, I'd say that I hope it distracts both countries from the magic, but I can imagine it's going to have a thing or two to say about that. We'll just have to make sure they don't have any success. Michael will not have that power. The King, in all his glory, is as a mute hawking on the street for alms. If he finds his voice, he'll deafen us before he knows it."

"Do you have another king in mind?" Jacopo asked, leaning forward, squinting.

Theodore said nothing. Frankly, Jacopo was tiring him, and he wanted to end the conversation quickly. The would-be lord did nothing, constantly on the cusp of speaking, held back by something unseen, so he was left giving proper thought at last. Too little, too late.

The Voice of Kings

"The fiasco with those foreigners isn't utterly lost to you," Jacopo brought up, seemingly to what he thought to be at his risk, judging by his cautiousness. "They found weapons and all sorts of paperwork in their lodging rooms, I hear? Let's call them incriminating papers: lots of things about Mürathneè all gathered together. Lots of things. And some lord or other smeared his name to the whole thing, more's the pity for the lord."

"Yes," Theodore said simply. Desperately unremarkable. Yet it needn't be, perhaps? He said nothing for a while. "Anything else?"

"Nothing good, nothing bad. I sent my men around the country to gather reports. Now that I think about it, I hope this talk of war doesn't change their perspectives."

His hands were at once fists, fingers pressing hard into his palms, and he stared darkly out the window. He could do little else with that face of his. Theodore tried to gather some subtleties from his muted anger and, to his shame, found none. His face fell into his hand.

~

"You didn't find anything did you?" Commander Leonardus anticipated.

"Not on display," his scout said as if it was obvious. It *was* obvious to be fair, but Cadro didn't care. That wasn't even the point.

Intimidating that lumbering idiot of a captain was more than a token fancy, and he didn't care how obvious it was, for he stood in the street in the armour he'd earned, prideful of it today as was required of him, and he avoided the shadows so that all could see him, his winged helm bright that it might really have been enchanted to fly him away. While it wasn't a style of law enforcement that appealed to his sensibilities, he had to admit it had its uses; usually for Leon, who already wore that persona like a second suit of armour. Martello Jacart emerged from the training yard, looked left to the sea, then right down the street to find the Commander of the Watch flaunting his authority without lifting a finger, through the magic of the captain's imagination. Several Watchmen backed him up, positioned against walls and behind him, no overt hint of aggression from any of them. Martello was bold, Martello was brooding, Martello stood down. Good for him.

Leon could do as he liked and would go far, so Cadro had no concerns there. Rayance would look for the traitor within the palace, so Cadro would search outside it, and no shortlist could be made without Captain Jacart right near the top.

Chapter Forty-three: The King of the Sterncastle

The Silver Star was a fragile living space. Not fragile in its construction, but rather that was what it induced into the soul, which if one was being remotely clever about, meant that travelling on any ship for so long was a sickening, claustrophobic, maddening affair of the same vein. Of all the ships out there, this was likely quite a good one to quell the frustrations, comparatively. The emptiness got to one after a while, Isaac experienced, or just him, perhaps. The water was meaningless after a while, just a sloshing mass of nothing: an illusion with no substance. It didn't help that he'd forgotten how much time had passed since their departure from port, with little in the way of land to satiate his needs. Fifteen, 16, 17 days were all very possible. One thing that made him start counting was how every morning a new sun stole the curve across the sky, each one crackling with malice, burning hotter and hotter, razing the clouds to the ether. Some of these other men were used to it, but none could shun its overbearing influence entirely.

For Isaac, the wind wasn't such a blessing either, not down on his knees scrubbing main deck, the fruits of his labour strewn out before his low sight as a shiny, salty sheen over pine boards. Dirty boots came down all across the deck to set back his task from Aventtari, the cleanliest of these men who placed a great deal of importance on hygiene, going so far as to actually wash himself, though whether the same could be said of his clothes was an optimistic assumption at best.

"I think that's clean," the first mate's coarsely worded opinion came out in an equally coarse tone, whisking Isaac into a two second fantasy of a dulcet voice soothing him. The first mate, Maevich, stank.

Being condescending was second nature to him, such that he didn't realise it half the time, Isaac guessed. Although it would grant him the opportunity of being free of the first mate's company, to reply with a slick humiliation would require effort on Isaac's part, which he found difficult to engage, and a tongue that didn't feel like cracked rock in his mouth, too. He said nothing, nodding subserviently to avoid trouble. For a time, he couldn't summon the energy to stand. The heat had locked his muscles into a stupor; his eyelids flickered to its will. The slop bucket was to be his aid, half-filled with water to surge coolness through him, so it was to his sorrow when, with sponge in grip, he plunged his hand into warm water. It would do some good, he assured himself, obscuring this world of invisible fire by pressing the sponge to his face, and as he lifted it, and the cloudless sky that echoed the eternity of the ocean assaulted his eyes, he finally arrived to his feet. The blue-black mass on his stomach embraced him like an old friend: an old friend that sincerely never wished to see him again, if that metaphor was to hold up. Soon it would get its wish, Isaac prayed. Like a weed shielded by a tall tree, it was definitely shrinking.

The Voice of Kings

He didn't let anyone see his pain as he headed for the main deck stairs with the bucket. They already had disgruntled looks saved for him, even if they weren't using them *for* him. It didn't help that he was wearing his suit: newly cleaned to the best of anyone's ability, and without the jacket so that the baggy white shirt would catch the wind better. He just couldn't stand wearing the clothes Lucian had bought for him anymore, and neither could Lucian his own, come to that, because with weeks of sweat embroidered into them, they smelt something like death. Before Isaac descended, he craned his neck so that the sails were before him. The ship was well-deserving of the name Silver Star, beautiful as it was. Real stars didn't have grubby pirates crawling all over them though. Fairness be, they were dirty, yes, but they were also scum of the earth who couldn't be trusted, and that deserved prominence in their evaluations.

The dark innards of the rocking wooden beast were better in some ways, worse in others. On the one hand, the baking yellow ball of malice was out of direct influence, while on the other, the lack of wind ensured that humidity could thrive. Briefly passing the open crew deck, he heard moaning from the sick individuals in their hammocks and prayed, as he found himself consistently doing, for them to recover to lighten the workload. To the bilge he went, where some of the barrels of food were stored. It made him uneasy to think that beyond every wall, the sea rose up several feet: something he decided not to think about as he cleaned.

At one end of the bilge, as poorly lit as the rest of it, the door to the mystery room beckoned, in a whisper of no words without a sound to be heard. Its call spoke rawer than that. Isaac's free hand fastened on the knob, waited, and pushed. It was locked. Again. The room he shared with Lucian didn't even have a lock as he'd requested, and here was a squalid little thing at the base of the ship that was never open. He knew there was something in there, because when a particularly powerful wave tipped the Silver Star, he could hear a slight scraping on the floor of something or other being moved. Logic dictated that it was stolen goods to be sold off. Logic had been known to fail before and, certainly of late, his expectations of it had been stretched. That wasn't the only thing he could hear right now.

The door that led out of the bilge was opened. In response, Isaac zipped away frantically, and began cleaning the wall. Apparently he'd been so absorbed by the secrets of the room beyond that he hadn't heard footsteps on the stairs.

"How are you?" Captain Aventtari said.

Isaac turned to see the bearded man skulking nimbly between barrels. He considered the question for what it was worth.

"You look thirsty," Aventtari said offhandedly before he could reply. "It's healthier to drink before you feel thirsty."

"That's not really going to happen, Captain; I'm always thirsty here."

"Hmm," Aventtari replied just as carelessly. "It's going to be like this for some time. We haven't altered course: it's still south for us. I have to decide which port I want to stop in at."

"What do you expect my brother and me to do?"

"Whatever you like."

"That's a reasonable proposition in theory, Captain. Like as not, that won't be an option, I fear. Aren't you breaching the trust of your employer in doing such?"

"I'm doing exactly what I was told to do, young master Isaac. I won't propose you join us in our endeavours on dry land because I know you'll decline on moral grounds. I'm aware of your opinion of my crew and me. It's your prerogative to ask me for that if you wish it, not the other way around."

He was rummaging in barrels with the utmost care, opening the lids as little as possible to preserve the food inside. The half-lit Isaac, meanwhile, was fixed to the spot, bitterness held back from Aventtari's view. The pirate captain grinned.

"It's not a death sentence, Isaac. Wherever we're stopping off will be somewhere I can stay comfortably without having to dig a trench to hide from the wind, or hide in a cave from the sun, and the same applies to you. There are plenty of choices you can make. There'll be women too, by the way. Living's about what you can do, not what you can't! If something can't be done, have a second think and see if you're not just being a pessimist."

He laughed raucously in a manner that suggested Isaac should join in, the opposite of Maevich in the sense of being completely ingenuous when he did so.

In the evening, Isaac slumped into the chair with a tankard of water, thanking the gods for the heat dying down for the night. Lucian was already in the chair across the table in much the same half-dead fashion, eyes shut.

"I've been thinking," Isaac began when his thirst was quenched. "What if Aventtari abandons us somewhere with this sort of weather, or worse? In civilisation or not, our bodies aren't suited for this."

"No," Lucian answered slowly, eyes still closed. They flung open. Resting his elbows on the table, he steepled his fingers. "Civilisation isn't a word I've heard used with regards to Mūrac as anything other than pure semantic. All considered, it's probably best we end up in Carlophinia. They may have regressed, but I've never heard anything about violence being ingrained in their culture so."

"Aventtari..." Isaac started, stopping breathlessly to listen for movement above, lowering his voice thereafter. "Aventtari could still be tempted to sell us as slaves; he hasn't got anyone to watch over him, or a moral compass for that matter."

"It could happen. Maybe he'll keep us and employ us in dangerous situations. Long have slaves been thrown at the forefront of violent disputes in Mūrac."

The Voice of Kings

Being forced to kill or be killed at a master's non-negotiable order, Isaac finished the sentence in his head. In the thick air, he shivered. *I stabbed a man through the shoulder*, he repeated to himself instinctively. *I drove it all the way through until the blade was soaked at every inch.* Or... no, that wasn't quite right. That potentially put his kill count up to two. Yet strain as he might, he could wring no memory of joy from that. His blood had pounded inside him, but it had stopped at that. Tamzin, quirky Tamzin: she could have been right at the first. There was no real way of ever knowing for sure. Lucian looked blankly into his soul, a bead of sweat trickling down his nose. He understood what was going on in there. Isaac surprised him with a broad smile, sickly all the same, because it had to be done once in a while.

The moon took its place in the sky. Then it vanished. Then the sun dominated those blue wastes.

The next day brought land almost within grasp. It was so close that in the fever of the eternal summer that they said held sway in this part of the world, it was just beyond the reach of him, if he were to lean over the port railing with arm pained by the effort of stretching. Captain Aventtari had been on puppis when Isaac emerged, blinking, into the morning light, shouting orders that none would disobey: the king of the sterncastle. Considering most, or all, had not been personally acquainted with the man before leaving Vilchentah, he'd reined in their loyalty admirably, with ferocity, and also humour when necessary: a force that couldn't be restrained by simple matters of temperature, at least not until he let it.

Isaac tried desperately to read him and always came to the conclusion that what he saw was what there was, and that would have been the end of it save for the niggling doubts he and Lucian harboured and uncovered every night. He wanted to believe Aventtari wasn't something else, but often he would jump to find the man just standing behind him, and when he smiled heartily across the deck at him, he presumed it carried a sinister ulterior message, one along the lines of, "You're mine".

No one stayed out for long that day though. Contact with the outside was minimised, which Maevich agreed to despite being stubborn near to the point of stupidity, and perhaps a bit closer than near, now that he thought about it.

"How much of a risk would jumping ship at the next sight of land be?" Isaac asked that evening, rubbing his hair after having poured a bucket of water over his head. It was drying quickly and he wanted to look presentable, if only for these evenings beside the tiny window. Sanity could only leave him if he abandoned all conceptions of his life prior to the Silver Star, they'd both decided on.

"It's out of the question, Isaac. In the near future, that may change. Just wait and see."

"I'm already doing both."

That elicited a half-smile from his tired older brother, tall and wan. It faded into the abyss, his mood turning dark and intense. If he was trying to make him uncomfortable, he would succeed if he kept that up for a couple of minutes longer.

"How much have you dreamed about your escape from Harth?"

"By which I take your meaning to be nightmares."

"That's what I mean," Lucian said patiently.

"Not as often as I'd dreaded, not that I recall."

Lucian, perhaps not believing him, gazed wistfully out the window, listening to the calm waves splashing against the hull, lips clamped like a seashell: all the signs that he was trying to say something profound, this being an occasion where Isaac's attention would be undivided.

"Do you know that you've frightened me before?"

"Are you going to regret saying this?" Isaac enquired edgily, to which he received a short smile.

"I was four years old the first time. Father sent me to accompany men gathering firewood from the tor, which I considered strange, but I was four so, naturally, I questioned everything. We worked harder than expected, myself and the others he sent, though of course I did nothing but pick up a few bits of wood, and I ran all the way home to tell all about it. I got as far as the doorstep when I heard Mother from inside, screaming. Now, in my twisted perception, I've never heard anything like it before or since, and windy, cloudy days have a tendency to dampen spirits enough. I believe I burst into tears right away. Father heard me and ran out to put me at ease. I heard her scream again, as she was bringing you into this world.

"Funny thing is, I remember one time, years later, when you scared her... because she hadn't heard you approaching, I should wager. What does it matter? I heard her yelp, and it all came back to me."

"Why?" Isaac demanded, angrier than he'd intended. "You didn't need to tell me that."

"We're out here with none other to trust than ourselves and each other, so I thought to give you something to relate with."

Lucian's strength had not diminished, nor had his capacity for playing a demure attitude, but the fever was seen on his face, and the struggle in his tired eyes. That aside, he'd just sat there and methodically recounted his experience, just more fiery than usual. He had that determined, wide-eyed expression that he generally reserved for more scathing discourses. After all, he'd just admitted something he never planned on revealing.

"Do you ever think about it?" Isaac said calmly, a question that was simply obligatory.

"No. Not in any disturbing context. Only for what it is: a memory."

"Are you telling me to change my perceptions too?"

"I'm not telling you to do anything. I was attempting to highlight how I've been vulnerable in the past."

"So?" Isaac prompted, smiling just enough to be noticed in the rocking light of the lantern.

"It doesn't define you. It's not a weakness; it is what it is."

"Some might call a hesitation to kill a strength."

"You didn't hesitate," Lucian put forward. "You did what you needed to, and you regretted that it had to be done afterwards, and that's fine. But necessary it was, and for that reason, your guilt is as irrational as flinching at Mother yelping at you surprising her, in a way. If the time comes when you must do it a third time, you will. We won't get caught by despair, not here!" Lucian growled, tapping a finger on the table as if to compensate for his own misgivings of his words. Never was it thus, but these were extraordinary times.

Isaac took those words at any rate, and moulded them for his own purposes, drumming his fingers on the desk all the while. Part of him vehemently opposed Lucian's stance, though he didn't know how to voice it. When he reached for that voice, it fled, leaving him thoughtless. He wiped sweat from his face and hung his arm out the window, ignoring his misgivings.

"What do you have in mind?"

"I'm still working this out."

"I'm thinking that Aventtari needs testing, Lucian. Father would never jump to conclusions without undergoing a process of trial and error. I suggest we find out if he really does have an obsession with us. I almost hope he does; at least, that way, we have an excuse to do something rash and not wait for him to sell us off on a whim."

"Very good," Lucian commended unceremoniously.

"If I go onto main deck and you watch from the darkness at the foot of the stairs, together we should be able to determine his interest, even if he doesn't completely leave his cabin, or if he sneaks around me as his wont seems to be."

"Do you want me to make some sort of noise?"

"Well, no. It's best if we stay as quiet as possible, in fact. Of course he's going to come out for a loud noise; that would just prove he won't stick his fingers in his ears when he's disturbed."

"That's the test you reserve for Maevich?" Lucian asked dryly, as if to emulate his humour, and succeeding better than expected.

"Quite."

It was decided that they would draw the captain from his hole, and so put their plan into action immediately. Isaac stood at the prow, in grey twilight permeated by the celestial bed shying into life overhead, twinkling dimly in the water below. He felt increasingly foolish, standing there goading for confirmation of his fever-induced dread, aware that the men on the rigging and the one relaxed by the wheel were probably prying at his back with their unpleasant glares. Hairs tingled on his back, not to warn him of them, but of soft footsteps bearing a presence close by.

"As fine an evening as you'll get round these parts," Aventtari observed. "If it's still too much, there's not much I can do."

"I'll take the all the blessings I can get, Captain," Isaac replied without turning.

Damn him, he was good. From experience, Isaac knew there were boards that creaked on main deck, so this man must have known where they all were to move around like that, and what boots he had were up for some very pointless speculation, because they must have been specially tailored for the job.

"I couldn't see much," Lucian admitted when he returned. "He wasn't sneaking, not overtly. I just saw his usual gait.

It wasn't enough to act upon, not by their father's standards that they had to consult, or rather the blurry outline of his standards which were difficult to place without him present, and with a summer haze sabotaging their every brain function. They'd have to make do.

The moon revealed itself. The sun followed with much resentment. Then the moon. Then the sun.

Isaac began to question the gods' imaginations, if truly they'd created or refined all things of Mura as some said. Yet in that time, Captain Aventtari perplexed him furthermore: everything he did started to seem like a trick, a play, a costume that began to peel away in the minor storm that swept through them the previous day. Something was peeling back, that was certain, whether in his head or Isaac's.

But he hadn't imagined the man sneaking by his chamber the previous night, for Lucian had heard it also, such that Lucian was the first to head for the door, finding nothing on the other side, to which they concluded, with some necessary trepidation, that none other would make such effort to be scarce when creaking the boards, nor would they be able to cause mere vibrations on the stairs.

Currently he stood on the port side of main deck, and mercifully the day was clear, foreboding no ill weather that would shake the Silver Star to bring him to the brink of vomiting. He was here because they passed close to land once more and had been doing so for a little while.

"Are we pulling into a port?" Isaac asked Maevich as the first mate walked by.

"Not so far as I know. From what I hear, it shouldn't matter to you one way or another."

"Usually when ships come out of open waters to pass land," Isaac went on, ignoring the comment, "they do it because their captain intends to stop off."

The Voice of Kings

"We're not stopping. I don't know when we will because I don't know where we're going. I know that that, there, is called The Tooth," he pointed out with the perceived wisdom of one who'd been here before, nodding at a great black piece of rock jutting from the sea, indeed curved just like a tooth.

At that declaration, Isaac went below deck with his head filled with finalities, and saw his brother there, but Lucian knew nothing of The Tooth or any landmarks along the coast of Mūrac.

"Do you think it's time we paid our captain a visit?" Isaac mused.

"I saw the men tenser than usual earlier," Lucian said. "They were fiddling with the cannons as if they're expecting an attack. My guess is that this is pirate territory, or that of King Alamier's patrol fleets. Now might be the perfect time to pay him a visit, yes."

"There is no perfect time, Lucian. Time can't take the blame for failure; we have to make it perfect ourselves."

Lucian laughed sombrely and gripped his shoulder firmly, such that it was close to hurting him. He looked as grim as he sounded, as someone preparing for a suicide march in the vanguard. He suggested they sneak into the armoury to equip themselves with a dagger each; a very tempting suggestion it was too, but Isaac feared for their well-being, for there could be no bluffing against a man like Aventtari.

"If he finds us with weapons, he'll slit our throats! I'm not going to wager my skill with a tiny little blade against him and his beloved sword, even if we draw first. If words are all we're seen to have, we're guaranteed to live longer."

"Very well," Lucian agreed grudgingly.

Feeling naked, Isaac put his royal blue jacket around him, and Lucian straightened the dark clothes he'd bought in Mürathneè with his hands, such that they could have been simply preparing for a meeting with local merchants in County Highlands. All save for the knot that wrapped around his stomach, screaming at him not to throw his life away. It was worse as he ascended the stairs onto main deck, Lucian at his side, for he felt naked at his waist where a dagger should have been concealed. Presently, the steel to inflict his third crippling blow was an option that was most attractive, the will to defend kicking in already. Irony was ever mocking.

They didn't stop before the doors of the captain's cabin, for it would have given them time to rethink this crazy scheme, or at least that was Isaac's reason. They flung the doors open and there he sat, the King of the Sterncastle, poring over a map behind his finely carved desk. The doors were shut; they were two, he was one.

"What can I do you for?" he pronounced in that slick, indefinable tone of his. When he looked up, he frowned. "What are you dressed up for? Going somewhere?"

Isaac stood at the right end of the desk while Lucian took to the left.

The King of the Sterncastle

"We'd like you to clear some things up for us," Lucian said resolutely, shaking slightly in the legs, which fortunately Aventtari could barely see. "We've reached some conclusions which can't be taken back."

"In short, please," Aventtari said, frown showing more concern.

"We'd like to know your interest in us," Isaac told him.

The captain flexed his arms and leaned back, looking back and forth between them. Suddenly he raised them a look of surprise, subdued, as if he expected this to happen eventually.

"There can't be any harm in telling you now," he relented.

Isaac nearly collapsed in astonishment at his concession to honesty, with a gaping expression that didn't go unnoticed. Aventtari smiled, but Isaac didn't like the look of it.

"Do take a seat, both of you."

"It's best we stand, Captain," Lucian said. "I hope you understand."

"Perfectly. Do as you will."

"Do you have another name we can call you?" Isaac asked. "Your real one, preferably."

"My real name is Maksym Beriddian." He smiled faintly, sharing a joke with himself. "I haven't used it in months. Satisfied?"

"Far from it. I trust that will change shortly."

Lucian scowled silently, disapproving of Isaac's forward interrogation style, and if truth were told, he, himself, felt the same way. His emotions had gotten the better of him, not to mention being lulled into a sense of security by Maksym's amicability.

"You're *very* interesting, actually," Maksym Beriddian went on. "Especially you, Isaac." Of course. He'd been led to believe he was the most fascinating man on the planet recently, for all the wrong reasons. "I've heard much regarding gods' magic where I live, the problem being that much is often said there and little is seen, so when I began to hear, more than usual, disturbing things, my King thought it a pertinent idea to investigate Mürathneè instead, and what do I find but you: the man hiding the key to secrets absolutely everyone wants."

"Everyone at once," Isaac said slowly, treading cautiously on the field of blades.

"Indeed. Myself included, I shan't lie. I need to be sure before it's too late. To cut a long story short, there are signs of what my King diplomatically labels as 'unusual behaviour' in Carlophinia, but you see, the other thing about Carlophinia is that there's already a lot of distractions in the wilderness. When griffins prowl the cliff tops, and bats half the height of a man rule the forests below, much superstition is invited into houses and castles alike, which isn't saying a lot, sadly."

"What do you need to know, precisely?" Lucian said. He had the right idea.

"Anything. Everything."

The Voice of Kings

"I can't help you there, because I don't know what you need." Isaac and Lucian were on the same page, he was sure of it. To withhold information could save their lives for the time being. "Am I answerable to you, not your King?"

"I hoped to have you answer to me without asking a single question, but then, you already know that," Maksym said, stroking his beard roughly, shaking his head from side to side disagreeably. The captain, the spy, whatever he was, looked suddenly professional, all grandeur locked away. "If we were back at Vilchentah, I'd think twice about it. I was given quite a start when I went to deal with the real captain of the Silver Star, which is to say, the original thief. What did I find but a token of my own inadequacies? I saw there, in his lodging, in the dead of night, a note from a previous intruder on the pillow on which he slept, pinned through with a knife, and it warned him not to lay a finger on either of you lest he be hunted down and burned into the abyss, Silver Star and all."

"Our friends at the palace haven't let us down yet," Lucian said.

"Friends at the palace," Maksym repeated plainly. He already knew. He knew they knew. "Of course, of course. He wouldn't have gotten this ship unless someone arranged it."

"You dealt with him," Isaac said, half-accusingly. He had no stake in that man's life, yet he needed to know, his bones told him so.

"He was a seasoned pirate: his criminal legacy could stretch to the moon if it was written down in a list. He won't be missed."

Maksym Beriddian pored over his map again, running a finger down the west coast of Mūrac, muttering something inaudibly. After a time, he nodded and slapped a hand on it, rising as he did so with the swiftness of a cat, and just as much finesse. Isaac always knew there was something special in his movements, in the agility he summoned to climb the rigging. He manoeuvred around the desk, Isaac drawing back alongside his brother as if pushed by Maksym's very presence. Maksym stopped and chuckled.

"You're smart, you two. I wouldn't trust me either."

"That's a fair analysis," Isaac agreed. "I'm wondering something, and I'd like to know if you're willing to divulge. Your accent isn't one I recognise. If it's a hybrid, then you must not have lived in Mūrathneè for a while, yet I hear Mūrathneèan tendencies clear as day."

"I *did* live in Mūrathneè. Being the last sane man of a diseased House, I just had to cut my losses and start anew."

If he was shamed by explaining this, he didn't expose it: not a hint. On the contrary, he sighed in relief afterwards and, seemingly ignoring them, went to the door. A knocking came upon it and, without checking his stride, he turned and gave them a conspiratorial glance, hand jumping to sword for a second before relaxing it again. Beyond it, the first mate glowed while Isaac accustomed himself to the full force of the sunlight, which sadly was the least of his worries.

"We need to change course," Maevich blurted out in terror.

The King of the Sterncastle

"Need?" the persona of Captain Aventtari replied sharply.

"The Devil's Jaw is a death trap," Maevich hissed.

Maksym was already halfway to the prow, not running but striding with his long, agile legs, with Isaac and Lucian not far behind. Devil's Jaw had been appropriately named, as Isaac saw, for in an oval inlet in the coastline some way ahead, there stood dozens of rocks, black as The Tooth they were, tall and curved, glistening with prideful menace above the three ships that were wrecked in their snare: ships as big as the Silver Star smashed within their clasp. Maksym was at the prow's very edge, crouched on one knee with the fingertips of both arms pressed to the wood as if preparing to spring from the ship. He rose suddenly, truly startled, because as Isaac had loath to believe, it was not the rocks alone that had been cause for worry.

"Those ships didn't just crash," Maksym said.

"Hard to starboard!" Maevich shouted.

"Belay that," Maksym snapped, fire in his eyes. "Steady the course, man the cannons."

The water was not calm anymore, not wholly. At random points, the blueness grew sick and white, frothing at the hold of creatures unseen. It spread like a plague so that in a great half-circle around them, the water pounded up, banging like obscene music, and encased in the shoots of foaming water, there beheld creatures like snakes, or so Isaac could see for all the water that cloaked them. The dance went on in haste, the creatures becoming more impatient, launching themselves up and smacking into the ocean so that it rippled all around.

"Serpents," Maksym said with utter loathing, curling his lips back and squinting. There was more than that though: genuine fear crossed him, helplessness even.

"What are they doing?" Isaac heard himself yell.

"I was hoping you'd tell me," Maksym told him, edgy now, dark eyebrows curving into arcs.

He remembered the wall that presented its glory to him in his youth, the beasts that glowed red that were wrought upon its surface. Of all of them, the serpent had never been forgotten, rearing mightily as they did now in their queer ceremony that sent chills deep through the men's spines, and he wondered if there was a connection; how could he not?

"Give them something to think about," Maksym ordered, swishing his tongue around his mouth, eyes hard set. Then he raised his voice to the men at starboard, clear and menacing: "Fire."

They heaved at winches on the cannons' sides and so it was lowered, the wide base taking the brunt of the weight, Isaac finally realising that it was the same design his father had presented to Sir Tristan Almaric all those years ago, or of the same cloth. In his momentary awe, he forgot himself, jolting at the blasts that rang out through the summer air: the flashes at the end of the metal contraptions, the immense rocking of their whole being, and not so far off, two huge splashes, first sucked beneath the waves before being reversed.

"Come on, load again!" Maksym encouraged, one hand behind his back while the other waved enthusiastically upwards. "We have a pathetic gunnery compliment as it is. If you're not all done in 70 seconds, there'll be watered ale tonight."

The men manning the cannons struggled to lift new cannonballs set into metal shelves at the deck's edge, but there were few of these on main deck, so other men rushed below to fetch more. It dawned on Isaac that he was now standing in the very centre of the deck, up against the main mast, the knot in his stomach so tight it was actually numbing. He stared everywhere there were disturbances in the sea, Lucian too. And still the serpents milled in scores ever expanding, heedless of the warning shots that might have injured or killed some of their brethren.

What came next was so well planned that Isaac thought, for a moment, he must be dreaming: the sea snakes raised themselves in the air, previously hidden beneath the ship, in rows of four and five, shooting from the waves so hard they might have been flying, for their slender shadows engulfed half the ship. Then the blackness beneath them shrank, their bodies seemed to grow, and down they came, crashing onto the railing where splinters flew like bees and fell like sharpened rain. Across the deck they reached, the nine of them. At his body's command, he dropped, leaped rather, to his stomach, just as Lucian made to drag him down anyway, and they rolled hard against the portside railing. Where his stomach constricted, he felt his eyes jam open so wide that blood welled up behind them, as, above his face contorted in terror, a serpent locked its teeth over a man's shoulder, dragging him to his knees. Its scales of pale green shined like silver, each one distinct on its body that scored ten feet in length, all of it out of water. Its fins were wide, its head was long, its frill around its head flapped taut, open like a mane. While its teeth wrestled with the man whose screams bore down above him, its tail writhed all about as if in pain, and beyond it there were more just the same, lashing despite their grief.

Crawling back, Isaac surveyed the area through bleary vision, getting used to the idea that he was in a waking nightmare. It was the rocking of the ship, the mindless gnashing of teeth beyond all practicality, and the scent of blood that made him feel alive, in all the worst ways. He stopped crawling, noticing that he was drawing too close to the prow where he might be an easier target, never taking his eyes off the nearest serpent that had succeeded in ripping its teeth through the man's arm, which was still attached but a shell of its former being. The beast went in for the kill at the face, lolling its body around the deck to what end couldn't be known, for it looked ill so out of the water, and yet was keen to torture itself.

"You two!" Maksym shouted from across the deck, where he, too, was hidden against the railing, with sword drawn, not baying for action as others were. "To the cannons!" he ordered.

The King of the Sterncastle

He nodded furiously to the cannons on their side, and feeling like he had a death wish, Isaac leapt up and ran. Lucian was behind him to ensure he didn't stop. There were four serpents on deck, Isaac noticed, their wet scales drying quickly on the boards, in the baking sun where they were never supposed to be. A fifth was slithering below deck while the others were falling back into the water, though not without some success, for the railings were tattered, the masts were scarred yet still standing, and the light bronze-coloured pine was spattered with streaks of red. Isaac found himself confronted with the girth of the serpent he just witnessed kill one of the crew: a serpent he tried to glide over, back first, with more success than he should have expected. It thrashed out at him with speed that surprised him, but a dying predator can be mighty indeed, Isaac was now reminded. It lurched forward, raising its head up and crashing it down to where Isaac was. As before, its shadow shrank and its head grew, catching the sun as it levelled, then crashed upon the deck when Isaac jumped from its range. Foolishly, he turned as he ran, looking into the eyes of the beast that were not thin like a snake's, but more the shape of a human's, but black with a large white pupil that seemed to probe him. Grow, it did, ever wider as its desperation became final.

He saw its teeth seem to sharpen as they gleamed, its headdress flap open, and spinal fin that ran down its body spring up. Like a legendary hero and not a spy, Maksym Beriddian entered his vision, steel no longer shining because it was drenched red. On his toes he was, and deftly like a dancer, he sprang forward, stabbed quickly into the mouth of the serpent, and was back where he started, having mildly wounded it. A tall man blurred on Isaac's left, incredibly familiar, the familiarity confirmed when his scrambled brain recognised it as Lucian, who now tugged him to the ground. There was a cannon right beside them, loaded and unmanned.

"Do it," Lucian hissed frantically.

He was nodding to the rod which was just within his reach. It was already in Isaac's hand, so ordinary a thing to look at, his saviour. It struck at the great contraption and did nothing. They stood, the two brothers, and were felled at once by a rocking from a place unseen: monsters in the abyss below. They tried again, Isaac slipping on blood but stamping his foot down, getting a grip with his fine boots, and together they hauled the cannon to point directly down where all was chaos. He blew on the rod cord and touched the cannon again.

A deafening blast sounded, and smoke rushed from the barrel and was tossed into his face by the wind, picking up now. A ball was flying through the air, just for a moment, then it was in the water. White foam surged out, and down, and up. White became red. Instinctively, Isaac fell to his knees at the booming of the second portside cannon, jolting violently back. His ears were ringing now. And through the ringing, a smooth voice declared itself to all.

677

The Voice of Kings

"Maevich, steer us into the rocks," Maksym commanded.

"Have you lost your mind?" the first mate retaliated.

Both of them rose, wearing the blood of the enemy upon them. Serpents writhed on deck, still dangerous but not an immediate threat.

"I intend to send this ship into oblivion, and if that makes me mad, then so be it."

"I will take the wheel," Maevich agreed, bounding up the steps with no need of encouragement. "Not to the rocks."

There was a twitch on Maksym's face. Just a twitch, but even now Isaac saw the desperation in it: a moment's helplessness, of fancying his chances in the sea. It went far away, and fire was his steed.

"Come on then!" Maksym bellowed, swinging his sword in the direction of his crew, spittle joining blood in taking flight. "You're just pirates! What's your combat experience, killing women and children? Do as I say, or you'll find yourselves emptying your bowels of 30 inches of steel!"

They backed off. They knew they were dealing with something very different than they'd imagined, and just the slightest hesitation was enough, given the circumstances. The man they'd accepted as captain with open arms shed his skin, and they couldn't be *positive* he wasn't bluffing, not in less than ten seconds of mayhem. Maevich was smart enough to understand this wasn't the ideal occasion for a mutiny, now obeying like a whipped dog.

Torn rigging from the main mast swung over Isaac's head; his hands gripped the rope for support, and thereby, he sprang to his feet. The mast creaked long and hoarse, as if sick, the water frothed anew, and of the whim of their unseen puppet masters, they thrashed wildly, those beasts, or so the play went on, for now Isaac was beginning to believe more deeply than he had in many a year. What he believed in was not relevant, only that faith welled inside him, putrid as it now was. Still they did not relent. If there was some physical representation of their madness, their strings would be twisted indeed. No such luck. None tangible.

"My desk," Maksym said hurriedly. Isaac jumped a little as he realised the gesture was for him. "Top drawer."

The captain slapped him hard on the back as he passed, causing him to run, as if he needed an incentive. As he went, he saw Maevich drawing in close, losing his opportunity, then back off, cursing under his breath. Lucian was ever shadowing him, for once something he was so grateful of he could cry; could if his body was capable of operating beyond the realm of absolute necessity and random inflections. His body barraged through the door, and Lucian wisely shut it behind them. And locked it, as seemed appropriate. It made him feel safe. He knew he wasn't.

Opening the top drawer of the desk, an obsessively shined flintlock glimmered on its dull wooden base, lead balls twinkling like dark stars around it. Hope, that grandest of all emotions at present, fired up as a tiny little ember. It didn't matter that loading and firing it were beyond him, let alone aiming it; it was a weapon, that's what mattered, being exactly what was needed right now, and only what was needed. More hope was thrown on the desk before him in the shape of a blade and hilt, then sapped by the screeches from the waves, guttural and with a distant echoic sound, as if played through a long metal pipe.

"What did Dorrin Santorellian do?" Isaac asked, frantically scrabbling with the curved lump of metal and powder in his shaking hands, oiled with sweat, learning the particulars in record time.

"I don't know," Lucian snapped, scratching at his forehead as if to physically procure the answer. He breathed. "They were chupacabras and the like, not comparable at all. He killed them, I'm sure, and kept doing it until there was nothing left to kill."

"Finality," Isaac muttered. "Everything has it."

As far as motivational endeavours went, this one left much to be desired, but it would have to do. As would his efforts with the pistol, which along with several lead balls, and the sword in his right hand, marked the end of his excursion, and so he saw what horrors he was returning to as he barged the door to open it. Pillars of black rock closed in on the ship at great speed, and serpents messily attempted to crawl onto the deck, snatching and biting, and slipping on their fallen brethren on a deck where the crew already had their hands full setting up a plan that would, as Maksym so aptly put it, cast them into the abyss. When they weren't dodging demonic jaws, tripping on blood and water, they heaved at the cannons; rather than turning them round, they spun the turret backwards so that all four faced inwards, pointing at one another: inanimate objects preparing to duel. By Maksym's hand, wine and oil was sloshed across the deck, seasoned with liberal applications of gunpowder. It wasn't the definition of finality he was looking for, or the eerie drumming of tail on water, of which immediate counting yielded none at all.

"Come," Maksym ordered, voice taking on a slippery texture when he raised it high. "Come on!" he shouted, impatient now.

The brothers were already running, straight down the centre, over the twitching, alcohol-soaked serpents, where those that still bayed at the sidelines would find it harder to reach. Not that it would save them. The Star would bow beneath them eventually, when enough had piled themselves upon the deck. The fell beasts would make it their mass grave, and so long as it was that of the crew also, then the surviving serpents would...die? Kill themselves? Lie in wait? Isaac found a powerful motivator in this, to rise in his stomach like the surf. He slipped once, twice, thrice, he felt his legs splay and a flash of pain shoot up: the feeling of veins splitting. But he never fell, not to his knees, for around him, four cracks had sounded, whip-like, and four flames swallowed four ropes that had been loosely strapped onto the cannons.

The Voice of Kings

"Everyone off," Maksym ordered, waving his free hand madly as he stood against a portside fragment of railing. A man stood reluctant at the edge, so Maksym pushed him off: a sacrifice, really, and there was no getting around that. And so Maksym Beriddian repeated: "Everyone off!"

Isaac held aloft the flintlock pistol as he ran, only for the captain to wave it away in disgust. *Had he ever wanted it?* Isaac wondered. He then grabbed it reluctantly, not knowing what he was doing, firing it into the water randomly. Seemingly he was more worried about his foot, as it was holding aloft a burning piece of rope, about to be left to react upon the wine-drenched boards. Maksym opened his mouth to speak, but somewhere unseen, rocks scraped against the hull of the ship, and beside him, Isaac fell. At least Lucian was falling too.

For a moment he was blind, then he almost wished he was. Vague shapes slithered about, dozens of them. There was a splash behind him, faint to his waterlogged ears, though he knew it was the captain, and so he braced himself. He pushed himself down into the depths of darkness. The darkness fled.

His ears could have been on fire, they stung as much, all the way inside, all the way to his brain: shaking, ringing. It was like a thousand sounds meshed together, of iron and wood, and colliding in the most devastating way possible. The snake wraiths around him became real, but only shortly, for a force slammed into him and dizzied him as he span, only orienting himself by the nightmare unfolding on the surface: the Silver Star becoming red hot vapour. A torn sail, silver aura gleaming onto the seabed, burned on the water's surface, and the fire fizzled out and scraps of black cloth drifted all around him. But fires still raged, he heard their crackling, such that Isaac dared not make for the surface. And Lucian was not with him.

He let the pain flush through him. If he could cry, he would, only tears were stopped short, crushed by the increasing pressure. He remembered again: Lucian wasn't with him... separated when disoriented. Singed serpents dropped like flies, but not his brother. He was nowhere to be seen. The tang of undefined blood was thick on his tongue, so thick the iron seemed to weigh at his lips, and though it was soon dispersed, the taste could not be washed clean, nor could he spit it out despite his body begging him so. The world was extreme darkness and extreme light, it was black rocky monoliths shimmering through his blurred vision, it was his hands flailing before him time and again, pushing on the teeth of the Jaw for support.

Then the world was only blackness, and when his hearing was a selection of bangs and hums, when driven by his body's raw functions and last energy, he glimpsed light; the world was something of an oddity for having things he could see. Somehow he found himself at the surface, and later washed up on dry land, spitting more water than he thought a human could contain, chest thumping such that the ground might give way beneath; indeed, it wasn't wholly solid. It shifted in his crawling wake, and a few seconds later, he realised it was sand.

His vision returned, in a way. He couldn't look left or right to check his surroundings; only the foreboding landscape ahead was his to see, foreboding in ways he couldn't understand, for when he wracked his brain, nothing in particular stuck out to him. It was just an overwhelming strangeness filling him, until from a black cloud it came: a single streak of lightning beyond the dunes in the distance, sanguine it was, and it roared at him. He struggled to understand it, and by that token, to understand why he thought he could understand it. Though dazed, he felt uneasy, as if standing before a crowd to give an important speech, and all their eyes were glaring at him, trying to figure him out. He squirmed, or did so inwardly, for he couldn't say what his body was doing. The imagined eyes wormed their judgements into his soul and... became bored. They retreated, vanished, to bother someone else.

Whether by dream or other influence, he heard voices within his head, images shooting by, various things becoming prominent for a moment before turning to dust. Most confounding of all, Kate's voice threatened to block all others.

"Why you?" Isaac asked in the confines of his mind.

"Why not?" she answered.

Sister Kate, timid Kate, silly Kate... ah, yes. Kate the Healer. The slightest stimuli spiralled out of control and elevated beyond reason. *Well, little sister*, he thought, *you may heal me in your own time.* Inwardly he laughed, still not grasping sanity. Outwardly he coughed violently, blowing sand onto his face. Isaac Brodie fought for life, there on the shores of Mūrac, and in time, his muddled brain told him, he would rise and return home, and all the nations of the world would know and understand what happened here, and take what meaning they would from it. But now he would rest.

He managed to pull a confused squint when, before his very eyes, a raven landed bearing the likeness of the sand in colour and roughness, now hopping along and onto his back. Isaac wondered if it was a harbinger of that red lightning or just a dream. He wondered little more, for his energy was spent. And so he rested.

Epilogue: The Leaden Crown

On the throne of Castle Türith, Walter Santorellian, the Prince of Frost as he was rather amusingly called for both good and ill, sat proudly with a grin that could not be vanquished; fine red wine sloshing in a gleaming goblet in his right hand, cheeky Ysallii on his lap, and Pazia sitting against his leg on the dais, only slighter lesser a lady than Ysallii, if he had to decide, which he didn't, on account of him being Prince Regent, but he had his preferences, and the classiest of them was right on top of him. Some people, mostly in robes too big for them, would think it inappropriate and negligent of him, of which he begged to differ. He presided over his little party now, and if something urgent or important presented itself, he would attend to it then, and properly, but only then.

"Put on the crown," Ysallii whispered into his ear, readjusting herself. She played with her platinum blonde locks absentmindedly. "Let's see what you look like as a king."

"This, dear, is a prince's crown. I will look no more a king in it than you do a chaste priestess. But since you insist."

His right hand exchanged the goblet for a bejewelled band of silver, not gold. He wasn't king yet, and may the honour of that elude him for as long as it pleased, Walter mused. All the same, it had a tiny lump of Sèhvorian steel, cut into a diamond shape, embedded into the crest at his order: a jewel which Ysallii prodded as if she'd never seen such a thing before. She had seen it on him previously, just never this close, apparently. Prince Walter was occupied by the sight of one of the heavy doors being opened from the other side. The commander of his household guard, Sir Virgil Malrk, abandoned his place at the foot of the dais and dodged wide around the dancers and other merrymakers to see to the disturbance, returning a moment later with two men in tow: couriers by the looks of them, both utterly bedraggled from the rain that had scoured this northern tip of Türithneè half the day.

With Sir Virgil in the lead, they doused the festive mood: he in his dark blue armour displaying the silhouette of Castle Türith on the breastplate, they in their wool and leather riding gear, fashioned with vaguely royal attention to detail. The minstrels played their songs all the same, and though men and women were distracted by the newcomers, the dancing and conversations weren't detracted so very much.

"Better give me some room," Walter told his lovemaker, grinning and winking.

She grinned back, a measure by which he gauged how handsome or charming he was, or both. At his feet she sat, and the prince, having adjusted his creased garments, raised his goblet in toast.

"House Santorellian welcomes you," he called, aware of being at least somewhat drunk; how much, he was too drunk to tell. Sir Virgil took to his side, briefly.

Epilogue

"More princely," his knight muttered, annoyed, from the corner of his mouth. Then, more loudly, "Important news, my Prince. It needs to be heard, even during parties."

When Virgil took himself away, the couriers came humbly forward, the first far more professional than the second, who looked cold and disgruntled.

"Dark tidings, actually," the first said.

"They had better be," Walter heard himself say. "We're busy."

"We didn't ride together," the second courier spoke up. "We just waited outside together. I didn't think to come in here so soon, actually."

"Well now you are. What's your news?" Walter said to the first man.

"*Royal* news."

A letter was held up in very official capacity beside a stern face, saying without words that he wasn't going to like it. Worriedly, Walter beckoned and took the letter, noting the royal seal stamped upon it. His finger went to slit it open, but stayed from its purpose at the last moment, playing with the wax. He became increasingly perplexed the more he stared at it, and the more his finger ran over the bumps, the more real it became. He took in the throne room's frivolities with an air of tired bitterness, biting hard down on his lip as the letter spiralled in his hands, appreciating the lack of interest of literally everyone. It was going to be a direct order of some displeasing fashion: a call for him to give up Castle Türith, or to marry, to which tricks of avoidance his father would be wise to this time. Or both. If he was to give up this life, he would prefer his own keep than living in the Palace of the Sun, grand as it was, because in those halls he would be on his father's leash. How this was perceived appropriate for a man of 20 years was beyond his guessing. One last time, he considered the envelope, letting his fears take dark wings that the truth could never surprise him, before very carefully placing it down on the table beside him, reverent as if to a dangerous creature in the wilds. His gaze fell on the second courier.

"What did you want?"

"I was looking for someone. Actually, I hadn't hoped to see you until the last straw."

"Good. Join the party if you wish. See if I care," Walter lazily permitted him with an air of passive aggressiveness. "You're going to have to tell me eventually."

"Spit it out, man," Sir Virgil contradicted him, somewhat to his annoyance.

Walter listened to gibberish about how the courier had been locating a rider from Burtal to trade news, because travelling over such time periods can often mean delivering unreliable information. Whatever his vocation was, lying wasn't it. It was insulting that, whilst drunk, he could detect the man's disingenuous speech.

It was also enough to bring him right forward, resting chin in hand, tapping an armrest with the other; being drunk, he couldn't be sure he wasn't just making a buffoon of his name, dallying on the throne, the Prince of Frost. It irked him. Only now, ironically.

"Sir Virgil, is this man lying?" he said forwardly.

The Voice of Kings

"I wouldn't presume either way. Shall I detain him?"

Walter held up a hand to halt his bodyguard pre-emptively, still eyeing the courier suspiciously: a big man with a silently aggressive reaction to being called dishonest.

"It's quite warm in here," Prince Walter told him. "You may remove your surcoat."

"Is this necessary?"

"I think it's quite warm in here," Walter repeated, looking around for support. "Lots of braziers and thick walls to keep the heat in and the cold out."

"Yes, my Prince, I have things beneath this coat," the courier answered, beaten. "They are not for you."

Metal glinted in a hand he withdrew from the coat, being a flintlock pistol, and time slowed to a crawl. There was no deliberation, no nothing. Walter's hand reached for the nearest object, and found a goblet which he hurled through the air, spraying red wine until the empty cup hit the courier on the head. In a flash, Virgil's sword was drawn, but even he was beaten to the chase, so to speak, by nearby guards jabbing either side of the man's belly in perfect synchronisation with their halberds. Time was back up to speed, now being the occasion for everything else to stop.

Glasses and instruments were dropped all at once, then stillness blanketed the hall. Prince Walter was already on his feet. He winked to his two whores cowering, disgusted as much as scared, before stalking vengefully to the courier. Steel tips only pierced him lightly, which the prince nodded approvingly at. A hand lifted the man's chin up, revealing a pleading face. Of course he was pleading; there was no lie there. The question was how it came to this. The coat was swung open now, residence of a second pistol and a dagger.

"They weren't for you," the courier said.

"They were for someone! Who? Who were you looking for? Was I involved, or was it a coincidence the trail took you here?"

"Murder was not on the cards, Prince. You are not involved."

"I am now. Why..." Walter sighed and stood back to study the pathetic man who was assuredly slipping into sleep, feeling sober yet unable to determine what was being implied. What Walter shouted next surprised him. "Fine. Out! Everyone out! Virgil, would you do the honours?"

"Prince?"

"Search everyone. Don't let them back in until they're clear."

The knight nodded and, along with his contingent of guards, herded up the poor guests who had probably done nothing wrong, and funnelled them out into the lobby, and beyond that, the courtyard. The throne room grew in the absence of inhabitants. It was somehow wrong without them. It didn't matter that they were party guests milling around inebriating themselves and telling bawdy jokes so much as their presence. Rarely did he find himself here with not a soul in sight.

Epilogue

"You'd better follow," Walter told his two women. "It won't look good if you don't. You'll have hot baths when you get back, I assure you.

They stood, they walked, they ran, they were gone. Walter Santorellian was the prince of nothing at that moment in time. He forced out a laugh and returned to his throne to view his non-existent subjects, there contemplating darkly the manner of sneaking weapons into here: three outer walls around the castle; guards at every one; watchtowers to spot intruders afar; pyres with which to reveal them. No one walked in here with weapons without permission.

On either side of the throne room, fires were lit in great stone sconces on the walls shaped like gauntlets, and on the walls above the balconies stretching the length of the hall on each side, stone men kept fires alive on staffs and in their hands. Realising that he'd been too focused on their likeness, eerie when alone, he became suddenly self-conscious again. Upon realising he'd been banging the sole of his boot against the ground, he decided he'd had enough and snatched the letter. One more lot of bad news, then to bed, and not alone.

And so the neat, thin words of his father's hand spoke terrible over and over again: the foreign lord paramount murdered, tensions boiling the air the country over, war on the way. A groan escaped him and he lowered the letter, having half-finished reading. The details were vague, deliberately so if he knew his father, though he could never tell for why until it was required of him. The subtext was clear enough: he was required to gather thousands of men and plan for a military campaign, and not only that, fund it for his part. How the hell was he supposed to pour money into a war? He'd done exactly as his liege father had suggested and initiated a new renaissance on top of the old one. Even now, he knew he'd spent too much. Excuses, then.

No, he could probably weave a good lie, but it wasn't going to help anyone. The money would have to come from somewhere, and he'd be the one to find it. Once more he sighed, once more. To the letter again: he read more with puzzlement as superstitious drivel rolled off the page, such that he wondered if the wine had temporarily wrecked his comprehension of the written word. The rumours he'd heard of his uncle were confirmed, now in full, by the King, his father.

The sheet of paper that was the letter whisked back and forth through the air, rid of Walter in form but not in essence. Damn it, damn his father for keeping him out of the loop, and most of all damn the halfwit who thought executing a foreign lord publicly on behalf of the country was at all clever. Suddenly the throne room took on a life of its own at last, and it was as if he'd given it the power. He felt powerful in that big chair by himself, like the King. Just then he *was* the King. This is what it was to be so. The crown was heavy on him. His thoughts raced through all the possibilities, all the potential of his coming decisions. Excitement was almost within his grasp; he should have been able to take it, but responsibility was so very heavy. Thoughts darkened, more vivid by the second, an

The Voice of Kings

underlying wrongness developing that couldn't quite be pinpointed. The winds howled, and the Sea of Everfrost opened up like a mouth and engulfed Castle Türith, the greatest siege fortress that ever was. Kings and queens floated without their crowns; their faces and fashion he didn't know. He was drifting with them, drowning. He blinked. He hadn't been dreaming, not exactly.

Indeed, something was wrong; he took heed of that now. There were whispers, quiet yet distant, half-frozen after riding the cold waters from north and west. And duty weighed heavy as the castle around him now. No, not that, something real. He buckled as if under a lead weight, eyes widening as a noise escaped his lips, somewhere between a yelp and a curse. He forced himself hard to the backrest of the throne to stop from falling. He *couldn't* be imagining it. The pain was real: it bled tears down his cheeks.

The crown. It's the crown.

In his hand it was as light as a feather, yet heavy enough to clang when tossed at the paving of the throne room. The clang echoed up into the high, curved ceiling, then slammed back into Walter. The silver band skittered like a stone on water, rolled on its edge, and stopped finally, sitting on its rim as a crown should.

When no one came, Walter jumped to his feet and took charge. Above the crown, he grimaced contemptuously. He was not a superstitious man, not really. His latest steed was a gift from the gods, he'd deemed, but only because it was easy to pass it off as such, because it didn't affect anything. Now tidings reached him from Harth, and he met magic in battle just the same, confused. But he was Walter Santorellian, the Prince of Frost, well liked and charismatic. He shrugged as if his disgust meant nothing.

The power of gods, then.

Milton Keynes UK
Ingram Content Group UK Ltd.
UKHW042212091224
452221UK00018B/197/J